SHOTGUN SHOWDOWN

A COZY MOUNTAIN TOWN MYSTERY - 2

TRENA REDDING

PROLOGUE

"*You* ou three idiots just don't get it. Do you?" I eased behind my desk as I spoke and sat in my custom designed chair. Costing me a fortune, my prized piece fit my body like a glove and intimidated like a throne. The cushion compressed as I settled in, and the leather groaned when I shifted to cross my legs. The smell of expensive Italian leather rose to surround me. Without taking my eyes from the goons standing before me, I pointed at my brother Fahid, slumped next to them. "I want her found and I want her dead. You hear me?"

I shifted my gaze to Fahid. He gulped like he had just eaten a fist full of dry crackers and his life depended on finding a drink to flush it down.

"We've tried boss, they sent her underground," interrupted the very large and very dumb looking thug closest to Fahid.

I wondered how I got anything done while surrounded by morons. And now I needed a smoke.

Not removing my gaze from my brother, I leaned forward to grab a Cohiba from the humidor on my desk. If this didn't soothe my nerves, I might have to kill someone. I blinked slowly. "Who is this suicidal idiot talking to me?" The interrupter looked as though he might pass out when I moved in his direction to grab my lighter.

Lighting a quality cigar should not be rushed. The feel of the cool wrap on the fingertips, the aromatic release of the luxurious cultivar after clipping the end, and that first drag... a heavenly, sensual experience. After taking a long drag of my cigar, I blew out a cloud of smoke. "How much are we paying our mole at the DEA?"

"A lot, brother."

"And we can't find her?"

"Abdul, I don't know what to tell you. He said he's trying. They've locked her down good. He can't find nothin'." Fahid leaned forward to open my box of Cubans.

"You touch my cigars and I'm going to bust your damned hand off."

Fahid yanked his hand back, his eyes wide and mouth open.

Big and Dumb leaned forward and placed his filthy paws on my desk. He chimed in again. "It's not his fault, boss. We will find her, I promise."

"You promise, do you?" I reached under my desk with my left hand and felt the welcoming coolness of cold steel in my hand. I pulled back the hammer on my forty-five as I whipped it out and pointed the barrel at his forehead. "You think you can touch my desk? And now, if you move a muscle, I'm going to end your miserable existence."

"Adbul, please," Fahid interjected.

He looked as though he might cry. I took a long, final drag from my cigar. The cherry on the end raged as I placed it over Big and Dumb's left hand, and he flinched. "Don't move." I raised my pistol.

His face flushed with a deep red, and his eyes welled with tears.

"Now," I said. "You two worthless human beings, listen to me. You're making my brother look bad. Even worse than he already does. And that's not easy. You find her. I don't care what you do. Squeeze that spineless mole at the DEA, search the entire country town by town if that's what it takes. I want her gone and nobody can know it was us. The last thing we need is more agents crawling up our butts. You can be damn sure that's what will happen when you kill agents."

"Agent Evans will not interrupt any more shipments of my product. And she damn sure will not take any more shots at my idiot brother. If you can't see to it, I will." I pointed to the door and reclined in my chair. "Now get out of my office. Do your job so I don't have to. I promise you will not like it if I do."

1

$\mathcal{R}$ough hospital sheets rubbed against my skin. My foggy brain registered muffled voices coming from nearby and the sound of footsteps approaching my bed.

My new friend, Rita, ambled over, her shoes making a soft shuffling sound on the hospital floor. She smoothed the sheets on the bed. "Look who is awake. How are you feeling, Ally?"

I pried my eyes open and gazed around me: vitals machine beeping in sync with my heartbeat, a blue curtain surrounding the bed, a rolling bedside table with a glass of water on top. "Actually, I am doing a lot better." I tried to keep the pain from showing in my voice.

I lifted my hand, fingertips dabbing the back of my sore head. "Ouch." Hard little pieces of dried blood remained glued to individual strands of hair.

"Oh, no dear. Don't touch it." Rita clucked at me like an old mother hen.

The sharp pain reminded me of being hit by a shovel. I grimaced at the unpleasant memory and winced at the touch. Carefully sitting on the edge of the bed, I rubbed my aching back. The room spun several times, causing me to clutch onto the bed rail for stability. The smell of strong disinfectants stung my throat and made me gag. "When did you guys get here?"

Helen joined Rita at the side of the bed, her vanilla perfume wafting in the air. "We just arrived about ten minutes ago." Her faced filled with a wide smile.

Rita placed her hand on top of my white knuckled grip. "We were so worried, dear. Dr. Handsome said you are free to go home!"

Home? Home was in Washington D.C., not Shotgun, Colorado, population roughly equal to the number of people that lived in my apartment complex back home.

Scooting forward, I put both feet on the cold floor. "Don't you two ever tire of trying to set me up with Dr. Dalton? Helen, why don't you focus on giving out more of Sheriff Riddle's business cards and forget about pushing me into Ky's arms. Besides, after working as a family doctor, surgeon and coroner extraordinaire, he doesn't have time for a girlfriend."

Gazing out the window, I studied majestic mountains in the west which were visible from every window on this side of the building. Tall evergreens, light green sagebrush and aspen trees speckled the ground, intermixed with terracotta-colored boulders of all shapes and sizes. The bright blue skies dotted with puffy, white cumulus clouds provided a stunning backdrop for the majestic scene. The sun shone through the window, warming my skin.

Rita strolled over to the bedside chair, grabbed my hospital bag containing my clothes, and tossed it on the mattress. "Get dressed. It's time for us to bust you out of here. We need your help with something." The fabric of the bag made a muffled thud as it hit the bed.

I caught the awkwardly shaped bag in time to avoid being hit in the head with my shoe. "Seriously, Rita, until we fix your coordination problem, you probably should keep things on the ground. You are still showing deficits after your stroke and I haven't cleared you to launch large objects at people. If you want to return to shooting guns, skiing and biking safely, then you will wait until I discharge you from physical therapy."

I leaned forward and placed the sack between my legs. "I was struck on the back of the head with a shovel last time you needed my help. Ronald Riley had a killer swing. No pun intended." The memories of the recent event still made my head ache.

Helen groaned. "Speaking of Ronald, I wonder how his dad, Chester, is doing after Ronald shot him in the shoulder?"

Rita fluffed the pillow on the bed. "Dr. Handsome said he is sending Chester home today, too. The bullet went straight through. The surgery went smoothly. He'll be in a sling for a while, but he'll be fine. Apparently, Ronald will go to jail. After he is stable enough to travel, he'll await trial."

Rita moved to the foot of the bed, her shoes creating a suctioning sound against the linoleum floor. "We'll wait out in the hallway while you dress." Her mouth moved rapidly as she chomped on a piece of gum. She sauntered out the door with Helen close behind, her walker wheels squeaking.

I sighed, the sound echoing in the quiet room. The sweet smell of my uneaten oatmeal mixed with the aroma of fresh flowers from the bouquet on the nightstand. *Now, what will they try to convince me to do?*

After I opened my door, I saw Rita stood in the hallway with a wheelchair. The metal frame of the chair glinted in the fluorescent lights, and the vinyl seat was cool to the touch. I shook my head fervently. "No way am I getting into that thing, especially with you driving. I've taken my fair share of risks riding in your sports car. Besides, I can walk. My legs are fine." Rita, Helen, and I quickly developed a playful way of interacting with each other.

When Rita grabbed my arm, her hand felt rough and calloused as she pulled me into the seat. The jolt sent a searing pain through my head, my vision blurring for a moment.

Rita flipped down the footrest of the wheelchair. "Every patient has to leave on wheels. It's hospital policy. You would think you would know, since you work in healthcare. I promised your nurse I would handle taking you out of the building safely. I can call her over here if you insist on doing things your way. She and I go way back. You are lucky she is letting me handle you. It's one of the perks of living in a small town with a small hospital."

I turned around and glared, the headache a sudden, stabbing pain. As the pounding sensation started again, I rubbed my temples to relieve the pressure. "My job as a home health physical therapist is to teach people how to stand and move their legs. I do not force people to use wheelchairs instead."

Lifting my feet onto the leg rests, I folded my arms across my chest tightly. "Now, push, and try not to run me into any walls or doors!"

Helen scurried down the hall, matching Rita's pace.

The front wheels of her walker squeaked and wobbled,

causing the device to shimmy from side to side. "Wow, Helen, maybe you should slow down before the front tires fall off of that thing. You just had your hip replaced recently and still have to be careful. I've never seen you move so fast."

Helen didn't decrease her pace. "I've been practicing. I don't want to be left in the car with you two experiencing all of the excitement. I have been walking without the dumb thing at home. Besides, I only have about six months before the ski slopes open."

As I rolled through the hospital hallway, the sound of two women's laughter roared and caught my attention. It was a full-bellied laugh that made me smile, and I couldn't help but feel envious of their carefree attitude. The sound echoed through the halls and mingled with the constant hum of machinery.

Helen took off in their direction, waving her arm in the air. "Excuse me, sweetheart! I have something to show you." She flipped up the seat of her rolling walker, pulled out a few business cards and handed each of the women one.

A tall, young blonde woman gazed at the card and smiled. "Isn't this the sheriff? He has no shirt on—not that I am complaining. Does he know you are giving out his private information to strangers? This even has his weight, height and eye color listed." She paused and grinned at the other women. "Is this his phone number?"

Helen touched the woman on the shoulder. "The number is not his, it's mine. You call me when you're ready to get to know my handsome son. I'll make sure we introduce you two in the proper way." She pivoted and walked past us.

I enjoyed watching Helen in action. "Frankly Helen, I admire your feistiness. I knew, when I first worked with you,

you would not follow my rules. You always say Sheriff Riddle is oblivious to your shenanigans."

When we arrived at the front, Rita paused. The sliding doors opened, creating a suctioning sound as warm summer air rushed in. The smell of fresh asphalt and blooming flowers wafted through the entrance.

Rita locked the brakes on the wheelchair, leaving me on the sidewalk. "I'll get my car."

I heard the engine revving up, mixing with the chatter of birds nesting in the trees. The scent of pine and sage reminded me of hiking on the hogback, a name used by locals to describe the surrounding mountains. I inhaled deeply, enjoying the contrast to the sterile, air-conditioned environment of the hospital. The hot, bright sun instantly warmed my skin, and its rays sent a searing pain through my eyes. I shielded my face with my hand. "So, will you tell me what is so important we had to race wheelchair against walker through the hospital?"

Helen jutted her chin and pulled her shoulders back. "The Shotgun Farmer's Market. Every summer, Rita and I run a booth selling her famous peach wine and my toilet artwork."

Sensing I should let the comment go, I almost didn't ask the question. "Toilet artwork?" My shoulders elevated and tightened as I awaited her response.

Helen smiled. "You gotta see my work. I've developed quite the talent for using scrap potty seats. The hobby started when I worked for Chester at his plumbing business. He had tons of old crappers sitting around, so I got creative. I decided making them visually pleasing would be better than crowding the landfill. They actually sell pretty well, especially to the out-of-town folks."

My nose wrinkled. "If that is the case, I'm afraid to see

what else sells at your markets. I am more hesitant to find out how you could need my help. I just got out of the hospital. I'm not sure Dr. Dalton would want me gallivanting around with two crazy women."

Rita pulled up to the curb in her navy-blue sports car wearing black leather driving gloves.

As she stopped, the tires squealed on the pavement and the smell of burning rubber filled the air. Luckily, the car missed my toes by a few inches. I stood, let my head clear, feeling the dizziness subside, and slid in the back, letting Helen have the front seat. The hot leather seat burned the back of my thighs. I shifted from side to side frantically, feeling the heat radiating from the leather, and pointed to the passenger seat. "Old ladies sit in the front row." I chuckled and gestured for her to climb into the vehicle.

Rita turned around; the sound of her seat creaking echoed in the car. "That's a bold statement, coming from someone who couldn't even dodge a shovel headed for her. You would think a highly trained agent would have a special Kung Fu move to avoid being hit."

The sudden movement made my eyes twitch as I tried to follow her action. My face flushed with frustration and my body tensed, the muscles in my jaw and neck tight. The scent of vinyl protectant mixed with the faint smell of pine trees coming from the air freshener dangling from the rearview mirror. On missions, I worked with highly trained partners. Knowing their next move and reading their body language was second nature. The tone in Rita's voice showed she was joking, but her comments reminded me of the frustration I experienced with errors made in the past. "Chester distracted me. Plus, this thin mountain air slowed my reaction time and dulled my senses. I don't know how you have survived here."

Rita's smile reflected in the rearview mirror, the sun shining directly on it, making it hard to look at. She raced out of the parking lot, the car's engine roaring as we sped up. "Probably because my reflexes and senses were better than yours from the start."

"Oh, I doubt it. If so, then the stroke REALLY did you in, judging by your recent performance. I still have a vivid memory of you getting fresh with the oak brush when you and Bryce ran away from Chester's house. You almost had buckshot in your booty. The image is likely to be locked in my brain." I leaned back in my seat, proud of myself for the witty retort. "What's with the driving gloves?"

Helen snorted. "They're part of her midlife crisis. She thinks they make her look younger."

Looking around, I noticed the vehicles on the highway were SUVs or trucks. Sportscars like Rita's were uncommon, and the sound of the car's engine made it stand out even more. "I'm still waiting for the answer to my question."

Rita swerved around a turning SUV. "What question?"

The sudden movement made me feel a little dizzy.

Helen reached out to grab the dashboard. "I already asked her about the farmer's market. She got weirded out because I told her about my talent."

RITA LAUGHED. "If it bothers you, you could opt out now. The toilet seats aren't her only projects."

Helen smacked Rita's arm with the back of her hand. "Bite me, Rita. Like getting people to buy booze in this area requires effort. At least, my product has character."

Looking out the window, I saw a hawk soaring in the air above a farmer's field. Its wing span massive, making its movement appear even more graceful. "Careful. Don't distract her. She might lose track of the steering wheel with her super-quick reaction time."

Helen reached back to give a high five.

The slap on my hand stung. "Now, seriously, what are you getting me into?"

2

*H*elen rotated to face the back seat, groaning. "Our town always holds the market in Eagle Park each year. The organizers designated sections as ten-by-ten areas lettered A to O. Booth A has belonged to the Palizzi Family Farm for a long time. The family started the festival eight years ago and currently sponsors the event. They grow the best peaches in the valley, and they only bring a few bushels to each market. A few of us compete for the space next to them because the convenient location brings us certain privileges."

I shifted in my seat to face Helen directly. "Privileges? What kind?"

"After people come through the entrance, they usually stop to taste the free slices of heaven first. The sound of fruit being sliced is almost magical. They walk right by our stand after Palizzi's instead of getting distracted by other vendors and missing ours completely." Helen licked her lips. "Mmmm, I can already taste the sweet goodness and feel the sticky juices dripping down my arms."

"So, why don't you just show up early and grab the spot first?" The solution seemed obvious.

The car in front of us made a turn without using the blinker. The sound of screeching tires and the smell of burning rubber filled the air.

Rita honked, then slammed on her brakes and uttered a few curse words. "If a simple answer to our problem existed, we wouldn't need you. They assigned the locations based on selecting letters the morning of the market. We need you to help rig the drawing."

My talents were used to chase drug lords over a week ago. Thanks to Director Sanchez, I'm relegated to helping two women cheat to win a space in a market. "Exactly how will I do such a thing?" As the car rapidly resumed the previous speed, I grabbed a hold of the Oh Crap handle. My vision blurred, and my stomach performed flips.

Helen released her hold on the dashboard as the vibration of the car gradually decreased. "Lily Jankins is the one in charge of the drawings."

"ARE YOU LADIES CRAZY?" I said. "Lily's husband is the district attorney, and I'm waiting for the moment she threatens to sue us. She is still mad at us for tricking her at the Bingo Hall. I'm shocked she didn't pull off one of her ivory high heels and chuck it. Plus, her hair is so poofy, even a Texas woman would be proud."

After interacting with her, I decided, if I wanted life to go smoothly, I should avoid running into her. Her voice sounded like nails on a chalkboard, grating and nasal.

Rita scratched the back of her head. "She uses the same wicker basket every time. She never leaves the stage until the selections are complete. The committee allows her to be in charge, even though she is one of the salespeople. She says the publicity helps people form a connection between the picture they see on their carts at Grocer's Market and the actual person."

Helen scoffed. "I place my purse in front of her face every time I shop, so I don't see her judgmental mug staring back while I pick out my food. I think she cheats to win the place she wants, but I don't have proof."

Rita glanced in the rearview mirror. "We want you to replace the container with the one we put together."

My hands tugged at the seatbelt to ease the tautness; the fabric squeaked against my skin. "Why me? I just got out of the hospital. Wouldn't the wise choice be to ask Bryce to perform the switch? He knows Lily and has a connection with his friend Sydney. He can get close to the stage without Lily suspecting anything."

I had the skills to go just about anywhere without being detected, and I'd taken part in multiple missions, with injuries, without missing a beat. Helping them rig a drawing put me in the position of potentially attracting unwanted attention, especially with Rita and Helen involved. The thought made my heart race and my palms sweat, and the car's air conditioning suddenly felt inadequate.

"Slugbug!" Helen smacked Rita's arm and used her other hand to point at the oncoming car. "We've tried to convince him to help us, but he won't. He is too worried about getting caught by the mom of his major crush. He thinks he has to be in good standing with Lily to win her daughter's affection. It's pretty logical thinking, if you ask me." Helen jutted her chin and pulled her shoulders back like a proud grandma.

As I watched their interaction, I felt relieved I did not sit up front. I always lost the same car game to my dad and ended up with a sore arm. "How do you plan on getting me close enough to the platform to make the switch? Isn't the park wide open?"

Helen leaned forward in her seat. "The drawing happens at noon. A port-a-potty housed inside a small, red wooden building stands about fifteen feet west of the gazebo. Be there by a quarter to twelve and watch the area. We'll draw her away so you can grab the one she brought and replace it with this." She held up a wicker basket. "Then get out of there. We will take care of the rest."

As I held the brown wicker basket in my lap, the earthy aroma of straw and natural fibers filled my nostrils. I ran my fingers over the rough surface, feeling the grooves and bumps of the woven material. When I reached inside to grab one of the folded papers, a tiny sliver of straw pricked my skin, and I winced at the sudden pain. I brought my finger to my lips, tasting the warm, salty tang of my blood. "You think I'm hiding in a rent-a-toilet to help you guys get your section? Maybe Ronald should have hit you in the head with the shovel. You're off your ever-aging rockers!"

"You don't have to hide inside of it, silly." Helen laughed. "Stand behind the building so she doesn't see you when she walks up."

My stomach flipped at the thought. "Oh, yes. I'm sure the stench of human waste will be a lot better from the back. Rita, why don't you do it? The physical exertion would be good practice for your rehabilitation. Running to the platform would work on your agility, reaction time, and all kinds of good things."

Rita shook a finger. "No can do. If I got caught, we would lose our slot at the farmer's market for the entire year. Plus, I am part of the distraction team responsible for luring her away from the area. I already have a job." She turned and winked at Helen.

"I SAW THAT. What is inside the basket that guarantees you the spot you wanted, anyway?" I tossed the pieces around to mix them.

Rita lowered the visor. "It has all the letters but B. When I reach in, I'll be palming the one we made, and I'll make it look like I pulled it out just then."

I nodded, the muscles in my shoulder tensing. The plan seemed simple enough, but I couldn't shake the feeling of unease that settled in the pit of my stomach. From what they described, the park seemed wide open, and I didn't know how we could pull off the switch without being detected. Letting someone else plan my missions was something I never did. For exactly this reason.

Gazing out the window, I admired the beauty of the Colorado River as water crashed against boulders and leaped into the air. My muscles relaxed, and I took a cleansing breath. "What if she already uses the same tactic and two of the same letters show up?"

Helen put a finger in the air. "We thought about the possibility already. We will draw first, so she won't have time to pull any stunts."

I shook my head and rolled my eyes. "Let's back up again. Why is this section so darned important? Don't people walk through the booths to check things out? I would think, if a customer shows up to a farmer's market, he would look around."

As we drove down the bumpy road, the car jostled us back and forth, making me feel queasy. I rubbed my forehead, trying to ease the motion sickness that was creeping up on me.

"We've discovered my wine sells better if I reach the people before they make their way to the other food tents," Rita explained. "I can convince them to try a sample before they head deep into the market."

A sharp clattering sound that accompanied Rita's words startled me. I realized she was tapping her nails on the steering wheel in a nervous rhythm.

Helen cranked her head to peer around the headrest with a crooked smile, and her eyebrows raised. "What she is really saying is she gets to shove sample cups of nose-burning alcohol in their faces before they know what hit them."

Rita snickered. "Only if Helen doesn't drink all the merchandise first. People are sidetracked by the toilet seats hanging on the walls of the tent and the smell of disinfectant. I need to draw their attention somehow." Rita drove down the rocky driveway of the old log cabin and came to a stop just before the porch.

Helen slid out and opened the passenger door. "Come on, old lady. Head inside and clean up. Make sure you put on good shoes and dark clothing. This is an undercover operation."

Grabbing the door frame, I stood and patted Helen's shoulder. "You really should watch less TV, Helen. You guys will owe me for this one. See you at the park."

Beano, an Australian Shepherd with black, brown and white fur, bounded down the steps to greet me and stuck his nose firmly in my crotch. His gesture made me feel slightly violated. To add to the assault, he went behind me and wedged himself between my legs, his wagging tail making my hips sway side to side. Beano belonged to the man who worked as the caller at the local Bingo Hall. He spent an excessive amount of time at the bar below the hall, so his dog looked for attention and companionship elsewhere. My house served as an additional residence, and I considered myself his adopted parent. He'd been a good watchdog, so far.

Stepping inside the mudroom, with Beano on my heels, I dropped my bag on the floor; the contents causing a thudding sound. A faint smell of peaches and cinnamon hovered in the air from the peach crisp I ate earlier. I walked into the living room and surveyed the environment: gas stove, firewood on an iron stand, tan couch, rustic wooden coffee table and end table, and a small tv on a stand. Everything remained the same as when I was last there. Crossing the room, I checked out the kitchen before I sat on a kitchen chair and petted Beano's soft, long fur. I contemplated how much my life had changed. Last week in D.C., they assigned me the task of taking down one of Abdul's suppliers before they made their delivery of drugs. A week later, I found myself involved with two middle-aged women in a scheme to help them sell peach wine and toilet artwork. Worse yet, I actually looked forward to the excitement it might provide, even if working with Helen and Rita didn't involve protecting our country and its citizens. I inwardly chastised myself for going soft before immediately deciding I didn't care.

The director told me I would be in hiding for a while, and I was happy to have friends. I think.

3

———

*C*urious about what this new adventure might hold, I climbed the stairs to the bedroom and stepped into a warm shower. Steamy mist enveloped and caressed me, and I could feel the heat penetrating my skin. The muscles in my back and shoulders eased, feeling soft and loose under my fingertips. The pain in my head melted until it was a dull ache. A light scent of mango body wash mingled with the steam and I inhaled, enjoying the refreshing aroma. Careful not to get my wound wet, I leaned my head back and closed my eyes. Medications dispensed by the nurse at the hospital helped to eliminate my pain, giving me an immense sense of relief. The hiss of the shower spray filled my ears with a comforting sound as I savored the sensation of the warm water cascading down my face and neck.

I pulled on stretchy, black leggings that hugged my legs, a running shirt, and my favorite pair of tennis shoes, which fit my feet like a glove. I opted for comfortable clothing in order to make quick, agile movements possible, so I felt ready for whatever might come my way.

After searching the kitchen to find something to eat, I discovered a surprise Rita left me: a pot of her "world famous" green chili. The lid held a yellow sticky note which read, *Eat up. You'll need some energy.* When I lifted the top, the robust scent of pork and roasted chilis filled my nose, causing my mouth to salivate. My eyes watered from the spice of the peppers.

According to Rita, her special concoction attracted people from all over town. Locals often begged her to make them their own batch, which kept Rita busy. Rita claimed the secret to great green chili was in the type and amount of peppers used in the recipe, but no way would she share which ones.

I ladled some into a bowl and put the dish in the microwave. I stood in front of it, staring as if it was a fire-place. The sound of the machine whirring filled the room, and I couldn't wait to taste the creation. After savoring the first spoonful, I understood the local's shameless behavior. The blending of flavors tasted like a scrumptious master-piece. The heat burned my lips and mouth, so I followed each bite with a drink of water as beads of sweat formed on my forehead. I could feel the spiciness creeping down my throat, making me feel alive. Inevitably, a stomachache would follow, but I didn't mind.

At eleven-thirty, I drove the SUV over to Eagle Park. Along the way, I passed Grocer's Market placed next to a small strip of stores and eateries. The aroma of baked bread flooded the air from the adjoining bakery. In the parking lot, the cleverly named Evergreen Bank illuminated signs claiming it to be open. Retail businesses lined the single road leading through town. The local hot spots included a McDonald's, a Subway sandwich shop, and a few small, private restaurants.

Across the street from the park stood a gas station, two hair salons, a small karate dojo, and a county library. I parked at the other end of the block, next to a seedy-looking bar called The Burning Mountain Saloon.

Lily's luxury car rested against the curb and I remembered seeing it at Chester Riley's house the previous day. She did not look up from the trunk as she removed items for the farmer's market.

With no effort, I slipped behind the taxidermy shop and felt the rough bricks of the wall with my fingertips. The shop, next to the park, displayed a sign with the sentiment, You shoot 'em, we stuff em. I shook my head and rolled my eyes. Only in a small, remote mountain town. The quote reminded me of the initial shock I experienced with being taken out of D.C. and dropped on an alien planet called Shotgun, Colorado, population 4,275. While I didn't understand the locals yet, I had found two friends to help me adjust.

Peering around the building, I started surveillance of the area: train tracks on the south side but no train in sight, the squeaking of swings moving back and forth as four young children played in the park to the east, the portable toilet bordered the park to the west, an elevated gazebo with a picnic table perched in the center of the park, two grassy regions divided by a sidewalk to the north. I could smell the cut grass mixed with the scent of flowers.

With the sun warming my skin, I waited patiently for the time to establish my position behind the enclosed port-a-potty. Three wooden walls surrounded the structure, leaving the front open to the street. Their presence seemed like an attempt to make it appear more aesthetically pleasing. Checking the time on my watch, I moved swiftly and silently behind the back wall, basket in hand. The rough wood scraped against my back. I convinced myself the foul stench of feces wafting from inside its walls could not be worse than the downtown D.C. streets. Using the camera on my phone to provide me with a view of the stage, I didn't have to risk exposing myself by peering around the corner. For a moment, I imagined I was back up on the roof of a high rise in D.C., planning my next move on a mission. The muscles in my body relaxed as my ears went on high alert, listening to the multitude of sounds in the area — birds chirping in the trees, and the distant sound of traffic coming from the interstate.

As I watched, Lily strolled up the paved path to the stage wearing navy pumps and a white linen pantsuit. The fabric billowed around her legs. She placed the basket, her backpack, and designer purse on the picnic table in the center of the gazebo before sitting down on the bench.

My keen, alert ears registered the faint sound of the creaking wood as she shifted her weight.

At eleven-thirty-five, Rita and Helen sauntered up the path with Beano on a leash. Rita's steps quickened as Beano tugged tightly.

Beano, a free-spirited creature, let them put a leash on him? Whose leash did they borrow? Wonders never cease. Helen's ability to persuade many creatures to do what she wanted astounded me.

Lily's eyes widened as she watched the two women and Beano approach. Immediately, she sprang to her feet at the top of the stairs leading to the platform, her hands on her hips and her feet firmly planted. "You know no dogs are allowed in the park! What do you two think you are doing?" Her voice reverberated in the open space of the gazebo.

"The market hasn't started yet, so we thought it would be okay to bring him for a stroll." Helen bent over and removed the leash from Beano, who stared in Lily's direction.

Beano dashed to greet Lily, his paws clicking on the pavement as he closed the distance between them. He halted, his nose twitching as he sniffed the air. His attention shifted to her belongings. In one swift move, he leaped over the stairs and snatched the pack, and jumped over the railing.

The display of his agility impressed me.

Lily ran down the stairs after him, her high heels clicking on the concrete. She stumbled into a stack of realtor signs leaning against the railing, metal crashing in a loud thunder. Lily shouted from where she laid on the ground. "Stop that damn dog! He has my stuff!"

Helen rushed to Lily's side and bent down to help her return to her feet. She grabbed Lily's shoulders, pivoted her away from the stage, and pretended to brush dirt off the back of her clothes.

Lily's arms flailed as she attempted to push Helen's moving hands away from her body.

Scurrying over to the targeted destination, I performed the switch faster than Houdini. Afterwards, I slipped behind the taxidermy shop and stashed my cargo in my SUV. Mission complete. I circled back around to the front of the shop and went in through the park's entranceway, looking as if I had just come. "What happened here?" I stepped onto the grass and reached down to set up the metal signs, but retracted my hand as the hot aluminum scorched my skin. Abandoning the good deed, I joined Helen and Rita on the sidewalk. "Helen, where is your walker?"

She waved her hand in a discarding manner. "I don't need the darn thing anymore. Now, shush. I want to hear this."

The rustling sound of Lily rummaging through her purse combined with low, unintelligible utterances.

As she glared in Helen's direction, she pulled out her phone. "I'm calling the sheriff. Your dog is a menace to society."

At the moment Lily began pushing buttons, a low rumbling sound grew, followed by a startling shrill whistle, hissing steam and screeching wheels of an oncoming train. As it passed by, the smell of burning coal mixed with sulfur and oil filled the air. Children on the playground screamed louder, competing with sounds of the train.

Lily stomped her foot and dropped her arms. Her mouth moved, but the sounds of the passing train made it impossible to know what she said.

I shared a smile with Rita and Helen, the irony of the train's timing amusing.

The sound of rocks crunching came from the direction of the playground. Sheriff Riddle crossed the play area holding Beano's stolen goods. The smart, furry thief did not return, which I figured meant the sheriff sent him home.

"I assume this belongs to you." He handed Lily her slobbery bag.

She yanked the straps out of his hand. "Sheriff Riddle! Thank God! These two imbeciles brought a beast into the park. If he did any damage, I'll press charges!"

Sheriff Riddle rubbed his recently assaulted hands together. "Take it easy, Lily. Obviously, the contents included something interesting enough to draw his attention."

A smile spread across Helen's face as she leaned in close to whisper in my ear. "Like a pig's ear."

I snickered in amusement. "I'm not even asking how you put that gross thing in her backpack."

Rita simply shrugged her shoulders.

Helen adjusted her hiked shirt sleeves. "You know I have my tricks."

Lily gestured to the sign at the entrance which declared, No Dogs Allowed and cleared her throat. "Dogs aren't allowed in the park during the market. Everyone knows the rule."

Rita lifted her wrist, showing her watch. "The market hasn't started yet. You wouldn't stand a chance in court against that pup. Judge Wally loves dogs."

Sheriff Riddle strutted towards his patrol car, shaking his head.

"So, you're not doing anything about it?" Lily called out after him.

Sheriff Riddle pivoted and stopped. "No damage occurred, other than ruffling your feathers. No need to take this matter further. It's time for the drawing, anyway. We'll need our full time to set up our booths. Let's get started."

Lily scowled with a furrowed brow and gritted teeth. "Figures you would side with them." She pointed towards Helen. "She's your mom. You would never stand up to her."

After noticing a wide smile spread across Helen's face, I turned to see other vendors trickling in. They whispered amongst themselves, gesturing towards the scene before them.

Lily huffed, snatched the basket, and perched on the top of the stairs. "I need everyone's attention."

A constant buzz of voices continued, like bees in a hive. A shrill whistle rang from somewhere in the crowd. Obediently, the group fell silent.

Helen and Rita stepped to the front of the line.

Lily glared at the two women as she declared that Suzie Ballcroft, who was running a homemade beef jerky stand, would be the first to draw the market.

Rita and Helen stood aside to allow Suzie in front of them.

She silently walked up to the steps and retrieved a letter. She handed the piece of paper to Lily.

"Suzie chose section F. Next owner." Lily set the scrap on the table.

Rita glided up to Lily, her right hand clasped by her side. She dove her fingers into the pile and lifted her arm above her head, then handed the slip to Lily.

Lily looked up from the piece of paper several times before making the announcement. "Rita and Helen get booth B." Lily's shoulders sagged.

With a wrinkled brow, Lily shook the letters with force and continued the process.

Twelve more booth owners received their spots, leaving only Lily to choose.

Lily drew in a breath and retrieved the final selection. "I have M." She pulled her shoulders back and jutted her chin. "Now, let's set up our booths."

The vendors quickly got their supplies out of their vehicles and began arranging their booths in the designated spots.

Finally, Lily grabbed her bags, took one last look at the basket before she slammed it down on the picnic table, and made her way over to her section.

Helping Rita and Helen unload their goods, I marveled at why people would want to buy a toilet seat with a painting of a mountain scene. Did they really hang the crazy artwork on their walls? The smell of juicy burgers from the nearby food truck made my mouth water and distracted me from my thoughts.

While Helen and Rita set up, Lily stalked over to their booth and roughly placed her hands on the table. "I know you two rigged the drawing somehow, and I will figure out what you did." She rushed away before anyone could respond.

Rita groaned. "Is it possible Lily uses the same palming technique to win? Otherwise, how would she know we did anything? Also, who wears high heels and a white linen pantsuit to a farmer's market? She's not only a pain in the butt, but she's also not smart. She doesn't realize she has a dirty brown spot on her backside. I want to be there to watch people's faces when she walks by. Maybe her heels will sink into the grass and she'll pitch forward onto her face!"

4

---

*A*s Rita and Helen giggled at the idea of Lily being a lawn stake, I plopped in a chair to watch all the organized chaos.

"You must be Ally," a stranger called from the nearby Palizzi Farm Stand, the name displayed on a truck with pictures of peaches and tomatoes.

A woman in her forties, with auburn hair and a slim, fit build, smiled from behind a table. "I am. And you are?" I stood and walked over to the edge of the booth.

"I'm Janie Palizzi. This stand belongs to my family. I've heard a lot about you from my friends. Welcome to town." Janie reached out to shake hands.

The firmness of her grip gained my immediate respect. "Nice to meet you, Janie! Hopefully, what your friends told you is not all bad stuff. I've only been in town less than a week." I pointed a thumb at Helen and Rita. "You can get a reputation pretty quickly associating with these two people."

Janie chuckled and nodded. "You should be careful with the company you keep."

Rita came over to join the conversation, carrying a bottle of her peach wine. "You will sell us the first two bushels of peaches today as your punishment for sassing off."

Janie began pulling tomatoes out of a box and setting them on the table. "I'll sell you what you want, but you'll have to wait. We put the peach boxes in the truck first, against the cab, in order to keep them safe from harm."

Rita opened the first bottle. "Oh, I can wait, and I'll even give you a sample of my peach wine. Maybe you'll give me a great price if you're a little tipsy."

The contents smelled like peach-flavored moonshine and made the hairs on my arms stand up.

Janie shivered. "I'm not easy, Rita. You'll have to save your tactic for your unsuspecting lovers."

I laughed, placing my hands on knees. "She's retired from dating. I think she's actually on disability."

Rita stuck her tongue out at us and resumed setting up her booth.

I placed my hand to my mouth, blew Rita a kiss, and then shifted my attention to Janie. "What did you hear about me?"

After Janie pulled a rotting tomato from the pile, she tossed it in a box. "You pulled off a miraculous rescue of Sydney Jankins from crazy Ronald Riley. They say you were amazingly brave."

I grimaced. *So much for keep a low profile.* "I don't know if what I did qualifies as remarkable. Rita is the one who knows how to handle a gun. She helped to save all of us."

Rita slowly turned her head, her eyes narrowing. Her gaze pinned us in a place like a butterfly to a display board. She had worked as an FBI agent on a potential homicide investigation before her stroke, and stuck around Shotgun for recovery before retiring. No one around here seemed to know Rita's past.

Janie tucked a strand of hair behind her ear. "Well, I guess I should hang out with you ladies more often. I'd feel a lot safer."

I leaned in. "What's there to worry about? This area is pretty secure, isn't it?"

Janie bowed her head, pursed her lips and cast her eyes downwards. "I thought so, but someone being chopped up and put into trash bags doesn't seem very safe. Crimes are more common here than we realize." Janie glanced over her shoulder towards an older couple working on unloading boxes.

The man appeared weathered and wore a cowboy hat, jean overalls, and a pair of well-used cowboy boots. His gray hair peeked out of the back of his hat, and he had a chiseled jawline which made him look stern. The woman, most likely in her seventies, wore skintight jeans and a pink lace shirt which hugged her breasts firmly. Her clothes gave the impression of someone not wanting to appear her age.

A man talked to the lady but did not assist with unloading the boxes. His belly hung over his pants and he had shoulder-length, unkempt blonde hair.

I tilted my head in their direction. "Are those people your parents?"

"The two working are my dad, Alvin, and my stepmom, Margaret. The other guy is my stepbrother, Seth Talis. My dad owns the farm. It's been in his family for three generations. After my mom died about thirty-two years ago, he married Margaret."

"Sorry to hear about your mom. The loss must have been very difficult. If you don't mind my asking, are you and Margaret close?"

Janie shook her head rapidly, frowning. "Not at all. She and Dad don't live in the same household. She didn't want to give up her place."

"They never shared the same house after marrying? At all?" I tried not to sound demeaning.

Janie periodically glanced over her shoulder. The strumming of guitar strings sounded in the distance as a band member tuned his instrument across the park.

Janie periodically glanced over her shoulder. "She insisted on maintaining her independence. It's a weird situation."

Her living environment seemed interesting and unique. "I'm glad you pointed out the obvious details first, so I don't have to sound rude. I guess the situation was awkward for you kids, since she was your stepmom but didn't live in the same household to help raise you. Some stepchildren would consider the setup a great situation. Your dad had a companion, and you guys didn't have to be with her all the time. Where did her kids stay?"

Janie rolled her eyes, her fingers fiddling with leaves from the tomato vine. "You mean where DO they stay? Seth and Troy still live in her house. My brother Greg and I are the only kids who stayed at dad's house. We both moved out at an appropriate age."

I shifted to the other leg and crossed my arms over my chest. "Math is not my major strong suit, but aren't they in their forties or fifties by now?"

"They have a simple life, so they won't move. They don't pay rent or buy groceries and can come and go as they please."

After stepping closer to her booth, I checked to see if Janie's parents had moved. "Don't they have wives or husbands?"

Janie pursed her lips. "Nope."

My eyebrows lifted as I shook my head. "I can't imagine dating anyone who still lives with their parents at their age. The situation would be a total turnoff."

"Her two boys dated, but their girlfriends didn't stick around for long." Janie stepped closer and leaned in. "Margaret has an interesting personality. She is very particular about things. Since he met her, my dad has let her run the show."

Before I responded, I contemplated why Janie chose me to divulge private family history. I tilted my head to the side. "If they are so different, why would he stay married all of this time if they are so different?"

"My husband, David, and I wondered the same thing for years. We joke sometimes that she knows something about his past and uses the information to blackmail him into staying married. Each time we talk about it, we come up with different scenarios. I know saying so sounds crazy, but their relationship is anything but conventional."

The clattering of a stack of toilet seats falling over interrupted our conversation.

After spinning towards Helen, I slowly shook my head and rotated back towards Janie. "What could she possibly know that would make him stay with such a unique woman?"

Janie placed the box she emptied under the table. "I don't know. I can't imagine him doing anything like committing a crime or keeping a dark secret. He's a simple gentleman farmer." Janie giggled and resumed speaking with wide eyes. "I hope I don't find out I'm actually adopted, and he doesn't want me to know. Sometimes, when I am pondering why he is with her, I let my mind consider crazy things."

I wondered if Janie thought I could give her the answer, which would make her relax. "What does your brother, Greg, think about all of this?"

"Greg works as a beer sales rep and travels. He gets frustrated with our family situation and stays away to keep from getting irritated. He suspects Margaret might be after my dad's land." Janie peered over her shoulder again.

Margaret moved toward the front of the booth with a stack of boxes on a hand truck. They unloaded boxes of fruit, cucumbers, more tomatoes, and other vegetables onto the tables.

The sweet smell of peaches made my mouth salivate. Instantly, I knew why Helen and Rita fought so hard for booth B.

Janie's stepbrother set up a lawn chair next to the truck and plopped down to watch while the others worked.

Margaret stopped briefly. "Hey Janie, can you help us load the tables?"

I noticed she didn't make the same request of her son, lazing in a chair and watching without lifting a finger to help the family.

Janie's shoulders drooped. "Gotta go help. Maybe, once we finish setting up, you and I can chat a little more."

Stepping back, I smiled. "I would like to talk more. Is there anything I can do to help?"

Janie shook her head. "Thanks for the offer, but Margaret would allow no one else to touch the product. She says she likes to do the work herself."

After watching Janie join her parents, I returned to where Rita and Helen worked. "How are you two ladies doing with setting up the liquor and crazy art store?"

Helen held up a seat with a painting of a bear. "Hilarious, and yes, we're just about done. I see you met Janie Palizzi."

Browsing their tent, I looked at the different scenes painted on the toilet seats—fish in a river, a meandering snake, deer in a meadow. "She seems really nice. She has an interesting family life."

Rita laid out a row of plastic sample cups. "I think you've made an accurate assessment. Who weds someone they supposedly love and then doesn't want to live in the same household? I know I sound like a hypocrite, but at least I decided against getting hitched altogether, rather than stringing a man along."

Reaching forward, I straightened one of the toilet seats. "It might make sense if Alvin is a wealthy man, but in my experience, most farmers aren't rich."

Helen assembled a white easel at the front corner of the booth. "Alvin is land rich. The Palizzis own property in various locations in our area. He also has mineral rights on his property and gets royalty checks from the oil companies each month. With all the recent development taking place in the region, his farm is worth three times more than when he inherited it. Also, he is a hard-working man who doesn't have time to spend his earnings. They go back into the farm except, I'm sure, for what Margaret spends camouflaging her age." Helen placed a small stool in front of the easel. "As if we don't see through all the layers she uses to cover up her flaws."

Helen, the queen of gossip. "How do you two know so much about this situation?"

As people entered through the gate, the sound of people laughing and talking grew louder. The smell of sweet and salty treats being prepared intensified. Kids squealed as they raced each other down the slide on the playground.

Rita looked up from her products. "It's a small town. If you want to know as much as we do, go back to the Bingo Hall. You'll learn all kinds of interesting things. Okay. Here we go." She retrieved a bottle of wine, opened the screw top, and poured into a row of sample cups. She snatched a few and rushed around to the front of the booth to offer them to potential customers.

Knowing Helen and Rita would provide an entertaining show, I grabbed a chair and placed the seat in a spot with the best view.

---

5

*R*ita interacted with each individual who perused her booth and took advantage of the free alcohol samples she offered. She called each one by name, a true master at her craft, as she convinced passers-by to purchase the elixir with its powerful scent.

Meanwhile, Helen sat on the stool in front of the easel with a white, clean toilet seat hanging from clamps. "I like to paint mountain scenes live, so the onlookers can witness my brilliance in action."

Interestingly, she made the process look fun and displayed a decent amount of talent. I leaned forward in my chair, wrinkling my nose at the smell of disinfectant coming from the toilet seats. "Next, maybe you could start doing family portraits instead of mountain scenes. It would give a whole new meaning to 'sitting' to have your picture painted."

She looked up from her project with a crinkled forehead, one eyebrow raised. "Actually, it's not a bad idea. I'll consider your suggestion."

Proud of the wit I displayed, I couldn't help but wonder if my comment went straight over Helen's head.

I looked at the small crowd gathered around Helen as my cell phone chimed in my pocket. The ringing came from the burner phone, which Director Sanchez issued for calls from the agency. "Hello?" I stepped away from the tent and found a private place for a conversation.

"Agent Evans, it's Cunningham. Just calling to check on how things are going in the colorful state of Colorado."

Cunningham, using my real last name, temporarily caught me off guard. I looked around before speaking. "Other than being dragged into schemes created by two crazy women to win drawings, I'm fine. Did you call to give me the good news? Can I return home?"

"Not yet. An unknown party hit a boat with a supply of cocaine Abdul had on route. Our sources say he and Fahid think the guilty person is you. Stay low. Our contact said they recruited some gangbangers from New York to join in the search for you."

Great! Abdul's influence reaches farther than I realized. I sighed and stomped my foot. "The best way to fight against an enemy is to get to them before they get to you. I feel like a sitting duck here. If you let me come back to D.C., I'll take care of this."

"You're a skilled agent, Evans. I can't afford to lose you. You will remain in Colorado. We'll contact you if we hear anything more. Director Sanchez is working on finding out who hit the boat so we can track where our intel went wrong. We'll be in touch."

He hung up before I could ask additional questions.

I stood for a moment, wrapping my brain around remaining in Colorado longer, feeling desperation followed by relief. The tension in my shoulders released as a thought occurred: I had Rita and Helen to help me survive. With the experiences so far, I knew life wouldn't be boring.

I wandered over to the booths to find Rita and Helen working to sell as much product as possible, like army ants bringing leaves back to their hill. Preoccupied with their business, the two women didn't acknowledge my return. I sauntered over to Janie's area, hoping to finish the conversation we started earlier.

She saw me approaching and stuck her index finger in the air. Janie packaged the woman's vegetables in a paper bag and met me halfway between the booths.

The sun beat down on my shoulders. "How are the sales going?"

Janie wiped the sweat off of her brow. "We always do well at this market. The townspeople love our peaches. Not to toot my own horn, but we have the best fruit in the state. The juices run down their forearms when they take a bite and they have to swallow a lot to keep from choking. They have to eat as fast as possible before the pit slips between their fingers. People end up sticky, but satisfied."

I turned my head to see Seth resting in the same position near the truck. He appeared to have fallen asleep while all the hard work took place without him. As I watched him, I had a familiar feeling of uneasiness, like being punched in the gut. Trusting my instincts during the many missions assigned by the agency became paramount to my success. Rarely was I wrong, so I continued to watch.

Janie still bragged about their produce, not looking to see what caught my attention.

As I watched Seth's body for signs of movement, I barely listened. "Hey Janie, I think Seth is doing a little more than sleeping."

She turned her head and shrugged her shoulders. "I'm

sure he is just snoozing. He is one of the laziest men I know. Margaret didn't force him to work around the house. Heck, he hasn't even had a job for five years. She always boasts she takes care of her boys."

"Maybe we should double-check. Just in case we are wrong." I already moved in his direction. "His chest hasn't risen in over sixty seconds." I stood next to his chair and put a hand on his shoulder.

His body pitched forward and fell to the ground with a thud.

Janie yelped and took a step back.

Margaret and Alvin glanced over from the booth and rushed to Seth's side, with Helen and Rita following on their heels.

Margaret rolled Seth onto his back. She gave his face several quick slaps. "Seth! Seth wake up!" She looked up at Alvin. "His skin is burning up!"

I reached from the side and felt for his pulse. Present, but sluggish. I glanced at Rita and Helen. "Call nine-one-one." As I assessed his status, he opened his eyes, turned his head to the side, and vomited. Jumping back to avoid being soaked by the vile liquid, I rolled him onto his side to prevent choking. Beads of sweat speckled his pale skin. The stench of feces filled the air.

Margaret sprang up and dashed away, crying and grabbing at her stomach.

Rita dialed for emergency services from her phone.

Within less than ten minutes, I heard a siren wailing closer as I continued to monitor his signs.

Seth spoke, but the words he used were unintelligible.

The ambulance arrived, and the paramedics rushed to Seth's body.

I stepped back to give them space to work and noticed Janie standing by her dad.

They both waited without speaking, embraced in each other's arms while watching the paramedics do their jobs.

People from nearby booths stopped what they were doing and murmured amongst themselves. Even the band stopped playing, making the park seem eerie, a stark contrast to just minutes ago.

I tried to make sense of what had happened as the medics loaded him into the ambulance.

Janie's eyes were wide, her jaw dropped, and her eyebrows lifted. "What do you think happened?"

I shrugged and shook my head. "I'm not sure at this point. His symptoms are typical of many conditions. Do you know if he had any health issues?"

Janie stepped closer. "Not that I'm aware of. He's not the best at taking care of himself, but Margaret feeds him home-cooked meals instead of junk food. I don't know any details about his health, since we weren't raised in the same home."

Margaret approached, her gaze darting and her head swiveling. "I'm going over to the hospital. Janie, you and Alvin clean up when the market is over and meet me at Shotgun Memorial. Make sure you count the money before you leave so we don't lose track of today's sales."

Alvin spun to face his wife. "Margaret, honey, we'll just close early and go to the hospital now. Whatever is happening to Seth is more important."

Shaking her head, Margaret placed her hands on her hips and planted her feet shoulder-width apart. "Stay and finish the market. We could make more money for this crop before it goes bad, and we need to earn as much as possible."

Stunned at her reaction to the situation, I resolved to ask

Rita and Helen questions about the Palizzi Family when I had a chance. When the market finished, I helped Janie and Alvin put the remaining vegetables and fruit in boxes and load them on the truck.

Janie closed the gate to the truck, the hinges squeaking in protest. "Ally, can you come to the hospital with dad and I? Since you work in healthcare, you'll know the right questions to ask."

Stepping closer, I put my hand on Janie's shoulder. "Of course. I'll help in any way I can."

Something about this situation makes little sense. Halleluiah. Another chance to draw attention to myself as I try to figure it out.

6

I entered Shotgun Community Hospital, eager to learn more about Seth's collapse.

An elderly volunteer who shuffled slowly, the sound of her shoes swishing against the linoleum, ushered us all to room fifteen.

Dr. Dalton, who shined a light in Seth's eyes, looked up at us and waved. He stepped outside of the room. "I didn't know you knew the Palizzi family."

He grabbed my hand between both of his.

After I noted Margaret's absence, my thoughts shifted as Dr. Dalton squeezed my hand gently for longer than I expected. Warmth coursed through my face. I hoped he didn't notice. "Janie and I just met at the farmer's market. I went with Rita and Helen to help them with their booth."

Dr. Dalton grinned. "So, they introduced you to overly potent peach wine and alternative toilet artwork. Sounds like you are really getting to know the area." His smile changed to a frown as he reached over and shook Alvin's hand. "Alvin. It's good to see you. Come on in, and we'll go over what we found so far."

Dr. Dalton placed his hand at the small of my back to guide me through the door. Instinctively, the muscles in my arms and legs tightened, my fists clenched. In my line of work, a man who touched my back, uninvited, ended up with his arm twisted behind his back and his face slammed into a wall. *Relax Ally. He is not a threat. He is just being polite. Besides, he smells so enticing.*

Seth laid on the bed with an IV in his right arm, oxygen tubing in his nose, and a blood pressure cuff attached to his left arm. His face looked pale; his respiration rate was low. Beeps and humming came from the vitals machine.

The sounds felt familiar and my stomach muscles tightened.

Once everyone crowded the room, Dr. Dalton picked up Seth's chart. "We've done a series of exams on Seth and, to be honest, have found nothing conclusive. We are working to rule out a possible stroke or neurological condition. The problem could also be some sort of poisoning, although I am not sure what type would cause his exact symptoms. We won't know more until all of our results come back. We'll keep him overnight to run more tests. He is fairly stable right now, but he is definitely not out of the woods."

Margaret entered the room, chocolate bar and chips in her hand. "What is everyone doing in Seth's room?" She turned to Alvin. "This is too many people in one room."

Alvin's mouth dropped, and his eyes widened. "We are checking to see how he is doing and to give him our love. What's wrong with us being here, honey?"

Margaret set the snacks down and moved around to the side of Seth's bed to adjust his sheets and blankets. "He doesn't need all of this attention. He's sick. If you make him more stressed, his body will have a hard time fighting against whatever ails him." She raised her top lip and gritted her teeth at Dr. Dalton. "What kind of hospital is this? As a doctor, you should know these distractions are not good for an ill patient!"

Dr. Dalton pushed a button on the vitals machine. "Visitors can help elevate a patient's mood, Margaret. I just gave them an update on his condition. Alvin is his stepfather and should be involved in his care."

Tears welled as she stepped closer to Dr. Dalton. "I'm worried about my son. I would like you to keep his room quiet and calm. Also, I don't want you distracted from figuring out what is wrong with my boy."

Dr. Dalton took a small step forward with his chest puffed. "Margaret, I know you are concerned, but Alvin is one of his parents. He needs to know what's happening."

Margaret looked in Alvin's direction. "Well, I need to know what you told them. Seth deserves his privacy."

Janie moved to Alvin's side. "Margaret, Dad did what you told him and brought us to the hospital. You asked for us to come. I think, if the cause of his illness is poisoning, we should all know. We can look for the source and protect everyone else from getting sick, too."

Margaret's head whipped around to face Dr. Dalton, her eyes wide. "You told them he was poisoned? Why would you say something so ludicrous? You told me his symptoms might show a stroke or a nerve problem."

Dr. Dalton closed his eyes and took a deep breath, exhaling slowly. His words came out deliberately and steadily. "Listen, Margaret. As a doctor with a lot of experience and education, I use a process called differential diagnosis." His words came out slowly and steadily. "This means I consider all possibilities which would cause his symptoms. Poisoning is one explanation."

Margaret spun on her heels to face the group and

pointed to the door. "Can you all please go? Taking care of Seth and dealing with all of you is too much."

Alvin didn't respond as he rushed towards the door and left the room.

Jumping to the side, I avoided being hit by his shoulder. Clearly, Alvin was used to Margaret taking control. I assumed he had seen this display many times in the last twenty years. I walked to the exit of the hospital with Janie following close behind. I knew if I verbalized my thoughts, my words would seem judgmental, so I kept my mouth shut. I needed to talk with Rita and Helen about the day's events. I knew they would already be at my house by the time I arrived home.

As I rolled up my driveway, I spotted Rita's sports car and a black pickup truck I didn't recognize. I stepped into the house, expecting to see a stranger sitting with Rita and Helen. My senses registered a familiar, pleasing scent just before Beano's cold, wet nose bumped my hand.

Helen and Rita sat alone at the kitchen table.

Scratching Beano behind the ear, I scanned the room. "Whose pickup is by your precious midlife crisis car?"

A timer beeped. Helen jumped up, scurried to the oven, and pulled out a dish. "The truck is mine. I can finally step onto the floorboard if I use a stool. I keep one in the back of the truck, so I have the handy tool wherever I go."

"You? I can't imagine you driving such a large vehicle." I went to the stove to see what she took from the oven. "Whatever you made smells fantastic! Is that what I think it is?"

Helen removed the foil. "It's a peach crisp. I remembered you said this is one of your favorites."

The aroma of peaches, cinnamon, and oats wafted through the air, causing my mouth to salivate.

Helen placed three servings on plates and distributed

them around the kitchen table. "I used some of our score from the Palizzi Farm Stand today. I told you major benefits exist when you get booth B at the market." She placed three servings on plates and distributed them around the kitchen table.

I closed my eyes after my first bite to enjoy the taste more. The fruit melted in my mouth, combining with the sugar and cinnamon. When I opened my eyes, I connected with both Rita's and Helen's stares. "What are you two looking at? I don't eat homemade food very often. When on missions, I dine out all the time. I'm savoring every moment of this."

Rita scraped the plate with her fork and shoved it in her mouth. "We've been waiting for the appropriate time before bombarding you with our questions. Helen came up with the idea. I wouldn't have hesitated at all. I want the information now."

I laughed. "I actually love that about you, Rita. You're a no-nonsense kind of woman. Where should I start?"

Rita looked at Helen and winked. "Start with what made Seth pitch onto his face and then throw up."

"Wow! No fluff needed, huh?" I took a second bite, wishing I had time to enjoy the flavors silently.

Rita licked her lips. "Seth is not really a likeable guy."

"Dr. Dalton, Ky, said he is looking at stroke, neurological deficit, or poisoning as the differential diagnoses," I said.

Rita and Helen smiled at each other from across the table.

Rolling my eyes, I shook my head. "Why are you both grinning like children? Did you already know what he suspected?"

Helen laid her fork across the plate. She dabbed her

mouth with a napkin. "We are happy you and Dr. Handsome are on a first name basis."

After rising from the table, I put my plate in the sink and leaned against the counter. The matchmaking attempts will never cease. "Look, we need to focus. Are we talking about Seth or not?"

Helen held up her hands. "All right, relax. I got lost after the word Ky. Could you please explain what you said in plain English?"

"He either had a stroke, a problem which relates to the nervous system, or he was poisoned. Ky, I mean, Dr. Dalton, said he was still running tests and didn't have a definite answer yet. He is keeping him stable for now."

Rita squinted her eyes and cocked her head to the side. "Poisoned. On accident or by someone else?"

I paused for a few moments before answering. "That's the big question here. If it wasn't an accident, then we're dealing with a case of attempted murder. Janie is a sweet person—I don't want her and her family to be in any kind of danger. Do you know anyone who might have a reason to poison Seth?"

7

*H*elen scooted her chair from the table. "I'm sure he ticked off many people in his life. Even though he has already made enemies in the past, he still engages in betting at the pool hall. From what I heard; he owes Reggie Nelson a large sum of money from previous losses. Everyone knows Reggie is not a patient guy."

Walking back to the table, I placed my hands on the table and leaned in. "How would poisoning Seth get him his money? A dead man doesn't pay his debts."

Helen shrugged. "Reggie concerns himself more with his reputation than money. If he let Seth get away with not settling his obligation, he risks losing the status he gained over many years. What kind of poison does the doc suspect?"

Plopping down in the chair, I admitted, "I don't know. He doesn't have a clear idea of what substance could make him sick so fast. As of now, I have very little information. All I know is Margaret got really upset when Dr. Dalton gave us the details. It seems like she wants to push away those who are trying to help her. It surprised me she acted anxious about Janie and Alvin finishing their work at the market and making money. Most moms would drop everything to rush their kid to the hospital, but Margaret wanted them to keep working."

Dishes clinked together as Helen gathered the rest of the plates from the table and took them to the sink.

Helen spun on her heels. "To be honest, I don't understand Margaret or the decisions she makes. She definitely likes to be in control of her environment. Perhaps her orders were a way of subduing the shock she felt. From what I know, she comes from an affluent family with money which was willed to her by her father. There's no desperation or poverty in her life." Helen paused for a moment before continuing. "Does their relationship have any substance when they don't live together? She seems to make Alvin do whatever she wants. We can only assume the reason is she's great in bed or something else is going on that we can't figure out."

Wow! The conversation took a fast turn. "Given the details I received so far, I understand Margaret's personality is one of a demanding person, but she cares about her boys deeply."

Rita wiped crumbs from the table onto the floor. "We think Troy and Seth turned out the way they did because of the way she treated them. They have no reason to live anywhere else. They come and go as they please and don't pay Margaret for food or rent."

"I think the reason is they know they will inherit a lot of dough if they stick around," Helen interjected. "Alvin's estate is substantial. When he dies, the property and money automatically transfer to Margaret as the surviving spouse. When she writes her will, she'll make sure her kids receive the bulk of the funds."

As the unfairness of the situation registered in my brain, my jaw dropped. "Can't Alvin create a document which designates certain estates, like the farm, to Janie and her brother, Greg?"

Helen shook her head. "Janie tried to convince Alvin to make a more specific will for years. He did nothing because Margaret talked him out of it. Since Alvin is getting older, Janie and her husband, David, offered to sell their house and move into Alvin's basement to take care of him. It's an 8,400 square foot house, and the basement is 4,000 more. The lower level has a separate entrance and its own kitchen. They could live there and still have their independence, as a married couple, and take care of Alvin. The space needs some work, but Janie says they would use the profit from the sale of their house to upgrade the basement. Doing so would allow them to be there to watch over Alvin and keep him safe. Margaret feels as though she can take care of Alvin herself."

A woman marrying into a family and ripping an inheritance away from the children is the recipe for future war. If I were Janie and David, I'd figure out a way to change the circumstances before Alvin passes away. "Didn't someone tell me Troy and Seth live in Margaret's house?"

Helen retrieved plastic wrap from inside a drawer and covered the leftover desert. "They sure do. Apparently, she can have her kids live with her, but Alvin cannot do the same. Janie's and Greg's names were listed as beneficiaries on the farm when their mom was alive. Janie, David and Greg think, since the property is now deeded joint tenancy with rights of survivorship, the land would still go to Margaret first."

Rita groaned. "I told them not to give up on convincing

Alvin. I've heard of many cases where tenants end up with squatters' rights."

A dog barked in the distance, distracting me briefly. "What are squatters' rights?"

Rita scooted away from the table and crossed her legs. "There have been owners who lease their property to someone who stops taking care of the place and ceases to honor the agreement. The landlord has a hell of a time evicting them because the laws favor the renters. I've heard of people living in a residence, without paying, and really trashing the place. The homeowner can't do a darn thing to get the deadbeats out. My thought is, if Janie and David already lived on the farm, getting them to leave could be harder for Margaret, since they would occupy the space. Their proximity to Alvin would give them time to change Alvin's mind about the will."

Leaning forward, I rested on my elbows. "I can't fathom why Alvin would leave Margaret in charge of his matters. He seems like a fairly intelligent man."

"We concur," Rita added. "We don't understand what is going on, either. Janie, David and Greg are concerned about the whole thing."

My gaze met Helen's. "None of them seem like a person who would want to hurt someone. Of course, I don't really know them, but I am familiar with how people behave when there is a large sum of money at stake. Greed can corrupt even the best people."

Helen's shoulder drooped. "Janie and David are decent people. I can't envision them harming an insect. Greg is a successful salesman, and he adores Janie immensely. Although it pains me to say, if I were in a similar scenario, I would strive to protect my inheritance no matter what."

"When the issue is money, even the nicest people

change. Considering my conversation with Janie at the market, it wouldn't surprise me if Greg has always had to protect Janie from Margaret's sons." Sighing, I reached my arms overhead and arched my back. "Well, I don't know about you two, but the peach crisp satisfied my belly enough to make me sleepy. Let's talk about this more tomorrow. My head is pounding again."

Rita yawned. "Me, too. We should all go to bed soon. We need to find a suitable spot for the fishing derby tomorrow, anyway."

As I stood, the words slowly registered in my brain. "The fishing derby? Why do I have the sense you two have more craziness planned?"

Helen rose and pushed her chair in. "Don't be so paranoid. We'll just be having fun. We already bought you an entrance ticket. You, Rita, Dr. Handsome, and I are all on the same team! We'll come by at eight-thirty a.m. to pick you up. Don't forget to put on sunscreen. It's easier to end up looking like a lobster in the mountains because you are closer to the sun. We'll see you then."

Rita and Helen rushed to the door, slamming it behind them.

I didn't get the chance to object to their plans. Grabbing both cell phones, I climbed the stairs to change into pajamas. My lack of skills and knowledge of fishing gave me anxiety. Add in the fact I would make a fool of myself in front of Ky. The last time Rita and Helen took me fishing, I ended up in the river, swimming in frigid waters because of Rita's poor boat driving skills. I assumed Rita and Helen forgot about the entire scene when they volunteered me to take part in a public fishing event. I would remind them about the mistake later.

After placing my nine on the nightstand, I pulled back

the covers and crawled into bed. Something soft brushed up against my leg. Bounding out of bed, I let out a high-pitched scream. Snatching my nine, I rolled once and came to my feet just under the light switch. I pointed my weapon at the bed and flipped on the light.

Unphased by all the chaos, Barley, my newly adopted cat, spun around in circles and curled up into a ball.

"How did you break in here? I put a screen on the window last week." I walked over and petted Barley's silky black fur.

He purred and rolled around, too lazy to stand.

"Of course. Helen and Rita. Those two will hear an earful tomorrow. You almost got shot!" I crawled in next to him and let the comforting sensation of stroking his smooth coat calm me. I enjoyed having him as a companion. The last time I owned a pet was as a child, and I missed having one around.

As I laid in bed, willing my body to relax, I thought about how to convince Rachel Roos, the executive assistant to Director Sanchez, to give me information about the location of Abdul's hired crew. If they made progress with finding me, I needed to be prepared.

8

I woke with a start when I realized I'd forgotten to set an alarm, and I had only thirty minutes to get ready. I sprang up in bed and searched my bedroom. Expecting to find Barley lazing on my queen-size bed with a pale blue and white quilt or sitting on top of my rustic nightstand or dresser, I found he was nowhere in sight. I eventually discovered him downstairs at the back door, patiently waiting to be let outside. I opened the door and gave him one last stroke down his back to the tip of his tail.

He meowed softly as he glided across the dirt towards the barn.

To avoid a repeat of the unfortunate "face plant in the river" incident, I dressed in layers. I chose a pair of canvas shorts, a quick-drying synthetic shirt, and some sandals with straps. To protect against possible rain, I added a light jacket and a pair of lightweight waterproof pants to my outfit. After Rita dumped me into the river, I got stuck wearing my soggy clothes to Chester Riley's house. So, this time, I prepared in advance to make sure I didn't repeat the same mistake.

Once downstairs, I chose a hat and sunglasses to protect my eyes, no matter the position of the sun. Attire picked out; I contemplated bringing a book because I knew fishing would be sinfully boring.

Multiple birds chirped in the trees just outside the kitchen window, like a well-rehearsed orchestral performance. I searched the kitchen for something to eat, my sandals squeaking with each step. As I scanned the empty cupboards and the leftovers in the refrigerator, I heard the roar of a vehicle rolling up the driveway. The sound of gravel crunching slowed and eventually stopped.

Rita and Helen briskly walked through the front door with coffee and banana nut bread from Coffee Hut.

I breathed in the aroma of coffee beans mixed with sweat cream and let out a sigh. "Thanks! I didn't realize Shotgun had a Coffee Hut."

Helen handed me a cool, iced drink. "Shotgun doesn't. I already went to Defiance today to buy some worms, lures, and bait. I figured you probably hadn't taken time to shop, so I brought you caffeine and breakfast."

Defiance, a neighboring town, held the local Bingo Hall where we played last week. The place provided a venue for town gossip to thrive.

Taking a sip of the cold liquid goodness, I let it slide down my throat. "You're right. I need to find time to restock because I am out of almost everything. I was just about to decide between leftover green chili and peach crisp for breakfast. Honestly, I try not to buy too much, just in case the director calls to tell me it's time to return to D.C. So, where is this derby taking place?"

Helen finished chewing a bite of banana nut bread before answering. "It's at Angler Lake. We need to leave now. Rita and I like to save the spot next to a fallen aspen tree.

The branches provide shade, and the fish hang out in a spot under the root system."

After taking a large bite of my slice of bread, I had to take a moment to finish chewing before speaking. "You guys are particular when it comes to taking part in events. First, we had to sit up front at Bingo. Then, you had to win booth B at the farmer's market. Now, we need a specific spot at a specific time by the lake." I gazed out the front window towards the driveway. "Where is Dr. Dalton? I thought he belonged on our team?"

Rita started towards the front door. "He's meeting us there because he usually goes mountain biking in the morning when he is not at the hospital. He'll ride his bike over. Let's go. We're taking my car."

Angler Lake, located in the middle of a residential area, had a full parking lot of cars and trucks. I marveled at how many people showed up for the event. I never imagined something like fishing could draw so many people out of their homes. A small bridge covered a creek, feeding the body of water. Adults, kids, grandmas, and grandpas milled about. Some children played tetherball just a short distance away from the water. The shrills of small, excited voices filled the air. Others ran with their dogs in the manicured grass nearby. The participants had their small areas set up next to the lake, with lawn chairs, coolers, umbrellas, and hibachi grills. Clearly, the derby ranked as an important town event.

Helen and Rita strutted over to the fallen aspen tree and began setting up.

A light breeze carried the smell of fish and slimy moss through the air. I inconspicuously scanned the crowd to see if I spotted Ky, but I had to be subtle in my search. I unfolded a chair and set the legs on a flat patch of dirt. "What exactly is a fishing derby?"

Helen unfolded her chair with a flick of the wrist. "It's basically just an event which allows people who like to fish a way to enjoy the sport together. Our town awards a prize to whoever catches the first one and another for the biggest trout. I've won for the last two years." Helen puffed up her chest.

Rita picked up some old fishing line left there by a previous untidy angler and placed the waste in her bag. "I'm pretty sure, if you check her cooler, you'll find a good-sized fish she bought from the grocery store. She always manages to hook one when I'm using the port-a-potty. It's a little too coincidental."

Helen turned towards Rita and placed her hands on her hips. "Listen here, you old windbag. I beat you fair and square. You can't blame me because you always drink too much beer and have to go to pee. Next time, you should bring your adult diaper so you don't have to leave. Then, you can witness a true fisherwoman in action." She plopped down in her seat.

Other participants trickled in and set up their equipment. The open spaces surrounding the lake quickly filled with people.

"Arguing already? I think you have set a new record."

I whirled around to see Ky in a tight-fitting blue bicycle jersey, padded black bicycle shorts, and cleats. He held his helmet in his hand, along with his fishing pole.

Helen looked up and smiled. "Hi, Dr. Handsome. Glad you didn't crash your bicycle so you could join us. We brought an extra seat for you to use. Do you want a brew?"

"Thanks, but not yet." He set his helmet down and squirted water from a bottle into his mouth. "I need to drink water first before getting into the hard stuff. I just got off of the mountain." He assembled his fishing rod within seconds.

Ky performed the task with ease and efficiency. Trying not to stare, I reached down and picked up my rod, spinning the rig around in my fingers. "Since you obviously know what you are doing, can you help me get my pole ready? This is only the second time I've fished, and the last time didn't go so well."

Rita chuckled. "She jumped in the river after the fish instead of using a hook."

I imagined playfully pushing Rita into the lake, but chose not to respond.

Ky grabbed my pole and put a lure on the line. "Did they at least try to teach you how to cast this?"

I took the rod from him, attempting to find the best hand placement. "Not really. They were busy drinking beers and gossiping."

Ky placed his hand next to mine. "Sounds about right. Stick your index finger right here to hold on to the fishing line while you depress this lever."

As he explained, he eased my fingers in place. He reached around my body and pressed his chest softly into my back. The musky, woody smell of sweat mixed with cologne filled my nose.

Ky pointed to a silver, metal, semi-circle. "When you are ready to cast, let go of this lever while you do, so the line will release. Try it once."

The sound of trickling water came from the creek feeding the lake. As I spread my feet, I looked over my shoulder and prepared to follow the steps Ky gave me.

From the other side of the lake, someone hollered, "Hey, you can't start yet. The whistle didn't blow."

I rotated my head forward and saw Lily Jankins sitting with a couple of other women. I noticed their bodies pressed together as she pointed my way. Slowly, I lowered the rod. "Relax, Lily. He's giving me lessons."

Gripping the reel firmly as Ky showed me, my hands shook. If my body performed the same way when I used my rifle to complete a mission, I never would have hit any of the targets assigned by Director Sanchez. I pulled my hand back, released the lever, and let the line go. I flung the rig as hard as I could, my shoulder straining with the effort. A low-pitched squeal came from behind me, and I spun around to see what made the noise.

Ky stared, wide eyed, down at his bike shorts. His jaw dropped.

My hook hung embedded in the front of his tight shorts, very close to his family jewels. Initially, I felt terrified but, when I saw his expression, I burst out laughing.

Rita and Helen stood and howled with laughter. They doubled over and placed their hands on their knees.

Not one person offered to help Ky pull out the hook.

He stood frozen like a child perched on the edge of a diving board for the first time, his face a dark shade of red. Reluctant to reach forward and help him myself, I paused. Our relationship had not progressed to the point of "handling" his bike shorts.

Rita put her hands on her cheeks and then clapped. "Nice performance, Ally. I don't think your catch will win you the award, though. Your fish is not big enough." She and Helen bent over, holding their stomachs and nearly pitched on their faces.

Ky frowned. "Very funny, Rita. You clearly are the one who taught her to fish. The method she used resembled your technique." He reached down and pulled on the hook, but the prongs dug in deeper, his eyes widening.

Grabbing the fishing pliers, I took a deep breath to calm myself and stopped laughing. "All right, you'll need to let me help you." Knowing I lacked the skills, I bent down and pinched the hook, deciding which way to pull to do the least amount of damage.

"In case no one mentioned the rules, this is a family fishing derby," Lily yelled with her hands surrounding her mouth. "You two need to take your shenanigans somewhere else."

I glanced up for a moment to see her expression. Judging by the scowl on her face, I assumed she meant what she said. If my hands were free, I would have flipped her the bird.

Helen rose from her lawn chair. "You're just jealous because no man has allowed you to hook him in years." She and Rita roared again and almost missed the blow of the horn to show the derby starting. They both instantly became straight faced, grabbed their rods, and tossed their lines into the lake. Apparently, they finished watching their lakeside entertainment.

---

9

*F*illed with embarrassment, I handed Ky the pliers and marched over to the cooler to find a beer. I turned just in time to see him exhale and smile as he pulled the hook loose. Squatting down, I grabbed another beer. Walking to his side, I reached out with the can in my hand. "Peace offering."

Ky popped the top, lifted the drink to his mouth and took a long swig. "Thanks. I guess we know each other a little better now."

I looked across the lake briefly and saw Lily and her friends staring at us and giggling. My attention returned to our conversation. "Ky, I'm really sorry. I didn't mean to catch you there with my hook. I have limited experience with fishing. It's a good thing you had on bike shorts. The extra padding probably saved you."

He grimaced. "I don't even want to think about the alternative. Now, let's try this again." He reached down, retrieved my rod, and extended it.

"No, thanks." I put my hands out and stepped back. "Maybe I'll sit this one out. I might try later, when my heart rate goes back to normal. I'd rather just relax and watch everyone else."

Ky set my pole down and grabbed his. He moved around the lake a few feet and tossed his line in the water with precision.

We were definitely not in the same league with fishing. I would need plenty of practice before the sport became an activity we both enjoyed. If ever. "So, how is Seth doing?"

Ky's eyes narrowed. "My staff are keeping a close eye on him."

I took a drink of cool beer and stared off in the distance at the children kicking a soccer ball in the field. "Did you figure out if he was poisoned?"

Ky reeled his line in slowly. "Ally, you know I can't tell you anything more. You're bound by the same HIPPA laws as I am."

"Sorry. I'm used to being able to talk freely about patients with other providers. Sometimes, I forget I am not the one working with a person." I kicked a rock into the lake. "When I saw Seth pitch forward in his chair, my 'therapist brain' started assessing the situation. Janie is a nice person and I wouldn't want her traumatized."

His reel clicked as he pulled in his line. His lure spun rapidly in the water, heading towards the shore. The sun periodically reflected off the silver medal. "We don't know enough about the situation yet to determine if anyone else is in danger of getting sick. I think I have the information I need, but I am still running a few more tests. I got lucky finding what I have so far."

After bending over to pick up a flat rock, I drew back my elbow to prepare to skip it across the water. "Or maybe you're just good at your job."

He reached forward and grabbed my hand. "You'll

scare away the fish." A smile spread across his face; his mouth full of straight, white teeth. "Last time you pulled information out of me, you ended up almost getting killed with a shovel. I've already learned to be more careful with what I tell you. It's hard not to be sucked in by such a pretty face."

His cell phone chimed in the pocket of his bike shirt.

Saved by the bell, or should I say a song by George Straight?

Ky peered at the screen. "I have to take this." He placed his rod on the ground and hustled away from the crowds, talking in a low tone.

Helen moved over to where I stood. "You know you'll have to fill us in on the details he gave you later. You guys seemed pretty involved in a juicy conversation."

Watching Ky's reactions to his call, I ignored her comment initially. "Juicy? I asked for intel on how Seth is doing. The situation with Janie's family is piquing my interest. She seemed like she had a lot on her mind when I first met her. Something is not right with her family, especially this poisoning."

Helen looked toward her chair and pole. "Oh, a lot of things are not right about the Palizzi family. Janie and Greg are about the only normal siblings in the..." After looking in Ky's direction, she stopped talking.

He started walking towards us, taking large strides.

He gently grasped both of my hands and leaned in to kiss me softly on the cheek. My face reddened from his overt display of affection. My defensive instinct almost made me push him away, but I wanted him to give me information when I needed. Plus, his touch felt comforting.

Ky dropped his hands and bent down to pick up his rod. He quickly disassembled the parts and placed his helmet on his head. "I have to go back to the hospital. Catch the biggest fish in the lake, so Lily doesn't win this year. She's impossible to deal with when she wins."

I saw an opportunity to avoid an awkward conversation with Helen and Rita. "Do you need a ride? I can probably convince Rita to let me borrow the sports car."

Rita straightened in her lawn chair and looked over her shoulder, shaking her head.

Ky grinned. "No thanks. From the expression on Rita's face, I might end up staying at the hospital longer to deal with her cardiac arrest. She doesn't like others driving her precious property. I can ride my bike to the hospital. The route doesn't take long, and my car is already there. You guys enjoy the derby." He climbed on his cycle, rode over the bridge, and disappeared around the corner.

Gazing around the lake at the other participants, a man and a woman standing toe to toe engaged in an animated conversation caught my attention. The man, a blonde who stood about five feet ten inches, had wide, muscular shoulders and tattoos running down both arms. A formidable character. The petite, attractive woman waved her hands in the air as she spoke. Their faces looked tense and others nearby watched them closely.

Rita whistled. "Ally, grab your chair and stroll on over here."

Picking up my gear, I carried the load next to the tree. I frequently assessed the scene between the couple across the lake as I walked. After setting my stuff on the ground, I pointed across the lake. "What's going on over there?"

Helen's eyes followed the direction I pointed. "Hard to say. That's Troy Talis and Leann Hall. He is Seth's brother. She practically lives at the Burning Mountain Saloon where the two men play pool. Leann used to date Troy but, from what I heard, he caught Seth and Leann together, doing more than just talking. Seth ended the affair, which didn't sit well with her. I wouldn't be surprised if they are arguing about their little love triangle."

Rita picked up her pole and tightened her line. "Maybe she thinks he had something to do with Seth getting sick. It's not the first time Seth got involved with one of Troy's girlfriends." Rita raised her eyebrows. "Or maybe Troy is accusing Leann of wanting to harm his brother. She has never been good at rejection."

Not taking my eyes off the scene, I lowered into my chair. "That would explain the look on Leann's face and her gestures. I think the situation will escalate. I've seen body language like that before."

Helen reeled in her line and cast far out into the water. "I doubt Leann would draw attention to herself. She's been in trouble with the law in the past for trying to stalk a previous boyfriend. She had a restraining order against her for over a year."

Leann stuck her finger in Troy's chest and leaned in close to his face, pivoted and marched towards the parking lot.

Troy watched Leann leave and picked up his equipment and left.

"There goes our show." Helen nudged my arm. "You and Dr. Handsome sure seem friendlier."

I leaned back in my chair, nearly tipping over backwards. My feet flew out in front of me to recover my balance. "If you call hooking him in the groin friendly, then yes, that's true."

Rita chuckled. "Your generation has a weird way of getting relationships started."

Regretting responding at all, I pointed toward the lake.

"Aren't you supposed to be catching a fish? Lily will end up winning, again."

Helen stared across the lake. "I can beat the pretentious woman with one hand tied behind my back, and my attention focused on you." She turned her head. "What was going on in your mind as you released the hook from his groin?"

I lightly shoved Helen's arm. "I don't share details of my life with nosy, dirty old ladies."

Helen steadied herself. "If that's what you call a love life, then things sure have changed from when I was on the prowl. If we wanted to touch some man's private parts, we—"

"Love life?" My face burned as I put my hands out. "Stop. I beg you not to finish your sentence."

Helen rotated her head toward the lake with surprising speed. The bobber disappeared below the water.

She bent forward, snatched her rod, and spun the line with impressive grace and efficiency. The whirling of the reel increased in speed with each second.

From the side of the lake, Lily stood and pulled in her line rapidly. She stepped closer to the lake and reached in. Just as she almost had the trout, her left foot slipped, throwing her sideways into the water.

The incident attracted the attention of the other contestants around her. Everyone stopped moving and watched Lily recover.

Two other women sitting with her leaped from their chairs and helped her stand while she continued to pull the line from the lake.

Focused on her catch, Helen expertly handled her rod until, finally, she had the fish to the shore. She lifted the trout up by its gills and extended her arm in front of her.

The silvery creature flipped side to side. "It's a rainbow." She yelled. "It's gotta be close to sixteen inches! I guess this means I won both prizes!"

Helen's voice seemed to echo over the entire open area.

Having picked her slimy victim out of the lake, Lily trudged to the shore and lifted her catch above her head. "You didn't win both prizes. I pulled in the first one. Yours might be bigger, but I got mine before you!"

Rita cupped her hands around her mouth. "Jumping in the lake to pull one out is not fishing. The rules state you have to use a pole, not pounce on the poor, unsuspecting creature and crush the thing to death." Rita slapped Helen's hand so hard they both almost ended up in the lake themselves.

Lily dropped her gear to the ground and stomped closer to the edge of the lake. "You two always have some excuse for swaying every competition your way. You can't handle the truth. I am a better angler than you are, so you have to make up your own rules. You probably bought yours at the store and pretended to pull the stupid thing out of the lake. You cheat at this event, just like you do at Bingo."

Helen lifted her catch in the air. "Fish-envy will get you nowhere, Lily. I beat you fair and square. Now, dry yourself off while I take mine to the judge to find out if my winnings are as substantial as this beauty." Helen pulled the hook out of the trout's mouth.

The sight made my stomach turn. I inwardly chastised myself for being able to shoot a drug dealer, but not handle watching a slimy creature headed for its inevitable death. *I need to get back to D.C. before I get soft.*

10

With the winner obvious, the other contestants talked and laughed. The air filled with the greasy smell of burgers and hot dogs cooking on the hibachi grills.

While Helen spent time at the judge's booth, I packed the chairs, poles, and coolers with Rita's help. I almost finished when I saw Janie hustling in our direction from the parking lot. Her head moved side to side, her arms crossed and her shoulders hunched.

Helen jumped in behind her. She moved fast enough to keep up, albeit with a slight limp.

Helen's recovery from her hip replacement happened faster than I expected. Determined, tough mountain women let little stop them from doing what they wanted. Helen deserved respect for being resilient.

Janie moved close to the chair. "Hi, guys. Who won the derby today?"

Helen stepped behind Janie. "I won the largest catch—"

Janie dropped her arms and spun. "You scared the poop out of me!"

Helen placed her hand on Janie's shoulder. "I didn't mean to frighten you. I should have won the First Catch of the Day, but the bleeding hearts gave the prize to Lily to shut her up."

"Congratulations, Helen! You seem to be good at a lot of things." Janie turned back. "Ally, I need to talk to you for a bit. Do you have time?"

Rita picked up the strap of a chair and slung it around her shoulder. "We are driving over to the Elk Creek Bar and Grill for a bite to eat and a beer. They'll be serving lunch, and we can talk there."

Eyes wide, Janie shifted her gaze back and forth between myself and Rita.

I picked up my gear and smiled at Janie. "It's okay. The three of us are kind of like the Three Musketeers. We make a good team when the issue involves solving complicated problems."

Janie exhaled loudly. "Well, I guess it's okay. As long as they can keep a secret." She turned to leave. "I haven't eaten all day, so a burger sounds nice."

I walked with the group to the parking lot and loaded the gear into Rita's vehicle. The tires on Rita's car squealed and rocks flew as she raced out of the parking lot.

Janie followed in her own vehicle, but not too close.

"Seriously Rita." I exclaimed. "A light touch on the petal works much better. At least for your passengers."

The Elk Creek Bar and Grill had a large, L-shaped counter made of all wood in the back by the kitchen. Rustic-looking backless oak stools surrounded the bar. Paintings created by local artists hung on the wall with stickers identifying their names and places of residence. Above the display of liquor bottles, a large photo of a mountain with steam peeking out of several small caves hung on the wall. Six high-top tables stood on an all-hardwood floor and had four stools surrounding each one.

The busty bartender with a dark blue bandana wrapped around braids leaned over the bar, engaged in a conversation. She barely looked up when we entered.

My feet suctioned to the sticky floor as I walked. The smell of sour, stale beer made my nose crinkle. I chose a lone table near the front window for privacy. I decided on a place to sit and waited my turn to use the bathroom so I could wash the dirt off of my hands.

At the bar, three men perched close together, watching a monster truck race on the television. They evidently spent a lot of time in the bar, since the bartender called them by their first names.

Helen sauntered out of the bathroom and stopped by the group of four, slapping one of the three guys on the back.

The bartender came around the bar and embraced her in a hug.

Rita strolled over to the table with Janie following.

I studied the beer list on the chalkboard attached to the wall. The artist accidentally erased part of the letters. "Helen sure knows everyone in town."

Rita looked over her shoulder. "She should know the three guys sitting at the bar. I'm pretty sure her son has arrested each of them at least two to three times."

Playing with a coaster on the table, I laughed. "They don't really look like hardened criminals. They seem more like bar flies."

Helen joined the table and plopped down in a seat. "Did you guys order me a lager?"

Rita shook her head. "We haven't talked to Jesse yet.

She's been over there talking to those guys since we arrived. And you."

Helen waved a hand in the air, drawing the attention of the bartender immediately. She worked as the only employee in the establishment, except for those in the kitchen whom I viewed through a small window.

I looked at Helen, slightly impressed she had such power. "Let me guess. Usually, when you walk in this joint, they all turn and yell, Helen!"

"Nice Cheers reference," Helen said. "When you live in the same place your whole life, you have time to learn more about the people in your town. Who wants wings and nachos?"

Rita rubbed her hands together. "Perfect."

The bartender arrived and slapped more coasters on the table. "Hi ladies. Sorry for making you wait. Charlene's brother was giving me a load of crap." She tilted her head toward the bar. "What can I get you?"

Her strong perfume, combined with the smell of cigarette smoke, made my eyes itch and water. I blocked my nose with my finger, holding back a sneeze.

Helen insisted we all have lagers made by a local brewery. She gave the order and asked for glasses of water as well.

I sat quietly for a few minutes with the girls, watching the different sports on the three TVs. As more people entered, the chatter in the bar grew. The volume in the room peaked and waned depending on the noises coming from the boys at the bar. The atmosphere didn't provide for any privacy, but I figured Janie knew what kind of decision she made when she agreed to have a conversation there.

I lifted my glass and pushed it towards the others. "Cheers to a solid win!" My glass met with the others — the sound quiet compared to the shouts of fans on the tv. "So, what did you want to talk about?"

She gazed around the bar at the other patrons and launched into her explanation. "My stepbrother, Seth, passed away. Dr. Dalton and his staff did everything they could, but they didn't save him."

Potential poisoning just became a possible homicide. "I'm so sorry to hear about your loss." I gently touched the soft skin of her arm. "His passing happened so fast."

Janie stared at her beer before taking a slow, lingering drink. "The thing is, I never liked him very much. Every Sunday, we had a family dinner at my dad's house. On Tuesdays and Thursdays, Dad and I went to Margaret's house after we got out of school. Seth and Troy treated me like crap. They got away with everything because Margaret took their word over mine. By the time I became a teenager, I avoided them, since they did things to make me look guilty. My dad defended me, but Margaret would talk with him privately. When they finished, I usually ended up grounded. Greg tried to protect me, but Margaret always had the last say."

Helen leaned in and placed her hand on top of Janie's. "Do you mind if I ask how he died?"

Janie put her hands in her lap. "Dr. Dalton, who also works as the coroner, said he is listing poisoning as the cause of death. From what I understand, the tests revealed something called Merilian Sulfide in his blood. The symptoms are hair loss, vomiting, and diarrhea. Apparently, the toxin causes problems with the nervous system, lungs, heart, and the liver. Frankly, the whole thing sounds awful."

Rita wiped the condensation from her glass on her pants. "Does he think someone deliberately poisoned him? If not, how did he get it? Is anyone else in the family at risk?"

A roar let out across the bar as the sport teams apparently did something good.

I placed my hands flat on the table and leaned towards Janie. "Listen. I know this situation is scary. Let's consider the information one bit at a time. Have you noticed anyone else in the household presenting with similar symptoms?"

She paused for a few minutes. "Although my dad doesn't live in the same house as Seth, he has not been feeling well. It's yet another reason my husband and I want to move in." She stopped talking and put her hand over her mouth. "You don't suppose he was poisoned, too?"

11

A momentary silence came over the table, contrasted by the constant buzz of voices and noises coming from the multiple televisions.

I sipped my lager, eager for the food to arrive and cure the feeling of an empty pit in my stomach. "First, we don't know how Seth ended up with poison in his system. We'll try to help you figure this out in any way we can. Second, don't panic. The Three Musketeers are here to help, but we should keep this between us, for now. If you involve too many other individuals, accurate information will be harder to get. The people in the valley gossip like a bunch of high schoolers." I raised my eyebrows and tilted my chin down as I looked at Helen.

"I think I'm feeling ill." Janie grabbed at her stomach. "Shouldn't we let the police handle the investigation? If he was intentionally poisoned, I wouldn't want you guys getting in trouble for trying to meddle in solving a crime."

Rita rubbed Janie's back. "No need to worry. Helen has a way of getting information to the sheriff without being obvious. Do you know of anyone who would want to harm Seth?"

Janie chewed on her thumbnail. "A better question is, who didn't want to harm Seth? He's been a jerk to others in this town for years. Margaret has spoiled those two boys so much it makes being around them difficult. They are snotty and entitled." She looked out the window, shaking her head. "Margaret will freak out when she finds out the cause of death was poison. Things will only get worse from here. Margaret's two boys always battled for her attention. She had a fondness for Seth, which was very upsetting for Troy. I can imagine he feels torn between being sad about his brother dying, but a little happy he'll finally be the center of Margaret's affection. Also, he'll be the only one in line to inherit what's left of her money and property."

As Janie talked, I searched the internet for information about the poison Janie mentioned. "It says here Merilian Sulfide is a chemical commonly used in rat poison and has been used to treat ringworm. In the past, the substance was used to give people a slow-acting poison because it creates symptoms that are like many other illnesses."

Janie inhaled, closed her eyes, and slowly exhaled. "My dad has chemicals to kill rats around the farm, but he is very careful where he stores the boxes. He doesn't want any of the other animals getting into them. He only places them deep in the back of the house cupboards. The rats come in from the fields looking for food. Most farmers have the same problem unless they keep an army of barn cats, but my dad is allergic to cats. Seth has never helped on the farm unless Margaret asked him to do a specific task or Margaret offered him money. I highly doubt he ever touched the stuff dad uses."

A man opened the front door, letting in a cloud of

cigarette smoke. My eyes watered and I held my breath briefly and slowly exhaled, hoping for a moment for the air to clear. "How much time does Seth spend at the farm?"

"He goes with Margaret twice a week when she takes Alvin his groceries, beer, and household goods. Alvin doesn't like shopping, and Margaret prefers to decide what he eats and drinks. She makes him dinners and delivers them when she drops off the groceries." Janie paused, looking off into the distance. "Now, as I am saying this all out loud, I realize how much control she has over my dad's life. He's prevented from going to the liquor store and buying his own beer. She buys him a twelve pack once a week. She says, if she purchases the alcohol, she can govern how much he consumes. Seth and Troy have had drinking problems, so she doesn't allow the substance in her own house."

It seemed unlikely Seth encountered the poison at Alvin's house, but I didn't discount the idea completely. The concept of him being poisoned by his brother, an angry pool hall shark, or a jilted girlfriend made more sense. I didn't share my thoughts immediately in order to prevent Helen and Rita from running out of the bar and asking questions around town.

Rita, who had been biting her lip, joined in the conversation. "As far as cause of death, I think we can rule out suicide for a few reasons. First, Seth and Troy have everything two men in middle age could ever want. They would be stupid to mess up a good thing. Second, even someone with less than a full head of brains wouldn't choose a slow-acting toxin to commit suicide. Death by poison is a terrible, painful way to die." She paused and gazed around the bar. "Which leaves us with accidental ingestion or homicide. We'll gather more intel before we decide which direction to take the investigation."

Janie raised her eyebrows. "Wow, Rita. You sure sound like someone who has done this before. If I didn't know better, I would assume you have experience in this type of work."

Fortunately, the waitress/bartender reappeared with our order.

The spice from the buffalo sauce made my eyes water and my nose tingle. The presence of food distracted me as I stared down and wondered the time required to not be rude before digging in.

"Thanks, Jessie." Helen grabbed a wing and dipped the end in the ranch. "Nothing like good food and drink to celebrate a win at the fishing derby. I wish you could have been there and seen the expression on Lily's face when I pulled the trout out of the water. She'll be whining about this one for days."

"I'm sure she will." Jessie laid down four small plates and some napkins. "Undoubtedly, I'll hear about the saga next time she is here. Congratulations! Enjoy the grub and let me know if you need anything else." Jessie returned to the bar and continued chatting with the guys.

After witnessing Helen attacking the wings, I dug into the delicious food in silence. I suspected we were all pondering what to do next. The deep, gruff voices of two guys at the bar raised in volume as they argued about which team might win. The crash of a tub of dropped dishes came from the kitchen, followed by profanity.

Licking the spicy wing sauce off of my fingers one at a time, I continued the conversation. "I think we have to find a place to start the investigation, which rules out the possibility Seth encountered the poison at home. Can we search both Margaret's house and Alvin's place? I think searching the farm will be pretty easy, but Margaret's residence is another story. If Margaret comes home, we can say I received orders to provide Alvin with physical therapy and wanted to meet with her first. It will provide us with a decent cover story. Janie, do you have the keys?"

Janie swallowed the bite in her mouth and cleared her throat. "Wow, Ally. You're like an amateur detective, jumping right into breaking and entering a person's house. I think you have been hanging out with Rita and Helen too much, but your idea makes sense. I have a key to Dad's house, but not Margaret's. She never gives them out. Even Dad doesn't have one."

Helen separated two bones of a wing and plucked the meat from between. "There's a big surprise. People who like to keep control do so in every aspect."

Janie grabbed a handful of nachos and placed them on her small plate. "I know where she keeps an emergency key case shaped like a rock. I saw Troy get into one once, when I gave him a ride home from the bar. He was tanked at The Burning Mountain Saloon and figuring out how to put his key in the lock on the door of his car. I stopped him before he could drive and offered him a ride home. When we arrived at their house, he went around the left corner, to the third bush, and took a secret storage rock from underneath. He forgot I took the keys away or thought he lost them, and I didn't want him to get angry with me when he remembered I had them."

"Perfect." I took a moment to commit the specific location of the key to memory. "So, now we figure out how to lure her and Troy away from the house long enough for us to search the place."

Janie dipped a chip in sour cream and salsa. "Actually, I think I can help with that detail, too. Today is Sunday. This is the day she and the boys, I mean Troy, go grocery shopping, stop at the liquor store, and take what she buys to Dad's house. She should be gone for quite a while. I'll offer to tag along so I can keep track of what they are doing. She'll think it's weird, but I'll make up some excuse about wanting to help after Seth's death. I'll do a group text to warn you if anything changes in her normal routine and she heads home. Doing so should give you enough time to get out of there before she arrives."

Helen leaned forward in her chair and rubbed her palms together. "I get to be a part of the good stuff this time, since my leg is feeling better and I can walk normally."

I exchanged glances with Rita as my brain calculated the additional risk of being detected with Helen along.

"What happens if we need to make a run for it?" Rita clucked at her friend like a protective mother hen.

As the fatigue set in from drinking a beer in the middle of the day after being in the sun, my eyelids drooped. "Yeah. And I've seen the way you drive. You park backwards, run up on curbs, and drive in the wrong direction on the street. You are not exactly the driver we need on an undercover mission." I attempted to make my tone sound playful, to not make Helen angry. In the back of my mind, I knew I meant what I said.

Helen stuck her tongue out. "Oh, give me a break. I had a hip replacement, but I'm not ninety years old. Even if they aren't as fast as they used to be, I can still think fast on my feet. I'll figure out how to make a quick getaway if I need to. And, as far as my driving skills, my son is the sheriff in town. Those nice deputies never pull me over."

The thought occurred to me whether the sheriff actually let Helen get away with her shenanigans or let her think she did in order to keep her quiet. Judging by my interactions with him, he seemed like a man who knew how to handle his job.

Rita picked up the last wing. "Let's be honest. You weren't very agile before your hip replacement. And now a few months have passed and you are even older. We might end up carrying you out of there. You'll slow us down."

Helen set her soiled napkin on her plate and took a large sip of her beer. "And you can't even take a step off of a curb without missing and almost falling on your face. I'd say we make a good team."

Janie scooted her chair away from the table. "Well, at any rate, we better get moving. Margaret usually goes to the store around two o'clock. I'll spontaneously show up at her house. If I call first, she'll find an excuse to not have me around."

Hopefully, Janie's part of the plan ends successfully. If not, Helen will need to convince her son, the sheriff, to keep my name off the records to avoid alerting Deputy Cunningham about my involvement with the law, again.

12

———

*H*elen paid for lunch and said goodbye to the other patrons.

I accompanied Janie to her car and made sure she had our correct cell phone numbers. The fresh air of the outdoors reminded me why I preferred to avoid crowded establishments.

Janie opened the car door and put one foot on the floorboard. "Wait until two-thirty before you approach the house, just in case she gets sidetracked with something. She drives an embarrassingly large, burgundy luxury car. If you don't see her vehicle in the driveway, it's safe. You can go inside." Janie drove off rapidly, her back tire thumping over the curb.

Rita exited the bar, followed by Helen. She laughed. "She drives like you, Helen."

Helen was still grumbling about her excellent driving skills when Rita dropped me off at my house so I could change and grab my nine. Searching Margaret's property unarmed seemed like a bad idea. Especially since Margaret and her son did not qualify as a "normal" family. The agency trained me to carry my weapon at all times.

Missing the comforting presence of Beano or Barley, I bound up the stairs to my bedroom. I chose a black shirt and black jeans, which seemed cliché for our purpose, but I had a habit of flying under the radar during missions. Pulling my hair up in a ponytail, I threw on my tennis shoes and a ball cap, and returned downstairs. With a few minutes to spare, I opened my email. I found a message from Music Lovers, a code name used by Rachel Roos, Deputy Cunningham's executive assistant. I opened the note, noticing my increased heart rate. The official communication gave me a tight sensation in my chest and butterflies in my stomach. Using my training, I took a moment and calmed my body's reaction. I longed for the adrenaline rush of my job, but I also wanted to find out if Seth's death was a homicide. In the few times I interacted with Janie, I had grown to like her and had a desire to help protect her future.

Hi Ally! I hope you are enjoying your trip. Everything here is going fine, but we are still waiting for the delivery order we placed a few days ago. Don't worry. We know you are eager for more details. We are writing to let you know we have not forgotten about you. Enjoy your time away. We will be in touch soon.

Closing my laptop a little too hard, I let out a sigh. Rachel's encrypted message let me know not much had changed in D.C., and they were monitoring the movement of Abdul's group. I felt torn between the friendship I was developing with Rita and Helen and my internal drive to return to my previous life. Seeing Rachel's email reminded me about my life, as it was just a little over a week ago.

Something moved outside the back window. Looking up, I saw a deer wander past the deck, acting like she owned the place. "Oh, no you don't!" I dropped the laptop on the couch like a hot potato and raced for the back door. I ran out onto the back deck just in time to catch the deer munching, with what seemed like a smile, on my newly planted baby cucumbers. "Shoo!" Waving my arms, I stomped toward the deer. "Shoo! Get out of here!"

Mouth moving side to side, the deer lifted her head to inspect me with big, oh-so-not-innocent brown eyes. Apparently, she decided I didn't present a threat because she lowered her head and yanked another of my starter cucumbers from the wet ground. The dirt still looked muddy from my earlier watering.

"Get! Go! Don't you dare eat that!" As ridiculous as I felt yelling at a deer, I felt twice as annoyed she had the nerve to rip a third cucumber from the ground and chew with her gaze focused on me like a dare.

"That's it." I should have gone for my gun, but didn't want to answer to the sheriff as he asked me about a hunting license. In the past, I fought hand-to-hand combat with men three times my size and ten times as mean. I could handle a sweet-faced, innocent little doe.

Arms whirling, I yelled nonsense and ran straight at her. As she sprinted to the edge of the tree line, her white bobtail bounced and disappeared. Satisfaction made me smirk.

My expression switched to a scream as my heel shifted in the soggy ground, my feet flew out from beneath me, and I landed on my back in the thick, slippery mud. "Damn it!" The cold muck soaked through my shirt, as well as my now-slimy backside.

Lying on the ground, I looked up at the bright blue sky and laughed out loud. I kept laughing until I caught sight of the deer on the opposite side of the yard, munching on the flowers.

Leaves and roots dangling from her mouth, she watched me with those same brown eyes, but I would swear the damn deer was mocking me. "I'm putting up a fence, just for you."

My threat didn't faze her. She defiantly pulled another flower up by the roots.

The sound of tires crunching gravel made me groan as I found a spot on the ground where I placed my hands without them sinking in above my fingers. Spreading my legs wide, I crawled my arms towards my feet like a drunk guy on ice.

After meeting Rita and Helen on the front porch, I told them I had to change, and ignored their laughter as I ran inside and up to my room. When I returned, the two ladies discussed our conversation with Janie. Helen's flushed pink cheeks and bright eyes looked a bit too excited.

Rita's arms lay across her chest. "Helen wanted to bring a shotgun."

Oh, dear. I believed decreased mobility should be my major concern.

"I've been shooting since I was in diapers." Helen crossed her arms over her chest like Rita.

"So, even longer than you've been driving." Rita put her hand over her mouth and covered her chuckle with a cough. "We've seen how well that goes."

Helen thumped Rita on the arm. "Before we begin our investigation, we must agree on the specifics in terms of our roles. Someone has to search the garage and barn. We'll need a body upstairs and downstairs in the house. We don't have a lookout, so I took care of the detail myself."

As if scripted in a movie, Bryce scurried up the driveway.

Helen walked down the steps, embraced him, and slapped him on the back. "You got my text. Atta boy! Always coming through for us when we need you. What did you tell your dad?"

"Hi, Grandma. I told him you asked for help to move your living room furniture around. It's the first thing I thought of, and he hates moving furniture."

Helen squeezed Bryce's hand. "You will make one heck of an investigator someday." She tousled his hair.

Bryce's smile spread from ear to ear, and his chest puffed. "How can I help?"

Helen grabbed Bryce by the arm. "We're headed over to Margaret Talis' house to look around. We need a lookout. Can you stand guard at the front door and warn us if anyone comes home? We have Janie working on the other end, but you know how the cell phone service is here. I don't trust it enough to rely on receiving a text."

Bryce leaned in to Helen. "I'm excited for another of Grandma's adventures. Just one question. You smell like alcohol. Are you sure you want to do this right now?"

Rita hurried down the steps. "It's now or never."

Following Rita, I tapped Bryce on the back. "We stopped at the pub for apps and a beer. Just one drink, so we are fine. We will search the house and look for boxes of rat poison, or bottles with labels which could show they contain Merilian Sulfide."

"I'm pretty sure I know why, so I won't ask for details. You should know my dad talked about performing an investigation himself. Once Dr. Dalton suggested homicide as a possibility, Dad started researching the poison. He knows what to look for now. You know how testy he gets about amateur investigators getting in his way."

Oh, yeah. I know how Sheriff Riddle gets. "Rita, you search upstairs and go through bathroom cabinets. I'll search the barn, shed, or any other outside structures.

Helen, the downstairs level is yours. Don't forget to check the refrigerator and freezer. You never know where you might find evidence."

Rita frowned. "You're right, but even if we find something, it won't be obvious how the poison ended up in his system? We need to talk to Dr. Handsome and determine if he examined the contents of Seth's stomach. Find out what else he ingested at the time. The information could help us narrow our search. I think it's time for another date."

I put my hand on her shoulder, tilted my chin down, and shook my head. "I'm not sure you are his type."

She flicked my hand away. "If I was twenty-five years younger, I would convince him I am. You know I meant for you to go on a date with him. Your last one served as a great way of getting information when we needed intel."

"Tomorrow is Monday, and I have to work. No one goes on a date on a Monday." I turned towards Bryce, hoping he would use his resources to help us like he did in the past. Aware doing so is illegal, I rationalized the need for gathering information rapidly as being more important. Not to mention, apparently the rules were only suggestions in small mountain areas. "Bryce, can't you pull the information out of your dad? I'm sure he has read the autopsy report."

"I can jump on his computer, but I can't try today." Bryce placed one foot on a step and leaned into the railing. "He's working on the yard and plans to be home all day. I can't risk getting caught, or he'll change his password and probably ground me."

Helen turned towards my vehicle. "And we can't wait. Janie's ruse might not work again."

She was right. "We'll take my SUV and park down the block. She doesn't know much about me or my vehicle. Also,

I can drive, which means we have a better chance of survival." I winked at Rita.

Helen walked down the driveway taking short, quick steps. "No way! It's my turn to drive. I know these roads better than both of you. You know, someday you must stop razzing me for my driving skills, or I'll find a way to run you over in a tragic accident. I'll use the hip replacement as an excuse, which will make the whole thing your fault."

I slapped my hand on my chest. "My fault?"

She shrugged. "Should have fixed my leg better."

Chuckling, I loaded into the passenger seat as Helen assumed her position as driver, which was a benefit, as she already knew the way to Margaret's house. There is no way I would admit my opinion if she asked.

Margaret lived in a neighborhood of large, expensive houses with professionally manicured landscaping. No uniformity existed with the designs; some houses were Victorian with steeply pitched roofs, while others were sleek modern designs with long horizontal lines. Each property had nearly a full acre of land, many of them with barns or sheds dotting the yards. There seemed to be an air of quiet privilege in these homes, which didn't strike me as surprising given my information about Margaret.

Just after Helen turned down Margaret's street, I noticed a one-way sign pointing in the opposite direction we traveled. "Helen! We're going the wrong way." I quickly slammed my foot down on the floorboard, trying to stop the car myself. My hands flew up to the warm dashboard.

"It'll be fine." She pressed the gas pedal and sped forward.

A car coming towards us honked as Helen swerved to avoid a head-on collision.

Tires screeched as she came to a stop, my forearms

straining to stop the forward momentum of my body. Two of the SUV's tires landed up on the curb, and I figured Helen didn't understand that all four tires should be in the street. I shook my head without saying a word as I slid out of the car and hurried up the street towards Margaret's house with Rita, Helen and Bryce trailing close behind. When I arrived at the entrance of the driveway, I did not see the car Janie mentioned earlier.

Margaret's property had a large, red barn with multiple grid windows and was located to the left of the house. A meandering sidewalk bordered by a freshly manicured lawn connected the two buildings. A gravel driveway stretched from the entrance of the property to the house, and midway, bifurcated, heading towards the barn. Several tall, Evergreen Trees bordered the front of the property, giving it a sense of privacy.

I surveyed the property for evidence of another's presence and, after concluding it to be vacant, proceeded to the barn. Peering inside, I saw they converted the space into a living area. Before going inside, I turned to see Helen, Rita and Bryce digging the fake rock with the key out from under a bush.

Helen and Rita disappeared after going in the front door.

Bryce followed them in and assumed his position in a window in the front room of the home, overlooking the driveway. He had binoculars in one hand and his cell phone in the other. I couldn't help but smile and think he would make a good sheriff, or possibly an agent someday.

Ok. Ally. It's time to search for evidence.

———————

13

*T*he door to the barn opened into a mudroom, which served as both Seth and Troy's makeshift closets. Shoes lay strewn across the floor and jackets hung from the wall. The stench of sweaty feet and body odor, combined with cheap cologne, smelled strong and gave me incentive to hurry as I surveyed the area for potential clues. I made a mental note to return to this room to check the cabinets for evidence later.

Making my way into the living room, I heard sounds of the demolition derby coming from the large TV covering half the wall. My hand reached for my nine as I crouched and listened for any movement coming from other parts of the barn—no sounds detected. I continued with my investigation. A bright red plaid couch looked as though a bomb had gone off in its cushions. Dishes and glasses littered the coffee table, along with several remotes. A horrible smell of rotting food filled the air. Seth and Troy spent a lot of time here, but I couldn't see anything useful in terms of evidence.

I walked to the back of the barn; I entered the kitchen. More dirty dishes filled the counters and the sink, which were not rinsed in days. The smell wafting from the garbage disposal made my stomach lurch. I put my hand to my nose to divert the odor and tried to breathe through my mouth. Unknown, caked-on substances covered the top of the stove.

 Searching each individual cupboard carefully, I kept an open mind about what I saw so I wouldn't miss a substance which might contain the poison. I opened the refrigerator and expected to find random condiments and beer, but then I remembered Margaret's restriction on alcohol consumption on her property. Soda replaced the normal staple for single men the age of Margaret's boys.

So far, I had found nothing which led me to believe any evidence of the substance used to poison Seth existed in this house. Gathering intel took me very little effort, and my patience waned.

I looked under the kitchen sink and found a box of rat poison in the far back corner. The container had a section on the top cut out, so an unsuspecting creature had easy access to its imminent death. Ky said the toxin found in Seth's blood was a component of rat poison. I took out my phone and snapped a picture of the product to use later when compiling information. I also took a picture of the box in the cupboard to show as evidence later if needed.

About to explore the rest of the barn, I heard a high-pitched scream from the direction of the house. I raced to the barn window to look.

Helen's head and shoulders appeared stuck halfway out a window, her eyes large, her teeth clenched. She clawed at the frame and curtains, attempting to slide, head first, through the opening without falling. She couldn't lift her leg up to the ledge for support and slipped all the way through with surprising speed. Helen landed, face up, in Margaret's landscaping, which included a large Kingcup

Cactus. I knew the name as I had several of them on my rental property and looked them up on the internet because of its beautiful, big, red flowers.

Cringing, I imagined the pain Helen experienced all over her back, legs, and arms. I rubbed my arms and felt concerned she may have injured her replaced hip. As I scanned the house looking for Rita and Bryce, I noticed Bryce's head peeking out the front door.

Bryce waved his cell phone in the air, eyes wide and saying something I could not hear.

I gazed down at my phone and realized I had a new text. The message read, "Get out! Margaret's on her way!" Surveying the driveway, I didn't see any vehicle coming. By the time I looked back to where Helen fell, I saw Bryce and Rita straining with all of their might to help Helen stand without impaling her with additional cactus needles. I checked the still-empty driveway one more time before going out the door I used to enter the barn. Seeing Helen walk like a penguin because of all the needles in her back-side, I ran back into the mudroom and retrieved a hand truck I saw earlier. I sprinted over to where they stood as the wheels wiggled back and forth, making me feel like a kid in a wheelbarrow race. "Get on!" I demanded.

Helen's eyes narrowed, and her jaw dropped. "Are you out of your mind? You'll kill me in that thing!"

I positioned my feet in a staggered stance and steadied the handles of the dolly with my hands. "Stand on the plat-form facing me and hold on tight. If you do, no pressure will be on the needles, and you won't have to walk."

Bryce hustled over, panting. "You better hurry, Grandma. Margaret's car just drove up the driveway!"

Helen stepped onto the dolly and grabbed hold of the handles next to where I placed my hands.

I tilted the bars towards me, bent my knees, and pushed to start the wheels rolling. The tires moved easier than I expected, and I sidestepped to gain control. I wheeled her around the back of the barn and found a smooth dirt path leading behind a row of houses and through a small wooded area.

The sound of Rita and Bryce's heavy breathing behind me registered in my ears.

"If you tip me over, these needles will puncture a lung, and I'm likely to die!" Helen's voice vibrated as she talked, and the skin on her knuckles blanched.

Rita stepped up beside us. "Stop freaking out and hold on, you old bat. It's your fault for going out the window, anyway."

Relieved we found a path which appeared flat, I felt exhausted by the minute. I said a prayer no one would walk down the path and witness the spectacle taking place. Leaves crunched under the weight of Helen's body, which made a quiet escape almost impossible.

Rita rushed ahead. "I'll run interference."

Fortunately, no one else came down the path, and I made my way to the SUV without being seen. I think. I set the dolly upright, almost pitching Helen onto her back.

Luckily, Bryce caught her before she lost her balance. "Now what? She can't sit down, or the needles will go in farther."

The back gate of the SUV protested with a high-pitched screech as I lowered it to the bumper. I lifted the window to open a space as large as possible. I laid down a soft, black blanket I kept in the back for emergencies. "Helen, you'll have to lie on your stomach and inch up to the front like a worm. This way, you can be in a less painful position for the ride home. Bryce, you and Rita slide into the backseat and each take a corner. Pull until she gets in far enough to allow me to close the gate."

Rita and Bryce both scooted the front seats as far forward as they could to give them more room to wedge their bodies in place. They crawled into the back, Bryce using his arms to fold his long legs into a small space.

I helped Helen lie on her stomach, trying not to touch any of the needles.

With each movement, Helen grunted and moaned.

Once her trunk cleared the gate, I grabbed the back two corners of the blanket to give her support around her legs.

"On my count," Bryce instructed. "One, two..."

Before Bryce counted to three, Rita yanked, causing Bryce and me to move faster than we planned.

My right elbow connected with the door frame, sending a shock wave throughout my arm. "Ouch! Crap, Rita."

Helen's body slid farther than we expected.

Rita fell backwards onto the front chair, pushing the backrest into the steering wheel and blasting the horn.

Fearing detection, my gaze darted around to see if our debacle drew attention from neighbors. "Bryce, help her up!" I urged.

Bryce sprinted to the other side of the SUV and pulled on Rita's arms to set her upright as quickly as possible. His face reddened with the effort and beads of sweat dripped down his forehead.

I lifted the gate and pushed until I heard a click. In order to avoid anyone seeing Helen lying in the back, I pulled the window closed. I moved the driver's seat back to my original setting and hopped in while the others rushed into their spots. I turned around in my seat. "Where to now?"

Helen lifted her head a few inches and groaned. "Let's go to your house. Rita, text Dr. Handsome and tell him to meet us at my house. In no way am I going to the hospital and answer a bunch of unwanted questions."

The advantages of living in a small town continued to surprise me. A doctor who makes house calls? In a city like D.C., they would charge a patient extra for that kind of service. Still, I couldn't help but notice a slight flutter in my chest at the idea of getting to see Ky again. Hopefully, I will have time to put on additional deodorant before he arrives. Pushing Helen around on a hand truck caused me to feel less than desirable.

14

———

*D*riving in silence the rest of the way home, I pondered how things ended up so complicated. Carefully, I obeyed the speed limit to avoid drawing attention. More of Helen's antics, that's how. I skillfully glided around potholes so I didn't cause Helen more pain than she had already experienced. Although, she might deserve the punishment after pulling the window stunt.

When I arrived at my house, I assumed the same position at the end of the blanket as before, as did Bryce and Rita. "This time, I will count!" I demanded. "We move AFTER I say three! One, two, three."

With Bryce and Rita's help, I slid Helen out far enough to help her safely get to her feet without falling.

Helen slowly waddled to the house and teetered up the stairs — each move she made deliberate and sluggish. Limping inside, she melted face down on the couch to await Dr. Dalton's arrival.

After hanging my keys on the hook, I sat on the coffee table. "Before Ky shows up, I think we should go over what we found. How did you guys make out?"

Rita flopped down on the loveseat with a loud exhale. "I found out it's a good thing Alvin doesn't live with her. Her choice of decorations would frustrate any hard-core, good-ole boy farmer. Everything has some type of flowers and most of the fabric has lace."

I pondered the FBI's definition of intel. "Sounds overly frilly, but not exactly the information I desired. Did you find anything to explain Seth's poisoning?"

Rita folded her arms behind her head. "I found a copy of some sort of will which leaves everything to her two sons. The document did not mention Alvin's kids, which doesn't surprise me. The one thing I found in her medicine cabinet had a label stating the drug treats ringworm. I am kind of surprised she would still have treatment for something so specific in her cabinet given the prescription expired a year ago. Wouldn't you think she would take all the pills and then discard the bottle?"

Helen attempted to roll onto her side, but stayed on her stomach. She lifted her head off the cushion. "Maybe she didn't finish the medication because the symptoms went away. Doesn't seem like anything, but we should keep track of things which are out of the ordinary. Did you take a picture?"

"I think you know by now I have skills," Rita chided. "Of course, I took a picture. And what did you find, Miss Private Investigator?"

Helen laid her head down and rubbed the back of her neck. "You don't need to be so testy. I'm just covering our bases. Besides, you can't pick on me. I'm an injured woman."

Rita put her feet up on the coffee table. "You're a lame duck because you act irrationally. Why the heck did you choose to go out the window? You could have gone out the back door instead. Margaret hadn't even shown up on the property yet. You had time to use a different exit."

Helen placed her balled up fists under her forehead. "You guys had all the fun with our investigations, and I was stuck at home or in the SUV as I waited for you to come out with information. I didn't think I would have difficulty getting out of the window. While I waited for you two to return from your journeys, I practiced similar moves in my head a billion times. I always visualize possible exits from dangerous situations. I've learned a thing or two from my son."

Rita waved her finger. "Well, maybe you should picture yourself making the stealthy move a few more times. You obviously forgot to include the part where you ended up on your back in a cactus."

I laughed. "All right, all right, can we return to the investigation? You two are like a bunch of snotty teenagers. Helen, what did you find?"

She turned her head to the side, leaning on the crook of her elbow. "I checked the refrigerator and freezer, but found nothing obvious. The stench of rotting vegetables assaulted me. We'd need to have everything tested for the poison, which is not an option. The only peculiar thing I found looked like a bottle capper and blank caps like a beer factory uses."

The doorbell chimed. As I walked to the door, I realized I still had on all black and probably appeared and reeked like I had just run a marathon. I quickly sniffed my armpits to make sure I didn't smell as bad as I looked. The odor was a combination of vanilla-scented deodorant and a skunk-like smell. Knowing I couldn't do much about my condition in such a short time, I opened the door with a smile, hoping to distract Ky with kindness. "Hi! Thanks so much for interrupting your day and coming over here to help us. I hope we didn't pull you away from an important patient."

He leaned in to brush a soft, warm kiss on the cheek. "No. Everything is under control at the hospital. Plus, I am curious about what you need that is so urgent."

Blushing, I stepped back, so I wasn't obstructing his view of the other three people in the room. "Actually, Helen is who needs you. Come on in." I waved my hand towards Helen like a talk show model.

Rita placed her feet on the floor and scooted to the edge of the loveseat. "Sorry to disappoint you, Doc, but I'm sure we can give you two some alone time a little later. Prickly Pear Helen needs your help. It seems she is not as agile as she likes to think she is. We were hiking, and she fell right into a Kingcup Cactus. She didn't want to go to the hospital because she would have to admit she was no longer a spring chicken."

Ky stepped over to where Helen lay sprawled and examined her wounds. He looked over at Bryce, who stood in the room's corner. "Son. Go out to my car and grab my bag, please."

Without saying a word, Bryce left the room as Ky asked.

"So, you three expect me to believe this happened on a hike?" Ky placed his hands on his hips and looked at each one of us from head to toe. "Before you decide on your answer, you should know I am already aware Sheriff Riddle had a call from Margaret Talis' house because of a potential breaking and entering. Nothing was taken, but her hidden key is missing, and her landscaping is damaged, including her favorite Kingcup Cactus. Now, you three wouldn't know anything about such a thing, would you? Seems like run-ins with Kingcup Cacti are on the rise."

Helen strained to look at Ky. "I know Margaret Talis is a unique person who is capable of telling all sorts of stories. It very well could have been Troy who took the hidden key after he lost his. Those two boys never have been responsible, not to speak ill of the dead." Helen lifted slightly to make the sign of the cross. "On multiple occasions, either Seth or Troy needed a ride home from the bar and couldn't go inside because they either had their keys taken away at the bar or lost them."

The front door slammed shut as Bryce returned with the doctor's equipment. He handed the bag to Ky.

Ky placed the bag on the coffee table. "My, oh my, Helen. If you aren't in everyone's business." He shook his head slowly. "And your explanation of the broken Kingcup Cactus?"

She shrugged. "Like Rita said. I fell while we were hiking. Must be a strange coincidence. The fact that her cactus ended up destroyed at the same time as my backside met up with one in the woods is weird, but stranger things have happened in them thar mountains."

A smile spread across my face as I marveled at Helen's attempt to distract Ky with her fake backwoods drawl. She had a way of interacting with the people of the town and clearly spent years perfecting her skills. Despite Helen's talents, I felt anxiety about Ky's involvement in our investigation. Most likely, he would push for more information now.

Ky moved closer to Helen. "Well, the truth doesn't really matter. The less I know, the better. I don't even want to know why you three went to her house to begin with. Now, unless you want your backside exposed in front of everyone in this room, I suggest I help you into the bedroom so I can start on the tedious task of pulling the needles out, one painful stab at a time." He uttered the last five words slowly, the words lingering in the air.

A thought occurred to me I should follow them into the room to make sure Helen didn't give Ky too many details under the stress of a painful needle extraction. I've seen fully grown men succumb to less torture. Knowing Helen wouldn't want me in the room, I pondered a cover story, just in case.

15

Several minutes passed as Helen moved like an inchworm to the edge of the couch and dropped one leg off the side.

Ky stuck his hands under her armpits and leaned back as he pulled her to a stand.

The guest room of the cabin I rented was small, just large enough to fit a futon, a coffee table, and a small television. I had never given it much thought, as I had never had a reason to use the space — until today.

I expected to hear a lot of screaming and grunting coming from the room, but only heard a low-pitched mumbling.

Rita scooted back on the loveseat and put her feet on the coffee table. "How will you start the conversation about Seth's stomach contents? If you ask too many questions, he will know we are investigating Seth's potential murder. Then Helen will look guilty for breaking and entering."

Trying to hear the conversation between Helen and Ky, I didn't answer immediately. I moved to the couch and sat down. "I don't really think we fooled him with our fake hiking story. Plus, he knows whatever information we find helps him. He just can't knowingly condone what we are doing, or he would look bad in front of the people in the town."

Bryce plopped down on the couch; the vibration reverberated in my still sensitive head. "Let's hope the doc doesn't let my dad know about my grandma's antics. He'll start asking me questions and won't stop until he thinks he has all the details. When it comes to hanging out with my grandma, I always feel like he is interrogating me."

After approximately thirty minutes, Ky returned to the living room, with Helen following.

Helen glided smoothly but slowly, the wrinkles in her forehead absent. "Whew. You would think they could invent floral-scented antibiotic cream. This stuff stinks!"

Ky walked within a few feet of Bryce. "Your grandma will be just fine. Most of the cactus needles imbedded in her clothes and didn't actually penetrate her skin. I removed all the embedded ones. Her wounds should heal pretty fast." He handed Bryce the sweatshirt Helen wore. "This shirt, however, will take longer to heal. The pins in the fabric are quite plentiful. If it belonged to me, I would just toss it."

Ky looked my direction. "Helen said you pushed her quite a distance on a dolly. You're in better shape than I am. I probably would have dumped her off the hand truck long before we arrived at our destination. Anyway, I have to go back to the hospital to finish my rounds. Do you think I could call you tomorrow?"

Ky and I went on a date recently, but I worried about getting involved, knowing Deputy Cunningham might pull me out of the town. I found him handsome but usually avoided going out with popular, powerful men. In my experience, they felt intimidated by my devotion to my career and the schedule the job required. Also, Helen mentioned previously, Ky was a magnet for multiple women in the area. Dating him would draw more focus towards me than I should. Oh, but looking at him is so fun. "I have to work, but call me anyway. If I am with a patient, you can leave a message, and I'll call you back in between visits. Thanks again for coming."

Ky performed a quick head nod and smiled. "My pleasure."

I rose from the couch and accompanied him to the front door and waited until he climbed in his car before I turned and went back into the living room.

Helen remained standing. "I'd say we are pretty lucky to have such a nice doctor in this town." She winked.

Straightening a blanket on the couch, I groaned. "When will you guys stop giving me such a hard time about my relationship with Ky?"

Helen crossed her arms. "Well, aren't you the egomaniac? I meant his coming over here to help me. Not everything can be about you. Besides, we don't always need you to be the one to find information about a case. I think I did pretty well on my own." She lifted her chin.

My arms dropped to my side. "What did you do now?"

"I managed to find out information about the contents of Seth's stomach." She put her hand out, looking at her fingernails.

Rita's jaw dropped. "You just asked him the question? You know you are asking him to violate HIPPA. Plus, you'll draw attention to us investigating Seth's death. You can't be so obvious with your approach."

Helen stepped behind Bryce and ran her fingers through his hair. "Just because I don't have FBI training doesn't mean I don't have skills. I simply asked him if he worried about

Seth contacting the poison by eating food from The Elk Creek Bar and Grill. I told him the three of us ate there earlier today and worried we could end up sick, too. He said Seth's digestive system did not show evidence of him consuming food within the last eight hours. Apparently, Seth had alcohol in his blood and Ky went by the saloon to inquire whether Seth had been there the day he died, and no one had seen him. Ky said the substance Seth ingested can be slow acting, depending on how much he consumed. It's impossible to tell for sure."

Rita rotated to face Helen. "I can't believe he told you all of that! So, where does it leave us now?"

Helen licked her fingers to slick down a rogue hair on Bryce's head. "He didn't exactly say all of what I just said. I sort of put the words in his mouth and he didn't deny they were the truth. I told you. I can get blood out of a turnip."

After being in Shotgun for only a short period, I discovered many differences exist between the handling of matters in the city and a small, mountain town: hospital policies, the handling of small, petty crimes, and giving out information which may violate HIPPA laws. I assumed the remoteness of the town contributed to the alternate rules. Despite my opinion, I felt certain Ky maintained his composure as the ultimate health care professional. Helen most likely embellished the story. I plopped down on the couch next to Bryce. "I think we need more information on where he spent his last few days. We should probably talk to Janie and see if she can help us figure out the details. She has the inside track, and we would most likely get the stiff arm from Margaret if we asked questions."

Helen started walking towards the front door. "I think you have a good idea. It's time for me to call it a day. I have had enough of prickly things for a while, and I'm exhausted.

Rita, take me home. I'm not sure how I'll sleep if I can't lie on my back, but I'll definitely try."

Bryce stood up and joined Helen. "I'm headed out, too. I hope your back feels better soon, Grandma. Let me know if you need any help."

All three left, and I breathed a sigh of relief at finally being alone, at least without other humans. After a brilliant idea entered my mind, I bolted upright and scooted to the couch's edge. I popped up and leaped up the stairs to change clothes. Solitude would have to wait.

The drive to the Burning Mountain Saloon took ten minutes. I hoped I picked the right time to catch Reggie in his usual hangout. Choosing a seat at the end of the bar with a view of the front door, I nonchalantly took in my surroundings. Not knowing what Reggie looked like, I opted to start with something to eat and have a casual conversation with the bartender.

The bartender, a rough, burly looking man in his forties, had long, shaggy hair and tattoos covering most of both arms. His appearance would have given me pause in the field, but is exactly what I expected in a small mountain town saloon. I ordered a bacon cheeseburger, fries and a lager.

He set the lager with a thud on the wooden bar. "Did you just move to town, or are you just visiting?"

His voice sounded low and raspy, like that of a person with a bad cold. I pulled the glass in close. "I've been here just a little over a week. My name is Ally. What's your name?" *Slow and easy, Ally. This is a casual environment.*

"I'm A.J. Nice to meet you. Welcome to our town."

Not having a lot of practice flirting these days, except for cautiously flirting with Ky, I did my best to give him my most flirtatious smile. "You too. Looks like these guys come here often." I tilted my head towards three men playing pool and bantering with each other.

After picking up a soiled glass, the bartender looked up at the pool table briefly and moved the dish in soapy water like a piston. "Yeah. That's Clate, Reggie and Doug. I'd say they are here often. It's like they never leave. Especially Reggie. He thinks he owns the place. The way he beats everyone at pool, he practically does."

Pretending to be distracted by the tv behind the bar, I took a sip of my beer, letting the foam rest on my top lip for a moment and set my glass down slowly. "Which one is Reggie? I'll make sure I never challenge him to a game." I smiled, wiping my mouth with the back of my hand.

"He's the one with the white ball in his hand, pacing around the table, looking like a lion circling his prey."

Mission accomplished!

He stopped doing dishes and stared for a minute. "You are an attractive woman, so you be safe, at least initially. Reggie doesn't like to lose. Just don't make a bet with him and take more than a week to pay him. That really sets him off."

The people in this town sure do like to talk about each other. "What do you mean, sets him off? Will he ask me to meet him outside for a brawl?" I winked, trying to appear playful.

"Oh, Reggie is more subtle when collecting his debts. He's more likely to make life miserable for you in a way you don't even notice at first. He's very tricky." The bartender quickly glanced at the group of guys and then continued cleaning.

A bell rang, indicating the bartender should retrieve my food order. When he returned with my cheeseburger, I inhaled deeply, enjoying the savory, greasy smell of freshly grilled ground beef. I always found it surprising how small, dumpy saloons make the best burgers. After taking my first bite, I watched the pool game, analyzing the behavior of all three players. Balls clacked together and rebounded off the bumper. It didn't take a trained eye to see who held the leadership position.

After learning of Reggie's vengeful, cunning side, I moved him to the top of my mental suspect list. Slowly poisoning someone would definitely qualify as making their life miserable. However, killing a person who owes money is not a way to get paid. Did he hope to affect Seth's mental status and manipulate him to get his money back without drawing the attention of the law? It seemed a pretty smart plan, actually. Deciding to bring the information up with Helen and Rita later, I finished my plate and headed home.

Walking into the quiet, still house, I missed the company of my furry friends. I opened the screen door and called for Beano and Barley. Barley sprang over the porch railing and ran between my legs. Peering around the side of the house, I didn't see Beano, so I closed the door. As my body relaxed, the muscles in my shoulders and neck slowly throbbed. After the day's events, I looked forward to having some time to decompress. I locked up the house and made butter-flavored microwave popcorn. Carefully carrying the scalding bag into the living room, I set it down on the coffee table and flipped on the television. Spending far too much time trying to find an interesting show, I settled on an old Friends episode.

Barley curled up on the back of the couch and kneaded the folded blanket in front of him. After a few moments, he jumped to the floor and disappeared. He returned with a purple, glittery puff ball like the kind used for crafts. Placing it down on the ground at my feet, he sat down and stared at me. He chirped twice and waited.

Reaching down, I stroked his satin fur. It took a moment before I realized what he requested. "Where did you get this? Are you teaching me to play fetch? Really! A cat who fetches like a dog?" I picked up the puff ball and held it in the air. "One, two." I moved my hand with each number.

Barley flinched and braced with each word, waiting for the ultimate release.

"Three!" My voiced sounded high pitched with the last number, and I flung the puff ball behind the couch.

Barley leaped onto the couch and to the floor with lightning speed. Within seconds, he returned to the same spot and set it down.

"Again?"

"Mat, mat." He chirped and braced to launch.

Giggling, I threw the toy three more times before he decided not to fetch it anymore.

He jumped on the back of the couch, turned in circles several times, and placed his head between his paws.

I couldn't help but wonder if he learned the game from the previous tenants or figured it out himself. Either way, I decided I liked even more now.

After finishing the show, I climbed the stairs and changed into soft pajamas. I needed to review my patient load for the morning, but wanted to get some sleep as soon as I had a plan for the day. I grabbed my laptop and crawled into bed. Within seconds, the soft pad of Barley's feet on the comforter registered in my ears. Waiting for him to settle in, I reviewed the first two scheduled patients before I fell asleep with the computer still in my lap and in the middle of stroking Barley's shiny, onyx fur.

The next morning, I stopped by the Mountain Tops

Home Health Agency office to check in and find out if they assigned me any new orders for physical therapy.

Amongst the list of new orders, I saw a name I recognized. Alvin Palizzi, Janie's dad, had an order, and I wondered why Janie didn't mention the script earlier. Most prescriptions came for individuals who were hospitalized for at least three nights because of a surgery, illness, or injury. I knew Alvin wasn't in the hospital because I met him at the farmer's market only two days ago. The paper listed my name specifically. I placed it in my day timer and walked to the car to call ahead to make an appointment. A female voice answered the phone. Surprised, my mouth filled with cotton. Margaret?

---

16

*S*till sitting in the company parking lot, I paused briefly before responding. "Hi! My name is Ally Justice, and I am a physical therapist who works for Mountain Tops Home Health Physical Therapy." My words initially came out with a stutter. "I received a prescription for Alvin Palizzi, and I would like to schedule an appointment to start treatment. Is he available to talk?"

"Ally! Hi! It's Janie. I'm so happy you received our request."

I took a deep breath and relaxed my grip on the phone. "Janie. Whew! I'm so glad you are the person on the other end. You scared me because I thought for sure the voice belonged to Margaret, and I wasn't really in the mood to go through her to help Alvin. I put your number on my phone when you gave it to me, but your name didn't show up on my screen. I'm not sure what happened."

"This isn't my cell phone," she explained. "This is Dad's landline. You won't believe this, but he finally agreed to let David and I live in the basement! We are rearranging the area right now to get ready for the move."

A mom and two small children walked in front of my car, one kid jumping on the back of the other playfully.

"What great news! How did you convince Margaret to agree?"

Janie cleared her throat. "Oh, she doesn't know about the plan yet. She has been so busy dealing with the break-in, she isn't micromanaging Dad's life. I can't believe we didn't come up with this idea sooner, or we would already live here. We convinced Dad the town was not as safe as the place once was, and it would be better if we stayed here to take care of him. The plan turned out to be a brilliant one!"

The roaring sound of a diesel engine from a passing truck caused me to pause before responding. The foul smell of exhaust penetrated the inside of my car. "I'm happy for you, Janie! So, what do you need from me as far as intervention?"

"Dad's safety and mobility are not as good as when he was younger. David and I realize, with the move and all, we will need some help in making sure Dad doesn't hurt himself. He has been acting kind of weird and doing things which put him at risk. We figured you would be the perfect person to whip him into shape. We called the agency and explained we would pay cash if they assigned you to him. They didn't give us a hard time at all. They said you would call us as soon as the office opened. And you did!" She giggled.

"I'm happy to help. How about eleven-thirty today? I have a patient up-valley and then will work my way down-valley. I can meet you then."

"Sounds great! We'll make sure he is ready."

When I ended the call, I knew this wouldn't be a simple task of helping a man in need. With this family, complications seemed unavoidable. However, Janie needed my help, and I planned to provide what she desired.

I drove to Rita's house for my first appointment of the day. Earlier, I planned for it to be her last visit, and I guaranteed her she was ready for discharge. I retrieved my equipment and ventured towards her house.

Rita stood on the front porch with one hand on her hip. "What took you so long?"

A wheel of my cart caught on a pebble and I wiggled the carrier loose. "What are you talking about? I am fifteen minutes early."

"Well, if you wanted a get out of jail free card, you would be anxious, too. Let's get this thing going!" She headed into the house and looked over her shoulder.

Retracting the handle, I carried the case up the stairs. "I know you are excited about your last day of therapy, but you should think about being nice because I might not provide you with your walking papers."

"I don't take too lightly to threats," Rita pivoted and halted. "How about we move this session out to the shooting range, and I'll show you how ready I am?"

"Oh, no. I'm not going with you near any sort of weapon in this mood. It's a lose-lose situation. If your coordination improved, you'll prove you can hit your target, which could be me. If you haven't, then I'm stuck working with you for a while longer." Shrugging, I presented open palms. "See? Lose-lose."

Rita opened the screen door. "At what point during our relationship did you start to be so snarky?"

Walking past Rita, I stepped into the house and turned around to wait for her to take the lead. "At the point where I realized hanging out with you and Helen is a matter of survival of the fittest. I count my blessings. I have the experience from my missions with the agency to call upon when I need to protect myself."

Rita's shoulders sagged, and she gazed at the ground. "All right. All right. I concede. What do I have to do to prove I am ready to be an ex-patient?"

"Let's start with a high-level balance test. The results will help me determine your level of progress." I took her through the test and several other assessments. Rita performed remarkably well. "Sticking your nose in other people's business has really helped you recover from your stroke."

Frankly, if the same thing happened to me, I would want chasing down bad guys to be my therapy, too.

"The law force in this town is small. They need my help. So, how did I do?"

"Actually, I think running around and solving crimes is the type of treatment which works best for you. I am officially ready to discharge you as of today. Congratulations! I wish I had a t-shirt to give you stating, *I survived physical therapy and lived to tell about it!*"

"I suspect few people would be running around town with the same t-shirt." Rita busted out laughing.

Let the torture recommence.

"Meanwhile, while you enjoy yourself at my expense, I have to pack to go to my next appointment. I am dying to share who my next patient is, but telling you would violate privacy."

Rita gave a crooked smile. "Don't worry. I already know you are seeing Alvin Palizzi. Janie told Betty, who told Helen, who told me."

Already in the middle of packing my equipment, I paused and rolled my eyes. "Oh, right. The good ol' mountain gossip chain. I keep forgetting."

Rita grabbed my tablet and handed it to me. "It's a small town with not a lot to do."

I pulled on the zipper of my luggage and extended the handle. "Obviously. Well, congratulations again. I'll chat with you later today."

Rita grabbed her keys off the table. "Wait! Maybe I can come with you and help." She stepped towards the front door.

"Not possible." I stretched out both hands, palms facing her. "Letting you tag along would definitely be a problem. He and his family are expecting to see only me. If you come too, I would have to explain how you knew he needed therapy. I don't want them to think I am part of your gossip chain. Don't worry. If I find any information which might help solve the Seth crime, I'll let you know." I waved behind me as I headed outside, the door slamming as a last gesture.

Driving to Alvin's house required some navigating. The roads between the farms must have come as an afterthought, since they really made no logical sense. The idea of using a grid clearly didn't cross their minds. I used the maps app on my phone, but the software didn't work as precisely as in the city. I passed his mailbox, which had his address on the side, three times before finally figuring out the container belonged to him. The letters on the box read PFF and the house numbers were so small, I had to squint to see them.

Two crabapple trees adorned the beginning of a long, dirt driveway which passed two barns and a horse stable. The smell of manure and hay wafted through my cracked driver's window. Alvin's house, a two story, beautiful, multi-pitch house, had large windows both front and back. Huge glass panes provided a view of the mountain behind the house. The structure had a wraparound balcony which sat above two full-sized garages with separate doors. The siding had a rustic, metal look, which made the house seem like the perfect mountain home. Several hundred yards behind the home stretched a vast field with probably seventy-five head of cattle grazing on the yellow, orange, and green grass.

As I parked the SUV, I noticed Janie strolling down the sidewalk to greet me. I crawled out of the driver's seat and opened the back door to retrieve my equipment bag.

She smiled and waved. "Hi. You found us. You didn't even have to call me to come get you and guide you in. Usually, people try for about fifteen minutes and then give up and cry for help."

I chuckled. "I can see why, but I guess I got lucky. This is an amazing property! I could disappear here and never be found again. Did Alvin design the place?"

Janie looked down at the ground with a frown. "My mom was the one who had the vision of how she wanted the homestead to look. She had a knack for design and practicality. A farmer's wife has to look well-bred and get muddy and dirty all in the same day. My mom did both really well."

"Well, she sounds like an amazing woman. My guess is, you take after her. Even in the short time I've known you, I can tell you are smart, practical, kind, and strong. Alvin is lucky to have you." I noticed tears in her eyes.

"Thanks." She looked off into the distance, wrinkles on her forehead, her mouth down-turned. "I'm really worried about my dad. Farmers let nothing bring them down, but he is acting differently than normal. I know he's getting older, but he is one of the toughest men I know. I can tell he is not himself. He has survived droughts and storms which threatened our entire livelihood, losing the woman of his dreams, water shortages, and diseases which took out half a herd of cattle, you name it. He came through all the tough times without even letting anyone know the experience affected him. But lately, he has been losing weight, and he never has an appetite."

I gently touched her arm, her skin slightly cool. "I can see how the change must be upsetting. You and David focus on finishing your move, and I'll take good care of your dad. He knows I'm coming, right?"

Janie bit her lower lip and didn't answer immediately. She looked over her shoulder after several cows mooed in the distance.

This should be interesting. I just became the key player is Janie's clever plan.

17

"We told him the doctor wants him to have physical therapy. I will warn you, old-time farmers don't accept help readily. I am a little worried he might develop some sort of dementia, and he won't remember us talking about you coming. When I walked into his bathroom earlier, he was talking to himself and pointing in the mirror. He is not usually like this. Maybe he acted like this for a while, and we didn't know since we weren't here as often as we wanted."

I grabbed the handle of my bag. "It's important to take one thing at a time. You already started the first step of moving you and David into this house permanently. Focus on finishing the transition, and I'll do my assessment and let you know about his specific needs. I'll help as much as I can to improve his quality of life. Now, go lift heavy boxes, bend your knees, and don't hurt your back."

Janie placed her hand on the small of my back and smiled. "You're right. Thank you so much. I don't know if I could handle this without you. If I do hurt my back, I have an amazing physical therapist as a friend to help me rehab.

Let me walk you in the house and reintroduce you to my dad." She led the way up the stairs to the main floor of the house. She walked through a large, open room with hardwood floors and a stone fireplace in the center.

The fireplace divided the room into two, one of which served as a sitting area and the other, a living room with a sectional couch, marble coffee table, and matching end tables. An oversized TV hung on the wall. The influence Janie's mother had in terms of the interior design impressed me. Colors of furniture, styles of wood, and room accents blended harmoniously. With me following, she continued through the rooms and entered the kitchen and dining room area.

Alvin rested at a large cherry wood table, drinking a cup of steaming coffee. He stood to greet me when Janie and I walked into the room and promptly plopped back down in his chair, nearly missing.

Janie moved to stand by his side and placed a hand on his shoulder. "Dad, this is Ally Justice. She is your new physical therapist. You met her at the farmer's market."

He stuck his hand out to shake mine — his skin cracked and dry. An indicator of a life of hard, physical work. "Pleasure to meet you, Ally. Thanks for coming, although I told Janie I don't need rehab. I would stand to shake your hand like a proper gentleman, but I am tuckered out and my balance isn't as good as it used to be. I'm sure you witnessed that already."

Alvin's face looked pale, his eyes red. He reached for his mug, his hands trembling. "Nice to meet you, Alvin. Working with me will help you feel stronger. Then standing from a chair to greet someone won't be so difficult. I can also improve your balance to keep you from falling out there in a field where someone might not find you right away. Let's do our assessment, and afterwards, I'll let you know if they are concerned for no reason. Since you are my patient and not David, Greg, or Janie, I can assure you I am on your side. Deal?"

Alvin gazed out the back windows and then returned his attention to me. "Deal."

Janie kissed him on the top of the head and left the room.

"What do I have to do?" Alvin asked.

Pulling my equipment bag closer, I retrieved my tablet. "Well, first I would like to ask you a few questions. Do you mind if I sit?"

"Of course not. Please. Have a seat."

The legs of the chair protested loudly as he pulled the armrest closer. I smiled and lowered into the seat. "Janie told me you've had problems with nausea and vomiting, and you've lost some weight. Has the doctor done tests to figure out what is causing these symptoms?" I opened the physical therapy application to record the details of the evaluation.

"I don't go to the doctor just because I feel a little sick," Alvin declared. "I figured something I ate made me ill. My symptoms haven't been bad enough to stop me from doing my work, but they slow me down. This is the prime season for our crops, and I have been very busy. I'm sure the weight loss is because I don't take enough time to eat when I am in the fields a lot."

The computer made a series of chiming noises as the system finished waking up. "Maybe. But I think a checkup with Dr. Dalton might be a good idea. In the meantime, I'll run you through a couple of tests to see what kind of help I can provide." I performed a thorough evaluation, which included balance tests and strength tests. I took his blood pressure and did a comprehensive check of his nervous system. He cooperated with everything I asked him to do without complaining.

When I finished with my assessment, I opted to involve Janie as I explained the results. I excused myself with Alvin and went in the same direction I saw Janie go earlier. I found the stairs leading to the basement and called out Janie's name as I descended. Hearing no response, I kept going, periodically calling out her name as I went. I found her and David in a back bedroom putting together a bedframe. David stood about six feet three inches tall, had wide muscular shoulders, blonde, clean-cut hair. He had on well-worn cowboy boots and jeans with a wide, silver belt buckle with a gold bronco. "Wow! You two could have a career in the moving business. I can't believe you got all of this done in such a short time."

David approached with his hand out. "You must be Ally. I'm David. Thanks for coming over to help Alvin."

I squeezed his hand firmly. "Nice to meet you, David. You're very welcome. Alvin is a nice man, even if he doesn't agree with my being here. I hoped you two would come upstairs and let me explain my findings to all of you at once."

"And get a break from all of this?" David swept both arms out to the side widely. "No problem." He and Janie headed for the stairs.

I followed close behind.

Janie stopped abruptly and pivoted. "My brother, Greg, should be here any moment. I told him about all the changes, and he wants to come and support us. He knows Margaret and Troy will not be happy about the changes and figures there is power in numbers." She continued ascending the remaining steps.

As we reached the top, a man with light brown, wavy

hair, a chiseled jaw and a commanding presence stepped in front of Janie and wrapped his arms around her.

Janie squeezed his waist. "Well, speak of the devil. When did you get here?"

Greg tousled Janie's hair and then reached for David's hand to shake. "Just walked in. How are you, David?"

David smiled, stepped forward, and put his hand on his shoulder. "It's great to see you, Greg. Glad you could come."

Janie smoothed her hair and pointed with an open palm. "Greg, this is Ally Justice. She is a physical therapist and is planning on working with Dad to help him get stronger."

Reaching for his hand, I appreciated the effect of how being raised on a farm impacted a man's body. His chest and arms were solid muscle. "Pleasure to meet you. We are headed to talk to your dad about the results from today's evaluation. Please join us."

David and Greg sat next to Alvin at the dining room table.

Janie circled behind Greg and stuck her finger in his ear. Smiling, she sat down next to him.

I chose the chair next to Alvin. "I did a very thorough workup of your dad, and I agree he has some things to work on decreasing his risk of having a fall. He also needs to regain some strength he has lost recently due to not feeling well. Improving strength takes a lot longer than the time to lose it. It's unfair, but it's the way our body works." I turned towards Alvin. "Sir, I realize you have probably never been to a gym, since slaving on a farm is all the hard work you've ever needed to stay fit. Our activities will be like farming, rather than asking you to do traditional exercises for the first time in your life. I also think it's important for Dr. Dalton to meet with you and do some blood tests to determine why you are getting nauseous, vomiting, and losing weight. I know your kids are very concerned. If you don't think there is a problem, please see Dr. Dalton just to put their minds at ease."

As a door slammed, I jumped in my seat and prepared to strike. The sounds of a commotion came from the front of the house.

Margaret and Troy entered the kitchen. Margaret scanned the table, her hands on her hips, a frown on her face. "What is going on in here?"

18

*E*ven the dogs barking across the field couldn't break the heavy silence in the room.

Margaret narrowed her eyes. "I said, what is going on here?"

Janie rushed to my side. "Ally is going to assess Dad's condition and give him a physical therapy exam. He's been having some issues, so I asked her to help."

"I'm Alvin's wife," Margaret spat. "Why wasn't I consulted about this? Obviously, I care about what my husband needs."

David stood from his chair. "Since we are living here now, we need to make sure Dad is well cared for."

I imagined Margaret's head spinning rapidly around in three circles.

"Living here! What do you mean, living here?" She faced Alvin directly, who had not spoken. "You let them move in? I thought I made myself very clear that your kids are not to stay with you. They have their own houses and don't need to be burdening you."

Janie's face reddened, and her lips pursed. "Burdening

him? We are here to help him. Seth and Troy have been living with you for years. How is this any different?"

Margaret pointed her finger at Janie. "Don't you dare speak ill of my dead son!"

Greg jumped up from his chair and moved in front of Janie with lightning speed. His eyes narrowed as he stared at Troy with his teeth clenched.

Wow! He could work for the agency with those reflexes.

Greg's gaze darted between Troy and Margaret. "She is not saying anything bad about Seth, Margaret. We are protecting our dad. His health is declining, and he did so much for us as kids. He deserves to be taken care of just like he took care of us after mom died."

Troy pushed closer to Margaret and puffed out his chest. He looked alternately at his mom and Greg.

Alvin attempted to stand. His eyes rolled back, and his body swayed. He abruptly plopped back down and grabbed the sides of the chair. "Please, stop this! Everybody sit down and let me talk!" He paused for a moment, blinked, and put his fingers on his temples. "Margaret, after the break-in at your house, I discovered I probably shouldn't be living alone right now. I haven't felt well lately, and living by myself is concerning me. The decision was tough, since I have never asked for help in my life. The determination is mine to make, and I made it. I am a grown man and can decide on my own."

Greg stepped forward and pointed his finger at Troy's chest. "Maybe if you and your brother were more responsible, our family situation could have been different. You are selfish and lazy. I wouldn't be surprised if you poisoned Seth so you could keep all our parent's inheritance to yourself."

Margaret scowled. "Back off, Greg! You're not even around enough to know what happens here daily. Of course,

Troy didn't poison his brother. He loved him just as I did... or do." A single tear ran down her cheek.

Margaret stomped across the kitchen. As she slammed the cabinet door, it rebounded. The buttons beeped on the refrigerator as she chose the water feature on the dispenser. The noises coming from the appliance were the only sound in the room.

She drank slowly during the silence, staring at everyone around the table. Her gaze finally landed on Alvin. "I think the answer is very clear, Alvin. You do not feel well since you have never spoken to me like you just did. You are admittedly not yourself."

Alvin leaned forward; his eyes narrowed. "I am still capable of making decisions and am letting Janie and David live here to help me out. My last will and testament designates this land is to be split between Janie and Greg equally after I die. It makes sense for Janie and David to stay here, since they can easily take over caring for the place after I am gone."

Margaret gasped. "This farm, like all of our property, goes to me when you die!"

Alvin sighed and took a deep breath. "I purposely did not add your name to the deed when we married because this property is the place where these kids grew up. After losing their mom, they didn't deserve to lose the home they shared, too. The place has great sentimental value for these kids. You have your own place to will to Troy and..."

Margaret slammed the glass down on the counter; some of the remaining water splashing over the edge. "You're obviously ill. I'll be nice and wait until you feel better and are more rational before we finish this discussion." She looked at Troy, who had backed up against the wall, his head moving back and forth like he watched a tennis game. "Let's go."

Janie leaned her hands on the tabletop. "Oh, he'll feel better after he sees Dr. Dalton. David and I will make sure he gets there. Don't worry."

Margaret grabbed Troy by the arm. "He doesn't need to visit Dr. Dalton. What he needs is to have you three to stop meddling in his life!" She yanked Troy in front of her and disappeared.

Janie slid back into her chair and placed her head in her hands. "Ally, I'm so sorry you had to witness the problems in my family. It's really embarrassing to have someone from the outside see how dysfunctional my family has become."

I leaned over to hug her. "Janie, I don't think I would recognize the difference between a normal family and a dysfunctional one. I'm sorry you experienced the drama when all you are doing is helping Alvin. I think we should stick to our plan of having Alvin see Dr. Dalton so we can figure out how to improve his health. In the meantime, I will work with him on strengthening and balance. You guys finish getting settled in, and the rest will fall into place."

Janie sniffled. "You are such a good friend to me already, and you hardly even know me. I can't imagine my dad being in better hands."

Her tears wet my cheek just before I dropped my arms. "It's easy to assist nice people like you. Now, you and David finish setting up your bed." I stood and pivoted towards Greg. "It was nice to meet you. It's time to move on to my next appointment. I'll have Dr. Dalton call and let Janie know when he can see Alvin." I turned to face Alvin, who looked at the ground, a blank stare in his eyes. "It was so nice to meet you, Alvin. I look forward to working with you. I'll be back on Wednesday, and we'll start then."

He reached up to shake my hand. "Thanks for coming, Ally. I would walk you out, but I just don't feel like I have the energy."

"You stay put. I'll show myself out. Have a great rest of your day." I picked up my equipment bag.

Greg assisted Alvin to stand and walked him into the living room.

Janie and David followed me out the door, remaining on the porch.

On the way to my car, I saw Janie and David embracing while Janie loudly sobbed. I felt a twinge of pain in my heart and vowed to rescue my new friend and find a happy balance in her life.

When I arrived back at the car, I saw a message in my texts to call Ky immediately. Excitement quickly changed to disappointment as I realized the text came from Sue Morrison, my direct supervisor, instead of Ky. The purpose of the call had to be business and not pleasure. Bummer. My call went straight through with one ring.

"This is Dr. Dalton."

"Hi, Ky. It's Ally. Sue sent me a message stating you wanted me to contact you immediately. I just finished with a patient and called you as soon as I saw the text. What's up?"

"I received a call recently from Margaret Talis, Alvin Palizzi's wife. She sounded very upset and gave me an earful about you forcing physical therapy on Alvin without her consent."

"Alvin is of sound mind and appeared very aware of what Janie did. Margaret showed up at the house after I finished the assessment and raised hell. The situation turned out to be a very uncomfortable moment for me, being an outsider. I can't help but wonder why Margaret wouldn't want Alvin to regain his strength and health."

"I don't know Margaret really well, but I know she likes to be in charge of everyone around her. She came to see me once and spent the entire twenty minutes telling me what kind of problem she had and how I should treat her. Like most people who are control-mongers, she already researched her symptoms on the Internet and decided exactly what she needed. She refused to listen to me."

Shifting in my seat, I leaned against the car door and pulled my leg underneath me. "She appeared more upset about Alvin agreeing to let Janie and David move in than about the physical therapy. The fact I said you would assess Alvin to see what is causing him to have nausea, vomiting, and weight loss clearly unsettled her."

I wondered, again, what motive Margaret possessed to control Alvin's living situation. Is this about money, love, or personal satisfaction? Time to dig deeper and find out.

19

*K*y sighed. "All right. You just gave me a lot of information in one breath. First, Janie and David are moving in at the farm? Don't they already have a house?"

A bead of sweat rolled down my back. I started the car in order to turn on the air conditioning. I hoped the roar of the engine wouldn't drown out my voice or make hearing Ky more difficult. "They do, but they have been wanting to move in with Alvin to help take care of him, and for other reasons, I'll explain later."

"And when did Alvin's symptoms begin?"

"I think they started about two to three weeks ago. Janie didn't tell me the exact timeline. Things felt a little chaotic at their house, as you can imagine. Do you have ideas on a diagnosis?"

"None, I want to say, but I would appreciate if you would call Janie and let her know I will be over to see Alvin within the next two hours."

"No problem. I'm still sitting in his driveway. Do you want me to meet you here?"

"No. I know you have another patient to see. I'll let you know later what I find out, since the information pertains to your treatment plan."

His reference to my earlier attempt at getting information out of him about Seth didn't go unnoticed. He hung up without saying goodbye. I continued to my next client's house, compiling the details I gathered today at Alvin's. I wondered what Ky thought as well.

When I finished with the client visit, I checked my phone to find out if Ky had left a message. I had ten missed calls and four voicemails. I noticed I had texts as well, but I started with the others first.

"Ally, it's Janie. Dr. Dalton came over to see my dad and decided he needed to be admitted to the hospital. I'm nervous and would love it if you call me back, please?" Her voice sounded desperate.

Rita's and Helen's messages parroted the information Janie gave.

The last one from Janie said she went to the hospital and was waiting for Dr. Dalton to come back to the room with results. She wanted to know if I could meet her and David there.

After looking at the texts, I drove to the hospital. I preferred to go home and change, but I knew I didn't have time for a pit stop. Plus, my curiosity overruled every other demand from my body.

Arriving at the hospital within thirty minutes, I messaged Janie to ask for Alvin's room number. When she responded, I entered the hospital, hoping I wouldn't have to encounter Margaret. I wasn't sure I could summon fake professionalism.

Janie, David, Rita, and Helen all gathered in Alvin's room, whispering in the corner.

Alvin lay asleep; the vitals machine monitoring his heart and lungs. The nurses had turned the lighting low and closed the curtains.

When I entered, Janie ran over and hugged me hard enough to take my breath away.

"How's he doing?" I turned to look at his last blood pressure, oxygen saturation, and heart rate.

"He's feeling fine. It's me who is a wreck. I'm worried sick. When Dr. Dalton decided my dad needed to stay, I flashed back to what happened to Seth. It's killing me to sit here and wait for Dr. Dalton to return and tell us what he found."

I wrapped my arms around Janie's shoulders. "I'm sure I would feel the same way, too. You should stay optimistic. If anyone can find out what is wrong with your dad, it's Dr. Dalton. He's very good at..."

The door squeaked open, and I watched Dr. Dalton walk across the room. The flush on my face gave away more information than I wanted.

"You can finish your sentence." Dr. Dalton smiled and winked. "I'll wait."

Janie rushed to his side and put her hand in the crook of his elbow. "Please, Dr. Dalton, can you tell us what you discovered? The wait is making me crazy!"

Dr. Dalton reached out to shake David's hand. "I understand. I'll have to ask Helen and Rita to leave the room. Sharing private information about Alvin with them would violate HIPPA."

Janie looked over her shoulder and turned back. "I don't mind if they stay. They are family friends, and Alvin is fond of both."

Ky pulled a chair to the end of the bed and sat. "Have a seat, and we'll talk." He waited for Janie and David to find a spot. Alvin's symptoms and tests matched someone else I've seen. I wanted to expand on those tests to prove my hunch is correct. The blood tests identified Merilian Sulfide in Alvin's bloodstream.

A collective gasp filled the room, followed by silence. The anxiety in the air felt palpable.

Details of the news flew through my head as I analyzed the information. Alvin and Seth both ingested the same poison. My immediate response: Alvin might die in the same way as his stepson. How did both get exposed and in what timeline? Was it an accident or is it time to ramp up the investigation before Janie gets hurt? Not wanting to voice my concerns verbally, I responded in the expected way. "Merilian Sulfide? The same poison found in Seth's blood?"

Ky nodded. "Exactly the same substance. Before you panic too much, the quantity is not near the concentration Seth had in his system. I'm administering an antidote called Pelican Blue. With the amount present in his body, the treatment should be enough to help him clear the toxin."

After waking Alvin up and explaining what he planned, Ky stood and reached into his pocket and pulled out a vial and a syringe. He injected the liquid into Alvin's IV.

Alvin responded to the doctor's instructions and answered his questions, but soon fell back asleep.

Afterwards, Ky turned to face the rest of us. "I will need to keep him here for a while longer to be sure the antidote is working. We'll do a repeat blood draw when the time is appropriate."

Janie's knee bounced up and down, and she nibbled at her fingernails. "Dr. Dalton, what are the chances that what you're doing won't work?" Her voice squeaked as she asked the question. "Is my dad going to make it?" Tears welled in Janie's eyes.

"I did some research after Seth died." Ky stared at the vitals machine. Afterwards, he pulled a flashlight out of his pocket, lifted Alvin's eyelid, and shined it in his eyes. "I think the chances are good we can rid Alvin's system of the poison. The nausea and vomiting should resolve, and he will feel like eating again. He'll regain strength and weight. As far as any problems with his nervous system or cardio-vascular system, we'll have to wait and see. I suggest you all stay for just a short while longer, and then let him rest. His body will need all of his energy to fight this. Let me know if you need me." He checked Alvin's vitals one more time, pushed buttons on the monitor, and left.

Janie sat in a chair and put her head in her hands.

David stood at her side, rubbing her back.

I remained quiet to let her have a moment.

She looked up a few minutes later with wrinkles on her forehead and rounded shoulders. "How did Seth and my dad end up with something in their systems used to kill a rat? I don't understand."

Helen went over to Janie's side and put a hand against Janie's face. "We don't know yet, but I can guarantee you the three of us will find out. In the meantime, you stay strong and focused so you can help your dad get through this."

Janie placed her hand on top of Helen's. "I'm not sure how much you can help. We don't even know where to start. I haven't even heard from Sheriff Riddle." She paused, looking up at Alvin's bed. "Thanks so much, Helen. I don't know how David and I would make it through this without you guys."

Rita touched Janie's shoulder. "We are here for you whenever you need us. Just text or call, anytime."

With Rita and Helen following, I left David and Janie to sit with Alvin alone. I waited until I stepped outside of the hospital before I spoke. "We now have two victims of poisoning. I think the likelihood of accidental ingestion is off the table."

Rita stopped walking and turned towards Helen and me. "I agree. The question is, who would have the motive to kill both Seth and Alvin?"

20

*H*elen surveyed the street before she said anything, her eyes sweeping like a radar. A man with a straw hat straddled a riding lawnmower and made calculated, tight turns in a small patch of grass. The wind generated by the blades sent a paper bag sailing through the air. Potted purple, yellow, and pink pansies lined the sidewalks. A local artist's painting of a black bear in a forest covered a large electrical box. Helen's tongue danced across her top lip, moistening it. "I think we should reconvene at my house to discuss this. We don't want anyone overhearing us. The gossip in this town spreads lightning fast."

I crossed my arms and cocked an eyebrow. "True, and, usually, you're the lightning bolt."

Helen just gave a shrug and walked towards the parking lot. "Everyone has their roles to play here. Information gathering is mine. Let's go."

When I arrived at Helen's house, I realized I couldn't think on an empty stomach.

She heated a tuna casserole she had made earlier. Light

brown bread crumbs covered the top with diced carrots and green peas peeking through. She opened three beers, passed them out to us, and sat down at the table.

I savored a sip of lager, something I acquired a taste for since moving to the area. As I rested for a moment, I held off before discussing the situation in more detail. The oceanic scent of the casserole teased my nose and made my stomach growl. Bitter hops sent chills down my spine as I took a deep breath.

The chime of the ringer on my phone startled me and brought me back to reality. I looked at the screen and saw Janie's number. "Hi Janie. Did you and David make the journey back home okay?"

Her breathing sounded quick and labored. "We did, but Margaret and Troy just pulled up in the driveway!"

"I don't think I can handle taking her on after experiencing the whole scare with my dad, and I'm a little worried David may react too strongly. Can you come over here, fast?"

"Of course. I'll be there as soon as I can." I hung up the phone and gazed longingly at the casserole boiling in the oven.

Helen scooted to the edge of her chair. "What's going on?"

I scooted my chair back and stood to grab my keys. "Margaret and Troy are at Alvin's farm. Janie wants me to come over to provide support. I'm going home to retrieve my nine. I left my piece at home since I couldn't take a weapon into the hospital. Rita, I hope you have something in your car. My instinct tells me we should hurry! Let's go!"

"Wait!" Helen attempted to stand twice before succeeding. "You don't need to go all the way home." She darted out of the room and returned with two pistols in one hand and her revolver in the other. She handed us each a gun.

As I turned the weapon around in my hand, I examined its components—three fifty-seven magnum, double action, six rounds, with a six-inch barrel. Nice. "Wow! I didn't know you had an entire arsenal in your home. You sure you don't mind if I use it? It's obviously registered in your name. If something goes wrong, they'll trace the gun back to you."

"Actually, I got this beauty as a gift. I never had to register the piece because it's not required in Colorado." She and Rita exchanged glances.

I knew better than to ask any further questions. Most of the time, the criminals I helped to take down had illegal weapons. Using an unregistered piece put me at more risk of getting in trouble with Director Sanchez.

Helen flipped off the oven, leaving the casserole for later.

The aroma of fresh baked bread and tuna lingered in the air. I inhaled deeply one more time, ignoring the hunger pang in my stomach. I drove the SUV, since I knew I would arrive there faster than letting Helen or Rita drive. After I climbed into my vehicle, I placed my weapon on the seat next to me. I looked over to see Helen cradling hers in her lap. On the way over to Janie's house, I considered the reason Margaret showed up at the farm, since Alvin remained at the hospital. "I think we might want to look around before we ring the doorbell."

I knew I didn't need to explain myself to Rita with her experience, but I wasn't sure about Helen.

Cutting the engine as I entered the driveway, I let the SUV coast the rest of the way. I hoped the people inside of the house were too busy talking to notice the sound of tires crunching gravel. Two vehicles lined the driveway, one of which I recognized as Margaret's burgundy luxury car Janie described earlier. I did not detect any movement on the outside of the house. The section of the home where I evaluated Alvin had lights on, but I couldn't see any figures from where I sat in the car.

Helen climbed out and pointed like a fire chief at an inferno. "I'll cover the back. Rita, you cover the east side of the house, since the west side is exposed. Ally, you check out the entrance and act like you've come alone."

I looked over at Rita and smiled. Even without the training, Helen turned out to be quite the asset. I slid out without making a sound, tucked the revolver in the back of my pants and went my assigned direction with no additional words exchanged.

When I peered through the front window leading to the sitting room and dining room, I saw both were empty. I wiggled the front doorknob, which was left unlocked, and let myself in quietly. Pausing for a moment, I listened to tense voices, but couldn't make out what they were saying. The sounds came from the kitchen, where the light glowed from inside. As I quietly glided forward, the individual voices became easier to identify.

Janie spoke rapidly as she explained why she and David moved in with Alvin.

Margaret interrupted her frequently, causing Janie to stutter.

As I pasted my body up against a wall, the rough surface caught the threads of my shirt. Unphased, I slowly peered around the corner into the kitchen. Instinctively and out of pure habit, I touched the cold pistol tucked into my back waistband. What I saw made alerts go off in my head and body as my muscles tightened and my pulse increased.

Margaret had Janie and David backed into the corner of the kitchen.

David stood in front of Janie in a protective stance, his feet wide.

Margaret held a pistol pointed at them.

I scanned the rest of the room, looking for Troy. He wasn't present in the room as far as I could see. The chance Margaret operated alone seemed slim. I listened again for sounds from other regions of the house, but could not distinguish any above the ones coming from Margaret's mouth.

"You two think you are so clever." Margaret spat as she talked. "You figure, if you are living here and pretending to help Alvin, you will take over this property when he dies. I have news for you, though. You don't have any idea who you are up against. I put up with taking care of your dad for over twenty years, and I am not letting you destroy all the work I've done. I will make sure I get what rightfully belongs to me and my kids." She paused, took a deep breath, and exhaled slowly. "Well, to the kids I have left."

David took a small step forward and put his hands in a position of surrender. "Look, Margaret, Janie and I are both sorry about what happened to Seth. His death is a tragedy. However, Janie and Greg are Alvin's children and deserve to benefit from all the hard work they put into this farm."

Margaret shook the pistol at him. "Get back. I can see what you are doing, and it's not working. You guys did your own thing for a lot of years. My boys stuck around to help me, but you two have hardly been here to see what things are like. Alvin's been having hallucinations and acting weird. You two think getting him to sign the deed over to you both as beneficiaries is legal, but it's not. He has to be of sound mind for such an act to hold up in court, and I have proof he is definitely not sane right now."

Janie peeked around David's shoulder — her eyes

squinted and teeth clenched. "He might be acting a little differently lately, but what do you expect from a man whose wife has been poisoning him?"

Knowing Margaret's behavior could escalate with such an accusation, I intervened. Taking several steps back into the living room, I called out Janie's name as though I had just arrived. I hastened into the kitchen.

Margaret shifted positions, her gaze shifting back and forth between Janie, David, and me. She held the gun down by her side. "We are having a private family meeting."

Janie started across the floor. "What are you doing here? Ally! Thank goodness! I am so glad you came."

"Don't move!" Margaret raised the pistol to shoulder height and aimed, alternating between targets. "I guess, since you interrupted our conversation, now you can make yourself useful." She leaned over a bag perched on the table, keeping her eyes trained on me, and tossed some ropes in my direction.

One of them painfully whipped my arm. The stinging sensation caused my anger to flare. I regained composure by controlling my breath.

Margaret pointed at Janie and David. "Tie these two up to the dining room chairs. I want this to look like a robbery Troy is upstairs, taking things of value. All I need is to call his name, and he'll be right here to help me."

Things just took a serious turn for the worse.

21

"*I* can't believe my dad married you, let alone stayed with you for these years." Janie stepped to the side of David but kept her hands on his shoulders. "I don't know how you convinced him to remain married. Just being around you as much as I have been forced to is hard enough. What did you say to keep him from leaving? We think you must have information which could cause him harm. Being with you must have been worse."

Margaret took a step closer to Janie and pointed her finger in her face. "You think you know so much? Your dad is gay, you naïve little idiot. He didn't want anyone to know about his homosexuality because the other farmers would never accept him. Our fake arrangement hid his little secret. You always thought of your family as a perfect little arrangement, but even your precious relatives have deep secrets."

Janie gasped and dropped her arms to her side.

Margaret lifted her top lip. "The problem is, I got tired of being married and giving up everything else. So, I figured out a way to improve my circumstances."

After easing Janie and David into the dining room

chairs, I tied their legs and arms with loose knots. I hoped they both took any opportunity to free themselves as soon as I distracted Margaret. As I worked, I surveyed the area for signs of Helen or Rita.

Margaret sidestepped to check the knots while still holding her gun on me.

In my mind, I calculated exactly two moves to take the weapon away from her, but feared she would lose control and accidentally shoot either Janie or David. I stood and waited. Patience in these situations came easy because of my vast experience.

Janie wiggled in her chair. "What do you mean, you found a way to make the circumstances better?"

Margaret stepped back and faced Janie and David. "Well, I hoped you would ask. I searched for a way to get rid of Alvin with no one knowing. I researched various toxins for a long time before deciding on the right one. Merilian sulfide has been used by others to slowly murder someone without getting caught. It's commonly found in rat poison, so I didn't have to worry about being a suspect. Everyone here keeps it around to eliminate the nasty creatures." Margaret leaned forward with a grin on her face. "And the best part of the plan? It's known as the Inheritance Powder!" She bent over and slapped her knee and laughed. "Isn't the name brilliant? What could be more perfect than a poison made specifically for my purposes?"

Janie hissed. "How did you sneak it to him?"

Margaret rolled her eyes and clucked her tongue. "See, that's exactly why I'm the one making all the decisions. Getting him to ingest the stuff was easy. I simply added a little to each of the beers I bought. The fact my plan worked is actually his fault for having such a stupid habit."

So that explains the bottle caps and bottles. "Next, are

you going to admit killing your own son as well?"

Margaret growled and pointed the gun at my head. "Listen here, you annoying, worthless, wannabe doctor! I did not intend for Seth to have any of the substance, and I did not kill my son! Apparently, Seth stole some of Alvin's beers without me knowing. He must have grabbed some after he carried them in the house and snuck them out without my knowing. After Seth's death, I spent quite a bit of time pondering how my precious boy ended up with the poison in his system. Then, I remembered Alvin complaining a few times about my shorting him several beers. At the time, I figured he forgot or the Inheritance Powder worked faster than the internet indicated. I figured him losing his memory was a good sign. Seth and Troy made a habit out of drinking, and the only way I could have any influence over them was to ban it from my home. I didn't want to draw more attention to our family. I was unaware he drank the beers until it was too late. Thinking Alvin drank them, I assumed he would be dead by now." Margaret stopped talking and her shoulders slumped. "Alvin should be a corpse and not my precious Seth. Trust me, I won't let a stupid thing like this happen again. Alvin will continue to decline, and you three ingrates can't help him, since you'll be shot during a breaking and entering gone bad. I am really brilliant at making—"

The clicking sound of footsteps came from the hallway. Troy rounded the corner. "Mama, how's it going in here?"

Eyes wide, Margaret quickly turned and pointed the gun in his direction. "Damn it Troy. You know better than to sneak up on me! There's no way Ally showed up without the other two--"

Perfect opportunity. I took two quick steps forward and performed a roundhouse kick with my right leg, knocking the gun out of Margaret's hand, and then swept her knees with my left.

Margaret slammed down forcefully on her back, hitting her head on the floor; a rush of air escaping her lungs.

I rolled to my left to grab her pistol. But before I returned to my feet, Troy had a gun pointed at my head.

Troy took a step forward. "Don't move an inch."

Annoyed at being outdone by a beginner, I slowly raised my hands above my head.

Helen rounded the corner of the hallway Troy came from and leveled a revolver on Troy. "Do you want your mama to lose two sons?"

Rita ran in behind Helen, her weapon lifted.

Wow. Helen has skills. Thank goodness for crazy women and their arsenals.

The distraction gave me enough time to recover from my position, pull Helen's gun out of my waistband, and place the muzzle against Troy's temple. "Now would be a good time to let go of your weapon."

Troy released the gun and bent over to help Margaret up.

"Rita, untie Janie and David," I instructed. "I'll need those chairs and ropes to detain Margaret and Troy until Sheriff Riddle can get here and take them in."

"Do you really think you can change my plan?" Margaret challenged. "Alvin will still die, and the property will be mine." She looked at Janie and David. "You two and your brother will end up with nothing!"

"Margaret, I hate to be the bearer of bad news, but they gave Alvin the antidote to the poison, and he is on the way to recovery. He should have no problems signing the divorce papers." I waved the gun at a chair. "Now, sit down right there. You too, Troy."

Rita and Helen efficiently secured Troy and Margaret to the dining room chairs, stepped back, wiping their hands together.

A shrill sound blared from outside. The sirens bellowed against the glass of the windowpanes. Flashes of red, blue, and white reflected off a mirror in the living room.

Helen disappeared from the kitchen for a few seconds and then returned with Sheriff Riddle in tow.

He surveyed the area slowly before he noticed Margaret and Troy restrained in the chairs. The sheriff turned his attention to Helen. "Let me guess. You three found trouble again. Exactly what happened here and, more importantly, why?"

Helen grinned and patted him on the shirt. "Wow, honey. Your uniform is wrinkled. Since that never happens, I can only hope you've found the mother of Bryce's future brother or sister."

Sheriff Riddle's face reddened. "Seriously, Mom. In front of these people? You're trying to distract me from the fact you are meddling in yet another investigation."

Janie stepped forward with a light laugh. "I think I can answer every one of your questions."

Sheriff Riddle placed his hand on his holster. "Stay put Janie and David. I am going to take these two down to the station." He pointed to Margaret and Troy. "I'll be back to take statements from each of you. Rita, Helen and Ally, you guys can go home. I'll be by later to get your reports." He untied Margaret and Troy and placed them in handcuffs. "Let's go."

Another official statement on the books. I may as well just show up on Abdul's doorstep and save him the trouble of trying to find me.

---

*a*fter Rita, Helen, Janie, and David went downstairs, I followed in order to take a moment to decompress. The stairs creaked under my weight as I descended, and a musty smell hit my nose as I reached the bottom. Haphazardly stacked boxes cluttered the living room, and six chairs sat between them.

David grabbed five beers and handed us each one.

The cold aluminum can felt slick against my palm and droplets of condensation dripped onto my fingers. When I opened the top, a faint aroma of hops and barley wafted from the can.

Rita sat slowly and stared down at her beer without moving. "I'm not sure we should drink these. How do we know they are safe?"

David laughed. "Don't worry. I just bought these today. There is no way Margaret tampered with them."

The sound of his laughter provided a welcome relief after the tense events of the night. I took a swig of mine without saying a word, enjoying the fizzy sensation on my tongue. The carbonation tickled my nose, and I felt a wave of relaxation wash over me as my nerves calmed. I sat on a chair which creaked under the weight of my body. "Thanks for the drink, guys. Janie, you accused Margaret of poisoning Alvin. How did you come to that conclusion?"

Janie sat next to Rita. "We didn't know for sure, but we noticed two things which made little sense—why my dad stayed married to a wretched woman and why his health declined so rapidly. We lay in bed one night discussing our questions, and David mentioned he wondered if Margaret could be slowly killing Alvin. At first, I thought he was crazy, but we were running out of ideas. We didn't know exactly how she would do it, but we knew something wasn't right."

"I'd say those are some pretty good reasoning skills." Rita leaned back and gulped her beer.

Smiling at Rita's chugging skills, I searched my brain for information. "Earlier, when we were at the bar, I researched the facts about Merilian Sulfide. The substance has can treat ringworm. It's possible the bottle Rita saw in Margaret's house could be what she put in the beer. I thought it unlikely she would keep the pills in her medicine cabinet, just in case someday she would need it. She seemed obsessed with organization. Janie and David, you should probably tell the sheriff you stumbled across some interesting items during one of your visits to her house. Warning him will save Rita, Helen, Bryce, and me from having to explain how we discovered them. Then we won't have to go down for breaking and entering."

"No problem." Janie scooted further back in her seat. "For you guys, I would say and do anything right now. I'm just so thankful you saved our lives. She planned to kill us. I'm just sad I have to tell my dad about her betrayal. He'll probably feel awful because the only reason she stayed with him was to take all the family's money. I think she saw an opportunity when she found out he was gay and pounced."

"I would like to see how he is doing." My voice sounded laced with concern. "How about I meet you guys at the hospital around nine o'clock, and I can help answer questions he might have? It'll put my mind at ease knowing he will really be okay."

"Sounds like a brilliant plan," Janie exclaimed. "As soon as Sheriff Riddle finishes his investigation, I would like to get some much-needed sleep."

The warm amber light from a nearby lamp illuminated the room, casting a cozy glow, enveloping us in its warmth. I could hear the gentle hum of a fridge in the background. "I should have known better than to drink a beer after all of this mess. It always makes me tired." Setting my beer down on a box, I rose from the chair. "We'll see you in the morning at the hospital. Call us if you need anything. Even if something else comes up tonight. My decompression process is a little lengthier than yours."

I headed back upstairs with Helen and Rita close behind. Our footsteps sounded like the hooves of horses going over a bridge.

The cool, refreshing air hit my face as I stepped outside, the soft crunch of gravel beneath my feet filling the silence.

After dropping my two friends at Helen's house, I went home looking forward to the soft comfort of my bed. The next day, I met Janie, Greg, and David at the hospital. The pungent smell of disinfectant brought back memories of my earlier stay. My stomach tightened slightly. I waited with the group for Alvin to wake up; the faint beeping of the machines and soft chatter of voices from the nearby nurse's station filled the room.

When he opened his eyes, he looked around the room

multiple times. His gaze darted around before finally settling on Jane.

"Look who is awake," Janie commented, standing at Alvin's bedside. "How are you feeling, Dad?"

"A lot less nauseous, but starving." He rubbed his eyes and pulled his blanket up to his chest.

David stood next to Janie. "I'd say hunger is a significant sign. How about we call the café and order us all food? They should know if you have any diet restrictions and we can all eat together. Maybe they'll make you a great, big Angus burger?"

Alvin grimaced. "Maybe I should start with some yogurt. I'm not sure my stomach could handle red meat right now."

Janie placed her hand on top of Alvin's. "Dad, do you remember the doctor telling you why you are sick?"

Alvin nodded, his gaze shifting to the window. The bright sun shone through the glass, casting a soft light across the room. "Doc said I have some poison in my system. He wasn't sure how the substance got there, but he gave me an antidote. He says the treatment is why I am feeling better."

Janie's chest heaved and a tear rolled down her face, leaving a trail on her flushed cheek. "Well, I know how the toxin got there. Margaret has been poisoning you for several weeks."

Alvin's face grew heavy as he sank into the bed, his shoulders slumping. "Oh, come on, now, Janie. I know you kids never really liked Margaret, but I don't think she would hurt me."

For a moment, the room seemed silent except for the sound of breathing. As I stepped closer to Alvin's bed, the faint smell of antiseptic on his skin filled my nostrils. I could see the crumpled sheets beneath him, creased and stained with sweat. "Sir, I know we just met, but Janie is telling the truth. Margaret put a poison called Merilian Sulfide in your beers when she brought them to your house. Seth died because he stole your beers and drank them. Margaret didn't realize he was thieving and assumed you ingested all the toxins. Last night, she showed up at the farm and held Janie and David at gunpoint. Her intention was to kill them. She figured you would die soon, and she would inherit the property. She set it up to look like a robbery. When you changed your will and let Janie and David move in, she was very frustrated. I think the news might have been the last straw."

He looked down at the bed. "I wondered how my beers disappeared. I figured I was losing my mind. Margaret never did actually care about me. I knew she planned to blackmail me, but I never thought she would try to kill me or my children."

Janie stroked Alvin's forehead. "Dad, she said you are gay. She told us she used the information to get you to do what she wanted. It's the reason you didn't let us move in earlier to take care of you, isn't it?"

The small wrinkles relaxed under Janie's touch. Alvin's eyes welled with tears. "She found out a long time ago when she saw me on a date in Shale. She convinced me she could help hide my issue from the other farmers in the area and keep me from being pushed out of town. I believed her and couldn't imagine she would go so far just to steal my money." Alvin balled his fists around the top of his sheet. "I'm an idiot."

Greg walked to the end of the bed, his footsteps clicking on the linoleum floor. He placed his hand on Alvin's leg. "No, you're not an idiot, Dad. You're an amazing, successful, and kind father. I don't care if other narrow-minded people won't accept you."

Janie laid down on the hospital bed next to Alvin and embraced him. "I just want you to be yourself and be happy, Dad." Janie laid down on the hospital bed next to Alvin and embraced him.

"Janie and Greg, I really loved your mom." A single tear escaped and dripped off the edge of his nose. "She was the only woman I ever treasured. She gave me you both and, for that, I will be eternally grateful."

Greg sniffled and his shoulders trembled with each inhale. "I love you, Dad. Let's just hope eternity turns out to be a lot longer now that you are recovering."

The air in the room felt heavy with emotion, and I could practically taste the saltiness of tears on my tongue.

Alvin kissed Janie on the head and reached out for Greg's hand, his fingers interlocking with his son's. He inhaled and let his breath out slowly. "So, what happened to Margaret and Troy?"

Helen clapped her hands from across the room; the sound echoed like thunder. "That's the best part. After Joey took them to jail, Margaret lost her mind. He plans to check her into a mental institution in Denver. Frankly, it's where she should have been living for a long time."

Alvin chuckled, his shoulders shaking. "I'd say you're absolutely right!"

I placed my hand on Alvin's shoulder. "Well, I think I have pretended to be a part of your family for long enough. I'm going to head home and check on my garden. I'm in a war with a deer who thinks she can outsmart me."

Janie scurried around the bed and opened her arms wide. Her eyes sparkled with unshed tears. "Can we go for a hike this Friday? I really need to blow off some steam."

I stepped into her embrace, and she squeezed my body tightly, causing me to gasp for air. The light scent of her perfume filled my nostrils, and I could feel the softness of her skin against mine. "A hike would be great. I'll call you Friday morning."

On my drive home, the memory of Ky comforting Alvin and his family played in my head. I remembered how his hand had felt on my back, the warmth of his skin a stark contrast to the coolness of the hospital room. His personality, and let's face it, his looks appealed to me. I didn't want to fully admit it to myself, but curiosity about what other special qualities he possessed got the best of me. Could we develop a relationship? Would it be one which could withstand long distance challenges?

As I walked through the front door, the ringing of my burner phone forced me back to reality. "The is Agent Evans."

"Evans, this is Deputy Cunningham. We have a recent development in the Abdul case."

Sighing, I plopped down on the couch. The springs squeaked under the weight of my body. What is this feeling inside of my chest? Is it fear or excitement? Torn between emotions, I inhaled deeply and slowly exhaled. "Ok, Deputy. Give it to me straight."

ALSO BY TRENA REDDING

A Cozy Mountain Town Mystery

Shotgun, Lies & Alibis

ABOUT THE AUTHOR

Trena Redding lives in the Rocky Mountains with her family, 2 dogs, 2 cats, and an adorable rabbit who wears a petite crown and reigns over the back yard. Her next cozy - another small town mystery set in Colorado - is coming soon!

Printed in Great Britain
by Amazon

DICTIONARY OF QUOTATIONS

DICTIONARY OF QUOTATIONS

Edited by Jonathan Hunt

HAMLYN
LONDON · NEW YORK · SYDNEY · TORONTO

First published in 1979 by
The Hamlyn Publishing Group Limited
London · New York · Sydney · Toronto
Astronaut House, Feltham, Middlesex, England

This edition published in 1981

ISBN 0 600 33214 4

Compiled by
Laurence Urdang Associates Ltd,
Aylesbury, Bucks.

7½ on 8½ point Intertype Fototronic
Times Roman

Printed in Great Britain by
Hazell Watson & Viney Ltd,
Aylesbury, Bucks.

Distributed in the U.S. by
Larousse & Co. Inc.,
572 Fifth Avenue, New York,
New York 10036.

INTRODUCTION

The quotations in this book have been selected primarily for their qualities of succinctness, perception, and wit. Many well-known quotations by major authors have been included, but the main criterion for the inclusion of a quotation has been that it should make an original or colourful observation about life. Such quotations, whether they are from speeches or plays, poetry or prose, are potentially useful to the writer or speaker who is looking for something to illustrate a point and is in need of an apt quotation. They also form an interesting introduction to the life, work, or personality of their authors, as well as providing entertaining reading.

An effort has been made to make this selection widely representative and fully up to date. Foreign quotations are given in English where they are best known in this form or in the original language (with a translation) where that is more familiar. Equal weight has been given to the humorous and the serious so as to reflect all aspects of life from the sternly philosophical to the broadly comical.

The quotations are arranged under their authors' names, which are listed alphabetically with a brief biographical description. Additional information is provided for quotations which are set in a specific context or which refer to a particular person or thing. The names of characters in plays and novels are given wherever such information is useful and references to the sources of quotations have been made as full as possible. Within the entry for each author, quotations are arranged in alphabetical order of sources in the case of novels, plays, poems, and other books, and in chronological order in the case of speeches, broadcasts, etc. In the entry for George Bernard Shaw, for example, quotations from the plays are listed first, then a quotation from a novel, and finally miscellaneous and attributed remarks.

Aylesbury, February 1979   Jonathan Hunt
                                                                John Daintith

HOW TO USE THIS BOOK

To assist the reader in finding a particular quotation, each author and each quotation has its own reference number. The author's number forms the first part of the reference number of each quotation by that author. Thus, 'Addison' bears the number '4' and the quotations by Addison are numbered '4.1', '4.2', '4.3', etc.

Each quotation is indexed under a number of key words to enable a fully or half remembered quotation to be traced easily. Key phrases from each quotation are listed in alphabetical order under the appropriate key word, and followed by the reference number of the full form of the quotation in the main text. An additional feature of the index is that some quotations which refer to a particular person or place have been indexed under the appropriate name, even though the the the name itself does not actually occur in the quotation. Thus 'Oxford' occurs in the index, even though Matthew Arnold does not refer to the 'city with her dreaming spires' by name at that point in his poem *Thyrsis*.

The reader may wish to consult the main section of the book directly in order to discover quotations by a particular author. He can use the index to discover the source of a particular quotation and also as a subject index to find quotations about, for example 'beauty', 'war', or 'time'. Browsing through both text and index will offer him the pleasures of variety, chance discovery, and the juxtaposition of the contradictory and the unexpected.

NOTE ON THE INDEX

The first part of a reference number refers to a particular author. The second part refers to the appropriate quotation by that author.

Plurals of nouns are indexed separately from the singular. Possessive forms, such as 'man's' or 'God's' will be found under 'man' and 'God'. Third person singular forms of verbs, such as 'makes' or 'hurries' are indexed separately from the plain form of that verb.

Foreign words are printed in italics. Index words which do not occur within a particular quotation are also printed in italics.

A

1 Acton, John Emerich Edward Dalberg, 1st Baron (1834-1902), English historian.
1.1
Power tends to corrupt, and absolute power corrupts absolutely. Great men are almost always bad men...There is no worse heresy than that the office sanctifies the holder of it.
Letter to Bishop Mandell Creighton, 5 Apr 1887

2 Adams, John Quincy (1767-1848), President of the United States.
2.1
Think of your forefathers! Think of your posterity! *Speech, Plymouth, Massachusetts, 22 Dec 1802*

3 Adcock, Sir Frank (1886-1968), English classicist.
3.1
That typically English characteristic for which there is no English name—*esprit de corps*. *Presidential address*

4 Addison, Joseph (1672-1719), English essayist and dramatist.
4.1
'Tis not in mortals to command success,
But we'll do more, Sempronius; we'll deserve it. *Cato, I:2*
4.2
The woman that deliberates is lost.
same, IV:1
4.3
When vice prevails, and impious men bear sway,
The post of honour is a private station.
same
4.4
Thus I live in the world rather as a Spectator of mankind, than as one of the species, by which means I have made myself a speculative statesman, soldier, merchant, and artisan, without ever meddling with any practical part of life.
The Spectator, 1 Mar 1711
4.5
Sunday clears away the rust of the whole week. *same, 9 July 1711*
4.6
[*Sir Roger*] told them, with the air of a man who would not give his judgment rashly,

that 'much might be said on both sides'.
same, 20 July 1711
4.7
A woman seldom asks advice until she has bought her wedding clothes.
same, 4 Sept 1712
4.8
We are always doing something for posterity, but I would fain see posterity do something for us. *same, 20 Aug 1714*
4.9
See in what peace a Christian can die.
Last words

5 Ady, Thomas (c. 1655), English poet.
5.1
Matthew, Mark, Luke and John,
The bed be blest that I lie on. *A Candle in the Dark*

6 Aesop, (c. 550 B.C.), Greek fabulist.
6.1
Beware that you do not lose the substance by grasping at the shadow. *Fables, 'The Dog and the Shadow'*
6.2
The gods help them that help themselves.
same, 'Hercules and the Waggoner'
6.3
It is not only fine feathers that make fine birds. *same, 'The Jay and the Peacock'*
6.4
Don't count your chickens before they are hatched. *same, 'The Milkmaid and her Pail'*

7 Agar, Herbert Sebastian (b. 1897), American poet and writer.
7.1
The truth that makes men free is for the most part the truth which men prefer not to hear. *A Time for Greatness*

8 Akins, Zoë (1886-1958), American dramatist.
8.1
The Greeks Had a Word for It. *Title of play*

9 Albee, Edward (b. 1928), American dramatist.
9.1
Who's Afraid of Virginia Woolf? *Title of play*
9.2
I have a fine sense of the ridiculous, but no sense of humour. *Who's Afraid of Virginia Woolf?, Act 1*

10 Alcuin, (735-804), English cleric and adviser of Charlemagne.
10.1
Vox populi, vox dei.
The voice of the people is the voice of God.
Letter to Charlemagne

11 Allainval, Abbé Lénor d' (1700-1753), French dramatist.
11.1
L'embarras des richesses.
A superfluity of good things. *Title of play*

12 Ambrose, Saint (340?-397?), Bishop of Milan.
12.1
When in Rome, live as the Romans do: when elsewhere, live as they live elsewhere.
Advice to St. Augustine

13 Amery, Leopold Stennett (1873-1955), English statesman.
13.1
[*To Neville Chamberlain, quoting Cromwell*] You have sat too long here for any good you have been doing. Depart, I say, and let us have done with you. In the name of God, *go!*
Speech, House of Commons, May 1940

14 Anouilh, Jean (b. 1910), French dramatist.
14.1
The object of art is to give life a shape.
The Rehearsal, I:2
14.2
What fun it would be to be poor, as long as one was *excessively* poor! Anything in excess is most exhilarating. *Ring Round the Moon, Act 2*

15 The Arabian Nights
15.1
Who will change old lamps for new ones?...new lamps for old ones?
The History of Aladdin
15.2
Open Sesame! *The History of Ali Baba*

16 Archimedes, (287-212 B.C.), Greek scientist.
16.1
Give me a firm place to stand, and I will move the earth. *On the Lever*
16.2
Eureka!
I have found it! *Remark on making a discovery*

17 Aristotle, (384-322 B.C.), Greek philosopher and scientist.
17.1
What we have to learn to do, we learn by doing. *Ethics, 2*
17.2
Man is by nature a political animal.
Politics, 1
17.3
Inferiors revolt in order that they may be equal and equals that they may be superior. Such is the state of mind which creates revolutions. *same, 5*
17.4
Plato is dear to me, but dearer still is truth.
Attributed

18 Armstrong, Neil (b. 1930), American astronaut.
18.1
[*Of his first step onto the moon*] That's one small step for man, one giant leap for mankind. *Remark, 21 July 1969*

19 Arnold, George (1834-1865), American poet and writer.
19.1
The living need charity more than the dead.
The Jolly Old Pedagogue

20 Arnold, Matthew (1822-1888), English poet and critic.
20.1
The sea is calm to-night,
The tide is full, the moon lies fair
Upon the Straits. *Dover Beach*
20.2
And we are here as on a darkling plain
Swept with confused alarms of struggle and flight,
Where ignorant armies clash by night.
same
20.3
Is it so small a thing
To have enjoy'd the sun,
To have lived light in the spring,
To have loved, to have thought, to have done? *Empedocles on Etna*
20.4
Come, dear children, let us away;
Down and away below.
The Forsaken Merman
20.5
She left lonely for ever
The kings of the sea. *same*
20.6
Who saw life steadily, and saw it whole:

The mellow glory of the Attic stage.
Sonnets to a Friend

20.7
Wandering between two worlds, one dead,
The other powerless to be born.
The Grand Chartreuse

20.8
Go, for they call you, Shepherd, from the hill. *The Scholar Gipsy*

20.9
All the live murmur of a summer's day.
same

20.10
Before this strange disease of modern life,
With its sick hurry, its divided aims.
same

20.11
Still nursing the unconquerable hope,
Still clutching the inviolable shade. *same*

20.12
Others abide our question, Thou art free,
We ask and ask: Thou smilest and art still,
Out-topping knowledge. *Shakespeare*

20.13
[*Of Oxford*] that sweet City with her dreaming spires
She needs not June for beauty's heightening.
Thyrsis

20.14
The pursuit of perfection, then, is the pursuit of sweetness and light. *Culture and Anarchy*

20.15
Thus we have got three distinct terms, Barbarians, Philistines, Populace, to denote roughly the three great classes into which our society is divided. *same*

20.16
[*Of Oxford*] Home of lost causes, and forsaken beliefs, and unpopular names, and impossible loyalties! *Essays in Criticism, First Series, Preface*

20.17
I am bound by my own definition of criticism: a disinterested endeavour to learn and propagate the best that is known and thought in the world. *same, Functions of Criticism at the Present Time*

20.18
Culture, the acquainting ourselves with the best that has been known and said in the world, and thus with the history of the human spirit. *Literature and Dogma, Preface*

21 Arnold, Thomas (1795-1842), English scholar and headmaster.

21.1
What we must look for here is, first, religious and moral principles; secondly, gentlemanly conduct; thirdly, intellectual ability.
Address to the Scholars at Rugby

21.2
My object will be, if possible to form Christian men, for Christian boys I can scarcely hope to make. *Letter on appointment as Headmaster of Rugby, 1828*

22 Ashburton, Baron see **Dunning, John**

23 Asquith, Herbert Henry, 1st Earl of Oxford and Asquith (1852-1928), British statesman.

23.1
Wait and see. *In various speeches, 1910*

24 Astor, John Jacob the third (b. 1918), American millionaire.

24.1
A man who has a million dollars is as well off as if he were rich. *Attributed*

25 Auden, Wystan Hugh (1907-1973), English poet.

25.1
Let us honour if we can
The vertical man
Though we value none
But the horizontal one. *Epigraph for Poems*

25.2
To save your world you asked this man to die:
Would this man, could he see you now, ask why? *Epitaph for an Unknown Soldier*

25.3
To us he is no more a person
Now but a whole climate of opinion.
In Memory of Sigmund Freud

25.4
In the nightmare of the dark
All the dogs of Europe bark,
And the living nations wait,
Each sequestered in its hate.
In Memory of W. B. Yeats

25.5
Intellectual disgrace
Stares from every human face,
And the seas of pity lie
Locked and frozen in each eye. *same*

25.6
Lay your sleeping head, my love,
Human on my faithless arm. *Lullaby*

25.7
To the man-in-the-street, who, I'm sorry to say

Is a keen observer of life,
The word Intellectual suggests straight away
A man who's untrue to his wife.　　*Note on*
Intellectuals
25.8
Our researchers into Public Opinion are
content
That he held the proper opinions for the
time of year;
When there was peace, he was for peace;
when there was war, he went.
The Unknown Citizen

26 Augustine, Saint (354-430), Bishop of
Hippo.
26.1
Give me chastity and continence, but not
yet.　　*Confessions, 8*

27 Austen, Jane (1775-1817), English
novelist.
27.1
EMMA. One half of the world cannot understand the pleasures of the other.
Emma, Ch. 9
27.2
MR WOODHOUSE. Nobody is healthy in
London, nobody can be.　　*same, Ch. 12*
27.3
JOHN KNIGHTLEY. Business, you know,
may bring money, but friendship hardly ever
does.　　*same, Ch. 34*
27.4
Let other pens dwell on guilt and misery.
Mansfield Park, Ch. 48
27.5
CATHERINE MORLAND. But are they all
horrid, are you sure they are all horrid?
Northanger Abbey, Ch. 6
27.6
A woman, especially if she have the misfortune of knowing anything, should conceal it
as well as she can.　　*same, Ch. 14*
27.7
One does not love a place the less for having
suffered in it, unless it has all been suffering,
nothing but suffering.　　*Persuasion, Ch. 20*
27.8
It is a truth universally acknowledged, that a
single man in possession of a good fortune
must be in want of a wife.　　*Pride and*
Prejudice, Ch. 1
27.9
Happiness in marriage is entirely a matter of
chance.　　*same, Ch. 6*
27.10
MR BENNET. For what do we live, but to

make sport for our neighbours, and laugh at
them in our turn?　　*same, Ch. 57*
27.11
MR DARCY. I have been a selfish being all
my life, in practice, though not in principle.
same, Ch. 58
27.12
What dreadful hot weather we have! It keeps
me in a continual state of inelegance.
Letter, 18 Sept 1796

28 Austin, Alfred (1835-1913), English
poet.
28.1
Across the wires the electric message came:
'He is no better, he is much the same.'
On the Illness of the Prince of Wales,
attributed

29 Ayer, Sir Alfred Jules (b. 1910), English
philosopher.
29.1
No morality can be founded on authority,
even if the authority were divine.　　*Essay on*
Humanism

B

30 Bacon, Francis, 1st Baron Verulam
(1561-1626), English writer, philosopher
and statesman.
30.1
If a man will begin with certainties, he shall
end in doubts, but if he will be content to
begin with doubts, he shall end in certainties.
The Advancement of Learning, I:5:8
30.2
What is truth? said jesting Pilate, and would
not stay for an answer.　　*Essays, 1, Of Truth*
30.3
Men fear death, as children fear to go in the
dark; and as that natural fear in children is
increased with tales, so is the other.
same, 2, Of Death
30.4
It is natural to die as to be born; and to a
little infant, perhaps, the one is as painful as
the other.　　*same*
30.5
All colours will agree in the dark.　　*same, 3,*
Of Unity in Religion

30.6
Revenge is a kind of wild justice; which the more man's nature runs to, the more ought law to weed it out. *same, 4, Of Revenge*

30.7
Prosperity doth best discover vice; but adversity doth best discover virtue.
same, 5, Of Adversity

30.8
The joys of parents are secret, and so are their griefs and fears. *same, 7, Of Parents and Children*

30.9
Children sweeten labours, but they make misfortunes more bitter. *same*

30.10
He that hath wife and children hath given hostages to fortune; for they are impediments to great enterprises, either of virtue or mischief. *same, 8, Of Marriage and Single Life*

30.11
Wives are young men's mistresses; companions for middle age; and old men's nurses.
same

30.12
He was reputed one of the wise men, that made answer to the question, when a man should marry? A young man not yet, an elder man not at all. *same, 8, Of Marriage and Single Life*

30.13
There is in human nature generally more of the fool than of the wise. *same, 12, Of Boldness*

30.14
If the hill will not come to Mahomet, Mahomet will go to the hill. *same*

30.15
In charity there is no excess. *same, 13, Of Goodness, and Goodness of Nature*

30.16
If a man be gracious and courteous to strangers, it shews he is a citizen of the world. *same*

30.17
Money is like muck, not good except it be spread. *same, 15, Of Seditions and Troubles*

30.18
The remedy is worse than the disease.
same

30.19
It were better to have no opinion of God at all, than such an opinion as is unworthy of him. *same, 17, Of Superstition*

30.20
Travel, in the younger sort, is a part of education; in the elder, a part of experience.
same, 18, Of Travel

30.21
It is a miserable state of mind to have few things to desire and many things to fear.
same, 19, Of Empire

30.22
Nothing destroyeth authority so much as the unequal and untimely interchange of power pressed too far, and relaxed too much.
same

30.23
Be so true to thyself, as thou be not false to others. *same, 23, Of Wisdom for a Man's Self*

30.24
He that will not apply new remedies must expect new evils: for time is the greatest innovator. *same, 24, Of Innovations*

30.25
To choose time is to save time.
same, 25, Of Dispatch

30.26
Whosoever is delighted in solitude is either a wild beast or a god. *same, 27, Of Friendship*

30.27
Cure the disease and kill the patient.
same

30.28
Riches are for spending. *same, 28, Of Expense*

30.29
Age will not be defied. *same, 30, Of Regiment of Health*

30.30
Suspicions amongst thoughts are like bats amongst birds, they ever fly by twilight.
same, 31, Of Suspicion

30.31
Nature is often hidden, sometimes overcome, seldom extinguished. *same, 38, Of Nature in Men*

30.32
A man that is young in years may be old in hours, if he have lost no time. *same, 42, Of Youth and Age*

30.33
Virtue is like a rich stone, best plain set
same, 43, Of Beauty

30.34
There is no excellent beauty that hath not some strangeness in the proportion.
same

30.35
Houses are built to live in, and not to look on. *same, 45, Of Building*

30.36

God Almighty first planted a garden. And indeed it is the purest of human pleasures.

same, 46, Of Gardens

30.37

Studies serve for delight, for ornament, and for ability. *same, 50, Of Studies*

30.38

Some books are to be tasted, others to be swallowed, and some few to be chewed and digested. *same*

30.39

Reading maketh a full man; conference a ready man; and writing an exact man.

same

30.40

Fame is like a river, that beareth up things light and swoln, and drowns things weighty and solid. *same, 53, Of Praise*

30.41

Nature, to be commanded, must be obeyed.

Novum Organum

30.42

I have taken all knowledge to be my province. *Letter to Lord Burleigh, 1592*

31 Bacon, Francis (b. 1909), Irish artist.

31.1

How can I take an interest in my work when I don't like it? *Francis Bacon (Sir John Rothenstein)*

32 Bagehot, Walter (1826-1877), English economist and journalist.

32.1

The Times has made many ministries.

The English Constitution, Ch. 1

32.2

It has been said that England invented the phrase, 'Her Majesty's Opposition'.

same, Ch. 2

32.3

Poverty is an anomaly to rich people. It is very difficult to make out why people who want dinner do not ring the bell.

Literary Studies, 2

33 Bairnsfather, Charles Bruce (1888-1959), English soldier and cartoonist.

33.1

Well, if you knows of a better 'ole, go to it.

Fragments from France, 1

34 Baldwin, James Arthur (b. 1924), American writer.

34.1

If the concept of God has any validity or use, it can only be to make us larger, freer, and more loving. If God cannot do this, then it is time we got rid of Him. *The Fire next Time*

34.2

Money, it turned out, was exactly like sex, you thought of nothing else if you didn't have it and thought of other things if you did. *Nobody Knows My Name*

34.3

The future is... black. *Observer 'Sayings of the Week', 25 Aug 1963*

35 Baldwin, Stanley (1867-1947), British statesman.

35.1

I would rather be an opportunist and float than go to the bottom with my principles round my neck. *Attributed*

35.2

The intelligent are to the intelligentsia what a man is to a gent. *Attributed*

36 Balfour, Arthur James (1848-1930), British statesman and philosopher.

36.1

It is unfortunate, considering that enthusiasm moves the world, that so few enthusiasts can be trusted to speak the truth. *Letter to Mrs Drew, 1918*

36.2

Nothing matters very much, and very few things matter at all. *Attributed*

37 Ball, John (?-1381), English priest and leader of the Peasants' Revolt.

37.1

When Adam delved and Eve span,
Who was then the gentleman? *Text for sermon*

38 Bankhead, Tallulah (1903-1968), American actress.

38.1

[*Of the revival of a play by Maeterlinck*] There is less in this than meets the eye.

Remark

38.2

I'm as pure as the driven slush.

Observer 'Sayings of the Week', 24 Feb 1957

39 Barnum, Phineas Taylor (1810-1891), American showman.

39.1

There's a sucker born every minute.

Attributed

40 Barrie, Sir James Matthew (1860-1937), Scottish novelist and dramatist.

40.1

When the first baby laughed for the first time, the laugh broke into a thousand pieces and they all went skipping about, and that was the beginning of fairies. *Peter Pan, Act 1*

40.2

Every time a child says 'I don't believe in fairies' there is a little fairy somewhere that falls down dead. *same*

40.3

One's religion is whatever he is most interested in, and yours is Success.
The Twelve-Pound Look

40.4

You've forgotten the grandest moral attribute of a Scotsman, Maggie, that he'll do nothing which might damage his career.
What Every Woman Knows, Act 2

40.5

There are few more impressive sights in the world than a Scotsman on the make.
same

40.6

I have always found that the man whose second thoughts are good is worth watching.
same, Act 3

40.7

Never ascribe to an opponent motives meaner than your own. *Rectorial Address, St. Andrews, 3 May 1922*

41 Barth, Karl (1886-1968), Swiss theologian.

41.1

Men have never been good, they are not good, they never will be good.
Time, 12 Apr 1954

42 Baruch, Bernard (1870-1965), American financier and public servant.

42.1

The cold war. *Saying*

42.2

I will never be an old man. To me, old age is always fifteen years older than I am.
Observer 'Sayings of the Week', 21 Aug 1955

43 Bayly, Thomas Haynes (1797-1839), English songwriter.

43.1

Absence makes the heart grow fonder,
Isle of Beauty, Fare thee well! *Isle of Beauty*

44 Beatty, David, 1st Earl Beatty (1871-1936), British admiral.

44.1

There's something wrong with our bloody ships today. *Remark during Battle of Jutland, 1916*

45 Beaumont, Francis (1584-1616) and **Fletcher, John** (1579-1625), English dramatists.

45.1

You are no better than you should be.
The Coxcomb, IV:3

45.2

It is always good
When a man has two irons in the fire.
The Faithful Friends, I:2

45.3

Let's meet, and either do, or die.
The Island Princess, II:2

45.4

I'll put a spoke among your wheels.
The Mad Lover, III:6

45.5

Those have most power to hurt us that we love. *The Maid's Tragedy, V:6*

45.6

All your better deeds
Shall be in water writ, but this in marble.
The Nice Valour, V:3

45.7

I'll have a fling. *Rule a Wife and have a Wife, III:5*

45.8

Kiss till the cow comes home.
Scornful Lady, II:2

45.9

Whistle and she'll come to you.
Wit Without Money, IV:4

46 Beauvoir, Simone Lucie de (b. 1908), French writer.

46.1

One is not born a woman, one becomes one.
The Second Sex, Ch.2

47 Beckett, Samuel (b. 1906), Irish novelist and dramatist.

47.1

CLOV. Do you believe in the life to come?
HAMM. Mine was always that. *Endgame*

47.2

ESTRAGON. Nothing happens, nobody comes, nobody goes, its awful! *Waiting for Godot, Act 1*

47.3

VLADIMIR. That passed the time.

ESTRAGON. It would have passed in any case.

VLADIMIR. Yes, but not so rapidly.   *same*

47.4

ESTRAGON....Let's go.

VLADIMIR. We can't.

ESTRAGON. Why not?

VLADIMIR. We're waiting for Godot.

same

47.5

We all are born mad. Some remain so.

same, Act 2

47.6

Habit is a great deadener.   *same, Act 3*

48 Beckford, William (1759-1844), English writer.

48.1

I am not over-fond of resisting temptation.

Vathek

49 Becon, Thomas (1512-1567), English cleric.

49.1

For when the wine is in, the wit is out.

Catechism, 375

50 Bee, Bernard Elliott (1823-1861), American Unionist soldier.

50.1

There is Jackson standing like a stone wall.

First Battle of Bull Run, 1861

51 Beerbohm, Sir Max (1872-1956), English writer and caricaturist.

51.1

Most women are not so young as they are painted.   *A Defence of Cosmetics*

51.2

There is always something rather absurd about the past.   *'1880'*

51.3

To give an accurate and exhaustive account of that period would need a far less brilliant pen than mine.   *same*

51.4

The lower one's vitality, the more sensitive one is to great art.   *Seven Men, 'Enoch Soames'*

51.5

Women who love the same man have a kind of bitter freemasonry.   *Zuleika Dobson, Ch.4*

51.6

You will find that the woman who is really kind to dogs is always one who has failed to inspire sympathy in men.   *same, Ch.6*

51.7

Beauty and the lust for learning have yet to be allied.   *same, Ch.7*

51.8

You will think me lamentably crude: my experience of life has been drawn from life itself.   *same, Ch.7*

51.9

You cannot make a man by standing a sheep on its hind legs. But by standing a flock of sheep in that position you can make a crowd of men.   *same, Ch.9*

51.10

She was one of the people who say, 'I don't know anything about music really, but I know what I like'.   *same, Ch.16*

52 Behan, Brendan (1923-1964), Irish writer.

52.1

He was born an Englishman and remained one for years.   *The Hostage, Act 1*

52.2

I wish I'd been a mixed infant.   *same, Act 2*

52.3

I am a sociable worker.   *same*

53 Behn, Aphra (1640-1689), English writer.

53.1

Love ceases to be a pleasure, when it ceases to be a secret.   *The Lover's Watch, Four o'clock*

53.2

Faith, Sir, we are here to-day, and gone to-morrow.   *The Lucky Chance, 4*

54 Bell, Clive (1881-1964), English critic.

54.1

It would follow that 'significant form' was form behind which we catch a sense of ultimate reality.   *Art, I:3*

54.2

I will try to account for the degree of my aesthetic emotion. That, I conceive, is the function of the critic.   *same, II:3*

54.3

Only reason can convince us of those three fundamental truths without a recognition of which there can be no effective liberty: that what we believe is not necessarily true; that what we like is not necessarily good; and that all questions are open.   *Civilization*

55 Belloc, Hilaire (1870-1953), Anglo-French author.

55.1

Child! do not throw this book about;

Refrain from the unholy pleasure
Of cutting all the pictures out!
Preserve it as your chiefest treasure.
The Bad Child's Book of Beasts,
Dedication
55.2
The Chief Defect of Henry King
Was chewing little bits of String.
Cautionary Tales, Henry King
55.3
'Oh, my Friends, be warned by me,
That Breakfast, Dinner, Lunch and Tea
Are all the Human Frame requires...'
With that the Wretched Child expires.
same
55.4
When I am dead, I hope it may be said:
'His sins were scarlet, but his books were
read.' *Epigrams, On His Books*
55.5
I'm tired of Love: I'm still more tired of
Rhyme.
But Money gives me pleasure all the Time.
Fatigue
55.6
The Microbe is so very small
You cannot make him out at all.
More Beasts for Worse Children, The
Microbe
55.7
I always like to associate with a lot of priests
because it makes me understand anti-clerical
things so well. *Letter to E. S. P. Haynes,*
9 Nov 1909

56 Bennett, Enoch Arnold (1867-1931),
English novelist.
56.1
'Ye can call it influenza if ye like, ' said Mrs
Machin. 'There was no influenza in my
young days. We called a cold a cold.'
The Card, Ch.8
56.2
Being a husband is a whole-time job. That is
why so many husbands fail. They cannot
give their entire attention to it.
The Title, Act 1

57 Benson, Arthur Christopher
(1862-1925), English writer.
57.1
Land of Hope and Glory, Mother of the
Free,
How shall we extol thee, who are born of
thee?
Wider still and wider shall thy bounds be
set;

God who made thee mighty, make thee
mightier yet. *Land of Hope and Glory*

58 Bentham, Jeremy (1748-1832), English
writer on jurisprudence and utilitarianism.
58.1
The greatest happiness of the greatest number
is the foundation of morals and legislation.
The Commonplace Book

59 Bentley, Edmund Clerihew (1875-1956),
English journalist, novelist and versifier.
59.1
When their lordships asked Bacon
How many bribes he had taken
He had at least the grace
To get very red in the face.
Baseless Biography, Bacon
59.2
The Art of Biography
Is different from Geography.
Geography is about Maps,
But Biography is about Chaps.
Biography for Beginners, Introductory
Remarks
59.3
Sir Christopher Wren
Said, 'I am going to dine with some men.
If anybody calls
Say I am designing St Paul's.' *same, Sir*
Christopher Wren
59.4
What I like about Clive
Is that he is no longer alive.
There is a great deal to be said
For being dead. *same, Clive*

60 Betjeman, Sir John (b. 1906), English
poet.
60.1
Phone for the fish knives Norman,
As Cook is a little unnerved;
You kiddies have crumpled the serviettes
And I must have things daintily served.
How to get on in Society
60.2
I know what I wanted to ask you;
Is trifle sufficient for sweet? *same*
60.3
Miss J. Hunter Dunn, Miss J. Hunter Dunn,
Furnish'd and burnish'd by Aldershot sun.
A Subaltern's Love song

61 Bevan, Aneurin (1897-1960), British
politician.
61.1
The language of priorities is the religion of

Socialism. *Aneurin Bevan (Vincent Brome),*
Ch.1

61.2
[*Of Churchill*] He is a man suffering from
petrified adolescence. *same, Ch.11*

61.3
We know what happens to people who stay
in the middle of the road. They get run over.
Observer 'Sayings of the Week', 9 Dec 1953

61.4
I read the newspaper avidly. It is my one
form of continuous fiction.
same, 3 Apr 1960

62 The Bible (Authorised Version,
1611)

62.1
In the beginning God created the heaven and
the earth.
And the earth was without form, and void.
Genesis, I:1-2

62.2
And God said, Let there be light: and there
was light. *same, I:3*

62.3
So God created man in his own image, in the
image of God created he him; male and
female created he them. *same, I:27*

62.4
For dust thou art, and unto dust shalt thou
return. *same, III:19*

62.5
Am I my brother's keeper? *same, IV:9*

62.6
His hand will be against every man, and
every man's hand against him.
same, XVI:12

62.7
Ye shall eat the fat of the land.
same, XLV:18

62.8
Unstable as water, thou shalt not excel.
same, XLIX:4

62.9
I have been a stranger in a strange land.
Exodus, II:22

62.10
A land flowing with milk and honey.
same, III:8

62.11
I AM THAT I AM. *same, III:14*

62.12
Let my people go, that they may serve me.
same, VIII:1

62.13
Thou shalt have no other gods before me.
same, XX:3

62.14
Thou shalt not make unto thee any graven
image. *same, XX:4*

62.15
Thou shalt not take the name of the Lord
thy God in vain. *same, XX:7*

62.16
Six days shalt thou labour, and do all thy
work:
But the seventh day is the sabbath of the
Lord thy God. *same, XX:8-10*

62.17
Honour thy father and thy mother: that thy
days may be long unto the land which the
Lord thy God giveth thee. *same, XX:12*

62.18
Thou shalt not kill. *same, XX:13*

62.19
Thou shalt not commit adultery.
same, XX:14

62.20
Thou shalt not steal. *same, XX:15*

62.21
Thou shalt not bear false witness against thy
neighbour. *same, XX:16*

62.22
Thou shalt not covet thy neighbour's house,
thou shalt not covet thy neighbour's wife,
nor his manservant, nor his maidservant, nor
his ox, nor his ass, nor any thing that is thy
neighbour's. *same, XX:17*

62.23
Thou shalt give life for life,
Eye for eye, tooth for tooth, hand for hand,
foot for foot. *same, XXI:23-24*

62.24
Thou shalt not suffer a witch to live.
same, XXII:18

62.25
Let him go for a scapegoat into the wilderness. *Leviticus, XVI:10*

62.26
Thou shalt love thy neighbour as thysefl.
same, XIX:18

62.27
Man doth not live by bread only, but by
every word that proceedeth out of the mouth
of the Lord doth man live.
Deuteronomy, VIII:3

62.28
For the poor shall never cease out of the
land. *same, XV:11*

62.29
He kept him as the apple of his eye.
same, XXXII:10

62.30
Hewers of wood and drawers of water.
Joshua, IX:21

62.31
Say now Shibboleth. *Judges, XII:6*
62.32
Out of the eater came forth meat, and out of the strong came forth sweetness.
same, XIV:14
62.33
Quit yourselves like men. *1 Samuel, IV:9*
62.34
Saul hath slain his thousands, and David his ten thousands. *same, XVIII:7*
62.35
How are the mighty fallen! *2 Samuel, I:19*
62.36
DAVID. [*Of Jonathan*] Thy love to me was wonderful, passing the love of women.
same, I:26
62.37
A still small voice. *1 Kings, XIX:12*
62.38
Naked came I out of my mother's womb, and naked shall I return thither: the Lord gave, and the Lord hath taken away; blessed be the name of the Lord. *Job, I:21*
62.39
Man that is born of a woman is of few days, and full of trouble. *same, XIV:1*
62.40
I am escaped with the skin of my teeth.
same, XIX:20
62.41
I know that my redeemer liveth.
same, XIX:25
62.42
Out of the mouth of babes and sucklings hast thou ordained strength. *Psalms, VIII:2*
62.43
What is man, that thou art mindful of him?
same, VIII:4
62.44
The fool hath said in his heart, There is no God. *same, XIV:1*
62.45
The heavens declare the glory of God; and the firmament sheweth his handywork.
same, XIX:1
62.46
The Lord is my shepherd, I shall not want.
same, XXIII:1
62.47
He maketh me to lie down in green pastures: he leadeth me beside the still waters.
same, XXIII:2
62.48
Yea, though I walk through the valley of the shadow of death, I will fear no evil: for thou art with me, thy rod and thy staff they comfort me. *same, XXIII:4*

62.49
Weeping may endure for a night, but joy cometh in the morning. *same, XXX:5*
62.50
Into thy hands I commend my spirit.
same, XXXI:6 (Book of Common Prayer version)
62.51
But the meek shall inherit the earth.
same, XXXVII:11
62.52
God is our refuge and strength, a very present help in trouble. *same, XLVI:1*
62.53
Oh that I had wings like a dove!
same, LV:6
62.54
For a thousand years in thy sight are but as yesterday when it is past, and as a watch in the night. *same, XC:4*
62.55
The days of our years are threescore years and ten; and if by reason of strength they be fourscore years, yet is their strength labour and sorrow; for it is soon cut off, and we fly away. *same, XC:10*
62.56
As for man, his days are as grass: as a flower of the field, so he flourisheth.
same, CIII:15
62.57
They that go down to the sea in ships, that do business in great waters. *same, CVII:23*
62.58
The fear of the Lord is the beginning of wisdom. *same, CXI:10*
62.59
The stone which the builders refused is become the head stone of the corner.
same, CXVIII:22
62.60
I will lift up mine eyes unto the hills, from whence cometh my help. *same, CXXI:1*
62.61
They that sow in tears shall reap in joy.
same, CXXVI:5
62.62
By the rivers of Babylon, there we sat down, yea, we wept, when we remembered Zion.
same, CXXXVII:1
62.63
Put not your trust in princes. *same, CXL:3*
62.64
Go to the ant, thou sluggard; consider her ways, and be wise. *Proverbs, VI:6*
62.65
For wisdom is better than rubies.
same, VIII:11

62.66
Stolen waters are sweet, and bread eaten in secret is pleasant.   *same, IX:17*

62.67
A wise son maketh a glad father: but a foolish son is the heaviness of his mother.
same, X:1

62.68
As a jewel of gold in a swine's snout, so is a fair woman which is without discretion.
same, XI:22

62.69
Hope deferred maketh the heart sick.
same, XIII:12

62.70
He that spareth his rod hateth his son: but he that loveth him chasteneth him betimes.
same, XIII:24

62.71
Pride goeth before destruction, and an haughty spirit before a fall.   *same, XVI:18*

62.72
Wealth maketh many friends.   *same, XIX:4*

62.73
Even a child is known by his doings.
same, XX:11

62.74
A good name is rather to be chosen than great riches.   *same, XXII:1*

62.75
If thine enemy be hungry, give him bread to eat; and if he be thirsty, give him water to drink:
For thou shalt heap coals of fire upon his head, and the Lord shall reward thee.
same, XXV:21-22

62.76
Whoso diggeth a pit shall fall therein.
same, XXVI:27

62.77
Open rebuke is better than secret love.
same, XXVII:5

62.78
Where there is no vision, the people perish.
same, XXIX:18

62.79
Vanity of vanities, saith the Preacher, vanity of vanities; all is vanity.   *Ecclesiastes, I:2*

62.80
There is no new thing under the sun.
same, I:9

62.81
For in much wisdom is much grief: and he that increaseth knowledge increaseth sorrow.
same, I:18

62.82
To every thing there is a season, and a time to every purpose under the heaven.
same, III:1

62.83
Be not righteous over much.   *same, VII:16*

62.84
Cast thy bread upon the waters: for thou shalt find it after many days.   *same, XI:1*

62.85
Of making many books there is no end; and much study is a weariness of the flesh.
same, XII:12

62.86
Fear God, and keep his commandments: for this is the whole duty of man.   *same, XII:13*

62.87
Let him kiss me with the kisses of his mouth: for thy love is better than wine.
The Song of Solomon, I:2

62.88
The flowers appear on the earth; the time of the singing of birds is come, and the voice of the turtle is heard in our land.   *same, II:12*

62.89
Love is strong as death; jealousy is cruel as the grave.   *same, VIII:6*

62.90
Many waters cannot quench love.
same, VIII:7

62.91
Though your sins be as scarlet, they shall be as white as snow.   *Isaiah, I:18*

62.92
They shall beat their swords into plowshares, and their spears into pruning-hooks: nation shall not lift up sword against nation, neither shall they learn war any more.   *same, II:4*

62.93
What mean ye that ye beat my people to pieces, and grind the faces of the poor?
same, III:15

62.94
The people that walked in darkness have seen a great light.   *same, IX:2*

62.95
For unto us a child is born, unto us a son is given: and the government shall be upon his shoulder: and his name shall be called Wonderful, Counsellor, The mighty God, The everlasting Father, The Prince of Peace.
same, IX:6

62.96
The wolf also shall dwell with the lamb, and the leopard shall lie down with the kid; and the calf and the young lion and the fatling together; and a little child shall lead them.
same, XI:6

62.97

Let us eat and drink; for to-morrow we shall die. *same, XXII:13*

62.98
All flesh is grass. *same, XL:6*

62.99
There is no peace, saith the Lord, unto the wicked. *same, XLVIII:22*

62.100
All we like sheep have gone astray. *same, LIII:6*

62.101
He is brought as a lamb to the slaughter. *same, LIII:7*

62.102
Can the Ethiopian change his skin, or the leopard his spots? *Jeremiah, XIII:23*

62.103
Remembering mine affliction and my misery, the wormwood and the gall. *Lamentations, III:19*

62.104
MENE, MENE, TEKEL, UPHARSIN. *Daniel, V:25*

62.105
Thou art weighed in the balances, and art found wanting. *same, V:27*

62.106
The law of the Medes and Persians, which altereth not. *same, VI:12*

62.107
The Ancient of days. *same, VII:13*

62.108
They have sown the wind, and they shall reap the whirlwind. *Hosea, VIII:7*

62.109
Your old men shall dream dreams, your young men shall see visions. *Joel, II:28*

62.110
Give not thy soul unto a woman. *Ecclesiasticus, IX:2*

62.111
Forsake not an old friend. *same, IX:10*

62.112
All wickedness is but little to the wickedness of a woman. *same, XXV:19*

62.113
Let us now praise famous men, and our fathers that begat us. *same, XLIV:1*

62.114
Rachel weeping for her children, and would not be comforted, because they are not. *St. Matthew, II:18*

62.115
The voice of one crying in the wilderness. *same, III:3*

62.116
O generation of vipers, who hath warned you to flee from the wrath to come? *same, III:7*

62.117
Man shall not live by bread alone, but by every word that proceedeth out of the mouth of God. *same, IV:4*

62.118
Blessed are the meek: for they shall inherit the earth. *same, V:5*

62.119
Blessed are the pure in heart: for they shall see God. *same, V:8*

62.120
Ye are the salt of the earth: but if the salt have lost his savour, wherewith shall it be salted? *same, V:13*

62.121
An eye for an eye, and a tooth for a tooth. *same, V:38*

62.122
Resist not evil: but whosoever shall smite thee on thy right cheek, turn to him the other also. *same, V:39*

62.123
Love your enemies. *same, V:44*

62.124
He maketh his sun to rise on the evil and on the good, and sendeth rain on the just and on the unjust. *same, V:45*

62.125
Let not thy left hand know what thy right hand doeth. *same, VI:3*

62.126
No man can serve two masters. *same, VI:24*

62.127
Ye cannot serve God and mammon. *same, VI:28*

62.128
Consider the lilies of the field, how they grow; they toil not, neither do they spin. *same, VI:28*

62.129
Sufficient unto the day is the evil thereof. *same, VI:34*

62.130
Judge not, that ye be not judged. *same, VII:1*

62.131
Neither cast ye your pearls before swine. *same, VII:6*

62.132
Beware of false prophets, which come to you in sheep's clothing, but inwardly they are ravening wolves. *same, VII:15*

62.133
What went ye out into the wilderness to see? A reed shaken with the wind? *same, XI:7*

13

62.134
He that is not with me is against me.

same, XII:30

62.135
One pearl of great price.   *same, XIII:46*

62.136
A prophet is not without honour, save in his own country.   *same, XIII:57*

62.137
If the blind lead the blind, both shall fall into the ditch.   *same, XV:14*

62.138
Get thee behind me, Satan.   *same, XVI:23*

62.139
If thine eye offend thee, pluck it out.

same, XVIII:9

62.140
For many are called, but few are chosen.

same, XXII:14

62.141
Render therefore unto Caesar the things which are Caesar's; and unto God the things that are God's.   *same, XXII:21*

62.142
Wars and rumours of wars.   *same, XXIV:6*

62.143
As a shepherd divideth his sheep from the goats.   *same, XXV:32*

62.144
Ye have the poor always with you.

same, XXVI:11

62.145
The spirit indeed is willing, but the flesh is weak.   *same, XXVI:41*

62.146
The sabbath was made for man, and not man for the sabbath.   *St. Mark, II:27*

62.147
If a house be divided against itself, that house cannot stand.   *same, III:25*

62.148
For what shall it profit a man, if he shall gain the whole world and lose his own soul?

same, VIII:36

62.149
What therefore God hath joined together, let not man put asunder.   *same, X:9*

62.150
Suffer the little children to come unto me, and forbid them not: for of such is the kingdom of God.   *same, X:14*

62.151
Before the cock crow twice, thou shalt deny me thrice.   *same, XIV:30*

62.152
Crucify him.   *same, XVI:13*

62.153
Physician, heal thyself.   *St. Luke, IV:23*

62.154
No man putteth new wine into old bottles.

same, V:37

62.155
The labourer is worthy of his hire.

same, X:7

62.156
He passed by on the other side.   *same, X:31*

62.157
Joy shall be in heaven over one sinner that repenteth, more than over ninety and nine just persons, which need no repentance.

same, XV:7

62.158
The crumbs which fell from the rich man's table.   *same, XVI:21*

62.159
Between us and you there is a great gulf fixed.   *same, XVI:26*

62.160
Father, forgive them; for they know not what they do.   *same, XXIII:34*

62.161
In the beginning was the Word, and the Word was with God, and the Word was God.   *St. John, I:1*

62.162
He came unto his own, and his own received him not.   *same, I:11*

62.163
The Word was made flesh, and dwelt among us.   *same, I:14*

62.164
Ye must be born again.   *same, III:7*

62.165
The wind bloweth where it listeth.

same, III:8

62.166
For God so loved the world, that he gave his only begotten Son, that whosoever believeth in him should not perish, but have everlasting life.   *same, III:16*

62.167
He that is without sin among you, let him first cast a stone at her.   *same, VIII:7*

62.168
I am the light of the world.   *same, VIII:12*

62.169
The good shepherd giveth his life for the sheep.   *same, X:11*

62.170
A new commandment I give unto you, That ye love one another.   *same, XIII:34*

62.171
Greater love hath no man than this, that a man lay down his life for his friends.

same, XV:13

62.172
Pilate saith unto him, What is truth?
same, XVIII:38
62.173
Blessed are they that have not seen, and yet
have believed. *same, XX:29*
62.174
It is hard for thee to kick against the pricks.
The Acts of the Apostles, IX:5
62.175
God is no respecter of persons. *same, X:34*
62.176
In him we live, and move, and have our
being. *same, XVII:28*
62.177
It is more blessed to give than to receive.
same, XX:35
62.178
These, having not the law, are a law unto
themselves. *Romans, II:14*
62.179
Death hath no more dominion over him.
same, VI:9
62.180
The wages of sin is death. *same, VI:23*
62.181
Vengeance is mine; I will repay, saith the
Lord. *same, XII:19*
62.182
Be not overcome of evil, but overcome evil
with good. *same, XII:21*
62.183
Absent in body, but present in spirit.
1 Corinthians, V:3
62.184
Know ye not that a little leaven leaveneth
the whole lump? *same, V:6*
62.185
All things to all men. *same, IX:22*
62.186
When I became a man, I put away childish
things. *same, XIII:11*
62.187
Now we see through a glass, darkly; but
then face to face. *same, XIII:12*
62.188
And now abideth faith, hope, charity, these
three; but the greatest of these is charity.
same, XIII:13
62.189
O death, where is thy sting? O grave, where
is thy victory? *same, XV:55*
62.190
The letter killeth, but the spirit giveth life.
2 Corinthians, III:6
62.191
For ye suffer fools gladly, seeing ye yourselves are wise. *same, XI:19*

62.192
A thorn in the flesh. *same, XII:7*
62.193
The right hands of fellowship.
Galatians, II:9
62.194
Ye are fallen from grace. *same, V:4*
62.195
Bear ye one another's burdens. *same, VI:2*
62.196
Be not deceived; God is not mocked: for
whatsoever a man soweth, that shall he also
reap. *same, VI:7*
62.197
Work out your own salvation with fear and
trembling. *Philippians, II:12*
62.198
The peace of God, which passeth all understanding. *same, IV:7*
62.199
Not greedy of filthy lucre. *1 Timothy, III:3*
62.200
Drink no longer water, but use a little wine
for thy stomach's sake and thine often infirmities. *same, V:23*
62.201
For we brought nothing into this world, and
it is certain we can carry nothing out.
same, VI:7
62.202
The love of money is the root of all evil.
same, VI:10
62.203
It is appointed unto men once to die, but
after this the judgment. *Hebrews, IX:27*
62.204
Faith is the substance of things hoped for,
the evidence of things not seen. *same, XI:1*
62.205
Jesus Christ the same yesterday, and today,
and for ever. *same, XIII:8*
62.206
Faith without works is dead. *James, II:20*
62.207
All flesh is as grass. *1 Peter, I:24*
62.208
Honour all men. Love the brotherhood. Fear
God. Honour the king. *same, II:17*
62.209
Charity shall cover the multitude of sins.
same, IV:8
62.210
God is love. *1 John, IV:8*
62.211
There is no fear in love; but perfect love
casteth out fear. *same, IV:18*
62.212

I am Alpha and Omega, the beginning and the ending. *Revelation, I:8*
62.213
Be thou faithful unto death, and I will give thee a crown of life. *same, II:10*
62.214
He shall rule them with a rod of iron. *same, II:27*
62.215
Behold a pale horse: and his name that sat on him was Death, and Hell followed with him. *same, VI:8*
62.216
And when he had opened the seventh seal, there was silence in heaven about the space of half an hour. *same, VIII:1*
62.217
The bottomless pit. *same, IX:1*
62.218
And I saw a new heaven and a new earth: for the first heaven and the first earth were passed away; and there was no more sea. *same, XXI:1*
62.219
The holy city, new Jerusalem, coming down from God out of heaven, prepared as a bride adorned for her husband. *same, XXI:2*
62.220
And God shall wipe away all tears from their eyes; and there shall be no more death, neither sorrow, nor crying, neither shall there be any more pain: for the former things are passed away. *same, XXI:4*

63 Bierce, Ambrose (1842?-1914), American journalist and humorist.
63.1
Bore, n. A person who talks when you wish him to listen. *The Devil's Dictionary*
63.2
Brain, n. An apparatus with which we think that we think. *same*
63.3
Debauchee, n. One who has so earnestly pursued pleasure that he has had the misfortune to overtake it. *same*
63.4
Egotist, n. A person of low taste, more interested in himself than in me. *same*
63.5
Future, n. That period of time in which our affairs prosper, our friends are true and our happiness is assured. *same*
63.6
Marriage, n. The state or condition of a community consisting of a master, a mistress and two slaves, making in all two. *same*

63.7
Patience, n. A minor form of despair, disguised as a virtue. *same*
63.8
Peace, n. In international affairs, a period of cheating between two periods of fighting. *same*

64 Binyon, Laurence Robert (1869-1943), English poet.
64.1
They shall grow not old, as we that are left grow old:
Age shall not weary them, nor the years condemn.
At the going down of the sun and in the morning
We will remember them. *For the Fallen (1914-1918)*

65 Blackstone, Sir William (1723-1780), English jurist.
65.1
The king never dies. *Commentaries on the Laws of England, I:7*
65.2
That the king can do no wrong, is a necessary and fundamental principle of the English constitution. *same, III:17*
65.3
It is better that ten guilty persons escape than one innocent suffer. *same, IV:27*

66 Blair, Eric, see Orwell, George

67 Blake, William (1757-1827), English poet, painter and engraver.
67.1
To see a World in a grain of sand,
And a Heaven in a wild flower,
Hold Infinity in the palm of your hand,
And Eternity in an hour. *Auguries of Innocence, 1*
67.2
A robin redbreast in a cage
Puts all Heaven in a rage. *same, 5*
67.3
Does the Eagle know what is in the pit
Or wilt thou go ask the Mole?
Can Wisdom be put in a silver rod,
Or love in a golden bowl? *The Book of Thel, Thel's Motto*
67.4
He who would do good to another must do it in Minute Particulars.
General Good is the plea of the scoundrel, hypocrite, and flatterer. *Jerusalem, 55*

67.5

I care not whether a man is Good or Evil;
   all that I care
Is whether he is a Wise Man or a Fool. Go!
   put off Holiness,
And put on Intellect.   *same, 91*

67.6

And did those feet in ancient time
Walk upon England's mountains green?
And was the holy lamb of God
On England's pleasant pastures seen?
                        Milton, Preface

67.7

I will not cease from mental fight,
Nor shall my sword sleep in my hand,
Till we have built Jerusalem
In England's green and pleasant land.
                                same

67.8

Mock on, mock on, Voltaire, Rousseau;
Mock on, mock on; 'tis all in vain!
You throw the sand against the wind,
And the wind blows it back again.
         Mock on, mock on, Voltaire, Rousseau

67.9

Love seeketh not itself to please,
Nor for itself hath any care,
But for another gives its ease,
And builds a Heaven in Hell's despair.
         *Songs of Experience, The Clod and the
                                Pebble*

67.10

Love seeketh only Self to please,
To bind another to its delight,
Joys in another's loss of ease,
And builds a Hell in Heaven's despite.
                                same

67.11

My mother groan'd, my father wept,
Into the dangerous world I leapt;
Helpless, naked, piping loud,
Like a fiend hid in a cloud.   *same, Infant
                                Sorrow*

67.12

Tiger! Tiger! burning bright
In the forests of the night,
What immortal hand or eye
Could frame thy fearful symmetry?
                        same, The Tiger

67.13

Piping down the valleys wild,
Piping songs of pleasant glee,
On a cloud I saw a child.   *Songs of
                        Innocence, Introduction*

67.14

'Pipe a song about a Lamb!'
So I piped with merry cheer.   *same*

67.15

Little Lamb, who made thee?
Dost thou know who made thee?
                        same, The Lamb

67.16

To Mercy, Pity, Peace, and Love
All pray in their distress.   *same, The Divine
                                Image*

67.17

For Mercy has a human heart,
Pity a human face,
And Love, the human form divine,
And Peace, the human dress.   *same*

67.18

'What, ' it will be questioned, 'when the sun
rises, do you not see a round disc of fire
somewhat like a guinea?' 'O no, no, I see an
innumerable company of the heavenly host
crying, "Holy, Holy, Holy is the Lord God
Almighty!"'   *Descriptive Catalogue, The
                        Vision of Judgment*

67.19

Without Contraries is no progression. Attraction and Repulsion, Reason and Energy,
Love and Hate, are necessary to Human
existence.   *The Marriage of Heaven and
                        Hell, The Argument*

67.20

Energy is Eternal Delight.   *same, The Voice
                        of the Devil*

67.21

The road of excess leads to the palace of
Wisdom.   *same, Proverbs of Hell*

67.22

He who desires but acts not, breeds
pestilence.   *same*

67.23

A fool sees not the same tree that a wise man
sees.   *same*

67.24

Damn braces. Bless relaxes.   *same*

67.25

Exuberance is Beauty.   *same*

67.26

If the doors of perception were cleansed
everything would appear to man as it is,
infinite.   *same, A Memorable Fancy*

68 Boethius, Anicius Manlius Severinus
(c. 475-524), Roman statesman and philosopher.

68.1

In every adversity of fortune, to have been
happy is the most unhappy kind of misfortune.   *De Consolatione Philosophiae, II:4*

69 Borges, Jorge Luis (b. 1899), Argentinian poet, writer and critic.

69.1

I have known uncertainty: a state unknown to the Greeks. *Ficciones, The Babylonian Lottery*

69.2

The visible universe was an illusion or, more precisely, a sophism. Mirrors and fatherhood are abominable because they multiply it and extend it. *same, Tlön, Uqbar, Orbis Tertius*

70 Borrow, George Henry (1803-1881), English writer.

70.1

Youth will be served, every dog has his day, and mine has been a fine one.

Lavengro, Ch. 92

71 Bosquet, Marshal Pierre (1810-1861), French soldier.

71.1

[*Of the Charge of the Light Brigade at the Battle of Balaclava, 1854*] C'est magnifique, mais ce n'est pas la guerre.

It is magnificent, but it is not war.

Remark

72 Bracken, Brendan (1901-1958), Irish journalist and politician.

72.1

It's a good deed to forget a poor joke.

Observer 'Sayings of the Week',
17 Oct 1943

73 Bradford, John (1510?-1555), English Protestant martyr.

73.1

[*On seeing some criminals being led to execution*] There, but for the grace of God, goes John Bradford. *Remark*

74 Brecht, Bertolt (1898-1956), German dramatist and poet.

74.1

What they could do with round here is a good war. *Mother Courage, Sc.1*

74.2

When he told men to love their neighbour, their bellies were full. Nowadays things are different. *same, Sc.2*

74.3

I don't trust him. We're friends. *same, Sc.3*

74.4

The finest plans have always been spoiled by the littleness of those that should carry them out. Even emperors can't do it all by themselves. *same, Sc.6*

74.5

A war of which we could say it left nothing to be desired will probably never exist.

same

74.6

What happens to the hole when the cheese is gone? *same*

74.7

War is like love, it always finds a way.

same

74.8

Don't tell me peace has broken out.

same

75 Bright, John (1811-1889), British radical statesman and orator.

75.1

[*Of the Crimean War*] The Angel of Death has been abroad thoughout the land; you may almost hear the beating of his wings.

Speech, House of Commons, 23 Feb 1855

75.2

England is the mother of parliaments.

Speech, Birmingham, 18 Jan 1865

75.3

Force is not a remedy.

Speech, Birmingham, 16 Nov 1880

76 Bronowski, Jacob (1908-1974), British scientist and writer.

76.1

The wish to hurt, the momentary intoxication with pain, is the loophole through which the pervert climbs into the minds of ordinary men. *The Face of Violence, Ch.5*

76.2

The world is made of people who never quite get into the first team and who just miss the prizes at the flower show.

same, Ch.6

77 Brontë, Emily (1818-1848), English poet and novelist.

77.1

No coward soul is mine,

No trembler in the world's storm-troubled sphere:

I see Heaven's glories shine,

And faith shines equal, arming me from fear.

Last Lines

77.2

Vain are the thousand creeds

That move men's hearts: unutterably vain;

Worthless as wither'd weeds. *same*

77.3

O! dreadful is the check—intense the agony—

When the ear begins to hear, and the eye begins to see;

When the pulse begins to throb—the brain to think again—

The soul to feel the flesh, and the flesh to feel the chain.   *The Prisoner*

78 Brooke, Rupert (1887-1915), English poet.
78.1
Just now the lilac is in bloom
All before my little room.
          The Old Vicarage, Grantchester
78.2
Stands the Church clock at ten to three?
And is there honey still for tea?   *same*
78.3
If I should die, think only this of me:
That there's some corner of a foreign field
That is forever England.   *The Soldier*

79 Brown, Thomas (1663-1704), English satirist.
79.1
I do not love thee, Doctor Fell,
The reason why I cannot tell;
But this alone I know full well,
I do not love thee, Doctor Fell.
          Translation of Martial's Epigrams, I:32

80 Brown, Thomas Edward (1830-1897), English poet.
80.1
A garden is a lovesome thing, God wot!
          My Garden

81 Browne, Charles Farrar, see Ward, Artemus

82 Browne, Sir Thomas (1605-1682), English doctor and writer.
82.1
He who discommendeth others obliquely commendeth himself.   *Christian Morals*
82.2
All things are artificial, for nature is the art of God.   *Religio Medici, I:16*
82.3
It is the common wonder of all men, how among so many million of faces, there should be none alike.   *same, II:2*
82.4
No man can justly censure or condemn another, because indeed no man truly knows another.   *same, II:4*
82.5
Charity begins at home, is the voice of the world.   *same, II:4*
82.6
Lord, deliver me from myself.   *same, II:10*
82.7
For the world, I count it not an inn, but an hospital, and a place, not to live, but to die in.   *same, II:12*
82.8
There is surely a piece of divinity in us, something that was before the elements, and owes no homage unto the sun.   *same, II:12*
82.9
Man is a noble animal, splendid in ashes, and pompous in the grave.
          Urn Burial, Ch.5

83 Browning, Robert (1812-1889), English poet.
83.1
So free we seem, so fettered fast we are!
          Andrea del Sarto
83.2
Ah, but a man's reach should exceed his grasp,
Or what's a heaven for?   *same*
83.3
Just when we are safest, there's a sunset-touch,
A fancy from a flower-bell, some one's death,
A chorus-ending from Euripides, —
And that's enough for fifty hopes and fears
As old and new at once as Nature's self,
To rap and knock and enter in our soul.
          Bishop Blougram's Apology
83.4
No, when the fight begins within himself,
A man's worth something.   *same*
83.5
Dauntless the slug-horn to my lips I set,
And blew. *Childe Roland to the Dark Tower came.*   *Childe Roland, 34*
83.6
Oh, to be in England
Now that April's there.
          Home-Thoughts, from Abroad
83.7
That's the wise thrush; he sings each song twice over,
Lest you should think he never could recapture
The first fine careless rapture!   *same*
83.8
I sprang to the stirrup, and Joris, and he;
I galloped, Dirck galloped, we galloped all three.   *How they brought the Good News from Ghent to Aix*
83.9
Just for a handful of silver he left us,
Just for a riband to stick in his coat.
          The Lost Leader
83.10
Never the time and the place

And the loved one all together! *Never the*
Time and the Place
83.11
Rats!
They fought the dogs and killed the cats,
And bit the babies in the cradles.
The Pied Piper of Hamelin, 2
83.12
'You threaten us, fellow? Do your worst,
Blow your pipe there till you burst!'
same, 9
83.13
The year's at the spring,
And day's at the morn;
Morning's at seven;
The hill-side's dew-pearled;
The lark's on the wing;
The snail's on the thorn;
God's in His heaven—
All's right with the world. *Pippa Passes, 1,*
Morning
83.14
Gr-r-r- there go, my heart's abhorrence!
Water your damned flower-pots, do!
Soliloquy of the Spanish Cloister
83.15
I the Trinity illustrate,
Drinking watered orange-pulp—
In three sips the Arian frustrate;
While he drains his at one gulp. *same*
83.16
There's a great text in Galatians,
Once you trip on it, entails
Twenty-nine distinct damnations,
One sure, if another fails. *same*
83.17
My scrofulous French novel
On grey paper with blunt type! *same*
83.18
What of soul was left, I wonder, when the
kissing had to stop? *A Toccata of*
Galuppi's
83.19
What's become of Waring
Since he gave us all the slip? *Waring*

84 Buchanan, Robert Williams
(1841-1901), British poet, novelist and
dramatist.
84.1
[*Of Swinburne, William Morris, D.G.*
Rossetti, etc.] The Fleshly School of Poetry.
Title of article in the Contemporary
Review, Oct 1871
84.2
She just wore
Enough for modesty—no more.
White Rose and Red, I:5

85 Buckingham, George Villiers, 2nd Duke
of (1628-1687), English royalist and
writer.
85.1
The world is made up for the most part of
fools and knaves. *To Mr. Clifford, on his*
Humane Reason
85.2
Ay, now the plot thickens very much upon
us. *The Rehearsal, III:1*

86 Buffon, Georges-Louis Leclerc, Comte
de (1707-1788), French naturalist.
86.1
Style is the man himself. *Discours sur le*
style

87 Buller, Arthur Henry Reginald
(1874-1944), English botanist.
87.1
There was a young lady named Bright,
Whose speed was far faster than light;
She set out one day
In a relative way,
And returned home the previous night.
Limerick

88 Bulwer-Lytton, Edward (1803-1873),
English novelist, poet and politician.
88.1
Beneath the rule of men entirely great,
The pen is mightier than the sword.
Richelieu, II:2

89 Buñuel, Luis (b. 1900), Mexican film
director.
89.1
I am an atheist still, thank God.
Luis Buñuel: an Introduction (Ado Kyrou)

90 Bunyan, John (1628-1688), English
writer and preacher.
90.1
As I walked through the wilderness of this
world. *Pilgrim's Progress, Part 1*
90.2
The name of the slough was Despond.
same
90.3
The gentleman's name that met him was Mr
Worldly Wiseman. *same*
90.4
It beareth the name of Vanity Fair, because
the town where 'tis kept is lighter than
vanity. *same*
90.5
A castle called Doubting Castle, the owner
whereof was Giant Despair. *same*

90.6
So I awoke, and behold it was a dream.
same

90.7
He that is down needs fear no fall;
He that is low, no pride.   *same, Shepherd*
Boy's Song

91   Burke, Edmund (1729-1797), British statesman and philosopher.

91.1
The concessions of the weak are the concessions of fear.   *Speech on Conciliation with*
America, 22 Mar 1775

91.2
The use of force alone is but *temporary*. It may subdue for a moment; but it does not remove the necessity of subduing again: and a nation is not governed, which is perpetually to be conquered.   *same*

91.3
I do not know the method of drawing up an indictment against an whole people.
same

91.4
All government, indeed every human benefit and enjoyment, every virtue, and every prudent act, is founded on compromise and barter.   *same*

91.5
The people are the masters.   *Speech on the*
Economical Reform, 11 Feb 1780

91.6
[*Of Pitt the Younger's first speech*] He was not merely a chip of the old block, but the old block itself.   *Remark, 26 Feb 1781*

91.7
There is, however, a limit at which forbearance ceases to be a virtue.
Observations on 'The Present State of the
Nation', 1769

91.8
But the age of chivalry is gone. That of sophisters, economists, and calculators, has succeeded; and the glory of Europe is extinguished for ever.   *Reflections on the*
Revolution in France

91.9
Man is by his constitution a religious animal.
same

91.10
Superstition is the religion of feeble minds.
same

91.11
Example is the school of mankind, and they will learn at no other.   *Letters on a Regicide*
Peace, 1, 1796

91.12
And having looked to government for bread, on the very first scarcity they will turn and bite the hand that fed them.   *Thoughts and*
Details on Scarcity

91.13
When bad men combine, the good must associate; else they will fall one by one, an unpitied sacrifice in a contemptible struggle.
Thoughts on the Cause of the Present
Discontents, 1770

91.14
Liberty, too, must be limited in order to be possessed.   *Letter to the Sherrifs of Bristol,*
1777

91.15
Among a people generally corrupt, liberty cannot long exist.   *same*

91.16
The greater the power, the more dangerous the abuse.   *Speech, House of Commons,*
7 Feb 1771

91.17
I am convinced that we have a degree of delight, and that no small one, in the real misfortunes and pains of others.
On the Sublime and Beautiful, I:14

92   Burnet, Gilbert (1643-1715), Bishop of Salisbury.

92.1
There was a sure way to see it lost, and that was to die in the last ditch.   *History of his*
own Times, 1

93   Burns, Robert (1759-1796), Scottish poet.

93.1
O Thou! Whatever title suit thee—
Auld Hornie, Satan, Nick, or Clootie.
Address to the Deil

93.2
Should auld acquaintance be forgot,
And never brought to min'?   *Auld Lang*
Syne

93.3
We'll tak a cup o' kindness yet,
For auld lang syne.   *same*

93.4
Gin a body meet a body
Coming through the rye;
Gin a body kiss a body,
Need a body cry?   *Coming through the Rye*

93.5
I wasna fou, but just had plenty.
Death and Doctor Hornbrook

93.6
On ev'ry hand it will allow'd be,

He's just—nae better than he should be.

A Dedication to Gavin Hamilton

93.7

A man's a man for a' that.   *For a' that and*
a' that

93.8

Green grow the rashes O,
Green grow the rashes O,
The sweetest hours that e'er I spend,
Are spent amang the lasses O!

Green Grow the Rashes

93.9

John Anderson my jo, John,
When we were first acquent,
Your locks were like the raven,
Your bonnie brow was brent.

John Anderson My Jo

93.10

Man's inhumanity to man
Makes countless thousands mourn!

Man was Made to Mourn

93.11

Wee, sleekit, cow'rin', tim'rous beastie,
O what a panic's in thy breastie!

To a Mouse

93.12

The best laid schemes o' mice an' men
Gang aft a-gley,
An' lea'e us nought but grief an' pain
For promis'd joy.   *same*

93.13

My heart's in the Highlands, my heart is not
here;
My heart's in the Highlands a-chasing the
deer;
Chasing the wild deer, and following the roe,
My heart's in the Highlands, wherever I go.

My Heart's in the Highlands

93.14

My love is like a red red rose
That's newly sprung in June:
My love is like the melodie
That's sweetly play'd in tune.   *A Red, Red*
Rose

93.15

Scots, wha hae wi' Wallace bled,
Scots, wham Bruce has aften led,
Welcome to your gory bed,
Or to victorie.   *Scots, Wha Hae*

93.16

Liberty's in every blow!
Let us do or die!   *same*

93.17

Ye banks and braes o' bonnie Doon,
How can ye bloom sae fresh and fair?
How can ye chant, ye little birds,
And I sae weary fu' o' care?   *Ye Banks and*
Braes

94 Burton, Robert (1577-1640), English
cleric and writer.

94.1

All my joys to this are folly,
Naught so sweet as Melancholy.

Anatomy of Melancholy, Abstract

94.2

Hinc quam sit calamus saevior ense patet.
From this it is clear how much more cruel
the pen is than the sword.   *same, 1*

94.3

England is a paradise for women, and hell
for horses: Italy a paradise for horses, hell
for women.   *same, 3*

94.4

One religion is as true as another.   *same*

95 Bussy-Rabutin, Roger, Comte de
(1618-1693), French soldier and writer.

95.1

Absence is to love what wind is to fire; it
extinguishes the small, it inflames the great.

Histoire Amoureuse des Gaules

96 Butler, Samuel (1612-1680), English
satirist.

96.1

When civil fury first grew high,
And men fell out they knew not why.

Hudibras, I:1:1

96.2

For every why he had a wherefore.

same, I:1:132

96.3

Love is a boy, by poets styl'd,
Then spare the rod, and spoil the child.

same, I:1:844

96.4

Through perils both of wind and limb,
Through thick and thin she follow'd him.

same, II:1:369

96.5

Oaths are but words, and words but wind.

same, II:2:107

96.6

What makes all doctrines plain and clear?
About two hundred pounds a year.

same, III:1:1277

96.7

He that complies against his will,
Is of his own opinion still.   *same, III:3:547*

96.8

The souls of women are so small,
That some believe they've none at all.

Miscellaneous Thoughts

97 Butler, Samuel (1835-1902), English
author, painter and musician.

97.1
It has been said that the love of money is the root of all evil. The want of money is so quite as truly. *Erewhon, Ch.20*

97.2
I keep my books at the British Museum and at Mudie's. *The Humour of Homer, Ramblings in Cheapside*

97.3
Life is one long process of getting tired. *Note-books, Life, 7*

97.4
Life is the art of drawing sufficient conclusions from insufficient premises. *same, 9*

97.5
All progress is based upon a universal innate desire on the part of every organism to live beyond its income. *same, 16*

97.6
The advantage of doing one's praising for oneself is that one can lay it on so thick and exactly in the right places. *The Way of All Flesh, Ch. 34*

97.7
'Tis better to have loved and lost than never to have lost at all. *same, Ch.77*

97.8
Brigands demand your money or your life; women require both. *Attributed*

98 Byron, George Gordon, 6th Baron (1788-1824), English poet.

98.1
In short, he was a perfect cavaliero,
And to his very valet seem'd a hero. *Beppo, 33*

98.2
I like the weather, when it is not rainy,
That is, I like two months of every year. *same, 48*

98.3
Adieu, adieu! my native shore
Fades o'er the waters blue. *Childe Harold's Pilgrimage, I:13*

98.4
My native Land—Good Night! *same, I:13*

98.5
War, war is still the cry, 'War even to the knife!' *same, I:85*

98.6
Hereditary bondsmen! know ye not
Who would be free themselves must strike the blow? *same, I:86*

98.7
There was a sound of revelry by night,
And Belgium's capital had gather'd then
Her Beauty and her Chivalry, and bright

The lamps shone o'er fair women and brave men. *same, III:21*

98.8
On with the dance! let joy be unconfined;
No sleep till morn, when Youth and Pleasure meet
To chase the glowing Hours with flying feet. *same, III:22*

98.9
While stands the Coliseum, Rome shall stand;
When falls the Coliseum, Rome shall fall;
And when Rome falls—the World. *same, IV:145*

98.10
There is a pleasure in the pathless woods,
There is a rapture on the lonely shore,
There is society, where none intrudes,
By the deep Sea, and music in its roar:
I love not Man the less, but Nature more. *same, IV:178*

98.11
What men call gallantry, and gods adultery,
Is much more common where the climate's sultry. *Don Juan, I:63*

98.12
Man's love is of man's life a thing apart,
'Tis woman's whole existence. *same, I:194*

98.13
Man, being reasonable, must get drunk;
The best of life is but intoxication. *same, II:179*

98.14
All tragedies are finish'd by a death,
All comedies are ended by a marriage. *same, III:9*

98.15
The isles of Greece, the isles of Greece!
Where burning Sappho loved and sung,
Where grew the arts of war and peace,
Where Delos rose, and Phoebus sprung!
Eternal summer gilds them yet,
But all, except their sun, is set. *same, III:86*

98.16
The mountains look on Marathon—
And Marathon looks on the sea:
And musing there an hour alone,
I dream'd that Greece might still be free. *same*

98.17
There is a tide in the affairs of women,
Which, taken at the flood, leads—God knows where. *same, VI:2*

98.18
A lady of a 'certain age', which means
Certainly aged. *same, VI:69*

98.19
Now hatred is by far the longest pleasure;
Men love in haste, but they detest at leisure.
same, XIII:6

98.20
Society is now one polish'd horde,
Form'd of two mighty tribes, the *Bores* and
Bored. *same, XIII:95*

98.21
'Tis strange—but true; for truth is always
strange;
Stranger than fiction: if it could be told,
How much would novels gain by the
exchange! *same, XIV:101*

98.22
I'll publish, right or wrong:
Fools are my theme, let satire be my song.
English Bards and Scotch Reviewers, 5

98.23
'Tis pleasant, sure, to see one's name in
print;
A book's a book, although there's nothing
in't. *same, 51*

98.24
A man must serve his time to every trade
Save censure—critics all are ready made.
same, 63

98.25
She walks in beauty, like the night
Of cloudless climes and starry skies;
And all that's best of dark and bright
Meet in her aspect and her eyes.
She Walks in Beauty

98.26
So, we'll go no more a roving
So late into the night,
Though the heart be still as loving,
And the moon be still as bright. *So,
we'll go no more a roving*

98.27
Though the night was made for loving,
And the day returns too soon,
Yet we'll go no more a roving
By the light of the moon. *same*

98.28
If I should meet thee
After long years,
How should I greet thee?—
With silence and tears. *When we two
parted*

98.29
[*After the publication of 'Childe Harold'*] I
awoke one morning and found myself
famous. *Entry in Memoranda*

99 Byron, Henry James (1834–1884),
English dramatist.

99.1
Life's too short for chess. *Our Boys, Act 1*

C

100 Caesar Augustus, (63 B.C.–A.D. 14),
Roman emperor.

100.1
[*Of Rome*] He so improved the city that he
justly boasted that he found it brick and left
it marble. *The Lives of the Caesars
(Suetonius), Augustus*

101 Julius Caesar, (102 B.C.?–44 B.C.),
Roman general, statesman and historian.

101.1
All Gaul is divided into three parts.
De Bello Gallico, I:1

101.2
Veni, vidi, vici.
I came, I saw, I conquered.
The Twelve Caesars (Suetonius)

101.3
The die is cast. *On crossing the Rubicon, 49
B.C.*

101.4
Et tu, Brute.
You too, Brutus? *Last words, attributed*

102 Camden, William (1551–1623), English
scholar, antiquary and historian.

102.1
Betwixt the stirrup and the ground
Mercy I asked, mercy I found. *Epitaph for
a Man killed by falling from his Horse*

103 Campbell, Roy (1902–1957), South
African poet and journalist.

103.1
Now Spring, sweet laxative of Georgian
strains,
Quickens the ink in literary veins,
The Stately Homes of England ope their
doors
To piping Nancy-boys and Crashing Bores.
The Georgiad, 1

104 Campbell, Thomas (1777–1844),
Scottish poet.

104.1
O leave this barren spot to me!

Spare, woodman, spare the beechen tree.
The Beech-Tree's Petition
104.2
'Tis distance lends enchantment to the view,
And robes the mountain in its azure hue.
Pleasures of Hope
104.3
Now Barabbas was a publisher.
Attributed

105 Campion, Thomas (1567-1620), English poet.
105.1
There is a garden in her face,
Where roses and white lilies grow.
There is a Garden in her Face
105.2
There cherries grow, which none may buy
Till 'Cherry Ripe' themselves do cry.
same

106 Camus, Albert (1913-1960), French writer.
106.1
Style, like sheer silk, too often hides eczema.
The Fall
106.2
A single sentence will suffice for modern man: he fornicated and read the papers.
same
106.3
How many crimes committed merely because their authors could not endure being wrong!
same
106.4
No man is a hypocrite in his pleasures.
same
106.5
Don't wait for the Last Judgement. It takes place every day. *same*
106.6
One cannot be a part-time nihilist.
The Rebel
106.7
What is a rebel? A man who says no.
same
106.8
All modern revolutions have ended in a reinforcement of the power of the State.
same
106.9
He who despairs over an event is a coward, but he who holds hopes for the human condition is a fool. *same*

107 Canning, George (1770-1827), English statesman.

107.1
I called the New World into existence to redress the balance of the Old.
Speech, 12 Dec 1826
107.2
But of all plagues, good Heaven, thy wrath can send,
Save me, oh, save me, from the candid friend. *New Morality*

108 Carey, Henry (1693?-1743), English poet and musician.
108.1
God save our Gracious King,
Long live our noble King,
God save the King.
Send him victorious,
Happy and glorious. *God Save the King*
108.2
Of all the girls that are so smart
There's none like pretty Sally;
She is the darling of my heart
And she lives in our alley. *Sally in our Alley*

109 Carlyle, Thomas (1795-1881), Scottish essayist and historian.
109.1
A witty statesman said, you might prove anything by figures. *Essay on Chartism*
109.2
The three great elements of modern civilization, Gunpowder, Printing, and the Protestant Religion. *Essay on German Literature*
109.3
History is the essence of innumerable biographies. *Essay on History*
109.4
A well-written Life is almost as rare as a well-spent one. *Essay on Richter*
109.5
Genius (which means transcendent capacity of taking trouble, first of all). *Frederick the Great, IV:3*
109.6
No great man lives in vain. The history of the world is but the biography of great men.
Heroes and Hero-Worship, 1
109.7
The true University of these days is a collection of books. *same, 5*
109.8
France was a long despotism tempered by epigrams. *History of the French Revolution, I:1:1*
109.9
A whiff of grapeshot. *same, I:5:3*

109.10

[*Of Robespierre*] The seagreen Incorruptible. *same, II:4:4*

109.11

Respectable Professors of the Dismal Science [*Political Economy*].

Latter-Day Pamphlets, 1

109.12

Nature admits no lie. *same, 5*

109.13

Captains of industry. *Past and Present, III:9*

109.14

No man who has once heartily and wholly laughed can be altogether irreclaimably bad.

Sartor Resartus.

109.15

I don't pretend to understand the Universe—it's a great deal bigger than I am...People ought to be modester.

Remark

109.16

MARGARET FULLER. I accept the universe.
CARLYLE. Gad! she'd better! *Attributed*

110 Carnegie, Dale (1888-1955), American writer.

110.1

How to Win Friends and Influence People.

Title of Book

111 Carroll, Lewis (**Charles Lutwidge Dodgson**) (1832-1898), English writer and mathematician.

111.1

'What is the use of a book, ' thought Alice, 'without pictures or conversation?'

Alice's Adventures in Wonderland, Ch. 1

111.2

'Curiouser and curiouser!' cried Alice.

same, Ch. 2

111.3

WHITE RABBIT. The Duchess! The Duchess! Oh my dear paws! Oh my fur and whiskers!

same, Ch. 4

111.4

'You are old, Father William, ' the young man said,
'And your hair has become very white;
And yet you incessantly stand on your head—
Do you think at your age, it is right?'

same, Ch. 5

111.5

'If everybody minded their own business, ' the Duchess said in a hoarse growl, 'the world would go round a deal faster than it does.' *same, Ch. 6*

111.6

HATTER. Twinkle, twinkle, little bat!
How I wonder what you're at! *same, Ch. 7*

111.7

'Take some more tea, ' the March Hare said to Alice, very earnestly.
'I've had nothing yet, ' Alice replied in an offended tone, 'so I can't take more.'
'You mean you can't take *less*, ' said the Hatter: 'it's very easy to take *more* than nothing.' *same, Ch. 7*

111.8

'Off with his head!' *same, Ch. 8*

111.9

DUCHESS. Everything's got a moral, if only you can find it. *same, Ch. 9*

111.10

DUCHESS. Take care of the sense, and the sounds will take care of themselves.

same, Ch. 9

111.11

MOCK TURTLE. Will you, won't you, will you, won't you, will you join the dance?

same, Ch. 10

111.12

MOCK TURTLE. Soup of the evening, beautiful Soup! *same, Ch. 10*

111.13

WHITE RABBIT. The Queen of Hearts, she made some tarts,
All on a summer day:
The Knave of Hearts, he stole those tarts,
And took them quite away! *same, Ch. 11*

111.14

'Where shall I begin, please your Majesty?' he asked.
'Begin at the beginning' the King said, gravely, 'and go on till you come to the end: then stop.' *same, Ch. 11*

111.15

'No, no!' said the Queen. 'Sentence first—verdict afterwards.' *same, Ch. 12*

111.16

For the Snark *was* a Boojum, you see.

The Hunting of the Snark

111.17

'Twas brillig, and the slithy toves
Did gyre and gimble in the wabe;
All mimsy were the borogoves,
And the mome raths outgrabe.

Through the Looking-Glass, Ch. 1

111.18

RED QUEEN. Now, *here*, you see, it takes all the running *you* can do, to keep in the same place. If you want to get somewhere else, you must run at least twice as fast as that!

same, Ch. 2

111.19

Tweedledum and Tweedledee

Agreed to have a battle;
For Tweedledum said Tweedledee
Had spoiled his nice new rattle.   *same, Ch. 4*

111.20
'Contrariwise, ' continued Tweedledee, 'if it was so, it might be; and if it were so, it would be: but as it isn't, it ain't. That's logic.'   *same, Ch. 4*

111.21
The Walrus and the Carpenter
Were walking close at hand;
They wept like anything to see
Such quantities of sand:
'If this were only cleared away, '
They said, 'it *would* be grand!'   *same, Ch. 4*

111.22
'The time has come, ' the Walrus said,
'To talk of many things:
Of shoes—and ships—and sealing-wax—
Of cabbages—and kings—
And why the sea is boiling hot—
And whether pigs have wings.'   *same, Ch. 4*

111.23
RED QUEEN. The rule is, jam tomorrow and jam yesterday—but never jam today.
    same, Ch. 5

111.24
'They gave it me, ' Humpty Dumpty continued thoughtfully, …'for an un-birthday present.'   *same, Ch. 6*

111.25
'When *I* use a word, ' Humpty Dumpty said in rather a scornful tone, 'it means just what I choose it to mean—neither more nor less.'
    same, Ch.6

111.26
WHITE KING. He's an Anglo-Saxon Messen-ger—and those are Anglo-Saxon attitudes.
    same, Ch. 7

111.27
HAIGHA. It's as large as life, and twice as natural!   *same, Ch. 7*

111.28
The Lion looked at Alice wearily. 'Are you animal—or vegetable—or mineral?' he said, yawning at every other word.   *same, Ch. 7*

111.29
WHITE KNIGHT. I'll tell thee everything I can;
There's little to relate.
I saw an aged aged man,
A-sitting on a gate.   *same, Ch. 8*

111.30
'Speak when you're spoken to!' the Red Queen sharply interrupted her.   *same, Ch. 9*

111.31
'You look a little shy; let me introduce you to that leg of mutton, ' said the Red Queen.
'Alice—Mutton; Mutton—Alice.'
    same, Ch. 9

111.32
RED QUEEN. It isn't etiquette to cut any one you've been introduced to. Remove the joint.   *same, Ch. 9*

112 Cary, Phoebe (1824-1871), American poet.

112.1
And though hard be the task,
'Keep a stiff upper lip.'   *Keep a Stiff Upper Lip*

113 Cato, Marcus Porcius (234-149 B.C.), Roman statesman and orator.

113.1
Delenda est Carthago.
Carthage must·be destroyed.   *Life of Cato (Plutarch)*

114 Catullus, Gaius Valerius (87-54? B.C.), Roman poet.

114.1
Vivamus, mea Lesbia, atque amemus.
Let us live, my Lesbia, and let us love.
    Carmina, 5

114.2
Odi et amo.
I hate and love.   *same, 85*

114.3
Atque in perpetuum, frater, ave atque vale.
And for ever, brother, hail and farewell!
    same, 101

115 Cavell, Edith (1865-1915), English nurse.

115.1
I realize that patriotism is not enough. I must have no hatred or bitterness towards anyone.   *Last Words*

116 Cervantes, Miguel de (1547-1616), Spanish writer.

116.1
Every man is as Heaven made him, and sometimes a great deal worse.
    Don Quixote, II:4

116.2
The best sauce in the world is hunger.
    same, II:5

116.3
There are only two families in the world, my old grandmother used to say, The *Haves* and the *Have-Nots*.   *same, II:20*

116.4

A private sin is not so prejudicial in the world as a public indecency.   *same, II:22*

116.5

Tell me what company thou keepest, and I'll tell thee what thou art.   *same, II:23*

117   Chamberlain, Joseph (1836-1914), British statesman.

117.1

Provided that the City of London remains as at present, the Clearing-house of the World.

Speech, Guildhall, London, 19 Jan 1904

117.2

The day of small nations has long passed away. The day of Empires has come.

Speech, Birmingham, 12 May 1904

118   Chamberlain, Neville (1869-1940), British statesman and prime minister.

118.1

In war, whichever side may call itself the victor, there are no winners, but all are losers.   *Speech, Kettering, 3 July 1938*

118.2

I believe it is peace for our time...peace with honour.   *Broadcast after Munich Agreement, 1 Oct 1938*

118.3

Hitler has missed the bus.   *Speech, House of Commons, 4 Apr 1940*

119   Chandler, John (1806-1876), English writer.

119.1

Conquering kings their titles take.   *Title of poem*

120   Chandler, Raymond (1888-1959), American writer.

120.1

It was a blonde. A blonde to make a bishop kick a hole in a stained-glass window.

Farewell, My Lovely, Ch. 13

120.2

She gave me a smile I could feel in my hip pocket.   *same, Ch. 18*

120.3

When I split an infinitive, god damn it, I split it so it stays split.   *Letter to his English publisher*

121   Chaplin, Charles (1889-1977), English film actor and director.

121.1

I am for people. I can't help it.

Observer 'Sayings of the week', 28 Sept 1952

121.2

All I need to make a comedy is a park, a policeman and a pretty girl.

My Autobiography

121.3

I remain just one thing, and one thing only—and that is a clown.

It places me on a far higher plane than any politician   *Observer 'Sayings of the Week', 17 June 1960*

122   Charles I, (1600-1649), King of England.

122.1

Never make a defence or apology before you be accused.   *Letter to Lord Wentworth, 3 Sept 1636*

123   Charles II, (1630-1685), King of England.

123.1

He had been, he said, a most unconscionable time dying; but he hoped that they would excuse it.   *History of England (Macaulay), I:4*

123.2

[*Of Presbyterianism*] Not a religion for gentlemen.   *History of My Own Time (Burnet), I:2:2*

123.3

[*Of Nell Gwynne*] Let not poor Nelly starve.   *Said on his death bed*

123.4

[*Of the House of Lords Debate on the Divorce Bill*] Better than a play.

Remark, 1670

124   Charles V, (1500-1558), Holy Roman Emperor.

124.1

I speak Spanish to God, Italian to women, French to men, and German to my horse.

Attributed

125   Charles, Prince of Wales (b. 1948), heir to the throne of the United Kingdom.

125.1

All the faces here this evening seem to be bloody Poms.   *Remark at Australia Day dinner, 1973*

125.2

British management doesn't seem to understand the importance of the human factor.

Speech, Parliamentary and Scientific Committee lunch, 21 Feb 1979

126   Charles, Hughie, see Parker, Ross

127 Chaucer, Geoffrey (1340?-1400), English poet.

127.1
Whan that Aprille with his shoures sote
The droghte of Marche hath perced to the
rote. *The Canterbury Tales, Prologue*

127.2
[*Of the knight*] He was a verray parfit gentil
knight. *same*

127.3
[*Of the squire*] He was as fresh as is the
month of May. *same*

127.4
[*Of the Prioress*] Ful wel she song the service
divyne,
Entuned in hir nose ful semely. *same*

127.5
A Clerk ther was of Oxenford also,
That un-to logik hadde longe y-go. *same*

127.6
As lene was his hors as is a rake. *same*

127.7
[*Of the Clerk*] Souninge in moral vertu was
his speche,
And gladly wolde he lerne, and gladly teche.
same

127.8
[*Of The Man of Law*] No-wher so bisy a
man as he ther nas,
And yet he semed bisier than he was.
same

127.9
[*Of The Doctor*] For gold in phisik is a
cordial,
Therfore he lovede gold in special. *same*

127.10
[*Of the Wife of Bath*] She was a worthy
womman al hir lyve,
Housbondes at chirche-dore she hadde fyve,
Withouten other companye in youthe.
same

127.11
The smyler with the knyf under the cloke.
The Knight's Tale

127.12
This world nis but a thurghfare ful of wo,
And we ben pilgrimes, passinge to and fro;
Deeth is an ende of every worldly sore.
same

127.13
So was hir joly whistle wel y-wet.
The Reve's Tale

127.14
Tragedie is to seyn a certeyn storie,
As olde bokes maken us memorie,
Of him that stood in greet prosperitee
And is y-fallen out of heigh degree

Into miserie, and endeth wrecchedly.
The Monk's Prologue

127.15
Mordre wol out, that see we day by day.
The Nun's Priest's Tale

127.16
The lyf so short, the craft so long to lerne,
Th'assay so hard, so sharp the conquering.
The Parlement of Foules

127.17
For of fortunes sharp adversitee
The worst kinde of infortune is this,
A man to have ben in prosperitee,
And it remembren, what is passed is.
Troilus and Criseyde, 3

127.18
Go, litel book, go litel myn tragedie.
O moral Gower, this book I directe To thee.
same, 5

128 Chesterfield, Philip Dormer Stanhope, 4th Earl of (1694-1773) English statesman and man of letters.

128.1
Be wiser than other people if you can, but do
not tell them so. *Letter to his son,
19 Nov 1745*

128.2
Whatever is worth doing at all is worth
doing well. *same, 10 Mar 1746*

128.3
An injury is much sooner forgotten than an
insult. *same, 9 Oct 1746*

128.4
Take the tone of the company you are in.
same, 9 Oct 1747

128.5
Do as you would be done by is the surest
method that I know of pleasing.
same, 16 Oct 1747

128.6
I recommend you to take care of the minutes:
for hours will take care of themselves.
same, 6 Nov 1747

128.7
Advice is seldom welcome; and those who
want it the most always like it the least.
same, 29 Jan 1748

128.8
Idleness is only the refuge of weak minds.
same, 20 July 1749

128.9
Women are much more like each other than
men: they have, in truth, but two passions,
vanity and love; these are their universal
characteristics. *same, 19 Dec 1749*

128.10
Every woman is infallibly to be gained by

every sort of flattery, and every man by one sort or other. *same, 16 Mar 1752*
128.11
A chapter of accidents. *same, 16 Feb 1753*
128.12
Religion is by no means a proper subject of conversation in a mixed company.

Letter to his godson

129 Chesterton, Gilbert Keith (1874-1936), English writer.
129.1
The strangest whim has seized me...After all
I think I will not hang myself today.

A Ballade of Suicide
129.2
The devil's walking parody
On all four footed things. *The Donkey*
129.3
Fools! For I also had my hour;
One far fierce hour and sweet;
There was a shout about my ears,
And palms before my feet. *same*
129.4
A great deal of contemporary criticism reads to me like a man saying: 'Of course I do not like green cheese: I am very fond of brown sherry.' *All I Survey*
129.5
The modern world...has no notion except that of simplifying something by destroying nearly everything. *same*
129.6
The rich are the scum of the earth in every country. *The Flying Inn*
129.7
The word 'orthodoxy' not only no longer means being right; it practically means being wrong. *Heretics, Ch. 1*
129.8
As enunciated today, 'progress' is simply a comparative of which we have not settled the superlative. *same, Ch. 2*
129.9
There is no such thing on earth as an uninteresting subject; the only thing that can exist is an uninterested person.

Heretics, Ch. 1
129.10
We ought to see far enough into a hypocrite to see even his sincerity. *same, Ch. 5*
129.11
Happiness is a mystery like religion, and should never be rationalized. *same, Ch. 7*
129.12
Charity is the power of defending that which we know to be indefensible. Hope is the power of being cheerful in circumstances which we know to be desperate. *same, Ch. 12*
129.13
Carlyle said that men were mostly fools. Christianity, with a surer and more reverend realism, says that they are all fools. *same*
129.14
A good novel tells us the truth about its hero; but a bad novel tells us the truth about its author. *same, Ch. 15*
129.15
The artistic temperament is a disease that afflicts amateurs. *same, Ch. 17*
129.16
The human race, to which so many of my readers belong. *The Napoleon of Notting Hill, I:1*
129.17
The madman is not the man who has lost his reason. The madman is the man who has lost everything except his reason.

Orthodoxy, Ch. 1
129.18
The cosmos is about the smallest hole that a man can hide his head in. *same*
129.19
Reason is itself a matter of faith. It is an act of faith to assert that our thoughts have any relation to reality at all. *same, Ch. 3*
129.20
Mr Shaw is (I suspect) the only man on earth who has never written any poetry.

same
129.21
All conservatism is based upon the idea that if you leave things alone you leave them as they are. But you do not. If you leave a thing alone you leave it to a torrent of change.

same, Ch. 7
129.22
Angels can fly because they take themselves lightly. *same*
129.23
Compromise used to mean that half a loaf was better than no bread. Among modern statesmen it really seems to mean that half a loaf is better than a whole loaf.

What's Wrong with the World
129.24
Mankind is not a tribe of animals to which we owe compassion. Mankind is a club to which we owe our subscription.

Daily News, 10 Apr 1906
129.25
A puritan's a person who pours righteous indignation into the wrong things.

Attributed

129.26
New roads: new ruts. *Attributed*

130 Chevalier, Maurice (1888-1972), French actor and singer.
130.1
I prefer old age to the alternative.
Remark, 1962

131 Churchill, Charles (1731-1764), English poet.
131.1
Be England what she will,
With all her faults, she is my country still.
The Farewell
131.2
The danger chiefly lies in acting well,
No crime's so great as daring to excel.
Epistle to William Hogarth
131.3
Keep up appearances; their lies the test
The world will give thee credit for the rest.
Night

132 Churchill, Lord Randolph Spencer (1849-1895), English statesman.
132.1
[*Of Gladstone*] An old man in a hurry.
Speech, June 1886
132.2
Ulster will fight; Ulster will be right.
Letter, 7 May 1886
132.3
The duty of an opposition is to oppose.
Lord Randolph Churchill (W. S. Churchill)
132.4
[*Of decimal points*] I never could make out what those damned dots meant *same*

133 Churchill, Winston Leonard Spencer (1874-1965), English statesman, writer and prime minister.
133.1
It cannot in the opinion of His Majesty's Government be classified as slavery in the extreme acceptance of the word without some risk of terminological inexactitude.
Speech, House of Commons, 22 Feb 1906
133.2
Men will forgive a man anything except bad prose. *Election speech, Manchester, 1906*
133.3
[*Over Irish Home Rule*] *The Times* is speechless and takes three columns to express its speechlessness. *Speech, Dundee, 14 May 1908*

133.4
[*Of Lord Charles Beresford*] He is one of those orators of whom it was well said, 'Before they get up they do not know what they are going to say; when they are speaking, they do not know what they are saying; and when they sit down, they do not know what they have said'. *Speech, House of Commons, 20 Dec 1912*
133.5
The maxim of the British people is 'Business as usual'. *Speech, Guildhall, 9 Nov 1914*
133.6
Labour is not fit to govern.
Election speech, 1920
133.7
[*Of the British*] They are the only people who like to be told how bad things are—who like to be told the worst. *Speech, 1921*
133.8
India is a geographical term. It is no more a united nation than the Equator.
Speech, Royal Albert Hall, 18 Mar 1931
133.9
We have sustained a defeat without a war.
Speech, House of Commons, 5 Oct 1938
133.10
I have nothing to offer but blood, toil, tears and sweat. *Speech, House of Commons, 13 May 1940*
133.11
Victory at all costs, victory in spite of all terror, victory however long and hard the road may be; for without victory there is no survival. *same*
133.12
We shall not flag or fail. We shall fight in France, we shall fight on the seas and oceans, we shall fight with growing confidence and growing strength in the air, we shall defend our island, whatever the cost may be, we shall fight on the beaches, we shall fight on the landing grounds, we shall fight in the fields and in the streets, we shall fight in the hills; we shall never surrender.
same, 4 June 1940
133.13
This was their finest hour.
same, 18 June 1940
133.14
The battle of Britain is about to begin.
same, 1 July 1940
133.15
Never in the field of human conflict was so much owed by so many to so few.
same, 20 Aug 1940
133.16

Give us the tools, and we will finish the job.
Radio Broadcast, 9 Feb 1941

133.17
You [*Hitler*] do your worst, and we will do our best. *Speech, 14 July 1941*

133.18
Do not let us speak of darker days; let us rather speak of sterner days. These are not dark days: these are great days—the greatest days our country has ever lived.
Address, Harrow School, 29 Oct 1941

133.19
When I warned them [*the French Government*] that Britain would fight on alone whatever they did, their Generals told their Prime Minister and his divided Cabinet: 'In three weeks England will have her neck wrung like a chicken.'
Some chicken! Some neck!
Speech, Canadian Parliament, 30 Dec 1941

133.20
[*Of the Battle of Egypt*] This is not the end. It is not even the beginning of the end. But it is, perhaps, the end of the beginning.
Speech, Mansion House, 10 Nov 1942

133.21
I have not become the King's First Minister in order to preside over the liquidation of the British Empire. *same*

133.22
There is no finer investment for any community than putting milk into babies.
Radio Broadcast, 21 Mar 1943

133.23
An iron curtain has descended across the Continent. *Address, Westminster College, Fulton, U.S.A., 5 Mar 1946*

133.24
We must build a kind of United States of Europe. *Speech, Zurich, 19 Sept 1946*

133.25
Perhaps it is better to be irresponsible and right than to be responsible and wrong.
Party Political Broadcast, London, 26 Aug 1950

133.26
By being so long in the lowest form [*at Harrow school*] I gained an immense advantage over the cleverest boys...I got into my bones the essential structure of the normal British sentence—which is a noble thing.
My Early Life, Ch. 2

133.27
Headmasters have powers at their disposal with which Prime Ministers have never yet been invested. *same, Ch. 2*

133.28

It is a good thing for an uneducated man to read books of quotations. *same, Ch. 9*

133.29
Those who can win a war well can rarely make a good peace and those who could make a good peace would never have won the war. *same, Ch. 26*

133.30
The redress of the grievances of the vanquished should precede the disarmament of the victors. *The Gathering Storm, Ch. 3*

133.31
I felt as if I were walking with destiny, and that all my past life had been but a preparation for this hour and this trial.
same, Ch. 38

133.32
No one can guarantee success in war, but only deserve it. *Their Finest Hour*

133.33
[*Of Dunkirk*] Wars are not won by evacuations. *same*

133.34
When I look back on all these worries I remember the story of the old man who said on his deathbed that he had had a lot of trouble in his life, most of which had never happened. *same*

133.35
I have only one purpose, the destruction of Hitler, and my life is much simplified thereby. If Hitler invaded Hell I would make at least a favourable reference to the Devil in the House of Commons.
The Grand Alliance, Ch. 20

133.36
Before Alamein we never had a victory. After Alamein we never had a defeat.
The Hinge of Fate, Ch. 33

133.37
Peace with Germany and Japan on our terms will not bring much rest....As I observed last time, when the war of the giants is over the wars of the pygmies will begin.
Triumph and Tragedy, Ch. 25

133.38
[*When asked whether the Niagara Falls looked the same as when he first saw them*] Well, the principle seems the same. The water still keeps falling over. *Closing the Ring, Ch. 5*

133.39
I said that the world must be made safe for at least fifty years. If it was only for fifteen to twenty years then we should have betrayed our soldiers. *same, Ch. 20*

133.40
We must have a better word than 'prefabri-

cated'. Why not 'ready-made'?
same, Appendix C
133.41
Everybody has a right to pronounce foreign names as he chooses. *Observer 'Sayings of the Week', 5 Aug 1951*
133.42
The nation had the lion's heart. I had the luck to give the roar. *Said on his 80th birthday*
133.43
[*Of Viscount Montgomery*] In defeat unbeatable; in victory unbearable.
133.44
[*Of Mr Baldwin*] It is a fine thing to be honest but it is also very important to be right.

134 Cibber, Colley (1671-1757), English actor and dramatist.
134.1
One had as good be out of the world, as out of the fashion. *Love's Last Shift, Act 2*
134.2
Stolen sweets are best. *The Rival Fools, Act 1*

135 Cicero, Marcus Tullius (106-43 B.C.), Roman statesman and orator.
135.1
There is nothing so absurd but some philosopher has said it.
De Divinatione, II:58
135.2
The good of the people is the chief law.
De Legibus, III:3
135.3
Summum bonum.
The greatest good. *De Officiis, I:2*
135.4
O tempora! O mores!
What times! What customs!
In Catilinam, I:1
135.5
Cui bono.
To whose profit. *Pro Milone, IV:9*

136 Clarke, John (*fl.* 1639), English writer.
136.1
Home is home, though it be never so homely.
Paroemiologia Anglo-Latina

137 Clay, Henry (1777-1852), American statesman.
137.1
I had rather be right than be President.
Speech, 1850

138 Clemens, Samuel Langhorne, see Twain, Mark

139 Clive, Lord Robert (1725-1774), English soldier.
139.1
By God, Mr Chairman, at this moment I stand astonished at my own moderation!
Reply during Parliamentary Inquiry, 1773

140 Clough, Arthur Hugh (1819-1861), English poet.
140.1
A world where nothing is had for nothing.
The Bothie of Tober-na-Vuolich, VIII:5
140.2
How pleasant it is to have money.
Dipsychus, I:4
140.3
Thou shalt have one God only; who
Would be at the expense of two?
The Latest Decalogue, 1
140.4
Thou shalt not kill; but needst not strive
Officiously to keep alive. *same, 11*
140.5
'Tis better to have fought and lost,
Than never to have fought at all.
Peschiera

141 Cobbett, William (1762-1835), English farmer, politician and writer.
141.1
To be poor and independent is very nearly an impossibility. *Advice to Young Men*
141.2
[*Of London*] But what is to be the fate of the great wen of all? *Rural Rides*

142 Coke, Desmond (1879-1931), English writer.
142.1
All rowed fast but none so fast as stroke.
Sandford of Merton (Popular quotation derived from the sentence: 'His blade struck the water a full second before any other... until... as the boats began to near the winning-post, his own was dipping into the water twice as often as any other.')

143 Coke, Sir Edward (1552-1634), English jurist.
143.1
A man's house is his castle. *Third Institute*

144 Coleridge, Samuel Taylor (1772-1834), English poet, philosopher and critic.

144.1
It is an ancient Mariner,
And he stoppeth one of three.
'By thy long grey beard and glittering eye,
Now wherefore stopp'st thou me?'
The Rime of the Ancient Mariner, I:1

144.2
The Sun came up upon the left,
Out of the sea came he!
And he shone bright, and on the right
Went down into the sea. *same, I:25*

144.3
The ice was here, the ice was there,
The ice was all around:
It cracked and growled, and roared and howled,
Like noises in a swound! *same, I:59*

144.4
With my cross-bow
I shot the albatross. *same, I:81*

144.5
We were the first that ever burst
Into that silent sea. *same, II:103*

144.6
Water, water, every where,
And all the boards did shrink;
Water, water, every where,
Nor any drop to drink. *same, II:119*

144.7
Alone, alone, all, all alone,
Alone on a wide wide sea!
And never a saint took pity on
My soul in agony. *same, IV:232*

144.8
The many men, so beautiful!
And they all dead did lie:
And a thousand thousand slimy things
Lived on; and so did I. *same, IV:236*

144.9
The moving Moon went up the sky,
And no where did abide:
Softly she was going up,
And a star or two beside. *same, IV:263*

144.10
Oh sleep! it is a gentle thing,
Beloved from pole to pole! *same, V:292*

144.11
Quoth he, 'The man hath penance done, And penance more will do.' *same, V:408*

144.12
Like one, that on a lonesome road
Doth walk in fear and dread,
And having once turned round walks on,
And turns no more his head;
Because he knows, a frightful fiend
Doth close behind him tread. *same, VI:446*

144.13

No voice; but oh! the silence sank
Like music on my heart. *same, VI:498*

144.14
He prayeth well, who loveth well
Both man and bird and beast.
same, VII:612

144.15
He prayeth best, who loveth best
All things both great and small;
For the dear God who loveth us,
He made and loveth all. *same, VII:614*

144.16
A sadder and a wiser man,
He rose the morrow morn. *same, VII:624*

144.17
A sight to dream of, not to tell!
Christabel, I:253

144.18
I may not hope from outward forms to win
The passion and the life, whose fountains are within. *Dejection: An Ode*

144.19
In Xanadu did Kubla Khan
A stately pleasure-dome decree:
Where Alph, the sacred river, ran
Through caverns measureless to man
Down to a sunless sea. *Kubla Khan*

144.20
A savage place! as holy and enchanted
As e'er beneath a waning moon was haunted
By woman wailing for her demon-lover!
same

144.21
Weave a circle round him thrice,
And close your eyes with holy dread,
For he on honey-dew hath fed,
And drunk the milk of Paradise. *same*

144.22
That willing suspension of disbelief for the moment, which constitutes poetic faith.
Biographia Literaria, Ch. 14

144.23
Our myriad-minded Shakespeare.
same, Ch. 15

144.24
Summer has set in with its usual severity.
Remark quoted in C. Lamb's letter to V. Novello, 9 May 1826

144.25
I wish our clever young poets would remember my homely definitions of prose and poetry; that is, prose = words in their best order;—poetry = the best words in the best order. *Table Talk*

144.26
No mind is thoroughly well organized that is deficient in a sense of humour. *same*

144.27

What comes from the heart, goes to the heart. *same*

145 Colette, Sidonie Gabrielle (1873-1954), French novelist.

145.1

Total absence of humour renders life impossible. *Chance Acquaintances*

145.2

When she raises her eyelids it's as if she were taking off all her clothes.

Claudine and Annie

145.3

My virtue's still far too small, I don't trot it out and about yet. *Claudine at School*

145.4

Don't ever wear artistic jewellery; it wrecks a woman's reputation. *Gigi*

145.5

Don't eat too many almonds; they add weight to the breasts *same*

146 Collins, Mortimer (1827-1876), English writer.

146.1

A man is as old as he's feeling,
A woman as old as she looks.

The Unknown Quantity

147 Colman, George (1762-1836), English dramatist and theatrical manager.

147.1

Mum's the word. *The Battle of Hexham, II:1*

147.2

Lord help you! Tell'em Queen Anne's dead.

Heir-at-Law, I:1

147.3

Not to be sneezed at. *same, II:1*

148 Colton, Charles Caleb (1780?-1832), English clergyman and writer.

148.1

Men will wrangle for religion; write for it; fight for it; anything but—live for it.

Lacon, I:25

148.2

When you have nothing to say, say nothing.

same, I:183

148.3

Imitation is the sincerest of flattery.

same, I:217

148.4

Examinations are formidable even to the best prepared, for the greatest fool may ask more than the wisest man can answer.

same, II:322

148.5

The debt which cancels all others.

same, II:66

149 The Book of Common Prayer

149.1

We have erred, and strayed from thy ways like lost sheep. *Morning Prayer, General Confession*

149.2

We have left undone those things which we ought to have done; and we have done those things we ought not to have done. *same*

149.3

As it was in the beginning, is now, and ever shall be: world without end. *same, Gloria*

149.4

Give peace in our time, O Lord.

same, Versicles

149.5

When two or three are gathered together in thy Name thou wilt grant their requests.

same, Prayer of St Chrysostom

149.6

Defend us from all perils and dangers of this night. *same*

149.7

All the deceits of the world, the flesh, and the devil. *same*

149.8

In the hour of death, and in the day of judgement. *same*

149.9

Read, mark, learn and inwardly digest.

Collect, 2nd Sunday in Advent

149.10

All our doings without charity are nothing worth. *Collect, Quinquagesima Sunday*

149.11

Renounce the devil and all his works.

Publick Baptism of Infants

149.12

Being now come to the years of discretion.

Order of Confirmation

149.13

If any of you know cause, or just impediment.

Solemnization of Matrimony

149.14

Let him now speak, or else hereafter for ever hold his peace. *same*

149.15

To have and to hold from this day forward, for better for worse, for richer for poorer, in sickness and in health, to love and to cherish, till death us do part. *same*

150 Confucius, (K'ung Fu-tse) (551-479 B.C.), Chinese philosopher.

150.1
Men's natures are alike; it is their habits that carry them far apart. *Analects*
150.2
Study the past, if you would divine the future. *same*
150.3
Learning without thought is labour lost; thought without learning is perilous. *same*
150.4
Fine words and an insinuating appearance are seldom associated with true virtue. *same*
150.5
Have no friends not equal to yourself. *same*
150.6
When you have faults, do not fear to abandon them. *same*
150.7
To be able to practise five things everywhere under heaven constitutes perfect virtue....gravity, generosity of soul, sincerity, earnestness, and kindness. *same*
150.8
The superior man is satisfied and composed; the mean man is always full of distress. *same*
150.9
The people may be made to follow a course of action, but they may not be made to understand it. *same*
150.10
Recompense injury with justice, and recompense kindness with kindness. *same*
150.11
The superior man is distressed by his want of ability. *same*
150.12
What you do not want done to yourself, do not do to others. *same*

151 Congreve, William (1670–1729), English dramatist.
151.1
She lays it on with a trowel.
The Double Dealer, III:10
151.2
See how love and murder will out.
same, IV:6
151.3
ALMERIA. Music has charms to soothe a savage breast. *The Mourning Bride, Act 1*
151.4
ZARA. Heaven has no rage like love to hatred turned,

Nor hell a fury like a woman scorned.
same, Act 3
151.5
Say what you will, 'tis better to be left than never to have been loved. *The Way of the World, II:1*
151.6
MRS MILLAMENT. I nauseate walking; 'tis a country diversion, I loathe the country and everything that relates to it. *same, IV:4*
151.7
LADY WISHFORT. I hope you do not think me prone to any iteration of nuptials.
same, IV:12
151.8
WAITWELL. O, she is the antidote to desire.
same, IV:14
151.9
Alack he's gone the way of all flesh.
Squire Bickerstaff Detected, attributed

152 Connell, James (1852–1929), English socialist and poacher.
152.1
Then raise the scarlet standard high!
Beneath its shade we'll live and die!
Though cowards flinch, and traitors jeer,
We'll keep the Red Flag flying here!
The Red Flag

153 Connolly, Cyril (1903–1974), English journalist and writer.
153.1
It is closing time in the gardens of the West.
The Condemned Playground
153.2
The ape-like virtues without which no one can enjoy a public school. *Enemies of Promise, Ch. 1*
153.3
An author arrives at a good style when his language performs what is required of it without shyness. *same, Ch. 3*
153.4
As repressed sadists are supposed to become policemen or butchers so those with irrational fear of life become publishers.
same
153.5
Literature is the art of writing something that will be read twice; journalism what will be grasped at once. *same*
153.6
Whom the gods wish to destroy they first call promising. *same*
153.7
There is no more sombre enemy of good art than the pram in the hall. *same*

153.8
I have always disliked myself at any given moment; the total of such moments is my life. *same, Ch. 18*
153.9
Boys do not grow up gradually. They move forward in spurts like the hands of clocks in railway stations. *same*
153.10
Better to write for yourself and have no public, than write for the public and have no self. *Turnstile One (edited by V. S. Pritchett)*
153.11
The man who is master of his passions is Reason's slave. *same*

154 Conrad, Joseph (1857-1924), English novelist.
154.1
Exterminate all brutes. *Heart of Darkness*
154.2
The horror! The horror! *same*
154.3
Mistah Kurtz—he dead. *same*
154.4
You shall judge of a man by his foes as well as by his friends. *Lord Jim, Ch. 34*
154.5
A work that aspires, however humbly, to the condition of art should carry its justification in every line. *The Nigger of the Narcissus, Preface*
154.6
The belief in a supernatural source of evil is not necessary; men alone are quite capable of every wickedness. *Under Western Eyes, Part 2*

155 Coolidge, Calvin (1872-1933), President of the United States.
155.1
The business of America is business.
Speech, Washington, 17 Jan 1925
155.2
[*Of the Boston police strike*] There is no right to strike against the public safety by anybody, anywhere, any time.
Remark, 14 Sept 1919
155.3
[*When asked what a clergyman had said in a sermon on sin*] He said he was against it.

156 Cooper, James Fenimore (1789-1851), American novelist.
156.1
The Last of the Mohicans. *Title of Novel*

157 Corbusier, Le (Charles Édouard Jeanneret) (1887-1965), Swiss architect.
157.1
A house is a machine for living in.
Towards an architecture

158 Corneille, Pierre (1606-1684), French dramatist.
158.1
We triumph without glory when we conquer without danger. *Le Cid, II:2*
158.2
Do your duty and leave the rest to the Gods.
Horace, II:8
158.3
The manner of giving is worth more than the gift. *Le Menteur, I:1*
158.4
A good memory is needed after one has lied.
same, IV:5

159 Cornuel, Anne-Marie Bigot de (1605-1694), Frenchwoman noted for her salon.
159.1
No man is a hero to his valet. *Lettres de Mlle Aissé, 13 Aug 1728*

160 Coubertin, Baron Pierre de (1863-1937), French founder of the modern Olympic games.
160.1
The most important thing in the Olympic Games is not winning but taking part....The essential thing in life is not conquering but fighting well. *Speech at Banquet to Officials of Olympic Games, London, 24 July 1908*

161 Coué, Émile (1857-1926), French doctor.
161.1
Tous les jours, à tous points de vue, je vais de mieux en mieux.
Every day, in every way, I am getting better and better. *Formula for a cure by auto-suggestion*

162 Cousin, Victor (1792-1867), French philosopher.
162.1
L'art pour l'art.
Art for art's sake. *Lecture at Sorbonne, 1818*

163 Coward, Sir Noel (1899-1973), English actor and dramatist.
163.1
Everybody was up to something, especially,

of course, those who were up to nothing.
Future Indefinite

163.2
The Stately Homes of England
How beautiful they stand,
To prove the upper classes
Have still the upper hand. *Operette, II:7,*
'The Stately Homes of England'

163.3
Strange how potent cheap music is.
Private Lives, Act 1

163.4
Very flat, Norfolk. *same*

163.5
Certain women should be struck regularly,
like gongs. *same, Act 2*

163.6
Never mind, dear, we're all made the same,
though some more than others.
The Café de la Paix

163.7
Sunburn is very becoming—but only when it
is even—one must be careful not to look like
a mixed grill. *The Lido Beach*

163.8
I've over-educated myself in all the things I
shouldn't have known at all. *Wild Oats*

163.9
Mad dogs and Englishmen go out in the
mid-day sun. *Title of song*

163.10
Don't put your daughter on the stage, Mrs
Worthington. *Title of song*

163.11
Twentieth-Century Blues. *Title of song*

163.12
Poor Little Rich Girl. *Title of song*

163.13
Don't let's be beastly to the Germans.
Title of song

163.14
Dance, dance, dance little lady. *Title of
song*

163.15
Mad about the boy. *Title of song*

163.16
Work is much more fun than fun.
Observer 'Sayings of the Week',
21 June 1963

164 Cowley, Abraham (1618-1667), Eng-
lish poet.
164.1
God the first garden made, and the first city
Cain. *The Garden*
164.2
Life is an incurable disease.
To Dr Scarborough

165 Cowper, William (1731-1800), English
poet.
165.1
We perish'd, each alone:
But I beneath a rougher sea,
And whelm'd in deeper gulphs than he.
The Castaway
165.2
He found it inconvenient to be poor.
Charity
165.3
God made the country, and man made the
town. *The Task*
165.4
England, with all thy faults, I love thee still,
My country. *same*
165.5
Variety's the very spice of life
That gives it all its flavour. *same*
165.6
While the bubbling and loud-hissing urn
Throws up a steamy column, and the cups,
That cheer but not inebriate, wait on each,
So let us welcome peaceful evening in.
same
165.7
Nature is but a name for an effect
Whose cause is God. *same*

166 Craig, Sir Edward Gordon
(1872-1966), English actor and stage
designer.
166.1
Farce is the essential theatre. Farce refined
becomes high comedy: farce brutalized
becomes tragedy. *The Story of my Days,*
Index

167 Crane, Stephen (1871-1900), American writer.
167.1
The Red Badge of Courage. *Title of novel*

168 Cranmer, Thomas (1489-1556),
English Archbishop.
168.1
This hand hath offended. *Memorials of*
Cranmer (Strype)

169 Creighton, Mandell (1843-1901),
English churchman and historian.
169.1
No people do so much harm as those who
go about doing good. *Life*

170 Croce, Benedetto (1866-1952), Italian
philosopher and critic.

170.1
Art is ruled uniquely by the imagination.
Esthetic, Ch. 1

171 Croker, John Wilson (1780-1857),
Irish politician.
171.1
A game which a sharper once played with a
dupe, entitled 'Heads I win, tails you lose.'
Croker Papers

172 Cromwell, Oliver (1599-1658), English
soldier and statesman.
172.1
I beseech you, in the bowels of Christ, think
it possible you may be mistaken.   *Letter to
the General Assembly of the Church of
Scotland, 3 Aug 1650*
172.2
What shall we do with this bauble? There,
take it away.   *Speech dismissing Parliament,
20 Apr 1653*
172.3
It is not fit that you should sit here any
longer!...you shall now give place to better
men.   *Speech to the Rump Parliament,
22 Jan 1654*
172.4
Warts and all.   *Anecdotes of Painting
(Horace Walpole), Ch. 12 (Popular
quotation derived from the sentence: 'Mr
Lely, I desire you would use all your skill
to paint my picture truly like me, and not
flatter me at all; but remark all these
roughnesses, pimples, warts, and
everything as you see me, otherwise I will
never pay a farthing for it.')*

173 Curran, John Philpot (1750-1817),
Irish orator.
173.1
The condition upon which God hath given
liberty to man is eternal vigilance.
*Speech on the Right of Election of Lord
Mayor of Dublin, 10 July 1790 vigilance*

D

174 The Daily Mail
174.1
Perhaps the real reason why we have always
been able to champion free speech in this
country is that we know perfectly well that
hardly anybody has got anything to say, and
that no one will listen to anyone that has.
Editorial (date unknown)

175 Dana, Charles Anderson (1819-1897),
American newspaper editor.
175.1
When a dog bites a man that is not news, but
when a man bites a dog, that is news.
The New York Sun, 1882

176 Dante, Alighieri (1265-1321), Italian
poet.
176.1
Abandon hope, all ye who enter here.
Divine Comedy, Inferno, III:9
176.2
There is no greater sorrow than to recall a
time of happiness when in misery.
same, V:121

177 Danton, Georges Jaques (1759-1794),
French politician.
177.1
Boldness, and again boldness, and always
boldness!   *Speech, French Legislative
Committee, 2 Sept 1792*

178 Darling, Charles John, 1st Baron
(1849-1936), English judge.
178.1
The Law of England is a very strange one; it
cannot compel anyone to tell the truth....But
what the Law can do is to give you seven
years for not telling the truth.
Lord Darling (D. Walker-Smith)

179 Darwin, Charles Galton (1887-1962),
English scientist.
179.1
The evolution of the human race will not be
accomplished in the ten thousand years of
tame animals, but in the million years of
wild animals, because man is and will always
be a wild animal.   *The Next Ten Million
Years, Ch. 4*

180 Darwin, Charles Robert (1809-1882),
English scientist.
180.1
Man with all his noble qualities...still bears
in his bodily frame the indelible stamp of his
lowly origin.   *The Descent of Man*
180.2
I have called this principle, by which each
slight variation, if useful, is preserved, by the

term of Natural Selection.   *The Origin of*
                                Species, Ch. 3
180.3
The expression often used by Mr Herbert
Spencer of the Survival of the Fittest is more
accurate, and is sometimes equally convenient.   *same*

181 Davies, William Henry (1871-1940),
English poet.
181.1
What is this life if, full of care,
We have no time to stand and stare?
                                        Leisure

182 Day-Lewis, Cecil (1904-1972), Eng-
lish poet.
182.1
It is the logic of our times,
No subject for immortal verse—
That we who lived by honest dreams
Defend the bad against the worse.
                            Where are the War Poets?

183 Decatur, Stephen (1779-1820), American naval commander.
183.1
Our country! In her intercourse with foreign
nations, may she always be in the right; but
our country, right or wrong.
                    Speech, Norfolk, Virginia, Apr 1816

184 Defoe, Daniel (1660?-1731), English
writer.
184.1
The good die early, and the bad die late.
                    Character of the late Dr. Annesley
184.2
I takes my man Friday with me.
                                Robinson Crusoe
184.3
And of all plagues with which mankind are
curst,
Ecclesiastic tyranny's the worst.
                    The True-Born Englishman, 2

185 Dekker, Thomas (1570?-1641?),
English dramatist.
185.1
Golden slumbers kiss your eyes,
Smiles awake you when you rise.
                            Patient Grissil, IV:2

186 Denman, Thomas, 1st Baron
(1779-1854), English judge.
186.1
Trial by jury itself, instead of being a security
to persons who are accused, will be a

delusion, a mockery, and a snare.
                    Judgment in O'Connell v The Queen,
                                    4 Sept 1844

187 Dennis, John (1657-1734), English
critic.
187.1
A man who could make so vile a pun would
not scruple to pick a pocket.
                    The Gentleman's Magazine, 1781

188 De Quincey, Thomas (1785-1859),
English writer.
188.1
Murder considered as one of the Fine Arts.
                                Title of Essay

189 Descartes, René (1596-1650), French
philosopher and mathematician.
189.1
Cogito, ergo sum.
I think, therefore I am.   *Le Discours de la*
                                    Méthode

190 De Vries, Peter (b. 1910), American
novelist.
190.1
We know the human brain is a device to
keep the ears from grating on one another.
                    Comfort me with Apples, Ch. 1
190.2
Gluttony is an emotional escape, a sign
something is eating us.   *same, Ch. 7*
190.3
Probably a fear we have of facing up to the
real issues. Could you say we were guilty of
Noel Cowardice?   *same, Ch. 8*
190.4
I wanted to be bored to death, as good a way
to go as any.   *same, Ch. 17*
190.5
It is the final proof of God's omnipotence
that he need not exist in order to save us.
                        The Mackerel Plaza, Ch. 2
190.6
Let us hope...that a kind of Providence will
put a speedy end to the acts of God under
which we have been labouring.   *same, Ch. 3*

191 Dickens, Charles (1812-1870), English
novelist.
191.1
'There are strings', said Mr Tappertit, 'in the
human heart that had better not be vibrated.'
                        Barnaby Rudge, Ch. 22
191.2
This is a London particular...A fog, miss.
                            Bleak House, Ch. 3

191.3

MISS FLITE. I expect a judgment. Shortly.

same

191.4

It is a melancholy truth that even great men have their poor relations. *same, Ch. 28*

191.5

'God bless us every one!' said Tiny Tim, the last of all. *A Christmas Carol*

191.6

'I am a lone lorn creetur, ' were Mrs Gummidge's words…'and everythink goes contrairy with me.' *David Copperfield, Ch. 3*

191.7

BARKIS. Barkis is willin'. *same, Ch. 5*

191.8

MICAWBER. Annual income twenty pounds, annual expenditure nineteen nineteen six, result happiness. Annual income twenty pounds, annual expenditure twenty pounds ought and six, result misery. *same, Ch. 12*

191.9

URIAH HEEP. We are so very 'umble. *same, Ch. 17*

191.10

MICAWBER. Accidents will occur in the best-regulated families. *same, Ch. 28*

191.11

MR PEGGOTTY. I'm Gormed—and I can't say no fairer than that. *same, Ch. 63*

191.12

CAPTAIN CUTTLE. When found, make a note of. *Dombey and Son, Ch. 15*

191.13

GRADGRIND. Now, what I want is Facts…Facts alone are wanted in life.

Hard Times, I:1

191.14

Whatever was required to be done, the Circumlocution Office was beforehand with all the public departments in the art of perceiving—HOW NOT TO DO IT.

Little Dorrit, I:10

191.15

MR PECKSNIFF. Let us be moral. Let us contemplate existence. *Martin Chuzzlewit, Ch. 10*

191.16

JONAS CHUZZLEWIT. Here's the rule for bargains: 'Do other men, for they would do you.' That's the true business precept.

same, Ch. 11

191.17

MRS GAMP. He'd make a lovely corpse.

same, Ch. 25

191.18

Every baby born into the world is a finer one than the last. *Nicholas Nickleby, Ch. 36*

191.19

GENTLEMEN IN THE SMALLCLOTHES. All is gas and gaiters. *same, Ch. 49*

191.20

MR BUMBLE. Oliver Twist has asked for more. *Oliver Twist, Ch. 2*

191.21

Known by the *sobriquet* of 'The artful Dodger.' *same, Ch. 8*

191.22

'If the law supposes that, ' said Mr Bumble…, 'the law is a ass— a idiot.'

same, Ch. 51

191.23

The question [*Mr. Podsnap asked himself*] about everything was, would it bring a blush to the cheek of a young person?

Our Mutual Friend, I:11

191.24

JINGLE. Kent, sir—everybody knows Kent—apples, cherries, hops and women.

Pickwick Papers, Ch. 2

191.25

JOE, THE FAT BOY. I wants to make your flesh creep. *same, Ch. 8*

191.26

It's always best on these occasions to do what the mob do.'

'But suppose there are two mobs?' suggested Mr Snodgrass.

'Shout with the largest, ' replied Mr Pickwick. *same, Ch. 13*

191.27

MR WELLER. Take example by your father, my boy, and be very careful o' vidders all your life. *same*

191.28

SAM WELLER. Poverty and oysters always seem to go together. *same, Ch. 22*

191.29

SAM WELLER. Wery glad to see you indeed, and hope our acquaintance may be a long 'un, as the gen'l'm'n said to the fi' pun' note. *same, Ch. 25*

191.30

MR WELLER. Poetry's unnat'ral; no man ever talked poetry 'cept a beadle on boxin' day. *same, Ch. 33*

191.31

STIGGINS. It's my opinion, sir, that this meeting is drunk. *same*

191.32

MR WELLER. Put it down a we, my lord, put it down a we! *same, Ch. 34*

191.33

SAM WELLER. Anythin' for a quiet life, as

the man said wen he took the sitivation at
the lighthouse. *same, Ch. 43*
191.34
SYDNEY CARTON. It is a far, far, better
thing that I do, than I have ever done; it is a
far, far, better rest that I go to, than I have
ever known. *A Tale of Two Cities, Ch. 15*

192 Dickinson, Emily (1830-1886), Ameri-
can poet.
192.1
Success is counted sweetest
By those who ne'er succeed. *Poems, 67*
192.2
Parting is all we know of heaven,
And all we need of hell. *same, 1732*

193 Diogenes, (412?-323? B.C.), Cynic
philosopher.
193.1
Stand a little less between me and the sun.
Life of Alexander (Plutarch)

194 Dionysius of Halicarnassus, (40?-8
B.C.), Greek historian and rhetorician.
194.1
History is philosophy teaching by examples.
Ars rhetorica, XI:2

**195 Disraeli, Benjamin, 1st Earl of
Beaconsfield** (1804-1881), English statesman and novelist.
195.1
I will sit down now, but the time will come
when you will hear me. *Maiden Speech,*
House of Commons, 7 Dec 1837
195.2
[*Of Sir Robert Peel*] The right honourable
gentleman caught the Whigs bathing, and
walked away with their clothes.
Speech, House of Commons, 28 Feb 1845
195.3
A Conservative government is an organized
hypocrisy. *Speech, 17 Mar 1845*
195.4
The question is this: Is man an ape or an
angel? I, my lord, am on the side of the
angels. *Speech, 25 Nov 1864*
195.5
Lord Salisbury and myself have brought you
back peace—but a peace I hope with honour.
Speech, House of Commons, 16 July 1878
195.6
[*Of Gladstone*] A sophistical rhetorician
inebriated with the exuberance of his own
verbosity. *Speech, 27 July 1878*
195.7

Youth is a blunder; manhood a struggle; old
age a regret. *Coningsby, III:1*
195.8
His Christianity was muscular.
Endymion, Ch. 14
195.9
Every woman should marry—and no man.
Lothair, Ch. 30
195.10
'My idea of an agreeable person, ' said Hugo
Bohun, 'is a person who agrees with me.'
same, Ch. 35
195.11
I was told that the Privileged and the People
formed Two Nations. *Sybil, IV:8*
195.12
[*Of his wife*] She is an excellent creature, but
she never can remember which came first,
the Greeks or the Romans. *Attributed*
195.13
When I want to read a novel I write one.
Attributed

196 Dobrée, Bonamy (b. 1891), English
scholar and critic.
196.1
It is difficult to be humble. Even if you aim
at humility, there is no guarantee that when
you have attained the state you will not be
proud of the feat. *John Wesley*

197 Dodgson, Charles Lutwidge, see
Carroll, Lewis

198 Donleavy, James Patrick (b. 1926),
American novelist.
198.1
I got disappointed in human nature as well
and gave it up because I found it too much
like my own. *Fairy Tales of New York*

199 Donne, John (1573-1631), English
poet.
199.1
And new Philosophy calls all in doubt,
The Element of fire is quite put out;
The Sun is lost, and th' earth, and no man's
wit
Can well direct him where to look for it.
An Anatomy of the World, 205
199.2
Come live with me, and be my love,
And we will some new pleasures prove
Of golden sands, and crystal brooks,
With silken lines, and silver hooks.
The Bait
199.3

For God's sake hold your tongue and let me
love.   *The Canonization*
199.4
Love built on beauty, soon as beauty, dies.
                           Elegies, 2, The Anagram
199.5
She, and comparisons are odious.   *same, 8,*
                                   The Comparison
199.6
Licence my roving hands, and let them go,
Before, behind, between, above, below.
                      same, 18, Love's Progress
199.7
O my America! my new-found-land,
My Kingdom, safeliest when with one man
man'd.   *same, 19, Going To Bed*
199.8
Death be not proud, though some have
called thee
Mighty and dreadful, for, thou art not so.
                              Holy Sonnets, 10
199.9
Go, and catch a falling star,
Get with child a mandrake root,
Tell me, where all past years are,
Or who cleft the Devil's foot.   *Song, Go*
                         and Catch a Falling Star
199.10
Busy old fool, unruly Sun,
Why dost thou thus,
Through windows and through curtains call
on us?   *The Sun Rising*
199.11
But I do nothing upon myself, and yet I am
mine own Executioner.   *Devotions, 12*
199.12
No man is an Island, entire of itself; every
man is a piece of the Continent, a part of the
main.   *same, 17*
199.13
Any man's death diminishes me, because I
am involved in Mankind; And therefore
never send to know for whom the bell tolls;
it tolls for thee.   *same, 17*

200   Dowson, Ernest   Christopher
(1867-1900), English poet.
200.1
I have been faithful to thee, Cynara! in my
fashion.   *Non Sum Qualis Eram Bonae*
                              Sub Regno Cynarae
200.2
I have forgot much, Cynara! gone with the
wind,
Flung roses, roses riotously with the throng.
                                        same
200.3
They are not long, the days of wine and

roses.   *Vitae Summa Brevis Spem Nos*
                          Vetat Incohare Longam

201   Doyle, Sir Arthur Conan (1859-1930),
English writer.
201.1
It is an old maxim of mine that when you
have excluded the impossible, whatever
remains, however improbable, must be the
truth.   *The Beryl Coronet*
201.2
You know my method. It is founded upon
the observance of trifles.
                    The Boscombe Valley Mystery
201.3
It has long been an axiom of mine that the
little things are infinitely the most important.
                              A Case of Identity
201.4
Depend upon it, there is nothing so unnatural
as the commonplace.   *same*
201.5
'Excellent!' I [*Dr Watson*] cried. 'Elementary, ' said he. [*Holmes*].   *same*
201.6
[*Of Professor Moriarty*] He is the Napoleon
of crime.   *The Final Problem*
201.7
It is quite a three-pipe problem.
                         The Red-Headed League
201.8
An experience of women which extends over
many nations and three continents.
                              The Sign of Four
201.9
'Is there any point to which you would wish
to draw my attention?'
'To the curious incident of the dog in the
night-time.'
'The dog did nothing in the night-time.'
'That was the curious incident, ' remarked
Sherlock Holmes.   *Silver Blaze*

202   Drake, Sir Francis (1540?-1596),
English navigator and naval commander.
202.1
[*Of the raid on Cadiz harbour*] I have singed
the Spanish king's beard.   *Remark, 1587*
202.2
[*On the Armada being sighted during a game
of bowls*] There is plenty of time to win this
game, and to thrash the Spaniards too.
                          Remark, 20 July 1588

203   Drayton, Michael (1563-1631), English poet.
203.1

Fair stood the wind for France
When we our sails advance.   *Agincourt*
203.2
Since there's no help, come let us kiss and
    part—
Nay, I have done, you get no more of me;
And I am glad, yea glad with all my heart
That thus so cleanly I myself can free.
                            Sonnets, 61

204 Drummond, Thomas (1797-1840),
Scottish engineer and statesman.
204.1
Property has its duties as well as its rights.
            Letter to the Earl of Donoughmore,
                                22 May 1838

205 Dryden, John (1631-1700), English
poet and dramatist.
205.1
In pious times, e'r Priest-craft did begin,
Before Polygamy was made a Sin.
            Absalom and Achitophel, I:1
205.2
What e'r he did was done with so much ease,
In him alone, 'twas Natural to please.
                            same, I:27
205.3
Great Wits are sure to Madness near alli'd
And thin Partitions do their Bounds divide.
                            same, I:163
205.4
Bankrupt of Life, yet Prodigal of Ease.
                            same, I:168
205.5
For Politicians neither love nor hate.
                            same, I:223
205.6
But far more numerous was the Herd of
    such,
Who think too little, and who talk too much.
                            same, I:533
205.7
A man so various, that he seem'd to be
Not one, but all Mankind's Epitome.
Stiff in Opinions, always in the wrong;
Was Everything by starts, and Nothing long.
                            same, I:545
205.8
Did wisely from Expensive Sins refrain,
And never broke the Sabbath, but for Gain.
                            same, I:587
205.9
During his Office, Treason was no Crime.
The Sons of Belial had a Glorious Time.
                            same, I:597
205.10
Nor is the Peoples Judgment always true:

The Most may err as grosly as the Few.
                            same, I:781
205.11
Beware the Fury of a Patient Man.
                            same, I:1005
205.12
None but the Brave deserves the Fair.
                        Alexander's Feast
205.13
All humane things are subject to decay,
And, when Fate summons, Monarchs must
    obey.   .   *Mac Flecknoe*
205.14
Happy the Man, and happy he alone,
He who can call to-day his own:
He who, secure within, can say,
Tomorrow do thy worst, for I have liv'd
    today.   *Translation of Horace, III:65*
205.15
Errors, like Straws, upon the surface flow;
He who would search for Pearls must dive
    below.   *All for Love, Prologue*
205.16
[*Of Shakespeare*] He was the man who of all
modern, and perhaps ancient poets had the
largest and most comprehensive soul.
                    Essay of Dramatic Poesy
205.17
[*Of Shakespeare*] He was naturally learned;
he needed not the spectacles of books to read
nature; he looked inwards, and found her
there.   *same*

206 Dumas, Alexandre (1803-1870),
French novelist.
206.1
All for one, and one for all.
                        The Three Musketeers

207 Dunning, John, Baron Ashburton
(1731-1783), English lawyer and politician.
207.1
The influence of the Crown has increased, is
increasing, and ought to be diminished.
            Motion passed by the House of Commons,
                                        1780

E

208 Eden, Sir Anthony, 1st Earl of Avon

(1897-1977), British statesman and prime minister.

208.1

Everybody is always in favour of general economy and particular expenditure.

Observer 'Sayings of the Week',
17 June 1956

208.2

We are not at war with Egypt. We are in an armed conflict. *Speech, House of Commons, 4 Nov 1956*

209 Edison, Thomas Alva (1847-1931), American inventor.

209.1

Genius is one per cent inspiration and ninety-nine per cent perspiration.

Newspaper interview

210 Edward III, (1312-1377), King of England.

210.1

[*Of the Black Prince*] Let the boy win his spurs. *Remark at the battle of Crécy, 1345*

211 Edward VIII, (Duke of Windsor) (1894-1972), King of Great Britain.

211.1

I have found it impossible to carry the heavy burden of responsibility and to discharge my duties as King as I would wish to do without the help and support of the woman I love.

Radio broadcast, 11 Dec 1936

212 Einstein, Albert (1879-1955), Swiss scientist.

212.1

I never think of the future. It comes soon enough. *Interview, 1930*

213 Eliot, George (Mary Ann Evans) (1819-1880), English novelist.

213.1

It's but little good you'll do a-watering the last year's crop. *Adam Bede, Ch. 18*

213.2

Animals are such agreeable friends—they ask no questions, they pass no criticisms.

Scenes of Clerical Life, 'Mr Gilfil's Love Story', Ch. 7

214 Eliot, Thomas Stearns (1888-1965), British poet, dramatist and critic.

214.1

Because I do not hope to turn again
Because I do not hope
Because I do not hope to turn.

Ash-Wednesday

214.2

Time present and time past
Are both perhaps present in time future,
And time future contained in time past.

Burnt Norton

214.3

Human kind
Cannot bear very much reality. *same*

214.4

Here I am, an old man in a dry month,
Being read to by a boy, waiting for rain.

Gerontion

214.5

We are the hollow men
We are the stuffed men
Leaning together
Headpiece filled with straw.

The Hollow Men

214.6

This is the way the world ends
Not with a bang but a whimper. *same*

214.7

Let us go then, you and I,
When the evening is spread out against the sky
Like a patient etherized upon a table.

The Love Song of J. Alfred Prufrock

214.8

In the room the women come and go
Talking of Michelangelo. *same*

214.9

I have measured out my life with coffee spoons. *same*

214.10

I grow old...I grow old...
I shall wear the bottoms of my trousers rolled. *same*

214.11

Shall I part my hair behind? Do I dare to eat a peach?
I shall wear white flannel trousers, and walk upon the beach.
I have heard the mermaids singing, each to each. *same*

214.12

The winter evening settles down
With smell of steaks in passageways.

Preludes, 1

214.13

'Put your shoes at the door, sleep, prepare for life.'
The last twist of the knife. *Rhapsody on a Windy Night*

214.14

Birth, and copulation, and death.
That's all the facts when you come to brass tacks. *Sweeney Agonistes, Fragment of an Agon*

214.15
The host with someone indistinct
Converses at the door apart,
The nightingales are singing near
The Convent of the Sacred Heart.
Sweeney among the Nightingales

214.16
April is the cruellest month, breeding
Lilacs out of the dead land, mixing
Memory and desire, stirring
Dull roots with spring rain.
The Waste Land, 'The Burial of the Dead'

214.17
Hell is oneself;
Hell is alone, the other figures in it
Merely projections. There is nothing to
escape from
And nothing to escape to. One is always
alone.   *The Cocktail Party, I:3*

214.18
THOMAS. The last temptation is the greatest
treason:
To do the right deed for the wrong reason.
Murder in the Cathedral, Act 1

214.19
No poet, no artist of any sort, has his
complete meaning alone. His significance,
his appreciation is the appreciation of his
relation to the dead poets and artists.
Tradition and the Individual Talent

215 Elizabeth I, (1533-1603), Queen of
England.
215.1
I will make you shorter by a head.
Sayings of Queen Elizabeth (Chamberlin)

215.2
I know I have the body of a weak and feeble
woman, but I have the heart and stomach of
a King, and of a King of England too.
*Speech at Tilbury on the Approach of the
Spanish Armada*

215.3
Though God hath raised me high, yet this I
count the glory of my crown: that I have
reigned with your loves.
The Golden Speech, 1601

215.4
All my possessions for a moment of time.
Last words

216 Ellis, Henry Havelock (1859-1939),
English psychologist.
216.1
What we call progress is the exchange of one
nuisance for another nuisance.
Remark

217 Éluard, Paul (Eugène Grindal)
(1895-1952), French poet.
217.1
Adieu tristesse
Bonjour tristesse
Tu es inscrite dans les lignes du plafond.
Farewell sadness
Good day sadness
You are written in the lines of the ceiling.
La Vie immédiate

218 Emerson, Ralph Waldo (1803-1882),
American poet and essayist.
218.1
Art is a jealous mistress.   *Conduct of Life,*
Wealth
218.2
Nothing great was ever achieved without
enthusiasm.   *Essays, Circles*
218.3
A Friend may well be reckoned the master-
piece of Nature.   *same, Friendship*
218.4
There is properly no history; only biography.
same, History
218.5
All mankind love a lover.   *same, Love*
218.6
The reward of a thing well done is to have
done it.   *same, New England Reformers*
218.7
Every man is wanted, and no man is wanted
much.   *same, Nominalist and Realist*
218.8
In skating over thin ice, our safety is in our
speed.   *same, Prudence*
218.9
Whoso would be a man must be a nonconformist.   *same, Self-Reliance*
218.10
To be great is to be misunderstood.   *same*
218.11
Every hero becomes a bore at last.
Representative Men, 'Uses of Great Men'
218.12
Hitch your wagon to a star.   *Society and*
Solitude, 'Civilization'
218.13
We boil at different degrees.
same, 'Eloquence'
218.14
America is a country of young men.
same, 'Old Age'
218.15
If a man write a better book, preach a better
sermon, or make a better mouse-trap than
his neighbour, though he build his house in

the woods, the world will make a beaten path to his door. *Attributed*

219 Estienne, Henri (1528-1598), French scholar and editor.
219.1
Si jeunesse savait; si vieillesse pouvait.
If only youth knew, if only age could.
Les Prémices

220 Euclid, (c. 300 B.C.), Greek mathematician.
220.1
Quod erat demonstrandum.
220.2
Which was to be proved. *Elements, I:5*

221 Euripides, (c. 485-406 B.C.), Greek dramatist.
221.1
Those whom God wishes to destroy, he first makes mad. *Fragment*

222 Everage, Dame Edna (Barry Humphries), 'Australian housewife and superstar'.
222.1
In the world of success and failure
Have you noticed the Genius Spark
Seems brightest in folk from Australia?
We all leave an indelible mark.
You just have to go to the Opera
Or an Art show, or glance at your shelves
To see in a trice that Australians
Have done *terribly* well for themselves.
Terribly Well
222.2
Did you know that Rolf Harris was Australian? *same*

F

223 Farquhar, George (1678-1707), Irish dramatist.
223.1
There's no scandal like rags, nor any crime so shameful as poverty.
The Beaux' Strategem, I:1
223.2
Lady Bountiful. *same*
223.3

Spare all I have, and take my life.
same, V:2

224 Ferdinand I, (1503-1568), Holy Roman Emperor.
224.1
Let justice be done, though the world perish.
Attributed

225 Fielding, Henry (1707-1754), English novelist.
225.1
These are called the pious frauds of friendship. *Amelia, III:4*
225.2
I am as sober as a Judge. *Don Quixote in England, III:14*
225.3
Oh! the roast beef of England,
And old England's roast beef.
The Grub Street Opera, III:3
225.4
Public schools are the nurseries of all vice and immorality. *Joseph Andrews, III:5*

226 Fields, William Claude (1879-1946), American actor and comedian.
226.1
It ain't a fit night out for man or beast.
The Fatal Glass of Beer, film
226.2
Anybody who hates children and dogs can't be all bad. *Attributed*
226.3
I am free of all prejudice. I hate everyone equally. *Attributed*

227 Firbank, Ronald (1886-1926), English novelist.
227.1
It is said, I believe, that to behold the Englishman at his *best* one should watch him play tip-and-run. *The Flower Beneath the Foot, Ch. 14*
227.2
To be sympathetic without discrimination is so very debilitating. *Vainglory, Ch.7*

228 Fitzgerald, Edward (1809-1883), English scholar, poet and translator.
228.1
Awake! for Morning in the Bowl of Night
Has flung the Stone that puts the Stars to Flight:
And Lo! the Hunter of the East has caught
The Sultan's Turret in a Noose of Light.
Rubáiyát of Omar Khayyám, 1

228.2
Come, fill the Cup, and in the Fire of Spring
The Winter Garment of Repentance fling:
The Bird of Time has but a little way
To fly — and Lo! the Bird is on the Wing.
same, 7

228.3
Here with a Loaf of Bread beneath the Bough,
A Flask of Wine, a Book of Verse—and Thou
Beside me singing in the Wilderness—
And Wilderness is Paradise enow.
same, 11

228.4
One thing is certain, that Life flies;
One thing is certain, and the Rest is Lies;
The Flower that once has blown for ever dies. *same, 26*

228.5
I came like Water, and like Wind I go.
same, 28

228.6
Ah, fill the Cup:—what boots it to repeat
How Time is slipping underneath our Feet:
Unborn TOMORROW, and dead YESTERDAY,

Why fret about them if TODAY be sweet!
same, 37

228.7
'Tis all a Chequer-board of Nights and Days
Where Destiny with Men for Pieces plays:
Hither and thither moves, and mates, and slays,
And one by one back in the Closet lays.
same, 49

228.8
The Moving Finger writes; and, having writ,
Moves on: nor all thy Piety nor Wit
Shall lure it back to cancel half a Line,
Nor all thy Tears wash out a Word of it.
same, 51

229 Fitzgerald, Francis Scott (1896-1940), American novelist.
229.1
Beware of the artist who's an intellectual also. The artist who doesn't fit. *This Side of Paradise, II:5*

229.2
'I know myself, ' he cried, 'but that is all.'
same

229.3
A big man has no time really to do anything but just sit and be big. *same, III:2*
229.4
FITZGERALD. The rich are different from us.

HEMINGWAY. Yes, they have more money.
Notebooks, E
229.5
All good writing is *swimming under water* and holding your breath. *Letter to Frances Scott Fitzgerald*
229.6
[*Of himself and his wife*] Sometimes I don't know whether Zelda and I are real or whether we are characters in one of my novels.
A Second Flowering (Malcolm Cowley)

230 Fitzsimmons, Robert Prometheus (1862-1917), British boxer.
230.1
The bigger they come the harder they fall.
Saying

231 Flecker, James Elroy (1884-1915), English poet.
231.1
For lust of knowing what should not be known,
We take the Golden Road to Samarkand.
Hassan, V:2

232 Fletcher, John see **Beaumont**, Francis

233 Florio, John (1553?-1625), English translator.
233.1
England is the paradise of women, the purgatory of men, and the hell of horses.
Second Fruits

234 Ford, Henry (1863-1947), American engineer and industrialist.
234.1
History is more or less bunk. It's tradition. We don't want tradition. We want to live in the present and the only history that is worth a tinker's damn is the history we make today. *Chicago Tribune, 25 May 1916*

235 Ford, John (c. 1586-c. 1640), English dramatist.
235.1
'Tis Pity She's a whore. *Title of play*

236 Forgy, Howell Maurice (b. 1908), American soldier.
236.1
Praise the Lord and pass the ammunition.
Said at Pearl Harbour, 7 Dec 1941

237 Forster, Edward Morgan (1879-1970), English novelist.

237.1
Only connect.   *Howard's End, Epigraph*
237.2
It is not that the Englishman can't feel—it is that he is afraid to feel. He has been taught at his public school that feeling is bad form. He must not express great joy or sorrow, or even open his mouth too wide when he talks—his pipe might fall out if he did.
Abinger Harvest, 'Notes on the English character'
237.3
Yes—oh dear, yes—the novel tells a story.
Aspects of the Novel, Ch. 2

238 Fosdick, Harry Emerson (1878-1969), American Baptist minister.
238.1
An atheist is a man who has no invisible means of support.   *Attributed*

239 Franklin, Benjamin (1706-1790), American statesman and scientist.
239.1
Remember that time is money.   *Advice to a Young Tradesman*
239.2
No nation was ever ruined by trade.
Essays, Thoughts on Commercial Subjects
239.3
We must indeed all hang together, or most assuredly, we shall all hang separately.
Remark on signing the Declaration of Independence, 4 July 1776
239.4
There never was a good war or a bad peace.
Letter to Josiah Quincy, 11 Sept 1783
239.5
In this world nothing is certain but death and taxes.   *Letter to Jean-Baptiste Leroy, 13 Nov 1789*

240 Frayn, Michael (b. 1933), British novelist and dramatist.
240.1
To be absolutely honest, what I feel really bad about is that I don't feel worse. There's the ineffectual liberal's problem in a nutshell.
Observer, 8 Aug 1965

241 Frederick the Great, (1712-1786), King of Prussia.
241.1
My people and I have come to an agreement which satisfies us both. They are to say what they please, and I am to do what I please.
Attributed

242 Freud, Sigmund (1856-1939), Austrian neurologist and psychoanalyst.
242.1
The psychic development of the individual is a short repetition of the course of development of the race.   *Leonardo da Vinci*
242.2
Religion is an illusion and it derives its strength from the fact that it falls in with our instinctual desires.
New Introductory Lectures on Psychoanalysis, 'A Philosophy of Life'
242.3
Conscience is the internal perception of the rejection of a particular wish operating within us.   *Totem and Taboo*
242.4
At bottom God is nothing more than an exalted father.   *same*
242.5
The great question...which I have not been able to answer, despite my thirty years of research into the feminine soul, is 'What does a woman want'?   *Psychiatry in American Life (Charles Rolo)*

243 Frost, Robert (1875-1963), American poet.
243.1
Most of the change we think we see in life
Is due to truths being in and out of favour.
The Black Cottage
243.2
Home is the place where, when you have to go there,
They have to take you in.   *The Death of the Hired Man*

244 Fry, Christopher (b. 1907), English dramatist.
244.1
THOMAS. Where in this small-talking world can I find
A longitude with no platitude?
The Lady's Not for Burning, Act 3
244.2
PRIVATE PETER ABLE. Try thinking of love, or something.
Amor vincit insomnia.   *A Sleep of Prisoners*

245 Fuller, Thomas (1608-1661), English writer and antiquarian.
245.1
There is a great difference between painting a face and not washing it.   *Church History, 7*

245.2
It is a silly game where nobody wins.
Gnomologia, 2880
245.3
A proverb is much matter decorated into few
words.   *The History of the Worthies of*
England, Ch. 2
245.4
Learning hath gained most by those books
by which the printers have lost.
The Holy and Profane State, 'Of Books'

G

246 Gabor, Zsa Zsa (b. 1923), American
actress.
246.1
I never hated a man enough to give him
diamonds back.   *Observer 'Sayings of the*
Week', 28 Aug 1957

247 Galbraith, John Kenneth (b. 1908),
Canadian economist.
247.1
Wealth is not without its advantages, and the
case to the contrary, although it has often
been made, has never proved widely
persuasive.   *The Affluent Society, Ch. 1*
247.2
Wealth has never been a sufficient source of
honour in itself. It must be advertised, and
the normal medium is obtrusively expensive
goods.   *same, Ch. 7*
247.3
Few things are as immutable as the addiction
of political groups to the ideas by which they
have once won office.   *same, Ch. 13*

248 Galilei, Galileo (1564-1642), Italian
astronomer.
248.1
[*Of the earth*] But it does move.
Remark made after his recantation of belief
in the Copernican system

249 Garbo, Greta (b. 1905), Swedish film
actress.
249.1
I want to be alone.   *Grand Hotel, film, 1932*

250 Gavarni, Paul (1801-1866), French
illustrator and caricaturist.

250.1
Les enfants terribles.
The embarrassing young.   *Title of series of*
prints

251 Gay, John (1685-1732), English poet
and dramatist.
251.1
PEACHUM. Do you think your mother and I
should have liv'd comfortably so long
together, if ever we had been married?
The Beggar's Opera, I:8
251.2
ASTARBE. She who has never loved has
never lived.   *Captives, I:2*
251.3
Life is a jest; and all things show it.
I thought so once; but now I know it.
My Own Epitaph

252 George, Dan (b. 1910?), Canadian
Indian chief and film actor.
252.1
When the white man came we had the land
and they had the Bibles; now they have the
land and we have the Bibles.   *Remark*

253 George, Daniel (b. 1890), English
writer and editor.
253.1
O Freedom, what liberties are taken in thy
name!   *The Perpetual Pessimist*

254 George II, (1683-1760), King of Great
Britain.
254.1
[*Of General Wolfe*] Oh! he is mad, is he?
Then I wish he would *bite* some other of my
generals.   *Remark*

255 Gibbon, Edward (1737-1794), English
historian.
255.1
[*Of his time at Oxford*] I spent fourteen
months at Magdalen College; they proved
the fourteen months the most idle and
unprofitable of my whole life.
Autobiography
255.2
[*Of London*] Crowds without company, and
dissipation without pleasure.   *same*
255.3
Corruption, the most infallible symptom of
constitutional liberty.   *Decline and Fall of*
the Roman Empire, Ch. 21
255.4
All that is human must retrograde if it does
not advance.   *same, Ch. 71*

256 Gibbons, Stella (b. 1902), English novelist.

256.1

Something nasty in the woodshed.

Cold Comfort Farm

257 Gilbert, Sir William Schwenk (1836-1911), English parodist and librettist.

257.1

DUKE OF PLAZA-TORO. He led his regiment from behind
He found it less exciting.

The Gondoliers, Act 1

257.2

CHORUS OF PEERS. Bow, bow, ye lower middle classes!
Bow, bow, ye tradesmen, bow, ye masses!

Iolanthe, Act 1

257.3

LORD CHANCELLOR. The Law is the true embodiment
Of everything that's excellent.
It has no kind of fault or flaw,
And I, my lords, embody the Law. *same*

257.4

PRIVATE WILLIS. I often think it's comical
How Nature always does contrive
That every boy and every gal
That's born into the world alive
Is either a little Liberal
Or else a little Conservative! *same, Act 2*

257.5

LORD MOUNTARARAT. The House of Peers, throughout the war,
Did nothing in particular,
And did it very well. *same*

257.6

LORD CHANCELLOR. For you dream you are crossing the Channel, and tossing about in a steamer from Harwich—
Which is something between a large bathing machine and a very small second-class carriage. *same*

257.7

Pooh-Bah (Lord High Everything Else)

The Mikado, Dramatis Personae

257.8

NANKI-POO. A wandering minstrel I—
A thing of shreds and patches,
Of ballads, songs and snatches,
And dreamy lullaby! *same, Act 1*

257.9

KO-KO. As some day it may happen that a victim must be found,
I've got a little list—I've got a little list
Of society offenders who might well be underground,

And who never would be missed—who never would be missed! *same*

257.10

YUM-YUM, PEEP-BO and PITTI-SING.
Three little maids from school are we,
Pert as a school-girl well can be,
Filled to the brim with girlish glee. *same*

257.11

MIKADO. My object all sublime
I shall achieve in time—
To let the punishment fit the crime—
The punishment fit the crime. *same, Act 2*

257.12

KO-KO. The flowers that bloom in the spring,
Tra la,
Have nothing to do with the case.
I've got to take under my wing,
Tra la,
A most unattractive old thing,
Tra la,
With a caricature of a face. *same*

257.13

KO-KO. On a tree by a river a little tom-tit
Sang 'Willow, titwillow, titwillow!' *same*

257.14

BUNTHORNE. If this young man expresses himself in terms too deep for *me*,
Why, what a very singularly deep young man this deep young man must be!

Patience, Act 1

257.15

CAPTAIN. I'm never, never sick at sea!
ALL. What, never?
CAPTAIN. No, never!
ALL. What, *never*?
CAPTAIN. Hardly ever!

HMS Pinafore, Act 1

257.16

SIR JOSEPH PORTER. When I was a lad I served a term
As office boy to an Attorney's firm.
I cleaned the windows and I swept the floor,
And I polished up the handle of the big front door.
I polished up that handle so carefullee
That now I am the Ruler of the Queen's Navee! *same*

257.17

MAJOR-GENERAL STANLEY. I am the very model of a modern Major-General,
I've information vegetable, animal and mineral,
I know the kings of England, and I quote the fights historical,
From Marathon to Waterloo, in order categorical. *The Pirates of Penzance, Act 1*

257.18

SERGEANT. When the foeman bares his steel,

Tarantara! tarantara!

We uncomfortable feel. *(same,) Act 2*

257.19

SERGEANT. When constabulary duty's to be done—

A policeman's lot is not a happy one.

same

257.20

JUDGE. She may very well pass for forty-three

In the dusk, with a light behind her!

Trial by Jury

257.21

Sir, I view the proposal to hold an international exhibition at San Francisco with an equanimity bordering on indifference.

Gilbert, His Life and Strife (Hesketh Pearson)

257.22

[*Of Irving's Hamlet*] Funny without being vulgar. *Attributed*

258 Gladstone, William Ewart (1809-1898), British prime minister.

258.1

You cannot fight against the future. Time is on our side. *Speech on Reform Bill, 1866*

258.2

All the world over, I will back the masses against the classes. *Speech, Liverpool, 28 June 1886*

258.3

We are part of the community of Europe, and we must do our duty as such.

Speech, Caenarvon, 10 Apr 1888

259 Glasse, Hannah (18th century), English habitmaker and writer.

259.1

First catch your hare. *Art of Cookery (Popular quotation derived from the recipe instruction: 'Take your hare when it is cased.')*

260 Goering, Hermann (1893-1946), German political and military leader.

260.1

Guns will make us powerful; butter will only make us fat. *Radio broadcast, 1936*

260.2

I herewith commission you [*Heydrich*] to carry out all preparations with regard to...a *total solution* of the Jewish question, in those territories of Europe which are under

German influence. *The Rise and Fall of the Third Reich (William Shirer)*

260.3

When I hear anyone talk of Culture, I reach for my revolver. *Attributed*

261 Goethe, Johann Wolfgang von (1749-1832), German poet, scientist and writer.

261.1

Dear friend, theory is all grey,

And the golden tree of life is green.

Faust, Part 1, Apprentice Scene

261.2

Two souls dwell, alas! in my breast.

same, Before the Gate

261.3

I am the spirit that always denies.

same, Study

261.4

A useless life is an early death.

Iphegenie, I:2

261.5

A talent is formed in stillness, a character in the world's torrent. *Torquato Tasso, I:2*

261.6

Mehr Licht!

More light! *Last words, attributed*

262 Goldsmith, Oliver (1728?-1774), Irish dramatist, novelist and poet.

262.1

The dog, to gain some private ends,

Went mad and bit the man. *Elegy on the Death of a Mad Dog*

262.2

The man recovered of the bite,

The dog it was that died. *same*

262.3

[*Of Garrick*] On the stage he was natural, simple, affecting;

'Twas only that when he was off he was acting. *same*

262.4

HARDCASTLE. I love everything that's old: old friends, old times, old manners, old books, old wine. *She Stoops to Conquer, Act 1*

262.5

HARDCASTLE. This is Liberty Hall, gentlemen. *same, Act 2*

262.6

Where wealth and freedom reign, contentment fails,

And honour sinks where commerce long prevails. *The Traveller, 91*

262.7

Laws grind the poor, and rich men rule the
law.   *same, 386*

262.8
I...chose my wife, as she did her wedding
gown, not for a fine glossy surface, but such
qualities as would wear well.   *The Vicar of
                                            Wakefield, Preface*

262.9
Let us draw upon content for the deficien-
cies of fortune.   *same, Ch. 3*

262.10
When lovely woman stoops to folly,
And finds too late that men betray,
What charm can soothe her melancholy,
What art can wash her guilt away?
                                                      same, Ch. 9

263 Goldwyn, Samuel (1882-1974), American film producer.

263.1
In two words: im - possible.   *Attributed*

263.2
Include me out.   *Attributed*

263.3
Anybody who goes to see a psychiatrist
ought to have his head examined.
                                                      Attributed

263.4
Every director bites the hand that lays the
golden egg.   *Attributed*

263.5
I'll give you a definite maybe.   *Attributed*

263.6
A verbal contract isn't worth the paper it's
written on.   *Attributed*

263.7
You ought to take the bull between the
teeth.   *Attributed*

263.8
We have all passed a lot of water since then.
                                                      Attributed

263.9
I read part of it all the way through.
                                                      Attributed

263.10
Let's have some new clichés.
                        *Observer 'Sayings of the Week',
                                            24 Oct 1948*

264 Grahame, Kenneth (1859-1932),
Scottish writer.

264.1
RAT. There is nothing—absolutely nothing—half so much worth doing as simply
messing about in boats.   *The Wind in the
                                            Willows, Ch. 1*

265 Grant, Ulysses Simpson (1822-1885),

American soldier and President of the
United States.

265.1
I know no method to secure the repeal of
bad or obnoxious laws so effective as their
stringent execution.   *Inaugural Address,
                                            4 Mar 1869*

266 Granville-Barker, Harley
(1877-1946), English actor, dramatist and
producer.

266.1
Rightly thought of there is poetry in
peaches...even when they are canned.
                                    The Madras House, Act 1

266.2
But oh, the farmyard world of sex!
                                                      same, Act 4

266.3
What is the prose for God?   *Waste, Act 1*

267 Graves, Robert (b. 1895), English poet
and novelist.

267.1
Goodbye to All That.   *Title of Book*

267.2
In love as in sport, the amateur status must
be strictly maintained.   *Occupation: Writer*

267.3
As for the Freudian, it is a very low, Central
European sort of humour.   *same*

267.4
To be a poet is a condition rather than a
profession.   *Horizon questionnaire, 1946*

267.5
The remarkable thing about Shakespeare is
that he is really very good—in spite of all the
people who say he is very good.
            Observer 'Sayings of the Week', 6 Dec 1964

268 Gray, Thomas (1716-1771), English
poet.

268.1
What female heart can gold despise?
What Cat's averse to fish?   *Ode on the
                                    Death of a Favourite Cat*

268.2
Not all that tempts your wand'ring eyes
And heedless hearts, is lawful prize;
Nor all, that glisters, gold.   *same*

268.3
Alas, regardless of their doom,
The little victims play!   *Ode on a Distant
                                    Prospect of Eton College*

268.4
Where ignorance is bliss
'Tis folly to be wise.   *same*

268.5
The Curfew tolls the knell of parting day,
The lowing herd winds slowly o'er the lea,
The plowman homeward plods his weary
way,
And leaves the world to darkness and to me.
Elegy written in a Country Church-Yard
268.6
Let not Ambition mock their useful toil,
Their homely joys, and destiny obscure;
Nor Grandeur hear with a disdainful smile,
The short and simple annals of the poor.
same

268.7
The paths of glory lead but to the grave.
same

268.8
Full many a gem of purest ray serene,
The dark unfathom'd caves of ocean bear:
Full many a flower is born to blush unseen,
And waste its sweetness on the desert air.
same

268.9
Some village-Hampden, that with dauntless
breast
The little Tyrant of his fields withstood;
Some mute inglorious Milton here may rest,
Some Cromwell guiltless of his country's
blood. *same*
268.10
Far from the madding crowd's ignoble strife.
same

269 Greely, Horace (1811-1872), American editor and politician.   ,
269.1
Go West, young man, and grow up with the
country. *Hints toward Reform*

270 Gregory I, (540-604), Roman Pope
and Saint.
270.1
[*On seeing a group of English captives being
sold at Rome*] Not Angles, but angels.
Attributed

271 Greville, Sir Fulke (1554-1628),
English poet.
271.1
Oh wearisome condition of humanity!
Born under one law, to another bound.
Mustapha, V:6

**272 Grey of Fallodon, Edward, 1st
Viscount** (1862-1933), British statesman.
272.1
[*On the eve of the Great War*] The lamps are
going out all over Europe; we shall not see

them lit again in our lifetime.
Remark, 3 Aug 1914

273 Grossmith, George (1847-1912),
English comedian and singer, and **Grossmith, Walter Weedon** (1854-1919), his
brother.
273.1
What's the good of a home, if you are never
in it? *The Diary of a Nobody, Ch. 1*

H

**274 Halifax, George Saville, 1st Marquis
of** (1633-1695), English statesman.
274.1
Men are not hanged for stealing horses, but
that horses may not be stolen.
*Political Thoughts and Reflections of
Punishment*

275 Hammerstein, Oscar (1895-1960),
American librettist and songwriter.
275.1
Ol' man river, dat ol' man river,
He must know sumpin', but don't say
nothin',
He just keeps rollin', he keeps on rollin'
along. *Ol' Man River*

276 Harcourt, Sir William (1827-1904),
British statesman.
276.1
We are all Socialists now. *Speech*

277 Hardy, Thomas (1840-1928), English
novelist and poet.
277.1
A local cult called Christianity.
The Dynasts, 1
277.2
My argument is that War makes rattling
good history; but Peace is poor reading.
same
277.3
A lover without indiscretion is no lover at
all. *The Hand of Ethelberta, Ch. 20*
277.4
Good, but not religious-good. *Under the
Greenwood Tree, Ch. 2*

278 Harington, Sir John (1561-1612), English courtier and translator.
278.1
Treason doth never prosper: what's the reason?
For if it prosper, none dare call it treason.
Epigrams, Of Treason

279 Haskell, Arnold (b. 1903), English writer on ballet.
279.1
[*Of Dame Nellie Melba*] Unlike so many who find success, she remained a 'dinkum hard-swearing Aussie' to the end.
Waltzing Matilda

280 Hay, Ian (John Hay Beith), (1876-1952), Scottish novelist and dramatist.
280.1
Funny peculiar, or funny ha-ha?
Housemaster, Act 3

281 Hazlitt, William (1778-1830), English essayist.
281.1
[*Of Coleridge*] He talked on for ever; and you wished him to talk on for ever.
Lectures on the English Poets, 8
281.2
The English (it must be owned) are rather a foul-mouthed nation. *On Criticism*
281.3
No young man believes he shall ever die.
On the Feeling of Immortality in Youth, 1
281.4
One of the pleasantest things in the world is going a journey; but I like to go by myself.
On Going a Journey
281.5
There is not a more mean, stupid, dastardly, pitiful, selfish, spiteful, envious, ungrateful animal than the public. It is the greatest of cowards, for it is afraid of itself.
On Living to Oneself
281.6
The art of pleasing consists in being pleased.
On Manner
281.7
We never do anything well till we cease to think about the manner of doing it.
On Prejudice
281.8
There is nothing good to be had in the country, or, if there is, they will not let you have it. *Observations on Wordsworth's 'Excursion'*

281.9
Well, I've had a happy life. *Last words*

282 Hegel, Georg Wilhelm Friedrich (1770-1831), German philosopher.
282.1
What experience and history teach is this—that people and governments never have learned anything from history, or acted on principles deduced from it.
Philosophy of History, Introduction

283 Heller, Joseph (b. 1923), American novelist.
283.1
There was only one catch and that was Catch-22, which specified that a concern for one's own safety in the face of dangers that were real and immediate was the process of a rational mind. *Catch-22, Ch. 5*
283.2
Some men are born mediocre, some men achieve mediocrity, and some men have mediocrity thrust upon them. With Major Major it had been all three. *same, Ch. 9*

284 Hemingway, Ernest (1898-1961), American novelist.
284.1
Bullfighting is the only art in which the artist is in danger of death and in which the degree of brilliance in the performance is left to the fighter's honour. *Death in the Afternoon, Ch. 9*

285 Henley, William Ernest (1849-1903), English poet and critic.
285.1
Under the bludgeonings of chance
My head is bloody, but unbowed.
Invictus
285.2
I am the master of my fate;
I am the captain of my soul. *same*

286 Henri IV, (1553-1610), King of France.
286.1
Paris is well worth a mass. *Attributed*
286.2
[*Of James I*] The wisest fool in Christendom.
Attributed

287 Henry II, (1133-1189), King of England.
287.1
[*Of Thomas à Becket*] Will no one free me of this turbulent priest? *Attributed*

288 Henry, Matthew (1662-1714), English Nonconformist minister.

288.1

They that die by famine die by inches.

Commentaries, Psalms, LIX:15

288.2

All this and heaven too. *Life of Philip Henry*

289 Henry, Patrick (1736-1799), American statesman.

289.1

I know not what course others may take; but as for me, give me liberty or give me death.

Speech in the Virginia Convention, 23 Mar 1775

290 Herbert, George (1593-1633), English poet.

290.1

I struck the board, and cried, 'No more;
I will abroad.'
What, shall I ever sigh and pine?
My lines and life are free; free as the road,
Loose as the wind, as large as store.

The Collar

290.2

But as I rav'd and grew more fierce and wild
At every word,
Methought I heard one calling, 'Child';
And I replied, 'My Lord.' *same*

290.3

Oh that I were an orange-tree,
That busy plant!
Then I should ever laden be,
And never want
Some fruit for Him that dressed me.

Employment

290.4

And now in age I bud again,
After so many deaths I live and write;
I once more smell the dew and rain,
And relish versing; O, my only Light,
It cannot be
That I am he
On whom Thy tempests fell all night.

The Flower

290.5

Death is still working like a mole,
And digs my grave at each remove.

Grace

290.6

Love bade me welcome; yet my soul drew back,
Guilty of dust and sin. *Love*

290.7

'You must sit down, ' says Love, 'and taste
My meat, '
So I did sit and eat. *same*

290.8

Sweet day, so cool, so calm, so bright,
The bridal of the earth and sky. *Virtue*

290.9

Only a sweet and virtuous soul,
Like season'd timber, never gives;
But though the whole world turn to coal,
Then chiefly lives. *same*

291 Herrick, Robert (1591-1674), English poet.

291.1

Cherry ripe, ripe, ripe, I cry.
Full and fair ones; come and buy.

Hesperides, Cherry Ripe

291.2

A sweet disorder in the dress
Kindles in clothes a wantonness.

same, Delight in Disorder

291.3

Fair daffodils, we weep to see
You haste away so soon:
As yet the early-rising sun
Has not attain'd his noon. *same, To Daffodils*

291.4

Whenas in silks my Julia goes
Then, then (methinks) how sweetly flows
That liquefaction of her clothes.

same, Upon Julia's Clothes

291.5

Gather ye rosebuds while ye may,
Old time is still a-flying:
And this same flower that smiles today
Tomorrow will be dying. *same, To the Virgins, to make much of Time*

292 Hewart, Gordon, Lord Hewart (1870-1943), British lawyer and statesman.

292.1

Justice should not only be done, but should manifestly and undoubtedly be seen to be done. *The Chief (R. Jackson)*

293 Heywood, Thomas (1574?-1641), English dramatist and poet.

293.1

A Woman Killed with Kindness. *Title of play*

294 Hickson, William Edward (1803-1870), educational writer.

294.1

If at first you don't succeed,
Try, try again. *Try and Try again*

295 Hill, Rowland (1744-1833), English preacher.
295.1
He did not see any good reasons why the devil should have all the good tunes.
Rev Rowland Hill (E. W. Broome)

296 Hippocrates, (460?-377? B.C.), Greek physician.
296.1
Art is long, but life is short. *Aphorisms, 1*

297 Hitler, Adolf (1889-1945), Chancellor and Führer of Germany.
297.1
All those who are not racially pure are mere chaff. *Mein Kampf, Ch. 2*
297.2
Only constant repetition will finally succeed in imprinting an idea on the memory of the crowd. *same, Ch. 6*
297.3
Germany will be either a world power or will not be at all. *same, Ch. 14*
297.4
In starting and waging a war it is not right that matters, but victory. *The Rise and Fall of the Third Reich (W. L. Shirer), Ch. 16*
297.5
The essential thing is the formation of the political will of the nation: that is the starting point for political action.
Speech, Düsseldorf, 27 Jan 1932
297.6
[*Of the invasion of Russia*] When Barbarossa commences, the world will hold its breath and make no comment. *Remark to General Franz Halder*

298 Hobbes, Thomas (1588-1679), English philosopher.
298.1
The condition of man...is a condition of war of everyone against everyone.
Leviathan, I:4
298.2
No arts; no letters; no society; and which is worst of all, continual fear and danger of violent death; and the life of man, solitary, poor, nasty, brutish, and short. *same, I:13*
298.3
The Papacy is not other than the Ghost of the deceased Roman Empire, sitting crowned upon the grave thereof. *same, IV:37*

298.4
I am about to take my last voyage, a great leap in the dark. *Last words*

299 Hoffman, Heinrich (1809-1874), German writer and illustrator.
299.1
But one day, one cold winter's day,
He screamed out, 'Take the soup away!'
Struwwelpeter, Augustus
299.2
Look at little Johnny there,
Little Johnny Head-in-Air. *same, Johnny Head-in-Air*
299.3
The door flew open, in he ran,
The great, long, red-legged scissor-man.
same, The Little Suck-a-Thumb
299.4
Anything to me is sweeter
Than to see Shock-headed Peter.
same, Shock-headed Peter

300 Holmes, Oliver Wendell (1809-1894), American writer and physician.
300.1
Man has his will, — but woman has her way.
The Autocrat of the Breakfast Table, Prologue
300.2
A thought is often original, though you have uttered it a hundred times. *same, Ch. 1*
300.3
The world's great men have not commonly been great scholars, nor great scholars great men. *same, Ch. 6*

301 Hoover, Herbert Clark (1874-1964), President of the United States.
301.1
The American system of rugged individualism. *Speech, New York, 22 Oct 1928*

302 Hopkins, Gerard Manley (1844-1899), English poet.
302.1
Not, I'll not, carrion comfort, Despair, not feast on thee;
Not untwist—slack they may be—these last strands of man
In me or, most weary, cry *I can no more.* I can;
Can something, hope, wish day come, not choose not to be. *Carrion Comfort*
302.2
That night, that year
Of now done darkness I wretch lay wrestling with (my God!) my God. *same*

302.3
The world is charged with the grandeur of
God. *God's Grandeur*
302.4
Glory be to God for dappled things—
For skies of couple-colour as a brinded cow;
For rose-moles all in stipple upon trout that
swim. *Pied Beauty*

303 Horace, (Quintus Horatius Flaccus)
(65-8 B.C.), Roman poet and satirist.
303.1
Carpe diem
Seize the day. *Ars Poetica, I:11:8*
303.2
Dulce et decorum est pro patria mori.
It is a sweet and seemly thing to die for one's
country. *same, III:2:13*

304 Housman, Alfred Edward
(1859-1936), English scholar and poet.
304.1
Loveliest of trees, the cherry now
Is hung with bloom along the bough,
And stands about the woodland ride
Wearing white for Eastertide.
A Shropshire Lad, 2
304.2
Here of a Sunday morning
My love and I would lie,
And see the coloured counties,
And hear the larks so high
About us in the sky. *same, 21*
304.3
Is my team ploughing,
That I was used to drive? *same, 27*
304.4
The goal stands up, the keeper
Stands up to keep the goal. *same*
304.5
With rue my heart is laden
For golden friends I had,
For many a rose-lipt maiden
And many a lightfoot lad. *same, 54*
304.6
Malt does more than Milton can
To justify God's ways to man. *same, 62*
304.7
We'll to the woods no more,
The laurels all are cut. *Last Poems,*
Introductory
304.8
The candles burn their sockets,
The blinds let through the day,
The young man feels his pockets
And wonders what's to pay. *same, 21*

305 Hoyle, Edmond (1672-1769), English
writer on card games.
305.1
When in doubt, win the trick.
Hoyle's Games, Whist, Twenty-four Short
Rules for Learners

306 Hubbard, Elbert (1856-1915), American writer and editor.
306.1
Life is just one damned thing after another.
A Thousand and One Epigrams
306.2
One machine can do the work of fifty
ordinary men. No machine can do the work
of one extraordinary man.
Roycroft Dictionary and Book of Epigrams
306.3
Little minds are interested in the extraordinary; great minds in the commonplace.
same

307 Hughes, Thomas (1822-1896), English
novelist.
307.1
Life isn't all beer and skittles.
Tom Brown's Schooldays, I:2
307.2
[*Of cricket*] It's more than a game. It's an
institution. *same, II:7*

308 Humphries, Barry (Dame Edna
Everage) (b. 1934), Australian actor and
writer.
308.1
[*Of 'Barry McKenzie'*] His favourite word to
describe the act of involuntary regurgitation
is the verb to chunder. This word is not in
popular currency in Australia, but the writer
recalls that ten years ago it was common in
Victoria's more expensive public schools. It
is now used by the Surfies, a repellent breed
of sun-bronzed hedonists who actually hold
chundering contests on the famed beaches of
the Commonwealth. I understand...that the
word derives from a nautical expression
'watch under', an ominous courtesy shouted
from the upper decks for the protection of
those below. *Times Literary Supplement,*
'Barry McKenzie', 16 Sept 1965

309 Hungerford, Margaret (1855?-1897),
Irish novelist.
309.1
Beauty is altogether in the eye of the
beholder. *Molly Bawn*

310 Huxley, Aldous Leonard (1894-1963), English novelist and essayist.

310.1
Since Mozart's day composers have learned the art of making music throatily and palpitatingly sexual. *Along the Road, 'Popular music'*

310.2
Christlike in my behaviour,
Like every good believer,
I imitate the Saviour,
And cultivate a beaver. *Antic Hay, Ch. 4*

310.3
He was only the Mild and Melancholy one foolishly disguised as a complete Man.
same, Ch. 9

310.4
There are few who would not rather be taken in adultery than in provincialism.
same, Ch. 10

310.5
The time of our Ford. *Brave New World, Ch. 3*

310.6
The proper study of mankind is books.
Chrome Yellow

310.7
We participate in a tragedy; at a comedy we only look. *The Devils of Loudon, Ch. 11*

310.8
Consistency is contrary to nature, contrary to life. The only completely consistent people are the dead. *Do What you Will, 'Wordsworth in the Tropics'*

310.9
Death…It's the only thing we haven't succeeded in completely vulgarizing.
Eyeless in Gaza, Ch. 31

310.10
Christianity accepted as given a metaphysical system derived from several already existing and mutually incompatible systems.
Grey Eminence, Ch. 3

310.11
The quality of moral behaviour varies in inverse ratio to the number of human beings involved. *same, Ch. 10*

310.12
'Bed, ' as the Italian proverb succinctly puts it, 'is the poor man's opera.' *Heaven and Hell*

310.13
I can sympathize with people's pains, but not with their pleasures. There is something curiously boring about somebody else's happiness. *Limbo, 'Cynthia'*

310.14
She was a machine-gun riddling her hostess with sympathy. *Mortal Coils, 'The Gioconda Smile'*

310.15
Most of one's life…is one prolonged effort to prevent oneself thinking. *same, 'Green Tunnels'*

310.16
She was one of those indispensables of whom one makes the discovery, when they are gone, that one can get on quite as well without them. *same, 'Nuns at Luncheon'*

310.17
Happiness is like coke - something you get as a by-product in the process of making something else. *Point Counter Point*

310.18
There is no substitute for talent. Industry and all the virtues are of no avail. *same*

310.19
Silence is as full of potential wisdom and wit as the unhewn marble of great sculpture.
same

310.20
A bad book is as much a labour to write as a good one; it comes as sincerely from the author's soul. *same*

310.21
That all men are equal is a proposition to which, at ordinary times, no sane individual has ever given his assent. *Proper Studies*

310.22
Those who believe that they are exclusively in the right are generally those who achieve something. *same*

310.23
Facts do not cease to exist because they are ignored. *same*

310.24
I'm afraid of losing my obscurity. Genuineness only thrives in the dark. Like celery.
Those Barren Leaves, I:1

310.25
'It's like the question of the authorship of the *Iliad*, ' said Mr Cardan. 'The author of that poem is either Homer or, if not Homer, somebody else of the same name.'
same, V:4

310.26
Knowledge is proportionate to being. …You know in virtue of what you are.
Time Must Have a Stop, Ch. 26

310.27
The aristocratic pleasure of displeasing is not the only delight that bad taste can yield. One can love a certain kind of vulgarity for its own sake. *Vulgarity in Literature, Ch. 4*

310.28
Defined in psychological terms, a fanatic is a

man who consciously over-compensates a secret doubt. *same*

311 Huxley, Julian Sorell (1887-1975), English biologist.
311.1
We all know how the size of sums of money appears to vary in a remarkable way according as they are being paid in or paid out. *Essays of a Biologist, 5*
311.2
Operationally, God is beginning to resemble not a ruler but the last fading smile of a cosmic Cheshire cat. *Religion without Revelation*

312 Huxley, Thomas Henry (1825-1895), English biologist.
312.1
It is the customary fate of new truths to begin as heresies and to end as superstitions.
The Coming of Age of the Origin of Species

I

313 Ibsen, Henrik (1828-1906), Norwegian dramatist and poet.
313.1
Fools are in a terrible, overwhelming majority, all the wide world over.
An Enemy of the People, Act 4
313.2
The minority is always right. *same*
313.3
A man should never put on his best trousers when he goes out to battle for freedom and truth. *same, Act 5*
313.4
What's a man's first duty? The answer's brief: To be himself. *Peer Gynt, IV:1*

314 Inge, William Ralph (1860-1954), English Churchman.
314.1
What we know of the past is mostly not worth knowing. What is worth knowing is mostly uncertain. Events in the past may roughly be divided into those which probably never happened and those which do not matter. *Assessments and Anticipations, 'Prognostications'*

314.2
The enemies of Freedom do not argue; they shout and they shoot. *The End of an Age, Ch. 4*
314.3
The effect of boredom on a large scale in history is underestimated. It is a main cause of revolutions, and would soon bring to an end all the static Utopias and the farmyard civilization of the Fabians. *same, Ch. 6*
314.4
Many people believe that they are attracted by God, or by Nature, when they are only repelled by man. *More Lay Thoughts of a Dean, II:1*
314.5
The proper time to influence the *character* of a *child* is about a *hundred* years before he is born. *Observer, 21 June 1929*
314.6
A nation is a society united by a delusion about its ancestry and by a common hatred of its neighbours.
The Perpetual Pessimist (Sagittarius and George)

315 Irving, Washington (1783-1859), American writer.
315.1
Whenever a man's friends begin to compliment him about looking young, he may be sure that they think he is growing old.
Bracebridge Hall, 'Bachelors'
315.2
A sharp tongue is the only edged tool that grows keener with constant use.
The Sketch Book, 'Rip Van Winkle'

316 Isherwood, Christopher William (b. 1904), English novelist.
316.1
I am a camera with its shutter open, quite passive, recording, not thinking.
A Berlin Diary
316.2
MR NORRIS. We live in stirring times—tea-stirring times. *Mr Norris Changes Trains (passim)*

J

317 James, Henry (1843-1916), American novelist.

317.1
It takes a great deal of history to produce a little literature. *Life of Nathaniel Hawthorne, Ch. 1*

317.2
[*Of Thoreau*] He was unperfect, unfinished, inartistic; he was worse than provincial—he was parochial. *same, Ch. 4*

317.3
Experience was to be taken as showing that one might get a five-pound note as one got a light for a cigarette; but one had to check the friendly impulse to ask for it in the same way. *The Awkward Age, IV:13*

317.4
Summer afternoon — summer afternoon; to me those have always been the two most beautiful words in the English language.
A Backward Glance (Edith Wharton), Ch. 10

318 James I, (1566-1625), King of England.

318.1
[*Of smoking*] A custom loathsome to the eye, hateful to the nose, harmful to the brain, dangerous to the lungs, and in the black, stinking fume thereof, nearest resembling the horrible Stygian smoke of the pit that is bottomless. *A Counterblast to Tobacco*

319 Jeans, Sir James Hopwood (1877-1946), English scientist and writer.

319.1
Life exists in the universe only because the carbon atom possesses certain exceptional properties. *The Mysterious Universe, Ch. 1*

320 Jefferson, Thomas (1743-1826), President of the United States.

320.1
We hold these truths to be self-evident: that all men are created equal; that they are endowed by their Creator with certain unalienable rights; that among these are life, liberty, and the pursuit of happiness.
Declaration of American Independence, 4 July 1776

321 Jerome, Jerome Klapka (1859-1927), English humorous writer.

321.1
Love is like the measles; we all have to go through with it. *Idle Thoughts of an Idle Fellow, 'On Being in Love'*

321.2
I like work; it fascinates me. I can sit and look at it for hours. I love to keep it by me; the idea of getting rid of it nearly breaks my heart. *Three Men in a Boat, Ch. 15*

322 Joad, Cyril Edwin Mitchinson (1891-1953), English philosopher.

322.1
It all depends what you mean by...
BBC Brains Trust, 1942-1948

323 Johnson, Samuel (1709-1784), English lexicographer, critic and poet.

323.1
When I took the first survey of my undertaking, I found our speech copious without order, and energetic without rules.
Dictionary of the English Language, Preface

323.2
Cricket.—A sport, at which the contenders drive a ball with sticks in opposition to each other. *same, Definitions*

323.3
Lexicographer.—A harmless drudge.
same

323.4
Network.—Any thing reticulated or decussated, at equal distances, with interstices between the intersections. *same*

323.5
Oats.—A grain, which in England is generally given to horses, but in Scotland supports the people. *same*

323.6
When two Englishmen meet their first talk is of the weather. *The Idler, 11*

323.7
For we that live to please, must please to live. *Prologue at the Opening of the Theatre in Drury Lane, 1747*

323.8
No place affords a more striking conviction of the vanity of human hopes, than a public library. *The Rambler, 23 Mar 1751*

323.9
Human life is every where a state in which much is to be endured, and little to be enjoyed. *Rasselas, Ch. 11*

323.10
The life of a solitary man will be certainly miserable, but not certainly devout.
same, Ch. 21

323.11
[*Of Lord Chesterfield*] This man I thought had been a Lord among wits; but, I find, he

is only a wit among Lords.
Boswell's Life of Johnson, 1754

323.12
If a man does not make new acquaintances as he advances through life, he will soon find himself left alone. A man, Sir, should keep his friendship in constant repair.
same, 1755

323.13
BOSWELL. I do indeed come from Scotland, but I cannot help it...
JOHNSON. That Sir, I find, is what a very great many of your countrymen cannot help.
same, 1763

323.14
The noblest prospect which a Scotchman ever sees, is the high road that leads him to England.
same

323.15
A man ought to read just as inclination leads him; for what he reads as a task will do him little good.
same

323.16
It is a sad reflection but a true one, that I knew almost as much at eighteen as I do now.
same

323.17
Your levellers wish to level down as far as themselves; but they cannot bear levelling up to themselves. They would all have some people under them; why not then have some people above them?
same

323.18
So far is it from being true that men are naturally equal, that no two people can be half an hour together, but one shall acquire an evident superiority over the other.
same, 1766

323.19
It matters not how a man dies, but how he lives.
same, 1769

323.20
I would not give half a guinea to live under one form of Government rather than another. It is of no moment to the happiness of an individual.
same, 1772

323.21
The mass of every people must be barbarous where there is no printing.
same

323.22
People seldom read a book which is given to them; and few are given. The way to spread a work is to sell it at a low price. No man will send to buy a thing that costs even sixpence, without an intention to read it.
same, 1773

323.23
There are few ways in which a man can be

more innocently employed than in getting money.
same

323.24
There may be other reasons for a man's not speaking in publick than want of resolution: he may have nothing to say.
same

323.25
Patriotism is the last refuge of a scoundrel.
same

323.26
Marriage is the best state for a man in general; and every man is a worse man, in proportion as he is unfit for the married state.
same, 1776

323.27
It is commonly a weak man, who marries for love.
same

323.28
Melancholy, indeed, should be diverted by every means but drinking.
same

323.29
No man but a blockhead ever wrote, except for money.
same

323.30
A man who has not been in Italy, is always conscious of an inferiority.
same

323.31
Depend upon it, Sir, when a man knows he is to be hanged in a fortnight, it concentrates his mind wonderfully.
same, 1777

323.32
You find no man, at all intellectual, who is willing to leave London. No, Sir, when a man is tired of London, he is tired of life; for there is in London all that life can afford.
same

323.33
BOSWELL. Is not the Giant's-Causeway worth seeing?
JOHNSON. Worth seeing? Yes; but not worth going to see.
same, 1779

323.34
Clear your mind of cant. You may talk as other people do: you may say to a man, 'Sir, I am your most humble servant.' You are *not* his most humble servant.
same, 1783

323.35
No man is a hypocrite in his pleasures.
same, 1784

323.36
I look upon every day to be lost, in which I do not make a new acquaintance.
same

323.37
[*Of a violinist's performance*] Difficult do you call it, Sir? I wish it were impossible.
Anecdotes by William Seward

323.38

The great source of pleasure is variety.
Lives of the English Poets, Butler
323.39
A man is in general better pleased when he has a good dinner upon his table, than when his wife talks Greek.
Johnsonian Miscellanies

324 Jolson, Al (1886-1950), American actor and singer.
324.1
You ain't heard nothin' yet, folks.
The Jazz Singer (the first talking film), 1927

325 Jonson, Ben (1573-1637), English poet and dramatist.
325.1
Drink to me only with thine eyes
And I will pledge with mine;
Or leave a kiss but in the cup
And I'll not look for wine.   *To Celia*
325.2
Thou hadst small Latin, and less Greek.
To the Memory of William Shakespeare
325.3
He was not of an age, but for all time!
same
325.4
Sweet Swan of Avon!   *same*
325.5
VOLPONE. Good morning to the day: and, next, my gold!—
Open the shrine, that I may see my saint.
Volpone, I:1
325.6
VOLPONE. Come, my Celia, let us prove,
While we can, the sports of love,
Time will not be ours for ever,
He, at length, our good will sever.
same, III:6
325.7
O rare Ben Jonson.   *Epitaph in Westminister Abbey*

326 Joyce, James (1882-1941), Irish novelist.
326.1
Ireland is the old sow that eats her farrow.
Portrait of the Artist as a Young Man
326.2
The snotgreen sea. The scrotumtightening sea.   *Ulysses*
326.3
When I makes tea I makes tea, as old mother Grogan said. And when I makes water I makes water.   *same*

326.4
History, Stephen said, is a nightmare from which I am trying to awake.   *same*

327 Jung, Carl Gustav (1875-1961), Swiss psychologist and psychiatrist.
327.1
Among all my patients in the second half of life...there has not been one whose problem in the last resort was not that of finding a religious outlook on life.   *Modern Man in Search of a Soul*
327.2
A man who has not passed through the inferno of his passions has never overcome them.   *Memories, Dreams, Reflections*
327.3
We need more understanding of human nature, because the only real danger that exists is man himself.... We know nothing of man, far too little. His psyche should be studied because we are the origin of all coming evil.   *Television Interview*

328 Junius, pseudonym of an anonymous writer (1768-1772) to the **London Public Advertiser.**
328.1
The Liberty of the press is the *Palladium* of all the civil, political and religious rights of an Englishman.   *Letters, Dedication*
328.2
There is a holy, mistaken zeal in politics, as well as religion. By persuading others we convince ourselves.   *Letter 35, 19 Dec 1769*

329 Juvenal, (**Decimus Junius Juvenalis**) (60-130? A.D.), Roman lawyer and satirist.
329.1
Quis custodiet ipsos custodes?
Who is to guard the guards themselves?
Satires, VI:347
329.2
The people long eagerly for just two things—bread and circuses.   *same, X:80*
329.3
Orandum est ut sit mens sana in corpore sano.
Your prayer must be for a sound mind in a sound body.   *same, X:356*

K

330 Kafka, Franz (1883-1924), Austrian novelist.
330.1
It's often safer to be in chains than to be free. *The Trial, Ch. 8*
330.2
Let me remind you of the old maxim: people under suspicion are better moving than at rest, since at rest they may be sitting in the balance without knowing it, being weighed together with their sins. *same*

331 Karr, Alphonse (1808-1890), French writer.
331.1
Plus ça change, plus c'est la même chose.
The more it changes, the more it is the same.
Les Guêpes, Jan 1849

332 Keats, John (1795-1821), English poet.
332.1
Season of mists and mellow fruitfulness,
Close bosom-friend of the maturing sun;
Conspiring with him how to load and bless
With fruit the vines that round the thatch-
eaves run. *To Autumn*
332.2
Where are the songs of Spring? Ay, where are they? *same*
332.3
Bright star, would I were steadfast as thou art. *Bright Star*
332.4
A thing of beauty is a joy for ever;
Its loveliness increases; it will never
Pass into nothingness. *Endymion, I:1*
332.5
St. Agnes' Eve—Ah, bitter chill it was!
The owl, for all his feathers, was a-cold;
The hare limp'd trembling through the frozen grass,
And silent was the flock in woolly fold.
The Eve of Saint Agnes, 1
332.6
And they are gone: aye, ages long ago
These lovers fled away into the storm.
same, 43
332.7
The Beadsman, after thousand aves told,
For aye unsought-for slept among his ashes cold. *same, 43*
332.8

Fanatics have their dreams, wherewith they weave
A paradise for a sect. *The Fall of Hyperion, I:1*
332.9
The poet and the dreamer are distinct,
Diverse, sheer opposite, antipodes.
The one pours out a balm upon the world,
The other vexes it. *same, I:199*
332.10
No stir of air was there,
Not so much life as on a summer's day
Robs not one light seed from the feather'd grass,
But where the dead leaf fell, there did it rest.
Hyperion, I:7
332.11
Oh what can ail thee, Knight at arms
Alone and palely loitering;
The sedge is wither'd from the lake,
And no birds sing. *La Belle Dame Sans Merci*
332.12
La belle Dame sans Merci
Hath thee in thrall! *same*
332.13
Love in a hut; with water and a crust,
Is—Love, forgive us!—cinders, ashes, dust;
Love in a palace is perhaps at last
More grievous torment than a hermit's fast.
Lamia, II:1
332.14
Do not all charms fly
At the mere touch of cold philosophy?
same, II:229
332.15
Thou still unravish'd bride of quietness,
Thou foster-child of silence and slow time.
Ode on a Grecian Urn
332.16
Heard melodies are sweet, but those unheard
Are sweeter; therefore, ye soft pipes, play on. *same*
332.17
Thou, silent form, dost tease us out of thought
As doth eternity: Cold Pastoral! *same*
332.18
'Beauty is truth, truth beauty,'—that is all
Ye know on earth, and all ye need to know.
same
332.19
No, no, go not to Lethe, neither twist
Wolf's-bane, tight-rooted, for its poisonous wine. *Ode on Melancholy*
332.20
Nor let the beetle, nor the death-moth be
Your mournful Psyche. *same*

332.21

Ay, in the very temple of delight
Veil'd Melancholy has her sovran shrine.
Though seen of none save him whose
    strenuous tongue
Can burst Joy's grape against his palate fine.
                same

332.22

My heart aches, and a drowsy numbness
    pains
My sense.   *Ode to a Nightingale*

332.23

O, for a draught of vintage! that hath been
Cool'd a long age in the deep-delved earth.
                same

332.24

O for a beaker full of the warm South,
Full of the true, the blushful Hippocrene,
With beaded bubbles winking at the brim,
And purple-stained mouth.   *same*

332.25

Fade far away, dissolve, and quite forget
What thou among the leaves hast never
    known,
The weariness, the fever, and the fret,
Here, where men sit and hear each other
    groan.   *same*

332.26

Now more than ever seems it rich to die,
To cease upon the midnight with no pain.
                same

332.27

Thou wast not born for death, immortal
    Bird!
No hungry generations tread thee down;
The voice I hear this passing night was heard
In ancient days by emperor and clown:
Perhaps the self-same song that found a path
Through the sad heart of Ruth, when sick
    for home,
She stood in tears amid the alien corn;
The same that oft-times hath
Charm'd magic casements, opening on the
    foam
Of perilous seas, in faery lands forlorn.
                same

332.28

Much have I travell'd in the realms of gold,
And many goodly states and kingdoms seen.
    On first looking into Chapman's Homer

332.29

Then felt I like some watcher of the skies
When a new planet swims into his ken;
Or like stout Cortez when with eagle eyes
He star'd at the Pacific—and all his men
Look'd at each other with a wild surmise—
Silent, upon a peak in Darien.   *same*

332.30

O soft embalmer of the still midnight.
                To Sleep

332.31

Turn the key deftly in the oiled wards,
And seal the hushed casket of my soul.
                same

332.32

A drainless shower
Of light is poesy; 'tis the supreme of power;
'Tis might half slumb'ring on its own right
    arm.   *Sleep and Poetry*

332.33

I am certain of nothing but the holiness of
the heart's affections and the truth of
imagination—what the imagination seizes as
beauty must be truth—whether it existed
before or not.   *Letter to Benjamin Bailey,*
                22 Nov 1817

332.34

O for a life of sensations rather than of
thoughts!   *same*

332.35

The excellence of every art is its intensity,
capable of making all disagreeables eva-
porate, from their being in close relationship
with beauty and truth.   *Letter to G. and T.*
              Keats, 21 Dec 1817

332.36

Negative Capability, that is, when a man is
capable of being in uncertainties, mysteries,
doubts, without any irritable reaching after
fact and reason.   *same*

332.37

If poetry comes not as naturally as leaves to
a tree it had better not come at all.
    Letter to John Taylor, 27 Feb 1818

332.38

Axioms in philosophy are not axioms until
they are proved upon our pulses; we read
fine things but never feel them to the full
until we have gone the same steps as the
author.   *Letter to J. H. Reynolds, 3 May 1818*

332.39

Love is my religion—I could die for that.
    Letter to Fanny Brawne, 13 Oct 1819

332.40

Here lies one whose name was writ in water.
                Epitaph

333   Kempis, Thomas À (1380–1471),
    German religious writer.

333.1

Man proposes but God disposes.
    The Imitation of Christ, I:19

333.2

Sic transit gloria mundi.

Thus the glory of the world passes away.
same, III:6

334 Keneally, Thomas (b. 1935), Australian novelist.
334.1
Pass a law to give every single wingeing bloody Pommie his fare home to England. Back to the smoke and the sun shining ten days a year and shit in the streets. Yer can have it.   *The Chant of Jimmy Blacksmith*

335 Kennedy, John Fitzgerald (1917-1963), President of the United States.
335.1
My fellow Americans: ask not what your country can do for you, ask what you can do for your country.   *Inaugural address, 20 Jan 1961*
335.2
We must use time as a tool, not as a couch.
Observer 'Sayings of the Week', 10 Dec 1961
335.3
The United States has to move very fast to even stand still.   *same, 21 July 1963*
335.4
When power narrows the areas of man's concern, poetry reminds him of the richness and diversity of his existence.   *Address at Dedication of the Robert Frost Library, 1963*
335.5
In free society art is not a weapon.... Artists are not engineers of the soul.   *same*

336 Kerouac, Jack (1922-1969), American novelist.
336.1
The beat generation.   *Expression*
336.2
You can't teach the old maestro a new tune.
On the Road, I:1
336.3
We're really all of us bottomly broke. I haven't had time to work in weeks.
same, I:7
336.4
I had nothing to offer anybody except my own confusion.   *same, II:3*

337 Keynes, John Maynard, 1st Baron (1883-1946), English economist.
337.1
It is better that a man should tyrannize over his bank balance than over his fellow citizens.
General Theory of Employment, VI:24

338 Khayyam, Omar, see **Fitzgerald, Edward**

339 King, Benjamin Franklin (1857-1894), American humorist.
339.1
Nothing to do but work,
Nothing to eat but food,
Nothing to wear but clothes,
To keep one from going nude.   *The Pessimist*

340 Kingsley, Charles (1819-1875), English writer.
340.1
More ways of killing a cat than choking her with cream.   *Westward Ho!, Ch. 20*

341 Kipling, Rudyard (1865-1936), English writer and poet.
341.1
Oh, East is East, and West is West, and never the twain shall meet.
The Ballad of East and West
341.2
And a woman is only a woman, but a good cigar is a smoke.   *The Betrothed*
341.3
But the Devil whoops, as he whooped of old:
'It's clever, but is it art?'
The Conundrum of the Workshops
341.4
For the female of the species is more deadly than the male.   *The Female of the Species*
341.5
You're a better man than I am, Gunga Din.
Gunga Din
341.6
If you can keep your head when all about you
Are losing theirs and blaming it on you.
If
341.7
If you can fill the unforgiving minute
With sixty seconds' worth of distance run,
Yours is the Earth and everything that's in it,
And—which is more—you'll be a Man, my son!   *same*
341.8
On the road to Mandalay
Where the flyin'-fishes play.   *Mandalay*
341.9
Take up the White Man's Burden.
The White Man's Burden
341.10
The silliest woman can manage a clever

man; but it needs a very clever woman to manage a fool.   *Plain Tales from the Hills, 'Three and—an Extra'*

341.11
The Light that Failed.   *Title of novel*

342 Knox, John (1505-1572), Scottish religious reformer.
342.1
The First Blast of the Trumpet Against the Monstrous Regiment of Women.   *Title of Pamphlet, 1558*

343 Knox, Ronald Arbuthnot (1888-1957), English theologian and essayist.
343.1
A loud noise at one end and no sense of responsibility at the other.   *Definition of a Baby*

344 Krushchev, Nikita (1894-1971), Russian statesman.
344.1
[*To British businessmen*] When you are skinning your customers, you should leave some skin on to grow so that you can skin them again.   *Observer 'Sayings of the Week', 28 May 1961*
344.2
If you start throwing hedgehogs under me, I shall throw two porcupines under you.
same, 10 Nov 1963

345 Kubrick, Stanley (b. 1928), American film director.
345.1
The great nations have always acted like gangsters, and the small nations like prostitutes.   *The Guardian, 5 Jan 1963*

L

346 Laing, Ronald David (b. 1927), Scottish psychiatrist.
346.1
The statesmen of the world who boast and threaten that they have Doomsday weapons are far more dangerous, and far more estranged from 'reality', than many of the people on whom the label 'psychotic' is affixed.   *The Divided Self, Preface (Pelican edition)*

346.2
Schizophrenia cannot be understood without understanding despair.   *same, Ch. 2*
346.3
We are effectively destroying ourselves by violence masquerading as love.
The Politics of Experience, Ch.13
346.4
Madness need not be all breakdown. It may also be break-through. It is potential liberation and renewal as well as enslavement and existential death.   *same, Ch.16*

347 Lamb, Lady Caroline (1785-1828), English novelist and lover of Byron.
347.1
[*Of Byron*] Mad, bad, and dangerous to know.   *Journal*

348 Lamb, Charles (Elia) (1775-1834), English essayist.
348.1
The human species, according to the best theory I can form of it, is composed of two distinct races, the men who borrow, and the men who lend.   *Essays of Elia, The Two Races of Men*
348.2
Borrowers of books—those mutilators of collections, spoilers of the symmetry of shelves, and creators of odd volumes.
same
348.3
I love to lose myself in other men's minds. When I am not walking, I am reading; I cannot sit and think. Books think for me.
Last Essays of Elia, Detached Thoughts on Books and Reading
348.4
Newspapers always excite curiosity. No one ever lays one down without a feeling of disappointment.   *same*
348.5
The greatest pleasure I know, is to do a good action by stealth, and to have it found out by accident.   *Table Talk by the late Elia, The Athenaeum, 4 Jan 1834*
348.6
I have had playmates, I have had companions
In my days of childhood, in my joyful schooldays—
All, all are gone, the old familiar faces.
The Old Familiar Faces

349 Langland, William (1330?-1400?), English poet.
349.1

In a somer season, when soft was the sonne.
Piers Plowman, B Text, Prologue, 1

350 Latimer, Hugh (1485?-1555), English Bishop.
350.1
[*While being burned at the stake with Ridley for heresy*] Be of good comfort, Master Ridley, and play the man; we shall this day light such a candle by God's grace in England, as I trust shall never be put out.
16 Oct 1555

351 Lawrence, David Herbert (1885-1930), English novelist and poet.
351.1
You may be the most liberal Liberal Englishman, and yet you cannot fail to see the categorical difference between the responsible and the irresponsible classes.
Kangaroo, Ch.1
351.2
Pornography is the attempt to insult sex, to do dirt on it. *Phoenix, 'Pornography and Obscenity'*
351.3
Away with all ideals. Let each individual act spontaneously from the for ever incalculable prompting of the creative wellhead within him. There is no universal law.
same, Preface to 'All Things are Possible', by Leo Shostov
351.4
It is no good casting out devils. They belong to us, we must accept them and be at peace with them. *same, 'The Reality of Peace'*
351.5
When I read Shakespeare I am struck with wonder
That such trivial people should muse and thunder
In such lovely language. *When I Read Shakespeare, 1*

352 Lawson, Henry Hertzberg (1867-1922), Australian writer.
352.1
Every true Australian bushman must try his best to tell a bigger outback lie than the last bush-liar. *Prose I:93, 'Stragglers'*

353 Leacock, Stephen Butler (1869-1944), Canadian economist and humorist.
353.1
If every day in the life of a school could be the last day but one, there would be little fault to find with it. *College Days, 'Memories and Miseries of a Schoolmaster'*

353.2
Get your room full of good air, then shut up the windows and keep it. It will keep for years. Anyway, don't keep using your lungs all the time. Let them rest. *Literary Lapses, 'How to Live to be 200'*
353.3
I detest life-insurance agents; they always argue that I shall some day die, which is not so. *same, 'Insurance. Up to Date'*
353.4
Lord Ronald said nothing; he flung himself from the room, flung himself upon his horse and rode madly off in all directions.
Nonsense Novels, 'Gertrude the Governess'
353.5
Golf may be played on Sunday, not being a game within the view of the law, but being a form of moral effort. *Other Fancies, 'Why I refuse to play Golf'*

354 Lear, Edward (1812-1888), English artist and writer.
354.1
On the Coast of Coromandel
Where the early pumpkins blow,
In the middle of the woods
Lived the Yonghy-Bonghy-Bò.
The Courtship of the Yonghy-Bonghy-Bò
354.2
The Dong!—the Dong!
The wandering Dong through the forest goes!
The Dong!—the Dong!
The Dong with a luminous Nose!
The Dong with a Luminous Nose
354.3
They went to sea in a sieve, they did
In a sieve they went to sea. *The Jumblies*
354.4
Far and few, far and few,
Are the lands where the Jumblies live;
Their heads are green, and their hands are blue,
And they went to sea in a sieve. *same*
354.5
The Owl and the Pussy-Cat went to sea
In a beautiful pea-green boat,
They took some honey, and plenty of money,
Wrapped up in a five-pound note.
The Owl and the Pussy-Cat

355 Lenin, Nikolai (1870-1924), Russian revolutionary and political leader.
355.1
Under capitalism we have a state in the proper sense of the word, that is, a special

machine for the suppression of one class by another. *The State and Revolution, V:2*
355.2
It is true that liberty is precious—so precious that it must be rationed. *Attributed*

356 Lessing, Doris (b. 1919), English novelist.
356.1
When a white man in Africa by accident looks into the eyes of a native and sees the human being (which it is his chief preoccupation to avoid), his sense of guilt, which he denies, fumes up in resentment and he brings down the whip. *The Grass is Singing, Ch.8*

357 Lévis, Duc de (1764-1830), French soldier.
357.1
Noblesse oblige.
Nobility has its own obligations. *Maximes et Réflexions*

358 Lewis, Clive Staples (1898-1963), English writer and academic.
358.1
Friendship is unnecessary, like philosophy, like art.... It has no survival value; rather it is one of those things that give value to survival. *The Four Loves, Friendship*
358.2
There is wishful thinking in Hell as well as on earth. *The Screwtape Letters, Preface*

359 Lewis, Sinclair (1885-1951), American novelist.
359.1
In other countries, art and literature are left to a lot of shabby bums living in attics and feeding on booze and spaghetti, but in America the successful writer or picture-painter is indistinguishable from any other decent business man. *Babbitt, Ch.14*
359.2
Our American professors like their literature clear and cold and pure and very dead. *'The American Fear of Literature', Nobel Prize Speech, 1930*

360 Lincoln, Abraham (1809-1865), President of the United States.
360.1
No man is good enough to govern another man without that other's consent. *Speech, 1854*
360.2

The ballot is stronger than the bullet. *Speech, 19 May 1856*
360.3
Those who deny freedom to others, deserve it not for themselves. *same*
360.4
What is conservatism? Is it not adherence to the old and tried, against the new and untried? *Speech, 27 Feb 1860*
360.5
I intend no modification of my oft-expressed personal wish that all men everywhere could be free. *Letter to Horace Greeley, 22 Aug 1862*
360.6
That this nation, under God, shall have a new birth of freedom; and that government of the people, by the people, and for the people, shall not perish from the earth. *Address at Dedication of National Cemetery, Gettysburg, 19 Nov 1863*
360.7
An old Dutch farmer, who remarked to a companion once that it was not best to swap horses in mid-stream. *Speech, 9 June 1864*
360.8
You can fool some of the people all the time and all the people some of the time; but you can't fool all the people all the time. *Attributed*
360.9
People who like this sort of thing will find this is the sort of thing they like. *Criticism of book*

361 Livy, (Titus Livius) (59 B.C.-A.D.17), Roman historian.
361.1
Vae victis.
Woe to the vanquished. *History, V:48*

362 Lloyd, Marie (1870-1922), English music-hall singer.
362.1
A little of what you fancy does you good. *Title of song*

363 Lloyd, Robert (1733-1764), English poet.
363.1
Slow and steady wins the race. *The Hare and the Tortoise*

364 Lloyd George, David, 1st Earl of Dwyfor, (1863-1945), British statesman and prime minister.
364.1
What is our task? To make Britain a fit

country for heroes to live in.

Speech, 24 Nov 1918

364.2

Every man has a House of Lords in his own head. Fears, prejudices, misconceptions—those are the peers, and they are hereditary. *Speech, Cambridge, 1927*

364.3

The world is becoming like a lunatic asylum run by lunatics. *Observer 'Sayings of Our Times', 31 May 1953*

365 Loos, Anita (b. 1893), American novelist and script-writer.

365.1

Gentlemen always seem to remember blondes. *Gentlemen Prefer Blondes, Ch.1*

365.2

So this gentleman said a girl with brains ought to do something else with them besides think. *same*

365.3

Kissing your hand may make you feel very very good but a diamond and safire bracelet lasts forever. *same, Ch.4*

366 Louis XIV, (1638-1715), King of France.

366.1

L'État c'est moi.

I am the State. *Attributed*

367 Louis XVIII, (1755-1824), King of France.

367.1

Punctuality is the politeness of kings.

Attributed

368 Lovelace, Richard (1618-1658), English poet.

368.1

Stone walls do not a prison make,

Nor iron bars a cage. *To Althea, from Prison*

369 Lover, Samuel (1797-1868), Irish artist, song-writer and novelist.

369.1

When once the itch of literature comes over a man, nothing can cure it but the scratching of a pen. *Handy Andy, Ch.36*

370 Lowry, Malcolm (1909-1957), English novelist.

370.1

How alike are the groans of love to those of the dying. *Under the Volcano, Ch.12*

371 Lucretius, (Titus Lucretius Carus) (c. 99-55 B.C.), Roman poet.

371.1

Nothing can be created out of nothing.

On the Nature of the Universe, I:155

372 Luther, Martin (1483-1546), German religious reformer.

372.1

Who loves not wine, woman and song,

Remains a fool his whole life long.

Attributed

373 Lutyens, Sir Edwin Landseer (1869-1944), English architect.

373.1

The answer is in the plural and they bounce.

Attributed

373.2

This piece of cod passes all understanding.

Attributed remark in restaurant

374 Lytton, 1st Earl of see **Meredith, Owen**

M

375 Macaulay, Thomas Babington, 1st Baron (1800-1859), British writer and historian.

375.1

The English Bible, a book which, if everything else in our language should perish, would alone suffice to show the whole extent of its beauty and power. *Essay on Dryden, Edinburgh Review.*

375.2

The gallery in which the reporters sit has become a fourth estate of the realm.

Essay on Hallam's Constitutional History, same

375.3

The Puritan hated bear-baiting, not because it gave pain to the bear, but because it gave pleasure to the spectators. *History of England, Ch.2*

376 MacCarthy, Sir Desmond (1878-1952), English writer and critic.

376.1

When I meet those remarkable people whose

company is coveted, I often wish they would show off a little more.   *Theatre, 'Good Talk'*

376.2
The whole of art is an appeal to a reality which is not without us but in our minds.
same, 'Modern Drama'

377 McLuhan, Marshall (b. 1911), Canadian writer on the mass media.
377.1
If the nineteenth century was the age of the editorial chair, ours is the century of the psychiatrist's couch.   *Understanding the Media, Introduction*

378 Macmillan, Sir Harold (b. 1894), English prime minister and publisher.
378.1
Most of our people have never had it so good.   *Speech, Bedford Football Ground, 20 July 1957*
378.2
When you're abroad you're a statesman: when you're at home you're just a politician.
Speech, 1958
378.3
The wind of change is blowing through the continent. Whether we like it or not, this growth of national consciousness is a political fact.   *Speech, South African Parliament, 3 Feb 1960*

379 Mao Tse-Tung, (1893-1976), Chinese communist leader.
379.1
All reactionaries are paper tigers.
Quotations from Chairman Mao Tse-Tung, 6
379.2
Letting a hundred flowers blossom and a hundred schools of thought contend is the policy for promoting the progress of the arts and the sciences.   *same, 32*

380 Marie-Antoinette, Josephe Jeanne (1755-1793), Queen of France.
380.1
[*When told that the people had no bread*] Let them eat cake.   *Attributed*

381 Marlowe, Christopher (1564-1593), English dramatist and poet.
381.1
GAVESTON. My men, like satyrs grazing on the lawns,
Shall with their goat-feet dance an antic hay.
Edward the Second, I:1:59

381.2
FAUSTUS. Was this the face that launch'd a thousand ships
And burnt the topless towers of Ilium?
Sweet Helen, make me immortal with a kiss.
Doctor Faustus, Sc.14
381.3
FAUSTUS. Now hast thou but one bare hour to live,
And then thou must be damn'd perpetually!
Stand still, you ever-moving spheres of heaven,
That time may cease, and midnight never come.   *same, Sc.16*
381.4
CHORUS. Cut is the branch that might have grown full straight,
And burned is Apollo's laurel-bough,
That sometime grew within this learned man.   *same*
381.5
BARABAS. And, as their wealth increaseth, so inclose
Infinite riches in a little room.   *The Jew of Malta, I:1*
381.6
FRIAR BARNARDINE. Thou hast committed—
BARABAS. Fornication: but that was in another country;
And beside the wench is dead.   *same, IV:1*
381.7
Come live with me, and be my love;
And we will all the pleasures prove
That hills and valleys, dales and fields,
Woods or steepy mountain yields.
The Passionate Shepherd to his Love

382 Marquis, Donald Robert (1878-1937), American writer.
382.1
To stroke a platitude until it purrs like an epigram.   *New York Sun, 'Sun Dial'*
382.2
An idea isn't responsible for the people who believe in it.   *same*

383 Marryat, Frederick (1792-1848), English naval officer and novelist.
383.1
NURSE. [*Of her illegitimate baby*] If you please, ma'am, it was a very little one.
Mr. Midshipman Easy, Ch.3
383.2
I never knows the children. It's just six of one and half-a-dozen of the other.
The Pirate, Ch.4

383.3

I think it much better that...every man
paddle his own canoe.   *Settlers in Canada,*
Ch.8

384 Marvell, Andrew (1621-1678), English
poet.

384.1

Had we but world enough, and time,
This coyness, lady, were no crime.
To his Coy Mistress

384.2

But at my back I always hear
Time's winged chariot hurrying near;
And yonder all before us lie
Deserts of vast eternity.   *same*

384.3

The grave's a fine and private place,
But none, I think, do there embrace.
same

384.4

How vainly men themselves amaze
To win the palm, the oak, or bays.
The Garden

384.5

Annihilating all that's made
To a green thought in a green shade.
same

384.6

So restless Cromwell could not cease
In the inglorious arts of peace.
An Horatian Ode upon Cromwell's
Return from Ireland

384.7

[*Of Charles I*] He nothing common did or
mean
Upon that memorable scene,
But with his keener eye
The axe's edge did try.   *same*

385 Marx, Groucho (1895-1977), American film comedian.

385.1

You're the most beautiful woman I've ever
seen, which doesn't say much for you.
Animal Crackers, film, 1930

385.2

One morning I shot an elephant in my
pajamas.
How he got into my pajamas I'll never
know.   *same*

385.3

What's a thousand dollars? Mere chicken
feed. A poultry matter.
The Cocoanuts, film, 1929

385.4

Your eyes shine like the pants of my blue
serge suit.   *same*

385.5

A child of five would understand this.
Send somebody to fetch a child of five.
Duck Soup, film, 1933

385.6

My husband is dead.
—I'll bet he's just using that as an excuse.
I was with him to the end.
—No wonder he passed away.
I held him in my arms and kissed him.
—So it was murder!   *same*

385.7

Go, and never darken my towels again!
same

385.8

There's a man outside with a big black
moustache.
—Tell him I've got one.   *Horse Feathers,*
film, 1932

385.9

You're a disgrace to our family name of
Wagstaff, if such a thing is possible.
same

385.10

You've got the brain of a four-year-old boy,
and I bet he was glad to get rid of it.
same

385.11

Look at me: I worked my way up from
nothing to a state of extreme poverty.
Monkey Business, film, 1931

385.12

I want to register a complaint. Do you know
who sneaked into my room at three o'clock
this morning?...
—Who?...
Nobody, and that's my complaint.   *same*

385.13

Do you suppose I could buy back my introduction to you?   *same*

385.14

Sir, you have the advantage of me.
—Not yet I haven't, but wait till I get you
outside.   *same*

385.15

Do they allow tipping on the boat?
—Yes, sir.
Have you got two fives?
—Oh, yes, sir.
Then you won't need the ten cents I was
going to give you.   *A Night at the Opera,*
film, 1935

385.16

The strains of Verdi will come back to you
tonight, and Mrs Claypool's cheque will
come back to you in the morning.   *same*

385.17

Send two dozen roses to Room 424 and put

'Emily, I love you' on the back of the bill.
A Night in Casablanca, film, 1945
385.18
I never forget a face, but I'll make an exception in your case.
The Guardian, 18 June 1965
385.19
[*On resigning from the Friar's Club, Hollywood*] Please accept my resignation. I don't want to belong to any club that will accept me as a member. *Telegram*
385.20
No, Groucho is not my real name. I'm breaking it in for a friend. *Attributed*
385.21
Whoever named it necking was a poor judge of anatomy. *Attributed*
385.22
A man is only as old as the woman he feels.
Attributed

386 Marx, Karl (1818–1883), German philosopher and founder of Communism.
386.1
Capitalist production begets, with the inexorability of a law of nature, its own negation.
Capital, Ch.15
386.2
From each according to his abilities, to each according to his needs. *Criticism of the Gotha Programme*
386.3
Religion…is the opium of the people.
Criticism of the Hegelian Philosophy of Right, Introduction
386.4
The history of all hitherto existing society is the history of class struggles. *Manifesto of the Communist Party, 1*
386.5
The workers have nothing to lose but their chains. They have a world to gain. Workers of the world, unite. *same, 4*

387 Mary Tudor, (1516–1558), Queen of England.
387.1
When I am dead and opened, you shall find 'Calais' lying in my heart.
Holinshed's Chronicles, III:1160

388 Maugham, William Somerset (1874–1965), English writer and dramatist.
388.1
Like all weak men he laid an exaggerated stress on not changing one's mind.
Of Human Bondage, Ch.37

388.2
People ask you for criticism, but they only want praise. *same, Ch.50*
388.3
Money is like a sixth sense without which you cannot make a complete use of the other five. *same, Ch.51*
388.4
The mystic sees the ineffable, and the psychopathologist the unspeakable.
The Moon and Sixpence, Ch.1
388.5
Impropriety is the soul of wit. *same, Ch.4*
388.6
You can't learn too soon that the most useful thing about a principle is that it can always be sacrificed to expediency.
The Circle, Act 3
388.7
It was such a lovely day I thought it was a pity to get up. *Our Betters, Act 2*
388.8
I would sooner read a time-table or a catalogue than nothing at all. They are much more entertaining than half the novels that are written. *The Summing Up*
388.9
Life is too short to do anything for oneself that one can pay others to do for one.
same
388.10
I've always been interested in people, but I've never liked them. *Observer 'Sayings of the Week', 28 Aug 1949*

389 Melba, Dame Nellie (1861–1931), Australian soprano.
389.1
[*To Clara Butt*] So you're going to Australia! Well, I made twenty thousand pounds on my tour there, but of course *that* will never be done again. Still, it's a wonderful country, and you'll have a good time. What are you going to sing? All I can say is—sing 'em muck! It's all they can understand!
Clara Butt: Her Life Story (W. H. Ponder)

390 Melbourne, William Lamb, 2nd Viscount (1779–1848), English statesman and prime minister.
390.1
Things have come to a pretty pass when religion is allowed to invade the sphere of private life. *Attributed*

391 Mellon, Andrew William (1855–1937), American financier.

391.1

A nation is not in danger of financial disaster merely because it owes itself money.

Remark, 1933

392 Mencken, Henry Louis (1880-1956), American philologist, editor and satirist.

392.1

Conscience is the inner voice that warns us somebody may be looking.

A Mencken Chrestomathy

392.2

It is now quite lawful for a Catholic woman to avoid pregnancy by a resort to mathematics, though she is still forbidden to resort to physics and chemistry.

Notebooks, 'Minority Report'

392.3

The chief contribution of Protestantism to human thought is its massive proof that God is a bore.　　　　　　　*same*

392.4　　　　　　　　　　·

The worst government is the most moral. One composed of cynics is often very tolerant and human. But when fanatics are on top there is no limit to oppression.　*same*

392.5

Poetry is a comforting piece of fiction set to more or less lascivious music.

Prejudices, Third Series, 'The Poet and his Art'

392.6

I've made it a rule never to drink by daylight and never to refuse a drink after dark.

New York Post, 18 Sept 1945

393 Meredith, George (1828-1909), English novelist and poet.

393.1

I expect that Woman will be the last thing civilized by Man.　*The Ordeal of Richard Feverel, Ch.1*

394 Meredith, Owen, Earl of Lytton (1831-1891), English poet and statesman.

394.1

Genius does what it must, and Talent does what it can.　*Last Words of a Sensitive Second-rate Poet*

395 Mikes, George (b. 1912), Hungarian-English writer.

395.1

On the Continent people have good food; in England people have good table manners.

How to be an Alien

395.2

An Englishman, even if he is alone, forms an orderly queue of one.　*same*

396 Mill, John Stuart (1806-1873), English philosopher.

396.1

All good things which exist are the fruits of originality.　*On Liberty, Ch.3*

396.2

The liberty of the individual must be thus far limited; he must not make himself a nuisance to other people.　*same*

396.3

The worth of a State in the long run is the worth of the individuals composing it.

same

397 Miller, Arthur (b. 1915), American dramatist.

397.1

A good newspaper, I suppose, is a nation talking to itself.　*Observer 'Sayings of the Week', 26 Nov 1961*

398 Miller, Jonathan (b. 1934), English academic, broadcaster, stage director and humorist.

398.1

I'm not really a Jew; just Jew-ish, not the whole hog.　*Beyond the Fringe, television review*

399 Milligan, Spike (b. 1918), English comic and writer.

399.1

—'Do you come here often?'
'Only in the mating season.'

The Goon Show, television programme

399.2

BLUEBOTTLE. I don't like this game.

same, passim

399.3

I'm walking backwards till Christmas

same

400 Milne, Alan Alexander (1882-1956), English writer and dramatist.

400.1

POOH. Time for a little something.

Winnie-the-Pooh, Ch.6

401 Milton, John (1608-1674), English poet.

401.1

Blest pair of Sirens, pledges of Heaven's joy,
Sphere-born harmonious sisters, Voice and Verse.　*At a Solemn Music*

401.2
Hence, vain deluding Joys,
The brood of Folly without father bred!
Il Penseroso, 1

401.3
[*Of the nightingale*] Sweet bird, that shunn'st
the noise of folly,
Most musical, most melancholy!   *same, 61*

401.4
Where glowing embers through the room
Teach light to counterfeit a gloom,
Far from all resort of mirth,
Save the cricket on the hearth.   *same, 79*

401.5
Where more is meant than meets the ear.
same, 120

401.6
Come, and trip it as you go
On the light fantastic toe.   *L'Allegro, 31*

401.7
Then to the spicy nut-brown ale.   *same, 100*

401.8
Or sweetest Shakespeare, Fancy's child,
Warble his native wood-notes wild.
same, 133

401.9
Yet once more, O ye laurels, and once more,
Ye myrtles brown, with ivy never sere,
I come to pluck your berries harsh and
crude,
And with forced fingers rude
Shatter your leaves before the mellowing
year.   *Lycidas, 1*

401.10
To sport with Amaryllis in the shade,
Or with the tangles of Neaera's hair?
same, 68

401.11
Fame is the spur that the clear spirit doth
raise
(That last infirmity of noble mind)
To scorn delights, and live laborious days.
same, 70

401.12
The hungry sheep look up, and are not fed,
But, swoln with wind and the rank mist they
draw,
Rot inwardly, and foul contagion spread.
same, 123

401.13
At last he rose, and twitched his mantle
blue:
To-morrow to fresh woods, and pastures
new.   *same, 192*

401.14
Of Man's first disobedience, and the fruit
Of that forbidden tree, whose mortal taste

Brought death into the World, and all our
woe...   *Paradise Lost, I:1*

401.15
What in me is dark
Illumine, what is low raise and support;
That, to the height of this great argument,
I may assert Eternal Providence,
And justify the ways of God to men.
same, I:22

401.16
What though the field be lost?
All is not lost—the unconquerable will,
And study of revenge, immortal hate,
And courage never to submit or yield:
And what is else not to be overcome?
same, I:105

401.17
A mind not to be changed by place or time.
The mind is its own place, and in itself
Can make a Heaven of Hell, a Hell of
Heaven.   *same, I:253*

401.18
To reign is worth ambition, though in Hell:
Better to reign in Hell than serve in Heaven.
same, I:262

401.19
From morn
To noon he fell, from noon to dewy eve,
A summer's day, and with the setting sun
Dropped from the zenith, like a falling star.
same, I:742

401.20
High on a throne of royal state, which far
Outshone the wealth of Ormus and of Ind,
Or where the gorgeous East with richest
hand
Showers on her kings barbaric pearl and
gold,
Satan exalted sat, by merit raised
To that bad eminence.   *same, II:1*

401.21
Which way I fly is Hell; myself am Hell;
And, in the lowest deep, a lower deep
Still threat'ning to devour me opens wide,
To which the Hell I suffer seems a Heaven.
same, IV:73

401.22
Farewell remorse! All good to me is lost;
Evil, be thou my Good.   *same, IV:180*

401.23
Now came still Evening on, and Twilight
grey
Had in her sober livery all things clad.
same, IV:598

401.24
Midnight brought on the dusky hour
Friendliest to sleep and silence.
same, V:667

401.25
In solitude
What happiness? who can enjoy alone,
Or, all enjoying, what contentment find?
same, VIII:364
401.26
Revenge, at first though sweet,
Bitter ere long back on itself recoils.
same, IX:171
401.27
The world was all before them, where to choose
Their place of rest, and Providence their guide:
They, hand in hand, with wandering steps and slow,
Through Eden took their solitary way.
same, XII:646
401.28
SAMSON. A little onward lend thy guiding hand
To these dark steps, a little further on.
Samson Agonistes, 1
401.29
SAMSON. Ask for this great deliverer now, and find him
Eyeless in Gaza at the mill with slaves.
same, 40
401.30
SAMSON. O dark, dark, dark, amid the blaze of noon,
Irrecoverably dark, total eclipse,
Without all hope of day! *same, 80*
401.31
How soon hath Time, the subtle thief of youth,
Stolen on his wing my three-and-twentieth year! *Sonnet, On being arrived at the age of twenty-three*
401.32
When I consider how my light is spent
Ere half my days in this dark world and wide,
And that one talent which is death to hide
Lodged with me useless. *Sonnet, On his Blindness*
401.33
God doth not need
Either man's work or his own gifts. Who best
Bear his mild yoke, they serve him best: his state
Is kingly; thousands at his bidding speed,
And post o'er land and ocean without rest;
They also serve who only stand and wait.
same
401.34

New Presbyter is but old Priest writ large.
Sonnet, On the new Forcers of Conscience under the Long Parliament
401.35
Who kills a man kills a reasonable creature, God's image; but he who destroys a good book, kills reason itself, kills the image of God, as it were in the eye. *Areopagitica*
401.36
A good book is the precious life-blood of a master spirit, embalmed and treasured up on purpose to a life beyond life. *same*
401.37
Let her and Falsehood grapple; who ever knew Truth put to the worse, in a free and open encounter? *same*
401.38
None can love freedom heartily, but good men; the rest love not freedom, but licence.
Tenure of Kings and Magistrates

402 Molière, (Jean Baptiste Poquelin) (1622-1673), French dramatist and actor.
402.1
One should eat to live, not live to eat.
L'Avare, III:5
402.2
Good heavens! I have been talking prose for over forty years without realizing it.
Le Bourgeois Gentilhomme, II:4
402.3
It is a public scandal that gives offence, and it is no sin to sin in secret. *Tartuffe, IV:5*

403 Montaigne, Michel de (1533-1592), French essayist.
403.1
The greatest thing in the world is to know how to be self-sufficient. *Essays, I:39*
403.2
A man must keep a little back shop where he can be himself without reserve. In solitude alone can he know true freedom. *same*
403.3
When I play with my cat, who knows whether she is not amusing herself with me more than I with her? *same, II:12*
403.4
Marriage is like a cage; one sees the birds outside desperate to get in, and those inside equally desperate to get out. *same, III:5*

404 More, Sir Thomas (1478-1535), English statesman and divine.
404.1
[*On mounting the scaffold*] I pray you, Master Lieutenant, see me safe up, and for

coming down let me shift for myself.
Life of Sir Thomas More (William Roper)

N

405 Morgan, Augustus de (1806-1871),
English mathematician.
405.1
Great fleas have little fleas upon their backs
to bite 'em,
And little fleas have lesser fleas, and so *ad
infinitum.*   *A Budget of Paradoxes*

406 Morris, Desmond (b. 1928), English
biologist and writer.
406.1
There are one hundred and ninety-three
living species of monkeys and apes. One
hundred and ninety-two of them are covered
with hair. The exception is a naked ape self-
named *Homo sapiens.*   *The Naked Ape,
Introduction*

407 Mosley, Sir Oswald (b. 1896), English
politician and fascist leader.
407.1
I am not and never have been, a man of the
right. My position was on the left and is now
in the centre of politics.
The Times, 26 Apr 1968

408 Motley, John Lothrop (1814-1877),
American historian and diplomat.
408.1
Give us the luxuries of life, and we will
dispense with its necessities.
*The Autocrat of the Breakfast Table (O.
W. Holmes), Ch.6*

409 Munro, Hector Hugh see Saki

410 Münster, Ernst Friedrich Herbert
(1766-1839), Hanoverian statesman.
410.1
[*Of the Russian Constitution*] Absolutism
tempered by assassination.   *Letter*

411 Mussolini, Benito (1883-1945), Italian
dictator.
411.1
[*Of Hitler's seizure of power*] Fascism is a
religion; the twentieth century will be known
in history as the century of Fascism.
Sawdust Caesar (George Seldes), Ch.24

412 Nabokov, Vladimir (1899-1977),
Russian novelist and lepidopterist.
412.1
Lolita, light of my life, fire of my loins. My
sin, my Soul.   *Lolita, I:1*
412.2
Spring and summer did happen in Cambridge
almost every year.   *The Real Life of
Sebastian Knight, Ch.5*
412.3
Literature and butterflies are the two sweetest
passions known to man.   *Radio Times, Oct
1962*

413 Napoleon Bonaparte, (1769-1821),
French emperor and general.
413.1
It is only a step from the sublime to the
ridiculous.   *After the retreat from Moscow,
1812*
413.2
England is a nation of shopkeepers.
Attributed
413.3
An army marches on its stomach.
Attributed

414 Nash, Ogden (1902-1971), American
writer of humorous verse.
414.1
A door is what a dog is perpetually on the
wrong side of.   *A Dog's Best Friend Is His
Illiteracy*
414.2
Home is heaven and orgies are vile
But you need an orgy, once in a while.
Home, 99.44/100% Sweet Home
414.3
Beneath this slab
John Brown is stowed.
He watched the ads
And not the road.   *Lather as You Go*
414.4
Children aren't happy with nothing to ignore,
And that's what parents were created for.
The Parents
414.5
I think that I shall never see
A billboard lovely as a tree.
Perhaps unless the billboards fall,
I'll never see a tree at all.   *Song of the Open
Road*

415   Nelson, Horatio, 1st Viscount
(1758-1805), English admiral.
415.1
England expects every man will do his duty.
Battle of Trafalgar
415.2
Kiss me, Hardy.   *Remark, Battle of*
Trafalgar, 1805

416   Newbolt, Sir Henry John (1862-1938),
English poet.
416.1
There's a breathless hush in the Close
tonight—
Ten to make and the match to win—
A bumping pitch and a blinding light,
An hour to play and the last man in.
Vitaï Lampada
416.2
But his captain's hand on his shoulder
smote—
'Play up! play up! and play the game!'
same

417   Newman, John Henry (1801-1890),
English Catholic theologian.
417.1
It is almost a definition of a gentleman to
say that he is one who never inflicts pain.
The Idea of a University, 'Knowledge and
Religious Duty'

418   Nicholas I, (1796-1855), Tsar of
Russia.
418.1
Russia has two generals in whom she can
confide—Generals Janvier and Février.
Punch, 10 Mar 1853

419   Nietzsche, Friedrich Wilhelm
(1844-1900), German philosopher and
critic.
419.1
When a man is in love he endures more than
at other times; he submits to everything.
The Antichrist, aphorism 23
419.2
God created woman. And boredom did
indeed cease from that moment—but many
other things ceased as well! Woman was
God's *second* mistake.   *same, 48*
419.3
I call Christianity the one great curse, the
one enormous and innermost perversion, the
one great instinct of revenge, for which no
means are too venomous, too underhand,
too underground and too petty—I call it the

one immortal blemish of mankind.
same, 62
419.4
My doctrine is: Live that thou mayest desire
to live again—that is thy duty—for in any
case thou wilt live again!
Eternal Recurrence, 27
419.5
I teach you the Superman. Man is something
that is to be surpassed.   *Thus Spake*
Zarathustra, Ch. 3

420   Nixon, Richard Milhous (b. 1913),
American politician and President of the
United States.
420.1
[*Of the first manned moon landing*] This is
the greatest week in the history of the world
since the creation.   *Remark, 24 July 1969*
420.2
I am not a crook.   *Remark, 17 Nov 1973*
420.3
There can be no whitewash at the White
House.   *Observer 'Sayings of the Week',*
30 Dec 1973

421   North, Christopher (**John Wilson**)
(1785-1854), Scottish poet, essayist and
critic.
421.1
His Majesty's dominions, on which the sun
never sets.   *Noctes Ambrosianae,*
20 Apr 1829
421.2
Laws were made to be broken.
same, 24 May 1830

O

422   Oates, Lawrence Edward Grace
(1880-1912), English explorer.
422.1 ˙
I am just going outside, and may be some
time.   *Last words: Recorded in Captain*
R. F. Scott's Antarctic Diary, 16 Mar 1912

423   O'Casey, Sean (1884-1964), Irish
dramatist.
423.1
There's no reason to bring religion into it. I
think we ought to have as great a regard for
religion as we can, so as to keep it out of as

many things as possible. *The Plough and the Stars, Act 1*

423.2
[*Of P. G. Wodehouse*] English literature's performing flea. *Remark*

424 Ochs, Adolph Simon (1858-1935), American newspaper publisher.
424.1
All the news that's fit to print. *Motto of New York Times*

425 O'Keefe, Patrick (1872-1934), American advertising agent.
425.1
Say it with flowers. *Slogan for Society of American Florists*

426 Orton, Joe (1933-1967), English dramatist.
426.1
I'd the upbringing a nun would envy and that's the truth. Until I was fifteen I was more familiar with Africa than my own body. *Entertaining Mr Sloane, Act 1*
426.2
It's all any reasonable child can expect if the dad is present at the conception. *same, Act 3*
426.3
The humble and meek are thirsting for blood. *Funeral Games, Act 1*
426.4
Every luxury was lavished on you—atheism, breast-feeding, circumcision. I had to make my own way. *Loot, Act 1*
426.5
Reading isn't an occupation we encourage among police officers. We try to keep the paper work down to a minimum. *same, Act 2*

427 Orwell, George (**Eric Blair**) (1903-1950), English novelist and essayist.
427.1
All animals are equal but some animals are more equal than others. *Animal Farm, Ch. 10*
427.2
Big Brother is watching you *Nineteen Eighty-Four*
427.3
War is Peace, Freedom is Slavery, Ignorance is Strength. *same*
427.4
Doublethink means the power of holding two contradictory beliefs in one's mind

simultaneously, and accepting both of them. *same, II:9*
427.5
[*Of the middle classes*] We have nothing to lose but our aitches. *The Road to Wigan Pier, Ch. 13*

428 Ovid, (**Publius Ovidius Naso**) (43 B.C.-17 A.D.), Latin poet.
428.1
Whether they give or refuse, women are glad to have been asked. *Ars Amatoria, 1*
428.2
Tu quoque.
You also. *Tristia*

429 Owen, Robert (1771-1858), Welsh social reformer.
429.1
[*Of his business partner, William Allen*] All the world is queer save thee and me, and even thou art a little queer. *Remark, 1828*

430 Owen, Wilfred (1893-1918), English poet.
430.1
Above all I am not concerned with Poetry. My subject is War, and the pity of War. The Poetry is in the pity. *Preface to Poems*
430.2
The old Lie: *Dulce et decorum est Pro patria mori.* *Dulce et decorum est*

P

431 Paine, Thomas (1737-1809), English philosopher and writer.
431.1
The sublime and the ridiculous are often so nearly related that it is difficult to class them separately. One step above the sublime makes the ridiculous; and one step above the ridiculous makes the sublime again. *The Age of Reason, Part 2*
431.2
Government, even in its best state, is but a necessary evil; in its worst state, an intolerable one. *Common Sense, Ch.1*

432 Palmerston, Henry John Temple, 3rd Viscount (1784-1865), English prime minister.

432.1

Die, my dear Doctor, that's the last thing I shall do! *Last words, attributed*

433 Parker, Dorothy (1893–1967), American writer.

433.1

How do people go to sleep? I'm afraid I've lost the knack. I might try busting myself smartly over the temple with the nightlight. I might repeat to myself, slowly and soothingly, a list of quotations beautiful from minds profound; if I can remember any of the damn things. *The Little Hours*

433.2

Men seldom make passes
At girls who wear glasses. *News Item*

433.3

Why is it no one ever sent me yet
One perfect limousine, do you suppose?
Ah no, it's always just my luck to get
One perfect rose. *One Perfect Rose*

433.4

Guns aren't lawful;
Nooses give;
Gas smells awful;
You might as well live. *Résumé*

433.5

Sorrow is tranquillity remembered in emotion. *Sentiment*

433.6

By the time you swear you're his,
Shivering and sighing,
And he vows his passion is
Infinite, undying—
Lady, make a note of this:
One of you is lying.
Unfortunate Coincidence

433.7

If all the young ladies who attended the Yale promenade dance were laid end to end, no one would be the least surprised.

While Rome Burns (Alexander Woollcott)

434 Parkinson, Cyril Northcote (b. 1909), English political scientist and writer.

434.1

Work expands so as to fill the time available for its completion. *Parkinson's Law*

435 Pascal, Blaise (1623–1662), French mathematician and theologian.

435.1

The heart has its reasons which reason does not know. *Pensées, IV:277*

436 Pater, Walter Horatio (1839–1894), English critic.

436.1

[*Of the Mona Lisa*] She is older than the rocks among which she sits.
The Renaissance, 'Leonardo da Vinci'

436.2

All art constantly aspires towards the condition of music. *same, 'The School of Giorgione'*

437 Peacock, Thomas Love (1785–1866), English novelist.

437.1

LADY CLARINDA. Respectable means rich, and decent means poor. I should die if I heard my family called decent.
Crotchet Castle, Ch.3

437.2

MR PORTPIPE. There are two reasons for drinking; one is, when you are thirsty, to cure it; the other, when you are not thirsty, to prevent it... Prevention is better than cure. *Melincourt, Ch.16*

438 Pepys, Samuel (1633–1703), English diarist.

438.1

And so to bed. *Diary, 6 May 1660 and passim*

438.2

Music and women I cannot but give way to, whatever my business is. *same, 9 Mar 1666*

438.3

To church; and with my mourning, very handsome, and new periwig, make a great show. *same, 31 Mar 1667*

439 Perón, Juan Domingo (1895–1974), Argentine soldier and president.

439.1

If I had not been born Perón, I would have liked to be Perón. *Observer 'Sayings of the Week', 21 Feb 1960*

440 Pétain, Henri Phillipe (1856–1951), French marshal.

440.1

[*Of the German army*] They shall not pass.
Verdun, Feb 1916

441 Peter, Laurence (b. 1919), Canadian writer and educationalist.

441.1

The Peter Principle: In a Hierarchy Every Employee Tends to Rise to his Level of Incompetence. *The Peter Principle, Ch.1*

441.2

Work is accomplished by those employees

who have not yet reached their level of incompetence. *same*

442 Petronius, (*fl.* 1st century A.D.), Latin writer.
442.1
Cave canem.
Beware of the dog.　　*Satyricon, XXIX:1*

443 Phelps, Edward John (1822-1900), American lawyer and diplomat.
443.1
The man who makes no mistakes does not usually make anything.　　*Speech, Mansion House, London, 24 Jan 1899*

444 Phillips, Wendell (1811-1884), American reformer.
444.1
One on God's side is a majority.
Speech, Brooklyn, 1 Nov 1859
444.2
Every man meets his Waterloo at last.
same

445 Picasso, Pablo (1881-1973), Spanish painter.
445.1
I hate that aesthetic game of the eye and the mind, played by these connoisseurs, these mandarins who 'appreciate' beauty. What *is* beauty, anyway? There's no such thing. I never 'appreciate', any more than I 'like'. I love or I hate.　　*Life with Picasso (Gilot and Lake), Ch.2*
445.2
Painting is a blind man's profession. He paints not what he sees, but what he feels, what he tells himself about what he has seen.
Journals (Jean Cocteau), 'Childhood'

446 Pinter, Harold (b. 1930), English dramatist.
446.1
DAVIES. If only I could get down to Sidcup! I've been waiting for the weather to break. He's got my papers, this man I left them with, it's got it all down there, I could prove everything.　　*The Caretaker, Act 1*

447 Pitt, William (1759-1806), English prime minister.
447.1
Necessity is the plea for every infringement of human freedom. It is the argument of tyrants; it is the creed of slaves.
Speech, House of Commons, 18 Nov 1783

447.2
[*On hearing of Napoleon's victory at the Battle of Austerlitz*] Roll up that map: it will not be wanted these ten years.
Remark, 1805
447.3
I think I could eat one of Bellamy's veal pies.　　*Last words, attributed*
447.4
Oh, my country! How I leave my country!
Last words, attributed

448 Plato, (429?-347? B.C.), Greek philosopher.
448.1
The good is the beautiful.　　*Lysis*
448.2
Our object in the construction of the state is the greatest happiness of the whole, and not that of any one class.　　*Republic, 4*

449 Pliny the Elder, (Gaius Plinius Secundus) (23-79), Roman soldier and writer.
449.1
In vino veritas.
Truth comes out in wine.
Historia Naturalis, XIV:141

450 Poe, Edgar Allan (1809-1849), American poet and writer.
450.1
Take thy beak from out my heart, and take thy form from off my door!
Quoth the Raven, 'Nevermore.'
The Raven

451 Pompadour, Madame de (1721-1764), mistress of Louis XV of France.
451.1
Après nous le déluge.
After us the deluge.　　*After the Battle of Rossbach, 1757*

452 Pope, Alexander (1688-1744), English poet.
452.1
The right divine of kings to govern wrong.
The Dunciad, IV:188
452.2
The Muse but serv'd to ease some friend, not Wife,
To help me through this long disease, my life.　　*Epistle to Dr. Arbuthnot, 131*
452.3
Damn with faint praise, assent with civil leer,

And, without sneering, teach the rest to sneer.
same, 201

452.4
Curst be the verse, how well so'er it flow,
That tends to make one worthy man my foe.
same, 283

452.5
Wit that can creep, and pride that licks the dust.
same, 333

452.6
In wit a man; simplicity a child.
Epitaph on Mr Gay

452.7
'Tis hard to say, if greater want of skill
Appear in writing or in judging ill.
An Essay on Criticism, 1

452.8
'Tis with our judgments as our watches, none
Go just alike, yet each believes his own.
same, 9

452.9
Of all the causes which conspire to blind
Man's erring judgment, and misguide the mind,
What the weak head with strongest bias rules,
Is Pride, the never-failing vice of fools.
same, 201

452.10
A little learning is a dangerous thing;
Drink deep, or taste not the Pierian spring:
There shallow draughts intoxicate the brain,
And drinking largely sobers us again.
same, 215

452.11
Whoever thinks a faultless piece to see,
Thinks what ne'er was, nor is, nor e'er shall be.
same, 253

452.12
True wit is nature to advantage dress'd;
What oft was thought, but ne'er so well express'd.
same, 297

452.13
True ease in writing comes from art, not chance,
As those move easiest who have learn'd to dance.
'Tis not enough no harshness gives offence,
The sound must seem an echo to the sense.
same, 362

452.14
Fondly we think we honour merit then,
When we but praise ourselves in other men.
same, 454

452.15
To err is human, to forgive, divine.
same, 525

452.16
For fools rush in where angels fear to tread.
same, 625

452.17
Hope springs eternal in the human breast;
Man never is, but always to be blest.
An Essay on Man, I:95

452.18
Know then thyself, presume not God to scan,
The proper study of Mankind is Man.
same, II:1

452.19
That true self-love and social are the same;
That virtue only makes our bliss below;
And all our knowledge is, ourselves to know.
same, IV:396

452.20
'Tis education forms the common mind,
Just as the twig is bent, the tree's inclined.
Moral Essays, I:149

452.21
Men, some to business, some to pleasure take;
But every woman is at heart a rake.
same, II:215

452.22
Woman's at best a contradiction still.
same, II:270

452.23
The ruling passion, be it what it will
The ruling passion conquers reason still.
same, III:153

452.24
I am His Highness' dog at Kew;
Pray tell me sir, whose dog are you?
On the collar of a dog given to Frederick, Prince of Wales

452.25
What dire offence from am'rous causes springs,
What mighty contests rise from trivial things.
The Rape of the Lock, I:1

452.26
Here thou great Anna! whom three realms obey,
Dost sometimes counsel take—and sometimes Tea.
The Rape of the Lock, III:7

452.27
Not louder shrieks to pitying heav'n are cast,
When husbands, or when lap-dogs breathe their last.
same, III:157

452.28
The hungry judges soon the sentence sign,
And wretches hang that jury-men may dine.
same, III:21

452.29
Coffee which makes the politician wise,

And see through all things with his half-shut eyes. *same, III:117*

453 Potter, Stephen (1900-1969), English writer and radio producer.
453.1
Gamesmanship or The Art of Winning Games Without Actually Cheating.
Title of book
453.2
How to be one up—how to make the other man feel that something has gone wrong, however slightly. *Lifemanship, Introduction*

454 Pound, Ezra Loomis (1885-1972), American poet and critic.
454.1
Winter is icummen in,
Lhude sing Goddamm,
Raineth drop and staineth slop
And how the wind doth ramm!
Sing: Goddamm. *Ancient Music*
454.2
Great Literature is simply language charged with meaning to the utmost possible degree.
How to Read

455 Powell, Anthony (b. 1905), English novelist.
455.1
'He fell in love with himself at first sight and it is a passion to which he has always remained faithful. Self-love seems so often unrequited.' *The Acceptance World, Ch.1*
455.2
Dinner at the Huntercombes' possessed 'only two dramatic features—the wine was a farce and the food a tragedy'. *same, Ch.4*

456 Prescott, William (1726-1795), American revolutionary soldier.
456.1
Don't fire until you see the whites of their eyes. *Bunker Hill,*

457 Proudhon, Pierre Joseph (1809-1865), French socialist.
457.1
Property is theft. *Qu'est-ce que la proprieté?, Ch.1*

458 Proust, Marcel (1871-1922), French novelist.
458.1
There can be no peace of mind in love, since the advantage one has secured is never anything but a fresh starting-point for further desires. *À l'Ombre des Jeunes Filles en Fleur*
458.2
As soon as one is unhappy one becomes moral. *same*
458.3
As soon as he ceased to be mad he became merely stupid. There are maladies we must not seek to cure because they alone protect us from others that are more serious.
Le Côté de Guermantes, 1
458.4
There is nothing like desire for preventing the thing one says from bearing any resemblance to what one has in mind.
same, 2
458.5
It has been said that the highest praise of God consists in the denial of Him by the atheist, who finds creation so perfect that he can dispense with a creator. *same*
458.6
I have a horror of sunsets, they're so romantic, so operatic. *Sodome et Gomorrhe, 2*
458.7
Everything great in the world is done by neurotics; they alone founded our religions and created our masterpieces.
The Perpetual Pessimist (Sagittarius and George)

Q

459 Quesnay, François (1694-1774), French physician and economist.
459.1
Laissez faire, laissez passer.
Let it be, let it pass. *Attributed*

R

460 Rabelais, Francois (1494?-1553?), French satirist.
460.1
Appetite comes with eating. *Gargantua, I:5*
460.2

83

Ring down the curtain, the farce is over.
> *Last words, attributed*

460.3
I am going in search of a great perhaps.
> *Last words, attributed*

461 Rae, John (b. 1931), English teacher and novelist.
461.1
War is, after all, the universal perversion. We are all tainted: if we cannot experience our perversion at first hand we spend our time reading war stories, the pornography of war; or seeing war films, the blue films of war; or titillating our senses with the imagination of great deeds, the masturbation of war.   *The Custard Boys, Ch. 6*

462 Raleigh, Sir Walter (1552?-1618), English courtier, navigator and writer.
462.1
Even such is Time, that takes in trust
Our youth, our joys, our all we have,
And pays us but with age and dust;
Who in the dark and silent grave,
When we have wandered all our ways,
Shuts up the story of our days;
But from this earth, this grave, this dust,
My God shall raise me up, I trust.
> *Written the night before his death*

462.2
[*On feeling the edge of the axe*] Tis a sharp remedy, but a sure one for all ills.
> *Remark made before his execution*

462.3
[*On laying his head on the block*] So the heart be right, it is no matter which way the head lies.   *same*

463 Raleigh, Sir Walter Alexander (1861-1922), English scholar and critic.
463.1
An anthology is like all the plums and orange peel picked out of a cake.   *Letter to Mrs. Robert Bridges, 15 Jan 1915*

464 Reade, Charles (1814-1884), English novelist.
464.1
Make 'em laugh; make 'em cry; make 'em wait.   *Advice to young writer*

465 Reed, Henry (b. 1914), English poet and dramatist.
465.1
Today we have naming of parts. Yesterday,
We had daily cleaning. And tomorrow morning

We shall have what to do after firing. But today,
Today we have naming of parts.
> *Naming of Parts*

465.2
They call it easing the Spring: it is perfectly easy
If you have any strength in your thumb: like the bolt,
And the breech, and the cocking-piece, and the point of balance,
Which in our case we have not got.   *same*

466 Reynolds, Sir Joshua (1723-1792), English portrait painter.
466.1
If you have great talents, industry will improve them: if you have but moderate abilities, industry will supply their deficiency.   *Discourses, 2*

467 Rhodes, Cecil John (1853-1902), South African statesman.
467.1
So little done, so much to do.   *Last words*

468 Rimsky-Korsakov, Nikolai (1844-1908), Russian composer.
468.1
[*Of Debussy's music*] I have already heard it. I had better not go: I will start to get accustomed to it and finally like it.
> *Conversations with Stravinsky (Robert Craft and Igor Stravinsky)*

469 Robinson, James Harvey (1863-1936), American historian and educator.
469.1
Partisanship is our great curse. We too readily assume that everything has two sides and that it is our duty to be on one or the other.   *The Mind in the Making*

470 Roche, Sir Boyle (1743-1807), English politician.
470.1
Mr Speaker, I smell a rat; I see him forming in the air and darkening the sky; but I'll nip him in the bud.   *Attributed*

471 Rochefoucauld, Duc de la (1613-1680), French writer.
471.1
Everyone complains of his memory, but no one complains of his judgement.
> *Les Maximes, 89*

471.2

The intellect is always fooled by the heart.
same, 102

471.3
Hypocrisy is the homage paid by vice to virtue. *same, 218*

471.4
The height of cleverness is to conceal one's cleverness. *same, 245*

471.5
In the misfortunes of our best friends, we find something that is not displeasing.
Maximes supprimées, 583

471.6
Self-love is the greatest of all flatterers.
Reflections, 2

471.7
We all have strength enough to endure the misfortunes of others. *same, 19*

471.8
We need greater virtues to sustain good fortune than bad. *same, 25*

471.9
If we had no faults of our own, we would not take so much pleasure in noticing those of others. *same, 31*

471.10
Self-interest speaks all sorts of tongues, and plays all sorts of roles, even that of disinterestedness. *same, 39*

471.11
We are never so happy nor so unhappy as we imagine. *same, 49*

471.12
To succeed in the world, we do everything we can to appear successful. *same, 50*

471.13
There are very few people who are not ashamed of having been in love when they no longer love each other. *same, 71*

471.14
The love of justice in most men is simply the fear of suffering injustice. *same, 78*

471.15
Silence is the best tactic for him who distrusts himself. *same, 79*

472 Rogers, Will (1879-1935), American actor and humorist.

472.1
You can't say civilization don't advance, however, for in every war they kill you a new way. *Autobiography, Ch. 12*

472.2
Everything is funny, as long as it's happening to somebody else. *The Illiterate Digest*

473 Rochester, John Wilmot, 2nd Earl of (1647-1680), English courtier and poet.

473.1
Here lies our sovereign lord the King,
Whose word no man relies on;
He never said a foolish thing,
Nor ever did a wise one. *Epitaph on Charles II A000*

474 Roland, Madame Marie Jeanne Philipon (1754-1793), French revolutionist.

474.1
[*On viewing the statue of Liberty*] Oh liberty, liberty, what crimes are committed in your name! *Remark from the scaffold*

475 Roosevelt, Franklin Delano (1882-1945), President of the United States.

475.1
I pledge you, I pledge myself, to a new deal for the American people. *Speech accepting nomination for Presidency, Chicago, 2 July 1932*

475.2
A radical is a man with both feet firmly planted in the air. *Broadcast, 26 Oct 1939*

475.3
We look forward to a world founded upon four essential human freedoms. The first is freedom of speech and expression—everywhere in the world. The second is freedom of every person to worship God in his own way—everywhere in the world. The third is freedom from want...everywhere in the world. The fourth is freedom from fear...anywhere in the world. *Speech to Congress, 6 Jan 1941*

475.4
We all know that books burn—yet we have the greater knowledge that books cannot be killed by fire. People die, but books never die. No man and no force can abolish memory...In this war, we know, books are weapons. *Message to American Booksellers Association, 23 Apr 1942*

475.5
More than an end to war, we want an end to the beginnings of all wars. *Speech written for broadcast, 13 Apr 1945 (the day after his death)*

476 Roosevelt, Theodore (1858-1919), President of the United States.

476.1
I wish to preach, not the doctrine of ignoble ease, but the doctrine of the strenuous life.
Speech, Chicago, 10 Apr 1899

476.2
There is no room in this country for

hyphenated Americanism. *Speech, New York, 12 Oct 1915*
476.3
No man is justified in doing evil on the ground of expediency. *The Strenuous Life*

477 Rosebery, Archibald Philip Primrose, 5th Earl of (1847-1929), British statesman.
477.1
The Empire is a Commonwealth of Nations. *Speech, Adelaide, 18 Jan 1884*
477.2
It is beginning to be hinted that we are a nation of amateurs. *Rectorial Address, Glasgow, 16 Nov 1900*

478 Ross, Alan Strode Campbell (b. 1907), English academic.
478.1
U and Non-U, An Essay in Sociological Linguistics. *Title of Essay in 'Noblesse Oblige', 1956*

479 Rossetti, Dante Gabriel (1828-1882), English poet and painter.
479.1
I have been here before.
But when or how I cannot tell:
I know the grass beyond the door,
The sweet keen smell,
The sighing sound, the lights around the shore. *Sudden Light*

480 Rouget de Lisle, Claude Joseph (1760-1836), French army officer.
480.1
Allons, enfants, de la patrie,
Le jour de gloire est arrivé.
Come, children of our native land,
The day of glory has arrived.
La Marseillaise

481 Rousseau, Jean Jacques (1712-1778), Swiss political philosopher.
481.1
Man was born free and everywhere he is in chains. *Du Contrat Social, Ch. 1*

482 Routh, Martin Joseph (1755-1854), English scholar.
482.1
Always verify your references. *Attributed*

483 Runyon, Damon (1884-1946), American writer and journalist.
483.1
More than somewhat. *Title of a collection of stories*
483.2
My boy...always try to rub up against money, for if you rub up against money long enough, some of it may rub off on you.
Furthermore, 'A Very Honourable Guy'

484 Ruskin, John (1819-1900), English writer and art critic.
484.1
If a book is worth reading, it is worth buying. *Sesame and Lilies*
484.2
Remember that the most beautiful things in the world are the most useless; peacocks and lilies for instance. *The Stones of Venice*
484.3
Fine art is that in which the hand, the head, and the heart of man go together. *The Two Paths*

485 Russell, Bertrand Arthur William, 3rd Earl (1872-1970), English philosopher and mathematician.
485.1
Three passions, simple but overwhelmingly strong, have governed my life: the longing for love, the search for knowledge, and unbearable pity for the suffering of mankind.
Autobiography, 1, Prologue
485.2
The megalomaniac differs from the narcissist by the fact that he wishes to be powerful rather than charming, and seeks to be feared rather than loved. To this type belong many lunatics and most of the great men of history.
The Conquest of Happiness, Ch. 1
485.3
Of all forms of caution, caution in love is perhaps the most fatal to true happiness.
Marriage and Morals
485.4
Mathematics possesses not only truth, but supreme beauty—a beauty cold and austere, like that of sculpture. *The Study of Mathematics*
485.5
Few people can be happy unless they hate some other person, nation or creed.
Attributed
485.6
Patriots always talk of dying for their country, and never of killing for their country.
Attributed

S

486   Saki, (Hector Hugh Munro)
(1870-1916), English novelist and short-
story writer.
486.1
The people of Crete unfortunately make
more history than they can consume locally.
The Jesting of Arlington Stringham
486.2
All decent people live beyond their incomes
nowadays, and those who aren't respectable
live beyond other people's. A few gifted
individuals manage to do both.
The Match Maker
486.3
I always say beauty is only sin deep.
Reginald's Choir Treat
486.4
The cook was a good cook, as cooks go; and
as cooks go she went.   *Reginald on*
Besetting Sins
486.5
People may say what they like about the
decay of Christianity; the religious system
that produced green Chartreuse can never
really die.   *Reginald on Christmas Presents*
486.6
I think she must have been very strictly
brought up, she's so desperately anxious to
do the wrong thing correctly.   *Reginald on*
Worries

487   Samuel, Herbert Louis, 1st Viscount
(1870-1963), English statesman and
writer.
487.1
It takes two to make a marriage a success
and only one a failure.   *A Book of*
Quotations
487.2
A truism is on that account none the less
true.   *same*
487.3
A library is thought in cold storage.
same
487.4
Without doubt the greatest injury...was
done by basing morals on myth, for sooner
or later myth is recognized for what it is, and
disappears. Then morality loses the foundation on which it has been built.
Romanes Lecture, 1947

488   Santayana, George (1863-1952),
American philosopher and poet.
488.1
The working of great institutions is mainly
the result of a vast mass of routine, petty
malice, self interest, carelessness, and sheer
mistake. Only a residual fraction is thought.
The Crime of Galileo
488.2
The young man who has not wept is a
savage, and the old man who will not laugh
is a fool.   *Dialogues in Limbo, Ch. 3*
488.3
Those who cannot remember the past are
condemned to repeat it.   *The Life of*
Reason, I:12
488.4
Happiness is the only sanction of life; where
happiness fails, existence remains a mad and
lamentable experiment.   *same*
488.5
Life is not a spectacle or a feast; it is a
predicament.   *The Perpetual Pessimist*
(Sagittarius and George)

489   Sartre, Jean-Paul (b. 1905), French
philosopher, dramatist and novelist.
489.1
I hate victims who respect their executioners.
Altona, 1
489.2
Things are entirely what they appear to be
and *behind them*...there is nothing.
Nausea
489.3
My thought is *me*: that is why I can't stop. I
exist by what I think...and I can't prevent
myself from thinking.   *same*
489.4
I know perfectly well that I don't want to do
anything; to do something is to create
existence — and there's quite enough
existence as it is.   *same*

490   Schelling, Friedrich William
(1775-1854), German philosopher.
490.1
Architecture in general is frozen music.
Philosophie der Kunst

491   Schweitzer, Albert (1875-1965),
French clergyman, musician and mis-
sionary.
491.1
[*To an African who refused to carry out a
humdrum task on the grounds that he was an
intellectual*] I too had thoughts once of being

an intellectual, but I found it too difficult.
Attributed

492 Scott, Robert Falcon (1868-1912), English Antarctic explorer.
492.1
[*Of the South Pole*] Great God! this is an awful place. *Journal, 17 Jan 1912*
492.2
Had we lived, I should have had a tale to tell of the hardihood, endurance, and courage of my companions which would have stirred the heart of every Englishman. These rough notes and our dead bodies must tell the tale.
Message to the Public

493 Scott, William, 1st Baron Stowell (1745-1836), English judge.
493.1
A dinner lubricates business.
Boswell's Life of Johnson, 1781

494 Selden, John (1584-1654), English historian and antiquary.
494.1
Preachers say, Do as I say, not as I do.
Table Talk
494.2
A king is a thing men have made for their own sakes, for quietness' sake. Just as if in a family one man is appointed to buy the meat. *Table Talk*
494.3
Every law is a contract between the king and the people and therefore to be kept.
same
494.4
Ignorance of the law excuses no man; not that all men know the law, but because 'tis an excuse every man will plead, and no man can tell how to confute him. *same*
494.5
Pleasure is nothing else but the intermission of pain. *same*

495 Sellar, Walter Carruthers (1898-1951) and **Yeatman, Robert Julian** (1897-1968), English humorous writers.
495.1
1066 And All That. *Title of Book*
495.2
The Roman Conquest was, however, a *Good Thing*, since the Britons were only natives at the time. *1066 And All That, Ch. 1*
495.3
Napoleon's armies used to march on their stomachs, shouting: 'Vive l'intérieur!'
same, Ch. 48

495.4
Do not on any account attempt to write on both sides of the paper at once. *same, Test Paper 5*

496 Service, Robert William (1874-1958), Canadian poet.
496.1
A promise made is a debt unpaid.
The Cremation of Sam McGee
496.2
This is the Law of the Yukon, that only the strong shall thrive;
That surely the weak shall perish, and only the Fit survive. *The Law of the Yukon*
496.3
When we, the Workers, all demand: 'What are we fighting for?'...
Then, then we'll end that stupid crime, that devil's madness—War. *Michael*

497 Shadwell, Thomas (1642?-1692), English dramatist.
497.1
Words may be false and full of art,
Sighs are the natural language of the heart.
Psyche, Act 3
497.2
'Tis the way of all flesh.
The Sullen Lovers, V:2
497.3
Every man loves what he is good at.
A True Widow, V:1

498 Shakespeare, William (1564-1616), English dramatist and poet.
498.1
HELENA. Our remedies oft in ourselves do lie,
Which we ascribe to heaven. *All's Well that End's Well, I:1:202*
498.2
2ND LORD. The web of our life is of a mingled yarn, good and ill together.
same, IV:3:67
498.3
KING. Th' inaudible and noiseless foot of Time. *same, V:3:41*
498.4
PHILO. The triple pillar of the world transform'd
Into a strumpet's fool. *Antony and Cleopatra, I:1:12*
498.5
ANTONY. There's beggary in the love that can be reckon'd. *same, I:1:15*
498.6

ANTONY. Where's my serpent of old Nile?
same, I:5:25

498.7

CLEOPATRA. My salad days,
When I was green in judgment, cold in blood,
To say as I said then! *same, I:5:73*

498.8

ENOBARBUS. The barge she sat in, like a burnish'd throne,
Burn'd on the water. The poop was beaten gold;
Purple the sails, and so perfumed that
The winds were love-sick with them; the oars were silver,
Which to the tune of flutes kept stroke and made
The water which they beat to follow faster,
As amorous of their strokes. For her own person,
It beggar'd all description. *same, II:2:195*

498.9

ENOBARBUS. Age cannot wither her, nor custom stale
Her infinite variety. Other women cloy
The appetites they feed, but she makes hungry
Where most she satisfies. *same, II:2:239*

498.10

ENOBARBUS. I will praise any man that will praise me. *same, II:6:88*

498.11

CLEOPATRA. Celerity is never more admir'd
Than by the negligent. *same, III:7:24*

498.12

ANTONY. To business that we love we rise betime,
And go to't with delight. *same, IV:4:20*

498.13

ANTONY. Unarm Eros; the long day's task is done,
And we must sleep. *same, IV:14:35*

498.14

ANTONY. I am dying, Egypt, dying; only
I here importune death awhile, until
Of many thousand kisses the poor last
I lay upon thy lips. *same, IV:15:18*

498.15

CLEOPATRA. O, wither'd is the garland of the war,
The soldier's pole is fall'n! Young boys and girls
Are level now with men. The odds is gone,
And there is nothing left remarkable
Beneath the visiting moon. *same, IV:15:64*

498.16

IRAS. The bright day is done,
And we are for the dark. *same, V:2:192*

498.17

CLEOPATRA. Dost thou not see my baby at my breast
That sucks the nurse asleep? *same, V:2:307*

498.18

CELIA. Well said; that was laid on with a trowel. *As You Like It, I:2:94*

498.19

TOUCHSTONE. I had rather bear with you than bear you. *same, II:4:9*

498.20

SILVIUS. If thou rememb'rest not the slightest folly
That ever love did make thee run into,
Thou hast not lov'd. *same, II:4:31*

498.21

AMIENS. Under the greenwood tree
Who loves to lie with me,
And turn his merry note
Unto the sweet bird's throat,
Come hither, come hither, come hither.
Here shall he see
No enemy
But winter and rough weather. *same, II:5:1*

498.22

JACQUES. And so, from hour to hour, we ripe and ripe,
And then, from hour to hour, we rot and rot;
And thereby hangs a tale. *same, II:7:26*

498.23

JACQUES. All the world's a stage,
And all the men and women merely players;
They have their exits and their entrances,
And one man in his time plays many parts,
His acts being seven ages. *same, II:7:139*

498.24

JACQUES. Last scene of all,
That ends this strange eventful history,
Is second childishness and mere oblivion;
Sans teeth, sans eyes, sans taste, sans every thing. *same, II:7:159*

498.25

AMIENS. Blow, blow, thou winter wind,
Thou art not so unkind
As man's ingratitude. *same, II:7:174*

498.26

AMIENS. Most friendship is feigning, most loving mere folly. *same, II:7:181*

498.27

CORIN. He that wants money, means, and content, is without three good friends.
same, III:2:23

498.28

ROSALIND. Do you not know I am a woman? When I think, I must speak.
same, III:2:234

498.29

498.30

ORLANDO. I do desire we may be better strangers. *same, III:2:243*

TOUCHSTONE. The truest poetry is the most feigning. *same, III:3:16*

498.31

ROSALIND. Men have died from time to time, and worms have eaten them, but not for love. *same, IV:1:94*

498.32

TOUCHSTONE. Your If is the only peacemaker; much virtue in If. *same, V:4:97*

498.33

ROSALIND. If it be true that good wine needs no bush, 'tis true that a good play needs no epilogue. *same, Epilogue*

498.34

CORIOLANUS. Custom calls me to't.
What custom wills, in all things should we do't,
The dust on antique time would lie unswept,
And mountainous error be too highly heap'd
For truth to o'erpeer. *Coriolanus, II:3:114*

498.35

CORIOLANUS. Like a dull actor now
I have forgot my part and I am out,
Even to a full disgrace. *same, V:3:40*

498.36

BELARIUS. O, this life
Is nobler than attending for a check,
Richer than doing nothing for a bribe,
Prouder than rustling in unpaid-for silk.
Cymbeline, II:3:21

498.37

IMOGEN. Society is no comfort
To one not sociable. *same, IV:2:12*

498.38

GUIDERIUS. Fear no more the heat o' th' sun
Nor the furious winter's rages;
Thou thy worldly task hast done,
Home art gone, and ta'en thy wages.
Golden lads and girls all must,
As chimney-sweepers, come to dust. *same, IV:2:259*

498.39

FRANCISCO. For this relief much thanks. 'Tis bitter cold,
And I am sick at heart. *Hamlet, I:1:8*

498.40

HAMLET. A little more than kin, and less than kind. *same, I:2:65*

498.41

HAMLET. But I have that within which passes show—
these but the trappings and the suits of woe. *same, I:2:85*

498.42

HAMLET. How weary, stale, flat, and unprofitable,
Seem to me all the uses of this world! *same, I:2:129*

498.43

HAMLET. Frailty, thy name is woman! *same, I:2:146*

498.44

HAMLET. It is not, nor it cannot come to good. *same, I:2:156*

498.45

HAMLET. 'A was a man, take him for all in all,
I shall not look upon his like again. *same, I:2:187*

498.46

OPHELIA. Do not, as some ungracious pastors do,
Show me the steep and thorny way to heaven,
Whiles, like a puff'd and reckless libertine,
Himself the primrose path of dalliance treads
And recks not his own rede. *same, I:3:47*

498.47

POLONIUS. Costly thy habit as thy purse can buy,
But not express'd in fancy; rich, not gaudy;
For the apparel oft proclaims the man. *same, I:3:70*

498.48

POLONIUS. Neither a borrower nor a lender be;
For loan oft loses both itself and friend,
And borrowing dulls the edge of husbandry.
This above all - to thine own self be true,
And it must follow, as the night the day,
Thou canst not then be false to any man. *same, I:3:75*

498.49

HAMLET. But to my mind, though I am native here
And to the manner born, it is a custom
More honour'd in the breach than the observance. *same, I:4:14*

498.50

MARCELLUS. Something is rotten in the state of Denmark. *same, I:4:90*

498.51

GHOST. Murder most foul, as in the best it is;
But this most foul, strange, and unnatural. *same, I:5:27*

498.52

HAMLET. There are more things in heaven and earth, Horatio,
Than are dreamt of in your philosophy. *same, I:5:166*

498.53

POLONIUS. Brevity is the soul of wit.

same, II:2:90

498.54

HAMLET. To be honest, as this world goes, is to be one man pick'd out of ten thousand.

same, II:2:177

498.55

POLONIUS. Though this be madness, yet there is method in't. *same, II:2:204*

498.56

HAMLET. There is nothing either good or bad, but thinking makes it so.

same, II:2:248

498.57

HAMLET. What a piece of work is a man! How noble in reason! how infinite in faculties! in form and moving, how express and admirable! in action, how like an angel! in apprehension, how like a god! the beauty of the world! the paragon of animals! And yet, to me, what is this quintessence of dust? Man delights not me—no, nor woman neither. *same, II:2:303*

498.58

HAMLET. The play, I remember, pleas'd not the million; 'twas caviare to the general.

same, II:2:429

498.59

HAMLET. Use every man after his desert, and who shall scape whipping?

same, II:2:523

498.60

HAMLET. The play's the thing Wherein I'll catch the conscience of the King. *same, II:2:600*

498.61

HAMLET. To be, or not to be — that is the question;
Whether 'tis nobler in the mind to suffer
The slings and arrows of outrageous fortune,
Or to take arms against a sea of troubles,
And by opposing end them? To die, to sleep—
No more; and by a sleep to say we end
The heart-ache and the thousand natural shocks
That flesh is heir to, 'tis a consummation
Devoutly to be wish'd. To die, to sleep;
To sleep, perchance to dream. Ay, there's the rub;
For in that sleep of death what dreams may come,
When we have shuffled off this mortal coil,
Must give us pause. *same, III:1:56*

498.62

HAMLET. The dread of something after death—

The undiscover'd country, from whose bourn
No traveller returns. *same, III:1:78*

498.63

HAMLET. Thus conscience does make cowards of us all;
And thus the native hue of resolution
Is sicklied o'er with the pale cast of thought.

same, III:1:83

498.64

CLAUDIUS. Madness in great ones must not unwatch'd go. *same, III:1:188*

498.65

HAMLET. It out-herods Herod.

same, III:2:14

498.66

HAMLET. Suit the action to the word, the word to the action; with this special observance, that you o'erstep not the modesty of nature. *same, III:2:17*

498.67

GERTRUDE. The lady doth protest too much, methinks. *same, III:2:225*

498.68

POLONIUS. Very like a whale.

same, III:2:372

498.69

HAMLET. A king of shreds and patches.

same, III:4:102

498.70

HAMLET. Some craven scruple
Of thinking too precisely on th' event.

same, IV:4:40

498.71

CLAUDIUS. When sorrows come, they come not single spies,
But in battalions! *same, IV:5:75*

498.72

CLAUDIUS. There's such divinity doth hedge a king
That treason can but peep to what it would.

same, IV:5:120

498.73

HAMLET. Alas, poor Yorick! I knew him, Horatio: a fellow of infinite jest, of most excellent fancy. *same, V:1:179*

498.74

HAMLET. There's a divinity that shapes our ends,
Rough-hew them how we will.

same, V:2:10

498.75

HAMLET. If thou didst ever hold me in thy heart,
Absent thee from felicity awhile,
And in this harsh world draw thy breath in pain,
To tell my story. *same, V:2:338*

498.76

HAMLET. The rest is silence.   *same, V:2:350*

498.77

PRINCE. If all the year were playing holidays,
To sport would be as tedious as to work.
Henry the Fourth, Part One, I:2:197

498.78

PRINCE. Falstaff sweats to death
And lards the lean earth as he walks along.
same, II:2:104

498.79

FALSTAFF. I have more flesh than another
man, and therefore more frailty.
same, III:3:167

498.80

FALSTAFF. Honour pricks me on. Yea, but
how if honour prick me off when I come on?
How then? Can honour set to a leg? No. Or
an arm? No. Or take away the grief of a
wound? No. Honour hath no skill in surgery,
then? No. What is honour? A word. What is
in that word? Honour. What is that honour?
Air.   *same, V:1:129*

498.81

HOTSPUR. But thoughts, the slaves of life,
and life, time's fool,
And time, that takes survey of all the world,
Must have a stop.   *same, V:4:81*

498.82

FALSTAFF. The better part of valour is
discretion; in the which better part I have
saved my life.   *same, V:4:120*

498.83

FALSTAFF. I am not only witty in myself,
but the cause that wit is in other men. I do
here walk before thee like a sow that hath
overwhelm'd all her litter but one.
King Henry the Fourth, Part Two, I:2:7

498.84

FALSTAFF. Well, I cannot last ever; but it
was always yet the trick of our English
nation, if they have a good thing, to make it
too common.   *same, I:2:200*

498.85

FALSTAFF. I can get no remedy against this
consumption of the purse; borrowing only
lingers and lingers it out, but the disease is
incurable.   *same, I:2:223*

498.86

HOSTESS. He hath eaten me out of house
and home.   *same, II:1:71*

498.87

POINS. Is it not strange that desire should so
many years outlive performance?
same, II:4:250

498.88

HENRY IV. Uneasy lies the head that wears
a crown.   *same, III:1:26*

498.89

FALSTAFF. We have heard the chimes at
midnight.   *same, III:2:210*

498.90

FEEBLE. I care not; a man can die but once;
we owe God a death.   *same, III:2:228*

498.91

Care I for the limb, the thews, the stature,
bulk, and big assemblance of a man! Give
me the spirit.   *same, III:2:251*

498.92

NYM. I dare not fight; but I will wink and
hold out mine iron.   *King Henry the Fifth,
II:1:6*

498.93

NYM. Though patience be a tired mare, yet
she will plod.   *same, II:1:24*

498.94

HOSTESS. His nose was as sharp as a pen,
and 'a babbl'd of green fields.
same, II:3:17

498.95

HENRY V. Once more unto the breach, dear
friends, once more;
Or close the wall up with our English dead.
same, III:1:1

498.96

BOY. Men of few words are the best men.
same, III:2:36

498.97

HENRY V. I think the King is but a man as I
am: the violet smells to him as it doth to me.
same, IV:1:101

498.98

HENRY V. Every subject's duty is the King's;
but every subject's soul is his own.
same, IV:1:175

498.99

HENRY V. Old men forget; yet all shall be
forgot,
But he'll remember, with advantages,
What feats he did that day.   *same, IV:3:49*

498.100

FLUELLEN. There is occasions and causes
why and wherefore in all things.
same, V:1:3

498.101

NORFOLK. Heat not a furnace for your foe
so hot
That it do singe yourself. We may outrun
By violent swiftness that which we run at,
And lose by over-running.   *King Henry the
Eighth, I:1:140*

498.102

ANNE. I would not be a queen
For all the world.   *same, II:3:45*

498.103

WOLSEY. Farewell, a long farewell, to all my greatness!
This is the state of man: to-day he puts forth
The tender leaves of hopes: to-morrow blossoms
And bears his blushing honours thick upon him;
The third day comes a frost, a killing frost,
And when he thinks, good easy man, full surely
His greatness is a-ripening, nips his root,
And then he falls, as I do.   *same, III:2:351*

498.104

WOLSEY. Had I but serv'd my God with half the zeal
I serv'd my King, he would not in mine age
Have left me naked to mine enemies.
same, III:2:455

498.105

GRIFFITH. Men's evil manners live in brass: their virtues
We write in water.   *same, IV:2:45*

498.106

SOOTHSAYER. Beware the ides of March.
Julius Caesar, I:2:18

498.107

CAESAR. Let me have men about me that are fat;
Sleek-headed men, and such as sleep o' nights.
Yond Cassius has a lean and hungry look;
He thinks too much. Such men are dangerous.   *same, I:2:192*

498.108

CASCA. For mine own part, it was Greek to me.   *same, I:2:283*

498.109

CAESAR. Cowards die many times before their deaths:
The valiant never taste of death but once.
same, II:2:32

498.110

CAESAR. *Et tu, Brute?*   *same, III:1:77*

498.111

CASSIUS. Why, he that cuts off twenty years of life
Cuts off so many years of fearing death.
same, III:1:102

498.112

ANTONY. O mighty Caesar! dost thou lie so low?
Are all thy conquests, glories, triumphs, spoils,
Shrunk to this little measure?
same, III:1:149

498.113

ANTONY. O, pardon me, thou bleeding piece of earth,

That I am meek and gentle with these butchers!
Thou art the ruins of the noblest man
That ever lived in the tide of times.
same, III:1:255

498.114

ANTONY. Cry 'Havoc!' and let slip the dogs of war.   *same, III:1:274*

498.115

BRUTUS. Not that I lov'd Caesar less, but that I lov'd Rome more.   *same, III:2:20*

498.116

ANTONY. Friends, Romans, countrymen, lend me your ears;
I come to bury Caesar, not to praise him.
The evil that men do lives after them;
The good is oft interred with their bones.
same, III:2:73

498.117

ANTONY. For Brutus is an honourable man;
So are they all, all honourable men.
same, III:2:82

498.118

ANTONY. Ambition should be made of sterner stuff.   *same, III:2:92*

498.119

ANTONY. If you have tears, prepare to shed them now.   *same, III:2:169*

498.120

ANTONY. For I have neither wit, nor words, nor worth,
Action, nor utterance, nor the power of speech,
To stir men's blood; I only speak right on.
same, III:2:221

498.121

CASSIUS. A friend should bear his friend's infirmities,
But Brutus makes mine greater than they are.   *same, IV:3:85*

498.122

BRUTUS. There is a tide in the affairs of men
Which, taken at the flood, leads on to fortune;
Omitted, all the voyage of their life
Is bound in shallows and in miseries.
On such a full sea are we now afloat,
And we must take the current when it serves,
Or lose our ventures.   *same, IV:3:216*

498.123

ANTONY. This was the noblest Roman of them all.
All the conspirators save only he
Did that they did in envy of great Caesar.
same, V:5:68

498.124

ANTONY. His life was gentle; and the elements

So mix'd in him that Nature might stand up
And say to all the world 'This was a man!'

same, V:5:73

498.125

BASTARD. Well, whiles I am a beggar, I will
rail
And say there is no sin but to be rich;
And being rich, my virtue then shall be
To say there is no vice but beggary.

King John, II:1:593

498.126

BASTARD. Bell, book, and candle, shall not
drive me back,
When gold and silver becks me to come on.

same, III:3:12

498.127

LEWIS. Life is as tedious as a twice-told tale
Vexing the dull ear of a drowsy man.

same, III:4:108

498.128

SALISBURY. To gild refined gold, to paint
the lily,
To throw a perfume on the violet,
To smooth the ice, or add another hue
Unto the rainbow, or with taper-light
To seek the beauteous eye of heaven to
garnish,
Is wasteful and ridiculous excess.

same, IV:2:11

498.129

KING JOHN. I beg cold comfort.

same, V:7:42

498.130

LEAR. Nothing will come of nothing. Speak
again. *King Lear, I:1:89*

498.131

EDMUND. This is the excellent foppery of
the world, that, when we are sick in fortune,
often the surfeits of our own behaviour, we
make guilty of our disasters the sun, the
moon, and stars. *same, I:2:112*

498.132

LEAR. Ingratitude, thou marble-hearted
fiend,
More hideous when thou show'st thee in a
child
Than the sea-monster! *same, I:4:259*

498.133

LEAR. O, let me not be mad, not mad, sweet
heaven!
Keep me in temper; I would not be mad!

same, I:5:43

498.134

KENT. Thou whoreson zed! thou unnecessary
letter! *same, II:2:58*

498.135

LEAR. *Hysterica passio*—down, thou climbing sorrow,
Thy element's below. *same, II:4:56*

498.136

LEAR. O, reason not the need! Our basest
beggars
Are in the poorest thing superfluous.
Allow not nature more than nature needs,
Man's life is cheap as beast's.

same, II:4:263

498.137

LEAR. Blow, winds, and crack your cheeks;
rage, blow.
You cataracts and hurricanoes, spout
Till you have drench'd our steeples, drown'd
the cocks. *same, III:2:1*

498.138

LEAR. Rumble thy bellyful. Spit, fire; spout
rain.
Nor rain, wind, thunder, fire, are my
daughters
I tax not you, you elements, with unkindness. *same, III:2:14*

498.139

LEAR. I am a man
More sinn'd against than sinning.

same, III:2:59

498.140

LEAR. Poor naked wretches, wheresoe'er
you are,
That bide the pelting of this pitiless storm,
How shall your houseless heads and unfed
sides,
Your loop'd and window'd raggedness,
defend you
From seasons such as these? *same, III:4:28*

498.141

LEAR. Take physic, pomp;
Expose thyself to feel what wretches feel.

same, III:4:33

498.142

CORNWALL. Out vile jelly!
Where is thy lustre now? *same, III:7:82*

498.143

EDGAR. The worst is not
So long as we can say 'This is the worst'.

same, IV:1:28

498.144

GLOUCESTER. As flies to wanton boys are
we to th' gods—
They kill us for their sport. *same, IV:1:37*

498.145

LEAR. Ay, every inch a king.

same, IV:6:107

498.146

LEAR. The wren goes to't, and the small
gilded fly
Does lecher in my sight. *same, IV:6:112*

498.147

LEAR. Through tatter'd clothes small vices
do appear;
Robes and furr'd gowns hide all.
same, IV:6:164

498.148

LEAR. Get thee glass eyes,
And, like a scurvy politician, seem
To see the things thou dost not.
same, IV:6:170

498.149

LEAR. When we are born, we cry that we are
come
To this great stage of fools.   *same, IV:6:183*

498.150

LEAR. Thou art a soul in bliss; but I am
bound
Upon a wheel of fire, that mine own tears
Do scald like molten lead.   *same, IV:7:46*

498.151

EDGAR. Men must endure
Their going hence, even as their coming
hither:
Ripeness is all.   *same, V:2:9*

498.152

LEAR. And my poor fool is hang'd! No, no,
no life!
Why should a dog, a horse, a rat have life,
And thou no breath at all? Thou'lt come no
more,
Never, never, never, never.   *same, V:3:305*

498.153

BEROWNE. At Christmas I no more desire a
rose
Than wish a snow in May's new-fangled
shows.   *Love's Labour's Lost, I:1:105*

498.154

SIR NATHANIEL. He hath never fed of the
dainties that are bred in a book; he hath not
eat paper, as it were; he hath not drunk ink;
his intellect is not replenished.
same, IV:2:22

498.155

BEROWNE. For where is any author in the
world
Teaches such beauty as a woman's eye?
Learning is but an adjunct to oneself.
same, IV:3:308

498.156

BEROWNE. A jest's prosperity lies in the ear
Of him that hears it, never in the tongue
Of him that makes it.   *same, V:2:849*

498.157

WINTER. When icicles hang by the wall,
And Dick the shepherd blows his nail,
And Tom bears logs into the hall,
And milk comes frozen home in pail,
When blood is nipp'd, and ways be foul,

Then nightly sings the staring owl:
'Tu-who;
Tu-whit, Tu-who'—A merry note,
While greasy Joan doth keel the pot.
same, V:2:899

498.158

MACBETH. So foul and fair a day I have not
seen.   *Macbeth, I:3:38*

498.159

MACBETH. This supernatural soliciting
Cannot be ill; cannot be good.
same, I:3:130

498.160

MACBETH. Come what come may,
Time and the hour runs through the roughest
day.   *same, I:3:146*

498.161

MALCOLM. Nothing in his life
Became him like the leaving it: he died
As one that had been studied in his death
To throw away the dearest thing he ow'd
As 'twere a careless trifle.   *same, I:4:7*

498.162

LADY MACBETH. Yet do I fear thy nature;
It is too full o' th' milk of human kindness
To catch the nearest way.   *same, I:5:13*

498.163

MACBETH. If it were done when 'tis done,
then 'twere well
It were done quickly.   *same, I:7:1*

498.164

MACBETH. That but this blow
Might be the be-all and the end-all here—
But here upon this bank and shoal of time—
We'd jump the life to come.   *same, I:7:4*

498.165

MACBETH. I have no spur
To prick the sides of my intent, but only
Vaulting ambition, which o'er-leaps itself,
And falls on th' other.   *same, I:7:25*

498.166

MACBETH. False face must hide what the
false heart doth know.   *same, I:7:82*

498.167

MACBETH. Sleep that knits up the ravell'd
sleave of care,
The death of each day's life, sore labour's
bath,
Balm of hurt minds, great nature's second
course,
Chief nourisher in life's feast.   *same, II:2:35*

498.168

PORTER. It provokes the desire, but it takes
away the performance. Therefore much drink
may be said to be an equivocator with
lechery.   *same, II:3:28*

498.169

LADY MACBETH. Nought's had, all's spent,

Where our desire is got without content.
'Tis safer to be that which we destroy,
Than by destruction dwell in doubtful joy.
same, III:2:4
498.170
MACBETH. I had else been perfect,
Whole as the marble, founded as the rock,
As broad and general as the casing air,
But now I am cabin'd, cribb'd, confin'd,
   bound in
To saucy doubts and fears. *same, II:4:21*
498.171
LADY MACBETH. Stand not upon the order
   of your going,
But go at once. *same, III:4:119*
498.172
MACBETH. I am in blood
Stepp'd in so far that, should I wade no
   more,
Returning were as tedious as go o'er.
same, III:4:136
498.173
LADY MACBETH. Out, damned spot! out, I
say! *same, V:1:33*
498.174
LADY MACBETH. Here's the smell of the
blood still. All the perfumes of Arabia will
not sweeten this little hand. *same, V:1:48*
498.175
MACBETH. I have liv'd long enough. My
   way of life
Is fall'n into the sear, the yellow leaf;
And that which should accompany old age,
As honour, love, obedience, troops of friends,
I must not look to have. *same, V:3:22*
498.176
MACBETH. I have supp'd full with horrors.
same, V:5:13
498.177
MACBETH. Tomorrow, and tomorrow, and
   tomorrow,
Creeps in this petty pace from day to day
To the last syllable of recorded time,
And all our yesterdays have lighted fools
The way to dusty death. Out, out, brief
   candle!
Life's but a walking shadow, a poor player,
That struts and frets his hour upon the stage,
And then is heard no more; it is a tale
Told by an idiot, full of sound and fury,
Signifying nothing. *same, V:5:17*
498.178
MACBETH. I gin to be aweary of the sun,
And wish th' estate o' th' world were now
undone. *same, V:5:49*
498.179
MACBETH. I bear a charmed life, which must
   not yield

To one of woman born.
MACDUFF. Despair thy charm;
And let the angel whom thou still hast serv'd
Tell thee Macduff was from his mother's
   womb
Untimely ripp'd. *same, V:8:12*
498.180
ISABELLA. But man, proud man
Dress'd in a little brief authority,
Most ignorant of what he's most assur'd,
His glassy essence, like an angry ape,
Plays such fantastic tricks before high heaven
As makes the angels weep. *Measure for
Measure, II:2:117*
498.181
ISABELLA. That in the captain's but a
   choleric word
Which in the soldier is flat blasphemy.
same, II:2:130
498.182
CLAUDIO. The miserable have no other
   medicine
But only hope. *same, III:1:12*
498.183
DUKE. Thou has nor youth nor age;
But, as it were, an after-dinner's sleep,
Dreaming on both. *same, III:1:32*
498.184
CLAUDIO. Ay, but to die, and go we know
   not where;
To lie in cold obstruction, and to rot;
This sensible warm motion to become
A kneaded clod; and the delighted spirit
To bathe in fiery floods or to reside
In thrilling region of thick-ribbed ice.
same, III:1:119
498.185
LUCIO. I am a kind of burr; I shall stick.
same, IV:3:173
498.186
DUKE. Haste still pays haste, and leisure
   answers leisure;
Like doth quit like, and Measure still for
Measure. *same, V:1:408*
498.187
GRATIANO. As who should say 'I am Sir
   Oracle,
And when I ope my lips let no dog bark'.
The Merchant of Venice, I:1:93
498.188
PORTIA. If to do were as easy as to know
what were good to do, chapels had been
churches, and poor men's cottages princes'
palaces. *same, I:2:11*
498.189
ANTONIO. The devil can cite Scripture for
his purpose. *same, I:3:93*

498.190

LAUNCELOT GOBBO. It is a wise father that knows his own child.   *same, II:2:69*

498.191

JESSICA. But love is blind, and lovers cannot see
The pretty follies that themselves commit.
same, II:6:36

498.192

NERISSA. The ancient saying is no heresy: Hanging and wiving goes by destiny.
same, II:9:82

498.193

SHYLOCK. Hath not a Jew eyes? Hath not a Jew hands, organs, dimensions, senses, affections, passions, fed with the same food, hurt with the same weapons, subject to the same diseases, healed by the same means, warmed and cooled by the same winter and summer, as a Christian is? If you prick us, do we not bleed? If you tickle us, do we not laugh? If you poison us, do we not die? And if you wrong us, shall we not revenge?
same, III:1:49

498.194

PORTIA. The quality of mercy is not strain'd; It droppeth as the gentle rain from heaven Upon the place beneath. It is twice blest; It blesseth him that gives and him that takes.
same, IV:1:179

498.195

JESSICA. I am never merry when I hear sweet music.   *same, V:1:69*

498.196

LORENZO. The man that hath no music in himself,
Nor is not mov'd with concord of sweet sounds,
Is fit for treasons, stratagems, and spoils.
same, V:1:83

498.197

PORTIA. How far that little candle throws his beams!
So shines a good deed in a naughty world.
same, V:1:90

498.198

PORTIA. For a light wife doth make a heavy husband.   *same, V:1:130*

498.199

PISTOL. Why, then the world's mine oyster, Which I with sword will open.
The Merry Wives of Windsor, II:2:4

498.200

FALSTAFF. They say there is divinity in odd numbers, either in nativity, chance, or death.
same, V:1:3

498.201

LYSANDER. For aught that I could ever read,
Could ever hear by tale or history,
The course of true love never did run smooth.
A Midsummer Night's Dream, I:1:132

498.202

HELENA. Love looks not with the eyes, but with the mind;
And therefore is wing'd Cupid painted blind.
same, I:1:234

498.203

SNUG. I am slow of study.   *same, I:2:59*

498.204

BOTTOM. A lion among ladies is a most dreadful thing; for there is not a more fearful wild-fowl than your lion living.
same, III:1:27

498.205

PUCK. Lord, what fools these mortals be!
same, III:2:115

498.206

THESEUS. The lunatic, the lover, and the poet,
Are of imagination all compact.
same, V:1:7

498.207

THESEUS. The poet's eye, in a fine frenzy rolling,
Doth glance from heaven to earth, from earth to heaven;
And as imagination bodies forth
The forms of things unknown, the poet's pen
Turns them to shapes, and gives to airy nothing
A local habitation and a name.
same, V:1:12

498.208

BENEDICK. Would you have me speak after my custom, as being a professed tyrant to their sex?   *Much Ado About Nothing,*
I:1:144

498.209

CLAUDIO. Friendship is constant in all other things
Save in the office and affairs of love.
same, II:1:154

498.210

CLAUDIO. Silence is the perfectest herald of joy: I were but little happy if I could say how much.   *same, II:1:275*

498.211

BENEDICK. Doth not the appetite alter? A man loves the meat in his youth that he cannot endure in his age.   *same, II:3:215*

498.212

DOGBERRY. To be a well-favoured man is the gift of fortune; but to write and read comes by nature.   *same, III:3:13*

498.213

VERGES. I thank God I am as honest as any man living that is an old man and no honester than I. *same, III:5:13*

498.214

DOGBERRY. Comparisons are odorous. *same, III:5:16*

498.215

DOGBERRY. Our watch, sir, have indeed comprehended two aspicious persons. *same, III:5:42*

498.216

DOGBERRY. Write down that they hope they serve God; and write God first; for God defend but God should go before such villains! *same, IV:2:17*

498.217

LEONATO. For there was never yet philosopher
That could endure the toothache patiently. *same, V:1:35*

498.218

DUKE. To mourn a mischief that is past and gone
Is the next way to draw new mischief on. *Othello, I:3:204*

498.219

IAGO. Put money in thy purse. *same, I:3:338*

498.220

IAGO. For I am nothing if not critical. *same, II:1:119*

498.221

IAGO. To suckle fools and chronicle small beer. *same, II:1:159*

498.222

CASSIO. Reputation, reputation, reputation! O, I have lost my reputation! I have lost the immortal part of myself, and what remains is bestial. *same, II:3:254*

498.223

IAGO. Good name in man and woman, dear my lord,
Is the immediate jewel of their souls:
Who steals my purse steals trash; 'tis something, nothing;
'Twas mine, 'tis his, and has been slave to thousands;
But he that filches from me my good name
Robs me of that which not enriches him
And makes me poor indeed. *same, III:3:159*

498.224

IAGO. O, beware, my lord, of jealousy;
It is the green-ey'd monster which doth mock
The meat it feeds on. *same, III:3:169*

498.225

OTHELLO. O curse of marriage,
That we can call these delicate creatures ours,
And not their appetites! I had rather be a toad,
And live upon the vapour of a dungeon,
Than keep a corner in the thing I love
For others' uses. *same, III:3:272*

498.226

OTHELLO. He that is robb'd, not wanting what is stol'n,
Let him not know't, and he's not robb'd at all. *same, III:3:346*

498.227

OTHELLO. Farewell the neighing steed and the shrill trump,
The spirit-stirring drum, th' ear-piercing fife,
The royal banner, and all quality.
Pride, pomp, and circumstance, of glorious war! *same, III:3:351*

498.228

OTHELLO. Put out the light, and then put out the light.
If I quench thee, thou flaming minister,
I can again thy former light restore,
Should I repent me; but once put out thy light,
Thou cunning'st pattern of excelling nature,
I know not where is that Promethean heat
That can thy light relume. *same, V:2:7*

498.229

OTHELLO Then must you speak
Of one that lov'd not wisely, but too well;
Of one not easily jealous, but, being wrought,
Perplexed in the extreme; of one whose hand,
Like the base Indian, threw a pearl away
Richer than all his tribe. *same, V:2:7*

498.230

PERICLES. Kings are earth's gods; in vice their law's their will. *Pericles, I:1:103*

498.231

3RD FISHERMAN. Master, I marvel how the fishes live in the sea.
1ST FISHERMAN. Why, as men do a-land—the great ones eat up the little ones. *same, II:1:27*

498.232

MOWBRAY. The purest treasure mortal times afford
Is spotless reputation; that away,
Men are but gilded loam or painted clay. *King Richard the Second, I:1:177*

498.233

GAUNT. Things sweet to taste prove in digestion sour. *same, I:3:236*

498.234

GAUNT. Teach thy necessity to reason thus:
There is no virtue like necessity.
same, I:3:275

498.235

GAUNT. This royal throne of kings, this
sceptred isle,
This earth of majesty, this seat of Mars,
This other Eden, demi-paradise,
This fortress built by Nature for herself
Against infection and the hand of war,
This happy breed of men, this little world,
This precious stone set in the silver sea,
Which serves it in the office of a wall,
Or as a moat defensive to a house,
Against the envy of less happier lands;
This blessed plot, this earth, this realm, this
England,
This nurse, this teeming womb of royal
kings,
Fear'd by their breed, and famous by their
birth.
same, II:1:40

498.236

RICHARD. Not all the water in the rough
rude sea
Can wash the balm from an anointed king;
The breath of worldly men cannot depose
The deputy elected by the Lord.
same, III:2:54

498.237

RICHARD. For God's sake let us sit upon the
ground
And tell sad stories of the death of kings:
How some have been depos'd, some slain in
war,
Some haunted by the ghosts they have
depos'd,
Some poison'd by their wives, some sleeping
kill'd,
All murder'd—for within the hollow crown
That rounds the mortal temples of a king
Keeps Death his court.
same, III:2:155

498.238

RICHARD. How sour sweet music is
When time is broke and no proportion kept!
So is it in the music of men's lives.
same, V:5:42

498.239

GLOUCESTER. Now is the winter of our
discontent
Made glorious summer by this sun of York.
King Richard III, I:1:1

498.240

CLARENCE. O Lord, methought what pain it
was to drown,
What dreadful noise of waters in my ears,
What sights of ugly death within my eyes!
same, I:4:21

498.241

RICHARD III. A horse! a horse ! my kingdom for a horse.
same, V:4:7

498.242

JULIET. O Romeo, Romeo! wherefore art
thou Romeo?
Romeo and Juliet, II:2:33

498.243

JULIET. What's in a name? That which we
call a rose
By any other name would smell as sweet.
same, II:2:43

498.244

JULIET. O, swear not by the moon, th'
inconstant moon,
That monthly changes in her circled orb,
Lest that thy love prove likewise variable.
same, II:2:109

498.245

JULIET. Good night, good night! Parting is
such sweet sorrow
That I shall say good night till it be morrow.
same, II:2:185

498.246

FRIAR LAWRENCE. Wisely and slow; they
stumble that run fast.
same, II:3:94

498.247

FRIAR LAWRENCE. Therefore love modera-
tely: long love doth so;
Too swift arrives as tardy as too slow.
same, II:6:14

498.248

MERCUTIO. A plague o' both your houses!
They have made worms' meat of me.
same, III:1:103

498.249

CAPULET. Thank me no thankings, nor proud
me no prouds.
same, III:5:152

498.250

SERVINGMAN. 'Tis an ill cook that cannot
lick his own fingers.
same, IV:2:6

498.251

TRANIO. No profit grows where is no
pleasure ta'en;
In brief, sir, study what you most affect.
The Taming of the Shrew, I:1:39

498.252

PETRUCHIO. This is a way to kill a wife with
kindness.
same, IV:1:192

498.253

PETRUCHIO. Our purses shall be proud, our
garments poor;
For 'tis the mind that makes the body rich;
And as the sun breaks through the darkest
clouds,
So honour peereth in the meanest habit.
same, IV:3:167

498.254

ARIEL. Full fathom five thy father lies;

Of his bones are coral made;
Those are pearls that were his eyes;
Nothing of him that doth fade
But doth suffer a sea-change
Into something rich and strange.

The Tempest, I:2:396

498.255

TRINCULO. When they will not give a doit
to relieve a lame beggar, they will lay out ten
to see a dead Indian.   *same, II:2:29*

498.256

TRINCULO. Misery acquaints a man with
strange bedfellows.   *same, II:2:38*

498.257

STEPHANO. He that dies pays all debts.

same, III:2:126

498.258

PROSPERO. Our revels now are ended. These
our actors,
As I foretold you, were all spirits, and
Are melted into air, into thin air;
And, like the baseless fabric of this vision,
The cloud-capp'd towers, the gorgeous
palaces,
The solemn temples, the great globe itself,
Yea, all which it inherit, shall dissolve,
And, like this insubstantial pageant faded,
Leave not a rack behind. We are such stuff
As dreams are made on; and our little life
Is rounded with a sleep.   *same, IV:1:148*

498.259

PROSPERO. I'll break my staff,
Bury it certain fathoms in the earth,
And deeper than did ever plummet sound
I'll drown my book.   *same, V:1:54*

498.260

MIRANDA. How beauteous mankind is! O
brave new world
That has such people in't!   *same, V:1:183*

498.261

CRESSIDA. That she belov'd knows nought
that knows not this:
Men prize the thing ungain'd more than it is.

Troilus and Cressida, I:2:278

498.262

ULYSSES. O, when degree is shak'd,
Which is the ladder of all high designs,
The enterprise is sick!   *same, I:3:101*

498.263

CRESSIDA. To be wise and love
Exceeds man's might.   *same, III:2:152*

498.264

ULYSSES. Time hath, my lord, a wallet at his
back,
Wherein he puts alms for oblivion,
A great-siz'd monster of ingratitudes.

same, III:3:145

498.265

THERSITES. Lechery, lechery! Still wars and
lechery! Nothing else holds fashion.

same, V:2:193

498.266

ORSINO. If music be the food of love, play
on,
Give me excess of it, that, surfeiting,
The appetite may sicken and so die.

Twelfth Night, I:1:1

498.267

SIR TOBY. Is it a world to hide virtues in?

same, I:3:123

498.268

FESTE. Many a good hanging prevents a bad
marriage.   *same, I:5:18*

498.269

SIR TOBY. Not to be abed after midnight is
to be up betimes.   *same, II:3:1*

498.270

FESTE. What is love? 'Tis not hereafter;
Present mirth hath present laughter;
What's to come is still unsure.
In delay there lies no plenty,
Then come kiss me, sweet and twenty;
Youth's a stuff will not endure.

same, II:3:46

498.271

SIR TOBY. Dost thou think, because thou art
virtuous, there shall be no more cakes and
ale?   *same, II:3:109*

498.272

VIOLA. She never told her love,
But let concealment, like a worm i' th' bud,
Feed on her damask cheek. She pin'd in
thought;
And with a green and yellow melancholy
She sat like Patience on a monument,
Smiling at grief.   *same, II:4:109*

498.273

MALVOLIO. Some are born great, some
achieve greatness, and some have greatness
thrust upon 'em.   *same, II:5:129*

498.274

OLIVIA. Love sought is good, but given
unsought is better.   *same, III:1:153*

498.275

FABIAN. If this were play'd upon a stage
now, I could condemn it as an improbable
fiction.   *same, III:4:121*

498.276

FABIAN. Still you keep o' th' windy side of
the law.   *same, III:4:156*

498.277

VIOLA. I hate ingratitude more in a man
Than lying, vainness, babbling drunkenness,
Or any taint of vice whose strong corruption
Inhabits our frail blood.   *same, III:4:338*

498.278

VALENTINE. Home-keeping youth have ever homely wits.   *The Two Gentlemen of Verona, I:1:2*

498.279

LUCETTA. I have no other but a woman's reason:
I think him so, because I think him so.
                            same, I:2:23

498.280

Who is Silvia? What is she,
That all our swains commend her?
Holy, fair, and wise is she.   *same, IV:2:38*

498.281

PAULINA. What's gone and what's past help
Should be past grief.   *The Winter's Tale, III:2:219*

498.282

Exit, pursued by a bear.   *same, Stage Direction, II:3:58*

498.283

SHEPHERD. I would there were no age between ten and three and twenty, or that youth would sleep out the rest; for there is nothing in the between but getting wenches with child, wronging the ancientry, stealing, fighting.   *same, III:3:59*

498.284

AUTOLYCUS. A snapper-up of unconsidered trifles.   *same, IV:3:26*

498.285

AUTOLYCUS. Though I am not naturally honest, I am so sometimes by chance.
                            same, IV:3:734

498.286

CLOWN. Though authority be a stubborn bear, yet he is oft led by the nose with gold.
                            same, IV:3:835

498.287

From fairest creatures we desire increase,
That thereby beauty's rose might never die.
                            Sonnet 1

498.288

Shall I compare thee to a summer's day?
Thou art more lovely and more temperate.
Rough winds do shake the darling buds of May,
And summer's lease hath all too short a date.   *Sonnet 18*

498.289

A woman's face, with Nature's own hand painted,
Hast thou, the Master Mistress of my passion.   *Sonnet 20*

498.290

When in disgrace with fortune and men's eyes
I all alone beweep my outcast state,
And trouble deaf heaven with my bootless cries,
And look upon myself, and curse my fate,
Wishing me like to one more rich in hope
Featur'd like him, like him with friends possess'd,
Desiring this man's art, and that man's scope,
With what I most enjoy contented least.
                            Sonnet 29

498.291

When to the sessions of sweet silent thought
I summon up remembrance of things past,
I sigh the lack of many a thing I sought,
And with old woes new wail my dear time's waste.   *Sonnet 30*

498.292

Not marble, nor the gilded monuments
Of princes, shall outlive this powerful rhyme.
                            Sonnet 55

498.293

Like as the waves make towards the pebbled shore,
So do our minutes hasten to their end.
                            Sonnet 60

498.294

That time of year thou mayst in me behold
When yellow leaves, or none, or few, do hang
Upon those boughs which shake against the cold,
Bare ruin'd choirs, where late the sweet birds sang.   *Sonnet 73*

498.295

Farewell! thou art too dear for my possessing,
And like enough thou know'st thy estimate:
The charter of thy worth gives thee releasing;
My bonds in thee are all determinate.
                            Sonnet 87

498.296

For sweetest things turn sourest by their deeds:
Lilies that fester smell far worse than weeds.
                            Sonnet 94

498.297

When in the chronicle of wasted time
I see descriptions of the fairest wights.
                            Sonnet 106

498.298

Let me not to the marriage of true minds
Admit impediments. Love is not love
Which alters when it alteration finds,
Or bends with the remover to remove.
O, no! it is an ever-fixed mark,
That looks on tempests and is never shaken.
                            Sonnet 116

Love alters not with his brief hours and weeks,

But bears it out even to the edge of doom.
If this be error, and upon me prov'd,
I never writ, nor no man ever lov'd.

same

498.299
Th' expense of spirit in a waste of shame
Is lust in action; and till action, lust
Is perjur'd, murd'rous, bloody, full of blame,
Savage, extreme, rude, cruel, not to trust;
Enjoy'd no sooner but despised straight.

Sonnet 129

498.300
My mistress' eyes are nothing like the sun;
Coral is far more red than her lips' red.

Sonnet 130

498.301
And yet, by heaven, I think my love as rare
As any she belied with false compare.

Sonnet 130

498.302
Two loves I have, of comfort and despair,
Which like two spirits do suggest me still;
The better angel is a man right fair,
The worser spirit a woman colour'd ill.

Sonnet 144

498.303
Crabbed age and youth cannot live together:
Youth is full of pleasure, age is full of care;
Youth like summer morn, age like winter
   weather;
Youth like summer brave, age like winter
   bare.   *The Passionate Pilgrim, 12*

498.304
Beauty itself doth of itself persuade
The eyes of men without an orator.

The Rape of Lucrece, I:29

499 Shaw, George Bernard (1856-1950),
Irish dramatist and critic.

499.1
All great truths begin as blasphemies.

Annajanska

499.2
One man that has a mind and knows it, can
always beat ten men who havnt and dont.

The Apple Cart, Act 1

499.3
I never resist temptation, because I have
found that things that are bad for me do not
tempt me.   *same, Act 2*

499.4
You can always tell an old soldier by the
inside of his holsters and cartridge boxes.
The young ones carry pistols and cartridges:
the old ones, grub.   *Arms and the Man, Act
1*

499.5

My father is a very hospitable man: he keeps
six hotels.   *same, Act 1*

499.6
I never apologize.   *same, Act 3*

499.7
You're not a man, you're a machine.

same, Act 3

499.8
Every genuine scientist must be ...a
metaphysician. *Back to Methuselah, Preface*

499.9
Well, as the serpent used to say, why not?

same, Act 2

499.10
When a stupid man is doing something he is
ashamed of, he always declares that it is his
duty.   *Caesar and Cleopatra, Act 3*

499.11
We have no more right to consume happiness
without producing it than to consume wealth
without producing it.   *Candida, Act 1*

499.12
Do you think that the things people make
fools of themselves about are any less real
and true than the things they behave sensibly
about?   *same, Act 1*

499.13
I'm only a beer teetotaller, not a champagne
teetotaller.   *same, Act 3*

499.14
Man can climb to the highest summits, but
he cannot dwell there long.   *same, Act 3*

499.15
The worst sin towards our fellow creatures is
not to hate them, but to be indifferent to
them.   *The Devil's Disciple, Act 2*

499.16
I never expect a soldier to think.   *same, Act
3*

499.17
All professions are conspiracies against the
laity.   *The Doctor's Dilemma, Act 1*

499.18
It's easier to replace a dead man than a good
picture.   *same, Act 2*

499.19
Morality consists in suspecting other people
of not being legally married.   *same, Act 3*

499.20
I don't believe in morality. I'm a disciple of
Bernard Shaw.   *same, Act 4*

499.21
You don't expect me to know what to say
about a play when I don't know who the
author is, do you?   *Fanny's First Play,
Epilogue*

499.22
What God hath joined together no man shall

ever put asunder: God will take care of that.
Getting Married

499.23
I cannot bear men and women.
Heartbreak House, Act 2

499.24
Go anywhere in England, where there are natural, wholesome, contented, and really nice English people; and what do you always find? That the stables are the real centre of the household. *same, Act 3*

499.25
Do you think the laws of God will be suspended in favour of England because you were born in it? *same, Act 3*

499.26
An Irishman's heart is nothing but his imagination. *John Bull's Other Island, Act 1*

499.27
What really flatters a man is that you think him worth flattering. *same, Act 4*

499.28
There are only two qualities in the world: efficiency and inefficiency; and only two sorts of people: the efficient and the inefficient. *same, Act 4*

499.29
We must be thoroughly democratic and patronize everybody without distinction of class. *same, Act 4*

499.30
The greatest of evils and the worst of crimes is poverty. *Major Barbara, Preface*

499.31
He is always breaking the law. He broke the law when he was born: his parents were not married. *same, Act 1*

499.32
I am a Millionaire. That is my religion.
same, Act 1

499.33
I cant talk religion to a man with bodily hunger in his eyes. *same, Act 1*

499.34
Nothing is ever done in this world until men are prepared to kill one another if it is not done. *same, Act 3*

499.35
Our political experiment of democracy, the last refuge of cheap misgovernment.
Man and Superman, Epistle Dedicatory

499.36
The more things a man is ashamed of, the more respectable he is. *same, Act 1*

499.37
A lifetime of happiness: no man alive could bear it: it would be hell on earth.
same, Act 1

499.38
The true artist will let his wife starve, his children go barefoot, his mother drudge for his living at seventy, sooner than work at anything but his art. *same, Act 1*

499.39
Is the devil to have all the passions as well as all the good tunes? *same, Act 1*

499.40
An Englishman thinks he is moral when he is only uncomfortable. *same, Act 3*

499.41
What is virtue but the Trade Unionism of the married? *same, Act 3*

499.42
I am a gentleman: I live by robbing the poor. *same, Act 3*

499.43
If you go to Heaven without being naturally qualified for it, you will not enjoy yourself there. *same, Act 3*

499.44
In the arts of peace Man is a bungler.
same, Act 3

499.45
There are two tragedies in life. One is not to get your heart's desire. The other is to get it.
same, Act 4

499.46
Do not do unto others as you would they should do unto you. Their tastes may not be the same. *same, Maxims for Revolutionists*

499.47
Beware of the man whose god is in the skies.
same

499.48
The golden rule is that there are no golden rules. *same*

499.49
Democracy substitutes election by the incompetent many for appointment by the corrupt few. *same*

499.50
Liberty means responsibility. That is why most men dread it. *same*

499.51
He who can, does. He who cannot, teaches.
same

499.52
Marriage is popular because it combines the maximum of temptation with the maximum of opportunity. *same*

499.53
The reasonable man adapts himself to the world: the unreasonable one persists in trying to adapt the world to himself. Therefore all progress depends on the unreasonable man
same

499.54
The man who listens to Reason is lost: Reason enslaves all whose minds are not strong enough to master her.   *same*

499.55
Home is the girl's prison and the woman's workhouse.   *same*

499.56
Every man over forty is a scoundrel.
      same

499.57
In heaven an angel is nobody in particular.
      same

499.58
Decency is Indecency's Conspiracy of Silence.   *same*

499.59
There is nothing so bad or so good that you will not find Englishmen doing it; but you will never find an Englishman in the wrong.
      The Man of Destiny

499.60
There is no satisfaction in hanging a man who does not object to it.   *same*

499.61
There is only one universal passion: fear.
      same

499.62
An English army led by an Irish general: that might be a match for a French army led by an Italian general.   *same*

499.63
The fickleness of the women I love is only equalled by the infernal constancy of the women who love me.   *The Philanderer, Act 2*

499.64
It is clear that a novel cannot be too bad to be worth publishing....It certainly is possible for a novel to be too good to be worth publishing.   *Plays Pleasant and Unpleasant, 1, Preface*

499.65
There is only one religion, though there are a hundred versions of it.   *same, 2, Preface*

499.66
It is impossible for an Englishman to open his mouth, without making some other Englishman despise him.
      Pygmalion, Preface

499.67
ELIZA DOOLITTLE. I dont want to talk grammar. I want to talk like a lady.
      same, Act 2

499.68
Not bloody likely.   *same, Act 2*

499.69
Assassination is the extreme form of censorship.   *The Rejected Statement, Act 1*

499.70
We were not fairly beaten, my lord. No Englishman is ever fairly beaten.
      St. Joan, Sc. 4

499.71
Must then a Christ perish in torment in every age to save those that have no imagination?   *same, Epilogue*

499.72
No woman can shake off her mother. There should be no mothers, only women.
      Too True to be Good

499.73
We dont bother much about dress and manners in England, because as a nation we don't dress well and we've no manners.
      You Never Can Tell, Act 1

499.74
My speciality is being right when other people are wrong.   *same, Act 2*

499.75
Money is indeed the most important thing in the world; and all sound and successful personal and national morality should have this fact for its basis.   *The Irrational Knot, Preface*

499.76
A man who has no office to go to—I don't care who he is—is a trial of which you can have no conception.   *same, Ch. 18*

499.77
Martyrdom is the only way in which a man can become famous without ability.
      Fabian Essays

499.78
People must not be forced to adopt me as their favourite author, even for their own good.   *Letter to Alma Murray, 20 Oct 1886*

499.79
We are a nation of governesses.
      New Statesman, 12 Apr 1913

499.80
Very few books of any nationality are worth reading.   *Table-Talk of George Bernard Shaw*

499.81
A coquette is a woman who rouses passions she has no intentions of gratifying.
      Attributed

499.82
If all economists were laid end to end, they would not reach a conclusion.   *Attributed*

500 Shelley, Percy Bysshe (1792-1822), English poet.

500.1

He has outsoared the shadow of our night;
Envy and calumny and hate and pain,
And that unrest which men miscall delight,
Can touch him not and torture not again;
From the contagion of the world's slow stain
He is secure, and now can never mourn
A heart grown cold, a head grown gray in
vain.   *Adonais, 352*

500.2

The One remains, the many change and
pass;
Heaven's light forever shines, Earth's
shadows fly;
Life, like a dome of many-coloured glass,
Stains the white radiance of Eternity.
                              same, 460

500.3

I never was attached to that great sect,
Whose doctrine is, that each one should
select
Out of the crowd a mistress or a friend,
And all the rest, though fair and wise,
commend
To cold oblivion.   *Epipsychidion, 149*

500.4

Good-night? ah! no; the hour is ill
Which severs those it should unite;
Let us remain together still,
Then it will be good night.   *Good-Night*

500.5

Most wretched men
Are cradled into poetry by wrong:
They learn in suffering what they teach in
song.   *Julian and Maddalo, 543*

500.6

I met Murder on the way—
He had a mask like Castlereagh.
                    The Mask of Anarchy, 5

500.7

O Wild West Wind, thou breath of Autumn's
being,
Thou, from whose unseen presence the leaves
dead
Are driven, like ghosts from an enchanter
fleeing,
Yellow, and black, and pale, and hectic red,
Pestilence-stricken multitudes.   *Ode to the*
                              West Wind, 1

500.8

Oh, lift me as a wave, a leaf, a cloud!
I fall upon the thorns of life! I bleed!
A heavy weight of hours has chained and
bowed
One too like thee: tameless, and swift, and
proud.   *same, 53*

500.9

If Winter comes, can Spring be far behind?
                              same, 66

500.10

'My name is Ozymandias, king of kings:
Look on my works, ye Mighty, and despair!'
Nothing beside remains. Round the decay
Of that colossal wreck, boundless and bare
The lone and level sands stretch far away.
                              Ozymandias

500.11

Hell is a city much like London—
A populous and a smoky city.   *Peter Bell*
                    the Third, Part 3, Hell, 1

500.12

Familiar acts are beautiful through love.
              Prometheus Unbound, IV:403

500.13

Hail to thee, blithe Spirit!
Bird thou never wert,
That from Heaven, or near it,
Pourest thy full heart
In profuse strains of unpremeditated art.
                              To a Skylark

500.14

Rarely, rarely, comest thou,
Spirit of Delight!   *Song, Rarely, Rarely,*
                              Comest Thou

500.15

Poetry lifts the veil from the hidden beauty
of the world, and makes familiar objects be
as if they were not familiar.   *A Defence of*
                              Poetry

500.16

Poets are the unacknowledged legislators of
the world.   *same*

501 Sheridan, Philip Henry (1831-1888),
American soldier.

501.1

The only good Indian is a dead Indian.
                              Attributed

502   Sheridan,   Richard   Brinsley
(1751-1816), English dramatist.

502.1

TILBURINA. An oyster may be crossed in
love.   *The Critic, III:1*

502.2

MRS MALAPROP. Thought does not become
a young woman.   *The Rivals, I:2*

502.3

MRS MALAPROP. Illiterate him, I say, quite
from your memory.   *same, I:2*

502.4

MRS MALAPROP. 'Tis safest in matrimony to
begin with a little aversion.   *same, I:2*

502.5

MRS MALAPROP. A supercilious knowledge in accounts. *same, I:2*

502.6

MRS MALAPROP. If I reprehend any thing in this world it is the use of my oracular tongue and a nice derangement of epitaphs.
same, III:3

502.7

MRS MALAPROP. As headstrong as an allegory on the banks of the Nile. *same*

502.8

ACRES. Too civil by half. *same, III:4*

502.9

SIR PETER TEAZLE. What is principle against the flattery of a handsome, lively young fellow? *same, IV:2*

502.10

[*Of Mr. Dundas*] The Right Honourable gentleman is indebted to his memory for his jests, and to his imagination for his facts.
Reply in the House of Commons

503   Sherman, William   Tecumseh (1820-1891), American general.

503.1

There is many a boy here today who looks on war as all glory, but, boys, it is all hell.
Speech, 1880

504 Sibelius, Jean (1865-1957), Finnish composer.

504.1

Pay no attention to what the critics say; no statue has ever been put up to a critic.
Attributed

505 Sidney, Algernon (1622-1683), English politician.

505.1

Liars ought to have good memories.
Discourses Concerning Government, Ch. 2, 15

506 Sidney, Sir Philip (1554-1586), English poet.

506.1

Biting my truant pen, beating myself for spite:
'Fool!' said my Muse to me, 'look in thy heart and write.' *Astrophel and Stella, Sonnet 1*

506.2

With a tale forsooth he cometh unto you, with a tale which holdeth children from play, and old men from the chimney corner.
The Defence of Poesy

506.3

[*On giving water to a dying soldier*] Thy

necessity is greater than mine. *After the battle of Zutphen, 1586*

507 Simpson, Norman Frederick (b. 1919), English dramatist.

507.1

I eat merely to put food out of my mind.
The Hole

507.2

It'll do him good to lie there unconscious for a bit. Give his brain a rest.
One Way Pendulum, 1

507.3

You should have thought of all this before you were born. *same*

507.4

We've got nothing against apes, Sylvia. As such. *same*

508   Sitwell, Sir Osbert (1892-1969), English writer and poet.

508.1

The British Bourgeoisie
Is not born,
And does not die,
But, if it is ill,
It has a frightened look in its eyes.
At the House of Mrs Kinfoot

509   Smedley, Francis   Edward (1818-1864), English novelist.

509.1

You are looking as fresh as paint.
Frank Fairleigh, Ch. 41

510 Smith, Adam (1723-1790), Scottish economist.

510.1

No society can surely be flourishing and happy, of which the far greater part of the members are poor and miserable.
The Wealth of Nations, I:8

510.2

To found a great empire for the sole purpose of raising up a people of customers may at first sight appear a project fit only for a nation of shopkeepers. It is, however, a project altogether unfit for a nation of shopkeepers; but extremely fit for a nation that is governed by shopkeepers.
same, II:4

511 Smith, Logan Pearsall (1865-1946), American writer.

511.1

The indefatigable pursuit of an unobtainable perfection, even though it consist in nothing more than in the pounding of an old piano, is what alone gives a meaning to our life on this unavailing star. *Afterthoughts*

511.2
Happiness is a wine of the rarest vintage, and seems insipid to a vulgar taste. *same*

511.3
There are few sorrows, however poignant, in which a good income is of no avail. *same*

511.4
The wretchedness of being rich is that you live with rich people. *same*

511.5
People say that Life is the thing, but I prefer Reading. *same*

511.6
How awful to reflect that what people say of us is true! *All Trivia*

511.7
Solvency is entirely a matter of temperament and not of income. *same*

511.8
There is more felicity on the far side of baldness than young men can possibly imagine. *same*

511.9
We need two kinds of acquaintances, one to complain to, while we boast to the others.
same

511.10
Thank heavens the sun has gone in, and I don't have to go out and enjoy it.
same, last words

511.11
A friend who loved perfection would be the perfect friend, did not that love shut his door on me. *Great Turnstile (edited by V. S. Pritchett)*

512 Smith, Sydney (1771-1845), English journalist, clergyman and wit.

512.1
Poverty is no disgrace to a man, but it is confoundedly inconvenient. *His Wit and Wisdom*

512.2
It requires a surgical operation to get a joke well into a Scotch understanding. Their only idea of wit...is laughing immoderately at stated intervals. *Lady Holland, Memoir, I:2*

512.3
[*When it was proposed to put a wooden pavement around St. Paul's*] Let the Dean and Canons lay their heads together and the thing will be done. *same*

512.4
Death must be distinguished from dying, with which it is often confused. *same*

512.5
No furniture so charming as books. *same*

512.6
Praise is the best diet for us, after all.
same

512.7
I never read a book before reviewing it; it prejudices a man so. *The Smith of Smiths (H. Pearson), Ch. 3*

512.8
I am convinced digestion is the great secret of life. *Letter to Arthur Kinglake, 30 Sept 1837*

512.9
I have no relish for the country; it is a kind of healthy grave. *Letter to Miss G. Harcourt, 1838*

513 Smollett, Tobias George (1721-1771), English novelist.

513.1
Some folk are wise, and some are otherwise.
Roderick Random, Ch. 6

513.2
I consider the world as made for me, not me for the world. It is my maxim therefore to enjoy it while I can, and let futurity shift for itself. *same, Ch. 45*

513.3
True patriotism is of no party.
Sir Launcelote Greavers

514 Snagge, John (b. 1904), English broadcaster.

514.1
I can't see who's ahead—it's either Oxford or Cambridge. *BBC Commentary on Boat Race, 1949*

515 Socrates, (469-399 B.C.), Athenian philosopher.

515.1
Having the fewest wants, I am nearest to the gods. *Diogenes Laertius, II:27*

515.2
There is only one good, knowledge, and one evil, ignorance. *same, II:31*

515.3
I know nothing except the fact of my ignorance. *same, II:32*

515.4
Bad men live that they may eat and drink, whereas good men eat and drink that they may live. *How a Young Man Ought to Hear Poems (Plutarch), 4*

515.5
I am not an Athenian or a Greek, but a

citizen of the world.
Of Banishment (Plutarch)

516 Solon, (640?-558? B.C.), Athenian lawgiver.
516.1
Call no man happy until he dies; he is at best fortunate. *Histories (Herodotus), I:32*

517 Soule, John Babsone Lane (1815-1891), American editor and writer.
517.1
Go west, young man. *Article in the Terre Haute Express, Indiana, 1851*

518 Spencer, Herbert (1820-1903), English philosopher.
518.1
Time: that which man is always trying to kill, but which ends in killing him.
Definitions
518.2
Science is organized knowledge.
Education, Ch. 2
518.3
The ultimate result of shielding men from the effects of folly is to fill the world with fools. *Essays, 'State Tamperings with Money Banks'*
518.4
Survival of the fittest. *Principles of Biology*
518.5
We all decry prejudice, yet are all prejudiced.
Social Statics, 2
518.6
Education has for its object the formation of character. *same, 2*
518.7
Hero-worship is strongest where there is least regard for human freedom. *same, 3*
518.8
Opinion is ultimately determined by the feelings, and not by the intellect. *same, 4*

519 Spenser, Edmund (1552?-1599), English poet.
519.1
Sleep after toil, port after stormy seas,
Ease after war, death after life does greatly please. *The Fairie Queen, I:9:40*
519.2
And as she looked about, she did behold,
How over that same door was likewise writ,
Be bold, be bold, and everywhere Be bold.
same, III:11:54
519.3
The gentle mind by gentle deeds is known,

For a man by nothing is so well bewrayed
As by his manners. *same, VI:3:1*
519.4
Sweet Thames! run softly, till I end my Song.
Prothalamion, 18
519.5
So now they have made our English tongue a gallimaufry or hodgepodge of all other speeches. *The Shepherd's Calendar, Letter to Gabriel Harvey*

520 Spooner, William Archibald (1844-1930), English clergyman and academic.
520.1
Sir, you have tasted two whole worms; you have hissed all my mystery lectures and have been caught fighting a liar in the quad; you will leave by the next town drain.
Attributed
520.2
Let us drink to the queer old Dean.
Attributed
520.3
I remember your name perfectly, but I just can't think of your face. *Attributed*

521 Squire, Sir John Collings (1884-1958), English writer.
521.1
But I'm not so think as you drunk I am.
Ballade of Soporific Absorption

522 Stanley, Sir Henry Morton (1841-1904), British explorer and journalist.
522.1
[*On meeting Livingstone*] Dr Livingstone, I presume? *Ujiji, Central Africa, 10 Nov 1871*

523 Staël, Madame de (1766-1817), French writer.
523.1
To know all makes one tolerant. *Corinne*
523.2
Love is the whole history of a woman's life, it is but an episode in a man's.
De l'Influence des Passions

524 Steele, Sir Richard (1672-1729), English essayist, dramatist and politician.
524.1
Among all the diseases of the mind there is not one more epidemical or more pernicious than the love of flattery.
The Spectator, No. 238
524.2

There are so few who can grow old with a good grace. *same, No. 263*

524.3
Reading is to the mind what exercise is to the body. *The Tatler, No. 147*

525 Stein, Gertrude (1874-1946), American writer.
525.1
In the United States there is more space where nobody is than where anybody is. That is what makes America what it is.
The Geographical History of America
525.2
Rose is a rose is a rose is a rose.
Sacred Emily
525.3
Just before she died she asked, 'What *is* the answer?' No answer came. She laughed and said, 'In that case what is the question?' Then she died. *G.S., a Biography of her Work (Duncan Sutherland), final words*

526 Stephen, James Kenneth (1859-1892), English writer of light verse.
526.1
Two voices are there: one is of the deep...
And one is of an old half-witted sheep
Which bleats articulate monotony
And indicates that two and one are three.
Lapsus Calami, Sonnet (Parody of Wordsworth)
526.2
When the Rudyards cease from kipling
And the Haggards ride no more. *same, To R.K.*

527 Sterne, Laurence (1713-1768), English novelist.
527.1
As an Englishman does not travel to see Englishmen, I retired to my room.
A Sentimental Journey, Preface
527.2
There are worse occupations in the world than feeling a woman's pulse.
same, The Pulse
527.3
So that when I stretched out my hand, I caught hold of the fille de chambre's—.
same, Last words
527.4
'L—d!' said my mother, 'what is all this story about?'
'A Cock and a Bull, ' said Yorick.
Tristram Shandy, III:11

528 Stevens, Wallace (1879-1955), American poet.
528.1
The only emperor is the emperor of ice-cream. *The Emperor of Ice-Cream*
528.2
Poetry is the supreme fiction, madame.
A High-toned Old Christian Woman

529 Stevenson, Robert Louis (1850-1894), Scottish writer.
529.1
Even if we take matrimony at its lowest, even if we regard it as no more than a sort of friendship recognised by the police.
Virginibus Puerisque, Part 1
529.2
Extreme busyness, whether at school or college, kirk or market, is a symptom of deficient vitality. *same, An Apology for Idlers*
529.3
There is no duty we so much underrate as the duty of being happy. *same*
529.4
To travel hopefully is a better thing than to arrive, and the true success is to labour.
same, El Dorado

530 Stravinsky, Igor (1882-1971), Russian composer.
530.1
Nothing is likely about masterpieces, least of all whether there will be any.
Conversations with Igor Stravinsky (Robert Craft)
530.2
My music is best understood by children and animals. *Observer, 'Sayings of the Week', 8 Oct 1961*

531 Suckling, Sir John (1609-1642), English poet.
531.1
Out upon it, I have loved
Three whole days together;
And am like to love three more,
If it prove fair weather. *A Poem with the Answer*

532 Suetonius, (Gaius Suetonius Tranquillus) (75?-150? A.D.), Roman biographer and antiquarian.
532.1
Festina lente.
Hasten slowly. *The Twelve Caesars, Augustus*

532.2
Hail, Emperor, those about to die salute you. *same, Claudius*

533 Surtees, Robert Smith (1803-1864), English sporting writer.
533.1
The only infallible rule we know is, that the man who is always talking about being a gentleman never is one. *Ask Mamma, Ch. 1*

533.2
He was a gentleman who was generally spoken of as having nothing a-year, paid quarterly. *Mr. Sponge's Sporting Tour, Ch. 24*

534 Svevo, Italo (Ettore Schmitz) (1861-1928), Italian novelist.
534.1
There are three things I always forget. Names, faces, and—the third I can't remember. *Attributed*

535 Swift, Jonathan (1667-1745), English satirist.
535.1
The two noblest of things, which are sweetness and light. *The Battle of the Books, Preface*

535.2
'Tis an old maxim in the schools,
That flattery's the food of fools;
Yet now and then your men of wit
Will condescend to take a bit. *Cadenus and Vanessa*

535.3
Yet malice never was his aim;
He lash'd the vice, but spared the name;
No individual could resent,
Where thousands equally were meant.
On the Death of Dr Swift, 512

535.4
Big-endians and small -endians.
Gulliver's Travels, Voyage to Lilliput, Ch. 4

535.5
Whoever could make two ears of corn or two blades of grass to grow upon a spot of ground where only one grew before would deserve better of mankind and do more essential service to his country than the whole race of politicians put together.
same, Voyage to Brobdingnag, Ch. 7

535.6
Proper words in proper places make the true definition of a style. *Letter to a young clergyman, 9 Jan 1720*

535.7
So, naturalists observe, a flea
Hath smaller fleas that on him prey,
And these have smaller fleas to bite 'em,
And so proceed *ad infinitum*. *On Poetry, 337*

535.8
The sight of you is good for sore eyes. *Polite Conversation, 1*

535.9
She's no chicken: she's on the wrong side of thirty, if she be a day. *same, 1*

535.10
She wears her clothes, as if they were thrown on her with a pitchfork. *same, 1*

535.11
He was a bold man that first eat an oyster. *same, 2*

535.12
That's as well said, as if I had said it myself. *same, 2*

535.13
She has more goodness in her little finger, than he has in his whole body. *same, 2*

535.14
Lord, I wonder what fool it was that first invented kissing! *same, 2*

535.15
I'll give you leave to call me anything, if you don't call me spade. *same, 2*

535.16
We have just enough religion to make us hate, but not enough to make us love one another. *Thoughts on Various Subjects*

535.17
Few are qualified to shine in company; but it is in most men's power to be agreeable. *same*

535.18
A nice man is a man of nasty ideas. *same*
535.19
[*Of 'A Tale of a Tub'*] Good God! What a genius I had when I wrote that book. *Attributed*

T

536 Talleyrand, Charles Maurice de (1754-1838), French statesman.
536.1
[*Of Napoleon's defeat at Borodino*] It is the

beginning of the end.   *Remark to Napoleon, 1813*

536.2
They have learnt nothing, and forgotten nothing.   *Attributed*

536.3
Speech was given to man to disguise his thoughts.   *Attributed*

536.4
Not too much zeal.   *Attributed*

536.5
War is much too serious a thing to be left to military men.   *Attributed*

537   Tarkington, Booth (1869-1946), American writer.

537.1
There are two things that will be believed of any man whatsoever, and one of them is that he has taken to drink.   *Penrod, Ch. 10*

538   Taylor, Alan John Percivale (b. 1906), English historian.

538.1
A racing tipster who only reached Hitler's level of accuracy would not do well for his clients.   *The Origins of the Second World War, Ch. 7*

538.2
They say that men become attached even to Widnes.   *Observer, 15 Sept 1963*

539   Tennyson, Alfred, 1st Baron (1809-1892), English poet.

539.1
For men may come and men may go
But I go on for ever.   *The Brook, 33*

539.2
Half a league, half a league,
Half a league onward,
All in the valley of Death
Rode the six hundred.   *The Charge of the Light Brigade*

539.3
Their's not to make reply,
Their's not to reason why,
Their's but to do and die.   *same*

539.4
Sunset and evening star,
And one clear call for me!
And may there be no moaning of the bar
When I put out to sea.   *Crossing the Bar*

539.5
God made the woman for the man,
And for the good and increase of the world.   *Edwin Morris, 43*

539.6
His honour rooted in dishonour stood,

And faith unfaithful kept him falsely true.   *Idylls of the King, Lancelot and Elaine, 871*

539.7
He makes no friend who never made a foe.   *same, 1082*

539.8
And slowly answer'd Arthur from the barge:
'The old order changeth, yielding place to new,
And God fulfils himself in many ways.'   *same, The Passing of Arthur, 407*

539.9
Our little systems have their day;
They have their day and cease to be.   *In Memoriam A.H.H., Prologue*

539.10
For words, like Nature, half reveal
And half conceal the Soul within.   *same, 5*

539.11
I hold it true, whate'er befall;
I feel it, when I sorrow most;
'Tis better to have loved and lost
Than never to have loved at all.   *same, 27*

539.12
Are God and Nature then at strife
That Nature lends such evil dreams?
So careful of the type she seems,
So careless of the single life.   *same, 55*

539.13
So many worlds, so much to do,
So little done, such things to be.   *same, 73*

539.14
One God, one law, one element,
And one far-off divine event,
To which the whole creation moves.   *same, 131*

539.15
Kind hearts are more than coronets,
And simple faith than Norman blood.   *Lady Clara Vere de Vere*

539.16
'The curse is come upon me, ' cried
The Lady of Shalott.   *The Lady of Shalott, 3*

539.17
In the Spring a young man's fancy lightly turns to thoughts of love.   *Locksley Hall, 20*

539.18
Music that gentlier on the spirit lies,
Than tir'd eyelids upon tir'd eyes.   *The Lotos Eaters*

539.19
Come into the garden, Maud,
For the black bat, night, has flown,
Come into the garden, Maud,
I am here at the gate alone.   *Maud, I:22*

539.20

But the churchmen fain would kill their church,
As the churches have kill'd their Christ.
same, V:2

539.21
The splendour falls on castle walls
And snowy summits old in story.
The Princess, IV, Song

539.22
Tears, idle tears, I know not what they mean,
Tears from the depth of some divine despair.
same, 2nd Song

539.23
Man is the hunter; woman is his game:
The sleek and shining creatures of the chase,
We hunt them for the beauty of their skins.
same, V:147

539.24
The moan of doves in immemorial elms,
And murmuring of innumerable bees.
same, VII:203

539.25
My strength is as the strength of ten,
Because my heart is pure.   *Sir Galahad*

539.26
The woods decay, the woods decay and fall,
The vapours weep their burthen to the ground,
Man comes and tills the field and lies beneath,
And after many a summer dies the swan.
Tithonus, 1

539.27
We are not now that strength which in old days
Moved earth and heaven; that which we are, we are;
One equal temper of heroic hearts,
Made weak by time and fate, but strong in will
To strive, to seek, to find, and not to yield.
Ulysses, 44

540 Terence, (**Publius Terentius Afer**) (c. 190-159 B.C.), Roman poet.
540.1
Fortune favours the brave.   *Phormio, 203*
540.2
So many men, so many opinions.
same, 454

541 Thackeray, William Makepeace (1811-1863), English novelist.
541.1
He who meanly admires mean things is a Snob.   *The Book of Snobs, Ch. 2*

541.2
It is impossible, in our condition of society, not to be sometimes a Snob.   *same, Ch. 3*
541.3
RICHARD STEELE. 'Tis not the dying for a faith that's so hard, Master Harry—every man of every nation has done that—'tis the living up to it that is difficult.
Henry Esmond, I:6
541.4
'Tis strange what a man may do, and a woman yet think him an angel.   *same, Ch. 7*
541.5
A woman with fair opportunities and without a positive hump, may marry whom she likes.
Vanity Fair, Ch. 4
541.6
BECKY SHARP. I think I could be a good woman if I had five thousand a year.
same, Ch. 36

542 Thomas, Brandon (1857-1914), English actor and dramatist.
542.1
LORD FANCOURT BABERLEY. I'm Charley's aunt from Brazil, where the nuts come from.   *Charley's Aunt, Act 1*

543 Thomas, Dylan (1914-1953), Welsh poet.
543.1
Do not go gentle into that good night,
Old age should burn and rave at close of day;
Rage, rage, against the dying of the light.
Do not go gentle into that good night
543.2
The force that through the green fuse drives the flower
Drives my green age.   *The Force that through the green Fuse drives the Flower*
543.3
After the first death, there is no other.
A Refusal to Mourn the Death, by Fire, of a Child in London
543.4
These poems, with all their crudities, doubts, and confusions, are written for the love of Man and in praise of God, and I'd be a damn' fool if they weren't.
Collected Poems, Note
543.5
[*Wales*] The land of my fathers. My fathers can have it.   *Dylan Thomas (John Ackerman)*
543.6
Too many of the artists of Wales spend too much time about the position of the artist of

Wales. There is only one position for an artist anywhere: and that is, upright.

New Statesman, 18 Dec 1964

544 Thomson, James (1700-1748), Scottish poet.

544.1
When Britain first, at Heaven's command,
Arose from out the azure main,
This was the charter of the land,
And guardian angels sung this strain:
'Rule, Britannia, rule the waves:
Britons never will be slaves.'   *Alfred: A Masque, II:5*

544.2
Oh! Sophonisba! Sophonisba! oh!

Sophonisba, III:2

545 Thoreau, Henry David (1817-1862), American essayist and poet.

545.1
The mass of men lead lives of quiet desperation.   *Walden, 'Economy'*

545.2
As for doing good, that is one of the professions which are full.   *same*

545.3
Things do not change; we change.   *same*

545.4
It is not all books that are as dull as their readers.   *same, 'Reading'*

545.5
Our life is frittered away by detail... Simplify, simplify.   *same, 'Where I Lived and What I Lived For'*

545.6
It takes two to speak the truth—one to speak, and another to hear.   *A Week on the Concord and Merrimack Rivers, Wednesday*

545.7
Not that the story need be long, but it will take a long while to make it short.   *Letter*

546 Thurber, James (1894-1961), American humorist and cartoonist.

546.1
Early to rise and early to bed makes a male healthy and wealthy and dead.   *Fables for Our Time, 'The Shrike and the Chipmunks'*

546.2
No man...who has wrestled with a self-adjusting card table can ever quite be the man he once was.   *Let Your Mind Alone, 'Sex ex Machina'*

546.3
You wait here and I'll bring the etchings down.   *Cartoon caption, 'Men, Woman, and Dogs'*

546.4
I said the hounds of spring are on winter's traces—but let it pass, let it pass!

Cartoon caption

546.5
Well, if I called the wrong number, why did you answer the phone?   *Cartoon Caption*

546.6
[*Of a play*] It had only one fault. It was kind of lousy.   *Remark*

546.7
The difference between our decadence and the Russians' is that while theirs is brutal, ours is apathetic.   *Observer 'Sayings of the Week', 5 Feb 1961*

547 Tolstoy, Leo (1828-1910), Russian writer.

547.1
All happy families resemble one another, each unhappy family is unhappy in its own way.   *Anna Karenina, I:1*

547.2
If you want to be happy, be.

Kosma Prutkov

547.3
Pure and complete sorrow is as impossible as pure and complete joy.   *War and Peace, XV:1*

548 Tree, Sir Herbert Beerbohm (1853-1917), English actor-manager.

548.1
I was born old and get younger every day. At present I am sixty years young

Beerbohm Tree (Hesketh Pearson), Ch. 1

548.2
[*To a man carrying a grandfather clock*] My poor fellow, why not carry a watch?

same

548.3
[*Of Israel Zangwill*] He is an old bore; even the grave yawns for him.   *same*

549 Trotsky, Leon (Lev Davidovich Bronstein) (1879-1940), Russian revolutionary.

549.1
The fundamental premise of a revolution is that the existing social structure has become incapable of solving the urgent problems of development of the nation.   *History of the Russian Revolution, III:6*

550 Trollope, Anthony (1815-1882), English novelist.

550.1
It's dogged as does it. It ain't thinking about it. *Last Chronicle of Barset, Ch. 61*
550.2
Three hours a day will produce as much as a man ought to write. *Autobiography, Ch. 15*

551 Truman, Harry S. (1884-1972), President of the United States.
551.1
The buck stops here. *Notice on the Presidential desk*
551.2
The President spends most of his time kissing people on the cheek in order to get them to do what they ought to do without getting kissed. *Observer 'Sayings of the Week', 6 Feb 1949*

552 Tuer, Andrew White (1838-1900), English publisher and writer.
552.1
English as she is Spoke, *Title of Portuguese-English Conversation Guide*

553 Twain, Mark (Samuel Langhorne Clemens) (1835-1910), American writer.
553.1
There are three kinds of lies: lies, damned lies, and statistics. *Autobiography*
553.2
Soap and education are not as sudden as a massacre, but they are more deadly in the long run. *The Facts concerning the Recent Resignation*
553.3
I must have a prodigious quantity of mind; it takes me as much as a week, sometimes, to make it up. *The Innocents Abroad, Ch. 7*
553.4
Familiarity breeds contempt—and children. *Notebooks*
553.5
Adam was but human—this explains it all. He did not want the apple for the apple's sake, he wanted it only because it was forbidden. *Pudd'nhead Wilson's Calendar, Ch. 2*
553.6
A classic is something that everybody wants to have read and nobody wants to read. *Speech, The Disappearance of Literature*
553.7
Reports of my death are greatly exaggerated. *Cable to the Associated Press*

554 Tynan, Kenneth (b. 1927), English theatre critic and producer.

554.1
William Congreve is the only sophisticated playwright England has produced; and like Shaw, Sheridan, and Wilde, his nearest rivals, he was brought up in Ireland. *Curtains, 'The Way of the World'*
554.2
A novel is a static thing that one moves through; a play is a dynamic thing that moves past one. *same*
554.3
What, when drunk, one sees in other women, one sees in Garbo sober. *Sunday Times, 25 Aug 1963*

U

555 Ustinov, Peter (b. 1921), English actor, dramatist and humorist.
555.1
GENERAL. As for being a General, well, at the age of four with paper hats and wooden swords we're all Generals. Only some of us never grow out of it. *Romanoff and Juliet, Act 1*
555.2
GENERAL. A diplomat these days is nothing but a head-waiter who's allowed to sit down occasionally. *same*

V

556 Vanbrugh, Sir John (1664-1726), English dramatist and architect.
556.1
Once a woman has given you her heart you can never get rid of the rest of her. *The Relapse, II:1*
556.2
No man worth having is true to his wife, or can be true to his wife, or ever was, or ever will be so. *same, III:2*

557 Vegetius, (Flavius Vegetius Renatus) (fl. 375 A.D.), Latin writer.
557.1

Let him who desires peace, prepare for war.
Epitoma Rei Militaris, 3, Prologue

W

558 Victoria, (1819-1901), Queen of England.
558.1
We are not amused. *Notebooks of a Spinster Lady, 2 Jan 1900*
558.2
[*Of Gladstone*] He speaks to Me as If I was a public meeting. *Collections and Recollections (Russell), Ch. 14*

559 Villon, François (1431-1485), French poet.
559.1
Mais où sont les neiges d'antan?
But where are the snows of yesteryear?
Ballade des Dames du Temps Jadis

560 Virgil, (Publius Vergilius Maro) (70-19 B.C.), Latin poet.
560.1
Arms and the man I sing. *Aeneid, I:1*
560.2
Woman is always fickle and changing. *same, IV:569*
560.3
The way down to Hell is easy. *same, VI:126*
560.4
Love conquers all, and we too succumb to love. *same, X:69*
560.5
Meanwhile, time is flying — flying, never to return. *same, III:284*

561 Voltaire, François Marie Arouet (1694-1778), French writer.
561.1
All is for the best in the best of possible worlds. *Candide, Ch. 1*
561.2
[*Of England*] In this country it is good to kill an admiral from time to time, to encourage the others. *same, Ch. 23*
561.3
'That is well said, ' replied Candide, 'but we must cultivate our garden.' *same, Ch. 30*
561.4
The best is the enemy of the good.
Dictionnaire Philosophique, 'Art Dramatique'
561.5
If God did not exist, it would be necessary to invent Him. *Épîtres, 96, À ' L'Auteur du livre des Trois Imposteurs*

562 Wallace, Lew (1827-1905), American soldier and writer.
562.1
Beauty is altogether in the eye of the beholder. *The Prince of India, III:6:78*

563 Walpole, Sir Robert, 1st Earl of Orford (1676-1745), English statesman.
563.1
The balance of power. *Speech, House of Commons, 1741*
563.2
All those men have their price. *Memoirs of Walpole (W. Coxe)*
563.3
Anything but history, for history must be false. *Walpoliana*

564 Walpole, Horace, 4th Earl of Orford (1717-1797), English writer.
564.1
It is charming to totter into vogue.
Letter to G. A. Selwyn, 1765
564.2
The world is a comedy to those who think, a tragedy to those who feel. *Letter to Sir Horace Mann, 1769*

565 Walton, Izaak (1593-1683), English writer.
565.1
Angling may be said to be so like the mathematics, that it can never be fully learnt.
The Compleat Angler, Epistle to the Reader
565.2
We may say of angling as Dr Boteler said of strawberries, 'Doubtless God could have made a better berry, but doubtless God never did.' *same, Ch. 5*

566 Ward, Artemus (Charles Farrar Browne) (1834-1867), American humorist.
566.1
I prefer temperance hotels—although they sell worse kinds of liquor than any other kind of hotels. *Artemus Ward's Lecture*
566.2
Why is this thus? What is the reason of this thusness? *same*
566.3
I am happiest when I am idle. I could live for months without performing any kind of

labour, and at the expiration of that time I should feel fresh and vigorous enough to go right on in the same way for numerous more months. *Pyrotechny*

567 Washington, George (1732-1799), first President of the United States.
567.1
Associate yourself with men of good quality if you esteem your own reputation; for 'tis better to be alone than in bad company.
Rules of Civility
567.2
Father, I cannot tell a lie. I did it with my little hatchet. *Attributed*

568 Watts, Isaac (1674-1748), English hymn-writer.
568.1
For Satan finds some mischief still
For idle hands to do. *Against Idleness*
568.2
'Tis the voice of the sluggard, I heard him complain:
'You have waked me too soon, I must slumber again.' *The Sluggard*

569 Waugh, Evelyn (1903-1966), English novelist.
569.1
I expect you'll be becoming a schoolmaster sir. That's what most of the gentlemen does sir, that gets sent down for indecent behaviour. *Decline and Fall, Prelude*
569.2
We class schools, you see, into four grades: Leading School, First-rate School, Good School, and School. *same, I:1*
569.3
Meanwhile you will write an essay on 'self-indulgence'. There will be a prize of half a crown for the longest essay, irrespective of any possible merit. *same, I:5*
569.4
I can't quite explain it, but I don't believe one can ever be unhappy for long provided one does just exactly what one wants to and when one wants to. *same, I:5*
569.5
Nonconformity and lust stalking hand in hand through the country, wasting and ravaging. *same, I:5*
569.6
'The Welsh, ' said the Doctor, 'are the only nation in the world that has produced no graphic or plastic art, no architecture, no drama. They just sing, ' he said with disgust,

'sing and blow down wind instruments of plated silver.' *same, I:8*
569.7
I have noticed again and again since I have been in the Church that lay interest in ecclesiastical matters is often a prelude to insanity. *same, I:8*
569.8
I have often observed in women of her type a tendency to regard all athletics as inferior forms of fox-hunting. *same, I:10*
569.9
I haven't been to sleep for over a year. That's why I go to bed early. One needs more rest if one doesn't sleep. *same, II:3*
569.10
There is a species of person called a 'Modern Churchman' who draws the full salary of a beneficed clergyman and need not commit himself to any religious belief. *same, II:4*
569.11
I came to the conclusion many years ago that almost all crime is due to the repressed desire for aesthetic expression. *same, III:1*
569.12
Anyone who has been to an English public school will always feel comparatively at home in prison. *same, III:4*
569.13
He was greatly pained at how little he was pained by the events of the afternoon.
same, III:4
569.14
Instead of this absurd division into sexes they ought to class people as static and dynamic. *same, III:7*
569.15
She had heard someone say something about an Independent Labour Party, and was furious that she had not been asked.
Vile Bodies, Ch. 4
569.16
All this fuss about sleeping together. For physical pleasure I'd sooner go to my dentist any day. *same, Ch. 6*
569.17
Assistant masters came and went.... Some liked little boys too little and some too much. *A Little Learning*
569.18
You never find an Englishman among the underdogs—except in England of course.
The Loved One
569.19
In the dying world I come from quotation is a national vice. It used to be the classics, now it's lyric verse. *same*

569.20
News is what a chap who doesn't care much about anything wants to read. And it's only news until he's read it. After that it's dead.
Scoop, I:5

569.21
Pappenhacker says that every time you are polite to a proletarian you are helping to bolster up the capitalist system. *same, I:5*

569.22
'I will not stand for being called a woman in my own house, ' she said. *same*

569.23
Other nations use 'force'; we Britons alone use 'Might'. *same, II:5*

569.24
Enclosing every thin man, there's a fat man demanding elbow-room. *Officers and Gentlemen, Interlude*

569.25
Manners are especially the need of the plain. The pretty can get away with anything.
Observer 'Sayings of the Year, ' 1962

570 Webb, Sidney, 1st Baron Passfield (1859-1947), English social reformer.
570.1
The inevitability of gradualness.
Presidential Address to Labour Party Conference, 1923

571 Webster, Daniel (1782-1852), American statesman.
571.1
[*When advised not to become a lawyer*] There is always room at the top. *Remark,*

571.2
The people's government, made for the people, made by the people, and answerable to the people. *Second Speech on Foote's Resolution, Jan 26 1830*

572 Webster, John (1580?-1625?), English dramatist.
572.1
BOSOLA. Other sins only speak; murder shrieks out. *The Duchess of Malfi, IV:2*
572.2
BIRD LIME. I saw him even now going the way of all flesh, that is to say towards the kitchen. *Westward Hoe, II:2*

573 Wellington, Arthur Wellesley, 1st Duke of (1769-1852), English general and statesman.
573.1
[*Of the British army*] Ours is composed of the scum of the earth. *Remark, 4 Nov 1831*
573.2
Up, Guards, and at 'em. *Order at the battle of Waterloo, 18 June 1815, attributed*
573.3
The battle of Waterloo was won on the playing fields of Eton. *Attributed*
573.4
Publish and be damned. *Attributed*

574 Wells, Herbert George (1866-1946), English writer.
574.1
The cat is the offspring of a cat and the dog of a dog, but butlers and lady's maids do not reproduce their kind. They have other duties.
Bealby, I:1
574.2
The Shape of Things to Come. *Title of Book*

575 Wesley, John (1703-1791), English founder of Methodism.
575.1
I look upon all the world as my parish.
Journal, 11 June 1739

576 West, Mae (1893-1980), American film actress.
576.1
Come up and see me sometime.
Diamond Lil, film, 1932
576.2
—My goodness those diamonds are lovely!
576.3
Goodness had nothing whatever to do with it. *same*
576.4
Beulah, peel me a grape. *I'm No Angel, film, 1933*
576.5
[*When asked what she wanted to be remembered for*] Everything. *Remark*
576.6
When I'm good I'm very good, but when I'm bad I'm better. *Remark*
576.7
Whenever I'm caught between two evils, I take the one I've never tried. *Remark*

577 Whistler, James Abbott McNeill (1834-1903), American painter.
577.1
I am not arguing with you—I am telling you.
The Gentle Art of Making Enemies
577.2
Nature is usually wrong. *same*

577.3
—I only know of two painters in the world: yourself and Velasquez. Why drag in Velasquez? *Whistler Stories (D. C. Seitz)*

577.4
You shouldn't say it is not good. You should say you do not like it; and then, you know, you're perfectly safe. *same*

577.5
—For two days' labour, you ask two hundred guineas?
No, I ask it for the knowledge of a lifetime. *same*

577.6
—This landscape reminds me of your work.
Yes madam, Nature is creeping up. *same*

577.7
OSCAR WILDE. I wish I had said that.
WHISTLER. You will, Oscar, you will. *Oscar Wilde (L. C. Ingleby)*

578 White, Elwyn Brooks (b. 1899), American journalist and humorist.

578.1
As in the sexual experience, there are never more than two persons present in the act of reading—the writer who is the impregnator, and the reader who is the respondent. *The Second Tree from the Corner*

578.2
To perceive Christmas through its wrapping becomes more difficult with every year. *same*

579 White, Patrick (b. 1912), Australian novelist.

579.1
But bombs *are* unbelievable until they actually fall. *Riders in the Chariot, I:4*

579.2
'I dunno, ' Arthur said. 'I forget what I was taught. I only remember what I've learnt.' *The Solid Mandala, Ch. 2*

579.3
All my novels are an accumulation of detail. I'm a bit of a bower-bird. *Southerly, 139*

579.4
Well, good luck to you, kid! I'm going to write the Great Australian Novel. *The Vivisector, 112*

580 Whitehead, Alfred North (1861-1947), English mathematician and philosopher.

580.1
There are no whole truths; all truths are half-truths. It is trying to treat them as whole truths that plays the devil. *Dialogues of Alfred North Whitehead (Lucien Price), 16*

580.2
Intelligence is quickness to apprehend as distinct from ability, which is capacity to act wisely on the thing apprehended. *same, 135*

580.3
Art is the imposing of a pattern on experience, and our aesthetic enjoyment is recognition of the pattern. *same, 228*

581 Whitlam, Gough (b. 1916), Australian prime minister.

581.1
I do not mind the Liberals, still less do I mind the Country Party, calling me a bastard. In some circumstances I am only doing my job if they do. But I hope you will not publicly call me a bastard, as some bastards in the Caucus have. *Speech to the Australian Labour Party, 9 June 1974*

582 Whitman, Walt (1819-1892), American poet.

582.1
If anything is sacred the human body is sacred. *I Sing the Body Electric, 8*

582.2
I celebrate myself, and sing myself,
And what I assume you shall assume. *Song of Myself, 1*

582.3
I think I could turn and live with animals, they're so placid and self-contain'd,
I stand and look at them long and long. *same, 32*

582.4
I have said that the soul is not more than the body,
And I have said that the body is not more than the soul,
And nothing, not God, is greater to one than one's self is. *same, 48*

582.5
Do I contradict myself?
Very well then I contradict myself,
(I am large, I contain multitudes). *same, 51*

582.6
No one will ever get at my verses who insists upon viewing them as a literary performance. *A Backward Glance O'er Travel'd Roads*

582.7
After you have exhausted what there is in business, politics, conviviality, and so on—have found that none of these finally

satisfy, or permanently wear—what remains?
Nature remains. *Specimen Days, 'New Themes Entered Upon'*

583 Wilcox, Ella Wheeler (1850–1919), American poet.
583.1
Laugh, and the world laughs with you;
Weep, and you weep alone,
For the sad old earth must borrow its mirth,
But has trouble enough of its own.
Solitude

584 Wilde, Oscar Fingall O'Flahertie Wills (1856–1900), Irish poet, dramatist and wit.
584.1
Yet each man kills the thing he loves,
By each let this be heard,
Some do it with a bitter look,
Some with a flattering word.
The coward does it with a kiss,
The bràve man with a sword!
The Ballad of Reading Gaol, I:7
584.2
Something was dead in each of us,
584.3
And what was dead was Hope.
same, III:31
584.4
For he who lives more lives than one
More deaths than one must die.
same, III:37
584.5
LORD GORING. To love oneself is the beginning of a lifelong romance.
An Ideal Husband, Act 3
584.6
ALGERNON. In married life three is company and two is none. *The Importance of Being Earnest, Act 1*
584.7
LADY BRACKNELL. Ignorance is like a delicate exotic fruit; touch it, and the bloom is gone. *same*
584.8
LADY BRACKNELL. To lose one parent, Mr Worthing, may be regarded as a misfortune; to lose both looks like carelessness. *same*
584.9
JACK. In a hand-bag.
LADY BRACKNELL. A hand-bag? *same*
584.10
GWENDOLEN. I never travel without my diary. One should always have something sensational to read in the train. *same, Act 2*
584.11
LADY BRACKNELL. No woman should ever be quite accurate about her age. It looks so calculating. *same, Act 3*
584.12
LORD DARLINGTON. It is absurd to divide people into good and bad. People are either charming or tedious. *Lady Windermere's Fan, Act 1*
584.13
LORD DARLINGTON. I can resist everything except temptation. *same*
584.14
LORD ILLINGWORTH. One knows so well the popular idea of health. The English country gentleman galloping after a fox—the unspeakable in full pursuit of the uneatable.
A Woman of No Importance, Act 1
584.15
LORD ILLINGWORTH. One should never trust a woman who tells one her real age. A woman who would tell one that, would tell one anything. *same*
584.16
LORD ILLINGWORTH. Moderation is a fatal thing, Lady Hunstanton. Nothing succeeds like excess. *same, Act 3*
584.17
All Art is quite useless. *The Picture of Dorian Gray, Preface*
584.18
There is only one thing in the world worse than being talked about, and that is not being talked about. *same, 1*
584.19
The only way to get rid of a temptation is to yield to it. *same, 2*
584.20
The man who sees both sides of a question is a man who sees absolutely nothing at all.
The Critic as Artist, Part 2
584.21
A little sincerity is a dangerous thing, and a great deal of it is absolutely fatal. *same*
584.22
Ah! don't say you agree with me. When people agree with me I always feel that I must be wrong. *same*
584.23
There is no sin except stupidity. *same*
584.24
Art is the most intense mode of individualism that the world has known. *The Soul of Man Under Socialism*
584.25
Over the piano was printed a notice: Please do not shoot the pianist. He is doing his best.
Impressions of America, Leadville
584.26

I have nothing to declare except my genius.
At New York Customs House

584.27

[*When told that an operation would be expensive*] I suppose that I shall have to die beyond my means.   *Life of Wilde (Sherard)*

584.28

Work is the curse of the drinking classes.
Attributed

585 Wilhelm II, (1859-1941), King of Prussia and German Emperor.

585.1

[*Of the British Expeditionary Force*] A contemptible little army.   *Remark, 1914*

586 William III, (1650-1702), King of Great Britain.

586.1

I will die in the last ditch.   *History of England (Hume)*

586.2

Every bullet has its billet.   *Journal (John Wesley), 6 June 1765*

587 William of Wykeham, (1324-1404), English churchman and statesman.

587.1

Manners maketh man.   *Motto of Winchester College and New College, Oxford, his foundations*

588 Wilson, Charles Erwin (1890-1961), American engineer and industrialist.

588.1

I thought what was good for the country was good for General Motors and vice versa.
Statement to U.S. Congressional Committee, 23 Jan 1953

589 Wilson, Sir Harold (b. 1916), British prime minister.

589.1

If I had the choice between smoked salmon and tinned salmon, I'd have it tinned. With vinegar.   *Observer 'Sayings of the Week', 11 Nov 1962*

589.2

From now, the pound is worth 14 per cent or so less in terms of other currencies. It does not mean, of course, that the pound here in Britain, in your pocket or purse or in your bank, has been devalued.   *Speech after devaluation of the pound, 20 Nov 1967*

589.3

One man's wage rise is another man's price increase.   *Observer 'Sayings of the Week', 11 Jan 1970*

590 Wilson, John, see **North, Christopher**

591   Wilson,   Thomas   Woodrow (1856-1924), President of the United States.

591.1

No nation is fit to sit in judgement upon any other nation.   *Address, Apr 1915*

591.2

There is such a thing as a man being too proud to fight.   *Address to foreign-born citizens, 10 May 1915*

591.3

[*To Congress, asking for a declaration of war*] The world must be made safe for democracy.   *Address, 2 Apr 1917*

592 Wodehouse, Pelham Grenville (1881-1975), English humorous novelist.

592.1

All the unhappy marriages come from the husbands having brains. What good are brains to a man? They only unsettle him.
The Adventures of Sally

592.2

It is no use telling me that there are bad aunts and good aunts. At the core they are all alike. Sooner or later, out pops the cloven hoof.   *The Code of the Woosters, Ch. 2*

592.3

I spent the afternoon musing on Life. If you come to think of it, what a queer thing Life is! So unlike anything else, don't you know, if you see what I mean.   *My Man Jeeves, 'Rallying Round Old George'*

592.4

The Right Hon. was a tubby little chap who looked as if he had been poured into his clothes and had forgotten to say 'When!'
Very Good Jeeves!, 'Jeeves and the Impending Doom'

592.5

The stationmaster's whiskers are of a Victorian bushiness and give the impression of having been grown under glass.
Wodehouse at Work (R. Usborne), Ch. 2

593 Wolsey, Thomas (1475?-1530), English cardinal and statesman.

593.1

Had I but served God as diligently as I have served the king, he would not have given me over in my gray hairs.   *To Sir William Kingston*

594   Wood, Mrs Henry (1814-1887), English novelist.

594.1
Dead! and...never called me mother.
*East Lynne (dramatized version; the words
do not occur in the novel)*

595 Wordsworth, William (1770–1850),
English poet.
595.1
The good die first,
And they whose hearts are dry as summer
dust
Burn to the socket.   *The Excursion, I:500*
595.2
I wandered lonely as a cloud
That floats on high o'er vales and hills,
When all at once I saw a crowd,
A host, of golden daffodils.
I Wandered Lonely as a Cloud
595.3
For oft, when on my couch I lie
In vacant or in pensive mood,
They flash upon that inward eye
Which is the bliss of solitude.   *same*
595.4
There was a time when meadow, grove, and
stream,
The earth, and every common sight,
To me did seem
Apparelled in celestial light,
The glory and the freshness of a dream.
*Ode, Intimations of Immortality from
Recollections of Early Childhood*
595.5
Our birth is but a sleep and a forgetting:
The Soul that rises with us, our life's Star,
Hath had elsewhere its setting,
And cometh from afar:
Not in entire forgetfulness,
And not in utter nakedness,
But trailing clouds of glory do we come
From God, who is our home:
Heaven lies about us in our infancy!
Shades of the prison-house begin to close
Upon the growing Boy.   *same*
595.6
To me the meanest flower that blows can
give
Thoughts that do often lie too deep for tears.
same
595.7
Have I not reason to lament
What man has made of man?
Lines Written in Early Spring
595.8
There is a comfort in the strength of love;
'Twill make a thing endurable, which else
Would overset the brain, or break the heart.
Michael, 448

595.9
The world is too much with us; late and
soon
Getting and spending, we lay waste our
powers:
Little we see in Nature that is ours.
Miscellaneous Sonnets, I:33
595.10
I'd rather be
A Pagan suckled in a creed outworn;
So might I, standing on this pleasant lea,
Have glimpses that would make me less
forlorn;
Have sight of Proteus rising from the sea;
Or hear old Triton blow his wreathèd horn.
same
595.11
Earth has not anything to show more fair:
Dull would he be of soul who could pass by
A sight so touching in its majesty:
This City now doth, like a garment, wear
The beauty of the morning; silent, bare,
Ships, towers, domes, theatres, and temples
lie
Open unto the fields, and to the sky;
All bright and glittering in the smokeless air.
same, II:36
595.12
Dear God! the very houses seem asleep;
And all that mighty heart is lying still!
same
595.13
The Child is father of the Man;
And I could wish my days to be
Bound each to each by natural piety.
My Heart leaps up
595.14
Bliss was it in that dawn to be alive,
But to be young was very Heaven!
The Prelude, II:108
595.15
Still glides the Stream, and shall for ever
glide;
The Form remains, the Function never dies.
The River Duddon, 34, After-Thought
595.16
A slumber did my spirit seal;
I had no human fears:
She seemed a thing that could not feel
The touch of earthly years.
595.17
No motion has she now, no force;
She neither hears nor sees;
Rolled round in earth's diurnal course,
With rocks, and stones, and trees.
A Slumber did my Spirit seal
595.18
Come forth into the light of things,

Let Nature be your Teacher.
The Tables Turned

595.19

One impulse from a vernal wood
May teach you more of man,
Of moral evil and of good,
Than all the sages can. *same*

595.20

That best portion of a good man's life,
His little, nameless, unremembered acts
Of kindness and of love. *Lines composed a*
few miles above Tintern Abbey, 33

595.21

That blessed mood,
In which the burthen of the mystery,
In which the heavy and the weary weight
Of all this unintelligible world,
Is lightened. *same, 37*

595.22

We are laid asleep
In body, and become a living soul:
While with an eye made quiet by the power
Of harmony, and the deep power of joy,
We see into the life of things. *same, 45*

595.23

I have learned
To look on nature, not as in the hour
Of thoughtless youth; but hearing often-
times
The still, sad music of humanity. *same, 88*

595.24

Nature never did betray
The heart that loved her. *same, 122*

595.25

Poetry is the spontaneous overflow of
powerful feelings: it takes its origin from
emotion recollected in tranquillity.
Lyrical Ballads, Preface

596 Wotton, Sir Henry (1568-1639),
English traveller, diplomatist and poet.

596.1

An Ambassador is an honest man sent to lie
abroad for his country. *Written in Mr*
Christopher Fleckamore's Album

597 Wren, Sir Christopher (1632-1723),
English architect.

597.1

If you seek my monument, look around you.
Inscription in St Paul's Cathedral, London

598 Wykeham, William of, see **William of**
Wykeham

X

599 Xenophon, (435?-354? B.C.), Greek
historian and soldier.

599.1

The sea! the sea! *Anabasis, IV:7*

600 Yeatman, Robert Julian, see **Sellar,**
Walter Carruthers

601 Yeats, William Butler (1865-1939),
Irish poet and dramatist.

601.1

O chestnut tree, great rooted blossomer,
Are you the leaf, the blossom or the bole?
O body swayed to music, O brightening
glance,
How can we know the dancer from the
dance? *Among School Children*

601.2

Now that my ladder's gone,
I must lie down where all the ladders start,
In the foul rag-and-bone shop of the heart.
The Circus Animals' Desertion

601.3

Though leaves are many, the root is one;
Through all the lying days of my youth
I swayed my leaves and flowers in the sun;
Now I may wither into the truth.
The Coming of Wisdom with Time

601.4

But Love has pitched his mansion in
The place of excrement. *Crazy Jane Talks*
with the Bishop

601.5

Wine comes in at the mouth
And love comes in at the eye;
That's all we shall know for truth
Before we grow old and die.
A Drinking Song

601.6

All changed, changed utterly:
A terrible beauty is born. *Easter 1916*

601.7

When I play on my fiddle in Dooney,
Folk dance like a wave of the sea.
The Fiddler of Dooney

601.8

For the good are always the merry,
Save by an evil chance,
And the merry love the fiddle,
And the merry love to dance *same*

601.9

But I, being poor, have only my dreams;
I have spread my dreams under your feet;

Tread softly because you tread on my dreams.
He Wishes for the Cloths of Heaven
601.10
I will arise and go now, and go to Innisfree,
And a small cabin build there, of clay and
    wattles made;
Nine bean rows will I have there, a hive for
    the honey bee,
And live alone in the bee-loud glade.
The Lake Isle of Innisfree
601.11
Never to have lived is best, ancient writers
    say;
Never to have drawn the breath of life, never
    to have looked into the eye of day
The second best's a gay goodnight and
    quickly turn away.   *Oedipus at Colonus*
601.12
In dreams begins responsibility.
Old Play, Epigraph, Responsibilities
601.13
A pity beyond all telling
Is hid in the heart of love.   *The Pity of Love*

601.14
Things fall apart; the centre cannot hold;
Mere anarchy is loosed upon the world,
The blood-dimmed tide is loosed, and every-
    where
The ceremony of innocence is drowned;
The best lack all conviction, while the worst
Are full of passionate intensity.
The Second Coming

602 Young, Edward (1683–1765), English
poet.
602.1
Some for renown, on scraps of learning dote,
And think they grow immortal as they quote.
Love of Fame, I:89
602.2
Be wise with speed,
A fool at forty is a fool indeed,
same, II:281
602.3
Procrastination is the thief of time.
Night Thoughts, I:393

INDEX

No stir of a. was there 332.10
waste its sweetness on the desert a. 268.8
Aitches nothing to lose but our a. 427.5
Alamein Before A. we never had a victory 133.36
Alarms confused a. of struggle and flight 20.2
Albatross I shot the a. 144.4
Aldershot burnish'd by A. sun 60.3
Ale no more cakes and a. 498.271
spicy nut-brown a. 401.7
Alice A. mutton; mutton A. 111.31
Alien amid the a. corn 332.27
Alike among so many million of faces... none a. 82.3
Alive Bliss was it in that dawn to be a. 595.14
he is no longer a. 59.4
needst not strive...to keep a. 140.4
All A. art is quite useless 584.17
A. for one, and one for a. 206.1
a. our yesterdays 498.177
A. things to a. men 62.185
are you sure they are a. horrid 27.5
man, take him for a. in a. 498.45
Ripeness is a. 498.151
To know a. makes one tolerant 523.1
Allegory a. on the banks of the Nile 502.7
Alley she lives in our a. 108.2
Almonds Don't eat too many a. 145.5
Alms a. for oblivion 498.264
Alone A., a., all, all a. 144.7
A. and palely loitering 332.11
better to be a. than in bad company 567.1
I am here at the gate a. 539.19
I want to be a. 249.1
Man shall not live by bread a. 62.117
No poet...has...meaning a. 214.19
One is always a. 214.17
Weep, and you weep a. 583.1
We perish'd, each a. 165.1
who can enjoy a. 401.25
Alph Where A., the sacred river, ran 144.19
Alpha I am A. and Omega 62.212
Also You a. 428.2
Alternative I prefer old age to the a. 130.1
Alters Love is not love which a. 498.298
Am I a. that I am 62.11
I think therefore I a. 189.1
Amaryllis sport with A. in the shade 401.10
Amateur In love...the a. status 267.2
Amateurs disease that afflicts a. 129.15
nation of a. 477.2
Amaze vainly men themselves a. 384.4
Ambassador A. is an honest man sent to lie abroad 596.1
Ambition A. should be made of sterner stuff 498.118
Vaulting a., which o'er-leaps itself 498.165
America A. is a country of young men 218.14
business of A. is business 155.1
my A.! my new-found-land 199.7
what makes A. what it is 525.1
American A. system of rugged individualism 301.1

Americanism hyphenated A. 476.2
Ammunition pass the a. 236.1
Amo Odi et a. 114.2
Amor A. vincit insomnia 244.2
Amused We are not a. 558.1
Amusing whether she is not a. herself 403.3
Anarchy a. is loosed upon the world 601.14
Anatomy poor judge of a. 385.21
Ancient a. Mariner 144.1
A. of days 62.107
Anderson John A. my jo 93.9
Angel a. is nobody in particular 499.57
A. of Death has been abroad 75.1
in action, how like an a. 498.57
Is man an ape or an a. 195.4
woman yet think him an a. 541.4
Angels A. can fly 129.22
Not Angles, but a. 270.1
where a. fear to tread 452.16
Angles Not A., but angels 270.1
Angling A. may be said to be so like the mathematics 565.1
Anglo-Saxon those are A. attitudes 111.26
Animal Are you a.—or vegetable—or mineral? 111.28
information vegetable, a. and mineral 257.17
man is and will always be a wild a. 179.1
Man is a noble a. 82.9
man is...a religious a. 91.9
Man is by nature a political a. 17.2
Animals All a. are equal 4
A. are such agreeable friends 213.2
I think I could...live with a. 582.3
paragon of a. 498.57
Anna great A.! whom three realms obey 452.26
Annals simple a. of the poor 268.6
Annihilating A. all that's made 384.5
Annual A. income twenty pounds 191.8
Anomaly Poverty is an a. to rich people 32.3
Another He who would do good to a. 67.4
Life is just one damned thing after a. 306.1
No man can...condemn a. 82.4
Answer more than the wisest man can a. 148.4
What *is* the a.? 525.3
why did you a. the phone? 546.5
would not stay for an a. 30.2
Ant Go to the a., thou sluggard 62.64
Antan les neiges d'a. 559.1
Anthology a. is like all the plums...out of a cake 463.1
Antic Hay dance an a. 381.1
Anti-clerical it makes me understand a. things 55.7
Antidote a. to desire '51.8
Anything call me a. i̱ you don't call me spade 535.15
pretty can get away with a. 569.25
Apart Man's love is...a thing a. 98.12
Things fall a. 601.14
Ape exception is a naked a. 406.1
Is man an a. or an angel 195.4
Ape-like a. virtues without which 153.2
Apes We've got nothing against a. 507.4

Apologize   I never a. 499.6

Apparel   a. oft proclaims the man 498.47

Appear   Things are...what they a. to be 489.2

Appearances   Keep up a. 131.3

Appetite   A. comes with eating 460.1
a. may sicken and so die 498.266

Apple   A. of his eye 62.29
want the a. for the a.'s sake 553.5

Appointment   a. by the corrupt few 499.49

Appreciate   I never a. 445.1

Apprehend   Intelligence is quickness to a. 580.2

Après   A. nous le déluge 451.1

April   A. is the cruellest month 214.16
Now that A.'s there 83.6

Aprille   Whan that A. with his shoures sote 127.1

Arabia   All the perfumes of A. 498.174

Architecture   A. in general is frozen music 490.1

Arguing   I am not a. with you 577.1

Arian   In three sips the A. frustrate 83.15

Arise   I will a. and go now 601.10

Arm   Human on my faithless a. 25.6

Armies   ignorant a. clash by night 20.2
Napoleon's a. used to march on their stomachs 495.3

Arms   A. and the man I sing 560.1

Army   a. marches on its stomach 413.3
contemptible little a. 585.1
English a. led by an Irish general 499.62

Arrive   travel...better thing than to a. 529.4

Art   a....aspires towards the condition of music 436.2
A. for a.'s sake 162.1
A. is a jealous mistress 218.1
A. is long 296.1
a. is not a weapon 335.5
A. is quite useless 584.16
A. is ruled uniquely by the imagination 170.1
A. is the imposing of a pattern 580.3
A. is the most intense mode of individualism 584.23
a....left to a lot of shabby bums 359.1
a. of pleasing consists 281.6
Bullfighting is the only a. in which the artist is in danger of death 284.1
Desiring this man's a. 498.290
excellence of every a. is its intensity 332.35
Fine a. is that in which the hand 484.3
It's clever but is it a. 341.3
more sensitive one is to great a. 51.4
nature is the a. of God 82.2
object of a. 14.1
sombre enemy of good a. 153.7
strains of unpremeditated a. 500.13
True ease in writing comes from a. 452.13
Welsh...produced no...a. 569.6
whole of a. is an appeal to a reality 376.2
Words...full of a. 497.1
work that aspires...to the condition of a. 154.5

Artful   a. Dodger 191.21

Artificial   All things are a. 82.2

Artist   Beware of the a. who's an intellectual 229.1
only one position for an a. anywhere 543.6
true a. will let his wife starve 499.38

Artistic   a. temperament is a disease that afflicts amateurs 129.15

Artists   A. are not engineers of the soul 335.5

Arts   inglorious a. of peace 384.6
Murder...one of the Fine A. 188.1

Ashamed   few people who are not a. of having been in love 471.13
man is doing something he is a. of 499.10
more things a man is a. of 499.36

Asked   furious that she had not been a. 569.15
women are glad to have been a. 428.1

Asleep   laid a. in body 595.21

Aspect   Meet in her a. 98.25

Aspicious   two a. persons 498.215

Ass   law is a a. 191.22

Assassination   Absolutism tempered by a. 410.1
A. is the extreme form of censorship 499.69

Assemblance   Care I for the ...a. of a man? 498.91

Associate   good must a. 91.13
I...like to a. with...priests 55.7

Assume   what I a. you shall a. 582.2

Astonished   a. at my own moderation 139.1

Astray   like sheep have gone a. 62.100

Asunder   let no man put a. 62.149
no man shall ever put a. 499.22

Asylum   world is...like a lunatic a. 364.3

Atheist   a. is a man who has no invisible means of support 238.1
denial of Him by the a. 458.5
I am an a. still, thank God 89.1

Athletics   a. as inferior forms of fox-hunting 569.8

Attached   men become a. even to Widnes 538.2

Attic   glory of the A. stage 20.6

Attitudes   Anglo-Saxon a. 111.26

Auld   a. acquaintance be forgot 93.2

Aunt   Charley's a. from Brazil 542.1

Aunts   bad a. and good a. 592.2

Aussie   dinkum hard-swearing A. 279.1

Australia   Genius Spark Seems brightest in folk from A. 222.1

Australian   Did you know that Rolf Harris was A.? 222.2
Every true A. bushman 352.1
Great A. Novel 579.4

Australians   A. Have done *terribly* well for themselves 222.1

Author   adopt me as their favourite a. 499.78
bad novel tells us...about its a. 129.14
when I don't know who the a. is 499.21

Authority   a. be a stubborn bear 498.286
man Dress'd in a little brief a. 498.180
No morality can be founded on a. 29.1
Nothing destroyeth a. so much 30.22

Authors   a. could not endure being wrong 106.3

Autumn   breath of A.'s being 500.7

Ave   A. atque vale 114.3

Aversion in matrimony to begin with a little a. 502.4

Aves Beadsman, after thousand a. told 332.7

Avon Sweet Swan of A. 325.4

Awake A. for Morning in the Bowl of Night 228.1

Away Take the soup a. 299.1

Aweary I gin to be a. of the sun 498.178

Awoke I a. one morning 98.29

Axe a.'s edge did try 384.7

Axioms A. in philosophy are not a. 332.38

B

Babbl'd 'a b. of green fields 498.94

Babes Out of the mouth of b. 62.42

Babies bit the b. in the cradles 83.11

  putting milk into b. 133.22

Baby b....loud noise at one end 343.1

  Every b. born into the world 191.8

  my b. at my breast 498.17

  When the first b. laughed 40.1

Babylon By the rivers of B. 62.62

Back But at my b. I always hear 384.2

Bacon When their lordships asked B. 59.1

Bad b. die late 184.1

  b. novel tells us the truth about its author 129.14

  Defend the b. against the worse 182.1

  never was a b. peace 239.4

  novel cannot be too b. 499.64

  too b. to be worth publishing 499.64

  what I feel really b. about 240.1

  When b. men combine 91.13

  when...I'm b. I'm better 576.6

Badge Red B. of Courage 167.1

Balance b. of power 563.1

Baiances weighed in the b. 62.105

Baldness felicity on the far side of b. 511.8

Baldwin fine thing to be honest 133.44

Ballot b. is stronger than the bullet 360.2

Balm wash the b. from an anointed king 498.236

Bang Not with a b. but a whimper 214.6

Bank b. and shoal of time 498.164

Bank balance better that a man should tyrannize over his b. 337.1

Bankrupt B. of Life 205.4

Banks Ye b. and braes 93.17

Bar no moaning of the b. 539.4

Barabbas B. was a publisher 104.3

Barbarians B., Philistines, Populace 20.15

Bargains rule for b. 191.16

Barge b. she sat in, like a burnish'd throne 498.8

Bark let no dog b. 498.187

Barkis B. is willin' 191.7

Bars Nor iron b. a cage 368.1

Based All progress is b. 97.5

Bastard I hope you will not...call me a b. 581.1

Bat black b., night, has flown 539.19

  Twinkle, twinkle, little b. 111.6

Bathing right honourable gentleman caught the Whigs b. 195.2

Bathing machine something between a large b. 257.6

Battalions not single spies but in b. 498.71

Battle b. of Britain 133.14

Bauble What shall we do with this b. 172.2

Bays To win the palm, the oak, or b. 384.4

Be If you want to b. happy, b. 547.2

  To b., or not to b. 498.61

Beaches we shall fight on the b. 133.12

Beadle b. on boxin' day 191.30

Beadsman B., after thousand aves told 332.7

Beaker b. full of the warm South 332.24

Be-all b. and the end-all here 498.164

Bean rows Nine b. will I have there 601.10

Bear authority be a stubborn b. 498.286

  B. ye one another's burdens 62.195

  Exit, pursued by a b. 498.282

  Human kind cannot b. 214.3

  I cannot b. men and women 499.23

  I had rather b. with you than b. you 498.19

  no man alive could b. it 499.37

  Thou shalt not b. false witness 62.21

Bear-baiting Puritan hated b. 375.3

Beard singed the Spanish king's b. 202.1

Beast for man or b. 226.1

  Man's life is cheap as b.'s 498.136

Beastie Wee, sleekit, cow'rin', tim'rous b. 93.11

Beastly Don't let's be b. to the Germans 163.13

Beaten We were not fairly b. 499.70

Beautiful good is the b. 448.1

  many men, so b. 144.8

  most b. things...are the most useless 484.2

Beauty B. and the lust for learning 51.7

  B. is...in the eye of the beholder 309.1

  B. is...in the eye of the beholder 562.1

  b. is only sin deep 486.3

  B. is truth, truth b. 332.18

  B. itself doth of itself persuade The eyes of men 498.304

  Exuberance is B. 67.24

  Love built on b. 199.4

  Mathematics possesses...b. 485.4

  She walks in b. 98.25

  Teaches such b. as a woman's eye 498.155

  terrible b. is born 601.6

  There is no excellent b. 30.34

  thing of b. is a joy for ever 332.4

  What *is* b., anyway? There's no such thing 445.1

Beaver And cultivate a b. 310.2

Becket this turbulent priest 287.1

Become What's b. of Waring? 83.19

Becoming Sunburn is very b. 163.7

Bed And so to b. 438.1

  b. be blest 5.1

  B....is the poor man's opera 310.12

Bedfellows Misery acquaints...strange b. 498.256
Beechen spare the b. tree 104.1
Beef roast b. of England 225.3
Beer chronicle small b. 498.221
  Life isn't all b. and skittles 307.1
  only a b. teetotaller 499.13
Bees murmuring of innumerable b. 539.24
Before I have been here b. 479.1
Begat and our fathers that b. us 62.113
Beggary b. in the love that can be reckon'd 498.5
  no vice but b. 498.125
Begin B. at the beginning 111.14
  If a man will b. with certainties 30.1
Beginning As it was in the b. 149.3
  Begin at the b. 111.14
  b. and the ending 62.212
  b. of fairies 40.1
  b. of the end 536.1
  end of the b. 133.20
  In the b. God 62.1
  In the b. was the Word 62.161
Beginnings end to the b. of all wars 475.5
Behaviour quality of moral b. varies 310.11
  sent down for indecent b. 569.1
Behind Get thee b. me, Satan 62.138
  In the dusk, with a light b. her 257.20
  led his regiment from b. 257.1
  part my hair b. 214.11
Behold b. it was a dream 90.6
  time of year thou mayst in me b. 498.294
Beholder Beauty is...in the eye of the b. 309.1
  Beauty is...in the eye of the b. 562.1
Being Knowledge is proportionate to b. 310.26
  live, and move, and have our b. 62.176
Belial Sons of B. 205.9
Beliefs holding two contradictory b. 427.4
Believe b. in the life to come 47.1
  I don't b. in fairies 40.2
  what we b. is not necessarily true 54.3
Believed two things that will be b. of any man 537.1
Bell B., book, and candle 498.126
  for whom the b. tolls 199.13
Bellamy B.'s veal pies 447.3
Bellies their b. were full 74.2
Bellyful Rumble thy b. 498.138
Belong I don't want to b. to any club 385.19
Below Down and away b. 20.4
Ben Jonson O rare B. 325.7
Berries I come to pluck your b. 401.9
Berry Doubtless God could have made a better b. 565.2
Beside star or two b. 144.9
Best all that's b. of dark and bright 98.25
  as in the b. it is 498.51
  b. is the enemy of the good 561.4
  b. lack all conviction 601.14
  b. of life is but intoxication 98.13
  b. of possible worlds 561.1
  b. that is known and thought in the world 20.17

Culture, the acquainting ourselves with the b. 20.18
  He is doing his b. 584.24
  Men of few words are the b. 498.96
  Never to have lived is b. 601.11
  Stolen sweets are b. 134.2
  we will do our b. 133.17
Bestial what remains is b. 498.222
Betimes to be up b. 498.269
Betray Nature never did b. the heart 595.23
Better b. strangers 498.29
  b. than a play 123.4
  b. to be alone 567.1
  b. to have loved and lost 539.11
  b. to have no opinion of God 30.19
  far, far, b. thing 191.34
  for b. for worse 149.15
  He is no b. 28.1
  I am getting b. and b. 161.1
  if you knows of a b. 'ole 33.1
  nae b. than he should be 93.6
  no b. than you should be 45.1
  when I'm bad I'm b. 576.6
Beulah B., peel me a grape 576.4
Beware B. of the artist who's an intellectual 229.1
  B. of the dog 442.1
Beyond live b. their incomes 486.2
Bible English B. 375.1
Bibles they have the land and we have the B. 252.1
Big b. man has no time 229.3
Big Brother B. is watching you 427.2
Big-endians B. and small-endians 535.4
Bigger b. they come 230.1
  it's a great deal b. than I am 109.15
Bill put 'Emily, I love you' on the back of the b. 385.17
Billboard b. lovely as a tree 414.5
Billet Every bullet has its b. 586.2
Biographies History...essence of...b. 109.3
Biography B. is about chaps 59.2
  no history; only b. 218.4
Bird B. is on the Wing 228.2
  B. thou never wert 500.13
Birds no b. sing 332.11
  that make fine b. 6.3
  where late the sweet b. sang 498.294
Birth B., and copulation, and death 214.14
  Our b. is but a sleep and a forgetting 595.5
Bishop blonde to make a b. kick a hole 120.1
Bisier he semed b. than he was 127.8
Bite b. some other of my generals 254.1
  b. the hand that fed them 91.12
Bites Every director b. the hand 263.4
  When a man b. a dog 175.1
Black future is...b. 34.3
Black Prince Let the boy win his spurs. 210.1
Blasphemies truths begin as b. 499.1
Blasphemy in the soldier is flat b. 498.181
Bled Scots wha hae wi' Wallace b. 93.15
Bleed If you prick us, do we not b. 498.193
Bless B. relaxes 67.23

God b. us, every one 191.5
Blessed   B. are the meek 62.118
B. are the pure in heart 62.119
B. are they that have not seen 62.173
b. be the name of the Lord 62.38
Blest   bed be b. 5.1
It is twice b. 498.194
Man never is, but always to be b. 452.17
Blind   If the b. lead the b. 62.137
love is b. 498.191
wing'd Cupid painted b. 498.202
Bliss   b. of solitude 595.3
B. was it in that dawn to be alive 595.14
Where ignorance is b. 268.4
Blithe   Hail to thee, b. Spirit 500.13
Block   chip of the old b. 91.6
Blockhead   No man but a b. ever wrote 323.29
Blonde   b. to make a bishop kick a hole 120.1
Blondes   Gentlemen always seem to remember
b. 365.1
Blood   b., toil, tears and sweat 133.10
humble and meek are thirsting for b. 426.3
I am in b. Stepp'd in so far 498.172
Bloody   All the faces...b. Poms 125.1
My head is b., but unbowed 285.1
Bloom   lilac is in b. 78.1
touch it, and the b. is gone 584.6
Blossom   letting a hundred flowers b. 379.2
Blossomer   great rooted b. 601.1
Blow   B., b., thou winter wind 498.25
B....till you burst 83.12
B., winds, and crack your cheeks 498.137
themselves must strike the b. 98.6
this b. Might be the be-all and the end-all
498.164
Bloweth   wind b. where it listeth 62.165
Blowing   b. through the continent 378.3
Blown   Flower that once has b. 228.4
Blows   meanest flower that b. 595.6
Blues   Twentieth-Century B. 163.11
Blunder   Youth is a b. 195.7
Blush   b. to the cheek of a young person 191.23
flower is born to b. unseen 268.8
Board   I struck the b. 290.1
Boat   beautiful pea-green b. 354.5
Boats   messing about in b. 264.1
Bodies   our dead b. must tell the tale 492.2
Body   Absent in b. 62.183
b. of a weak and feeble woman 215.2
human b. is sacred 582.1
laid asleep In b. 595.21
mind that makes the b. rich 498.253
more familiar with Africa than my own b.
426.1
O b. swayed to music 601.1
soul is not more than the b. 582.4
than he has in his whole b. 535.13
what exercise is to the b. 524.3
Boil   b. at different degrees 218.13
Bold   Be b., be b., and everywhere Be b. 519.2
Boldness   B., and again b., and always b. 177.1
Bolster   helping to b. up the capitalist system
569.21

Bombs   b. *are* unbelievable 579.1
Bones   Of his b. are coral made 498.254
Bonjour   B. tristesse 217.1
Bono   Cui b. 135.5
Bonum   Summum b. 135.3
Boojum   Snark was a B. 111.16
Book   bad b. is as much a labour to write
310.20
Bell, b., and candle 498.126
b.'s a b., although there's nothing in't 98.23
dainties that are bred in a b. 498.154
do not throw this b. about 55.1
Go, litel b. 127.18
good b. is the precious life-blood 401.36
he who destroys a good b., kills reason 401.35
If a b. is worth reading 484.1
I'll drown my b. 498.259
People seldom read a b. which is given 323.22
What a genius I had when I wrote that b.
535.19
What is the use of a b. 111.1
Books   b. by which the printers have lost 245.4
b. cannot be killed by fire 475.4
B. think for me 348.3
Borrowers of b. 348.2
but b. never die 475.4
few b....are worth reading 499.80
His b. were read 55.4
I keep my b. at the British Museum 97.2
No furniture so charming as b. 512.5
not all b. that are as dull as their readers
545.4
Of making many b. there is no end 62.85
proper study of mankind is b. 310.6
Some b. are to be tasted 30.38
true University is a collection of b. 109.7
We all know that b. burn 475.4
Bore   B., a person who talks 63.1
Every hero becomes a b. 218.11
He is an old b. 548.3
proof that God is a b. 392.3
Bored   Bores and B. 98.20
I wanted to be b. to death 190.4
Boredom   effect of b. on a large scale 314.3
Bores   B. and Bored 98.20
Boring   something...b.   about...happiness
310.13
Born   B. under one law 271.1
British Bourgeoisie Is not b. 508.1
He broke the law when he was b. 499.31
He was b. an Englishman 52.1
I was b. old 548.1
Man that is b. of a woman 62.39
Man was b. free 481.1
natural to die as to be b. 30.4
One is not b. a woman 46.1
one of woman b. 498.179
powerless to be b. 20.7
Some are b. great 498.273
Some men are b. mediocre 283.2
sucker b. every minute 39.1
terrible beauty is b. 601.6
thought of all this before you were b. 507.3

take the b. between the teeth 263.7
Bullet ballot is stronger than the b. 360.2
  Every b. has its billet 586.2
Bullfighting B. is the only art 284.1
Bums art…left to a lot of shabby b. 359.1
Bungler Man is a b. 499.44
Bunk History is more or less b. 234.1
Burden White Man's B. 341.9
Burdens Bear ye one another's b. 62.195
Burr kind of b.; I shall stick 498.185
Burst Blow your pipe there till you b. 83.12
  first that ever b. 144.5
Burthen b. of the mystery 595.21
Bury I come to b. Caesar 498.116
Bus Hitler has missed the b. 118.3
Bush good wine needs no b. 498.33
Bush-liar bigger outback lie than the last b. 352.1
Bushman Every true Australian b. 352.1
Business B. as usual 133.5
  B.…may bring money 27.3
  b. of America is b. 155.1
  dinner lubricates b. 493.1
  do b. in great waters 62.57
  If everybody minded their own b. 111.5
  That's the true b. precept 191.16
  To b. that we love we rise betime 498.12
Busyness b.…symptom of deficient vitality 529.2
Butlers b. and lady's maids do not reproduce 574.1
Butter b. will only make us fat 260.1
Buy I could b. back my introduction 385.13
Buying book…is worth b. 484.1
Byron Mad, bad, and dangerous 347.1

C

Cabbages c. and kings 111.22
Cabin small c. build there 601.10
Cabin'd c., cribb'd, confin'd, bound in 498.170
Caesar C.! dost thou lie so low 498.112
  I come to bury C. 498.116
  Not that I lov'd C. less 498.115
  Render therefore unto C. 62.141
Cage Marriage is like a c. 403.4
  Nor iron bars a c. 368.1
  robin redbreast in a c. 67.2
Cain first city C. 164.1
Cake anthology…plums…picked out of a c. 463.1
  Let them eat c. 380.1
Cakes no more c. and ale 498.271
Calais C. lying in my heart 387.1
Call leave to c. me anything 535.15
  one clear c. for me 539.4
Called c. a cold a cold 56.1
  many are c. 62.140
  never c. me mother 594.1
Calm sea is c. to-night 20.1

Cambridge ahead…either Oxford or C. 514.1
  Spring and summer did happen in C. 412.2
Came I c., I saw, I conquered 101.2
  I c. like Water 228.5
Camera I am a c. 316.1
Can cry c. no more. I c. 302.1
  He who c., does 499.51
  Talent does what it c. 394.1
Cancel c. half a Line 228.8
Cancels debt which c. all others 148.5
Candid save me, from the c. friend 107.2
Candle Bell, book, and c. 498.126
  little c. throws his beams 498.197
  Out, out, brief c. 498.177
  we shall this day light such a c. 350.1
Canem *Cave c.* 442.1
Canoe every man paddle his own c. 383.3
Cant Clear your mind of c. 323.34
Capability Negative C. 332.36
Capitalism c.…machine for the suppression 355.1
Capitalist C. production begets…its own negation 386.1
  helping to bolster up the c. system 569.21
Captain I am the c. of my soul 285.2
Captains C. of industry 109.13
Carbon c. atom possesses certain exceptional properties 319.1
Card table wrestled with a self-adjusting c. 546.2
Care age is full of c. 498.303
  Sleep that knits up the ravell'd sleave of c. 498.167
Career nothing which might damage his c. 40.4
Careful be very c. of vidders 191.27
Careless first fine c. rapture 83.7
Carelessness to lose both looks like c. 584.7
Carpe C. *diem* 303.1
Carpenter Walrus and the C. 111.21
Carriage very small second-class c. 257.6
Carry why not c. a watch? 548.2
Carthage C. must be destroyed 113.1
Carthago *delenda est* C. 113.1
Case in our c. we have not got 465.2
Casements Charm'd magic c. 332.27
Casket seal the hushed c. of my soul 332.31
Cassius C. has a lean and hungry look 498.107
Cast die is c. 101.3
  pale c. of thought 498.63
Casting It is no good c. out devils 351.4
Castle c. called Doubting C. 90.5
  man's house is his c. 143.1
Cat c. is the offspring of a c. 574.1
  God…a cosmic Cheshire c. 311.2
  More ways of killing a c. 340.1
  What C.'s averse to fish 268.1
  When I play with my c. 403.3
Catch First c. your hare 259.1
  Go, and c. a falling star 199.9
  only one c. and that was C.-22 283.1

Catholic lawful for a C. woman to avoid pregnancy 392.2

Caught I c. hold of the fille de chambre's...527.3

Causes dire offence from amorous c. 452.25
Home of lost c. 20.16

Caution c. in love is...fatal 485.3

Cavaliero perfect c. 98.1

Cave C. *canem* 442.1

Caverns c. measureless to man 144.19

Caviare c. to the general 498.58

Cease c. upon the midnight 332.26
have their day and c. to be 539.9
I will not c. from mental fight 67.7
poor shall never c. 62.28

Ceases forbearance c. to be a virtue 91.7

Celebrate I c. myself 582.2

Celerity C. is never more admir'd 498.11

Celia Come, my C., let us prove 325.6

Censorship Assassination is...form of c. 499.69

Centre c. cannot hold. 601.14
stables are the real c. 499.24

Cents you won't need the ten c. 385.15

Century twentieth c....c. of Fascism 411.1

Ceremony c. of innocence is drowned 601.14

Certain nothing is c. but death and taxes 239.5
One thing is c. 228.4

Certainties begin with c. 30.1

Chain flesh to feel the c. 77.3

Chains It's often safer to be in c. 330.1
Man...everywhere he is in c. 481.1
nothing to lose but their c. 386.5

Champagne not a c. teetotaller 499.13

Chance bludgeonings of c. 285.1
honest...sometimes by c. 498.285

Change If you leave a thing alone you leave it to a torrent of c. 129.21
Most of the c. we think we see 243.1
Plus ça c., plus c'est la même chose 331.1
Things do not c.; we c. 545.3
wind of c. is blowing through the continent 378.3

Changed All c., c. utterly 601.6

Changeth old order c. 539.8

Changing stress on not c. one's mind 388.1

Channel dream you are crossing the C. 257.6

Chapels c. had been churches 498.188

Chaps Biography is about C. 59.2

Chapter c. of accidents 128.11

Character c. in the world's torrent 261.5
Education...formation of c. 518.6
time to influence the c. of a child 314.5

Characteristic typically English c. 3.1

Characters c. in one of my novels 229.6

Chariot Time's winged c. hurrying near 384.2

Charity C. begins at home 82.5
C. is the power of defending...indefensi ble 129.12
C. shall cover the multitude of sins 62.209
faith, hope, c. 62.188
greatest of these is c. 62.188
In c. there is no excess 30.15

living need c. 19.1
without c. are nothing worth 149.10

Charles I He nothing common did or mean 384.7

Charley I'm C.'s aunt from Brazil 542.1

Charming People are either c. or tedious 584.11

Chastity Give me c. and continence 26.1

Cheating Winning Games Without...C. 453.1

Check dreadful is the c. 77.3

Cheek c., turn to him the other also 62.122

Cheeks Blow, winds, and crack your c. 498.137

Cheer cups, That c. but not inebriate 165.6

Cheese I do not like green c. 129.4
when the c. is gone 74.6

Cheque Mrs Claypool's c. will come back to you 385.16

Chequer-board C. of Nights and Days 228.7

Cherry C. ripe, ripe, ripe 291.1
C. Ripe themselves do cry 105.2
Loveliest of trees, the c. 304.1

Chess Life's too short for c. 99.1

Chewing c. little bits of String 55.2

Chicken mere c. feed 385.3
She's no c. 535.9
Some c. 133.19

Chickens Don't count your c. 6.4

Child all any reasonable c. can expect 426.2
C.! do not throw this book about 55.1
C. is father of the Man 595.13
c. is known by his doings 62.73
c. of five would understand this 385.5
getting wenches with c. 498.283
I heard one calling C. 290.2
In...simplicity a c. 452.6
little c. shall lead them 62.96
proper time to influence the *character* of a c. is 314.5
spoil the c. 96.3
unto us a c. is born 62.95
wise father that knows his own c. 498.190

Childe C. Roland to the Dark Tower 83.5

Childish I put away c. things 62.186

Childishness second c. 498.24

Children Anybody who hates c. and dogs 226.2
C. aren't happy with nothing to ignore 414.4
c. fear to go in the dark 30.3
C. sweeten labours 30.9
Come dear c. 20.4
Familiarity breeds...c. 553.4
My music is best understood by c. 530.2
Rachel weeping for her c. 62.114
Suffer the little c. to come unto me 62.150
tale which holdeth c. from play 506.2

Chill! bitter c. it was 332.5

Chimes c. at midnight 498.89

Chimney corner holdeth...old men from the c. 506.2

Chimney-sweepers As c., come to dust 498.38

Chip c. of the old block 91.6

Chirche-dore housbondes at c. 127.10

Chivalry age of c. is gone 91.8

Choirs   Bare ruin'd c. 498.294

Chosen   few are c. 62.140

Christ   churches have kill'd their C. 539.20
I beseech you, in the bowels of C. 172.1
Must then a C. perish in torment 499.71

Christendom   wisest fool in C. 286.2

Christian   in what peace a C. can die 4.9
object...to form C. men 21.2

Christianity   C. accepted...a metaphysical
system 310.10
C. one great curse 419.3
C....says that they are all fools 129.13
decay of C. 486.5
His C. was muscular 195.8
local cult called C. 277.1

Christmas   At C. I no more desire a rose
498.153
I'm walking backwards till C. 399.3
To perceive C. through its wrapping 578.2

Chronicle   c. of wasted time 498.297
c. small beer 498.221

Chunder   His favourite word...c. 308.1

Churches   chapels had been c. 498.188
c. have kill'd their Christ 539.20

Churchill   a man suffering from petrified
adolescence 61.2

Churchman   species of person called a 'Modern
C.' 569.10

Cigar   good c. is a smoke 341.2

Circle   Weave a c. round him thrice 144.21

Circumcision   Every luxury...atheism, breast-
feeding, c. 426.4

Circumlocution Office   C. 191.14

Circumstance   Pride, pomp, and c. 498.227

Circuses   bread and c. 329.2

Citizen   c. of the world 30.16
I am...a c. of the world 515.5

City   C. now doth, like a garment 595.11
first c. Cain 164.1

Civil   Too c. by half 502.8

Civilization   You can't say c. don't advance
472.1

Civilized   Woman will be the last thing c. 393.1

Class   history of c. struggles 386.4
machine for the suppression of one c. 355.1
patronize...without distinction of c. 499.29

Classes   back the masses against the c. 258.2
curse of the drinking c. 584.27
responsible and the irresponsible c. 351.1

Classic   c. is something that everybody wants
to have read 553.6

Clearing-house   C. of the World 117.1

Clerk   C. ther was of Oxenford also 127.5

Clever   It's c., but is it art? 341.3

Cleverness   height of c. is to conceal 471.4

Clichés   Let's have some new c. 263.10

Climate   common where the c.'s sultry 98.11
whole c. of opinion 25.3

Clive   What I like about C. 59.4

Clock   Stands the Church c. at ten to three?
78.2

Clocks   hands of c. in railway stations 153.9

Cloke   knyf under the c. 127.11

Clootie   Satan, Nick, or C. 93.1

Close   breathless hush in the C. tonight 416.1

Closing time   c. in the gardens of the West
153.1

Clothes   as if she were taking off all her c.
145.2
bought her wedding c. 4.7
c....thrown on her with a pitchfork 535.10
Nothing to wear but c. 339.1
walked away with their c. 195.2

Clothing   in sheep's c. 62.132

Cloud   fiend hid in a c. 67.11
I wandered lonely as a c. 595.2

Clouds   trailing c. of glory 595.5

Clown   I remain...a c. 121.3

Club   I don't want to belong to any c. 385.19
Mankind is a c. 129.24

Coals   heap c. of fire upon his head 62.75

Cock   Before the c. crow twice 62.151
C. and a Bull 527.4

Cod   piece of c. passes all understanding 373.2

Coffee   C. which makes the politician wise
452.29
measured out my life with c. spoons 214.9

Cogito   C., ergo sum 189.1

Coil   shuffled off this mortal c. 498.61

Coke   Happiness is like c. 310.17

Cold   c. in blood 498.7
C. Pastoral 332.17
c. war 42.1
I beg c. comfort 498.129
We called a c. a c. 56.1

Coleridge   He talked on for ever 281.1

Coliseum   While stands the C., Rome shall
stand 98.9

Collections   those mutilators of c. 348.2

Colour'd   woman c. ill 498.302

Colours   All c. will agree in the dark 30.5

Combine   When bad men c. 91.13

Come   bigger they c. 230.1
Do you c. here often? 399.1
men may c. and men may go 539.1
Shape of Things to C. 574.2
Thou'lt c. no more 498.152
Whistle and she'll c. to you 45.9

Comedies   c. are ended by a marriage 98.14

Comedy   All I need to make a c. 121.2
at a c. we only look 310.7
Farce refined becomes high c. 166.1
world is a c. 564.2

Comfort   c. in the strength of love 595.8
I beg cold c. 498.129
I'll not, carrion c., Despair 302.1
rod and thy staff c. me 62.48
Society is no c. 498.37
Two loves I have, of c. and despair 498.302

Coming   C. through the rye 93.4

Command   mortals to c. success 4.1
When Britain first, at Heaven's c. 544.1

Commanded   Nature, to be c. 30.41

Commandment   new c. I give unto you 62.170

Commandments   keep his c. 62.86

Commendeth   obliquely c. himself 82.1

Commerce   honour sinks where c. long prevails 262.6

Common   good thing, to make it too c. 498.84
He nothing c. did or mean 384.7

Commonplace   great minds in the c. 306.3
nothing so unnatural as the c. 201.4

Commonwealth   C. of Nations 477.1

Community   We are part of the c. of Europe 258.3

Company   better to be alone than in bad c. 567.1
Crowds without c. 255.2
few are qualified to shine in c. 535.17
In married life three is c. 584.5
people whose c. is coveted 376.1
Take the tone of the c. 128.4
Tell me what c. thou keepest 116.5

Companye   other c. in youthe 127.10

Comparative   progress is simply a c. 129.8

Compare   any she belied with false c. 498.301
c. thee to a summer's day 498.288

Comparisons   c. are odious 199.5
C. are odorous 498.214

Complains   No one c. of his judgement 471.1

Complaint   I want to register a c. 385.12

Complete   disguised as a C. Man 310.3

Comprehended   c. two aspicious persons 498.215

Compromise   C. used to mean that half a loaf 129.23
government...is founded on c. 91.4

Conceal   words...half c. 539.10

Concealment   c., like a worm i' th' bud 498.272

Concept   If the c. of God has 34.1

Conception   dad is present at the c. 426.2

Concern   power narrows the areas of man's c. 335.4

Concessions   c. of the weak are the c. of fear 91.1

Conclusion   they would not reach a c. 499.82

Conclusions   Life is the art of drawing...c. 97.4

Condemn   No man can justly censure or c. another 82.4

Condition   c. of man...is a c. of war 298.1
hopes for the human c. 106.9
To be a poet is a c. 267.4
wearisome c. of humanity 271.1

Confin'd   cabin'd, cribb'd, c. 498.170

Conflict   We are in an armed c. 208.2

Confusion   nothing to offer anybody except my own c. 336.4

Congreve   C. is the only sophisticated playwright 554.1

Connect   Only c. 237.1

Conquer   when we c. without danger 158.1

Conquered   I came, I saw, I c. 101.2

Conquering   C. kings 119.1
not c. but fighting well 160.1

Conquers   Love c. all 560.4

Conquest   Roman C. was, however, a *Good Thing* 495.2

Conscience   c. does make cowards of us all 498.63
C. is the inner voice 392.1
C. is the...rejection of a particular wish 242.3
I'll catch the c. of the King 498.60

Conservatism   c....adherence to the old and tried 360.4
c. is based upon the idea 129.21

Conservative   C. government is an organized hypocrisy 195.3
Or else a little C. 257.4

Consistency   C. is contrary to nature 310.8

Conspiracies   All professions are c. 499.17

Conspiracy   Indecency's C. of Silence 499.58

Conspirators   All the c. 498.123

Constabulary   When c. duty's to be done 257.19

Constancy   infernal c. of the women who love me 499.63

Constant   Friendship is c. in all other things 498.209

Consume   more history than they can c. locally 486.1
no more right to c. happiness 499.11

Consummation   c. Devoutly to be wish'd 498.61

Consumption   this c. of the purse 498.85

Contagion   c. of the world's slow stain 500.1

Contain   I c. multitudes 582.5

Contemptible   c. little army 585.1

Contend   hundred schools of thought c. 379.2

Content   desire is got without c. 498.169
draw upon c. for the deficiencies of fortune 262.9

Contented   With what I most enjoy c. least 498.290

Contests   mighty c. rise from trivial things 452.25

Continence   Give me chastity and c. 26.1

Continent   On the C. people have good food 395.1

Continents   which extends over many nations and three c. 201.8

Continual   c. state of inelegance 27.12

Contract   Every law is a c. 494.3
verbal c. isn't worth the paper 263.6

Contradict   Do I c. myself 582.5

Contradiction   Woman's at best a c. 452.22

Contrairy   everythink goes c. with me 191.6

Contraries   Without C. is no progression 67.18

Contrariwise   'C.,' continued Tweedledee 111.20

Convent   C. of the Sacred Heart 214.15

Conversation   proper subject of c. 128.12

Conviction   best lack all c. 601.14

Cook   C. is a little unnerved 60.1
c. was a good c., as cooks go 486.4
ill c. that cannot lick his own fingers 498.250

Copulation   Birth, and c., and death 214.14

Coquette   c. is a woman who rouses passions 499.81

Coral   C. is far more red 498.300
Of his bones are c. made 498.254

Cordial   gold in phisik is a c. 127.9

Corn amid the alien c. 332.27
  Whoever could make two ears of c. 535.5
Corner c. in the thing I love 498.225
  head stone of the c. 62.59
  some c. of a foreign field 78.3
Coromandel On the Coast of C. 354.1
Coronets Kind hearts are more than c. 539.15
Corpse He'd make a lovely c. 191.17
Correctly anxious to do the wrong thing c. 486.6
Corrupt Among a people generally c. 91.15
  Power tends to c. 1.1
Corruption C....symptom of constitutional liberty 255.3
Cosmos c. is about the smallest hole 129.18
Couch century of the psychiatrist's c. 377.1
  time as a tool not as a c. 335.2
Counsel sometimes c. take—and sometimes Tea 452.26
Count Don't c. your chickens 6.4
Counties see the coloured c. 304.2
Country ask not what your c. can do for you 335.1
  c. diversion 151.6
  c. from whose bourn no traveller returns 498.62
  c.; it is a kind of healthy grave 512.9
  c. of young men 218.14
  Fornication...in another c. 381.6
  God made the c. 165.3
  How I leave my c. 447.4
  I love thee still, my c. 165.4
  loathe the c. 151.6
  nothing good...in the c. 281.8
  our c., right or wrong 183.1
  save in his own c. 62.136
  she is my c. still 131.1
  undiscover'd c. 498.62
  what was good for the c. 588.1
Countrymen Friends, Romans, c. 498.116
Courage c. never to submit or yield 401.16
  Red Badge of C. 167.1
  tale...of...c. of my companions 492.2
Course c. of true love never did run smooth 498.201
  earth's diurnal c. 595.16
Courteous If a man be...c. to strangers 30.16
Covet Thou shalt not c. thy neighbour's house 62.22
Cow till the c. comes home 45.8
Coward c. does it with a kiss 584.1
  No c. soul is mine 77.1
Cowardice we were guilty of Noel C. 190.3
Cowards C. die many times 498.109
  public...is the greatest of c. 281.5
  Thus conscience does make c. of us all 498.63
Coyness This c., lady, were no crime 384.1
Cradled c. into poetry by song 500.5
Cradles bit the babies in the c. 83.11
Craft c. so long to lerne 127.16
Cream choking her with c. 340.1
Created c. man in his own image 62.3
Creation greatest week...since the c. 420.1

Creatures call these delicate c. ours 498.225
  From fairest c. we desire increase 498.287
Creed suckled in a c. outworn 595.10
Creeds Vain are the thousand c. 77.2
Creep I wants to make your flesh c. 191.25
  Wit that can c. 452.5
Creeping Nature is c. up 577.6
Creetur lone lorn c. 191.6
Crete people of C....make more history 486.1
Cricket C. A sport, at which the contenders drive a ball with sticks 323.2
  c. on the hearth 401.4
  c. It's more than a game 307.2
Crime coyness, lady, were no c. 384.1
  c. is...desire for aesthetic expression 569.11
  Napoleon of c. 201.6
  no...c. so shameful as poverty 223.1
  punishment fit the c. 257.11
  Treason was no C. 205.9
Crimes how many c. committed 106.3
  liberty, what c. are committed in thy name 474.1
  worst of c. is poverty 499.30
Critic function of the c. 54.2
  no statue has ever been put up to a c. 504.1
Critical nothing if not c. 498.220
Criticism great deal of contemporary c. 129.4
  my own definition of c. 20.17
  People ask you for c. 388.2
Critics c. all are ready made 98.24
Cromwell restless C. could not cease 384.6
  Some C. guiltless 268.9
Crook I am not a c. 420.2
Crop watering last year's c. 213.1
Cross-bow With my c. I shot 144.4
Crowd Far from the madding c. 268.10
  select Out of the c. a mistress or a friend 500.3
Crowds C. without company 255.2
Crown influence of the C. has increased 207.1
  I will give thee a c. of life 62.213
  Uneasy lies the head that wears a c. 498.88
  within the hollow c. 498.237
Crucify C. him 62.152
Cruellest April is the c. month 214.16
Crumbs c. which fell from the rich man's table 62.158
Cry make 'em c. 464.1
Crying one c. in the wilderness 62.115
Cui C. bono 135.5
Cult local c. called Christianity 277.1
Cultivate c. our garden 561.3
Culture C., the acquainting ourselves with the best 20.18
  When I hear anyone talk of C. 260.3
Cup Ah, fill the C. 228.6
  Come, fill the C. 228.2
  tak a c. o' kindness yet 93.3
Cupid wing'd C. painted blind 498.202
Cups c., that cheer but not inebriate 165.6
Cure C. the disease 30.27
  maladies we must not seek to c. 458.3
  Prevention is better than c. 437.2

Curfew   C. tolls the knell of parting day 268.5
Curiosity   Newspapers always excite c. 348.4
Curious   That was the c. incident 201.9
Curiouser   C. and c. 111.2
Curse   Christianity the one great c. 419.3
   c. is come upon me 539.16
   Partisanship is our great c. 469.1
Curst   C. be the verse 452.4
Curtain   iron c. has descended across the
   Continent 133.23
   Ring down the c. 460.2
Custodes   Quis custodiet ipsos c.? 329.1
Custom   C. calls me to't 498.34
   c. loathsome to the eye 318.1
   c. More honour'd in the breach than the
   observance 498.49
   c. stale Her infinite variety 498.9
Customers   raising up a people of c. 510.2
   When you are skinning your c. 344.1
Cut   It isn't etiquette to c. any one 111.32
   laurels all are c. 304.7
Cuts   he that c. off twenty years of life 498.111
Cynara   faithful to thee, C. 200.1

D

Dad   if the d. is present at the conception 426.2
Daffodils   Fair d., we weep to see 291.3
   host, of golden d. 595.2
Dainties   d. that are bred in a book 498.154
Dalliance   primrose path of d. 498.46
Damage   nothing which might d. his career
   40.4
Dame   La belle D. sans Merci 332.12
Damn   D. braces 67.24
   D. with faint praise 452.3
Damnations   Twenty-nine distinct d. 83.16
Damn'd   thou must be d. perpetually 381.3
Damned   Publish and be d. 573.4
Dance   D., d., d. little lady 163.14
   Folk d. like a wave of the sea 601.7
   know the dancer from the d. 601.1
   merry love to d. 601.8
   On with the d. 98.8
   those move easiest who have learn'd to d.
   452.13
   will you join the d.? 111.11
Dancer   know the d. from the dance 601.1
Danger   d....lies in acting well 131.2
   only real d. that exists is man 327.3
   when we conquer without d. 158.1
Dangerous   little learning is a d. thing 452.10
   little sincerity is...d. 584.20
   Mad, bad, and d. to know 347.1
   more d. the abuse 91.16
Dappled   Glory be to God for d. things 302.4
Dare   d. to eat a peach 214.11
Darien   Silent, upon a peak in D. 332.29
Daring   d. to excel 131.2
Dark   children fear...the d. 30.3

colours will agree in the d. 30.5
Genuineness only thrives in the d. 310.24
great leap in the d. 298.4
never to refuse a drink after d. 392.6
nightmare of the d. 25.4
O d., d., d., amid the blaze of noon 401.30
we are for the d. 498.16
What in me is d. Illumine 401.15
Darken   never d. my towels again 385.7
Darkling   as on a d. plain 20.2
Darkly   through a glass, d. 62.187
Darkness   people that walked in d. 62.94
Daughter   Don't put your d. on the stage
   163.10
David   D. his ten thousands 62.34
Dawn   Bliss was it in that d. to be alive 595.14
Day   bright d. is done 498.16
   compare thee to a summer's d. 498.288
   d. returns too soon 98.27
   every d....lost, in which I do not make a new
   acquaintance 323.36
   every dog has his d. 70.1
   from this d. forward 149.15
   Good morning to the d.: and, next, my gold
   325.5
   If every d. in the life of a school 353.1
   in the d. of judgement 149.8
   It takes place every d. 106.5
   It was such a lovely d. 388.7
   live murmur of a summer's d. 20.9
   long d.'s task is done 498.13
   Our little systems have their d. 539.9
   runs through the roughest d. 498.160
   Seize the d. 303.1
   So foul and fair a d. 498.158
   Sufficient unto the d. 62.129
   Sweet d., so cool, so calm 290.8
   Without all hope of d. 401.30
Daylight   rule never to drink by d. 392.6
Days   Ancient of d. 62.107
   d. of wine and roses 200.3
   Do not let us speak of darker d. 133.18
   his d. are as grass 62.56
   live laborious d. 401.11
   loved three whole d. together 531.1
   Shuts up the story of our d. 462.1
   Six d. shalt thou labour 62.16
Dead   American professors like their litera-
   ture...d. 359.2
   D....never called me mother 594.1
   fairy somewhere...falls down d. 40.2
   great deal to be said for being d. 59.4
   healthy and wealthy and d. 546.1
   It's easier to replace a d. man 499.18
   Mistah Kurtz—he d. 154.3
   Queen Anne's d. 147.2
   Something was d. in each of us 584.2
Deadener   Habit is a great d. 47.6
Deadly   female...is more d. 341.4
   Soap and education...are more d. 553.2
Deal   new d. for the American people 475.1
Dean   drink to the queer old D. 520.2

Let the D. and Canons lay their heads together 512.3
Dear too d. for my possessing 498.295
Dearer d. still is truth 17.4
Death After the first d., there is no other 543.3
Angel of D. has been abroad 75.1
Any man's d. diminishes me 199.13
artist is in danger of d. 284.1
Be thou faithful unto d. 62.213
Birth, and copulation, and d. 214.14
cuts off...fearing d. 498.111
d. after life does greatly please 519.1
D. be not proud 199.8
D. hath no more dominion 62.179
D. is still working like a mole 290.5
D. must be distinguished from dying 512.4
D....we haven't succeeded in vulgarizing 310.9
dread of something after d. 498.62
give me liberty or give me d. 289.1
I here importune d. awhile 498.14
I wanted to be bored to d. 190.4
Love is strong as d. 62.89
Men fear d. 30.3
nothing is certain but d. and taxes 239.5
O d., where is thy sting 62.189
one that had been studied in his d. 498.161
Reports of my d. are greatly exaggerated 553.7
sad stories of the d. of kings 498.237
Thou wast not born for d. 332.27
till d. us do part 149.15
tragedies are finished by a d. 98.14
useless life is an early d. 261.4
valiant never taste of d. but once 498.109
valley of the shadow of d. 62.48
wages of sin is d. 62.180
way to dusty d. 498.177
we owe God a d. 498.90
Deaths More d. than one must die 584.3
Debauchee D., one who has...pursued pleasure 63.3
Debt d. which cancels all others 148.5
promise made is a d. unpaid 496.1
Debts He that dies pays all d. 498.257
Decadence difference between our d. and the Russians' 546.7
Decay All humane things are subject to d. 205.13
woods d. and fall 539.26
Deceived Be not d. 62.196
Decency D. is Indecency's Conspiracy of Silence 499.58
Decent d. means poor 437.1
Declare nothing to d. except my genius 584.25
Decorated proverb...much matter d. 245.3
Decorum Dulce et d. est 303.2
Dulce et d. est 430.2
Deed good d. in a naughty world 498.197
good d. to forget a poor joke 72.1
right d. for the wrong reason 214.18
Deeds better d. shall be in water writ 45.6
Deep beauty is only sin d. 486.3

one is of the d. 526.1
Thoughts...too d. for tears 595.6
what a very singularly d. young man 257.14
Deeper d. than did ever plummet sound 498.259
whelm'd in d. gulphs 165.1
Deeth D. is an ende of every worldly sore 127.12
Defeat d. without a war 133.9
In d. unbeatable 133.43
Defect Chief D. of Henry King 55.2
Defence Never make a d. or apology 122.1
Deferred Hope d. maketh the heart sick 62.69
Defied Age will not be d. 30.29
Definite d. maybe 263.5
Definition true d. of a style 535.6
Degree d. of delight 91.17
when d. is shak'd 498.262
Degrees we boil at different d. 218.13
Delenda D. est Carthago 113.1
Deliberates woman that d. is lost 4.2
Delight degree of d. 91.17
Energy is Eternal D. 67.20
go to't with d. 498.12
Spirit of D. 500.14
Studies serve for d. 30.37
unrest...men miscall d. 500.1
very temple of d. 332.21
Delighted Whosoever is d. in solitude 30.26
Delights Man d. not me 498.57
To scorn d. 401.11
Deliver d. me from myself 82.6
Déluge Après nous le d. 451.1
Delved When Adam d. 37.1
Democracy D. substitutes election by the incompetent 499.49
d., the last refuge of cheap misgovernment 499.35
world must be made safe for d. 591.3
Democratic We must be...d. and patronize 499.29
Demon woman wailing for her d.-lover 144.20
Demonstrandum Quod erat d. 220.1
Denies spirit that always d. 261.3
Denmark rotten in the state of D. 498.50
Dentist For physical pleasure I'd sooner go to my d. 569.16
Deny Those who d. freedom 360.3
thou shalt d. me thrice 62.151
Derangement nice d. of epitaphs 502.6
Descriptions d. of the fairest wights 498.297
Desert Use every man after his d. 498.59
Deserts D. of vast eternity 384.2
Deserves None but the Brave d. 205.12
Designing I am d. St. Paul's 59.3
Desire antidote to d. 151.8
d. is got without content 498.169
d. should so many years outlive performance 498.87
It provokes the d. 498.168
like d. for preventing the thing one says 458.4
not to get your heart's d. 499.45
to have few things to d. 30.21

universal innate d. 97.5

Desired   war which...left nothing to be d. 74.5

Desires   He who d. but acts not 67.22
starting-point for further d. 458.1

Despair   Giant D. 90.5
I'll not...D., not feast on thee 302.1
Patience, a minor form of d. 63.7
some divine d. 539.22
without understanding d. 346.2

Despairs   He who d. over an event is a coward 106.9

Desperation   lives of quiet d. 545.1

Despise   making some other Englishman d. him 499.66

Despond   name of the slough was D. 90.2

Despotism   France was a long d. 109.8

Destiny   I were walking with d. 133.31

Destroy   whom God wishes to d. 221.1
Whom the gods wish to d. 153.6

Destruction   one purpose...d. of Hitler 133.35
Pride goeth before d. 62.71

Detail   life is frittered away by d. 545.5
novels are an accumulation of d. 579.3

Detest   they d. at leisure 98.19

Devil   cleft the D.'s foot 199.9
d. can cite Scripture 498.189
d. should have all the good tunes 295.1
d.'s madness—War 496.3
d.'s walking parody 129.2
Is the d. to have all the passions 499.39
Renounce the d. 149.11
world, the flesh, and the d. 149.7

Devils   It is no good casting out d. 351.4

Diamond   d....bracelet lasts forever 365.3

Diamonds   goodness, those d. are lovely! 576.3
to give him d. back 246.1

Diary   I never travel without my d. 584.9

Die   appointed unto men once to d. 62.203
Before we grow old and d. 601.5
books never d. 475.4
Cowards d. many times 498.109
d. in the last ditch 92.1
d. in the last ditch 586.1
d. is cast 101.3
D....last thing I shall do 432.1
either do, or d. 45.3
good d. first 595.1
If I should d. 78.3
in what peace a Christian can d. 4.9
I shall have to d. beyond my means 584.26
It is natural to d. 30.4
Let us do or d. 93.16
man can d. but once 498.90
More deaths than one must d. 584.3
No young man believes he shall ever d. 281.3
place...to d. in 82.7
save your world you asked this man to d. 25.2
seems it rich to d. 332.26
Their's but to do and d. 539.3
they...argue that I shall some day d. 353.3
They that d. by famine 288.1
those about to d. salute you 532.2
to d., and go we know not where 498.184

tomorrow we shall d. 62.97

Died   dog it was that d. 262.2
Men have d. from time to time 498.31

Diem   *Carpe d.* 303.1

Dies   Call no man happy until he d. 516.1
Function never d. 595.15
He that d. pays all debts 498.257
It matters not how a man d. 323.19
king never d. 65.1

Diet   Praise is the best d. 512.6

Different   rich are d. 229.4

Difficult   D. do you call it, Sir? I wish it were impossible 323.37
intellectual...found it too d. 491.1
It is d. to be humble 196.1

Digest   mark, learn, and inwardly d. 149.9

Digestion   d. is the great secret of life 512.8
Things sweet to taste prove in d. sour 498.233

Diggeth   Whoso d. a pit 62.76

Diminished   ought to be d. 207.1

Dine   wretches hang that jury-men may d. 452.28

Dinkum   d. hard-swearing Aussie 279.1

Dinner   Breakfast, D., Lunch and Tea 55.3
d. lubricates business 493.1
D....possessed only two dramatic features 455.2
man is...better pleased when he has a good d. 323.39

Diplomat   d. these days is nothing but a head-waiter 555.2

Directions   rode madly off in all d. 353.4

Director   Every d. bites the hand 263.4

Disarmament   precede the d. of the victors 133.30

Disaster   nation is not in danger of financial d. 391.1

Disbelief   willing suspension of d. 144.22

Disc   round d. of fire 67.17

Disciple   d. of Bernard Shaw 499.20

Discommendeth   He who d. others 82.1

Discontent   winter of our d. 498.239

Discretion   better part of valour is d. 498.82
years of d. 149.12

Discrimination   sympathetic without d. 227.2

Disease   Cure the d. 30.27
Life is an incurable d. 164.2
remedy is worse than the d. 30.18
strange d. of modern life 20.10
this long d., my life 452.2

Diseases   d. of the mind 524.1

Disgrace   d. to our family name of Wagstaff 385.9
Intellectual d. 25.5
Poverty is no d. to a man 512.1

Disguise   Speech...to d. his thoughts 536.3

Dishonour   honour rooted in d. 539.6

Disliked   I have always d. myself 153.8

Dismal   D. Science 109.11

Disobedience   Of Man's first d. 401.14

Disorder   sweet d. in the dress 291.2

Displeasing   misfortunes...not d. 471.5

Disposes   God d. 333.1

Dissipation d. without pleasure 255.2
Dissolve Fade far away, d. 332.25
Distance d. lends enchantment 104.2
Distress All pray in their d. 67.16
  mean man is always full of d. 150.8
Distrusts him who d. himself 471.15
Ditch die in the last d. 92.1
  die in the last d. 586.1
Dive search for Pearls must d. below 205.15
Diversion 'tis a country d. 151.6
Divide absurd to d. people into good and bad 584.11
Divided If a house be d. 62.147
Divine to forgive d. 452.15
Divinity d. in odd numbers 498.200
  d. that shapes our ends 498.74
  piece of d. in us 82.8
  There's such d. doth hedge a king 498.72
Division absurd d. into sexes 569.14
Do D. as I say, not as I d. 494.1
  D. as you would be done by 128.5
  D. not d. unto others 499.46
  d. other men 191.16
  either d., or die 45.3
  far, far, better thing that I d. 191.34
  I am to d. what I please 241.1
  If to d. were as easy as to know what were good to d. 498.188
  Let us d. or die 93.16
  so much to d. 467.1
  so much to d., So little done 539.13
  they would d. you 191.16
  to d. something is to create existence 489.4
  what you can d. for your country 335.1
Doctor I do not love thee, D. Fell 79.1
Doctrine d. of the strenuous life 476.1
Doctrines What makes all d. plain 96.6
Dodger artful D. 191.21
Does He who can, d. 499.51
  It's dogged as d. it 550.1
Dog Beware of the d. 442.1
  curious incident of the d. in the night-time 201.9
  d. it was that died 262.2
  d., to gain some private ends, Went mad and bit the man 262.1
  door is what a d. is...on the wrong side of 414.1
  every d. has his day 70.1
  His Highness' d. at Kew 452.24
  I ope my lips let no d. bark 498.187
  When a d. bites a man 175.1
  whose d. are you 452.24
Dogged It's d. as does it 550.1
Dogs All the d. of Europe bark 25.4
  Anybody who hates children and d. 226.2
  let slip the d. of war 498.114
  Mad d. and Englishmen 163.9
  Rats...fought the d. 83.11
  woman who is...kind to d. 51.6
Doing we learn by d. 17.1
  Whatever is worth d. 128.2
Doings All our d. without charity 149.10

child is known by his d. 62.73
Dollars What's a thousand d.? 385.3
Dominion Death hath no more d. 62.179
Done bright day is d. 498.16
  do as you would be d. by 128.5
  d. those things...we ought not 149.2
  If it were d. when 'tis d. 498.163
  Justice...should...be seen to be d. 292.1
  Let justice be d. 224.1
  let us have d. with you 13.1
  long day's task is d. 498.13
  Nothing is ever d. 499.34
  so little d. 539.13
  thy worldly task hast d. 498.38
  What you do not want d. to yourself 150.12
Dong D. with a luminous Nose 354.2
Doom even to the edge of d. 498.298
  regardless of their d. 268.3
Doon banks and braes o' bonnie D. 93.17
Dooney my fiddle in D. 601.7
Door d. is what a dog is perpetually on the wrong side of 414.1
  world will make a beaten path to his d. 218.15
Doors d. of perception were cleansed 67.26
Dots I never could make out what those damned d. 132.4
Doublethink D. means the power of holding two contradictory beliefs 427.4
Doubt fanatic...over-compensates a secret d. 310.28
  new Philosophy calls all in d. 199.1
  When in d., win the trick 305.1
Doubting castle called D. Castle 90.5
Doubtless D. God could have made a better berry 565.2
Doubts end in d. 30.1
Dove wings like a d. 62.53
Doves moan of d. in immemorial elms 539.24
Down He that is d. 90.7
  I'll bring the etchings d. 546.3
  put it d. a we 191.32
Drag Why d. in Velasquez? 577.3
Drain you will leave by the next town d. 520.1
Dramatic Dinner...two d. features 455.2
Draught O, for a d. of vintage 332.23
Drawers d. of water 62.30
Dread close your eyes with holy d. 144.21
  most men d. it 499.50
Dreadful d. is the check 77.3
  some have called thee Mighty and d. 199.8
Dream behold it was a d. 90.6
  glory and the freshness of a d. 595.4
  old men shall d. dreams 62.109
  sight to d. of 144.17
  To sleep, perchance to d. 498.61
  you d. you are crossing the Channel 257.6
Dreamer poet and the d. are distinct 332.9
Dreaming after-dinner's sleep, d. on both 498.183
  d. spires 20.13
Dreams Fanatics have their d. 332.8
  In d. begins responsibility 601.12
  We are such stuff As d. are made on 498.258

Egotist E., a person...more interested in himself 63.4

Egypt I am dying, E., dying 498.14
We are not at war with E. 208.2

Eighteen I knew almost as much at e. as I do now 323.16

Element One God, one law, one e. 539.14

Elementary 'E.,' said he 201.5

Elements I tax not you, you e., with unkindness 498.138
something that was before the e. 82.8

Elephant I shot an e. in my pajamas 385.2

Elms moan of doves in immemorial e. 539.24

Else Lord High Everything E. 257.7

Embalmer soft e. of the still midnight 332.30

Embarras e. des richesses 11.1

Embody I, my lords, e. the Law 257.3

Embrace none, I think, do there e. 384.3

Emily E., I love you 385.17

Emotion degree of my aesthetic e. 54.2
e. recollected in tranquillity 595.24
Sorrow is tranquillity...in e. 433.5

Emperor e. of ice-cream 528.1

Emperors e. can't do it all by themselves 74.4

Empire E. is a Commonwealth 477.1

Empires day of E. has come. 117.2

Employee E....Rise to his Level of Incompetence 441.1

Enchantment lends e. to the view 104.2

Encourage to e. the others 561.2

End all economists were laid e. to e. 499.82
beginning of the e. 536.1
Big-e.ians and small-e.ians 535.4
e. of the beginning 133.20
e. to the beginnings of all wars 475.5
he shall e. in doubts 30.1
I was with him to the e. 385.6
our minutes hasten to their e. 498.293
world without e. 149.3
young ladies...were laid e. to e. 433.7

Ending beginning and the e. 62.212

Ends divinity that shapes our e. 498.74

Endurable 'Twill make a thing e. 595.8

Endure Men must e. their going 498.151
Youth's a stuff will not e. 498.270

Endured Human life...is to be e. 323.9

Endures man is in love he e. more 419.1

Enemies e. of Freedom 314.2
Love your e. 62.123

Enemy best is the e. of the good 561.4
If thine e. be hungry 62.75
No e. but winter 498.21
no more sombre e. of good art 153.7

Energy E. is Eternal Delight 67.20

Enfants Allons, e., de la patrie 480.1
Les e. terribles 250.1

Engineers Artists are not e. of the soul 335.5

England Be E. what she will 131.1
E. expects every man will do his duty 415.1
E. is a nation of shopkeepers 413.2
E. is a paradise for women 94.3
E. is the mother of parliaments 75.2
E. is the paradise of women 233.1

E.'s green and pleasant land 67.7
E.'s pleasant pastures 67.6
E., with all thy faults 165.4
in E. people have good table manners 395.1
Law of E. is a very strange 178.1
Oh, to be in E. 83.6
roast beef of E. 225.3
Stately Homes of E. 163.2
suspended in favour of E. 499.25
that is forever E. 78.3
this realm, this E. 498.235
We dont bother much about dress and manners in E. 499.73

English E. as she is Spoke 552.1
E. (it must be owned) are rather a foul-mouthed nation 281.2
our E. nation, if they have a good thing...make it too common 498.84
our E. tongue a gallimaufry or hodgepodge 519.5
typically E. characteristic 3.1

Englishman E. does not travel to see Englishmen 527.1
E....is afraid to feel 237.2
E....queue of one 395.2
E. thinks he is moral 499.40
He was born an E. 52.1
impossible for an E. to open his mouth 499.66
never find an E. among the underdogs 569.18
No E. is ever fairly beaten 499.70
tale...which would have stirred...E. 492.2
to behold the E. at his best 227.1
You may be the most liberal Liberal E. 351.1
you will never find an E. in the wrong 499.59

Englishmen Englishman does not travel to see E. 527.1
Mad dogs and E. 163.9
nothing so bad...you will not find E. doing it 499.59
When two E. meet 323.6

Enjoy I don't have to go out and e. it 511.10

Enjoyed much is to be endured and little to be e. 323.9

Enough It comes soon e. 212.1
patriotism is not e. 115.1

Enslaves Reason e. all 499.54

Enthusiasm Nothing great was ever achieved without e. 218.2

Enthusiasts so few e. can be trusted 36.1

Entrances their exits and their e. 498.23

Entuned E. in hir nose 127.4

Epigram it purrs like an e. 382.1

Epigrams long despotism tempered by e. 109.8

Epilogue good play needs no e. 498.33

Episode Love...but an e. in a man's 523.2

Epitaphs nice derangement of e. 502.6

Epitome all Mankind's E. 205.7

Equal All animals are e. 427.1
all men are created e. 320.1
Inferiors revolt...that they may be e. 17.3
So far is it from being true that men are naturally e. 323.18

some...are more e. than others 427.1
That all men are e. is a proposition 310.21
Equally   I hate everyone e. 226.3
Equanimity   e. bordering on indifference 257.21
Equivocator   drink...e. with lechery 498.168
Eros   Unarm E. 498.13
Err   To e. is human 452.15
Erred   We have e., and strayed from thy ways 149.1
Errors   E., like Straws upon the surface 205.15
Escape   Gluttony is an emotional e. 190.2
There is nothing to e. from 214.17
Esprit de corps   English characteristic... 3.1
Essay   e. on 'self-indulgence' 569.3
Estate   e. o' th' world were now undone 498.178
fourth e. of the realm 375.2
État   *L'é. c'est moi* 366.1
Etchings   I'll bring the e. down 546.3
Eternal   Hope springs e. in the human breast 452.17
Eternity   Deserts of vast e. 384.2
E. in an hour 67.1
white radiance of E. 500.2
Ethiopian   E. change his skin 62.102
Etiquette   It isn't e. to cut any one 111.32
Eton   won on the playing fields of E. 573.3
Eureka   16.2
Europe   All the dogs of E. bark 25.4
glory of E. is extinguished 91.8
lamps are going out all over E. 272.1
part of the community of E. 258.3
United States of E. 133.24
Evacuations   Wars are not won by e. 133.33
Eve   St. Agnes' E.—Ah, bitter chill it was 332.5
Evening   e. is spread out against the sky 214.7
Now came still E. on 401.23
Soup of the e. 111.12
Event   one far-off divine e. 539.14
thinking too precisely on th' e. 498.70
Events   E. which...never happened 314.1
Ever   for e. hold his peace 149.14
I go on for e. 539.1
thing of beauty is a joy for e. 332.4
What, *never*? Hardly e. 257.15
Every   E. day in e. way 161.1
God bless us, e. one 191.5
Everybody   E. is always in favour of general economy 208.1
E. was up to something 163.1
Everyone   e. against e. 298.1
I hate e. equally 226.3
Everything   destroying nearly e. 129.5
E. 576.5
E. by starts 205.7
E. is funny 472.2
E.'s got a moral 111.9
sans e. 498.24
Evil   belief in a supernatural source of e. 154.6
E., be thou my Good 401.22
e. that men do lives after them 498.116
Government...is...a necessary e. 431.2
I will fear no e. 62.48
love of money is the root of all e. 62.202

Men's e. manners live in brass 498.105
No man is justified in doing e. 476.3
one e., ignorance 515.2
overcome e. with good 62.182
Sufficient unto the day is the e. 62.129
we are the origin of all coming e. 327.3
Evils   greatest of e....is poverty 499.30
He...must expect new e. 30.24
Whenever I'm caught between two e. 576.7
Evolution   e. in...ten thousand years 179.1
Exaggerated   Reports of my death are greatly e. 553.7
Example   E. is the school of mankind 91.11
Excel   daring to e. 131.2
thou shalt not e. 62.8
Excellent   everything that's e. 257.3
Exception   I'll make an e. in your case 385.18
Excess   e. is most exhilarating 14.2
Give me e. of it 498.266
In charity there is no e. 30.15
Nothing succeeds like e. 584.15
road of e. 67.21
Exciting   He found it less e. 257.1
Excluded   when you have e. the impossible 201.1
Excrement   place of e. 601.4
Excuse   bet he's just using that as an e. 385.6
Executioner   I am mine own E. 199.11
Executioners   victims who respect their e. 489.1
Exercise   e. is to the body 524.3
Exhausted   e. what there is in business, politics, conviviality, and so on 582.7
Exist   Facts do not cease to e. 310.23
I e. by what I think 489.3
If God did not e. 561.5
liberty cannot long e. 91.15
Existence   Let us contemplate e. 191.15
to do something is to create e. 489.4
woman's whole e. 98.12
Exit   E., pursued by a bear 498.282
Exits   They have their e. and their entrances 498.23
Expands   Work e. to fill the time 434.1
Expect   I e. a judgment 191.3
Expediency   evil on the ground of e. 476.3
principle...sacrificed to e. 388.6
Expenditure   annual e. nineteen nineteen 191.8
in favour of particular e. 208.1
Expense   who Would be at the e. of two 140.3
Experience   e. of women which extends 201.8
my e. of life has been drawn from life itself 51.8
Experiment   existence remains...e. 488.4
Express'd   but ne'er so well e. 452.12
Expression   crime is due to...desire for...e. 569.11
Exterminate   E. all brutes 154.1
Extinguished   glory of Europe is e. 91.8
Nature is...seldom e. 30.31
Extraordinary   Little minds are interested in the e. 306.3
Exuberance   E. is Beauty 67.25
Eye   apple of his e. 62.29

Beauty is...in the e. of the beholder 562.1
e. for an e. 62.121
E. for e. 62.23
flash upon that inward e. 595.3
his keener e. The axe's edge did try 384.7
less in this than meets the e. 38.1
love comes in at the e. 601.5
such beauty as a woman's e. 498.155
thine e. offend thee, pluck it 62.139
Eyeless   E. in Gaza 401.29
Eyelids   tir'd e. upon tir'd eyes 539.18
When she raises her e. 145.2
Eyes   Drink to me only with thine e. 325.1
fortune and men's e. 498.290
lift up mine e. unto the hills 62.60
Love looks not with the e. 498.202
pearls that were his e. 498.254
sight of you is good for sore e. 535.8
whites of their e. 456.1
Your e. shine like the pants 385.4

F

Fabric   baseless f. of this vision 498.258
Face   f. that launch'd a thousand ships 381.2
False f. must hide 498.166
garden in her f. 105.1
I just can't think of your f. 520.3
painting a f. and not washing 245.1
then f. to f. 62.187
To get very red in the f. 59.1
Faces   All, all are gone, the old familiar f. 348.6
among so many million of f. 82.3
grind the f. of the poor 62.93
Factor   importance of the human f. 125.2
Facts   F. alone are wanted in life 191.13
F. do not cease to exist 310.23
his imagination for his f. 502.10
Failed   Light that F. 341.11
Fair   Brave deserves the F. 205.12
Earth has not anything...more f. 595.11
F. stood the wind for France 203.1
man right f. 498.302
name of Vanity F. 90.4
So foul and f. a day 498.158
Faire   Laissez f. 459.1
Fairer   I can't say no f. than that 191.11
Fairies   beginning of f. 40.1
I don't believe in f. 40.2
Faith   f., hope, charity 62.188
F. is the substance of things hoped for 62.204
f. unfaithful kept him falsely true 539.6
F. without works is dead 62.206
Reason itself is a matter of f. 129.19
'Tis not the dying for a f. 541.3
Faithful   Be thou f. unto death 62.213
I have been f. to thee 200.1
Fall   harder they f. 230.1
Pride goeth...before a f. 62.71
Fallen   How are the mighty f. 62.35

Ye are f. from grace 62.194
y-f. out of heigh degree 127.14
False   be not f. to others 30.23
F. face must hide what the f. heart 498.166
history must be f. 563.3
Thou canst not then be f. 498.48
Words may be f. 497.1
Falsehood   Let her and F. grapple 401.37
Falstaff   F. sweats to death 498.78
Fame   F. is like a river 30.40
F. is the spur 401.11
Familiar   f. objects be as if they were not f. 500.15
old f. faces 348.6
Familiarity   F. breeds contempt—and children 553.4
Families   All happy f. resemble one another 547.1
best-regulated f. 191.10
There are only two f. in the world 116.3
Famine   They that die by f. 288.1
Famous   I awoke...found myself f. 98.29
Martyrdom...way...a man can become f. 499.77
Fanatic   f....over-compensates   a...doubt 310.28
Fanatics   F. have their dreams 332.8
when f. are on top there is no limit to oppression 392.4
Fancy   In the Spring a young man's f. 539.17
little of what you f. does you good 362.1
Fantastic   light f. toe 401.6
Far   F. from the madding crowd 268.10
Farce   f. is over 460.2
F. is the essential theatre 166.1
wine was a f. 455.2
Farewell   F., a long f., to all my greatness 498.103
F.! thou art too dear for my possessing 498.295
hail and f. 114.3
Farmyard   f. world of sex 266.2
Fascism   F. is a religion 411.1
Fashion   as good be out of f. 134.1
faithful to thee, Cynara! in my f. 200.1
Nothing else holds f. 498.265
Fast   none so f. as stroke 142.1
they stumble that run f. 498.246
U.S. has to move very f. 335.3
Faster   world would go round a deal f. 111.5
Fat   butter will only make us f. 260.1
f. of the land 62.7
Let me have men about me that are f. 498.107
Fatal   caution in love is...f. 485.3
Moderation is a f. thing 584.15
sincerity is...f. 584.20
Fate   I am the master of my f. 285.2
when F. summons 205.13
Father   brood of Folly without f. 401.2
Child is f. of the Man 595.13
F., I cannot tell a lie 567.2
f. is a very hospitable man 499.5
Full fathom five thy f. lies 498.254
God is...an exalted f. 242.4

Five

Honour thy f. and mother 62.17
wise f. that knows his own child 498.190
wise son maketh a glad f. 62.67
Fatherhood Mirrors and f. are abominable 69.2
Fathers land of my f. 543.5
our f. that begat us 62.113
Fathom Full f. five thy father lies 498.254
Fault only one f.. It was…lousy 546.6
Faultless Whoever thinks a f. piece to see 452.11
Faults England, with all thy f. 165.4
f., do not fear to abandon them 150.6
If we had no f. of our own 471.9
When you have f. 150.6
Favour truths being in and out of f. 243.1
Fear concessions of f. 91.1
F. God 62.86
F. no more the heat o' th' sun 498.38
f. of suffering injustice 471.14
f. of the Lord is the beginning 62.58
freedom from f. 475.3
have…many things to f. 30.21
I do f. thy nature 498.162
I will f. no evil 62.48
love casteth out f. 62.211
no f. in love 62.211
one universal passion: f. 499.61
those with f. of life become publishers 153.4
Fearful thy f. symmetry 67.12
Fears enough for fifty hopes and f. 83.3
Feast Chief nourisher in life's f. 498.167
life is not…a f. 488.5
Feathers not only fine f. 6.3
Fed bite the hand that f. them 91.12
he on honey-dew hath f. 144.21
hungry sheep look up and are not f. 401.12
Feel Englishman…is afraid to f. 237.2
f. what wretches f. 498.141
tragedy to those who f. 564.2
what I f. really bad about 240.1
Feeling man is as old as he's f. 146.1
Feelings Opinion is…determined by the f. 518.8
spontaneous overflow of powerful f. 595.24
Fools as old as the woman he f. 385.22
Feet both f. firmly planted in the air 475.2
spread my dreams under your f. 601.9
those f. in ancient time 67.6
Feigning Most friendship is f. 498.26
truest poetry is the most f. 498.30
Felicity Absent thee from f. awhile 498.75
more f. on the far side of baldness 511.8
Fell Doctor F. 79.1
From morn to noon he f. 401.19
men f. out 96.1
where the dead leaf f. 332.10
Fellow f. of infinite jest 498.73
Fellowship right hands of f. 62.193
Female f. of the species is more deadly 341.4
What f. heart can gold despise 268.1
Festina F. lente 532.1
Fettered so f. fast we are 83.1

Few appointment by the corrupt f. 499.49
err as grossly as the F. 205.10
f. are chosen 62.140
f. are qualified to shine 535.17
f. who can grow old with a good grace 524.2
owed by so many to so f. 133.15
Fickle Woman is always f. 560.2
Fickleness f. of the women I love 499.63
Fiction an improbable f. 498.275
one form of continuous f. 61.4
Poetry is a comforting piece of f. 392.5
Poetry is the supreme f. 528.2
Stranger than f. 98.21
Fiddle When I play on my f. in Dooney 601.7
Field flower of the f. 62.56
some corner of a foreign f. 78.3
Fields 'a babbl'd of green f. 498.94
Fiend f. hid in a cloud 67.11
frightful f. Doth close behind him tread 144.12
Ingratitude, thou marble-hearted f. 498.132
Fight I dare not f. 498.92
I will not cease from mental f. 67.7
too proud to f. 591.2
Ulster will f. 132.2
we shall f. on the beaches 133.12
when the f. begins within 83.4
You cannot f. against the future 258.1
Fighting f. a liar in the quad 520.1
not conquering but f. 160.1
What are we f. for 496.3
Figures prove anything by f. 109.1
Fille de chambre I caught hold of the f.'s— 527.3
Filthy f. lucre 62.199
Financial in danger of f. disaster 391.1
Find to f., and not to yield 539.27
Fine f. feathers that make f. birds 6.3
Finer every baby…is a f. one 191.18
Finest their f. hour 133.13
Finger more goodness in her little f. 535.13
Moving F. writes 228.8
Fingers ill cook that cannot lick his own f. 498.250
Fire bound Upon a wheel of f. 498.150
two irons in the f. 45.2
what wind is to f. 95.1
Firmament f. sheweth his handywork 62.45
First good die f. 595.1
If at f. you don't succeed 294.1
which came f., the Greeks or the Romans 195.12
Fish What Cat's averse to f. 268.1
Fishes f. live in the sea 498.231
Fish knives Phone for the f. Norman 60.1
Fit It is not f. that you should sit here 172.3
let the punishment f. the crime 257.11
only the F. survive 496.2
Fittest Survival of the F. 180.3
Survival of the f. 518.4
Five child of f. would understand this 385.5
practise f. things 150.7

Five pound note gentlemen said to the f. 191.29

get a f. as...a light for a cigarette 317.3

Flag keep the Red F. flying here 152.1

Flash f. upon that inward eye 595.3

Flat Very f., Norfolk 163.4

Flatterers Self-love...greatest of all f. 471.6

Flattering think him worth f. 499.27

Flatters What really f. a man 499.27

Flattery f.'s the food of fools 535.2

Imitation is the sincerest of f. 148.3

more pernicious than the love of f. 524.1

What is principle against the f. 502.9

woman...to be gained by...f. 128.10

Flea f. Hath smaller fleas that on him prey 535.7

performing f. 423.2

Fleas flea hath smaller f. that on him prey 535.7

Great f. have little f. upon their backs 405.1

Flee f. from the wrath to come 62.116

Flesh All f. is as grass 62.207

All f. is grass 62.98

f. is weak 62.145

f. to feel the chain 77.3

going the way of all f. 572.2

I have more f. than another man 498.79

I wants to make your f. creep 191.25

thorn in the f. 62.192

way of all f. 151.9

way of all f. 497.2

Word was made f. 62.163

world, the f., and the devil 149.7

Fleshly F. School of Poetry 84.1

Flies As f. to wanton boys 498.144

certain, that Life f. 228.4

Fling I'll have a f. 45.7

Float rather be an opportunist and f. 35.1

Flood Which, taken at the f. 498.122

Flower f. of the field 62.56

F. that once has blown 228.4

many a f. is born to blush unseen 268.8

meanest f. that blows 595.6

Flowers f. appear on the earth 62.88

f. that bloom in the spring 257.12

Letting a hundred f. blossom 379.2

Say it with f. 425.1

Flowing f. with milk and honey 62.10

Flung he f. himself from the room 353.4

Fly small gilded f. Does lecher 498.146

Flying time is f. 560.5

Foam f. Of perilous seas 332.27

Foe Heat not a furnace for your f. 498.101

He...who never made a f. 539.7

make one worthy man my f. 452.4

Foeman When the f. bares his steel 257.18

Foes You shall judge of a man by his f. 154.4

Fog London particular...a f. 191.2

Follies lovers cannot see the pretty f. 498.191

Folly brood of F. without father 401.2

shielding men from the effects of f. 518.3

slightest f. That ever love did make thee run into 498.20

'Tis f. to be wise 268.4

When lovely woman stoops to f. 262.10

Fond f. of resisting temptation 48.1

Fonder Absence makes the heart grow f. 43.1

Food eat...to put f. out of my mind 507.1

f. a tragedy 455.2

Nothing to eat but f. 339.1

On the Continent...good f. 395.1

Fool Busy old f., unruly Sun 199.10

f. at forty is a f. indeed 602.2

f. hath said in his heart 62.44

f. his whole life long 372.1

f. sees not the same tree 67.23

f....the people 360.8

greatest f. may ask more 148.4

He who holds hopes...is a f. 106.9

more of the f. than of the wise 30.13

needs a very clever woman to manage a f. 341.10

old man who will not laugh is a f. 488.2

strumpet's f. 498.4

what f. it was that first invented kissing 535.14

Wise Man or a F. 67.5

wisest f. in Christendom 286.2

Foolish He never said a f. thing 473.1

Fools Christianity...says they are all f. 129.13

fill the word with f. 518.3

flattery's the food of f. 535.2

F. are in a terrible, overwhelming majority 313.1

For f. rush in 452.16

Pride the...vice of f. 452.9

things people make f. of themselves about 499.12

this great stage of f. 498.149

To suckle f. and chronicle 498.221

what f. these mortals be 498.205

ye suffer f. gladly 62.191

Foot noiseless f. of Time 498.3

Foppery excellent f. of the world 498.131

Forbearance f. ceases to be a virtue 91.7

Forbidden he wanted it only because it was f. 553.5

Force f. alone is but temporary 91.2

F. is not a remedy 75.3

F. that through the green fuse 543.2

Other nations use 'f.' 569.23

Ford time of our F. 310.5

Forefathers Think of your f. 2.1

Foreign pronounce f. names as he chooses 133.41

Forests f. of the night 67.12

Forever diamond...bracelet lasts f. 365.3

That is f. England 78.3

Forget Fade far away, dissolve, and...f. 332.25

I f. what I was taught 579.2

I never f. a face, but I'll make an exception 385.18

Old men f. 498.99

three things I always f. 534.1

Forgetting birth is but a sleep and a f. 595.5

Forgive Father, f. them 62.160

Men will f. a man 133.2
to f., divine 452.15
Forgot   I have f. my part 498.35
old acquaintance be f. 93.2
Forgotten   They have...f. nothing 536.2
Forlorn   faery lands f. 332.27
Form   F. remains 595.15
significant f. 54.1
Formation   Education...f. of character 518.6
Formidable   Examinations are f. 148.4
Forms   from outward f. to win 144.18
Fornicated   f. and read the papers 106.2
Fornication   F.: but that was in another country 381.6
Forsake   F. not an old friend 62.111
Fortress   f. built by Nature 498.235
Fortunate   he is at best f. 516.1
Fortune   deficiences of f. 262.9
f. and men's eyes 498.290
F. favours the brave 540.1
F.'s sharp adversitee 127.17
greater virtues to sustain good f. 471.8
hostages to f. 30.10
slings and arrows of outrageous f. 498.61
Forty   Every man over f. is a scoundrel 499.56
fool at f. is a fool 602.2
Forty-three   She may very well pass for f. 257.20
Foster-child   f. of silence and slow time 332.15
Fou   I wasna f. 93.5
Fought   better to have f. and lost 140.5
Foul   Murder most f. 498.51
So f. and fair a day 498.158
Foul-mouthed   English...are rather a f. nation 281.2
Found   he f. it brick 100.1
I have f. it 16.2
When f., make a note of 191.12
Four   at the age of f....we're all Generals 555.1
f. essential human freedoms 475.3
Four-year-old   brain of a f. boy 385.10
Fox-hunting   athletics...inferior forms of f. 569.8
Frailty   F., thy name is woman 498.43
more flesh...more f. 498.79
Frame   all the Human F. requires 55.3
France   Fair stood the wind for F. 203.1
F. was a long despotism 109.8
Frauds   pious f. of friendship 225.1
Free   all men everywhere could be f. 360.5
Greece might still be f. 98.16
Man was born f. 481.1
Mother of the F. 57.1
safer to be in chains than to be f. 330.1
So f. we seem 83.1
Thou art f. 20.12
truth that makes men f. 7.1
Who would be f. 98.6
Freedom   enemies of F. 314.2
F. is Slavery 427.3
F., what liberties are taken in thy name 253.1
In solitude alone can he know f. 403.2
least regard for human f. 518.7

Necessity is the plea for every infringement of human f. 447.1
new birth of f. 360.6
None can love f. heartily, but good men 401.38
Those who deny f. to others 360.3
Freedoms   four essential human f. 475.3
Freemasonry   kind of bitter f. 51.5
French   I speak F. to men 124.1
Frenzy   poet's eye, in a fine f. rolling 498.207
Fresh   as f. as paint 509.1
f. as is the month of May 127.3
Fret   weariness, the fever, and the f. 332.25
Freudian   F., it is a very low, Central European sort of humour 267.3
Friend   Forsake not an old f. 62.111
F....masterpiece of Nature 218.3
f. should bear his f.'s infirmities 498.121
f. who loved perfection 511.11
He makes no f. 539.7
save me, from the candid f. 107.2
would be the perfect f. 511.11
Friends   Animals are such agreeable f. 213.2
F., Romans, countrymen 498.116
Have no f. not equal 150.5
honour, love, obedience, troops of f. 498.175
How to Win F. 110.1
I don't trust him. We're f. 74.3
In the misfortunes of our best f. 471.5
man lay down his life for his f. 62.171
Once more unto the breach, dear f. 498.95
Wealth maketh many f. 62.72
without three good f. 498.27
Friendship   f. hardly ever does 27.3
F. is constant in all other things 498.209
F. is unnecessary 358.1
man, Sir, should keep his f. in constant repair 323.12
matrimony...f. recognised by the police 529.1
Most f. is feigning 498.26
pious frauds of f. 225.1
Frittered   life is f. away by detail 545.5
Front door   polished up the handle of the big f. 257.16
Fruit   f. Of that forbidden tree 401.14
Ignorance is like a...f. 584.6
Fruitfulness   Season of...mellow f. 332.1
Frustrate   In three sips...Arian f. 83.15
Full   one of the professions which are f. 545.2
Reading maketh a f. man 30.39
Fun   Work is much more f. than f. 163.16
Function   F. never dies 595.15
f. of the critic 54.2
Funny   Everything is f. 472.2
F. peculiar, or f. ha-ha 280.1
F. without being vulgar 257.22
Fur   Oh my f. and whiskers 111.3
Furious   f. that she had not been asked 569.15
Furnace   Heat not a f. for your foe 498.101
Furniture   No f. so charming as books 512.5
Fury   full of sound and f. 498.177
F. of a Patient Man 205.11
Fuse   force that through the green f. 543.2

Fuss f. about sleeping together 569.16
Future f. is...black 34.3
  F., that period of time in which 63.5
  if you would divine the f. 150.2
  I never think of the f. 212.1
  You cannot fight against the f. 258.1
Futurity let f. shift for itself 513.2

G

Gain g. the whole world 62.148
  never broke the Sabbath, but for g. 205.8
Gained learning hath g. most 245.4
Gaiters gas and g. 191.19
Galatians great text in G. 83.16
Gall wormwood and the g. 62.103
Gallantry What men call g. 98.11
Gallery g. in which the reporters sit 375.2
Gallimaufry English...g....of all other spee-
  ches 519.5
Galloped I g., Dirck g. 83.8
Game I don't like this g. 399.2
  It is a silly g. 245.2
  It's more than a g.. It's an institution 307.2
  play up! and play the g.! 416.2
  win this g. and thrash the Spaniards 202.2
  woman is his g. 539.23
Gamesmanship G. or The Art of Winning
  Games 453.1
Gangsters great nations have always acted like
  g. 345.1
Garbo one sees in G. sober 554.3
Garden Come into the g., Maud 539.19
  cultivate our g. 561.3
  g. is a lovesome thing 80.1
  God Almighty first planted a g. 30.36
  God the first g. made 164.1
  There is a g. in her face 105.1
Gardens closing time in the g. of the West
  153.1
Garland wither'd is the g. of the war 498.15
Garment City now doth, like a g., wear 595.11
Garrick G. On the stage he was natural 262.3
Gas g. and gaiters 191.19
  G. smells awful 433.4
Gate aged...man a-sitting on a g. 111.29
  I am here at the g. alone 539.19
Gathered two or three are g. together 149.5
Gaul G. is divided into three 10!.1
Gave Lord g. 62.38
Gaza Eyeless in G. 401.29
General caviare to the g. 498.58
  French army led by an Italian g. 499.62
General Motors what was...good for G. 588.1
Generals at the age of four... we're all G.
  555.1
  Russia has two g. 418.1
  wish he would bite...my g. 254.1
Generation O g. of vipers 62.116

Generations No hungry g. tread thee down
  332.27
Genius G....capacity of taking trouble 109.5
  G. does what it must 394.1
  G. is one per cent inspiration 209.1
  nothing to declare except my g. 584.25
  What a g. I had when I wrote that book
  535.19
Gent what a man is to a g. 35.2
Gentil verray parfit g. knight 127.2
Gentle Do not go g. into that good night 543.1
  g. mind by g. deeds is known 519.3
Gentleman g....I live by robbing the poor
  499.42
  g....is one who never inflicts pain 417.1
  g. said to the five pound note 191.29
  man who is always talking about being a g.
  533.1
  Who was then the g. 37.1
Gentlemanly secondly, g. conduct 21.1
Gentlemen G....remember blondes 365.1
  religion for g. 123.2
Genuineness G. only thrives in the dark 310.24
Geographical India is a g. term 133.8
Geography G. is about Maps 59.2
Georgian sweet laxative of G. strains 103.1
German I speak G. to my horse 124.1
Germans Don't let's be beastly to the G.
  163.13
Get up I thought it was a pity to g. 388.7
Ghosts g. from an enchanter fleeing 500.7
Giant owner whereof was G. Despair 90.5
Giants war of the g. is over 133.37
Giant's-Causeway Is not the G. worth seeing?
  323.33
Gift giving is worth more than the g. 158.3
Gild To g. refined gold 498.128
Girl g. with brains 365.2
  Home is the g.'s prison 499.55
  park, a policeman and a pretty g. 121.2
  Poor Little Rich G. 163.12
Girls g. who wear glasses 433.2
Give g. me liberty or g. me death 289.1
  more blessed to g. than to receive 62.177
Giving g. is worth more than the gift 158.3
Glade live alone in the bee-loud g. 601.10
Gladstone inebriated with...own verbosity
  195.6
Glass impression of having been grown under
  g. 592.5
  Life, like a dome of many-coloured g. 500.2
  through a g., darkly 62.187
Glasses girls who wear g. 433.2
Glimpses g. that would make me less forlorn
  595.10
Glisters Nor all that g. gold 268.2
Globe great g. itself 498.258
Gloire Le jour de g. est arrivé 480.1
gloria Sic transit g. mundi 333.2
Glorious Happy and g. 108.1
Glory G. be to God for dappled things 302.4
  g. of Europe is extinguished for ever 91.8
  Land of Hope and G. 57.1

paths of g. lead but to the grave 268.7
trailing clouds of g. 595.5
Gluttony   G. is an emotional escape 190.2
Go   as cooks g. she went 486.4
In the name of God, g. 13.1
Let my people g. 62.12
Let's g. 47.4
Let us g. then, you and I 214.7
like Wind I g. 228.5
to die and g. we know not where 498.184
Goal   g. stands up 304.4
Goats   divideth his sheep from the g. 62.143
God   an atheist still, thank G. 89.1
Are G. and Nature then at strife 539.12
better to have no opinion of G. 30.19
but for the grace of G. goes 73.1
charged with the grandeur of G. 302.3
concept of G. has any validity 34.1
dear G. who loveth us 144.15
Doubtless G. could have made a better berry 565.2
effect whose cause is G. 165.7
either a wild beast or a g. 30.26
Fear G. 62.86
Fear G. 62.208
'G. bless us every one!' 191.5
G. disposes 333.1
G....first planted a garden 30.36
G. is beginning to resemble...a cosmic Cheshire cat 311.2
G. is love 62.210
G. is nothing more than an exalted father 242.4
G. is not mocked 62.196
G. is our refuge and strength 62.52
G. made the country 165.3
G....need not exist...to save us 190.5
G. save our gracious King 108.1
G. should go before such villains 498.216
G.'s in His heaven 83.13
G. so loved the world 62.166
G. the first garden made 164.1
G. will take care of that 499.22
Had I but serv'd my G. with half the zeal I serv'd my King 498.104
Had I but served G. as diligently 593.1
heavens declare the glory of G. 62.45
highest praise of G. consists in the denial of Him 458.5
If G. did not exist 561.5
In the beginning G. created 62.1
In the name of G., go! 13.1
justify the ways of G. to men 401.15
laws of G. will be suspended in favour of England 499.25
lay wrestling with my G.! my G. 302.2
lovesome thing, God wot 80.1
man whose g. is in the skies 499.47
Many people believe that they are attracted by G. 314.4
mighty G. 62.95
nature is the art of G. 82.2
One G., one law, one element 539.14

One on G.'s side is a majority 444.1
poems...for the love of Man and in praise of G. 543.4
presume not G. to scan 452.18
proof that G. is a bore 392.3
prose for G. 266.3
Providence will...end...acts of G. 190.6
serve G. and mammon 62.127
There is no G. 62.44
they shall see G. 62.119
Thou shalt have one G. only 140.3
unto G. the things that are G.'s 62.141
we owe G. a death 498.90
What...G. hath joined 62.149
What G. hath joined together 499.22
whom G. wishes to destroy 221.1
Woman was G.'s second mistake 419.2
Goddamm   Lhude sing G. 454.1
Godot   waiting for G. 47.4
Gods   g. adultery 98.11
g. help them 6.2
I am nearest to the g. 515.1
Kings are earth's g. 498.230
leave the rest to the G. 158.2
Thou shalt have no other g. 62.13
Whom the g. wish to destroy 153.6
Going   Men must endure Their g. hence 498.151
not worth g. to see 323.33
Stand not upon the order of your g. 498.171
Gold   For g. in phisik is a cordial 127.9
gild refined g. 498.128
Good morning to the day: and next my g. 325.5
led by the nose with g. 498.286
Nor all that glisters g. 268.2
travell'd in the realms of g. 332.28
What female heart can g. despise 268.1
Golden   G. Road to Samarkand 231.1
G. slumbers kiss your eyes 185.1
there are no g. rules 499.48
Golf   G....a form of moral effort 353.5
Gone   g. with the wind 200.2
here today and g. tomorrow 53.2
sun has g. in 511.10
Gongs   women should be struck...like g. 163.5
Good   All g. writing 229.5
As for doing g. 545.2
best is the enemy of the g. 561.4
Every man loves what he is g. at 497.3
Evil, be thou my G. 401.22
General G. is the plea of the scoundrel 67.4
g. are always the merry 601.8
G., but not religious-g. 277.4
g. die early 184.1
g. die first 595.1
g. for sore eyes 535.8
g. is oft interred with their bones 498.116
g. is the beautiful 448.i
g. must associate 91.13
g. novel tells us the truth 129.14
g. of the people 135.2
greatest g. 135.3

He who would do g. to another 67.4
If to do were as easy as to know what were g. 498.188
it cannot come to g. 498.44
little of what you fancy does you g. 362.1
Men have never been g. 41.1
never was a g. war 239.4
nothing g. to be had in the country 281.8
only g. Indian is...dead 501.1
only one g., knowledge 515.2
our people have never had it so g. 378.1
overcome evil with g. 62.182
Roman Conquest...a G. Thing 495.2
those who go about doing g. 169.1
What's the g. of a home? 273.1
what was g. for the country was g. for General Motors 588.1
You shouldn't say it is not g. 577.4
Goodbye G. to All That 267.1
Goodness G. had nothing whatever to do with it 576.3
more g. in her little finger 535.13
Goodnight second best's a gay g. 601.11
Then it will be g. 500.4
Gormed I'm G. 191.11
Got Tell him I've g. one 385.8
Which in our case we have not g. 465.2
Govern Labour is not fit to g. 133.6
No man is good enough to g. another man 360.1
Governesses nation of g. 499.79
Government G....is but a necessary evil 431.2
g....is founded on compromise 91.4
g. of the people, by the people 360.6
one form of G. rather than another 323.20
people's g. 571.2
worst g. is the most moral 392.4
Gower moral G. 127.18
Grace but for the g. of God, goes 73.1
fallen from g. 62.194
few who can grow old with a good g. 524.2
Grades We class schools...into four g. 569.2
Gradually Boys do not grow up g. 153.9
Gradualness inevitability of g. 570.1
Grammar I dont want to talk g. 499.67
Grandeur g. of God 302.3
Grape Beulah, peel me a g. 576.4
Grapeshot whiff of g. 109.9
Grasp man's reach should exceed his g. 83.2
Grass All flesh is as g. 62.207
All flesh is g. 62.98
his days are as g. 62.56
Gratifying passions she has no intention of g. 499.81
Grave country...a kind of healthy g. 512.9
g.'s a fine and private place 384.3
g. yawns for him 548.3
jealousy is cruel as the g. 62.89
O g., where is thy victory 62.189
paths of glory lead but to the g. 268.7
Graven any g. image 62.14
Great All things both g. and small 144.15
Everything g....is done by neurotics 458.7

fate of the g. wen 141.2
g. men have not...been g. scholars 300.3
g. ones eat up the little ones 498.231
Some are born g. 498.273
To be g. is to be misunderstood 218.10
Great Australian Novel write the G. 579.4
Greater g. the power 91.16
Thy necessity is g. than mine 506.3
Greatest g. good 135.3
g. happiness of the g. number 58.1
Greatness long farewell to all my g. 498.103
some achieve g. 498.273
some have g. thrust upon 'em 498.273
Greece G. might still be free 98.16
isles of G. 98.15
Greek it was G. to me 498.108
Greeks G. Had a Word 8.1
uncertainty: a state unknown to the G. 69.1
which came first, the G. or the Romans 195.12
Green g. thought in a g. shade 384.5
G. grow the rashes O 93.8
I was g. in judgment 498.7
tree of life is g. 261.1
Green Chartreuse religious system that produced G. 486.5
Green-ey'd jealousy...g. monster 498.224
Greenwood Under the g. tree 498.21
Grey theory is all g. 261.1
Grief in much wisdom is much g. 62.81
Should be past g. 498.281
Grievances redress of the g. of the vanquished 133.30
Grill be careful not to look like a mixed g. 163.7
Grind g. the faces of the poor 62.93
Groan men sit and hear each other g. 332.25
Groans How alike...g. of love to...dying 370.1
Groucho No, G. is not my real name 385.20
Grow Green g. the rashes O 93.8
They shall g. not old 64.1
Grown whiskers...g. under glass 592.5
Grow out some of us never g. 555.1
Grub old ones, g. 499.4
Guarantee No one can g. success in war 133.32
Guard Who is to g. the guards? 329.1
Guards Up, G., and at 'em 573.2
Who is to guard the g. themselves? 329.1
Guerre *ce n'est pas la g.* 71.1
Guilt pens dwell on g. and misery 27.4
Guilty better that ten g. persons escape 65.3
g. of Noel Cowardice 190.3
Guinea round disc of fire somewhat like a g. 67.18
Gulf there is a great g. fixed 62.159
Gulphs whelm'd in deeper g. than he 165.1
Gunga Din better man than I am, G. 341.5
Gunpowder G., Printing, and the Protestant Religion 109.2
Guns G. aren't lawful 433.4
G. will make us powerful 260.1

H

Habit   H. is a great deadener 47.6
honour peereth in the meanest h. 498.253
Habitation   to airy nothing A local h. 498.207
Habits   h. that carry them far apart 150.1
Hae   Scots, wha h. 93.15
Haggards   H. ride no more 526.2
Ha-ha   funny h. 280.1
Hail   h. and farewell 114.3
H. to thee, blithe Spirit 500.13
Hair   part my h. behind 214.11
Hairs   given me over in my gray h. 593.1
Half   H. a league onward 539.2
h. a loaf is better than a whole 129.23
One h....cannot understand...the other 27.1
Too civil by h. 502.8
Half-a-dozen   six of one and h. of the other 383.2
Half-truths   all truths are h. 580.1
Hampden   Some village-H. 268.9
Hand   bite the h. that fed them 91.12
His h. will be against every man 62.6
h., the head, and the heart 484.3
Let not thy left h. know 62.125
little onward lend they guiding h. 401.28
sweeten this little h. 498.174
This h. hath offended 168.1
what thy right h. doeth 62.125
Hand-bag   A h. 584.8
Handful   for a h. of silver he left us 83.9
Handle   h. of the big front door 257.16
Hands   Into thy h. I commend my spirit 62.50
Licence my roving h. 199.6
mischief...for idle h. to do 568.1
right h. of fellowship 62.193
Handsome   with my mourning, very h. 438.3
Handywork   firmament sheweth his h. 62.45
Hang   I will not h. myself today 129.1
We must indeed all h. together 239.3
wretches h. that jury-men may dine 452.28
Hanged   Men are not h. for stealing 274.1
when a man knows he is to be h. 323.31
Hanging   h. a man who does not object 499.60
h. prevents a bad marriage 498.268
H. and wiving goes by destiny 498.192
Happened   most of which had never h. 133.34
Happening   h. to somebody else 472.2
Happens   Nothing h. 47.2
Happiest   I am h. when I am idle 566.3
Happiness   greatest h. of the greatest number 58.1
greatest h. of the whole 448.2
h. fails, existence remains...experiment 488.4
H. in marriage 27.9
H. is a mystery like religion 129.11
H. is a wine of the rarest vintage 511.2
H. is like coke 310.17
In solitude what h. 401.25

life, liberty, and the pursuit of h. 320.1
lifetime of h. 499.37
recall a time of h. when in misery 176.2
result h. 191.8
something curiously boring about somebody else's h. 310.13
We have no more right to consume h. 499.11
Happy   Call no man h. until he dies 516.1
duty of being h. 529.3
Few people can be h. unless they hate 485.5
h. families resemble each other 547.1
H. the Man 205.14
If you want to be h., be 547.2
I've had a h. life 281.9
I were but little h. 498.210
No society can be...h. 510.1
policeman's lot is not a h. one 257.19
to have been h. 68.1
We are never so h....as we imagine 471.11
Harder   h. they fall 230.1
Hardy   Kiss me, H. 415.2
Hare   First catch your h. 259.1
Harm   No people do so much h. 169.1
Haste   Men love in h. 98.19
Hasten   H. slowly 532.1
Hatched   chickens before they are h. 6.4
Hatchet   did it with my little h. 567.2
Hate   enough religion to make us h. 535.16
Few people can be happy unless they h. 485.5
I h. and love 114.2
I h. everyone equally 226.3
I love or I h. 445.1
worst sin...is not to h. 499.15
Hated   I never h. a man enough 246.1
Hates   Anybody who h. children and dogs 226.2
Hatred   h. is...the longest pleasure 98.19
Haunted   e'er beneath a waning moon was h. 144.20
Have   My fathers can h. it 543.5
To h. and to hold 149.15
Haves   H. and the have-nots 116.3
Havoc   Cry 'H.' and let slip the dogs 498.114
Hay   dance an antic h. 381.1
Head   heap coals of fire upon his h. 62.75
If you can keep your h. 341.6
Lay your sleeping h. 25.6
My h. is bloody but unbowed 285.1
no matter which way the h. lies 462.3
Off with his h. 111.8
ought to have his h. examined 263.3
shorter by a h. 215.1
Uneasy lies the h. that wears a crown 498.88
you incessantly stand on your h. 111.4
Head-in-Air   Little Johnny H. 299.2
Headmasters   H. have powers 133.27
Headpiece   h. filled with straw 214.5
Heads   Dean and Canons lay their h. together 512.3
H. I win 171.1
Head-waiter   diplomat...is nothing but a h. 555.2
Heal   Physician, h. thyself 62.153

Healthy h. and wealthy and dead 546.1
  Nobody is h. in London 27.2
Hear ear begins to h. 77.3
  time will come when you will h. me 195.1
  truth which men prefer not to h. 7.1
Heard I have already h. it 468.1
  You ain't h. nothin' yet 324.1
Heart Absence makes the h. grow fonder 43.1
  Because my h. is pure 539.25
  Blessed are the pure in h. 62.119
  'Calais' lying in my h. 387.1
  hand, the head, and the h. 484.3
  h. and stomach of a King 215.2
  h. has its reasons 435.1
  hid in the h. of love 601.13
  holiness of the h.'s affections 332.33
  Hope deferred maketh the h. sick 62.69
  I am sick at h. 498.39
  intellect is always fooled by the h. 471.2
  Irishman's h. is...his imagination 499.26
  look in thy h. and write. 506.1
  mighty h. is lying still 595.12
  My h. aches 332.22
  my h.'s abhorrence 83.14
  My h.'s in the Highlands 93.13
  Nature never did betray the h. 595.24
  not to get your h.'s desire 499.45
  Once a woman has given you her h. 556.1
  rag-and-bone shop of the h. 601.2
  Sighs...language of the h. 497.1
  So the h. be right 462.3
  strings...in the human h. 191.1
  What comes from the h. 144.27
  With rue my h. is laden 304.5
Hearth cricket on the h. 401.4
Hearts h. are dry as summer dust 595.1
  Kind h. are more than coronets 539.15
  One equal temper of heroic h. 539.27
  Queen of H. 111.13
Heat fear no more the h. o' th' sun 498.38
Heaven all H. in a rage 67.2
  All this and h. too 288.2
  go to H. without being naturally qualified
    499.43
  H. in Hell's despair 67.9
  H. in a wild flower 67.1
  H. lies about us in our infancy 595.5
  Hell I suffer seems a H. 401.21
  make a H. of Hell, a Hell of H. 401.17
  man is as H. made him 116.1
  more things in h. and earth 498.52
  new h. and a new earth 62.218
  Parting is all we know of h. 192.2
  steep and thorny way to h. 498.46
  to be young was very H. 595.14
  what's a h. for 83.2
Heavens h. declare the glory of God 62.45
Hedgehogs If you start throwing h. under me
  344.2
Hell all we need of h. 192.2
  Better to reign in H. 401.18
  Heaven of H., a H. of Heaven 401.17
  h. a fury like a woman 151.4

H. in Heaven's despite 67.10
H. is a city much like London— 500.11
H. is oneself 214.17
h. of horses 233.1
Italy...h. for women 94.3
it would be h. on earth 499.37
war is...all h. 503.1
way down to H. is easy 560.3
Which way I fly is H.; myself am H. 401.21
wishful thinking in H. 358.2
Help gods h. them that h. themselves 6.2
  Since there's no h. 203.2
  very present h. in trouble 62.52
Herd H. of such, Who think too little 205.6
Here h. today and gone tomorrow 53.2
Heresies new truths begin as h. 312.1
Hero Every h. becomes a bore 218.11
  No man is a h. to his valet 159.1
  to his very valet seem'd a h. 98.1
Herod It out-h.'s H. 498.65
Heroes fit country for h. to live in 364.1
Hero-worship H. is strongest 518.7
Hewers H. of wood 62.30
Hidden Nature is often h. 30.31
Hide Robes and furr'd gowns h. all 498.147
  talent which is death to h. 401.32
High civil fury first grew h. 96.1
Highlands My heart's in the H. 93.13
Hill h. will not come to Mahomet 30.14
  they call you...from the h. 20.8
Hills lift up mine eyes unto the h. 62.60
Himself back shop where he can be h. 403.2
  Egotist...more interested in h. 63.4
  He fell in love with h. 455.1
Hippocrene blushful H. 332.24
Hire labourer is worthy of his h. 62.155
Hissed you have h. all my mystery lectures
  520.1
History deal of h. to produce...literature 317.1
  for h. must be false 563.3
  H...is a nightmare from which I am trying to
    awake 326.4
  H. is more or less bunk 234.1
  H. is philosophy teaching by examples 194.1
  H. is the essence of innumerable biographies
    109.3
  h....is the h. of class struggles 386.4
  h. of the human spirit 20.18
  h. of the world is but the biography 109.6
  Love...h. of a woman's life 523.2
  more h. than they can consume locally 486.1
  no h.; only biography 218.4
  people...never have learned anything from h.
    282.1
  War makes...good h. 277.2
Hitch H. your wagon to a star 218.12
Hither Come h., come h. 498.21
Hitler H. has missed the bus 118.3
  H. You do your worst 133.17
  one purpose, the destruction of H. 133.35
  tipster who...reached H.'s level of accuracy
    538.1

Hodgepodge English h.... of all other speeches 519.5

Hog not the whole h. 398.1

Hold centre cannot h. 601.14
h. your tongue and let me love 199.3
To have and to h. 149.15

Holder office sanctifies the h. 1.1

Hole if you knows of a better h. 33.1
smallest h.... man can hide his head in 129.18
What happens to the h. when the cheese is gone? 74.6

Holiness h. of the heart's affections 332.33
put off H. 67.5

Hollow We are the h. men 214.5
within the h. crown 498.237

Holmes 'Elementary', said he 201.5

Home at h. you're just a politician 378.2
Charity begins at h. 82.5
eaten me out of house and h. 498.86
feel... at h. in prison 569.12
H. is heaven 414.2
H. is h. 136.1
H. is the girl's prison 499.55
H. of lost causes 20.16
H.... where... they have to take you in 243.2
till the cow comes h. 45.8
What's the good of a h. 273.1

Home-keeping h. youth 498.278

Homely be never so h. 136.1
h. wits 498.278

Homer author of that poem is either H. 310.25

Homo sapiens naked ape... H. 406.1

Honest fine thing to be h. 133.44
I am as h. as any man living 498.213
Though I am not naturally h. 498.285
To be h., as this world goes 498.54

Honey flowing with milk and h. 62.10
h. still for tea 78.2
They took some h., and plenty of money 354.5

Honey bee hive for the h. 601.10

Honey-dew he on h. hath fed 144.21

Honour His h. rooted in dishonour 539.6
H. all men 62.208
H. pricks me on 498.80
h. sinks where commerce long prevails 262.6
H. thy father and thy mother 62.17
Let us h. if we can 25.1
peace I hope with h. 195.5
prophet is not without h. 62.136
So h. peereth in the meanest habit 498.253
What is h.? A word. 498.80

Honour'd custom more h. in the breach 498.49

Hoof out pops the cloven h. 592.2

Hope Abandon h., all ye who enter here 176.1
faith, h., charity 62.188
H. deferred maketh the heart sick 62.69
H. is the power of being cheerful 129.12
H. springs eternal 452.17
I do not h. to turn 214.1
Land of H. and Glory 57.1
no other medicine but only h. 498.182
unconquerable h. 20.11

what was dead was H. 584.2

Hoped Faith is the substance of things h. for 62.204

Hopefully To travel h. is a better thing 529.4

Hopes enough for fifty h. and fears 83.3

Horde Society is now one polish'd h. 98.20

Horizontal we value none But the h. one 25.1

Horn Triton blow his wreathèd h. 595.10

Hornie Auld H., Satan, Nick 93.1

Horrid are they all h.? 27.5

Horror h.! The h. 154.2
I have a h. of sunsets 458.6

Horrors I have supp'd full with h. 498.176

Horse Behold a pale h. 62.215
my kingdom for a h. 498.241

Horses England... hell for h. 94.3
England... hell of h. 233.1
swap h. in mid-stream 360.7

Hospital world, I count it not an inn, but an h. 82.7

Host h., of golden daffodils 595.2
h. with someone indistinct 214.15

Hostages h. to fortune 30.10

Hotels he keeps six h. 499.5
I prefer temperance h. 566.1

Hounds I said the h. of spring 546.4

Hour h. is ill Which severs those 500.4
I also had my h. 129.3
In the h. of death 149.8
Midnight brought on the dusky h. 401.24
one bare h. to live 381.3
their finest h. 133.13
Time and the h. runs through 498.160

Hours h. will take care of themselves 128.6
Three h. a day 550.2

Housbondes H. at chirche-dore 127.10

House being called a woman in my own h. 569.22
h. is a machine for living in 157.1
If a h. be divided against itself 62.147
man's h. is his castle 143.1
not covet thy neighbour's h. 62.22

Household stables... centre of the h. 499.24

House of Lords Every man has a H. in his own head 364.2

Houses H. are built to live in 30.35
plague o' both your h. 498.248

Hue native h. of resolution 498.63

Human Adam was but h. 553.5
All that is h. must retrograde 255.4
H. kind cannot bear 214.3
h. nature... more of the fool 30.13
H. on my faithless arm 25.6
h. race to which... my readers belong 129.16
I got disappointed in h. nature 198.1
importance of the h. factor 125.2
Mercy has a h. heart 67.17
To err is h. 452.15

Humanity Oh wearisome condition of h. 271.1
still, sad music of h. 595.22

Humble h. and meek are thirsting for blood 426.3
It is difficult to be h. 196.1

Humour   deficient in a sense of h. 144.26
  Freudian...low...sort of h. 267.3
  Total absence of h. 145.1
Hump   woman...without a positive h. 541.5
Hunger   best sauce...is h. 116.2
  talk religion to a man with bodily h. 499.33
Hungry   If thine enemy be h. 62.75
  she makes h. Where most she satisfies 498.9
Hunter   Man is the h. 539.23
  Miss J. H. Dunn 60.3
Hurricanoes   You cataracts and h. 498.137
Hurry   old man in a h. 132.1
Hurt   Those have most power to h. 45.5
  wish to h. 76.1
Husband   Being a h. is a whole-time job 56.2
  light wife doth make a heavy h. 498.198
  My h. is dead 385.6
Husbandry   borrowing dulls the edge of h.
  498.48
Hush   breathless h. in the Close tonight 416.1
Hut   Love in a h. 332.13
Hyphenated   h. Americanism 476.2
Hypocrisy   Conservative government is an
  organized h. 195.3
  H. is the homage paid by vice to virtue 471.3
Hypocrite   h. in his pleasures 106.4
  No man is a h. in his pleasures 323.35
  We ought to see far enough into a h. 129.10
Hysterica   H. passio 498.135

I

I   I am for people 121.1
  I am that I am 62.11
  I also had my hour 129.3
Ice   i. was all around 144.3
  i. was here, the i. was there 144.3
  skating over thin i. 218.8
Ice-cream   emperor of i. 528.1
Icicles   When i. hang by the wall 498.157
Icummen   Winter is i. in 454.1
Idea   constant repetition...in imprinting an i.
  297.2
  i. isn't responsible for the people 382.2
Ideals   Away with all i. 351.3
Ideas   addiction of political groups to the i.
  247.3
  nice man is a man of nasty i. 535.18
Ides   Beware the I. of March 498.106
Idiot   tale told by an i. 498.177
Idle   I am happiest when I am i. 566.3
Idleness   I. is only the refuge of weak minds
  128.8
If   I. you can keep your head 341.6
  much virtue in I. 498.32
Ignorance   I. is like a delicate exotic fruit 584.6
  I. is Strength 427.3
  I know nothing except the fact of my i. 515.3
  I. of the law excuses 494.4
  one evil, i. 515.2

Where i. is bliss 268.4
Ill   Cannot be i.; cannot be good 498.159
  woman colour'd i. 498.302
  writing or in judging i. 452.7
Illiterate   I. him, I say, quite from your memory
  502.3
Ills   sharp remedy...for all i. 462.2
Illumine   What in me is dark, i. 401.15
Illusion   Religion is an i. 242.2
  visible universe was an i. 69.2
Image   created man in his own i. 62.3
  Thou shalt not make unto thee any graven i.
  62.14
Imagination   Art is ruled...by the i. 170.1
  his i. for his facts 502.10
  Irishman's heart is...i. 499.26
  of i. all compact 498.206
  to save those that have no i. 499.71
  truth of i. 332.33
Imagine   never so happy...as we i. 471.11
Imitate   I i. the Saviour 310.2
Imitation   I. is the sincerest of flattery 148.3
Immortal   I have lost the i. part 498.222
  make me i. with a kiss 381.2
  think they grow i. as they quote 602.1
Immutable   Few things are as i. 247.3
Impediment   cause, or just i. 149.13
Important   little things are the most i. 201.3
  Money...most i. thing in the world 499.75
Impossible   complete sorrow is as i. 547.3
  Difficult...I wish it were i. 323.37
  In two words: i. 263.1
  when you have excluded the i. 201.1
Improbable   an i. fiction 498.275
Impropriety   I. is the soul of wit 388.5
Impulse   i. from a vernal wood 595.18
Inch   every i. a king 498.145
Incident   curious i. of the dog 201.9
Inclination   man ought to read just as i. leads
  323.15
Include   I. me out 263.2
Income   Annual i. twenty pounds 191.8
  live beyond its i. 97.5
  sorrows...in which a good i. is of no avail
  511.3
Incomes   people live beyond their i. 486.2
Incompetence   Employee Tends to Rise to his
  Level of I. 441.1
Incompetent   Democracy...election by the i.
  499.49
Inconvenient   He found it i. to be poor 165.2
Incorruptible   seagreen I. 109.10
Increase   another man's price i. 589.3
  from fairest creatures we desire i. 498.287
Increased   influence of the Crown has i. 207.1
Indecency   I.'s Conspiracy of Silence 499.58
  prejudicial as a public i. 116.4
Indecent   sent down for i. behaviour 569.1
Independent   something about an I. Labour
  Party 569.15
  To be poor and i. 141.1
India   I. is a geographical term 133.8
Indian   base I., threw a pearl away 498.229

lay out ten to see a dead I. 498.255
only good I. is a dead I. 501.1
Indictment i. against an whole people 91.3
Indifference equanimity bordering on i. 257.21
Indifferent worst sin…to be i. 499.15
Indignation puritan pours righteous i. 129.25
Indiscretion lover without i. 277.3
Indispensables She was one of those i. 310.16
Indistinguishable in America the successful
writer or picture-painter is i. 359.1
Individual No i. could resent 535.3
psychic development of the i. 242.1
Individualism American system of rugged i.
301.1
Art is the most intense mode of i. 584.23
Individuals worth of the i. composing it 396.3
Industry Captains of i. 109.13
i. will supply their deficiency 466.1
Ineffable mystic sees the i. 388.4
Inefficiency efficiency and i. 499.28
Inelegance a continual state of i. 27.12
Inevitability i. of gradualness 570.1
Inexactitude terminological i. 133.1
Infancy Heaven lies about us in our i. 595.5
Infant mixed i. 52.2
Inferiority man…is always conscious of an i.
323.30
Inferiors I. revolt in order that they may be
equal 17.3
Infinite everything would appear…i. 67.26
Infinitive When I split an i. 120.3
Infinity I. in the palm of your hand 67.1
Infirmities friend should bear his friend's i.
498.121
Infirmity last i. of noble mind 401.11
Influence How to…I. People 110.1
i. of the Crown has increased 207.1
Influenza call it i. if ye like 56.1
Infortune worst kinde of i. is this 127.17
Inglorious mute i. Milton 268.9
Ingratitude I hate i. more in a man 498.277
I., thou marble-hearted fiend 498.132
man's i. 498.25
Inherit meek shall i. the earth 62.51
they shall i. the earth 62.118
Inhumanity Man's i. to man 93.10
Injury i. is much sooner forgotten 128.3
Recompense i. with justice 150.10
Injustice fear of suffering i. 471.14
Innisfree go to I. 601.10
Innocence ceremony of i. 601.14
Innocent one i. suffer 65.3
Innocently few ways in which a man can be
more i. employed 323.23
Innovator time is the greatest i. 30.24
Insanity lay interest in ecclesiastical matters is
often a prelude to i. 569.7
Insipid Happiness…seems i. 511.2
Insomnia *Amor vincit i.* 244.2
Inspiration Genius is one per cent i. 209.1
Institution more than a game. It's an i. 307.2
Institutions working of great i. 488.1
Insult sooner forgotten than an i. 128.3

Intellect by the feelings, not by the i. 518.8
his i. is not replenished 498.154
i. is…fooled by the heart 471.2
put on I. 67.5
Intellectual artist who's an i. 229.1
I had thoughts once of being an i. 491.1
I. disgrace 25.5
thirdly, i. ability 21.1
word I. suggests 25.7
Intelligence I. is quickness to apprehend 580.2
Intelligent i. are to the intelligentsia 35.2
Intelligentsia intelligent are to the i. 35.2
Intensity excellence of every art is its i. 332.35
worst are full of passionate i. 601.14
Intent prick the sides of my i. 498.165
Interest How can I take an i. in my work? 31.1
lay i. in ecclesiastical matters 569.7
Interested always been i. in people 388.10
Intérieur *Vive l'i.* 495.3
Intoxication best of life is…i. 98.13
momentary i. with pain 76.1
Introduce let me i. you to that leg of mutton
111.31
Introduction buy back my i. to you 385.13
Intrudes society, where none i. 98.10
Invent it would be necessary to i. Him 561.5
Investment There is no finer i. 133.22
Inviolable i. shade 20.11
Invisible no i. means of support 238.1
Inwards he looked i., and found her 205.17
Ireland I. is the old sow 326.1
Irishman I.'s heart is nothing but his imagina-
tion 499.26
Iron i. curtain has descended across the
Continent 133.23
rule them with a rod of i. 62.214
wink and hold out mine i. 498.92
Irons two i. in the fire 45.2
Irresponsible better to be i. and right 133.25
Island No man is an I. 199.12
Isle this sceptred i. 498.235
Isles i. of Greece 98.15
Italian I speak I. to women 124.1
Italy man who has not been in I. 323.30
I. a paradise for horses 94.3
Itch i. of literature 369.1
Iteration i. of nuptials 151.7
Itself Love seeketh not i. to please 67.9

J

Jackson J. standing like a stone wall 50.1
Jam rule is, j. tomorrow and j. yesterday
111.23
James I wisest fool in Christendom 286.2
Jealous Art is a j. mistress 218.1
Jealousy j. is cruel as the grave 62.89
j.; It is the green-ey'd monster 498.224
Jelly Out vile j. 498.142
Jerusalem holy city, new J. 62.219

Till we have built J. 67.7
Jest   fellow of infinite j. 498.73
  j.'s prosperity lies in the ear 498.156
  Life is a j. 251.3
Jesting   j. Pilate 30.2
Jests   his memory for his j. 502.10
Jesus Christ   J. the same yesterday 62.205
Jew   Hath not a J. eyes? 498.193
  I'm not really a J.; just Jew-ish 398.1
Jewel   j. of gold in a swine's snout 62.68
Jewellery   Don't ever wear artistic j. 145.4
  j. wrecks a woman's reputation 145.4
Jewish   total solution of the J. question 260.2
Jo   John Anderson my j. 93.9
Joan   greasy J. doth keel the pot 498.157
Job   Being a husband is a whole-time j. 56.2
  we will finish the j. 133.16
John   Beneath this slab J. Brown is stowed
    414.3
  but for the grace of God goes J. Bradford 73.1
  J. Anderson my jo 93.9
  Matthew, Mark, Luke and J. 5.1
Johnny   Little J. Head-in-Air 299.2
Join   will you...j. the dance? 111.11
Joined   What God hath j. together 499.22
  What therefore God hath j. together 62.149
Joke   good deed to forget a poor j. 72.1
  to get a j....into a Scotch understanding
    512.2
Journalism   j. what will be grasped at once
    153.5
Journey   One of the pleasantest things in the
    world is going a j. 281.4
Joy   as impossible as complete j. 547.3
  j. cometh in the morning 62.49
  let j. be unconfined 98.8
  Silence is the perfectest herald of j. 498.210
  thing of beauty is a j. for ever 332.4
Joys   Hence, vain deluding J. 401.2
  j. of parents are secret 30.8
Judge   J. not, that ye be not judged 62.130
  j. of a man by his foes 154.4
Judged   Judge not, that ye be not j. 62.130
Judgement   day of j. 149.8
  Don't wait for the Last J. 106.5
  green in j. 498.7
  No nation is fit to sit in j. 591.1
  no one complains of his j. 471.1
Judging   in j. ill 452.7
Judgment   after this the j. 62.203
  I expect a j. 191.3
Judgments   'Tis with our j. as our watches
    452.8
Julia   Whenas in silks my J. goes 291.4
Jumblies   far and few, Are the lands where the
    J. live 354.4
Jump   We'd j. the life to come 498.164
Jury   Trial by j. itself...will be a delusion 186.1
Jury-men   wretches hang that j. may dine
    452.28
Just   rain on the j. and on the unjust 62.124
Justice   J. should not only be done 292.1
  Let j. be done 224.1

love of j. in most men 471.14
Recompense injury with j. 150.10
Revenge is a kind of wild j. 30.6
Justified   No man is j. in doing evil 476.3
Justify   j. the ways of God to men 401.15

K

Keep   K. up appearances 131.3
Keeper   k. stands up 304.4
  my brother's k. 62.5
Keepest   what company thou k. 116.5
Ken   when a new planet swims into his k.
    332.29
Kent   K., sir—everybody knows K. 191.24
Kew   I am His Highness' dog at K. 452.24
Key   turn the k. deftly 332.31
Kick   k. against the pricks 62.174
Kid   leopard shall lie down with the k. 62.96
Kiddies   k. have crumpled the serviettes 60.1
Kill   churchmen fain would k. their church
    539.20
  good to k. an admiral 561.2
  k. a wife with kindness 498.252
  k. the patient 30.27
  k. us for their sport 498.144
  men are prepared to k. one another 499.34
  they k. you a new way 472.1
  Thou shalt not k. 62.18
  Time: that which man is...trying to k. 518.1
Killeth   letter k. 62.190
Killing   More ways of k. a cat 340.1
  Patriots never talk of...k. 485.6
Kills   each man k. the thing he loves 584.1
  Who k. a man k. a reasonable creature 401.35
Kin   more than k., and less than kind 498.40
Kind   more than kin, and less than k. 498.40
Kindness   cup o' k. yet 93.3
  full o' th' milk of human k. 498.162
  kill a wife with k. 498.252
  little...unremembered acts of k. 595.19
  recompense k. with k. 150.10
  Woman Killed with K. 293.1
Kinds   We need two k. of acquaintances 511.9
King   as diligently as I have served the k. 593.1
  conscience of the K. 498.60
  every inch a k. 498.145
  Every subject's duty is the K.'s 498.98
  God save our Gracious K. 108.1
  half the zeal I serv'd my K. 498.104
  heart and stomach of a K. 215.2
  Here lies our sovereign lord the K. 473.1
  I think the K. is but a man 498.97
  k. can do no wrong 65.2
  k. is a thing 494.2
  k. never dies 65.1
  k. of shreds and patches 498.69
  Ozymandias, k. of kings 500.10
  such divinity doth hedge a k. 498.72
  wash the balm from an anointed k. 498.236

Kingdom   my k. for a horse 498.241
  of such is the k. of God 62.150
Kings   Conquering k. their titles take 119.1
  K. are earth's gods 498.230
  politeness of k. 367.1
  sad stories of the death of k. 498.237
  teeming womb of royal k. 498.235
  This royal throne of k. 498.235
Kipling   Rudyards cease from k. 526.2
Kiss   come let us k. and part 203.2
  coward does it with a k. 584.1
  K. me, Hardy 415.2
  K. till the cow comes home 45.8
  Let him k. me with the kisses 62.87
  make me immortal with a k. 381.2
  Then come k. me, sweet and twenty 498.270
Kissed   I held him in my arms and k. him 385.6
Kissing   President spends most of his time k.
    551.2
  what fool first invented k.? 535.14
  when the k. had to stop 83.18
Kitchen   way of all flesh…k. 572.2
Knaves   world is made up…of fools and k.
    85.1
Knew   I k. him, Horatio 498.73
Knife   last twist of the k. 214.13
  War even to the k. 98.5
Knight   verray parfit gentil k. 127.2
Knight at arms   what can ail thee, K.? 332.11
Know   all our knowledge is, ourselves to k.
    452.19
  all Ye k. on earth 332.18
  I k. myself 229.2
  I k. nothing except…my ignorance 515.3
  I k. what I like 51.10
  K. then thyself 452.18
  Mad, bad, and dangerous to k. 347.1
  they k. not what they do 62.160
  To k. all makes one tolerant 523.1
  What we k. of the past 314.1
  You k.…what you are 310.26
Knowing   woman…if she have the misfortune
    of k. anything 27.6
Knowledge   all k. to be my province 30.42
  all our k. is, ourselves to know 452.19
  he that increaseth k. increaseth sorrow 62.81
  K. is proportionate to being 310.26
  k. of a lifetime 577.5
  only one good, k. 515.2
  Out-topping k. 20.12
  Science is organized k. 518.2
  search for k. 485.1
Knows   One man that has a mind and k. it
    499.2
Kubla Khan   In Xanadu did K. 144.19

L

Labour   L. is not fit to govern 133.6
  Six days shalt thou l. 62.16

  true success is to l. 529.4
Labourer   l. is worthy of his hire 62.155
Labour Party   Independent L. 569.15
Labours   Children sweeten l. 30.9
Lad   many a lightfoot l. 304.5
Ladders   lie down where all the l. start 601.2
Ladies   lion among l. 498.204
Lady   Dance, dance, dance little l. 163.14
  I want to talk like a l. 499.67
  L. Bountiful 223.2
  l. doth protest too much 498.67
  l. of a certain age 98.18
  young l. named Bright 87.1
Laid   all the young ladies…were l. end to end
    433.7
  l. on with a trowel 498.18
Laissez   L. *faire* 459.1
Laity   conspiracies against the l. 499.17
Lake   sedge is wither'd from the l. 332.11
Lamb   as a l. to the slaughter 62.101
  Little L., who made thee? 67.15
  Pipe a song about a L. 67.14
  wolf also shall dwell with the l. 62.96
Lament   Have I not reason to l.? 595.7
Lamps   l. are going out all over Europe 272.1
  new l. for old ones 15.1
Land   England's green and pleasant l. 67.7
  fat of the l. 62.7
  L. of Hope and Glory 57.1
  l. of my fathers 543.5
  My native L. 98.4
  stranger in a strange l. 62.9
  they have the l. and we have the Bibles 252.1
Lands   in faery l. forlorn 332.27
  l. where the Jumblies live 354.4
Language   l. of priorities 61.1
  l. performs…without shyness 153.3
Lap-dogs   when l. breathe their last 452.27
Lards   l. the lean earth as he walks 498.78
Large   old Priest writ l. 401.34
Lash'd   he l. the vice 535.3
Last   Die…l. thing I shall do 432.1
  Don't wait for the L. Judgement 106.5
  l. day but one 353.1
  L. of the Mohicans 156.1
Late   So l. into the night 98.26
Latin   small L., and less Greek 325.2
Laugh   L., and the world laughs with you 583.1
  Make 'em l. 464.1
  old man who will not l. 488.2
Laughed   No man who has once heartily…l.
    109.14
  When the first baby l. 40.1
Laughing   idea of wit…is l. immoderately 512.2
Laughter   present l. 498.270
Launch'd   face that l. a thousand ships 381.2
Laurel-bough   burned is Apollo's l. 381.4
Laurels   l. all are cut 304.7
  once more, O ye l. 401.9
Law   Born under one l. 271.1
  Every l. is a contract 494.3
  He broke the l. when he was born 499.31
  Ignorance of the l. 494.4

l. is a ass 191.22
L. is the true embodiment 257.3
L. of England is a very strange one 178.1
l. of the Medes and Persians 62.106
L. of the Yukon 496.2
l. unto themselves 62.178
rich men rule the l. 262.7
There is no universal l. 351.3
windy side of the l. 498.276
Laws L. grind the poor 262.7
L. were made to be broken 421.2
repeal of bad or obnoxious l. 265.1
Laxative sweet l. of Georgian strains 103.1
Lay L. your sleeping head 25.6
Lays l. it on with a trowel 151.1
Lea standing on this pleasant l. 595.10
Lead little child shall l. them 62.96
Leadeth l. me beside the still waters 62.47
Leaf l., the blossom or the bole 601.1
sear, the yellow l. 498.175
where the dead l. fell, there did it rest 332.10
League half a l., Half a l. onward 539.2
Leap great l. in the dark 298.4
one giant l. for mankind 18.1
Leapt Into the dangerous world I l. 67.11
Learn What we have to l. to do 17.1
Learned He was naturally l. 205.17
people...never have l. anything from history 282.1
Learning beauty and the lust for l. 51.7
L. hath gained most 245.4
L. is but an adjunct 498.155
L. without thought is labour lost 150.3
little l. is a dangerous thing 452.10
on scraps of l. dote 602.1
Learnt I only remember what I've l. 579.2
They have l. nothing 536.2
Leaven little l. leaveneth the whole lump 62.184
Leaves If poetry comes not as naturally as l. 332.37
Though l. are many 601.3
Leaving became him like the l. it 498.161
Lecher small gilded fly does l. 498.146
Lechery drink...an equivocator with l. 498.168
Still wars and l. 498.265
Led l. by the nose with gold 498.286
Left for a handful of silver he l. us 83.9
Let not thy l. hand know 62.125
'tis better to be l. 151.5
Legislators Poets are the unacknowledged l. 500.16
Leisure Men...detest at l. 98.19
Lend men who l. 348.1
Lender Neither a borrower nor a l. be 498.48
Lene As l. was his hors as is a rake 127.6
Lente Festina l. 532.1
Leopard l. his spots 62.102
l. shall lie down with the kid 62.96
Lerne gladly wolde he l. 127.7
Lesbia Let us live, my L. 114.1
Vivamus, mea L. 114.1
Less found it l. exciting 257.1

I love not man the l. 98.10
l. in this than meets the eye 38.1
Lethe go not to L. 332.19
Letter l. killeth 62.190
thou unnecessary l. 498.134
Levellers Your l. wish to level down 323.17
Lever firm place to stand 16.1
Lexicographer L. harmless drudge 323.3
Liar fighting a l. in the quad 520.1
Liars L. ought to have good memories 505.1
Liberal either a little L. 257.4
ineffectual l.'s problem 240.1
most l. L. Englishman 351.1
Liberation Madness...is potential l. 346.4
Liberties Freedom, what l. are taken 253.1
Liberty condition upon which God hath given l. 173.1
Corruption...symptom of constitutional l. 255.3
give me l. or give me death 289.1
l. cannot long exist 91.15
life, l., and the pursuit of happiness 320.1
l. is precious 355.2
L. means responsibility 499.50
l. of the individual must be thus far limited 396.2
L. of the press 328.1
L., too, must be limited 91.14
l., what crimes are committed in your name 474.1
Liberty Hall This is L., gentlemen 262.5
Library l. is thought in cold storage 487.3
vanity of human hopes...a public l. 323.8
Licence L. my roving hands 199.7
rest love not freedom, but l. 401.38
Licht Mehr L. 261.6
Lick ill cook that cannot l. his own fingers 498.250
Lie Ambassador...sent to l. abroad 596.1
Father, I cannot tell a l. 567.2
My love and I would l. 304.2
Nature admits no l. 109.12
old L. 430.2
tell a bigger outback l. 352.1
to l. down in green pastures 62.47
Who loves to l. with me 498.21
Lied good memory is needed after one has l. 158.4
Lies l., damned l., and statistics 553.1
which way the head l. 462.3
Life Anythin' for a quiet l. 191.33
Bankrupt of l. 205.4
believe in the l. to come 47.1
best of l. is but intoxication 98.13
cuts off twenty years of l. 498.111
digestion is the great secret of l. 512.8
doctrine of the strenuous l. 476.1
essential thing in l. 160.1
fourteen months the most idle...of my l. 255.1
give l. a shape 14.1
Human l. is...to be endured 323.9
I fall upon the thorns of l. 500.8

L. and butterflies are the two sweetest passions 412.3
L. is simply language charged with meaning 454.2
L....something that will be read twice 153.5
Little it was a very l. one 383.1
 l. of what you fancy 362.1
 l. things are infinitely the most important 201.3
Littleness l. of those that should carry them out 74.4
Liv'd I have l. today 205.14
Live anything but l. for it 148.1
 Come l. with me 199.2
 Come l. with me 381.7
 country for heroes to l. in 364.1
 good men eat...that they may l. 515.4
 Houses are built to l. in 30.35
 In him is not l., and move 62.176
 in Rome, l. as the Romans 12.1
 Let us l., my Lesbia 114.1
 l. beyond its income 97.5
 L. that thou mayest desire to l. again 419.4
 Man shall not l. by bread alone 62.117
 not l. to eat 402.1
 not suffer a witch to l. 62.24
 one bare hour to l. 381.3
 people l. beyond their incomes 486.2
 we l. but to make sport 27.10
 we that l. to please 323.7
 You might as well l. 433.4
Lived Never to have l. is best 601.11
 She...has never l. 251.2
 slimy things l. on 144.8
Lives he who l. more l. than one 584.3
 l. of quiet desperation 545.1
Liveth my redeemer l. 62.41
Living faith...l. up to it 541.3
 house is a machine for l. in 157.1
 l. need charity 19.1
Livingstone Dr L., I presume 522.1
Loaf half a l. is better than a whole l. 129.23
Loathe I l. the country 151.6
Logic l. of our times 182.1
Logik un-to l. hadde longe y-go 127.5
Loitering Alone and palely l. 332.11
Lolita L., light of my life 412.1
London Hell is a city much like L. 500.11
 L....Clearing-house of the World 117.1
 L....the great wen? 141.2
 Nobody is healthy in L. 27.2
 when a man is tired of L. 323.32
Lonely She left l. for ever 20.5
Lonesome one, that on a l. road 144.12
Long Art is l. 296.1
 Not that the story need be l. 545.7
 You have sat too l. here 13.1
Longing l. for love 485.1
Longitude l. with no platitude 244.1
Look Cassius has a lean and hungry l. 498.107
 frightened l. in its eyes 508.1
 If you seek my monument, l. around you 597.1

I have learned to l. on nature 595.22
Looking somebody may be l. 392.1
Looks woman as old as she l. 146.1
Lord blessed be the name of the L. 62.38
 fear of the L. 62.58
 I replied My L. 290.2
 L. among wits 323.11
 L. High Everything Else 257.7
 L. is my shepherd 62.46
 Praise the L. and pass the ammunition. 236.1
Lorn lone l. creetur,' 191.6
Lose l. his own soul 62.148
 l. the substance 6.1
 nothing to l. but our aitches 427.5
 nothing to l. but their chains 386.5
 tails you l. 171.1
 To l. one parent...a misfortune 584.7
Losers In war...all are l. 118.1
Lost All is not l. 401.16
 better to have loved and l. 539.11
 by which the printers have l. 245.4
 Home of l. causes 20.16
 never to have l. at all 97.7
 'Tis better to have fought and l. 140.5
 woman that deliberates is l. 4.2
Lot policeman's l. is not a happy one 257.19
Lousy only one fault. It was kind of l. 546.6
Lov'd I never writ, nor no man ever l. 498.298
 Of one that l. not wisely, but too well 498.229
Love Absence is to l. 95.1
 alike are the groans of l. to...dying 370.1
 All mankind l. a lover 218.5
 And l. comes in at the eye 601.5
 ashamed of having been in l. 471.13
 caution in l. is...fatal 485.3
 Come live with me, and be my l. 381.7
 comfort in the strength of l. 595.8
 corner in the thing I l. 498.225
 Familiar acts are beautiful through l. 500.12
 folly...l. did make thee run into 498.20
 God is l. 62.210
 Greater l. hath no man 62.171
 He fell in l. with himself 455.1
 help...of the woman I l. 211.1
 he told men to l. their neighbour 74.2
 hid in the heart of l. 601.13
 hold your tongue and let me l. 199.3
 I do not l. thee, Doctor Fell 79.1
 If music be the food of l. 498.266
 I hate and l. 114.2
 I l. or I hate 445.1
 I'm tired of l. 55.5
 In l....the amateur status 267.2
 I think my l. as rare 498.301
 let us prove...the sports of l. 325.6
 live with me, and be my l. 199.2
 longing for l. 485.1
 l. and murder will out 151.2
 l. a place the less 27.7
 L. bade me welcome 290.6
 L. built on beauty 199.4
 L. ceases to be a pleasure 53.1
 L. conquers all 560.4

L. has pitched his mansion 601.4
l. in a golden bowl 67.3
L. in a hut 332.13
L. in a palace 332.13
L. is a boy 96.3
l. is blind 498.191
L. is like the measles 321.1
L. is my religion 332.39
L. is not l. Which alters 498.298
L. is strong as death 62.89
L. is the whole history of a woman's life 523.2
L. looks not with the eyes 498.202
l. of justice in most men 471.14
l. of money is the root of all evil 62.202
L. seeketh not itself to please 67.9
L. seeketh only Self to please 67.10
L. sought is good 498.274
L., the human form divine 67.17
l. thy neighbour as thyself 62.26
L. your enemies 62.123
man is in l. he endures more 419.1
Man's l. is of man's life 98.12
Many waters cannot quench l. 62.90
Men l. in haste 98.19
My l. and I would lie 304.2
My l. is like a red red rose 93.14
not enough to make us l. 535.16
office and affairs of l. 498.209
One can l....vulgarity 310.27
oyster may be crossed in l. 502.1
passing the l. of women 62.36
perfect l. casteth out fear 62.211
rebuke is better than secret l. 62.77
She never told her l. 498.272
That ye l. one another 62.170
There can be no peace of mind in l. 458.1
Those have most power to hurt us that we l. 45.5
thy l. is better than wine 62.87
Thy l. to me was wonderful 62.36
To be wise and l. 498.263
To business that we l. we rise betime 498.12
true l. never did run smooth 498.201
Try thinking of l. 244.2
turns to thoughts of l. 539.17
unremembered acts of...l. 595.19
vanity and l....universal characteristics 128.9
violence masquerading as l. 346.3
War is like l. 74.7
weak man, who marries for l. 323.27
What is l.? 'Tis not hereafter 498.270
worms have eaten them, but not for l. 498.31
Loved And the l. one all together 83.10
better to have l. and lost 97.7
For God so l. the world 62.166
I have l. Three whole days together 531.1
l., to have thought, to have done 20.3
never to have been l. 151.5
She who has never l. has never lived 251.2
'Tis better to have l. and lost 539.11
Loveliest L. of trees, the cherry 304.1
Lover All mankind love a l. 218.5
l. without indiscretion is no l. 277.3

lunatic, the l., and the poet 498.206
Lovers l. cannot see The pretty follies 498.191
l. fled away into the storm 332.6
Loves each man kills the thing he l. 584.1
Every man l. what he is good at 497.3
I have reigned with your l. 215.3
Two l. I have, of comfort and despair 498.302
Lovesome garden is a l. thing 80.1
Loveth He prayeth best who l. best 144.15
Loving most l. mere folly 498.26
night was made for l. 98.27
Low Caesar! dost thou lie so l.? 498.112
He that is l. 90.7
Lower l. one's vitality 51.4
Lubricates dinner l. business 493.1
Luck l. to give the roar 133.42
Lucre filthy l. 62.199
Luminous Dong with a l. Nose 354.2
Lump leaveneth the whole l. 62.184
Lunatic l., the lover, and the poet 498.206
word is...like a l. asylum 364.3
Lungs don't keep using your l. all the time 353.2
Lust Beauty and the l. for learning 51.7
l. in action 498.299
Nonconformity and l. stalking hand in hand 569.5
Luxuries Give us the l. of life 408.1
Luxury Every l. was lavished on you 426.4
Lyf l. so short 127.16
Lying mighty heart is l. still 595.12
One of you is l. 433.6

M

Macduff M. was from his mother's womb 498.179
Machine house is a m. for living in 157.1
not a man, you're a m. 499.7
One m. can do the work of fifty ordinary men 306.2
Machine-gun m. riddling her hostess 310.14
Mad he first makes m. 221.1
let me not be m. 498.133
M. about the boy 163.15
M., bad, and dangerous to know 347.1
soon as he ceased to be m. he became merely stupid 458.3
We all are born m. 47.5
Madding Far from the m. crowd 268.10
Made Annihilating all that's m. 384.5
Little Lamb, who m. thee? 67.15
we're all m. the same 163.6
What man has m. of man 595.7
Madman m. is not the man who has lost his reason 129.17
Madness devil's m.—War 496.3
M. in great ones 498.64
M. need not be all breakdown 346.4
m., yet there is method in't 498.55

Wits are sure to M. near alli'd 205.3

Maestro You can't teach the old m. a new tune 336.2

Magnifique c'est m., mais 71.1

Mahomet If the hill will not come to M. 30.14

Maids Three little m. from school 257.10

Majesty Her M.'s Opposition 32.2
This earth of m. 498.235

Major-General very model of a modern M. 257.17

Majority Fools are in a terrible...m. 313.1
One on God's side is a m. 444.1

Make Scotsman on the m. 40.5

Maladies m. we must not seek to cure 458.3

Malice m. never was his aim 535.3

Malt M. does more than Milton 304.6

Mammon cannot serve God and m. 62.127

Man Ambassador is an honest m. 596.1
another m.'s price increase 589.3
apparel oft proclaims the m. 498.47
Arms and the m. I sing 560.1
'A was a m., take him for all in all 498.45
big m. has no time 229.3
bold m. that first eat an oyster 535.11
Brutus is an honourable m. 498.117
Child is father of the M. 595.13
condition of m. is a condition of war 298.1
created m. in his own image 62.3
disguised as a complete M. 310.3
dog...went mad and bit the m. 262.1
Enclosing every thin m....fat m. 569.24
Every m. is as Heaven made him 116.1
Every m. is wanted 218.7
for m. or beast 226.1
God made the woman for the m. 539.5
Go West, young m. 269.1
hanging a m. who does not object 499.60
Happy the m. 205.14
hate ingratitude more in a m. 498.277
I care not whether a m. is Good 67.5
If a m. be gracious and courteous 30.16
I love not M. the less 98.10
In wit a m. 452.6
It matters not how a m. dies 323.19
King is but a m. 498.97
life of a solitary m. 323.10
M....always to be blest 452.17
M., being reasonable, must get drunk 98.13
m. can die but once 498.90
M. delights not me 498.57
M. doth not live by bread only 62.27
M. has his will 300.1
m. has made of m. 595.7
m. hath penance done 144.11
M. is a bungler 499.44
M. is a noble animal 82.9
M. is...a political animal 17.2
m. is...a religious animal 91.9
m. is as old as he's feeling 146.1
m. is...a wild animal 179.1
m. is in love he endures more 419.1
m. is only as old as the woman 385.22
M. is something that is to be surpassed 419.5

M. is the hunter 539.23
m. knows he is to be hanged 323.31
m. made the town 165.3
m. meets his Waterloo 444.2
m. must serve his time to every trade 98.24
Manners maketh m. 587.1
M. proposes 333.1
m. right fair 498.302
m.'s a m. for a' that 93.7
M.'s first disobedience 401.14
m. should never put on his best trousers 313.3
M.'s inhumanity to m. 93.10
M.'s life is cheap as beast's 498.136
M.'s love is of m.'s life a thing apart 98.12
m. so various 205.7
M....still bears the stamp of his...origin 180.1
m.'s worth something 83.4
m. that hath no music in himself 498.196
M. that is born of a woman 62.39
m. that is young in years 30.32
M. was born free 481.1
m. who could make so vile a pun 187.1
m. who...had the largest...soul 205.16
m. who has...laughed 109.14
m. who has no office to go to 499.76
m. who has not been in Italy 323.30
m. who has not passed through the inferno of his passions 327.2
m. who listens to Reason is lost 499.54
m. who makes no mistakes 443.1
m. whose god is in the skies 499.47
m. whose second thoughts are good 40.6
m. who's untrue to his wife 25.7
Marriage is the best state for a m. 323.26
mean m. is always full of distress 150.8
No m....ever wrote, except for money 323.29
No m. is a hypocrite in his pleasures 106.4
No m. is an Island 199.12
No m. is good enough to govern another 360.1
no m. who has wrestled with a...card table 546.2
no m. worth having 556.2
not a m., you're a machine 499.7
not m. for the sabbath 62.146
No young m. believes he shall ever die 281.3
old m. in a dry month 214.4
old m. who will not laugh 488.2
one m. pick'd out of ten thousand 498.54
one small step for m. 18.1
Painting is a blind m.'s profession. 445.2
play the m. 350.1
proper study of Mankind is M. 452.18
real danger...is m. himself 327.3
say to all the world 'This was a m.' 498.124
silliest woman can manage a clever m. 341.10
single sentence...for modern m. 106.2
Style is the m. himself 86.1
superior m. is distressed by his want of ability 150.11
superior m. is satisfied 150.8
teach you more of m. 595.18

This is the state of m. 498.103
'Tis strange what a m. may do 541.4
To the m.-in-the-street, who 25.7
uneducated m. to read books of quotations 133.28
weak m....marries for love 323.27
what a m. is to a gent 35.2
What a piece of work is a m. 498.57
what a very singularly deep young m. 257.14
What is m. 62.43
when a m. bites a dog 175.1
When a stupid m. is doing something 499.10
whether he is a Wise M. or a Fool 67.5
Whoso would be a m. 218.9
Women who love the same m. 51.5
you asked this m. to die 25.2
You cannot make a m. by standing a sheep 51.9
you'll be a M., my son 341.7
young m. feels his pockets 304.8
young m. not yet 30.12
young m. who has not wept 488.2
You're a better m. than I am 341.5
Management   British m. doesn't seem to understand 125.2
Mandalay   On the road to M. 341.8
Mandrake   Get with child a m. root 199.9
Man Friday   I takes my m. with me 184.2
Manhood   m. a struggle 195.7
Mankind   all M.'s epitome 205.7
 Example is the school of m. 91.11
 giant leap for m. 18.1
 M. is a club 129.24
 M. is not a tribe of animals 129.24
 proper study of m. is books 310.6
 proper study of M. is Man 452.18
 Spectator of m. 4.4
Manner   to the m. born 498.49
Manners   as a nation...we've no m. 499.73
 in England people have...m. 395.1
 man...by his m. 519.3
 M. are especially the need of the plain 569.25
 M. maketh man 587.1
Mansion   Love has pitched his m. 601.4
Many   m. are called 62.140
 m. change and pass 500.2
 So m. men, so m. opinions 540.2
 so much owed by so m. 133.15
Map   Roll up that m. 447.2
Maps   Geography is about M. 59.2
Marathon   mountains look on M. 98.16
Marble   he...left it m. 100.1
 Not m., nor the gilded monuments 498.292
March   Beware the ides of M. 498.106
 Napoleon's armies used to m. on their stomachs 495.3
Marche   droghte of M. 127.1
Mare   Though patience be a tired m. 498.93
Mariner   It is an ancient M. 144.1
Mark   ever-fixed m. 498.298
 We all leave an indelible m. 222.1
Marriage   comedies are ended by a m. 98.14
 hanging prevents a bad m. 498.268

Happiness in m. 27.9
It takes two to make a m. 487.1
Let me not to the m. of true minds 498.298
M.,...a community...making in all two. 63.6
M. is like a cage 403.4
M. is the best state for a man 323.26
M....maximum of temptation 499.52
Married   if ever we had been m. 251.1
 not being legally m. 499.19
 parents were not m. 499.31
 virtue...Trade Unionism of the m. 499.41
Marry   Every woman should m. 195.9
 when a man should m. 30.12
 woman...may m. whom she likes 541.5
Mars   seat of M. 498.235
Martyrdom   M. is the only way in which a man can become famous 499.77
Mask   He had a m. like Castlereagh 500.6
Mass   m. of men lead lives 545.1
 Paris is well worth a m. 286.1
Masses   I will back the m. against the classes 258.2
Master   I am the m. of my fate; 285.2
 M. Mistress of my passion 498.289
Masterpiece   m. of Nature 218.3
Masterpieces   Nothing is likely about m. 530.1
Masters   Assistant m. came and went 569.17
 No man can serve two m. 62.126
 people are the m. 91.5
Masturbation   m. of war 461.1
Mates   moves, and m., and slays 228.7
Mathematics   Angling...like the m. 565.1
 M. possesses not only truth, but supreme beauty 485.4
 pregnancy...resort to m. 392.2
Mating   only in the m. season 399.1
Matrimony   in m. to begin with a little aversion 502.4
 m....friendship recognised by the police 529.1
Matter   poultry m. 385.3
 proverb is much m. decorated 245.3
Matters   Nothing m. very much 36.2
Matthew   M., Mark, Luke and John, 5.1
Maud   Come into the garden, M. 539.19
May   as fresh as is the month of M. 127.3
 darling buds of M. 498.288
 wish a snow in M.'s...shows 498.153
Maybe   I'll give you a definite m. 263.5
Me   between m. and the sun 193.1
 I consider the world as made for m. 513.2
 My thought is m. 489.3
 think only this of m. 78.3
Meadow   There was a time when m., grove 595.4
Mean   He who meanly admires m. things is a Snob 541.1
 It all depends what you m. by... 322.1
 it means just what I choose it to m. 111.25
 tears, I know not what they m. 539.22
Meaner   motives m. than your own 40.7
Meaning   Literature is...language charged with m. 454.2
Means   die beyond my m. 584.26

m. just what I choose it to mean 111.25

no invisible m. of support 238.1

Meant   more is m. than meets the ear 401.5

Measles   Love is like the m. 321.1

Measure   M. still for M. 498.186

Shrunk to this little m. 498.112

Measureless   caverns m. to man 144.19

Meat   man loves the m. in his youth 498.211

one man is appointed to buy the m. 494.2

Out of the eater came forth m. 62.32

Medes   law of the M. and Persians 62.106

Medicine   miserable have no other m. 498.182

Mediocre   Some men are born m. 283.2

Meek   Blessed are the m. 62.118

m. shall inherit the e?rth 62.51

Meet   never the twain shall m. 341.1

Meeting   as If I was a public m. 558.2

this m. is drunk 191.31

Megalomaniac   m....seeks to be feared 485.2

Melancholy   M. has her sovran shrine 332.21

M., indeed, should be diverted by every means 323.28

Most musical, most m. 401.3

so sweet as M. 94.1

Melba   *M.* dinkum hard-swearing Aussie 279.1

Melodies   Heard m. are sweet 332.16

Member   club that will accept me as m. 385.19

Memories   Liars ought to have good m. 505.1

Memory   Everyone complains of his m. 471.1

good m. is needed after one has lied 158.4

Illiterate him...from your m. 502.3

indebted to his m. for his jests 502.10

Men   all m. are created equal 320.1

All things to all m. 62.185

All those m. have their price 563.2

Do other m. 191.16

England...purgatory of m. 233.1

give place to better m. 172.3

Great m. are almost always bad m. 1.1

happy breed of m. 498.235

I cannot bear m. and women 499.23

justify the ways of God to m. 401.15

Let us now praise famous m. 62.113

many m., so beautiful 144.8

mass of m. lead lives 545.1

m. about me that are fat 498.107

M. are not hanged for stealing horses 274.1

m....capable of every wickedness 154.6

m. everywhere could be free 360.5

M. fear death 30.3

M. have never been good 41.1

m. may come and m. may go 539.1

M. must endure their going 498.151

M. of few words are the best m. 498.96

M. seldom make passes 433.2

M.'s natures are alike 150.1

m. who borrow, and the m. who lend 348.1

old m. shall dream dreams 62.109

One machine can do the work of fifty...m. 306.2

Quit yourselves like m. 62.33

rich m. rule the law 262.7

schemes o' mice an' m. 93.12

So far...from being true that m. are...equal 323.18

So many m., so many opinions 540.2

Such m. are dangerous 498.107

That all m. are equal 310.21

tide in the affairs of m. 498.122

to form Christian m. 21.2

We are the hollow m. 214.5

Wives are young m.'s mistresses 30.11

young m. shall see visions 62.109

Mene   *M., M., Tekel, Upharsin* 62.104

Mens   *m. sana in corpore sano* 329.3

Merci   La Belle Dame Sans M. 332.12

Mercy   For M. has a human heart 67.17

m. I asked, m. I found 102.1

quality of m. is not strain'd 498.194

To M., Pity, Peace, and Love 67.16

Mermaids   I have heard the m. singing 214.11

Merry   good are always the m. 601.8

I am never m. when I hear sweet music 498.195

Message   electric m. came 28.1

Messing   m. about in boats 264.1

Metaphysician   scientist must be m. 499.8

Method   madness, yet there is m. in't 498.55

You know my m. 201.2

Mice   schemes o' m. an' men 93.12

Michelangelo   Talking of M. 214.8

Microbe   M. is so very small 55.6

Mid-day   go out in the m. sun 163.9

Middle   people who stay in the m. of the road 61.3

Middle classes   Bow, bow, ye lower m. 257.2

Midnight   cease upon the m. with no pain 332.26

chimes at m. 498.89

M. brought on the dusky hour 401.24

m. never come 381.3

Not to be abed after m. 498.269

soft embalmer of the still m. 332.30

Mid-stream   best to swap horses in m. 360.7

Might   Britons alone use 'M.' 569.23

m. half slumb'ring 332.32

Mightier   pen is m. than the sword 88.1

Mighty   How are the m. fallen 62.35

Look on my works, ye M. 500.10

Milk   And drunk the m. of Paradise 144.21

flowing with m. and honey 62.10

putting m. into babies 133.22

too full o' th' m. of human kindness 498.162

Mill   at the m. with slaves 401.29

Million   man who has a m. dollars 24.1

Millionaire   I am a M.. That is my religion 499.32

Milton   Malt does more than M. can 304.6

mute inglorious M. 268.9

Mimsy   All m. were the borogoves 111.17

Mind   clear your m. of cant 323.34

diseases of the m. 524.1

education forms the common m. 452.20

exaggerated stress on not changing one's m. 388.1

I eat...to put food out of my m. 507.1

Mortals   what fools these m. be 498.205

Most   M. may err as grosly 205.10

Mother   m. of parliaments 75.2
M. of the Free 57.1
never called me m. 594.1

Mothers   There should be no m., only women 499.72

Motion   No m. has she now 595.16

Motives   m. meaner than your own 40.7

Mountains   England's m. green 67.6
m. look on Marathon 98.16

Mourn   countless thousands m. 93.10
To m. a mischief that is past 498.218

Mourning   with my m., very handsome 438.3

Mouse-trap   If a man...make a better m. than his neighbour 218.15

Moustache   man outside with a big black m. 385.8

Mouth   impossible for an Englishman to open his m. 499.66
of the m. of God 62.117
Out of the m. of babes 62.42
Wine comes in at the m. 601.5

Move   But it does m. 248.1
Those m. easiest who have learn'd 452.13

Moves   m., and mates, and slays 228.7
novel...one m. through 554.2

Moving   M. Finger writes 228.8
people under suspicion are better m. 330.2

Much   m....said on both sides 4.6
righteous over m. 62.83
So little done, so m. to do 467.1
so m. owed by so many to so few 133.15

Muck   Money is like m. 30.17
sing 'em m. 389.1

Multitudes   I contain m. 582.5
Pestilence-stricken m. 500.7

Mum   M.'s the word 147.1

Mundi   Sic transit gloria m. 333.2

Murder   I met M. on the way 500.6
love and m. will out 151.2
M. considered as one of the Fine Arts 188.1
M. most foul 498.51
m. shrieks out 572.1
M. will out 127.15
So it was m. 385.6

Murmur   live m. of a summer's day 20.9

Murmuring   m. of innumerable bees 539.24

Muscular   His Christianity was m. 195.8

Music   Architecture...is frozen m. 490.1
art aspires towards...m. 436.2
how potent cheap m. is 163.3
How sour sweet m. is 498.238
If m. be the food of love 498.266
making m. throatily and palpitatingly sexual 310.1
man that hath no m. in himself 498.196
more or less lascivious m. 392.5
M. and women I cannot but give way to 438.2
M. has charms to soothe 151.3
M. that gentlier on the spirit lies 539.18
My m. is best understood by children and animals 530.2

never merry when I hear sweet m. 498.195
silence sank like m. 144.13
still, sad m. of humanity 595.22

Musical   Most m., most melancholy 401.3

Must   Genius does what it m. 394.1

Mutton   Alice m.; m. Alice 111.31

Myriad-minded   Our m. Shakespeare 144.23

Myself   as well said as if I had said it m. 535.12
coming down let me shift for m. 404.1
deliver me from m. 82.6
I celebrate m., and sing m. 582.2
I have always disliked m. 153.8
I know m. 229.2
I like to go by m. 281.4
I've over-educated m. 163.8
not only witty in m. 498.83

Mystery   burthen of the m. 595.20
Happiness is a m. like religion 129.11
hissed all my m. lectures 520.1

Mystic   m. sees the ineffable 388.4

Myth   basing morals on m. 487.4

N

Naked   N. came I out of my mother's womb 62.38
Poor n. wretches 498.140

Name   family n. of Wagstaff 385.9
Good n. in man and woman 498.223
good n. is rather to be chosen than great riches 62.74
Groucho is not my real n. 385.20
I remember your n. perfectly 520.3
lash'd the vice, but spared the n. 535.3
local habitation and a n. 498.207
one whose n. was writ in water 332.40
rose by any other n. 498.243
take the n. of the Lord thy God in vain 62.15
What's in a n. 498.243

Naming   Today we have n. of parts 465.1

Napoleon   N. of crime 201.6

Narcissist   megalomaniac differs from the n. 485.2

Nasty   Something n. in the woodshed 256.1

Nation   England is a n. of shopkeepers 413.2
n. had the lion's heart 133.42
n. is a society united by a delusion 314.6
n. is not in danger of financial disaster 391.1
n. of amateurs 477.2
n. shall not lift up sword against n. 62.92
No n. is fit to sit in judgement 591.1
No n. was ever ruined by trade 239.2
project unfit for a n. of shopkeepers 510.2
We are a n. of governesses 499.79

Nations   Commonwealth of N. 477.1
The day of small n. has long passed away 117.2
great n. have always acted like gangsters 345.1
small n. like prostitutes 345.1

Privileged and the People formed Two N. 195.11

Native My n. Land—Good Night 98.4
white man...looks into the eyes of a n. 356.1

Natives Britons were only n. 495.2

Natural It is n. to die 30.4
N. Selection 180.2
'twas N. to please 205.2

Naturally Though I am not n. honest 498.285

Nature Allow not n. more than n. needs 498.136
but N. more 98.10
Consistency is contrary to n. 310.8
fortress built by N. 498.235
Friend...masterpiece of N. 218.3
God and N. then at strife 539.12
I got disappointed in human n. 198.1
I have learned To look on n. 595.22
Let N. be your Teacher 595.17
Little we see in N. that is ours 595.9
N. admits no lie 109.12
N. is but a name for an effect 165.7
N. is creeping up 577.6
N. is often hidden 30.31
n. is the art of God 82.2
N. is usually wrong 577.2
N. never did betray The heart 595.23
N. remains 582.7
n. to advantage dress'd 452.12
N., to be commanded 30.41
o'erstep not the modesty of n. 498.66
spectacles of books to read n. 205.17
to write and read comes by n. 498.212

Natures Men's n. are alike 150.1

Naught N. so sweet as melancholy 94.1

Nauseate I n. walking 151.6

Navy Ruler of the Queen's N. 257.16

Nearest I am n. to the gods 515.1

Necessities we will dispense with its n. 408.1

Necessity N. is the plea for...infringement of...freedom 447.1
no virtue like n. 498.234
Thy n. is greater than mine 506.3

Neck go to the bottom with my principles round my n. 35.1
Some n. 133.19

Necking Whoever named it n. 385.21

Need reason not the n. 498.136

Needs to each according to his n. 386.2

Negation Capitalist production begets...its own n. 386.1

Negative N. Capability 332.36

Negligent Celerity...admir'd...by the n. 498.11

Neiges *les n. d'antan* 559.1

Neighbour better mouse-trap than his n. 218.15
love thy n. as thyself 62.26
not covet thy n.'s house 62.22
told men to love their n. 74.2

Neighbours make sport for our n. 27.10

Nelly let not poor N. starve 123.3

Network N. Any thing reticulated or decussated 323.4

Neurotics Everything great in the world is done by n. 458.7

Never N., n., n., n. 498.152
n. to have been loved 151.5
N. to have lived is best 601.11
n. to have loved at all 539.11
What n....hardly ever 257.15

Nevermore Quoth the Raven, 'N.' 450.1

New fresh woods and pastures n. 401.13
He that will not apply n. remedies 30.24
n. deal for the American people 475.1
n. heaven and a n. earth 62.218
N. roads: n. ruts 129.26
no n. thing under the sun 62.80

New-found-land my n. 199.7

News And it's only n. until he's read it 569.20
man bites a dog, that is n. 175.1
N. is what a chap...wants to read 569.20
n. that's fit to print 424.1

Newspaper good n. is a nation talking to itself 397.1
I read the n. avidly 61.4

Newspapers N. always excite curiosity 348.4

Nice n. man is a man of nasty ideas 535.18

Nick Satan, N., or Clootie 93.1

Night as a watch in the n. 62.54
black bat, n., has flown 539.19
Do not go gentle into that good n. 543.1
ignorant armies clash by n. 20.2
It ain't a fit n. out 226.1
Morning in the Bowl of N. 228.1
n. was made for loving 98.27
outsoared the shadow of our n. 500.1
perils...of this n. 149.6
returned home the previous n. 87.1
So late into the n. 98.26
sound of revelry by n. 98.7
Weeping may endure for a n. 62.49

Nightingales n. are singing 214.15

Nightmare History...is a n. 326.4

Nights Chequer-board of N. and Days 228.7

Nihilist part-time n. 106.6

Nile allegory on the banks of the N. 502.7
my serpent of old N. 498.6

Nip I'll n. him in the bud 470.1

No rebel...man who says n. 106.7

Noblesse *N. oblige* 357.1

Noblest n. Roman of them all 498.123
two n. of things 535.1

Nobody In heaven an angel is n. 499.57
N., and that's my complaint 385.12
silly game where n. wins 245.2

Noise dreadful n. of waters in my ears 498.240
loud n. at one end 343.1

Noises Like n. in a swound 144.3

Nonconformist man must be a n. 218.9

Nonconformity N. and lust stalking hand in hand 569.5

Non-U U and N. 478.1

Noon dark, amid the blaze of n. 401.30
from n. to dewy eve 401.19

Nooses N. give 433.4

Norfolk Very flat, N. 163.4

Nose Dong with a luminous N. 354.2
  Entuned in hir n. ful semely 127.4
  led by the n. with gold 498.286
Not as the serpent used to say, why n. 499.9
  how n. to do it 191.14
Note make a n. of 191.12
Nothing behind them...there is n. 489.2
  book's a book, although there's n. 98.23
  from n. to a state of extreme poverty 385.11
  he may have n. to say 323.24
  House of Lords...Did n. in particular 257.5
  m. who sees absolutely n. at all 584.19
  n. a-year, paid quarterly 533.2
  N. can be created out of n. 371.1
  n. either good or bad 498.56
  N. happens 47.2
  n. if not critical 498.220
  n. is certain but death and taxes 239.5
  N. is ever done in this world 499.34
  N. long 205.7
  N. matters very much 36.2
  N. to do but work 339.1
  n. to do with the case 257.12
  N. will come of n. 498.130
  Signifying n. 498.177
  take more than n. 111.7
  They have learnt n., and forgotten n. 536.2
  those who were up to n. 163.1
  we brought n. into this world 62.201
  When you have n. to say, say n. 148.2
  world where n. is had 140.1
  You ain't heard n. yet 324.1
Nought N.'s had, all's spent 498.169
Nourisher Chief n. in life's feast 498.167
Novel good n. tells us the truth 129.14
  Great Australian N. 579.4
  n. cannot be too bad to be worth publishing 499.64
  n. is a static thing 554.2
  n. tells a story 237.3
  scrofulous French n. 83.17
  When I want to read a n. 195.13
Novels characters in one of my n. 229.6
  more entertaining than half the n. 388.8
  my n. are an accumulation of detail 579.3
Now We are all Socialists n. 276.1
Nude To keep one from going n. 339.1
Nuisance exchange of one n. for another n. 216.1
Number if I called the wrong n., why did you answer 546.5
Numbers divinity in odd n. 498.200
Numbness drowsy n. pains My sense 332.22
Nun upbringing a n. would envy 426.1
Nuptials prone to any iteration of n. 151.7
Nurse sucks the n. asleep 498.17
Nurseries n. of all vice 225.4
Nut-brown spicy n. ale 401.7
Nuts Brazil, where the n. come from 542.1

O

Oaths O. are but words 96.5
Oats O. A grain, which in England 323.5
Obey great Anna! whom three realms o. 452.26
  Monarchs must o. 205.13
Obeyed Nature...must be o. 30.41
Object hanging a man who does not o. 499.60
  o. of art 14.1
  o. to form Christian men 21.2
Oblige Noblesse o. 357.1
Oblivion alms for o. 498.264
  rest...commend to cold o. 500.3
Observance More honour'd in the breach than the o. 498.49
  o. of trifles 201.2
Occupations worse o. in the world than feeling a woman's pulse 527.2
Occur Accidents will o. 191.10
Odds o. is gone 498.15
Odi O. et amo 114.2
Odious comparisons are o. 199.5
Odorous Comparisons are o. 498.214
O'er Returning were as tedious as go o. 498.172
O'er-leaps Vaulting ambition, which o. itself 498.165
Off O. with his head 111.8
Offence dire o. from am'rous causes springs 452.25
Offend If thine eye o. thee 62.139
Offended This hand hath o. 168.1
Offer nothing to o....except my own confusion 336.4
Office man who has no o. to go to 499.76
  o. of a wall 498.235
  o. sanctifies the holder 1.1
Often Do you come here o. 399.1
Oh O.! Sophonisba! 544.2
Old few who can grow o. with a good grace 524.2
  for o. lang syne 93.3
  I grow o.... I grow o. 214.10
  I love everything that's o. 262.4
  I was born o. 548.1
  I will never be an o. man 42.2
  man...as o. as the woman he feels 385.22
  o. acquaintance be forgot 93.2
  o. familiar faces 348.6
  O. men forget 498.99
  redress the balance of the O. 107.1
  They shall grow not o. 64.1
  they think he is growing o. 315.1
  You are o., Father William 111.4
Old age I prefer o. to the alternative 130.1
  o. a regret 195.7
  o. is...older than I am 42.2
Older she is o. than the rocks 436.1
Oliver Twist O. has asked for more 191.20
Olympic Games most important thing in the O. 160.1
Omega Alpha and O. 62.212

Omnipotence final proof of God's o. 190.5
On O. with the dance 98.8
Once journalism...be grasped at o. 153.5
  O. more unto the breach, dear friends 498.95
  Yet o. more, O ye laurels 401.9
One All for o. and o. for all 206.1
  O. on God's side is a majority 444.1
  O. remains 500.2
  root is o. 601.3
Oneself Hell is o. 214.17
  To love o. is the beginning of a lifelong
  romance 584.4
One up How to be o. 453.2
Only O. connect 237.1
Onward Half a league o. 539.2
  little o. lend thy guiding hand 401.28
Open all questions are o. 54.3
  O. Sesame 15.2
Opera Bed...is the poor man's o. 310.12
Operatic sunsets, they're so...o. 458.6
Operation o. to get a joke well into a Scotch
  understanding 512.2
Opinion better to have no o. of God 30.19
  of his own o. still 96.7
  O. is ultimately determined by the feelings
  518.8
  whole climate of o. 25.3
Opinions proper o. for the time of year 25.8
  So many men, so many o. 540.2
Opium Religion...is the o. of the people 386.3
Opponent Never ascribe to an o. motives
  meaner than your own 40.7
Opportunist rather be an o. and float 35.1
Oppose duty...to o. 132.3
Opposition duty of an o. 132.3
  Her Majesty's O. 32.2
Oppression fanatics...no limit to o. 392.4
Oracle I am Sir O. 498.187
Orange-tree Oh that I were an o. 290.3
Order old o. changeth 539.8
  speech copious without o. 323.1
  upon the o. of your going 498.171
  words in the best o. 144.25
Orgies o. are vile 414.2
Orgy you need an o. 414.2
Origin indelible stamp of his lowly o. 180.1
Original thought is often o. 300.2
Originality All good things which exist are the
  fruits of o. 396.1
Orthodoxy O. not only no longer means being
  right 129.7
Oscar You will, O., you will 577.7
Others anything...one can pay o. to do 388.9
  By persuading o. we convince ourselves 328.2
  corner...for o.' uses 498.225
  delight in...misfortunes...of o. 91.17
  do not do to o. 150.12
  Do not do unto o. as you would they 499.46
  some more than o. 163.6
  strength enough to endure the misfortunes of
  o. 471.7
  to encourage the o. 561.2
  who discommendeth o. 82.1

Otherwise some are o. 513.1
Ours Little we see in Nature that is o. 595.9
Ourselves all our knowledge is, o. to know
  452.19
  By persuading others we convince o. 328.2
  remedies oft in o. do lie 498.1
  we but praise o. in other men 452.14
Out Include me o. 263.2
  love and murder will o. 151.2
  Mordre will o. 127.15
  O., damned spot 498.173
Outlive o. this powerful rhyme 498.292
Outlook religious o. on life 327.1
Outside wait till I get you o. 385.14
Outsoared o. the shadow of our night 500.1
Outward I may not hope from o. forms 144.18
Overcome And what is else not to be o. 401.16
  o. evil with good 62.182
Over-educated I've o. myself in all the things
  163.8
Overflow spontaneous o. of powerful feelings
  595.24
Owe We o. God a death 498.90
Owl O. and the Pussy-Cat went to sea 354.5
Own He who can call to-day his o. 205.14
  his o. received him not 62.162
  mine o. Executioner 199.11
Oxenford Clerk...of O. 127.5
Oxford City with her dreaming spires 20.13
  Home of lost causes 20.16
Oyster bold man that first eat an o. 535.11
  o. may be crossed in love 502.1
  world's mine o. 498.199
Oysters Poverty and o. 191.28
Ozymandias O., king of kings 500.10

P

Pace this petty p. from day to day 498.177
Paddle p. his own canoe 383.3
Pagan I'd rather be A P. 595.10
Pageant insubstantial p. faded 498.258
Pain draw thy breath in p. 498.75
  gentleman...never inflicts p. 417.1
  momentary intoxication with p. 76.1
  Pleasure is...intermission of p. 494.5
  what p. it was to drown 498.240
Pained p. at how little he was p. by 569.13
Pains I can sympathize with people's p. 310.13
Paint as fresh as p. 509.1
  to p. the lily 498.128
Painted women...not so young as...p. 51.1
Painting great difference between p. a face
  245.1
  P. is a blind man's profession 445.2
Pair Blest p. of Sirens 401.1
Pajamas shot an elephant in my p. 385.2
Palladium Liberty of the press is the P.
  of...rights 328.1
Palm To win the p., the oak 384.4

Palms   p. before my feet 129.3
Pants   p. of my blue serge suit 385.4
Papacy   P. is...the Ghost of the deceased Roman Empire 298.3
Paper   isn't worth the p. it's written on 263.6
reactionaries are p. tigers 379.1
Papers   fornicated and read the p. 106.2
Paper work   keep the p. down to a minimum 426.5
Paradise   drunk the milk of p. 144.21
England is a p. for women 94.3
England is the p. of women 233.1
p. for a sect 332.8
Wilderness is P. enow 228.3
Paragon   p. of animals 498.57
Parent   To lose one p....a misfortune 584.7
Parents   his p. were not married 499.31
joys of p. are secret 30.8
what p. were created for 414.4
Paris   P. is well worth a mass 286.1
Parish   all the world as my p. 575.1
Parliaments   England...mother of p. 75.2
Parody   devil's walking p. 129.2
Part   I have forgot my p. 498.35
let us kiss and p. 203.2
read p. of it all the way 263.9
till death us do p. 149.15
Particular   angel is nobody in p. 499.57
did nothing in p. 257.5
London p....A fog 191.2
Particulars   Minute P. 67.4
Parting   P. is all we know of heaven 192.2
P. is such sweet sorrow 498.245
Partisanship   P. is our great curse 469.1
Parts   one man in his time plays many p. 498.23
Today we have naming of p. 465.1
Part-time   p. nihilist 106.6
Party   True patriotism is of no p. 513.3
Pass   but let it p., let it p. 546.4
many change and p. 500.2
p. for forty-three 257.20
p. the ammunition 236.1
They shall not p. 440.1
Passageways   smell of steaks in p. 214.12
Passed   He p. by on the other side 62.156
That p. the time 47.3
We have all p. a lot of water 263.8
Passes   Men seldom make p. 433.2
Passeth   p. all understanding 62.198
Passio   Hysterica p. 498.135
Passion   Master Mistress of my p. 498.289
p. and the life, whose fountains are within 144.18
ruling p. conquers reason still 452.23
Passions   coquette...rouses p. 499.81
devil to have all the p. 499.39
Literature and butterflies...two sweetest p. 412.3
man who has not passed through the inferno of his p. 327.2
man who is master of his p. 153.11
Three p....have governed my life 485.1

Women...have...but two p. 128.9
Past   remembrance of things p. 498.291
something...absurd about the p. 51.2
Study the p. 150.2
Those who cannot remember the p. 488.3
Time present and time p. 214.2
what's p. help Should be p. grief 498.281
What we know of the p. is 314.1
Pastoral   Cold P. 332.17
Pastures   fresh woods and p. new 401.13
lie down in green p. 62.47
Patches   king of shreds and p. 498.69
thing of shreds and p. 257.8
Path   primrose p. of dalliance 498.46
world will make a...p. to his door 218.15
Patience   like P. on a monument, Smiling at grief 498.272
P., a minor form of despair 63.7
Though p. be a tired mare 498.93
Patient   Fury of a P. Man 205.11
kill the p. 30.27
Like a p. etherized upon a table 214.7
Patrie   Allons, enfants, de la p. 480.1
Patriotism   p. is not enough 115.1
P. is the last refuge of a scoundrel 323.25
True p. is of no party 513.3
Patriots   P....never talk of killing 485.6
Patronize   p. everybody without distinction of class 499.29
Pattern   Art is the imposing of a p. 580.3
p. of excelling nature 498.228
Pay   wonders what's to p. 304.8
Peace   hereafter for ever hold his p. 149.14
inglorious arts of p. 384.6
In the arts of p. 499.44
in what p. a Christian can die 4.9
Let him who desires p., prepare for war 557.1
never was a good war or a bad p. 239.4
no p. of mind in love 458.1
no p., saith the Lord, unto the wicked 62.99
P....a period of cheating 63.8
p. for our time 118.2
p. has broken out 74.8
p. I hope with honour 195.5
p. in our time 149.4
P. is poor reading 277.2
p. of God, which passeth 62.198
P., the human dress 67.17
p. with honour 118.2
Prince of P. 62.95
those who could make a good p. 133.29
War is P. 427.3
When there was p., he was for p. 25.8
Peace-maker   If is the only p. 498.32
Peach   dare to eat a p. 214.11
Peaches   poetry in p. 266.1
Peak   Silent, upon a p. in Darien 332.29
Pearl   base Indian, threw a p. away 498.229
One p. of great price 62.135
Pearls   cast ye your p. before swine 62.131
He who would search for P. 205.15
p. that were his eyes 498.254
Peculiar   Funny p. 280.1

Peel   *P*. caught the Whigs bathing 195.2
  p. me a grape 576.4
Peers   Fears,   prejudices,
  misconceptions—those are the p. 364.2
Pen   how much more cruel the p. 94.2
  less brilliant p. than mine 51.3
  nothing can cure it but the scratching of a p.
  369.1
  p. is mightier than the sword 88.1
Penance   man hath p. done 144.11
Pens   Let other p. dwell on guilt 27.4
People   always been interested in p. 388.10
  good of the p. 135.2
  government of the p. by the p. 360.6
  I am for p. 121.1
  indictment against an whole p. 91.3
  Let my p. go 62.12
  mass of every p. must be barbarous 323.21
  p....are attracted by God 314.4
  P. are either charming or tedious 584.11
  p. are the masters 91.5
  p. may be made to follow a course of action
  150.9
  P. must not be forced to adopt me as their
  favourite author 499.78
  p. perish 62.78
  P. seldom read a book which is given to them
  323.22
  p.'s government, made for the p., made by the
  p. 571.2
  p. under suspicion are better moving 330.2
  p. who...just miss the prizes 76.2
  P. who like this sort of thing 360.9
  p. whose company is coveted 376.1
  p. who stay in the middle of the road 61.3
  Religion...opium of the p. 386.3
  talk as other p. do 323.34
Perception   doors of p. were cleansed 67.26
Perfection   friend who loved p. 511.11
  pursuit of an unobtainable p. 511.1
  pursuit of p. 20.14
Performance   desire should...outlive p. 498.87
  it takes away the p. 498.168
  viewing them as a literary p. 582.6
Performing   p. flea 423.2
Perfumes   All the p. of Arabia 498.174
Perhaps   I am going in search of a great p.
  460.3
Perils   all p. and dangers of this night 149.6
Perish   everything else in our language should
  p. 375.1
  no vision...people p. 62.78
  though the world p. 224.1
  weak shall p. 496.2
Periwig   new p. 438.3
Perón   If I had not been born P. 439.1
Perpetually   damn'd p. 381.3
Persians   law of the Medes and P. 62.106
Person   idea of an agreeable p. 195.10
  only thing that can exist is an uninterested p.
  129.9
  to the cheek of a young p. 191.23
  To us he is no more a p. 25.3

Persons   never more than two p. present
  in...reading 578.1
  ninety and nine just p. 62.157
  no respecter of p. 62.175
  two aspicious p. 498.215
Persuade   Beauty...doth...p. the eyes of men
  498.304
Perversion   War is...universal p. 461.1
Pervert   p. climbs into the minds 76.1
Pestilence   He who...acts not, breeds p. 67.22
Pestilence-stricken   P. multitudes 500.7
Peter   Shock-headed P. 299.4
Philistines   Barbarians, P., Populace 20.15
Philosopher   never yet p. That could endure
  the toothache 498.217
  some p. has said it 135.1
Philosophy   Axioms in p. are not axioms 332.38
  dreamt of in your p. 498.52
  History is p....by examples 194.1
  mere touch of cold p. 332.14
  new P. calls all in doubt 199.1
Phone   why did you answer the p. 546.5
Physic   Take p., pomp 498.141
Physician   P., heal thyself 62.153
Pianist   Please do not shoot the p. 584.24
Piano   pounding of an old p. 511.1
Pick   man...would not scruple to p. a pocket
  187.1
Picture   easier to replace...than a good p.
  499.18
Pictures   book without p. 111.1
Piece   p. of cod passes all understanding 373.2
  p. of divinity in us 82.8
  thou bleeding p. of earth 498.113
  What a p. of work is a man 498.57
  Whoever thinks a faultless p. to see 452.11
Pies   I could eat one of Bellamy's veal p. 447.3
Pigs   And whether p. have wings 111.22
Pilate   jesting P. 30.2
Pillar   triple p. of the world 498.4
Pious   p. frauds of friendship 225.1
Pipe   Blow your p. there 83.12
Piping   Helpless, naked, p. loud 67.11
  P. down the valleys wild 67.13
Pit   bottomless p. 62.217
  Whoso diggeth a p. 62.76
Pitchfork   clothes...thrown on her with a p.
  535.10
Pity   P. a human face 67.17
  p. beyond all telling 601.13
  p. for the suffering of mankind 485.1
  Poetry is in the p. 430.1
  seas of p. lie 25.5
  'Tis p. She's a whore 235.1
Place   firm p. to stand 16.1
  grave's a fine and private p. 384.3
  Home is the p. where 243.2
  mind is its own p. 401.17
  Never the time and the p. 83.10
  p. of excrement 601.4
  running...to keep in the same p. 111.18
  this is an awful p. 492.1
  Upon the p. beneath 498.194

you shall now give p. to better men 172.3
Placid   animals...so p. and self-contain'd 582.3
Plague   p. o' both your houses! 498.248
Plagues   of all p. with which mankind are curst 184.3
Plain   best p. set 30.33
   Manners are...need of the p. 569.25
Planet   When a new p. swims into his ken 332.29
Plans   finest p. have always been spoiled 74.4
Platitude   longitude with no p. 244.1
   To stroke a p. until it purrs 382.1
Plato   P. is dear to me 17.4
Play   behold the Englishman...p. tip-and-run 227.1
   Better than a p. 123.4
   good p. needs no epilogue 498.33
   know what to say about a p. 499.21
   little victims p. 268.3
   p., I remember, pleas'd not the million 498.58
   p. is a dynamic thing 554.2
   p.'s thing 498.60
   p. the man 350.1
   p. up! and p. the game 416.2
   tale which holdeth children from p. 506.2
Player   poor p., That struts and frets his hour 498.177
Players   men and women merely p. 498.23
Playing fields   won on the p. of Eton 573.3
Playwright   Congreve...only sophisticated p. 554.1
Pleasant   How p. it is to have money 140.2
Please   death after life does...p. 519.1
   I...do what I p. 241.1
   Love seeketh not itself to p. 67.9
   must p. to live 323.7
   Natural to p. 205.2
   They...say what they p. 241.1
Pleased   man is in general better p. when he has a good dinner 323.39
Pleasing   art of p. consists in 281.6
Pleasure   Debauchee...One who has...pursued p. 63.3
   dissipation without p. 255.2
   for...p. I'd sooner go to my dentist 569.16
   gave p. to the spectators 375.3
   greatest p....to do a good action 348.5
   great source of p. is variety 323.38
   hatred is by far the longest p. 98.19
   Love ceases to be a p. 53.1
   Money gives me p. 55.5
   No profit grows where is no p. 498.251
   p. in the pathless woods 98.10
   P. is...intermission of pain 494.5
   Youth is full of p. 498.303
Pleasure-dome   stately p. decree 144.19
Pleasures   No man is a hypocrite in his p. 323.35
   One half...cannot understand the p. 27.1
   purest of human p. 30.36
Plenty   but just had p. 93.5
Plods   plowman homeward p. his weary way 268.5

Plot   p. thickens 85.2
Ploughing   Is my team p. 304.3
Plowman   p. homeward plods his weary way 268.5
Plowshares   beat their swords into p. 62.92
Pluck   eye offend thee, p. it out 62.139
Plural   in the p. and they bounce 373.1
Plus   *P. ça change, p. c'est la même chose* 331.1
Pocket   pound...in your p. 589.2
   smile I could feel in my hip p. 120.2
Pockets   young man feels his p. 304.8
Poems   p....for the love of Man and in praise of God 543.4
Poesy   drainless shower of light is p. 332.32
Poet   lunatic, the lover, and the p. 498.206
   No p., no artist of any sort, has his complete meaning alone 214.19
   p. and the dreamer are distinct 332.9
   p.'s eye, in a fine frenzy 498.207
   To be a p. is a condition 267.4
Poetry   If p. comes not as naturally as leaves 332.37
   Mr Shaw...never written any p. 129.20
   no man ever talked p. 191.30
   P. is a comforting piece of fiction 392.5
   P. is in the pity 430.1
   P. is the spontaneous overflow of powerful feelings 595.24
   P. is the supreme fiction 528.2
   P. lifts the veil from the hidden beauty 500.15
   p. reminds him of the richness 335.4
   P.'s unnatural 191.30
   p. = the best words in the best order 144.25
   there is p. in peaches 266.1
   truest p. is the most feigning 498.30
   wretched men Are cradled into p. by wrong 500.5
Poets   P. are the unacknowledged legislators 500.16
Pole   Beloved from p. to p. 144.10
Police   friendship recognised by the p. 529.1
   Reading...among p. officers 426.5
Policeman   p.'s lot is not a happy one 257.19
Policemen   repressed sadists...become p. 153.4
Polite   every time you are p. to a proletarian 569.21
Politeness   Punctuality is the p. of kings 367.1
Political   addiction of p. groups to ideas 247.3
   formation of the p. will of the nation 297.5
Political Economy   Dismal Science 109.11
Politician   at home you're just a p. 378.2
   Coffee, which makes the p. wise 452.29
   like a scurvy p. 498.148
Politicians   P. neither love nor hate 205.5
   race of p. put together 535.5
Polygamy   P. was made a Sin 205.1
Pommie   every...P....his fare home 334.1
Pomp   Pride, p., and circumstance 498.227
   Take physic, p. 498.141
Pompous   p. in the grave 82.9
Poms   All the faces...bloody P. 125.1

Pooh-Bah P. (Lord High Everything Else) 257.7

Poor decent means p. 437.1
  great men have their p. relations 191.4
  grind the faces of the p. 62.93
  I live by robbing the p. 499.42
  inconvenient to be p. 165.2
  Laws grind the p. 262.7
  p. always with you 62.144
  P. Little Rich Girl 163.12
  p. shall never cease 62.28
  short and simple annals of the p. 268.6
  To be p. and independent 141.1
  What fun it would be to be p. 14.2

Populace Barbarians, Philistines, P. 20.15

Populi vox p., vox dei 10.1

Porcupines I shall throw two p. under you 344.2

Pornography P. is the attempt to insult sex 351.2
  p. of war 461.1

Position only one p. for an artist 543.6

Possessing too dear for my p. 498.295

Possessions p. for a moment of time 215.4

Post p. of honour is a private station 4.3

Posterity doing something for p. 4.8
  Think of your p. 2.1

Pot greasy Joan doth keel the p. 498.157

Potent how p. cheap music is 163.3

Poultry p. matter 385.3

Pound p. here in Britain, in your pocket 589.2

Pounds two hundred p. a year 96.6

Poured he had been p. into his clothes 592.4

Pouvait si vieillesse p. 219.1

Poverty crime so shameful as p. 223.1
  from nothing to...extreme p. 385.11
  greatest of evils...is p. 499.30
  P. and oysters 191.28
  P. is an anomaly to rich people 32.3
  P. is no disgrace to a man 512.1

Power balance of p. 563.1
  greater the p. 91.16
  P. tends to corrupt 1.1
  When p. narrows the areas of man's concern 335.4

Powerful Guns will make us p. 260.1

Powerless p. to be born 20.7

Powers Headmasters have p. 133.27
  we lay waste our p. 595.9

Practical meddling with any p. part of life 4.4

Praise bury Caesar, not to p. him 498.116
  Damn with faint p. 452.3
  highest p. of God...denial 458.5
  I will p. any man that will p. me 498.10
  Let us now p. famous men 62.113
  People...only want p. 388.2
  P. is the best diet 512.6
  P. the Lord 236.1
  we but p. ourselves in other men 452.14

Praising advantage of...p....oneself 97.6

Pram sombre enemy of good art than the p. 153.7

Prayeth He p. well 144.14

Preachers P. say, Do as I say 494.1

Precisely thinking too p. on th' event 498.70

Predicament life is...a p. 488.5

Prefabricated better word than p. 133.40

Prefer I p. Reading 511.5

Pregnancy It is now quite lawful for a Catholic woman to avoid p. 392.2

Prejudice I am free of all p. 226.3
  We all decry p. 518.5

Prejudices it p. a man so 512.7

Prelude p. to insanity 569.7

Premise fundamental p. of a revolution 549.1

Presbyter P. is but old Priest writ large 401.34

Present P. mirth hath p. laughter 498.270
  Time p. and time past 214.2

President P. spends...time kissing people 551.2
  rather be right than be P. 137.1

Presume Dr Livingstone, I p.? 522.1

Pretty p. can get away with anything 569.25

Prevention P. is better than cure 437.2

Price All those men have their p. 563.2
  pearl of great p. 62.135

Prick If you p. us, do we not bleed? 498.193
  p. the sides of my intent 498.165

Pricks Honour p. me on 498.80
  kick against the p. 62.174

Pride Is P., the never-failing vice of fools 452.9
  P. goeth before destruction 62.71
  p. that licks the dust 452.5

Priest Presbyter is but old P. writ large 401.34
  this turbulent p. 287.1

Priest-craft e'r P. did begin 205.1

Priests I always like to associate with a lot of p. 55.7

Prince P. of Peace 62.95

Princes Put not your trust in p. 62.63

Principle p....can always be sacrificed to expediency 388.6
  p. seems the same 133.38
  What is p. against the flattery 502.9

Principles my p. round my neck 35.1

Print news that's fit to p. 424.1
  pleasant, sure, to see one's name in p. 98.23

Printers those books by which the p. have lost 245.4

Printing Gunpowder, P., and the Protestant Religion 109.2
  mass...must be barbarous...no p. 323.21

Priorities language of p. is 61.1

Prison comparatively at home in p. 569.12
  Home is...girl's p. 499.55
  Stone walls do not a p. make 368.1

Prison-house Shades of the p. begin to close 595.5

Prize Men p. the thing ungain'd 498.261
  Not all that tempts your wand'ring eyes...is lawful p. 268.2

Prizes people who...just miss the p. 76.2

Problem ineffectual liberal's p. 240.1
  three-pipe p. 201.7

Procrastination P. is the thief of time 602.3

Prodigal P. of Ease 205.4

Q

Queue Englishman...forms an orderly q. of one 395.2
Quiet Anythin' for a q. life 191.33
Quietness unravish'd bride of q. 332.15
Quintessence this q. of dust 498.57
Quit Q. yourselves like men 62.33
Quod q. erat demonstrandum 220.2
Quoque Tu q. 428.2
Quotation q. is a national vice 569.19
Quotations good thing...to read books of q. 133.28
q. beautiful from minds profound 433.1
Quote think they grow immortal as they q. 602.1

R

Race Slow and steady wins the r. 363.1
Races human species...composed of two distinct r. 348.1
Rachel R. weeping for her children 62.114
Racially those who are not r. pure 297.1
Rack Leave not a r. behind 498.258
Radiance white r. of Eternity 500.2
Radical r. is a man 475.2
Rag-and-bone foul r. shop of the heart 601.2
Rage all Heaven in a r. 67.2
R., r., against the dying of the light 543.1
Rags no scandal like r. 223.1
Rain droppeth as the gentle r. 498.194
r. on the just and on the unjust 62.124
Rainy when it is not r. 98.2
Raise My God shall r. me up 462.1
Rake every woman is at heart a r. 452.21
lene...as is a r. 127.6
Rapidly but not so r. 47.3
Rapture first fine careless r. 83.7
r. on the lonely shore 98.10
Rare O r. Ben Jonson 325.7
Rarely R., r., comest thou 500.14
Rashes Green grow the r. O 93.8
Rat Mr Speaker, I smell a r. 470.1
Rationed liberty...must be r. 355.2
Rats R.! They fought the dogs 83.11
Raven Quoth the R., 'Nevermore' 450.1
Reach man's r. should exceed his grasp 83.2
Reactionaries r. are paper tigers 379.1
Read classic...nobody wants to r. 553.6
His books were r. 55.4
I never r. a book before reviewing it 512.7
only news until he's r. it 569.20
r. just as inclination leads 323.15
R., mark, learn and inwardly digest 149.9
sooner r. a time-table...than nothing 388.8
When I want to r. a novel 195.13
Readers human race, to which so many of my r. belong 129.16
not all books...are as dull as their r. 545.4
Reading few books...are worth r. 499.80
If a book is worth r. 484.1

I prefer R. 511.5
Peace is poor r. 277.2
R. isn't an occupation we encourage among police officers 426.5
R. is to the mind 524.3
R. maketh a full man 30.39
two persons...in the act of r. 578.1
When I am not walking I am r. 348.3
Ready made critics all are r. 98.24
Why not 'r.' 133.40
Real whether Zelda and I are r. 229.6
Reality art...r. in our minds 376.2
Cannot bear very much r. 214.3
Realms travell'd in the r. of gold 332.28
Reap they shall r. in joy 62.61
they shall r. the whirlwind 62.108
whatsoever a man soweth that shall he also r. 62.196
Reason he who destroys a good book kills r. 401.35
madman...has lost his r. 129.17
man...is R.'s slave 153.11
man who listens to R. is lost 499.54
no r. to bring religion into it 423.1
Only r. can convince us 54.3
right deed for the wrong r. 214.18
R. is itself a matter of faith 129.19
r. not the need 498.136
r. of this thusness 566.2
ruling passion conquers r. 452.23
Their's not to r. why 539.3
woman's r. 498.279
Reasonable r. man adapts himself to the world 499.53
Reasons heart has its r. 435.1
two r. for drinking 437.2
Rebel What is a r. 106.7
Rebuke Open r. is better than secret love 62.77
Recall r....happiness...in misery 176.2
Receive more blessed to give than to r. 62.177
Received his own r. him not 62.162
Reckon'd beggary in the love that can be r. 498.5
Recoils back on itself r. 401.26
Recollected emotion r. in tranquility 595.24
Recompense R. injury with justice 150.10
Red Coral is far more r. 498.300
keep the R. Flag flying 152.1
R. Badge of Courage 167.1
To get very r. in the face 59.1
Redeemer my r. liveth 62.41
Reed r. shaken by the wind 62.133
References Always verify your r. 482.1
Reflection It is a sad r. but a true one 323.16
Refuge God is our r. 62.52
only r. of weak minds 128.8
Refuse never r. a drink 392.6
Regardless r. of their doom 268.3
Regiment led his r. from behind 257.1
Monstrous R. of Women 342.1
Regret old age a r. 195.7
Reign Better to r. in Hell 401.18

Reigned   I have r. with your loves 215.3
Relations   great men have their poor r. 191.4
Relaxes   Bless r. 67.24
Relief   For this r. much thanks 498.39
Religion   Fascism is a r. 411.1
  I am a Millionaire. That is my r. 499.32
  just enough r. to make us hate 535.16
  Love is my r. 332.39
  Men will wrangle for r. 148.1
  no reason to bring r. into it 423.1
  One r. is as true as another 94.4
  r. for gentlemen 123.2
  r. is allowed to invade the sphere of private
  life 390.1
  R. is an illusion 242.2
  R. is by no means a proper subject 128.12
  R....is the opium of the people 386.3
  r. of feeble minds 91.10
  r. of Socialism 61.1
  r....yours is Success 40.3
  talk r. to a man with bodily hunger in his eyes
  499.33
  There is only one r. 499.65
Religious   first, r. and moral principles 21.1
  not r.-good 277.4
  r. animal 91.9
  r. outlook on life 327.1
Remains   Form r. 595.15
  One r. 500.2
  what r.? Nature r. 582.7
Remarkable   nothing left r. Beneath the visiting
  moon 498.15
Remedies   He that will not apply new r. 30.24
  Our r. oft in ourselves do lie 498.1
Remedy   Force is not a r. 75.3
  r. is worse than the disease 30.18
  Tis a sharp r., but a sure one 462.2
Remember   I only r. what I've learnt 579.2
  third I can't r. 534.1
  Those who cannot r. the past 488.3
  We will r. them 64.1
Remembrance   r. of things past 498.291
Render   R. unto Caesar 62.141
Repair   m. should keep his friendship in...r.
  323.12
Repay   I will r., saith the Lord 62.181
Repeal   method to...r. bad...laws 265.1
Repentance   persons, which need no r. 62.157
  Winter Garment of R. 228.2
Repenteth   one sinner that r. 62.157
Repetition   constant r....imprinting an idea
  297.2
Replenished   His intellect is not r. 498.154
Reply   Their's not to make r. 539.3
Reprehend   If I r. any thing in this world 502.6
Reproduce   butlers and lady's maids do not r.
  574.1
Reputation   it wrecks a woman's r. 145.4
  R., r., r.! O, I have lost my r. 498.222
  spotless r. 498.232
Requests   thou wilt grant their r. 149.5
Requires   all the Human Frame r. 55.3
Resemble   happy families r. one another 547.1

Resent   no individual could r. 535.3
Resist   r. everything except temptation 584.12
Resisting   fond of r. temptation 48.1
Resolution   native hue of r. 498.63
Respectable   more r. he is 499.36
  R. means rich 437.1
Respecter   no r. of persons 62.175
Responsibility   In dreams begins r. 601.12
  Liberty means r. 499.50
  no sense of r. at the other 343.1
Responsible   idea isn't r. for the people 382.2
  r. and the irresponsible classes 351.1
Rest   get rid of the r. of her 556.1
  Give his brain a r. 507.2
  leave the r. to the Gods 158.2
  One needs more r. if one doesn't sleep 569.9
  r....commend To cold oblivion 500.3
  r. is silence 498.76
Reticulated   Any thing r. or decussated 323.4
Retrograde   All that is human must r. 255.4
Return   unto dust shalt thou r. 62.4
Returning   R. were as tedious as go o'er 498.172
Reveal   words...half r. and half conceal 539.10
Revelry   sound of r. by night 98.7
Revels   Our r. now are ended 498.258
Revenge   if you wrong us, shall we not r.
  498.193
  R., at first though sweet 401.26
  R. is a...wild justice 30.6
Reviewing   I never read a book before r. it
  512.7
Revolution   fundamental premise of a r. 549.1
Revolutions   All modern r. have ended 106.8
  state of mind which creates r. 17.3
Revolver   I reach for my r. 260.3
Reward   r. of a thing well done 218.6
Rhyme   outlive this powerful r. 498.292
Rich   as well off as if he were r. 24.1
  no sin but to be r. 498.125
  Poor Little R. Girl 163.12
  Poverty is an anomaly to r. people 32.3
  Respectable means r. 437.1
  r. are different from us 229.4
  r. are the scum of the earth 129.6
  seems it r. to die 332.26
  wretchedness of being r. 511.4
Richer   for r. for poorer 149.15
  R. than all his tribe 498.229
Riches   good name...than great r. 62.74
  Infinite r. in a little room 381.5
  R. are for spending 30.28
Richesses   *l'embarras des r.* 11.1
Rid   glad to get r. of it 385.10
  never get r. of the rest 556.1
  only way to get r. of a temptation 584.18
Ride   Haggards r. no more 526.2
Ridiculous   fine sense of the r. 9.2
  sublime and the r. 431.1
Right   All's r. with the world 83.13
  better to be irresponsible and r. 133.25
  I am not and never have been, a man of the r.
  407.1
  I had rather be r. than be President 137.1

minority is always r. 313.2
My speciality is being r. 499.74
no r. to strike against public safety 155.2
orthodoxy no longer means...r. 129.7
our country, r. or wrong 183.1
publish, r. or wrong 98.22
r. divine of kings to govern wrong 452.1
so the heart be r. 462.3
Those who believe that they are exclusively
in the r. 310.22
Ulster will be r. 132.2
very important to be r. 133.44
Righteous   Be not r. over much 62.83
Ring   R. down the curtain 460.2
Ripe   Cherry R. 105.2
Cherry r. 291.1
we r. and r. 498.22
Ripeness   R. is all 498.151
Ripp'd   mother's womb untimely r. 498.179
Rise   Early to r. and early to bed 546.1
One man's wage r. is another man's 589.3
River   Alph, the sacred r. ran 144.19
Fame is like a r. 30.40
Old man r. 275.1
Ol' man r. 275.1
Rivers   By the r. of Babylon 62.62
Road   Golden R. to Samarkand 231.1
On the r. to Mandalay 341.8
people who stay in the middle of the r. 61.3
r. of excess 67.21
Roads   New r.: new ruts 129.26
Roar   I had the luck to give the r. 133.42
Robb'd   He that is r., not wanting what is
stol'n 498.226
Robbing   I live by r. the poor 499.42
Robes   R. and furr'd gowns hide all 498.147
Robespierre   seagreen Incorruptible 109.10
Robin   r. redbreast in a cage 67.2
Rocks   older than the r. among which she sits
436.1
With r., and stones, and trees 595.17
Rod   He that spareth his r. hateth his son 62.70
rule them with a r. of iron 62.214
spare the r. 96.3
thy r. and thy staff they comfort me 62.48
Rode   r. madly off in all directions 353.4
Roland   Childe R. to the Dark Tower came
83.5
Rolf Harris   Did you know that R. was
Australian? 222.2
Rolled   bottoms of my trousers r. 214.10
Rollin'   he keeps on r. along 275.1
Roman   noblest R. of them all 498.123
Papacy...Ghost of the...R. Empire 298.3
Romance   love oneself...a lifelong r. 584.4
Romans   Friends, R., countrymen, lend me
your ears 498.116
Rome   I lov'd R. more 498.115
R. found it brick and left it marble 100.1
When in R. 12.1
when R. falls—the World 98.9
Romeo   R.! wherefore art thou R. 498.242
Room   always r. at the top 571.1

before my little r. 78.1
Infinite riches in a little r. 381.5
who sneaked into my r. at three o'clock
385.12
Root   love of money is the r. of all evil 62.202
r. is one 601.3
Rose   At Christmas I no more desire a r.
498.153
One perfect r. 433.3
r. By any other name 498.243
R. is a r. is a r. is a r. 525.2
Roses   days of wine and r. 200.3
Flung r., r. riotously 200.2
Send two dozen r. to Room 424 385.17
Rot   lie in cold obstruction, and to r. 498.184
we r. and r. 498.22
Rotten   r. in the state of Denmark 498.50
Rough-hew   R. them how we will 498.74
Roving   we'll go no more a r. 98.26
Rowed   All r. fast 142.1
Rub   there's the r. 498.61
try to r. up against money 483.2
Rubies   wisdom is better than r. 62.65
Rudyards   When the R. cease from kipling
526.2
Rue   With r. my heart is laden 304.5
Ruined   r. by trade 239.2
Rule   R. Britannia 544.1
r. them with a rod of iron 62.214
Ruler   I am the R. of the Queen's Navee
257.16
Rules   energetic without r. 323.1
there are no golden r. 499.48
Ruling   r. passion conquers reason 452.23
Rumble   R. thy bellyful 498.138
Rumours   Wars and r. of wars 62.142
Running   it takes all the r....to keep in the
same place 111.18
Rush   For fools r. in 452.16
Rushes   Green grow the r. O 93.8
Russia   R. has two generals 418.1
Russians   our decadence and the R.' 546.7
Rust   r. of the whole week 4.5
Rustling   r. in unpaid-for silk 498.36
Ruts   New roads: new r. 129.26
Rye   Coming through the r. 93.4

S

Sabbath   never broke the S. 205.8
s. was made for man 62.146
seventh day is the s. 62.16
Sacred   human body is s. 582.1
Sacred Heart   Convent of the S. 214.15
Sadder   s. and a wiser man 144.16
Sadists   repressed s. are supposed to become
policemen 153.4
Safe   world must be made s. for democracy
591.3
Safest   Just when we are s. 83.3

Safety   s. is in our speed 218.8
Sages   Than all the s. can 595.18
Said   great deal to be s. For being dead 59.4
    I wish I had s. that 577.7
    they do not know what they have s. 133.4
    well s., as if I had said it myself 535.12
Saint   never a s. took pity on My soul 144.7
Sakes   king...men have made for their own s.
    494.2
Salad   My s. days 498.7
Sally   There's none like pretty S. 108.2
Salmon   choice between smoked s. and tinned
    s. 589.1
Salt   Ye are the s. of the earth 62.120
Salute   those about to die s. you 532.2
Salvation   Work out your own s. 62.197
Samarkand   Golden Road to S. 231.1
Same   he is much the s. 28.1
    principle seems the s. 133.38
    Their tastes may not be the s. 499.46
    we're all made the s. 163.6
Sana   mens s. in corpore sano 329.3
Sand   Such quantities of s. 111.21
    throw the s. against the wind 67.8
    World in a grain of s. 67.1
Sans   S. teeth, s. eyes, s. taste, s. every thing
    498.24
Sappho   Where burning S. loved 98.15
Sat   we s. down, yea, we wept 62.62
    You have s. too long here 13.1
Satan   Get thee behind me, S. 62.138
    S. exalted sat, by merit raised 401.20
    S. finds some mischief 568.1
    S., Nick, or Clootie 93.1
Satisfied   superior man is s. 150.8
Sauce   best s. in the world 116.2
Saul   S. hath slain his thousands 62.34
Savage   s. place! as holy and enchanted 144.20
    soothe a s. breast 151.3
    young man who has not wept is a s. 488.2
Savait   Si jeunesse s. 219.1
Save   he need not exist in order to s. us 190.5
    s. those that have no imagination 499.71
Saviour   I imitate the S. 310.2
Savour   if the salt have lost his s. 62.120
Saw   I came, I s., I conquered 101.2
Say   hardly anybody has got anything to s.
    174.1
    Preachers say, Do as I s. 494.1
    S. it with flowers 425.1
    They are to s. what they please 241.1
    they do not know what they are going to s.
    133.4
    what people s. of us is true 511.6
    When you have nothing to s. 148.2
Saying   they do not know what they are s.
    133.4
Says   desire for preventing the thing one s.
    458.4
Scandal   It is a public s. that gives offence
    402.3
    There's no s. like rags 223.1
Scape   who shall s. whipping 498.59

Scapegoat   Let him go for a s. 62.25
Scarlet   His sins were s. 55.4
    sins be as s. 62.91
Scene   Upon that memorable s. 384.7
Sceptred   this s. isle 498.235
Schemes   best laid s. o' mice an' men 93.12
Schizophrenia   S. cannot be understood 346.2
Scholars   great men have not commonly been
    great s. 300.3
School   Anyone who has been to an English
    public s. 569.12
    Example is the s. of mankind 91.11
    fleshly s. of Poetry 84.1
    If every day in the life of a s. 353.1
    Three little maids in s. 257.10
Schoolmaster   you'll be becoming a s. sir 569.1
Schools   hundred s. of thought contend 379.2
    We class s., you see, into four grades 569.2
Science   S. is organized knowledge 518.2
Scientist   genuine s. must be ...a metaphysician
    499.8
Scissor-man   great, long, red-legged s. 299.3
Scope   this man's art, and that man's s. 498.290
Scorned   fury like a woman s. 151.4
Scotch   get a joke well into a S. understanding
    512.2
Scotchman   noblest prospect which a S. ever
    sees 323.14
Scotland   I...come from S., but I cannot help
    it 323.13
Scots   S., wha hae wi' Wallace bled 93.15
Scotsman   grandest moral attribute of a S. 40.4
    S. on the make 40.5
Scoundrel   General Good is the plea of the s.
    67.4
    man over forty is a s. 499.56
    Patriotism...last refuge of a s. 323.25
Scratching   s. of a pen 369.1
Scripture   devil can cite S. 498.189
Scrofulous   s. French novel 83.17
Scum   rich are the s. of the earth 129.6
    s. of the earth 573.1
Sea   Alone on a wide wide s. 144.7
    Down to a sunless s. 144.19
    fishes live in the s. 498.231
    go down to the s. in ships 62.57
    I'm never, never sick at s. 257.15
    Into that silent s. 144.5
    kings of the s. 20.5
    Out of the s. came he 144.2
    Owl and the Pussy-Cat went to s. 354.5
    precious stone set in the silver s. 498.235
    Proteus rising from the s. 595.10
    s. is calm to-night 20.1
    s.! the s.! 599.1
    snotgreen s. The scrotumtightening s. 326.2
    there was no more s. 62.218
    They went to s. in a sieve 354.3
    why the s. is boiling hot 111.22
Sea-change   doth suffer a s. 498.254
Seagreen   s. Incorruptible 109.10
Seal   And when he had opened the seventh s.
    62.216

slumber did my spirit s. 595.16
Sear My way of life Is fall'n into the s., the
    yellow leaf 498.175
Search in s. of a great perhaps 460.3
    s. for knowledge 485.1
Seas s. of pity lie 25.5
Season Only in the mating s. 399.1
    To every thing there is a s. 62.82
Second best s.'s a gay goodnight 601.11
Secret digestion...s. of life 512.8
    joys of parents are s. 30.8
    to sin in s. 402.3
    when it ceases to be a s. 53.1
Sect attached to that great s. 500.3
    paradise for a s. 332.8
Sedge s. is wither'd from the lake 332.11
See change we think we s. 243.1
    Come up and s. me sometime 576.1
    s....into a hypocrite 129.10
    seem to s. things thou dost not 498.148
    they shall s. God 62.119
Seeing Is not the Giant's-Causeway worth s.
    323.33
Seek To strive, to s....and not to yield 539.27
Seen Blessed are they that have not s. 62.173
    Justice should...be s. to be done 292.1
    most beautiful woman I've ever s. 385.1
Sees fool s. not the same tree 67.23
    man who s. absolutely nothing 584.19
    What, when drunk, one s. in other women
    554.3
Seize S. the day 303.1
Selection term of Natural S. 180.2
Self nothing, not God, is greater to one than
    one's s. 582.4
    to thine own s. be true 498.48
Self-adjusting No man...who has wrestled
    with a s. card table 546.2
Self-indulgence essay on s. 569.3
Self-interest S. speaks all sorts of tongues
    471.10
Selfish I have been a s. being 27.11
Self-love S. is the greatest of all flatterers 471.6
    S. seems so often unrequited 455.1
    true s. and social are the same 452.19
Self-sufficient know how to be s. 403.1
Semed he s. bisier than he was 127.8
Sensational something s. to read in the train
    584.9
Sensations life of s. rather than of thoughts
    332.34
Sense drowsy numbness pains my s. 332.22
    fine s. of the ridiculous 9.2
    Money is like a sixth s. 388.3
    sound must seem an echo to the s. 452.13
    Take care of the s. 111.10
Sensibly things they behave s. about 499.12
Sensitive more s. one is to great art 51.4
Sentence S. first—verdict afterwards 111.15
    structure of the British s. 133.26
Serious War is much too s....to be left to
    military men 536.5
Serpent as the s. used to say, why not 499.9

my s. of old Nile 498.6
Servant You are *not* his most humble s. 323.34
Serv'd s. my God with half the zeal I s. my
    King 498.104
Serve No man can s. two masters 62.126
    They also s. who only stand and wait 401.33
Served I must have things daintily s. 60.1
    Youth will be s. 70.1
Serviettes kiddies have crumpled the s. 60.1
Sesame Open S. 15.2
Sessions s. of sweet silent thought 498.291
Set all, except their sun, is s. 98.15
    best plain s. 30.33
Sets dominions, on which the sun never s.
    421.1
Setting had elsewhere its s. 595.5
Seven his acts being s. ages 498.23
Sex farmyard world of s. 266.2
    Money...was exactly like s. 34.2
    Pornography is the attempt to insult s. 351.2
    professed tyrant to their s. 498.208
Sexes this absurd division into s. 569.14
Sexual music throatily s. 310.1
Shade inviolable s. 20.11
    sport with Amaryllis in the s. 401.10
Shadow lose the substance by grasping at the
    s. 6.1
Shak'd when degree is s. 498.262
Shakespeare myriad-minded S. 144.23
    S. he was naturally learned 205.17
    S. is...really very good 267.5
    S. man who... had the largest...soul 205.16
    S. Out-topping knowledge 20.12
    S. small Latin and less Greek 325.2
    S....Warble his...wood-notes wild 401.8
    When I read S. I am struck 351.5
Shame expense of spirit in a waste of s. 498.299
Shape to give life a s. 14.1
Shapes divinity that s. our ends 498.74
Shaw disciple of Bernard S. 499.20
    Mr S....has never written any poetry 129.20
She s. is my country still 131.1
    S. who has never loved 251.2
Shed tears, prepare to s. them 498.119
Sheep All we like s. have gone astray 62.100
    divideth his s. from the goats 62.143
    hungry s. look up, and are not fed 401.12
    in s.'s clothing 62.132
    like lost s. 149.1
    make a man by standing a s. 51.9
    one is of an old half-witted s. 526.1
    shepherd giveth his life for the s. 62.169
Shepherd Go, for they call you, S., from the
    hill 20.8
    good s. giveth his life for the sheep 62.169
    Lord is my s. 62.46
Sherry I am very fond of...s. 129.4
Shibboleth Say now S. 62.31
Shielding s. men from...folly 518.3
Shift coming down let me s. for myself 404.1
    let futurity s. for itself 513.2
Shine eyes s. like the pants of my...suit 385.4
    Few are qualified to s. in company 535.17

Shining

Shining sun s. ten days a year 334.1
Ships face that launch'd a thousand s. 381.2
go down to the sea in s. 62.57
S., towers, domes, theatres 595.11
something wrong with our bloody s. 44.1
Shit s. in the streets 334.1
Shock-headed S. Peter 299.4
Shocks s. That flesh is heir to 498.61
Shoes s. and ships and sealing wax 111.22
Shoot Please do not s. the pianist 584.24
Shop man must keep a little back s. 403.2
Shopkeepers altogether unfit for a nation of s. 510.2
England is a nation of s. 413.2
Shore adieu! my native s. 98.3
rapture on the lonely s. 98.10
waves make towards the pebbled s. 498.293
Short it will take a long while to make it s. 545.7
life is s. 296.1
Life is too s. to do anything...one can pay others to do 388.9
lyf so s. 127.16
Shorter s. by a head 215.1
Should nae better than he s. be 93.6
no better than you s. be 45.1
Show I have that within which passes s. 498.41
Show off I often wish they would s. a little more 376.1
Shreds thing of s. and patches 257.8
Shrieks murder s. out 572.1
Shrine Melancholy has her...s. 332.21
Shrink all the boards did s. 144.6
Shuffled s. off this mortal coil 498.61
Shyness language performs...without s. 153.3
Sick I am s. at heart 498.39
I'm never, never s. at sea 257.15
Sidcup If only I could get down to S. 446.1
Side He passed by on the other s. 62.156
on the wrong s. of thirty 535.9
Time is on our s. 258.1
windy s. of the law 498.276
Sides Do not...write on both s. of the paper 495.4
man who sees both s. of a question 584.19
said on both s. 4.6
We...assume that everything has two s. 469.1
Sieve They went to sea in a s. 354.3
Sighs S. are the natural langauge of the heart 497.1
Sight s. of you is good for sore eyes 535.8
s. to dream of 144.17
thousand years in thy s. 62.54
Sights few more impressive s. in the world 40.5
Significant s. form 54.1
Signifying S. nothing 498.177
Silence foster-child of s. and slow time 332.15
Friendliest to sleep and s. 401.24
rest is s. 498.76
S. is as full of potential wisdom 310.19
S. is the best tactic 471.15
S. is the perfectest herald of joy 498.210

s. sank Like music 144.13
was s. in heaven 62.216
With s. and tears 98.28
Silk rustling in unpaid-for s. 498.36
s., too often hides eczema 106.1
Silks Whenas in s. my Julia goes 291.4
Silver for a handful of s. 83.9
Silvia Who is S.? What is she 498.280
Simplicity In...s. a child 452.6
Simplify S., s. 545.5
Simultaneously two contradictory beliefs...s. 427.4
Sin beauty is only s. deep 486.3
He that is without s. among 62.167
it is no s. to s. in secret 402.3
no s. but to be rich 498.125
no s. except stupidity 584.22
private s. is not so prejudicial 116.4
wages of s. is death 62.180
worst s. towards our fellow creatures is not to hate 499.15
Sincerest Imitation...s. of flattery 148.3
Sincerity hypocrite...even his s. 129.10
s. is a dangerous thing 584.20
Sing Arms and the man I s. 560.1
s. 'em muck 389.1
Welsh...just s. 569.6
Singed s. the Spanish king's beard 202.1
Singing nightingales are s. near 214.15
Single s. man...must be in want of a wife 27.8
Sinn'd More s. against than sinning 498.139
Sinner one s. that repenteth 62.157
Sinning more sinn'd against than s. 498.139
Sins Charity shall cover the multitude of s. 62.209
from Expensive S. refrain 205.8
His s. were scarlet 55.4
Other s. only speak 572.1
Though your s. be as scarlet 62.91
Sir I am S. Oracle 498.187
Sirens Blest pair of S. 401.1
Sit I will s. down now 195.1
men s. and hear each other groan 332.25
not fit that you should s. here 172.3
So I did s. and eat 290.7
Six s. of one and half-a-dozen of the other 383.2
Six hundred Rode the s. 539.2
Skating s. over thin ice 218.8
Skies man whose god is in the s. 499.47
Skill greater want of s. 452.7
Skin Ethiopian change his s. 62.102
s. of my teeth 62.40
Skinning When you are s. your customers 344.1
Skins beauty of their s. 539.23
Skittles Life isn't all beer and s. 307.1
Sky evening is spread out against the s. 214.7
moon went up the s. 144.9
Slaughter as a lamb to the s. 62.101
Slave man...is Reason's s. 153.11
Slavery Freedom is S. 427.3
Slaves at the mill with s. 401.29

Britons never will be s. 544.1
Slays   moves, and mates, and s. 228.7
Sleave   ravell'd s. of care 498.167
Sleep   an after-dinner's s. 498.183
How do people go to s. 433.1
One needs more rest if one doesn't s. 569.9
our little life Is rounded with a s. 498.258
S. after toil 519.4
s.! it is a gentle thing 144.10
S. that knits up the ravell'd sleave 498.167
To s., perchance to dream 498.61
we must s. 498.13
youth would s. out the rest 498.283
Sleeping   All this fuss about s. together 569.16
Slimy   thousand thousand s. things 144.8
Slings   s. and arrows of outrageous fortune 498.61
Slip   he gave us all the s. 83.19
Slipping   Time is s. underneath 228.6
Slough   s. was Despond 90.2
Slow   I am s. of study 498.203
S. and steady wins the race 363.1
too swift arrives as tardy as too s. 498.247
Slowly   Hasten s. 532.1
Sluggard   Go to the ant, thou s. 62.64
'Tis the voice of the s. 568.2
Slug-horn   s. to my lips I set 83.5
Slumber   I must s. again 568.2
s. did my spirit seal 595.16
Slumbers   Golden s. kiss your eyes 185.1
Slumb'ring   might half s. 332.32
Slush   pure as the driven s. 38.2
Small   Microbe is so very s. 55.6
souls of women are so s. 96.8
still s. voice 62.37
virtue's still far too s. 145.3
Small-endians   Big-endians and s. 535.4
Small-talking   Where in this s. world 244.1
Smell   I once more s. the dew and rain 290.4
I s. a rat 470.1
rose...would s. as sweet 498.243
Smile   s. I could feel in my hip pocket 120.2
Smite   whosoever shall s. thee on thy right cheek 62.122
Smoking   s. custom loathsome to the eye 318.1
Smooth   course of true love never did run s. 498.201
Smyler   s. with the knyf 127.11
Snail   s.'s on the thorn 83.13
Snapper-up   s. of unconsidered trifles 498.284
Snark   For the S. was a Boojum 111.16
Sneaked   who s. into my room 385.12
Sneer   teach the rest to s. 452.3
Sneezed   Not to be s. at 147.3
Snob   He who meanly admires...is a S. 541.1
impossible...not to be sometimes a S. 541.2
Snotgreen   s. sea 326.2
Snow   as white as s. 62.91
wish a s. in May's new-fangled shows 498.153
Snows   s. of yesteryear 559.1
Soap   S. and education...are more deadly 553.2
Sober   as s. as a Judge 225.2
one sees in Garbo s. 554.3

Sociable   I am a s. worker 52.3
Society is no comfort to one not s. 498.37
Social   true self-love and s. are the same 452.19
Socialism   religion of S. 61.1
Socialists   We are all S. now 276.1
Society   nation is a s. united by a delusion 314.6
No s. can surely be flourishing and happy 510.1
S. is no comfort To one not sociable 498.37
S. is now one polish'd horde 98.20
s., where none intrudes 98.10
Socket   Burn to the s. 595.1
Softly   Tread s. because 601.9
Soldier   I never expect a s. to think 499.16
in the s. is flat blasphemy 498.181
You can always tell an old s. 499.4
Soliciting   supernatural s. 498.159
Solitude   In s. alone can he know true freedom 403.2
In s. What happiness 401.25
Which is the bliss of s. 595.3
Whosoever is delighted in s. 30.26
Solution   total s. of the Jewish question 260.2
Solvency   S. is a matter of temperament 511.7
Some   s. more than others 163.6
You can fool s. of the people all the time 360.8
Somer   In a s. season 349.1
Something   Everybody was up to s. 163.1
simplifying s. by destroying nearly everything 129.5
S. nasty in the woodshed 256.1
Time for a little s. 400.1
Sometime   Come up and see me s. 576.1
Somewhat   More than s. 483.1
Son   gave his only begotten S. 62.166
He that spareth his rod hateth his s. 62.70
wise s. maketh a glad father 62.67
you'll be a Man, my s. 341.7
Song   learn in suffering what they teach in s. 500.5
run softly, till I end my S. 519.4
Who loves not wine, woman and s. 372.1
Songs   Where are the s. of Spring 332.2
Sonne   when soft was the s. 349.1
Sons   S. of Belial had a Glorious Time 205.9
Soon   day returns too s. 98.27
Sophonisba   Oh! S.! S.! oh 544.2
Sorrow   down, thou climbing s. 498.135
increaseth knowledge increaseth s. 62.81
Parting is such sweet s. 498.245
Pure and complete s. is as impossible 547.3
S. is tranquillity remembered in emotion 433.5
There is no greater s. 176.2
Sorrows   few s....in which a good income is of no avail 511.3
When s. come, they come not single spies 498.71
Sort   like this s. of thing 360.9
Sought   Love s. is good 498.274
Soul   Artists are not engineers of the s. 335.5

become a living s. 595.21
Dull would he be of s. 595.11
Give not thy s. unto a woman 62.110
half conceal the S. within 539.10
I am the captain of my s. 285.2
largest and most comprehensive s. 205.16
lose his own s. 62.148
My s. in agony 144.7
No coward s. is mine 77.1
seal the hushed casket of my s. 332.31
s. is not more than the body 582.4
s. like season'd timber 290.9
subject's s. is his own 498.98
Souls   s. of women are so small 96.8
Two s. dwell, alas! in my breast 261.2
Sound   deeper than did ever plummet s. 498.259
full of s. and fury 498.177
s. mind in a s. body 329.3
s. must seem an echo to the sense 452.13
Sounds   s. will take care of themselves 111.10
Soup   S. of the evening, beautiful S. 111.12
Take the s. away 299.1
Sour   How s. sweet music is 498.238
Sourest   sweetest things turn s. 498.296
South   beaker full of the warm S. 332.24
Sow   Ireland is the old s. 326.1
like a s. that hath overwhelm'd all her litter 498.83
they that s. in tears 62.61
Soweth   whatsoever a man s., that shall he also reap 62.196
Sown   They have s. the wind 62.108
Space   In the United States there is more s. where nobody is 525.1
Spade   if you don't call me s. 535.15
Spaniards   time to win this game, and to thrash the S. 202.2
Spanish   I speak S. to God 124.1
singed the S. king's beard 202.1
Spare   S. all I have 223.3
s. the rod 96.3
Spareth   He that s. his rod 62.70
Speak   I only s. right on 498.120
Let him now s. 149.14
Other sins only s. 572.1
s. when you're spoken to 111.30
When I think, I must s. 498.28
Speciality   My s. is being right 499.74
Species   s. of person called a 'Modern Churchman' 569.10
Spectacle   Life is not a s. 488.5
Spectator   S. of mankind 4.4
Spectators   pleasure to the s. 375.3
Speech   freedom of s. and expression 475.3
real reason...we...champion free s. 174.1
S. was given to man to disguise his thoughts 536.3
Speechless   *The Times* is s. 133.3
Speed   Be wise with s. 602.2
safety is in our s. 218.8
s. was faster than light 87.1
Spending   Getting and s. 595.9
Riches are for s. 30.28

Spent   Nought's had, all's s. 498.169
When I consider how my light is s. 401.32
Spice   Variety's the very s. of life 165.5
Spies   sorrows...come not single s. 498.71
Spin   they toil not, neither do they s. 62.128
Spires   dreaming s. 20.13
Spirit   Give me the s. 498.91
Hail to thee, blithe S. 500.13
haughty s. before a fall 62.71
history of the human s. 20.18
Into thy hands I commend my s. 62.50
life-blood of a master s. 401.36
Music that gentlier on the s. lies 539.18
present in s. 62.183
slumber did my s. seal 595.16
s. giveth life 62.190
s. indeed is willing 62.145
S. of Delight 500.14
s. that always denies 261.3
Th' expense of s. in a waste of shame 498.299
Splendour   s. falls on castle walls 539.21
Split   when I s. an infinitive...it stays s. 120.3
Spoil   s. the child 96.3
Spoiled   finest plans have always been s. 74.4
Spoke   English as she is S. 552.1
s. among your wheels 45.4
Spoken   Speak when you're s. to 111.30
Spoons   measured out my life with coffee s. 214.9
Sport   kill us for their s. 498.144
s. with Amaryllis 401.10
s. would be as tedious as to work 498.77
to make s. for our neighbours 27.10
Spot   Out, damned s. 498.173
Spotless   s. reputation 498.232
Spots   leopard his s. 62.102
Sprang   I s. to the stirrup 83.8
Spread   not good except it be s. 30.17
Spring   flowers that bloom in the s. 257.12
If Winter comes, can S. be far behind 500.9
In the S. a young man's fancy 539.17
I said the hounds of s. 546.4
lived light in the s. 20.3
S....did happen in Cambridge 412.2
S., sweet laxative 103.1
They call it easing the S. 465.2
Where are the songs of S. 332.2
year's at the s. 83.13
Spur   Fame is the s. 401.11
Spurs   Let the boy win his s. 210.1
Spurts   They move forward in s. 153.9
St Paul's   I am designing S. 59.3
Stables   s. are the real centre of the household 499.24
Staff   I'll break my s. 498.259
Stage   All the world's a s. 498.23
Attic s. 20.6
Don't put your daughter on the s. 163.10
If this were play'd upon a s. 498.275
On the s. he was natural, simple, affecting 262.3
this great s. of fools 498.149
Stain   contagion of the world's slow s. 500.1

Stand   firm place to s. 16.1
    no time to s. and stare 181.1
    s. a little less 193.1
    s. not upon the order of...going 498.171
    that house cannot s. 62.147
    They also serve who only s. and wait 401.33
Standard   raise the scarlet s. high 152.1
Stands   S. the Church clock 78.2
Star   Bright s., would I were steadfast 332.3
    Go, and catch a falling s. 199.9
    Hitch your wagon to a s. 218.12
    our life's S. 595.5
    s. or two beside 144.9
    Sunset and evening s. 539.4
Stare   no time to stand and s. 181.1
Stars   Stone that puts the S. to Flight 228.1
Starting-point   s. for further desires 458.1
Starve   artist will let his wife s. 499.38
    Let not poor Nelly s. 123.3
State   I am the S. 366.1
    object in the construction of the s. 448.2
    reinforcement of the power of the S. 106.8
    s. in the proper sense of the word 355.1
    worth of a S. 396.3
Stately Homes   S. of England 163.2
    S. of England ope their doors 103.1
Statesman   abroad you're a s. 378.2
Statesmen   s....estranged from reality 346.1
Static   class people as s. and dynamic 569.14
    novel is a s. thing 554.2
Station   honour is a private s. 4.3
Statistics   lies, damned lies, and s. 553.1
Statue   no s. has ever been put up to a critic 504.1
Steadfast   would I were s. as thou art 332.3
Steaks   smell of s. in passageways 214.12
Steal   Thou shalt not s. 62.20
Stealing   hanged for s. horses 274.1
Steals   Who s. my purse, trash 498.223
Stealth   do a good action by s. 348.5
Steamer   tossing about in a s. from Harwich 257.6
Steel   When the foeman bares his s. 257.18
Steeples   Till you have drench'd our s. 498.137
Step   one small s.for man 18.1
    s. from the sublime to the ridiculous 413.1
Stepp'd   in blood s. in so far 498.172
Stick   kind of burr; I shall s. 498.185
Stiff   s. upper lip 112.1
Still   of his own opinion s. 96.7
Stillness   talent is formed in s. 261.5
Sting   death, where is thy s. 62.189
Stirring   We live in s. times 316.2
Stirrup   Betwixt the s. and the ground 102.1
    I sprang to the s. 83.8
Stolen   not wanting what is s. 498.226
    S. sweets are best 134.2
Stomach   army marches on its s. 413.3
    little wine for thy s.'s sake 62.200
Stomachs   Napoleon's armies used to march on their s. 495.3
Stone   head s. of the corner 62.59
    Jackson standing like a s. wall 50.1

    let him first cast a s. at her 62.167
    precious s. set in the silver sea 498.235
    s. which the builders refused 62.59
    virtue is like a rich s. 30.33
Stoops   When lovely woman s. to folly 262.10
Stop   come to the end: then s. 111.14
    time...must have a s. 498.81
    when the kissing had to s. 83.18
Stoppeth   he s. one of three 144.1
Stops   buck s. here 551.1
Storage   library is thought in cold s. 487.3
Storm   lovers fled away into the s. 332.6
Story   Not that the s. need be long 545.7
    novel tells a s. 237.3
    snowy summits old in s. 539.21
Straight   branch that might have grown full s. 381.4
Strain'd   quality of mercy is not s. 498.194
Strange   truth is always s. 98.21
Strangeness   s. in the proportion 30.34
Stranger   s. in a strange land 62.9
    S. than fiction 98.21
Strangers   better s. 498.29
Straw   Headpiece filled with s. 214.5
Straws   Errors, like S. 205.15
Strayed   s. from thy ways 149.1
Streets   shit in the s. 334.1
Strength   Ignorance is S. 427.3
    My s. is as the s. of ten 539.25
    We are not now that s. 539.27
Strenuous   doctrine of the s. life 476.1
Strife   God and Nature then at s. 539.12
Strike   no right to s. against the public safety 155.2
    themselves must s. the blow 98.6
String   chewing little bits of S. 55.2
Strings   'There are s.', said Mr Tappertit, 'in the human heart' 191.1
Strive   Thou shalt not kill; but needst not s. 140.4
    To s., to seek, to find, and not to yield 539.27
Stroke   none so fast as s. 142.1
Strong   out of the s. came forth sweetness 62.32
    s. shall thrive 496.2
Stronger   ballot is s. than the bullet 360.2
Strongest   Hero-worship is s. 518.7
Struck   Certain women should be s. regularly 163.5
    I s. the board 290.1
Structure   essential s. of the normal British sentence 133.26
Struggle   manhood a s. 195.7
Struggles   history of class s. 386.4
Strumpet   s.'s fool 498.4
Struts   player that s. and frets 498.177
Studies   S. serve for delight 30.37
Study   I am slow of s. 498.203
    much s. is a weariness of the flesh 62.85
    proper s. of Mankind 452.18
    s. what you most affect 498.251
Stuff   Ambition should be made of sterner s. 498.118
    such s. as dreams are made on 498.258

Stuffed   We are the s. men 214.5
Stumble   they s. that run fast 498.246
Stupidity   no sin except s. 584.22
Style   s. is the man himself 86.1
   s....often hides eczema 106.1
   true definition of a s. 535.6
Subject   Every s.'s duty is the King's 498.98
Sublime   step from the s. to the ridiculous
   413.1
   s. and the ridiculous 431.1
Substance   lose the s. by grasping at the shadow
   6.1
Substitute   no s. for talent 310.18
Succeed   If at first you don't s. 294.1
   those who ne'er s. 192.1
   To s....appear successful. 471.12
Succeeds   Nothing s. like excess 584.15
Success   not in mortals to command s. 4.1
   religion...yours is S. 40.3
   S. is counted sweetest 192.1
   true s. is to labour 529.4
   two to make a marriage a s. 487.1
Successful   we do everything we can to appear
   s. 471.12
Such   nothing against apes...As s. 507.4
Sucker   s. born every minute 39.1
Suckle   To s. fools 498.221
Suckled   s. in a creed outworn 595.10
Sucklings   babes and s. 62.42
Sucks   s. the nurse asleep 498.17
Suffer   S. the little children to come unto me
   62.150
   ye s. fools gladly 62.191
Suffering   pity for the s. of mankind 485.1
   unless it has all been s. 27.7
Sufficient   Is trifle s. for sweet? 60.2
   S. unto the day 62.129
Sultry   common where the climate's s. 98.11
Sum   Cogito, ergo s. 189.1
Summer   after many a s. dies the swan 539.26
   All on a s. day 111.13
   Made glorious s. 498.239
   S. afternoon...most beautiful words 317.4
   S. has set in 144.24
   s.'s day 401.19
Summits   Man can climb to the highest s.
   499.14
   snowy s. old in story 539.21
Summum   S. bonum 135.3
Sun   all, except their s. is set 98.15
   aweary of the s. 498.178
   between me and the s. 193.1
   Busy old fool, unruly S. 199.10
   Fear no more the heat o' th' s. 498.38
   go out in the mid-day s. 163.9
   no new thing under the s. 62.80
   nothing like the s. 498.300
   on which the s. never sets 421.1
   S. came up upon the left 144.2
   s. has gone in 511.10
   s. shining ten days a year 334.1
   this s. of York 498.239
   To have enjoy'd the s. 20.3

Sunburn   S. is very becoming 163.7
Sunday   S. clears away the rust 4.5
Sunless   Down to a s. sea 144.19
Sunset   S. and evening star 539.4
   s.-touch 83.3
Sunsets   I have a horror of s. 458.6
Supercilious   s. knowledge in accounts 502.5
Superlative   we have not settled the s. 129.8
Superman   I teach you the S. 419.5
Supernatural   This s. soliciting 498.159
Superstition   S. is the religion of feeble minds
   91.10
Superstitions   new truths...end as s. 312.1
Supp'd   I have s. full with horrors 498.176
Support   atheist...no invisible means of s. 238.1
Suppression   capitalism...machine for the s.
   355.1
Surmise   with a wild s. 332.29
Surpassed   Man is...to be s. 419.5
Surrender   we shall never s. 133.12
Survival   Friendship...has no s. value 358.1
   S. of the Fittest 180.3
   S. of the fittest 518.4
   without victory there is no s. 133.11
Survive   only the Fit s. 496.2
Suspended   laws of God will be s. 499.25
Suspension   willing s. of disbelief 144.22
Suspicion   people under s. are better moving
   330.2
Suspicions   S. among thoughts 30.30
Swains   all our s. commend her 498.280
Swan   after many a summer dies the s. 539.26
   Sweet S. of Avon 325.4
Swap   s. horses in mid-stream 360.7
Swear   s. not by the moon 498.244
Sweat   blood, toil, tears and s. 133.10
Sweats   Falstaff s. to death 498.78
Sweet   Heard melodies are s. 332.16
   if today is s. 228.6
   Is trifle sufficient for s. 60.2
   Revenge, at first though s. 401.26
   rose...would smell as s. 498.243
   so s. as melancholy 94.1
   Stolen waters are s. 62.66
   S. day, so cool, so calm 290.8
Sweetest   s. things turn sourest 498.296
   Success is counted s. 192.1
Sweetness   out of the strong...s. 62.32
   pursuit of s. and light 20.14
   s. and light 535.1
   waste its s. on the desert air 268.8
Sweets   Stolen s. are best 134.2
Swift   Too s. arrives as tardy as too slow
   498.247
Swimming   s. under water 229.5
Swine   cast ye your pearls before s. 62.131
   jewel...in a s.'s snout 62.68
Sword   brave man with a s. 584.1
   more cruel...the pen than the s. 94.2
   pen is mightier than the s. 88.1
   s. sleep in my hand 67.7
Swords   beat their s. into plowshares 62.92
Swound   Like noises in a s. 144.3

Symmetry thy fearful s. 67.12
Sympathetic To be s. without discrimination 227.2
Sympathy failed to inspire s. in men 51.6
machine-gun riddling her hostess with s. 310.14
Syne For auld lang s. 93.3
System Christianity accepted...a metaphysical s. 310.10
Systems Our little s. have their day 539.9

T

Table crumbs...from the rich man's t. 62.158
patient etherized upon a t. 214.7
Tactic Silence is the best t. 471.15
Tails t. you lose 171.1
Take T. care of the sense 111.10
They have to t. you in 243.2
Taken Lord hath t. away 62.38
Taking not winning but t. part 160.1
Tale Life is as tedious as a twice-told t. 498.127
our dead bodies must tell the t. 492.2
t. Told by an idiot 498.177
t. to tell of the hardihood, endurance, and courage of my companions 492.2
t. which holdeth children from play 506.2
thereby hangs a t. 498.22
Talent T. does what it can 394.1
t. is formed in stillness 261.5
that one t. which is death to hide 401.32
There is no substitute for t. 310.18
Talents If you have great t., industry will improve them 466.1
Talk Herd...who t. too much 205.6
I dont want to t. grammar 499.67
t. as other people do 323.34
when I hear anyone t. of Culture 260.3
Talked He t. on for ever 281.1
one thing in the world worse than being t. about 584.17
Talking always t. about being a gentleman 533.1
good newspaper...nation t. to itself 397.1
T. of Michelangelo 214.8
Tarts she made some t. 111.13
Task long day's t. is done 498.13
Taste Drink deep or t. not 452.10
Things sweet to t. prove...sour 498.233
Tasted Some books are to be t. 30.38
t. two whole worms 520.1
Tastes Their t. may not be the same 499.46
Taught I forget what I was t. 579.2
Taxes nothing is certain but death and t. 239.5
Tea Dinner, Lunch and T. 55.3
honey still for t. 78.2
sometimes counsel take—and sometimes T. 452.26
Take some more t. 111.7
t.-stirring times 316.2

When I makes t. I makes t. 326.3
Teach t. you more of man 595.18
Teacher Let Nature be your T. 595.17
Teaches He who cannot, t. 499.51
Team Is my t. ploughing 304.3
Tears blood, toil, t. and sweat 133.10
God shall wipe away all t. 62.220
If you have t., prepare to shed them 498.119
mine own t. Do scald 498.150
T., idle t. 539.22
They that sow in t. 62.61
too deep for t. 595.6
With silence and t. 98.28
Teche gladly wolde he lerne and gladly t. 127.7
Tedious People are either charming or t. 584.11
Teeth skin of my t. 62.40
take the bull between the t. 263.7
Teetotaller I'm only a beer t. 499.13
Tell do not t. them so 128.1
Father, I cannot t. a lie 567.2
Telling I am t. you 577.1
pity beyond all t. 601.13
Temperament artistic t. is a disease 129.15
Solvency is a matter of t. 511.7
Temperance I prefer t. hotels 566.1
Tempests That looks on t. 498.298
Temple in the very t. of delight 332.21
Temples Ships, towers, domes, theatres, and t. lie 595.11
tempora O t.! O mores 135.4
Temporary force alone is but t. 91.2
Tempt things that are bad for me do not t. me 499.3
Temptation I never resist t. 499.3
last t. 214.18
Marriage is popular because it combines the maximum of t. 499.52
only way to get rid of a t. 584.18
over-fond of resisting t. 48.1
resist everything except t. 584.12
Ten as the strength of t. 539.25
Ten-sixty-six T. And All That 495.1
Terminological t. inexactitude 133.1
Terribles Les enfants t. 250.1
Text great t. in Galatians 83.16
Thames Sweet T.! run softly 519.4
Thank T. me no thankings 498.249
Thanks For this relief much t. 498.39
That Goodbye to All T. 267.1
1066 And All T. 495.1
Theatre Farce is the essential t. 166.1
Theft Property is t. 457.1
Themselves law unto t. 62.178
Theory t. is all grey 261.1
Thick Through t. and thin 96.4
Thickens plot t. 85.2
Thief Procrastination...t. of time 602.3
Time...t. of youth 401.31
Thin Enclosing every t. man, there's a fat man 569.24
Through thick and t. 96.4
Thing beauty...no such t. 445.1

Things

It is a far, far, better t. that I do 191.34
Life is the t. 511.5
play's the t. 498.60
Things former t. are passed away 62.220
good t.... are the fruits of originality 396.1
Shape of T. to Come 574.2
T. are entirely what they appear to be 489.2
T. fall apart 601.14
To talk of many t. 111.22
We see into the life of t. 595.21
Think apparatus with which we t. 63.2
Books t. for me 348.3
comedy to those who t. 564.2
Herd... who t. too little 205.6
I cannot sit and t. 348.3
I exist by what I t. 489.3
I just can't t. of your face 520.3
I'm not so t. as you drunk I am 521.1
I never t. of the future 212.1
I t. him so, because I t. him so 498.279
I t., therefore I am 189.1
never expect a soldier to t. 499.16
T. of your posterity 2.1
t. only this of me 78.3
Thinking It ain't t. about it 550.1
one prolonged effort to prevent oneself t. 310.15
There is wishful t. in Hell 358.2
t.makes it so 498.56
try t. of love 244.2
Thirsty when you are t., to cure it 437.2
Thirty on the wrong side of t. 535.9
This All t. and heaven too 288.2
Thorn t. in the flesh 62.192
Thorns I fall upon the t. of life 500.8
Thou Book of Verse—and T. 228.3
Thought green t. in a green shade 384.5
Learning without t. is labour lost 150.3
My t. is me 489.3
pale cast of t. 498.63
residual fraction is t. 488.1
sessions of sweet silent t. 498.291
silent form, dost tease us out of t. 332.17
T. does not become a young woman 502.2
t. in cold storage 487.3
t. is often original 300.2
t. without learning is perilous 150.3
What oft was t. 452.12
You should have t. of all this before you were born 507.3
Thoughts man whose second t. are good 40.6
sensations rather than of t. 332.34
Speech... to disguise... t. 536.3
Suspicions amongst t. 30.30
t.... too deep for tears 595.6
Thousand I could be a good woman if I had five t. 541.6
Thousands Saul hath slain his t. 62.34
t. at his bidding speed 401.33
Where t. equally were meant 535.3
Three he stoppeth one of t. 144.1
In married life t. is company 584.6
t. fundamental truths 54.3

T. little maids from school 257.10
t. things I always forget 534.1
we galloped all t. 83.8
Three-pipe t. problem 201.7
Threescore t. years and ten 62.55
Thrice circle round him t. 144.21
thou shalt deny me t. 62.151
Thrive strong shall t. 496.2
Throne barge... like a burnished t. 498.8
High on a t. of royal state 401.20
royal t. of kings 498.235
Through part of it all the way t. 263.9
Throw do not t. this book about 55.1
t. away the dearest thing he ow'd 498.161
Thrown t. on her with a pitchfork 535.10
Thrush That's the wise t. 83.7
Thrust greatness t. upon them 498.273
Thus Why is this t. 566.2
Thusness reason of this t. 566.2
Thyself Be so true to t. 30.23
Know then t. 452.18
love thy neighbour as t. 62.26
Tide blood-dimmed t. is loosed 601.14
lived in the t. of times 498.113
t. in the affairs of men 498.122
t. in the affairs of women 98.17
t. is full 20.1
Tiger T.! T.! burning bright 67.12
Tigers reactionaries are paper t. 379.1
Timber soul like season'd t. 290.9
Time And t.... Must have a stop 498.81
big man has no t. 229.3
chronicle of wasted t. 498.297
Even such is T. 462.1
Had we but world enough, and t. 384.1
I haven't had t. to work 336.3
inaudible and noiseless foot of T. 498.3
moment of t. 215.4
Never the t. and the place 83.10
no t. to stand and stare 181.1
not of an age, but for all t. 325.3
peace for our t. 118.2
peace in our t., O Lord 149.4
Procrastination... thief of t. 602.3
That passed the t. 47.3
There was a t. when meadow, grove 595.4
this bank and shoal of t. 498.164
those feet in ancient t. 67.6
T. and the hour runs through 498.160
t. as a tool not as a couch 335.2
T. for a little something 400.1
t. has come,' the Walrus said 111.22
T. hath, my lord, a wallet at his back 498.264
t. is flying 560.5
t. is money 239.1
T. is on our side 258.1
T. is slipping underneath our Feet 228.6
t. is the greatest innovator 30.24
T. present and t. past 214.2
T.'s winged chariot 384.2
T.: that which man is always trying to kill 518.1
T., the subtle thief of youth 401.31

t. to every purpose 62.82
t. will come when you will hear me 195.1
To choose t. is to save t. 30.25
Work expands...to fill the t. 434.1
Times lived in the tide of t. 498.113
logic of our t. 182.1
tea-stirring t. 316.2
The T. has made many ministries 32.1
The T. is speechless 133.3
We live in stirring t. 316.1
Time-table I would sooner read a t. 388.8
Tim'rous Wee,...t. beastie 93.11
Tinned I'd have it t. 589.1
Tip-and-run watch him play t. 227.1
Tipping Do they allow t. on the boat? 385.15
Tipster racing t. who only reached Hitler's
level of accuracy 538.1
Tired I'm t. of Love 55.5
Life...process of getting t. 97.3
when a man is t. of London 323.32
To-day here t., and gone tomorrow 53.2
He who can call t. his own 205.14
if t. be sweet 228.6
I have lived t. 205.14
Toe light fantastic t. 401.6
Together And the loved one all t. 83.10
We must...all hang t. 239.3
Toil Ambition mock their useful t. 268.6
they t. not, neither do they spin 62.128
Tolerant To know all makes one t. 523.1
Tolls for whom the bell t. 199.13
To-morrow for t. we shall die 62.97
here today and gone t. 53.2
T., and t., and t. 498.177
T. do thy worst 205.14
Tom-tit little t. sang Willow 257.13
Tone t. of the company you are in 128.4
Tongue him whose strenuous t. Can burst
Joy's grape 332.21
hold your t. and let me love 199.3
sharp t. is the only...tool 315.2
Tongues Self-interest speaks all sorts of t.
471.10
Tool sharp tongue is the only edged t. 315.2
time as a t., not as a couch 335.2
Tools Give us the t. 133.16
Too much Not t. zeal 536.4
Tooth t. for a t. 62.121
t. for t. 62.23
Toothache philosopher that could endure the
t. 498.217
Top always room at the t. 571.1
Torrent character in the world's t. 261.5
Total t. eclipse 401.30
t. solution of the Jewish question 260.2
Totter t. into vogue 564.1
Touch mere t. of cold philosophy 332.14
sunset t. 83.3
t. of earthly years 595.16
Toves slithy t. did gyre 111.17
Towels never darken my t. again 385.7
Tower Childe Roland to the Dark T. 83.5
Towers cloud-capp'd t. 498.258

Town man made the t. 165.3
next t. drain 520.1
Trade man must serve his time to every t.
98.24
no nation was ever ruined by t. 239.2
Trade Unionism virtue T....of the married
499.41
Tradition It's t.. We don't want t. 234.1
Tragedie go litel myn t. 127.18
T. is to seyn a certeyn storie 127.14
Tragedies t. are finish'd by a death 98.14
two t. in life 499.45
Tragedy Farce brutalized becomes t. 166.1
food a t. 455.2
We participate in a t. 310.7
world is...a t. to those who feel 564.2
Train something sensational to read in the t.
584.9
Tranquillity emotion recollected in t. 595.24
Sorrow is t. remembered in emotion 433.5
Transit Sic t. gloria mundi 333.2
Trappings the t. and the suits of woe 498.41
Trash Who steals my purse steals t. 498.223
Travel To t. hopefully is a better thing than to
arrive 529.4
T., in the younger sort 30.20
Traveller from whose bourn no t. returns
498.62
Tread frightful fiend...behind him t. 144.12
where angels fear to t. 452.16
you t. on my dreams 601.9
Treason T. doth never prosper 278.1
T. was no Crime 205.9
Treasure Preserve it as your chiefest t. 55.1
purest t. mortal times afford 498.232
Tree billboard lovely as a t. 414.5
chestnut t....great rooted blossomer 601.1
same t. that a wise man sees 67.23
spare the beechen t. 104.1
that forbidden t. 401.14
t. of life is green 261.1
t.'s inclined 452.20
Under the greenwood t. 498.21
Trees Loveliest of t., the cherry 304.1
With rocks, and stones, and t. 595.16
Trial T. by jury...a delusion 186.1
t. of which you can have no conception
499.76
Tribe Mankind is not a t. 129.24
Richer than all his t. 498.229
Trick When in doubt, win the t. 305.1
Tried conservatism...adherence to the old and
t. 360.4
I take the one I've never t. 576.7
Trifle Is t. sufficient for sweet 60.2
Trifles observance of t. 201.2
snapper-up of unconsidered t. 498.284
Trinity I the T. illustrate 83.15
Tristesse Bonjour t. 217.1
Triton hear old T. blow his wreathèd horn
595.10
Triumph We t. without glory 158.1
Trot I don't t. it out and about 145.3

Trouble   Genius...capacity of taking t. 109.5
  lot of t. in his life 133.34
  very present help in t. 62.52
Troubles   take arms against a sea of t. 498.61
Trousers   bottoms of my t. rolled 214.10
  I shall wear white flannel t. 214.11
  man should never put on his best t. 313.3
Trowel   laid on with a t. 498.18
  lays it on with a t. 151.1
True   Be so t. to thyself 30.23
  faith unfaithful kept him falsely t. 539.6
  No man worth having is t. to his wife 556.2
  One religion is as t. as another 94.4
  to thine own self be t. 498.48
  truism is...none the less t. 487.2
  what people say of us is t. 511.6
  what we believe is not necessarily t. 54.3
Truism   t. is on that account none the less true
  487.2
Trust   I don't t. him. We're friends 74.3
  Put not your t. in princes 62.63
Truth   all we shall know for t. 601.5
  Beauty is t., t. beauty 332.18
  dearer still is t. 17.4
  few enthusiasts...speak the t. 36.1
  it cannot compel anyone to tell the t. 178.1
  It takes two to speak the t. 545.6
  T. comes out in wine 449.1
  t. is always strange 98.21
  t. of imagination 332.33
  t. that makes men free 7.1
  t. universally acknowledged 27.8
  whatever remains, however improbable, must
  be the t. 201.1
  What is t. 30.2
  What is t. 62.172
  who ever knew T. put to the worse 401.37
  wither into the t. 601.3
Truths   new t. begin as heresies 312.1
  no whole t. 580.1
  those three fundamental t. 54.3
  t. begin as blasphemies 499.1
  t. being in and out of favour 243.1
Try   axe's edge did t. 384.7
  T., t. again 294.1
Tu   *Et t., Brute* 101.4
  Et t., Brute 498.110
  T. quoque 428.2
  T.-whit, T.-who 498.157
Tune   You can't teach the old maestro a new t.
  336.2
Tunes   devil should have all the good t. 295.1
Turbulent   this t. priest 287.1
Turn   I do not hope to t. 214.1
Turtle   voice of the t. is heard 62.88
Twain   never the t. shall meet 341.1
Tweedledee   Tweedledum said T. Had spoiled
  his nice new rattle 111.19
Tweedledum   T. and Tweedledee Agreed to
  have a battle 111.19
Twentieth   T. Century Blues 163.11
Twenty   sweet and t. 498.270
Twenty-nine   t. distinct damnations 83.16

Twice   Literature...will be read t. 153.5
  t. as natural 111.27
Twig   as the t. is bent 452.20
Twilight   T. grey 401.23
Twinkle   T. t. little bat 111.6
Twist   last t. of the knife 214.13
Two   It takes t. to speak the truth 545.6
  t. things that will be believed of any man
  537.1
Tyrannize   man should t. over his bank balance
  337.1
Tyranny   Ecclesiastic t.'s the worst 184.3
Tyrant   professed t. to their sex 498.208

U

U   U and Non-U 478.1
Ulster   U. will fight; U. will be right 132.2
Umble   We are so very u. 191.9
Unbelievable   bombs are u. 579.1
Un-birthday   u. present 111.24
Uncertainty   I have known u. 69.1
Uncomfortable   when he is only u. 499.40
Unconfined   let joy be u. 98.8
Unconquerable   u. hope 20.11
Unconscionable   most u. time dying 123.1
Unconscious   It'll do him good to lie there u.
  507.2
Under   chunder...watch u. 308.1
Underdogs   find an Englishman among the u.
  569.18
Underestimated   effect of boredom is...u. 314.3
Underrate   no duty we so much u. 529.3
Understand   It's all they can u. 389.1
  makes me u. anti-clerical things 55.7
  people...may not be made to u. 150.9
Understanding   passeth all u. 62.198
  piece of cod passes all u. 373.2
  well into a Scotch u. 512.2
Understood   Schizophrenia cannot be u. 346.2
Undone   estate o' th' world were now u. 498.178
  left u. those things 149.2
Uneasy   U. lies the head that wears a crown
  498.88
Uneatable   unspeakable in full pursuit of the u.
  584.13
Unforgiving   fill the u. minute 341.7
Ungain'd   Men prize the thing u. more 498.261
Unhappy   I don't believe one can ever be u. for
  long 569.4
  most u. kind of misfortune 68.1
  u. family is u. in its own way 547.1
  u. one becomes moral 458.2
Uninteresting   no...u. subject 129.9
Unite   Workers of the world, u. 386.5
United States   U. has to move very fast 335.3
  U. of Europe 133.24
Universal   There is no u. law 351.3
Universe   I accept the u. 109.16
  I don't pretend to understand the U. 109.15

Life exists in the u. 319.1
visible u. was an illusion 69.2
University true U. of these days 109.7
Unjust rain on the just and on the u. 62.124
Unkind Thou art not so u. 498.25
Unkindness I tax not you, you elements, with u. 498.138
Unlike Life...u. anything else 592.3
Unnatural so u. as the commonplace 201.4
Unpaid promise...debt u. 496.1
Unprofitable How weary, stale, flat, and u. 498.42
Unrequited Self-love seems so often u. 455.1
Unrest u. which men miscall delight 500.1
Unsettle They only u. him 592.1
Unspeakable psychopathologist the u. 388.4
u. in full pursuit of the uneatable 584.13
Unstable U. as water 62.8
Unwatched Madness...must not u. go 498.64
Up U., Guards, and at 'em 573.2
Upbringing u. a nun would envy 426.1
Upper u. classes Have still the u. hand 163.2
Upright position for an artist...u. 543.6
Use what is the u. of a book 111.1
Useless All Art is quite u. 584.16
most beautiful things...are the most u. 484.2
Uses all the u. of this world 498.42
Usual Business as u. 133.5
Utterly All changed...u. 601.6

V

Vae victis V. 361.1
Vain name of the Lord...in v. 62.15
No great man lives in v. 109.6
V. are the thousand creeds 77.2
vale ave atque v. 114.3
Valet No man is a hero to his v. 159.1
to his very v. seem'd a hero 98.1
Valiant v. never taste of death but once 498.109
Valley All in the v. of Death 539.2
v. of the shadow of death 62.48
Valleys Piping down the v. wild 67.13
Valour better part of v. is discretion 498.82
Value Friendship...has no survival v. 358.1
Vanity name of V. Fair 90.4
v. and love...universal characteristics 128.9
v. of human hopes 323.8
v. of vanities; all is v. 62.79
Vanquished redress of the grievances of the v. 133.30
Woe to the v. 361.1
Varies quality of moral behaviour v. 310.11
Variety custom stale her infinite v. 498.9
great source of pleasure is v. 323.38
V.'s the very spice of life 165.5
Various man so v., that he seem'd to be 205.7
Vary money appears to v. 311.1
Veal Bellamy's v. pies 447.3
Vegetable animal or v. or mineral 111.28

Veil Poetry lifts the v. 500.15
Velasquez Why drag in V. 577.3
Vengeance V. is mine 62.181
Verbal v. contract isn't worth the paper 263.6
Verbosity inebriated with...his own v. 195.6
Verdi strains of V. will come back to you tonight 385.16
Verdict Sentence first—v. afterwards 111.15
Verify Always v. your references 482.1
Veritas In vino v. 449.1
Verse Curst be the v. 452.4
Verses No one will ever get at my v. 582.6
Versing I once more... relish v. 290.4
Versions hundred v. of it 499.65
Vertical v. man 25.1
Vice He lash'd the v., but spared the name 535.3
homage paid by v. to virtue 471.3
no v. but beggary 498.125
Pride...v. of fools 452.9
Prosperity doth best discover v. 30.7
public schools are the nurseries of all v. 225.4
quotation is a national v. 569.19
When v. prevails 4.3
Vices small v. do appear 498.147
Victim v. must be found 257.9
Victims little v. play 268.3
v. who respect their executioners 489.1
Victis Vae v. 361.1
Victorious Send him v. 108.1
Victory Before Alamein we never had a v. 133.36
grave, where is thy v. 62.189
in v. unbearable 133.43
In war it is not right that matters, but v. 297.4
V. at all costs 133.11
without v. there is no survival 133.11
Vidders be very careful o' v. 191.27
Vieillesse si v. pouvait 219.1
View lends enchantment to the v. 104.2
Vigilance condition upon which God hath given liberty...is eternal v. 173.1
Villains God should go before such v. 498.216
Vino In v. veritas 449.1
Vintage O, for a draught of v. 332.23
Violence v. masquerading as love 346.3
Vipers generation of v. 62.116
Virginia Woolf Who's Afraid of V.? 9.1
Virtue adversity doth best discover v. 30.7
Fine words...seldom associated with v. 150.4
forbearance ceases to be a v. 91.7
homage paid by vice to v. 471.3
much v. in If 498.32
My v.'s still far too small 145.3
no v. like necessity 498.234
to practise five things...constitutes perfect v. 150.7
V. is like a rich stone 30.33
v....Trade Unionism of the married 499.41
Virtues ape-like v. without which 153.2
greater v. to sustain good fortune 471.8
v. We write in water 498.105
world to hide v. in 498.267

Vision   Where there is no v. 62.78
Visions   young men shall see v. 62.109
Vitality   busyness…is a symptom of deficient
   v. 529.2
   lower one's v. 51.4
Vogue   totter into v. 564.1
Voice   still small v. 62.37
   v. of the people is the v. of God 10.1
   v. of the turtle is heard 62.88
Voices   Two v. are there 526.1
Vox populi, vox dei 10.1
Vulgar   Funny without being v. 257.22
Vulgarity   One can love a certain kind of v.
   310.27
Vulgarizing   Death…we haven't succeeded in
   completely v. 310.9

W

Wabe   gyre and gimble in the w. 111.17
Wages   ta'en thy w. 498.38
   w. of sin is death 62.180
Wagon   Hitch your w. to a star 218.12
Wagstaff   disgrace to our family name of W.
   385.9
Wait   They also serve who only stand and w.
   401.33
   W. and see 23.1
Waiting   We're w. for Godot 47.4
Waked   You have w. me too soon 568.2
Walking   I'm w. backwards till Christmas 399.3
   I nauseate w. 151.6
   I were w. with destiny 133.31
   When I am not w., I am reading 348.3
Walks   She w. in beauty 98.25
Wall   office of a w. 498.235
   There is Jackson standing like a stone w. 50.1
Wallace   Scots wha hae wi' W. bled 93.15
Wallet   Time hath…a w. at his back 498.264
Walls   splendour falls on castle w. 539.21
   Stone w. do not a prison make 368.1
Walrus   W. and the Carpenter 111.21
Wandered   I w. lonely as a cloud 595.2
Wandering   w. minstrel I 257.8
Want   freedom from w. 475.3
   I shall not w. 62.46
   w. of money is so 97.1
   What does a woman w. 242.5
Wanted   Every man is w. 218.7
   it will not be w. these ten years 447.2
Wanting   art found w. 62.105
Wants   Having the fewest w. 515.1
   one does just exactly what one w. 569.4
War   cold w. 42.1
   defeat without a w. 133.9
   him who desires peace, prepare for w. 557.1
   in every w. they kill you 472.1
   In starting and waging w. it is not right that
   matters, but victory 297.4
   In w.…there are no winners 118.1

let slip the dogs of w. 498.114
My subject is W., and the pity of W. 430.1
neither shall they learn w. any more 62.92
never was a good w. 239.4
No one can guarantee success in w. 133.32
that devil's madness—W. 496.3
Those who can win a w. well 133.29
W. even to the knife 98.5
W. is, after all, the universal perversion 461.1
w. is…all hell 503.1
W. is like love 74.7
W. is much too serious a thing to be left to
   military men 536.5
W. is Peace 427.3
W. makes rattling good history 277.2
w. of the giants is over 133.37
w. which…left nothing to be desired 74.5
We are not at w. with Egypt 208.2
What they could do with round here is a
   good w. 74.1
when there was w., he went 25.8
Warble   W. his…wood-notes wild 401.8
Wards   key deftly in the oiled w. 332.31
Waring   What's become of W. 83.19
Warned   my Friends, be w. by me 55.3
Wars   end to the beginnings of all w. 475.5
   Still w. and lechery 498.265
   W. and rumours of w. 62.142
   W. are not won by evacuations 133.33
Washing   painting a face and not w. 245.1
Waste   we lay w. our powers 595.9
Watch   as a w. in the night 62.54
   why not carry a w. 548.2
Watches   'Tis with our judgments as our w.
   452.8
Water   better deeds Shall be in w. writ 45.6
   drawers of w. 62.30
   I came like W. 228.5
   name was writ in w. 332.40
   Unstable as w. 62.8
   virtues we write in w. 498.105
   We have all passed a lot of w. 263.8
   when I makes w. I makes w. 326.3
   w. still keeps falling over 133.38
   W., w., every where 144.6
Watering   a-w. the last year's crop 213.1
Waterloo   Every man meets his W. 444.2
   W. was won on the playing fields of Eton
   573.3
Waters   Cast thy bread upon the w. 62.84
   do business in great w. 62.57
   dreadful noise of w. in my ears 498.240
   leadeth me beside the still w. 62.47
   Stolen w. are sweet 62.66
   w. cannot quench love 62.90
Wave   Folk dance like a w. of the sea 601.7
   lift me as a w. 500.8
Waves   Britannia rule the w. 544.1
   w. make towards the pebbled shore 498.293
Way   catch the nearest w. 498.162
   going the w. of all flesh 572.2
   I met Murder on the w. 500.6
   in every war they kill you a new w. 472.1

plowman homeward plods his weary w. 268.5
There was a sure w. to see it lost 92.1
Through Eden took their solitary w. 401.27
War...always finds a w. 74.7
w. down to Hell is easy 560.3
w. of all flesh 151.9
w. of all flesh 497.2
w. to dusty death 498.177
woman has her w. 300.1
Ways   consider her w. 62.64
strayed from thy w. 149.1
We   put it down a w. 191.32
w. are for the dark 498.16
Which...w. have not got 465.2
Weak   concessions of the w. 91.1
flesh is w. 62.145
only refuge of w. minds 128.8
surely the w. shall perish 496.2
Wealth   Outshone the w. of Ormus and of Ind
401.20
W. is not without its advantages 247.1
W. maketh many friends 62.72
W....must be advertised 247.2
Weapon   art is not a w. 335.5
Weapons   books are w. 475.4
Wear   City now doth, like a garment, w. 595.11
I...chose my wife...for...qualities as would
w. well 262.8
Weariness   much study is a w. 62.85
w., the fever, and the fret 332.25
Weary   Age shall not w. them 64.1
Weather   Englishmen...first talk is of the w.
323.6
I like the w. 98.2
winter and rough w. 498.21
Web   w. of our life is of a mingled yarn 498.2
Wee   W.,...tim'rous beastie 93.11
Weeds   Lilies that fester smell far worse than
w. 498.296
Worthless as wither'd w. 77.2
Week   greatest w. in the history of the world
420.1
Weep   Fair daffodils, we w. to see 291.3
W., and you w. alone 583.1
Weeping   W. may endure for a night 62.49
Weighed   w. in the balances 62.105
Welcome   Advice is seldom w. 128.7
Love bade me w. 290.6
Well   lov'd wisely, but too w. 498.229
nothing...and did it very w. 257.5
reward of a thing w. done 218.6
We never do anything w. 281.7
worth doing w. 128.2
Well off   as w. as if he were rich 24.1
Well-written   w. Life is almost as rare 109.4
Welsh   W....just sing 569.6
Wen   fate of the great w. 141.2
Wench   w. is dead 381.6
Went   as cooks go she w. 486.4
Wept   They w. like anything to see 111.21
we sat down, yea, we w. 62.62
young man who has not w. 488.2
Wert   Bird thou never w. 500.13

West   East is East, and W. is W. 341.1
Go W., young man 269.1
Go w., young man 517.1
West Wind   O Wild W. 500.7
Wet   joly whistle wel y-w. 127.13
Whale   Very like a w. 498.68
What   W. is truth? 30.2
Wheel   bound upon a w. of fire 498.150
Wheels   spoke among your w. 45.4
When   had forgotten to say 'W.!' 592.4
w. a man should marry 30.12
Where   to die, and go we know not w. 498.184
Wherefore   For every why he had a w. 96.2
There is occasions and causes why and w.
498.100
w. art thou Romeo 498.242
Whiff   w. of grapeshot 109.9
Whigs   caught the W. bathing 195.2
Whim   strangest w. 129.1
Whimper   not with a bang but a w. 214.6
Whipping   who shall scape w. 498.59
Whirlwind   reap the w. 62.108
Whiskers   Oh my fur and w. 111.3
w....grown under glass 592.5
Whistle   So was hir joly w. wel y-wet 127.13
W. and she'll come to you 45.9
White   w. as snow 62.91
White House   no whitewash at the W. 420.3
White man   When a w. in Africa 356.1
When the w. came we had the land 252.1
W.'s Burden 341.9
Whites   until you see the w. of their eyes 456.1
Whitewash   no w. at the White House 420.3
Who   W. is Silvia? 498.280
Whole   greatest happiness of the w. 448.2
Whom   for w. the bell tolls 199.13
Whore   'Tis Pity She's a w. 235.1
Whoreson   w. zed 498.134
Whoso   W. would be a man 218.9
Why   For every w. 96.2
occasions and causes w. and wherefore
498.100
Their's not to reason w. 539.3
they knew not w. 96.1
Wicked   no peace...unto the w. 62.99
Wickedness   men alone are quite capable of
every w. 154.6
w. of a woman 62.112
Widnes   men become attached even to W.
538.2
Wife   artist will let his w. starve 499.38
chose my w. for...qualities as would wear
well 262.8
light w. doth make a heavy husband 498.198
man who's untrue to his w. 25.7
No man worth having is true to his w. 556.2
single man...must be in want of a w. 27.8
Wilderness   one crying in the w. 62.115
W. is Paradise enow 228.3
w. of this world 90.1
Wild-fowl   more fearful w. than your lion
498.204
Will   complies against his w. 96.7

formation of the political w. of the nation 297.5
Man has his w. 300.1
You w., Oscar, you w. 577.7
William You are old, Father W. 111.4
Willin Barkis is w.'. 191.7
Willing spirit indeed is w. 62.145
Willow W., titwillow, titwillow 257.13
Win Heads I w. 171.1
Let the boy w. his spurs 210.1
Those who can w. a war 133.29
Wind Blow, blow, thou winter w. 498.25
Fair stood the w. for France 203.1
gone with the w. 200.2
like W. I go 228.5
of w. and limb 96.4
reed shaken with the w. 62.133
sown the w. 62.108
throw the sand against the w. 67.8
what w. is to fire 95.1
w. bloweth where it listeth 62.165
w. of change is blowing 378.3
words but w. 96.5
Wine days of w. and roses 200.3
Flask of W. 228.3
for its poisonous w. 332.19
good w. needs no bush 498.33
Happiness is a w. 511.2
love is better than w. 62.87
new w. into old bottles 62.154
Truth comes out in w. 449.1
use a little w. for thy stomach's sake 62.200
Who loves not w., woman and song 372.1
W. comes in at the mouth 601.5
w. is in, the wit is out 49.1
w. was a farce 455.2
Wing Bird is on the W. 228.2
Wings whether pigs have w. 111.22
w. like a dove 62.53
Wink I will w. and hold out mine iron 498.92
Winners In war...there are no w. 118.1
Winning Gamesmanship...Art of W. Games 453.1
not w. but taking part 160.1
Wins silly game where nobody w. 245.2
steady w. the race 363.1
Winter furious w.'s rages 498.38
If W. comes, can Spring be far behind? 500.9
w. and rough weather 498.21
W. is icummen in 454.1
w. of our discontent 498.239
Wisdom beginning of w. 62.58
in much w. is much grief 62.81
palace of W. 67.21
Silence is full of potential w. 310.19
W. be put in a silver rod 67.3
w. is better than rubies 62.65
Wise Be w. with speed 602.2
Coffee, which makes the politician w. 452.29
more of the fool than of the w. 30.13
Nor ever did a w. one 473.1
Some folk are w. 513.1
'Tis folly to be w. 268.4

To be w. and love 498.263
Wisely lov'd not w., but too well 498.229
Wiseman Mr Worldly W. 90.3
Wiser Be w. than other people 128.1
sadder and a w. man 144.16
Wish Conscience is...rejection of a w. 242.3
w. to hurt 76.1
Wished consummation devoutly to be w. 498.61
Wishful w. thinking in Hell 358.2
Wit Brevity is the soul of w. 498.53
cause that w. is in other men 498.83
idea of w....is laughing immoderately 512.2
I have neither w., nor words, nor worth 498.120
Impropriety is the soul of w. 388.5
In w. a man 452.6
True w. is nature to advantage 452.12
wine is in, the w. is out 49.1
w. among Lords 323.11
W. that can creep 452.5
Witch suffer a w. to live 62.24
With He that is not w. me is against me 62.134
Wither Age cannot w. her 498.9
w. into the truth 601.3
Wither'd w. is the garland of the war 498.15
Within that w. which passes show 498.41
when the fight begins w. himself 83.4
Witness Thou shalt not bear false w. 62.21
Wits Great W....to Madness near alli'd 205.3
homely w. 498.278
Witty I am not only w. in myself 498.83
Wives W. are young men's mistresses 30.11
Wiving Hanging and w. goes by destiny 498.192
Woe suits of w. 498.41
W. to the vanquished 361.1
Wolf w. also shall dwell with the lamb 62.96
Wolfe I wish he would bite...my generals 254.1
Wolf's-bane neither twist W. 332.19
Wolves inwardly they are ravening w. 62.132
Woman being called a w. in my own house 569.22
body of a weak and feeble w. 215.2
every w. is at heart a rake 452.21
Every w. is infallibly to be gained 128.10
Every w. should marry 195.9
fair w. which is without discretion 62.68
Frailty, thy name is w. 498.43
Give not thy soul unto a w. 62.110
God made the w. for the man 539.5
good w. if I had five thousand 541.6
hell a fury like a w. scorned 151.4
help and support of the w. I love 211.1
I am a w.? When I think, I must speak 498.28
Love...history of a w.'s life 523.2
Man that is born of a w. 62.39
most beautiful w. I've ever seen 385.1
needs a very clever w. to manage a fool 341.10
never trust a w. who tells one her real age 584.14

nor w. neither 498.57
No w. should ever be quite accurate about her age 584.10
Once a w. has given you her heart 556.1
One is not born a w. 46.1
one of w. born 498.179
silliest w. can manage a clever man 341.10
such beauty as a w.'s eye 498.155
Thought does not become a...w. 502.2
What does a w. want 242.5
When lovely w. stoops to folly 262.10
Who loves not wine, w. and song 372.1
wickedness of a w. 62.112
w. as old as she looks 146.1
w. colour'd ill 498.302
w. has her way 300.1
W. is always fickle 560.2
w. is his game 539.23
w. is only a w. 341.2
w. killed with kindness 293.1
w....knowing anything 27.6
W.'s at best a contradiction 452.22
w. seldom asks advice 4.7
w.'s reason 498.279
w.'s whole existence 98.12
w. that deliberates is lost 4.2
W. was God's *second* mistake 419.2
w. who is really kind to dogs 51.6
W. will be the last thing civilized by Man 393.1
w....without a positive hump 541.5
w. yet think him an angel 541.4
wrecks a w.'s reputation 145.4
Womb mother's w. Untimely ripp'd 498.179
Naked...out of my mother's w. 62.38
teeming w. of royal kings 498.235
Women England...paradise for w. 94.3
experience or w. 201.8
fickleness of the w. I love 499.63
Monstrous Regiment of W. 342.1
Music and w. I cannot but give way to 438.2
no mothers, only w. 499.72
passing the love of w. 62.36
souls of w. are so small 96.8
tide in the affairs of w. 98.17
w. are glad to have been asked 428.1
W. are much more like each other 128.9
w. come and go 214.8
w....not so young as...painted 51.1
w. require both 97.8
w. should be struck...like gongs 163.5
W. who love the same man 51.5
Womman worthy w. al hir lyve 127.10
Wonder common w. of all men 82.3
Wood Hewers of w. 62.30
impulse from a vernal w. 595.18
Woodman w. spare the beechen tree 104.1
Wood-notes Warble his native w. wild 401.8
Woods fresh w., and pastures new 401.13
pleasure in the pathless w. 98.10
We'll to the w. no more 304.7
w. decay, the w. decay and fall 539.26
Woodshed Something nasty in the w. 256.1

Word better w. than pre-fabricated 133.40
by every w. that proceedeth 62.117
every w. that proceedeth out of the mouth of the Lord 62.27
Greeks had a W. for It 8.1
In the beginning was the W. 62.161
in the captain's but a choleric w. 498.181
Mum's the w. 147.1
Suit the action to the w. 498.66
What is honour? A w. 498.80
when I use a w. 111.25
W. was made flesh 62.163
Words best w. in the best order 144.25
Fine w. and an insinuating appearance 150.4
For w., like Nature, half reveal 539.10
In two w.: im - possible 263.1
Men of few w. are the best 498.96
neither wit, nor w., nor worth 498.120
w. but wind 96.5
W. may be false and full of art 497.1
Wore w. enough for modesty 84.2
Work How can I take an interest in my w. 31.1
I haven't had time to w. in weeks 336.3
I like w.; it fascinates me 321.2
To sport would be as tedious as to w. 498.77
W. expands so as to fill the time available 434.1
W. is accomplished 441.2
W. is much more fun than fun 163.16
W. is the curse of the drinking classes 584.27
W. out your own salvation 62.197
w. that aspires to...art 154.5
Worked I w. my way up...to...poverty 385.11
Worker sociable w. 52.3
Workers W. of the world, unite 386.5
Workhouse Home is...woman's w. 499.55
Working w. of great institutions 488.1
Works all his w. 149.11
Faith without w. 62.206
Look on my w., ye Mighty 500.10
World All's right with the w. 83.13
all the uses of this w. 498.42
all the w. as my parish 575.1
All the w. is queer 429.1
All the w.'s a stage 498.23
brave new w. That has such people in't 498.260
citizen of the w. 30.16
estate o' th' w. were now undone 498.178
excellent foppery of the w. 498.131
fill the w. with fools 518.3
gain the whole w. 62.148
God so loved the w. 62.166
good deed in a naughty w. 498.197
greatest week in the history of the w. 420.1
Had we but w. enough, and time 384.1
I am...a citizen of the w. 515.5
I am the light of the w. 62.168
I called the New W. into existence 107.1
I consider the w. as made for me 513.2
Into the dangerous w. I leapt 67.11
Laugh, and the w. laughs 583.1

One had as good be out of the w. 134.1
queen for all the w. 498.102
reasonable man adapts himself to the w. 499.53
say to all the w. 'This was a man' 498.124
This is the way the w. ends 214.6
this little w. 498.235
This w. nis but a thurghfare 127.12
though the w. perish 224.1
triple pillar of the w. 498.4
we brought nothing into this w. 62.201
where in this small-talking w. 244.1
wilderness of this w. 90.1
w., I count it...but an hospital 82.7
W. in a grain of sand 67.1
w. is a comedy to those who think 564.2
w. is becoming like a lunatic asylum 364.3
w. is charged with the grandeur of God 302.3
w. is made of people who 76.2
w. is made up for the most part of fools 85.1
w. is too much with us 595.9
w. must be made safe for at least fifty years 133.39
w. must be made safe for democracy 591.3
w.'s mine oyster 498.199
w., the flesh, and the devil 149.7
w. to hide virtues in 498.267
w. was all before them 401.27
w. where nothing is had for nothing 140.1
w. will make a...path to his door 218.15
w. without end 149.3
w. would go round...faster 111.5
Worldly   Mr. W. Wiseman 90.3
Worlds   best of possible w. 561.1
    So many w. 539.13
    Wandering between two w. 20.7
Worm   concealment, like a w. i' th' bud 498.272
Worms   w. have eaten them, but not for love 498.31
    you have tasted two whole w. 520.1
Wormwood   w. and the gall 62.103
Worse   Defend the bad against the w. 182.1
    for better for w. 149.15
    one thing...w. than being talked about 584.17
    Truth put to the w. 401.37
Worship   freedom of every person to w. God 475.3
Worst   we can say This is the w. 498.143
    w. Are full of passionate intensity 601.14
    w. kinde of infortune is 127.17
Worth   man's w. something 83.4
    Whatever is w. doing 128.2
    w. of a State 396.3
Worthington   daughter on the stage, Mrs W. 163.10
Wrapping   To perceive Christmas through its w. 578.2
Wrath   flee from the w. to come 62.116
Wren   Sir Christopher W. Said 59.3
    w. goes to't 498.146
Wrestling   I wretch lay w. with (my God!) my God 302.2
Wretchedness   w. of being rich 511.4

Wretches   feel what w. feel 498.141
    Poor naked w. 498.140
    w. hang that jury-men may dine 452.28
Writ   I never w., nor no man ever lov'd 498.298
Write   as much as a man ought to w. 550.2
    bad book is...a labour to w. 310.20
    Better to w. for yourself 153.10
    Do not...w. on both sides of the paper at once 495.4
    look in they heart and w. 506.1
    w. and read comes by nature 498.212
Writer   successful w....is indistinguishable 359.1
Writes   Moving Finger w. 228.8
Writing   All good w. is swimming under water 229.5
    ease in w. comes from art 452.13
    in w....ill 452.7
    w. an exact man 30.39
Wrong   anxious to do the w. thing correctly 486.6
    cradled into poetry by w. 500.5
    Nature is usually w. 577.2
    our country, right or w. 183.1
    right deed for the w. reason 214.18
    right divine...to govern w. 452.1
    something w. with our bloody ships 44.1
    That the king can do no w. 65.2
    their authors could not endure being w. 106.3
    When people agree with me...I must be w. 584.21

X,Y,Z

Xanadu   In X. did Kubla Khan 144.19
Yarn   web of our life is of a mingled y. 498.2
Yawns   grave y. for him 548.3
Year   all the y. were playing holidays 498.77
    nothing a-y. 533.2
    That time of y. thou mayst in me behold 498.294
    two months of every y. 98.2
    y.'s at the spring 83.13
Years   After long y. 98.28
    he that cuts off twenty y. of life 498.111
    thousand y. in thy sight 62.54
    threescore y. and ten 62.55
    touch of earthly y. 595.16
    world must be made safe for...fifty y. 133.39
    y. of discretion 149.12
Yesterday   Jesus Christ the same y. 62.205
Yesterdays   And all our y. 498.177
Yesteryear   snows of y. 559.1
Yet   but not y. 26.1
    young man not y. 30.12
Yield   temptation...y. to it 584.18
    To strive, to seek...and not to y. 539.27
Yorick   Alas, poor Y. 498.73
York   this sun of Y. 498.239
You   Y. also 428.2